You want the story of Poitiers, messieurs? Well, I was there, and no mistake. It was warmer there – I fought in the south for several years, and I can tell you that the folds of Gascony are no place to farm, but a fine place to fight. Perhaps that's why the Gascons are such good fighters.

Par dieu. When I began the path that would take me to chivalry, I was what? Fifteen? My hair was still red then and my freckles were ruddy instead of brown and I thought that I was as bad as Judas. I played Judas in the passion play – shall I tell you of that? Because however you may pour milk on my reputation, I was an apprentice boy in London. And in the passion plays, it's always some poor bastard with red hair, and that described me perfectly as a boy: a poor bastard with red hair.

Christian Cameron is a writer, re-enactor and military historian, and the author of *Alexander: God of War* as well as the acclaimed Tyrant and Long War series. He has a degree in Medieval History, and is a veteran of the United States Navy, where he served as both an aviator and an intelligence officer. He lives in Toronto where he is currently writing his next novel. Visit his website at www.hippeis.com

By Christian Cameron

THE TYRANT SERIES

Tyrant
Tyrant: Storm of Arrows
Tyrant: Funeral Games
Tyrant: King of the Bosporus
Tyrant: Destroyer of Cities

THE LONG WAR SERIES

Killer of Men
Marathon
Poseidon's Spear
The Great King

OTHER NOVELS

Washington and Caesar
Alexander: God of War
The Ill-Made Knight

EBOOK EXCLUSIVES

Tom Swan and the Head of St George Parts One–Six

CHRISTIAN CAMERON

An Orion paperback

First published in Great Britain in 2013
by Orion
This paperback edition published in 2014
by Orion Books,
an imprint of The Orion Publishing Group Ltd,
Orion House, 5 Upper St Martin's Lane,
London WC2H 9EA

An Hachette UK company

1 3 5 7 9 10 8 6 4 2

A CIP catalogue record for this book
is available from the British Library.

ISBN 978-1-4091-3750-4

Printed and bound in Great Britain by
CPI Group (UK) Ltd, Croydon, CR0 4YY

The Orion Publishing Group's policy is to use papers that
are natural, renewable and recyclable products and
made from wood grown in sustainable forests. The logging
and manufacturing processes are expected to conform to
the environmental regulations of the country of origin.

www.orionbooks.co.uk

*For Dr Richard Kaeuper, my mentor into
the world of the fourteenth century.*

Glossary

Arming sword – A single-handed sword, thirty inches or so long, with a simple cross guard and a heavy pommel, usually double-edged and pointed.

Arming coat – A doublet either stuffed, padded, or cut from multiple layers of linen or canvas to be worn under armour.

Alderman – One of the officers or magistrates of a town or *commune*.

Basinet – A form of helmet that evolved during the late middle ages, the basinet was a helmet that came down to the nape of the neck everywhere but over the face, which was left unprotected. It was almost always worn with an aventail made of maille, which fell from the helmet like a short cloak over the shoulders. By 1350, the basinet had begun to develop a moveable visor, although it was some time before the technology was perfected and made able to lock.

Brigands – A period term for foot soldiers that has made it into our lexicon as a form of bandit – brigands.

Burgher – A member of the town council, or sometimes, just a prosperous townsman.

Commune – In the period, powerful towns and cities were called communes and had the power of a great feudal lord over their own people, and over trade.

Coat of plates – In period, the plate armour breast and back plate were just beginning ot appear on European battlefields by the time of Poitiers – mostly due to advances in metallurgy which allowed larger chunks of steel to be produced in furnaces. Because large pieces of steel were comparatively rare at the beginning of William Gold's career, most soldiers wore a coat of small plates – varying from a breastplate made of six or seven carefully formed plates, to a jacket made up of hundreds of very small plates riveted to a leather or linen canvas backing. The protection offered was superb, but the garment was heavy and the junctions of the plates were not resistant to a strong thrust, which had a major impact on the sword styles of the day.

Cote – In the novel I use the period term cote to describe what might then have been called a gown – a man's over-garment worn atop shirt and doublet or pourpoint or jupon, sometimes furred, fitting tightly across the shoulders and then dropping away like a large bell. They could go all the way to the floor with buttons all the way, or only to the middle of the thigh. They were sometimes worn with fur, and were warm and practical.

Demesne – The central holdings of a lord – his actual lands, as opposed to lands to which he may have political rights but not taxation rights or where he does not control the peasantry.

Donjon – The word from which we get dungeon.

Doublet – A small garment worn over the shirt, very much like a modern vest, that held up the hose and sometimes to which armour was attached. Almost every man would have one. Name comes from the requirement of the Paris Tailors' guild that the doublet be made – at the very least – of a piece of linen doubled, thus heavy enough to hold the grommets and hold the strain of the laced-on hose.

Gauntlets – Covering for the hands was essential for combat. Men wore *maille* or scale gauntlets or even very heavy leather gloves, but by William Gold's time, the richest men wore articulated steel gauntlets with fingers.

Gown – An over-garment worn in Northern Europe (at least) over the kirtle, it might have dagged or magnificently pointed sleeves and a very high collar and could be worn belted to be warm, or open, to daringly reveal the kirtle. Sometimes lined in fur, often made of wool.

Haubergeon – Derived from hauberk, the haubergeon is a small, comparatively light maille shirt. It does not go down past the thighs, nor does it usually have long sleeves, and may sometimes have had leather reinforcement at the hems.

Helm or haum – The great helm had become smaller and slimmer since the thirteenth century, but continued to be very popular, especially in Italy, where a full helm that covered the face and head was part of most harnesses until the armet took over in the early fifteenth century. Edward III and the Black Prince both seem to have worn helms. Late in the period, helms began to have moveable visors like basinets.

Hobilar – A non-knightly man-at-arms in England.

Horses – Horses were a mainstay of medieval society, and they were expensive, even the worst of them. A good horse cost many days wages for a poor man; a war horse cost almost a year's income for a knight, and the loss of a warhorse was so serious that most mercenary companies specified in their contracts (or *condottas*) that the employer would replace the horse. A second level of horse was the lady's palfrey – often smaller and finer, but the medieval warhorse was *not* a giant farm horse, but a solid beast like a modern Hanoverian. Also, ronceys, which are generally inferior, smaller horses ridden by archers.

Hours – The medieval day was divided – at least in most parts of Europe – by the canonical periods observed in churches and religious houses. The day started with matins very early, past nonnes in the middle of the day, and came around to vespers towards evening. This is a vast simplification, but I have tried to keep to the flavor of medieval time by avoiding minutes and seconds.

Jupon – A close-fitting garment, in this period often laced, and sometimes used to support other garments. As far as I can tell, the term is almost interchangeable with doublet and with pourpoint. As fashion moved from loose garments based on simply cut squares and rectangles to the skintight, fitted clothes of the mid-to-late 14th century, it became necessary for men to lace their hose (stockings) to their upper garment – to hold them up! The simplest doublet (the term comes from the guild requirement that they be made of two thicknesses of linen or more, 'doubled') was a skin-tight vest worn over a shirt, with lacing holes for 'points' that tied up the hose. The pourpoint (literally, For Points) started as the same garment. The pourpoint became quite elaborate, as you can see by looking at the original that belonged to Charles of Blois online. A jupon could also be worn as a padded garment to support armour (still with lacing holes, to which armour attach) or even over armour, as a tight-fitting garment over the breastplate or coat of plates, sometimes bearing the owner's arms.

Kirtle – A women's equivalent of the doublet or pourpoint. In Italy, young women might wear one daringly as an outer garment. It is skintight from neck to hips, and then falls into a skirt. Fancy ones were buttoned or laced from the navel. Moralists decried them.

Leman – A lover.

Longsword – One of the period's most important military innovations, a double-edged sword almost forty-five inches long, with a sharp, armour-piercing point and a simple cross guard and heavy pommel. The cross guard and pommel could be swung like an axe, holding the blade – some men only sharpened the last foot or so for cutting. But the main use was the point of the weapon which, with skill, could puncture maille or even coats of plates.

Maille – I use the somewhat period term maille to avoid confusion. I mean what most people call chain mail or ring mail. The manufacturing process was very labor intensive, as real mail has to have each ling either welded closed or riveted. A fully armoured man-at-arms would have a haubergeon and aventail of maille. Riveted maille was almost proof against the cutting power of most weapons – although concussive damage could still occur! And even the most strongly made *maille* is ineffective against powerful archery, spears, or well-thrust swords in period.

Malle – Easy to confuse with maille, malle is a word found in Chaucer and other sources for a leather bag worn across the back of a horse's saddle – possibly like a round-ended portmanteau, as we see these for hundreds of years in English art. Any person travelling, be he or she pilgrim or soldier or monk, needed a way to carry clothing and other necessities. Like a piece of luggage, for horse travel.

Partisan – A spear or light glaive, for thrusting but with the ability to cut.

Pater Noster – A set of beads, often with a tassle at one end and a cross at the other – much like a modern rosary, but straight rather than in a circle.

Pauldron or Spaulder – Shoulder armour.

Prickers – Outriders and scouts.

Rondel Dagger – A dagger designed with flat, round plates of iron or brass (rondels) as the guard and the pommel, so that, when used by a man wearing a gauntlet, the rondels close the space around the fingers and make the hand invulnerable. By the late 14th century, it was not just a murderous weapon for prying a knight out of plate armour, it was a status symbol – perhaps because it is such a very useless knife for anything like cutting string or eating …

Sabatons – The 'steel shoes' worn by a man-at-arms in full harness, or full armour. They were articulated, something like a lobster tail, and allowed a full range of foot movement. They are also very light, as no fighter would expect a heavy, aimed blow at his feet. They also helped a knight avoid foot injury in a close press of mounted mêlée – merely from other horses and other mounted men crushing against him.

Shift – A woman's innermost layer, like a tight-fitting linen shirt at least down to the knees, worn under the kirtle. Women had support garments, like bras, as well.

Tow – The second stage of turning flax into linen, tow is a fibrous, dry mass that can be used in most of the ways we now use paper towels, rags and toilet paper. Biodegradable, as well.

Yeoman – A prosperous countryman. Yeoman families had the wealth to make their sons knights or squires in some cases, but most yeoman's sons served as archers, and their prosperity and leisure time to practice gave rise to the dreaded English archery. Only a modestly well-to-do family could afford a six-foot yew bow, forty or so cloth yard shafts with steel heads, as well as a haubergeon, a sword, helmet and perhaps even a couple of horses; all required for military service.

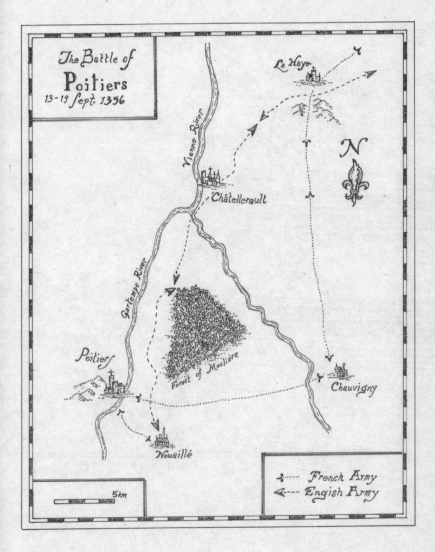

The Battle of
Poitiers
13-19 Sept. 1356

La Haye

N

Vienne River

Châtellerault

Gartempe River

Forest of Moulière

Poitiers

Chauvigny

Nouaillé

5 km

⚔······ French Army
⚔---- English Army

Prologue

Calais, June, 1381

The sound of iron-shod hooves rang on the cobbles of the gatehouse road like the sound of weapons hitting armour. As the cavalcade passed into the gatehouse with the arms of England in painted and gilded stone, the soldiers on the gate stood still, and the gate captain bowed deeply as the lord passed at the head of his retinue. He was dressed entirely in red and black; his badge, a spur rowel, repeated endlessly on his velvet gown, his swordbelt, his cloak and his horse's magnificent red, black and gold barding, all of which was cloth covered, though it could not conceal the small fortune in plate armour he wore. By his side rode his squire, equally resplendent in red, black and gold, carrying his knight's helmet and lance. Behind them rode a dozen professional men-at-arms, in full harness, their new Italian steel armour gleaming despite a cold, rainy day on the outskirts of Bruges. Behind the men-at-arms rode another dozen English archers who wore almost as much armour as the men-at-arms, and behind them rode another dozen pages. Then came four wagons, and behind the wagons rode servants, also armed. Every man in the column wore the red and black; every man had a gold spur rowel badge on his cloak.

The knight of the spur rowels returned the salute of the gate captain, raising a small wooden baton to his forehead and bowing slightly in the saddle. He smiled, which in return coaxed a smile from the scarred face of the gate captain.

He reined in. 'John,' he said. 'The captain will want to see our letters of passage and our passes.'

His squire handed the helmet and lance to a page and reached into his belt pouch.

The gate captain bowed. 'My lord. All of us know the arms of

Sir William Gold.' He accepted the papers. 'The Duke of Burgundy informed us you were en route.'

Sir William Gold made an odd facial movement – half a smile, with only the left side of his mouth moving. 'How kind of him,' he said. 'I'd be wary of forty armed men on my roads, too.' He leaned down from the saddle. 'You're English.'

'Yes, my lord,' the man said.

'I know you. Giles something. Something Giles.' Sir William took the hood hat from his head and shook the rain off it.

The man's smile became broader. 'Anselm Saint-Gilles, my lord.'

'You were with – damn it, I'm an old man, Saint-Gilles – Brignais. You were at Brignais, with—'

'Nay, my lord, but I wish I had been. I was Sir Robert Knolly's man.' He was obviously pleased to have been recognized. 'I was an archer, then.'

'And now a man-at-arms – well done, Saint-Gilles.' Sir William reached down and offered his hand to clasp, and the gate captain took it.

'Tell an old war-horse where the best wine is? I don't know Calais, and I've a four-day wait for a ship to England.' Sir William's eyes seemed to twinkle.

'My lord, the White Swan is not the largest inn, but it has the most courteous keeper, the best wine, and it is' – the man raised his eyebrows expressively – 'convenient to the baths.' He bowed again and handed up the leather roll that contained their passports and letters from a dozen kings and independent lords and *communes*. The Count of Savoy, the Duke of Milan, the Republic of Florence and the Duke of Burgundy were all represented. 'Please enjoy Calais, my lord,' he ventured.

'White Swan – that's a badge I'll know. Come and drink a cup of wine with me, Master Saint-Gilles.' Sir William saluted again with his baton and, without any outward sign, his horse stepped off into the great city.

Behind him, the disciplined men who'd waited silently in the rain while he chatted wiped the rain from their helmets and pressed their mounts into motion.

When they were clear of the gate, the squire leaned forward. 'My lord?'

'Speak, John.'

'We have a letter from the Duke of Lancaster sending us to the

White Swan, my lord.' His tone said, *you already knew where we were going*. John de Blake was a well-born Englishman of seventeen – an age at which he tried to know everything but understood all too little.

'It never hurts to ask,' Sir William said with his odd half-smile. 'Sometimes, you learn something, John.'

'Yes, my lord,' John said.

Forty men do not just dismount and hand over their horses at an inn. Even an inn that is six tall buildings of whitewashed stone surrounding a courtyard that wouldn't disgrace a great lord's palace. The courtyard featured a horse fountain and a small garden behind a low wall, with a wrought-iron gate that was gilded and painted. The inn's doors – twelve of them – were painted a beautiful heraldic blue, and the windows on the courtyard had their frames whitewashed so carefully they seemed to sparkle in the rain, while their glass – very expensive glass too – gave the impression of well-set jewels.

The master of the inn came out into the yard as soon as his gate opened. He bowed, and a swarm of servants fell on his troop like an ambush of friendship.

'My lord,' he said in Flemish-English.

Sir William bowed courteously in his saddle. 'You are the master of the White Swan?'

'I have that honour. Henri, my lord, at your service. We had word of your coming.'

Sir William's retinue filled the courtyard. Horses moved and grunted, but the men on their backs were silent and no one made a move to dismount. The servants had moved to take the horses, but hesitated at the armed silence.

'I pray you, be welcome here,' the innkeeper said.

Sir William looked back over his troop, his left fist on the rump of his horse. 'Gentlemen!' he called out. 'It seems we've fallen soft. Eat and drink your fill. This is a good house, and we'll do nothing to change its name, eh? Am I understood, gentles?'

There was a chorus of grunts and steel-clad nods. A horse farted, and men smiled.

Sir William sighed and threw an armoured leg over his horse's broad back. He pressed his breastplate against the red leather of his war saddle and slid neatly to the ground, his golden spurs chiming like the bell for Communion. He handed his war horse's reins to his page and turned to his squire.

'There are few places more like heaven on earth for a soldier,' he said, 'than a good inn.'

John de Blake allowed himself a nod of agreement.

'By nightfall, one of our archers will be in Ghent, and another will be so drunk he'll sell his bow and a third will try and force some girl and get a knife in his gizzard.' Sir William gave his half-smile.

From the expression on his face, de Blake didn't think he was supposed to answer that.

'Other guests?' Sir William asked of the master of the inn.

'My lord? I have two gentlemen en route to the convocation in Paris. Monsieur Jean Froissart, and Monsieur Geoffrey Chaucer. On the young King's business.'

At the name Chaucer, the half-smile appeared.

Innkeepers do not rise in their profession without the ability to read faces. 'You know Master Chaucer, my lord?'

Sir William Gold's dark-green eyes looked off into the middle distance. 'Since we were boys,' he said. 'Does he know I am here?'

The innkeeper bowed.

'Well, then.' Sir William nodded. 'Let's get these men out of the rain, shall we, good master?'

Great lords do not, generally, sit in the common room of inns – even inns that cater to princes. Good inns have rooms and rooms and yet more rooms – they are, in effect, palaces for rent, where lords can hold court, order food and have the use of servants without bringing their own.

Vespers rang, and men went to hear Mass. There was a fine new church across the tiny square from the White Swan, and every man in Gold's retinue attended. They stood in four disciplined rows and heard the service in English Latin, which made some of his Italians squirm.

After the service, they filled the common room and wine flowed like blood on a stricken battlefield. The near roar of their conversation rose around them to fill the place. Sir William broke with convention and took a small table with his squire and raised a cup to his retinue.

Before the lights were lit, there were dice and cards on most tables. A voice – pitched a little too harshly, a little too loud, like the voice of a hectoring wife in a farce – came from the stairs: 'That will be Gold's little army. If you want to hear the latest from Italy, stop preening and come down!'

Half a smile from Sir William.

He had time to finish his wine. A pretty woman – the only serving woman in the room – appeared with a flagon.

Sir William brushed the greying red hair from his forehead and smiled at her.

Her effort to return his smile was marred by obvious fear. She curtsied. 'This wine, my lord?' she asked.

He put a hand on her arm. 'Ma petite – no one here will touch you. Breathe easy. We're not fiends from hell, only thirsty Englishmen and a handful of Italians. How many years have you?'

She curtsied again. 'Sixteen, my lord.' Despite the hand on her arm, or perhaps because of it, she was as tense as a hunting dog with a scent.

'And your father asked you to wait on me?' Sir William asked.

She curtsied a third time.

'By St John! That is hospitable,' Sir William said, and his eyes sparkled in a way that made the young woman blush. 'Listen, ma petite. Serve the wine and don't linger at table, and no one can reproach you – or grab you. Yes? I served a table or two. A hand reaches for you, you move through it and pretend nothing happened, yes?'

She nodded. 'This is what my father says.'

'Wise man. Just so. On your way, ma petite.' Sir William's odd green eyes met hers before she could look down.

Later, she told a friend it was like looking into the eyes of a wolf.

The knight got to his feet as she moved away and bowed. 'Ah, Master Chaucer, the sele of the day to you.' He offered a hand. 'You are a long way from London.'

Chaucer had a narrow face and a curling beard that made him look like the statues of Arabs in the cathedrals, or like a sprite or elf, to the old wives. He took the knight's hand and they exchanged a kiss of peace – carefully.

'The king's business,' Chaucer said. His answering smile could have meant anything.

Sir William nodded. 'Of course. As always, eh?' He turned to the other man – a tall, blond man, almost gangly in his height, with golden hair. 'You are a Hainaulter, unless I miss my guess, monsieur.'

Chaucer indicated his companion. 'Monsieur de Froissart.'

Sir William offered his hand and Froissart bowed deeply. 'One is ... deeply moved to meet so famous a knight.'

Sir William shrugged. 'Oh, as to that,' he said.

'You *must* know he's writing a book of all the great deeds of arms of our time,' Chaucer said.

Froissart bowed again. 'Master Chaucer is too kind. One makes every attempt to chronicle the valour, the prowess. The ... chivalry.'

Sir William's green eyes strayed to Chaucer's. 'Not your sort of book at all,' he said.

Chaucer's eyes were locked on Sir William's. 'No,' he said. 'If I wrote such a chronicle, it would not be about valour. Or prowess.'

The two men looked at each other for too long. Long enough for John de Blake to move, worried there might be violence; for Aemilie, the innkeeper's daughter, dressed in her very best clothes, to flatten herself against the plastered wall, and for Monsieur de Froissart to worry that he had said something out of place. He looked back and forth between the two men.

'We could sit,' Sir William said. The room had fallen quiet, but with these words, games of cards and dice sprang back into action and conversations resumed.

'How have you kept, Geoffrey? When did we last meet? Milan?' Sir William asked.

'The wedding of Prince Lionel,' Chaucer said. 'No thanks to you.'

Sir William laughed. 'You have me all wrong, Master Chaucer. I was not against you. The French were against us both.'

Chaucer frowned. 'Perhaps.' He collected himself. 'What takes you to England?' he asked.

Sir William smiled, eyes lidded. 'The King's business,' he said.

Chaucer threw back his head and laughed. 'Damn me, I had that coming. Very well, William. I promised Monsieur Froissart that you were the man to tell him about Italy.'

Froissart leaned forward like an eager dog. 'My lord will understand that one collects tales of arms. Deeds of arms – battles, wars, tournaments. At the court of the young King, one hears many tales of Crecy and Poitiers and the wars in France, but one hears little of Italy. That is,' – he hurried on – 'that is, one hears a great deal of rumour, but one has never had the chance to bespeak a famous knight who has served—' he paused. 'My lord.'

Sir William was laughing softly. 'Well, I love to talk as I love a pretty face,' he said.

'By our lord, that's the truth,' Chaucer observed.

'What is your name, ma petite?' the knight asked the serving maid.

'Aemilie, my lord,' she said, with another stiff-backed curtsey.

Sir William had begun to turn away, but he froze and his eyes went back to hers, and she trembled.

'That is a name of great value to me, ma petite. I have loved a lady *par amours*, and that is her name.' He nodded. 'Fetch us two more of the same, if you will be so kind.'

She curtseyed and walked away, trying to glide in her heavy skirts.

'If you want Italy, then you will not want France,' he said. 'How do I begin?'

Froissart shook his head. 'When talk turns to feats of arms, one is all attention,' he said. 'One is as interested in Poitiers as any other passage of arms. It was, perhaps, the greatest feat of arms of our time.'

Sir William glared at him. 'So kind of you to say so,' he snapped.

Froissart paled.

'Don't come it the tyrant, William!' Chaucer said. 'He means no harm. It is merely his way. He's a connoisseur of arms, as other men are of art or letters.' He put a hand out. 'I saw your sister a week or more ago.'

Gold smiled. 'In truth, I cannot wait to see her. Is she well?'

Chaucer nodded. 'I cannot say she's plump, but she had her sisters well in hand. She was en route to Clerkenwell to deliver her accounts, I think.'

Sir William turned to Froissart. 'My sister is a prioress of the Order of St John, monsieur.' He said it with sufficient goodwill that Froissart relaxed.

'I would be most pleased if you would share with me your experiences at Poitiers,' Froissart continued. 'Another knight's account would only help—'

Chaucer and Gold laughed together.

Aemilie appeared at the table with her father and two men, and they began to place small pewter dishes on the table – a dish of sweet meats, a dish of saffroned cakes, and a beautiful glazed dish of dates, as well as two big-bellied flagons of wine.

Sir William rose and bowed to the master of the house. 'Master, your hospitality exceeds anything in Italy; it is like a welcome home to England.'

The innkeeper flushed at the praise. 'Calais is England, my lord,' he acknowledged.

Sir William indicted his companions. 'I'm going to bore these two poor men with a long story,' he said. 'Please keep the wine coming.'

Chaucer rose. 'William, I'm for my bed. I know your stories.'

'I'll tell him all your secrets,' Gold said.

Chaucer smiled his thin, elven smile. 'We're in the same business,' he said. 'He *knows* all my secrets.'

Again, the silence.

This time, Chaucer broke it. 'Will I see you in London?'

Sir William nodded. 'I shall look forward to it. Will your business be long?'

Chaucer shook his head. 'I hope not, *par dieu*. I'm too old to be a courier.' He gave a sketchy bow and headed for the stairs.

Froissart, left almost alone with the knight, had a little of Aemilie's look. John de Blake watched his master. 'Shall I withdraw?' he asked.

Gold gave a half-smile to his squire. 'Only if you want to go, John.'

De Blake settled himself in his seat and poured himself more wine.

Aemilie crossed from her counter to the wall and stood against it, ready to serve.

Sir William drank some wine and glanced at the young woman. Then he turned back to Froissart. 'Do you really want to hear about Poitiers, monsieur?' he asked.

Froissart sat up. 'Yes!' he replied.

Gold nodded. 'I wasn't a knight then,' he said.

Poitiers 1356

Men trod on their own guts and spat out their teeth; many were cloven to the ground or lost their limbs while on their feet. Dying men fell in the blood of their companions and groaned under the weight of corpses until they gave out their last breath. The blood of serfs and Princes flowed in one stream into the river.

Geoffrey le Baker, *Chronicon*

You want the story of Poitiers, messieurs? Well, I was there, and no mistake. It was warmer there – I fought in the south for several years, and I can tell you that the folds of Gascony are no place to farm, but a fine place to fight. Perhaps that's why the Gascons are such good fighters.

Par dieu. When I began the path that would take me to chivalry, I was what? Fifteen? My hair was still red then and my freckles were ruddy instead of brown and I thought that I was as bad as Judas. I played Judas in the passion play – shall I tell you of that? Because however you may pour milk on my reputation, I was an apprentice boy in London. And in the passion plays, it's always some poor bastard with red hair, and that described me perfectly as a boy: a poor bastard with red hair.

It shouldn't have been that way. My parents were properly wed. My da' had a coat of arms from the King. We owned a pair of small manors – not a knight's fee; not by a long chalk – but my mother was of the De Vere's and my father was a man-at-arms in Wales. I needn't have been an apprentice. In fact, that was my first detour from a life of arms, and it almost took me clear for ever.

I imagine I'm one of the few knights you'll meet who's so old that he remembers the plague. No, not the plague. The Great Plague. The year everyone died. I went to play in the fields, and when I came home, my mother was dead and my father was going.

It changes you, death. It takes everything away. I lost my father and mother and all I had left was my sister.

I'll tell you of knighthood – and war, and Poitiers, and everything, but with God's help, and in my own time.

*

My father's brother was a goldsmith. In my youth, a lot of the young gentry went off to London and went to the guilds. Everything was falling apart. You know what I'm telling you? No? Well, monsieur, the aristocracy – let's be frank: knighthood, chivalry – was dying. Taxes, military service and grain prices. Everything was against us. I remember it, listening to my father, calm and desperate, telling my mother we'd have to sell our land. Maybe the plague saved them. I can't see my mother in a London tenement, her husband some mercer's worker. She was a lady to her finger's ends.

My uncle came and got us. Given what happened, I don't know why he came – he was a bad man and I was afraid of him from the first. He had no Christian charity whatsoever in him, and may his soul burn in hell for ever.

You are shocked, but I mean it. May he burn – in – hell.

He came and fetched us. I remember my uncle taking my father's great sword down from where it hung on the wall. And I remember that he sold it.

He sold our farms, too.

I remember riding a tall wagon to London with my sister pressed against my side. Sometimes she held my hand. She was a little older and very quiet.

I remember entering London on that wagon, sitting on a small leather trunk of my clothes, and the city was a wonder that cut through my grief. I remember pointing to the sights that I knew from my mother and father – the Tower, and the Priory of the Knights at Clerkenwell, and all the ships ... My uncle's wife was as quiet as my sister. My uncle had beaten all the noise out of her – he bragged about it. My pater used to say that only a coward or a peasant hit a woman, and now I think he had his brother in mind, because Guillaulm the Goldsmith was a coward *and* a peasant.

His wife was Mary. She took us into her house. Her eyes were blank. I can't remember what colour they were – I don't think she ever looked me in the eye.

Before the sun had set a finger's width, I discovered that we were to be servants, not children.

It wasn't the end of the world. I had waited tables for gentlemen visiting our house –my mother was trying to bring me up gently, even though we lacked the money or influence to have me placed as a page. I could carve and I could serve, so I hid my dismay and did my best.

It's a long time ago, but he beat me before the day was out, and he liked it. I remember his breath, his face red. Licking his lips. I took it. I think I cried, but I took it. But later on he tried to beat my sister, and I bit him.

I had years of it. I doubt a day went by when he didn't hit me, and some days – some days he beat me badly.

Bah. This isn't what you want to hear.

I went to the church school – he did that much for me – and the monks liked me, and I liked them. Without them, I think I'd be a much worse man. They doctored me when he beat me too badly, and they prayed with me. Praying – it's always helped me. I know there's men-at-arms who spit at God. I think they're fools.

I learned some Latin. Saved my life later.

I also learned to cook. My uncle wasn't just a bad man, he was a nasty-minded miser who wouldn't buy good food or pay a cook. He bought old meat and the last vegetables in the market. It was like a compulsion for him, not to spend money. And his poor wife was too broken to do more than throw it all in a pot and boil it. I was tired of this, and hungry, and when I complained I was beaten. Well, I'm not the only boy to be beaten for complaining about food, but I may be one of the few who decided on the spot to learn to cook. I asked men in pot houses and taverns, and women who worked in great houses, and I learned a few things. As you will see. The path of arms, for me, included many beatings, a little Latin and cooking.

A boy can grow used to anything, eh? I served in the house; I ran errands for the shop; I did apprentice work like polishing silver and pewter and cleaning the files and saws; I went to Mass and to matins; I learned my letters and I cooked. And on Sundays, after church . . .

If you three were Londoners, you'd know what we do on Sunday after church.

The girls dance in the squares.

And the lads take a sword and a buckler and fight.

By the gentle Christ, I loved to fight. I never minded the split knuckles, the broken fingers, the gash in the head. Daily beatings from my uncle made me hard. I had to borrow a sword – it was years before I had one of my own – but there was this fellow who was like a god to us youngers; he was an apprentice goldsmith to the big shop that served the court, and he had woollen clothes and a fine sword and he was such a pleasant fellow that he let little things like me use it. Thomas Courtney, he was. Long dead. I'll wager he is *not* burning in hell.

Thomas Courtney was my hero from very young. And *par dieu*, messieurs, he would have been a good knight. He was ill-sorted for the life of a draper, and he was an example of everything that I could be.

I'd like to say I grew better, but I was too young to wield a man's sword properly – it was all I could do to block a blow – but I learned how to move, and how to avoid one. One of the monks was a good blade, and he taught me, too. He was a lusty bastard, a terror with the virgins as well as being quite fast with his fists, and he taught me some of that, too. Brother John. A bad monk, but not such a bad man. Nor a good one, as you'll hear.

And there was wrestling. Everyone in London – every man and boy and no few women – can wrestle. Out in the fields, we'd gather in packs, peel off our hose and have at it.

I loved to fight, and there were many teachers. It was just as well. I grew fast, and I had red hair.

When I was eleven, I came in from an errand and couldn't find my sister. She should have been helping the cook, who was my friend in the house. Cook hadn't seen her. I went up to the rooftrees and I found her, with my uncle trying to get between her legs.

He'd tried his member on me several times, and I'd learned to knee him in the groin. So I wasn't as shocked as I might have been.

I hit him.

He beat the living hell out of me, his parts hanging out of his braes. He chased me around the attic, pounding me with his fists.

But he didn't finish what he was about.

After that, I never left my sister alone in the house. I went to my aunt and told her, and she turned her head away and said nothing.

So I went to the monks. An eleven-year-old boy needs an ally.

Brother John took me to the Abbott, and the Abbott went to the guild of goldsmiths, and that was the end of it.

A week later, my uncle came home late, with his face puffy and his lip and eyebrows cut from punches. Footpads had set on him, taken his purse and pounded him.

Next day, Brother John had two sets of split knuckles, and so did Brother Bartholomew. Perhaps they'd had a dust up.

For a year, things were better. But better is an odd word to a boy who has to fear everything and everyone, and who has to fight every day. I'm not making excuses for what came later. Just saying.

I'm coming to Poitiers in my own time. Listen, messieurs. When you face the arrow storm, when you face a big man in the lists or on the battlefield, when you stand knee deep in mud and your sword is broken and you cannot catch your breath and you have two bloody wounds – then you need to have something. Some men get it from their fathers. Some get it from God.

So just listen.

I always wanted to be a knight. In my boy's head, my pater had been a knight – not strictly true, but a boy's dreams are golden and that's how it was. And yet, such is youth, when the Guildhall sent for me and I was entered as an apprentice – at the insistence of the Abbott, I think – I was puffed like an adder, over the moon with delight. I intended to be the best goldsmith since the Romans, and I worked like a slave. I went to another shop. My sister was working every day for the sisters of St John, serving the poor and thus safe from my uncle, so I could go and work the whole day with a free heart.

As apprentices, we had thirty-five feast days a year. My master was John de Villers, and he beat me when I broke things. I never heard a word of praise from him, and I got a ration of curses, but that was only his way. He wasn't a money-grubbing louse. He was a fine craftsman, and he didn't make the cheap crap you see in the streets. He made nothing but scabbard fittings for the nobility, and he made things that caused me, as a boy, to gawk. Enamel blue, whorls of gold like the tracery on a cathedral – by St John, friends, he had the true gift of making, and all his bad temper didn't stop him from teaching us. In fact, he liked his apprentices better than some apparently kinder men – most of his boys made their grade and got their mark.

I worked in copper and learned my way. I did a lot more low work – I remember that I spent a week cleaning his stable shed, which can't have taught me a thing about metal work – but he took the time to show me some things, and I loved the work, and I could tell that he could feel my enthusiasm.

I made a set of clasps and hinges for a Bible for the monks, and Master de Villers said they were good enough. That was a great day for me. As far as I know, the monks still use that Bible – I saw it on the lectern in King Richard's day.

Oh, aye, messieurs, I'm older than dirt. I can remember Caesar. You asked for this story – fill my cup or go to your bed.

That's better.

I was getting bigger. I had a little money. I finally bought a tuck – a sword. It probably wasn't so much, but *par dieu*, gentlemen, it was the world to me, and I wore it out on Sundays' under my buckler – a fine buckler with copper and bronze studs and a fine iron rim, all my work or my friends' work. And when I swaggered swords with another boy, girls watched me.

Well. When they danced, I watched them.

And glances became looks, and looks became visits, and visits became hands brushing, and perhaps clasping, and then there was kissing . . .

Heh, I'll assume you know whereof I speak. So you know what comes next. I'm a sinful man, and lust has always had a place for me. A pretty face, a pair of breasts, a fine leg shown when tying a garter, and by our saviour, I'm off like a greyhound. I started young, and I'm not sure that I'm finished. But a chivalrous man is a lover of women – Lancelot was a lover of women, and Sir Tristan, and all the great knights. The priests clip us too close. There's very little harm in a little love, eh?

Any gate, by the time I was fourteen I was ready to be wed, and my chosen mate was Nan Steadman, whose da' was an alderman. He thought me beneath her, but she had him wrapped around her fingers. She wed another, and I have a different life, but we still share a cup when I'm in London, Nan and I. Fifty years and more.

Bah, I'm old. What I'm trying to say is that I had a life, a fine life. Hard, but I was making it, and with gentle manners and a good craft skill, there were no limits to what I might be. A fine life. I haven't really said what an advantage my mother's work on my manners were. But I spoke like a gentleman, English or French, and I could bow, carve, pour wine, read or speak a prayer. These may not seem like great achievements, but by our lady, without them you are doomed to be a certain kind of man. I had them, and as the alderman said, if I wasn't hanged, I'd be Lord Mayor.

I had everything required to succeed, in London.

And in two afternoons, I fucked it away.

I was learning to ride and joust and use the bow. Nay, don't shake your heads – the Londoners over there nodding know that by law any free man of London, and that includes an apprentice, may bear arms and ride the joust – eh? Just so, messieurs. And such was my passion for it that I took Nan to see some foreign worthies fight at barriers in the meadows – knights and squires. There were Frenchmen and Germans and Englishmen and even a Scot. We fought the French, but we *hated* the Scots. But the Scottish knight was *preux*, and he fought well, and the French knights fought brilliantly – one of them like the god Mars incarnate – and one of the Brabanters was no great swordsman, but he was brave and spirited and I admired him. He was in the Queen's retinue, I thought – she was a Hainaulter, and she brought more than a few of them with her.

Things were different then, and when he was in his pavilion disarming, I walked in, bowed and paid my compliments on his fighting. He was older than I thought, and he was very pleased to have his fighting complimented by any man; it was nothing to him that I was an apprentice, and we talked for some time and I was served wine like a gentle. I think it went to my head, the wine and the company.

There were other men about, and my Nan, looking a tad embarrassed as women are want to be when out of their element. But Sir Otto, as he was called, was courtly to her, and she blushed.

A young English knight came in. They'd fought three blows of the sword, and they embraced, and I saw that the knight knew me. And I knew him. He was a cousin, on my mother's side. A De Vere. He winced when I said I was a goldsmith.

We might have had hot words, but then he shrugged. I didn't want to admire him, but I did; he was everything I wasn't, and suddenly he, by existing, burned my happiness to the ground.

I didn't want to be a goldsmith. I wanted to be a knight.

He was Edward. Well, everyone was Edward in those days. He was a little too courtly to Nan, who ate his admiration the way a glutton eats pork. He had fine clothes, beautiful manners and he'd just fought in armour. Every one of you knows that a man never, ever looks better than when he's just fought in harness. His body is as light as air. Fighting is a proper penance for sin – a man who has endured the harness and the blows is as stainless as a virgin for a little while. Edward had golden hair and a golden belt, and even then and there, I couldn't resent Nan's attention.

Besides, after some initial hesitation, he treated me as family, and that only made me seem higher. I was glad. Nan would go home to her father and say we'd been served wine by gentlemen who were my relatives.

The French knights came – they were prisoners of the war in France, waiting in England for ransom. The older knight was courtly to Nan and quite polite to me – no foolish distance. His name was Geoffrey de Charny, and if my cousin Edward looked like a true knight, De Charny looked like a paladin from the chansons. He was as tall as me – and damned few men are – a good six feet in his hose, and maybe a finger more. He had a face carved from marble, and hair the colour of silver-gilt, with blue eyes. He looked like the saint of your choice. He was the best fighter in armour that I ever saw, and he had the most perfect manners, and the reputation of being the fiercest man in the field. In fact, he was considered the greatest knight of his generation – some men say the greatest knight of all time.

You know of him, messieurs, I'm sure. Well, I will have more to say of that noble gentleman.

The other man knight was as young as me, or Nan, but he wore the whole value of my master's shop on his back. The first *silk* arming jacket I ever saw, with silk cords pointed in figured gold – and this a garment meant to be worn *under* armour and unseen.

Nan was the only woman in the tent, and she received a great deal of attention, and I tried not to be angry or jealous. I was so busy hanging on de Charny's every word that I scarcely noticed her. But young men are fools, and she blushed and smiled a great deal, and eventually came and stood by me, and Messire de Charny told her that she was very beautiful. She still tells that story, and well she might. He asked her for a lace from her sleeve, and promised to wear it the next time he fought.

I admired him so much that I restrained my jealousy and managed to smile.

We had too much wine, and on the way home we found a lane and we dallied. She had never been so willing – grown men know about women and wine, but young ones don't know yet. She was liquorice, and I was hot for her. Her mouth tasted of cloves. We played long, but we stayed just inside the bounds, so to speak.

I took her to her door, begged her mother's forgiveness for the hour and escaped alive. Just.

So when I came home to my uncle's house, I thought I was safe and whole, relatively sinless.

He was raping my sister. She was crying – whimpering and pleading. I could hear them from the back door, and all the while I climbed the stairs I knew he had her and was using her, and that as a knight, I had failed, because I had not been there to protect her. Climbing those stairs still comes to me in nightmares. Up and up the endless, narrow, rickety stair, my sister begging him to stop, the sound of his fist striking her, the wet sound as he moved inside her.

Eventually I made the top. We lived in the attic, under the eaves, and he had her on my pallet. I went for him. I wasn't ten years old any more, and he never trained to arms.

I'll make this brief – you all want to hear about Poitiers.

I beat him badly.

I dragged him off her, and locked one of his arms behind his back, using it to hold him, then I smashed his face with my fists until I broke his nose. As he fell to the floor, arse in the air, I kicked him. I made his member black by kicking him there fifteen or twenty times.

The next day, he stayed abed. I had to mind *his* shop, and I sent a boy round to my true master and said my uncle was sick. It was evil fate riding me hard.

The French knight Geoffrey de Charny – the one who had fought so well the day before – came to the shop. The younger knight was with him. De Charny had a dagger, a fine thing, all steel – steel rondels, steel grip, steel blade – and better than anything I'd seen in London. It was a wicked, deadly thing that shouted murder across the room. He laid it on the counter and asked how much it would cost to put it in a gold-mounted scabbard.

After I named a price, he looked down his nose at me. In French, he asked me if he hadn't seen me at the passage of arms the day before.

I spoke French well, or so I thought until I went to France, so I nodded and bowed and said that yes, I had been present.

He pursed his lips. 'With the very handsome woman, yes?' he asked. He looked at the younger knight, who grinned.

I nodded. I didn't like that grin.

'And the English knight, Sir Edward, is your cousin?' he asked.

'Yes, my lord,' I said.

'But you are in a dirty trade. Your hands are not clean.' He made a face. 'Why do you betray your blood like this?'

Perhaps my anger showed in my eyes, but he shrugged. 'You English,' he said. 'I have insulted you, and truly, I mean no insult. You look like a healthy boy who would not be useless in arms. Why not turn your back on this dirt and do something worthy?'

I had no answer for that. I do not think that trade is dirty. Good craft still makes my heart sing like sweet music, but something he said seemed to me to be from God. Why was I intending to be a goldsmith?

You might ask why I wasn't seeking the law and revenge for my sister. I'm telling this badly. In fact, I spent the morning taking her to the nuns before I opened the shop. I went to Nan's father and swore a complaint. I did all that, and the French knight's visit was, if anything, a pleasant diversion from my thoughts. Perhaps I should have killed my uncle myself. That's what a man-of-arms does – he is justice. He carries justice in his scabbard. But in London, in the year of our lord 1355, an apprentice went meekly to the law, because the King's courts were fair courts, because the Mayor and Aldermen, despite being rich fucks, were mostly fair men, and because I believed then – and still do, friends – that the rule of law is better than the rule of the sword, at least in England.

My uncle wasn't bound by such rules.

When I closed the shop, I didn't want to spend another minute under his roof, so I went to evensong, and then I walked. I'd been in the great passion play at the hospital as Judas – I already mentioned that – and I knew a few of the knights, that is, the Knights of the Order. They sometimes allowed me to watch them while they practised their arms, and my sister worked there. Now my sister was lying on a bed among the sisters, so my feet took me out Clerkenwell way to the hospital priory. I saluted the porter and went to find my sister. I sat on her bed for three quarters of an hour by the bells, listening to the sound of sheep cropping grass, and to the squawking of hens and the barking of dogs and the sounds of a Knight of the Order riding his war horse, practising, in the yard. Twice I went and watched him.

The Hospitallers – the Knights of St John – have always, to me, been the best men, the best fighters, the very epitome of what it means to be a knight. So even while my sister wept with her face to the wall, I watched the knight in the yard.

When I went back to her bedside and tried to hold her hand, she shrank into a ball.

After some time, I gave up and went back to get some sleep. I walked up to the servant's door of my uncle's house, and two men came out of the shadows and ordered me to hand over my sword.

I did.

And I was taken.

I want you, gentlemen, to see how I came to a life of arms, but I'll cut this part short. I was taken for theft. My uncle swore a warrant against me for the theft of the knight's dagger. I never touched it – I swear on my sword – but that boots nothing when a Master Goldsmith swears a case against an apprentice. I was taken. I wasn't ill used, and all they did was lock me in a plain room of the sheriff's house. I had a bed.

The next day, I went for trial.

Nothing went as I expected. I have always hated men of law, and my trial for theft confirmed what every apprentice knows: the men of law are the true enemy. I could tell from the way they spoke that none of them – not one – believed me guilty. It was like the passion play, they acted out the parts of accuser and accused. My uncle said that I had always been bad and that I had stolen the dagger. The French knight, Sir Geoffrey, appeared merely to say the dagger had been his. He looked at me a long time. When the court thanked him formally for attending, he bowed and then said, in French, that my case was what came of forcing a nobly born boy to ignoble pursuits.

Given it was a court of merchants and craftsmen, I'm fairly sure his words did me no good. Most of the court talk was in Norman French, which I understood well enough. My advocate wasn't much older than me, and seemed as willing to see me hanged as my accuser. No one seemed to care when I shouted that my uncle had raped my sister.

I was found guilty and condemned to be branded.

They branded me right here, on my right hand. See? Of course you can't, messieurs. I was branded with a cold iron, because Brother John and the Abbott appeared as if from a machine and told the court that I was in lower orders. I read one of the psalms in Latin when the Abbott ordered me to. It was like having a fever – I scarcely understood what was happening.

I was dismissed from the guild.

My uncle burned all my clothes and all my belongings. He had the right to do so, but he made me a beggar.

Nan's father told me never to come to his house, but in truth he was decent about it. He didn't say it in words, but he made it clear that he knew I was no thief. And yet ...

And yet, my life was done.

I went and slept on the floor of the monks' chapel, where I swept their floors. I was there three days, and they gave me some cast-off clothes, while the Abbott made me a reader – I read the gospel two mornings – so as not to have lied in court.

I'll *never* forget those mornings, reading the gospel to the monks. I am a man of blood, but for two whole days, I loved Jesus enough to be a monk. I considered it and the Abbott invited me.

But the third day, Brother John came and took me on a walk.

We walked a long way. I was still so shattered I had no conversation, and he merely walked along, greeting all who looked at him, winking at the maidens and sneering at the men. We walked along the river to the Tower and back.

Just short of our chapel, having walked the whole of London, he stopped. 'I'm giving up the habit,' he said suddenly.

I doubt I looked very interested.

'The Prince is taking an army to Gascony,' he said. 'The indentures to raise the troops are written – it's spoken of in every tavern. I'm not cut out for a monk, and I mean to try my hand at war.'

I suppose I nodded. Nothing he said touched me at all.

He put his hand on my shoulder.

'Come with me, lad,' he said. 'If you stay here, you'll be a thief in truth soon enough.'

I see you all smile, and I'll smile with you. It is the hand of God. I was born to be a man-of-arms, and then the plague and the devil and my uncle came to stop me. But every work of the devil rebounds to God in the end. The Abbott taught me that. My uncle tried to hurt me, and instead he made me tough. Later, he made me a criminal, and because of him ...

I went to France.

Brother John and I left the monks without a goodbye and walked across the river at the bridge. I had to pass my former master's shop, but no one recognized me. We walked out into the meadow, and there were the city archery butts – really, they belonged to Southwark, but we all used them. And John – no longer brother

John – walked straight up to an old man with a great bow and proclaimed himself desirous of taking service.

The old man – hah, twenty years younger than I am now, but everyone looks ancient when you are fifteen – looked at John and handed him his bow.

'Just bend it,' he said. 'And don't loose her dry or I'll break your head.'

John took the bow which, to me, looked enormous – the middle of the bow was as thick as my wrist. It was a proper war bow, not like the light bows I'd shot. A good war bow of Spanish yew was worth, well, about as much as a fine rondel dagger.

John took it, tested the string, and then he took up an odd posture, almost like a sword stance, pointed the bow at the ground and raised it, drawing all the while.

He didn't get the whole draw. I was no great archer, but I knew he should have pulled the string to his cheek and he only got it back to his mouth, and even then he was straining. He grunted, exhaled and let the string out gradually.

'Too heavy for me, master,' he confessed.

The old man took an arrow from his belt and turned to face the butt. He took his bow back the way a man might receive his wife back from a guardian at the end of a long trip. His right hand stroked the wood.

Then he seized the grip, pointed the bow down as John had, lifted it and loosed his arrow in one great swinging motion. His right hand went back almost to his ear, and the arrow sang away to bury itself in the butt – it was no great shot, yet done so effortlessly as to show mastery, just as a goldsmith or cordwainer might do some everyday craft so that you'd see their skill.

An armourer once told me that any man might make *one* fine helmet, but that a master armourer made one every day just as good.

At any rate, the master archer watched his arrow a moment. 'You know how to shoot,' he admitted to John. 'Have your own bow?'

'No,' John confessed.

The old man nodded. Spat. 'Armour?' he asked.

'No,' John said.

'Sword?' he asked.

'No.' John was growing annoyed.

'Buckler?' the old man pressed on.

'No!' John said.

'Rouncey?' the old man asked. 'I am only taking for a retinue. We ride.'

'No!' John said, even more loudly.

The old man laughed; it was a real laugh, and I liked him instantly. He laughed and clapped John on the shoulder. 'Then you shall have to owe me your pay for many days, young man,' he said. 'Come and I'll buy you a cup of wine, then we'll go and find you some harness.'

'I'd like to come to France,' I said.

He nodded. 'Can you pull a bow?' he asked.

I hung my head. 'Not a war bow,' I admitted. 'But I can fight.'

'Of course you can. God's pity on those who cannot. Can you ride?' he asked.

'Yes.'

That stopped him. He paused and turned back. 'You can ride, boy?' he asked.

'I can joust. A little,' I admitted. 'I can use a sword. My father was a knight.' The words came unbidden.

'But you have no gear.'

I nodded.

He looked at me. 'You are a big lad, and no mistake, and if your hair is any sign of your fire, you'll burn hot. I misdoubt that my lord will take you as a man-at-arms with no arms of your own, but you look likely to me. Can you cook?'

Here I was, being measured as a potential killer of men, and suddenly I was being asked if I could cook. I could, though.

'I can cook and serve. I can carve. I know how to use spices.' I shrugged. It was true enough.

He reached into his purse and handed me flint and a steel. 'Can ye start a fire, lad?'

'I could if I had dry tow, some bark and some char,' I said. 'Only Merlin could start a fire with flint and steel alone.'

He nodded and pulled out some charred linen and a good handful of dry tow.

I dug a shallow hole with my heel because of the wind and gathered twigs. I found two sticks and made a little shelter for my bird's nest of fire makings, and laid some char cloth on my nest of tow. Then I struck the steel sharply down on the flint, with a piece of char sitting on the flint. I peeled minute strips of metal off the face of the steel with the flint – that's really what a spark of metal is, as any swordsman can see, just a red-hot piece of metal, too small to see. A few sparks fell on my charred linen and it caught. I laid it on my nest and blew until I had flame, and laid the burning nest on the ground and put twigs on top.

The old man put out my fire with one stomp of his booted foot. 'Can you do it in the rain?' he asked.

'Never tried,' I admitted.

'I like you,' he said. 'You ain't a rat. Too many little rats in the wars. If I take you to France to help cook, you'll still get to France. Understand me, boy?'

'Will I fight?' I asked.

He smiled. It was a horrible smile. 'In France, everyone fights,' he said.

So I went to France as the very lowest man in a retinue: the cook's boy.

It's true. In Italy, they still call me Guillermo le Coq – William the Cook. It's not some social slur. When I started fighting in Italy, I was riding with men who could remember when I was their cook's boy.

Because in France, everyone fights.

We're almost to Poitiers, so hold your horses. I went and said goodbye to my sister. She wanted to be a nun, but we were too poor – convents required money for women who wanted to take orders – and the Sisters of St John, the women who served with the knights, were very noble indeed, and didn't take women without more quarters of arms than my sister would ever be able to muster. But they were good women, for all that, and they accepted her as a serving sister, a sort of religious servant. It was low, but so was the rank of 'cook's boy'. I was lucky I wasn't visibly branded a thief; she was lucky she wasn't spreading her legs in Southwark five times a day. And we both knew it.

Before I saw her, the lady of the house came in person. I gave her my best bow and the sele of the day, and she was courteous. She spoke beautifully. She was the daughter of one of the northern lords, and she spoke like the great aristocrat she was.

'Your sister has been grievously misused,' the lady said.

I kept my eyes down.

'She has a real vocation, I think. And my sisters and I would, if certain conditions were met, be delighted to accept her.' She honoured me with a small smile.

I bowed again. I was a convicted felon and my sister was a

raped woman. A gentleman knows, but among peasants, rape is the woman's fault, isn't it? At any rate, I had the sense to keep my mouth shut.

'It is possible that you will, ahem, improve yourself,' she said, her eyes wandering the room. 'If that were to happen, with a small donation, we would be delighted to accept your sister as our sister.' She rose. 'Even without a donation, I will make it a matter of my own honour that she is safe here.'

I bowed again.

The lady's words – and her unsolicited promise on her honour – are probably what prevented me from murdering my uncle on the last night I was in England. Before God, I thought of it often enough.

Her suggestion fired my blood and helped set me on the road to recovering from the darkness that surrounded me. Remember, gentles, I had lost my girl, my sister's honour and my own.

I had nothing and I *was* nothing. Brother John was right: I'd have been a sneak thief in days.

But the lady gave me an odd hope, a sense of mission. I would take a ransom in France and buy my sister grace.

My sister had recovered some in three days. She was sorry to see me go, but truly happy to be staying with the sisters, even as a servant. She managed to embrace me and wish me well, and gave me a little cap she'd made me of fine linen, with the cross of her order worked into it. She saved my life with that cap. It may be the finest gift I ever got. At the time, I was so happy to hear her speak without whimpering that I paid it no heed.

At the gate, there was a Knight of the Order chatting with the porter. He smiled at me. He was one tough-looking bastard, with a tan so dark he looked like a Moor, a white line from his brow across one eye and across his nose. He wore a black arming coat with the eight pointed cross-worked in thread and black hose. I bowed.

'You must be Mary's brother,' he said.

I bowed again. 'Yes, sir.'

'She says you go to France. To war.' He fingered his beard.

I nodded, awestruck to be talking to one of the athletes of Christ. 'I want to be a knight,' I said suddenly.

He put his hand on my head and spoke a blessing. 'Fight well,' he said. His eyes had a look, as though he could see through me. 'May the good shepherd show you a path to knighthood.'

We sailed for France in a ship so large I could have got lost in the holds. The ship was assigned to Lord Stafford and some young men-at-arms. John had two doublets, a fine fustian-covered jack, a dented basinet and a pair of boots that were like leather hose. His sword was rusty and his buckler wasn't as nice as the one my uncle had robbed me of.

I spent all my time on the boat fixing his gear. I'd done some sewing – how John, who'd been a monk, had avoided sewing is a mystery to me, but he wouldn't sew a stitch. I begged needles and thread from some of the women. All the older archers had women –some were mere whores, but others were solid matrons, married to their archers. Two were dressed like ladies. A master archer after Crécy might have more money than a moneylender and could dress his lady as well as many knights.

Any gate, I was pretty enough, and by the standards of a company of archers, I had excellent manners, so they cosseted me and loaned me needles and thread, and I mended everything John owned. Our first night in Gascony, I took his helmet to an armourer – the castle was ringed with them after so many years of English armies coming – and begged the use of the man's anvil and a mushroom stake. You don't need a hammer to take the dent out of a helmet.

The armourer was kindness itself. I've often noticed that people will be friendly to the young where they might be stiff to an older man. So he fed me some cheap wine, and watched while I unpicked the liner of the helmet, laid it aside (filthy, ill kept and needing repair) and carefully bashed the dent against the stake – from the inside.

I couldn't budge the dent.

Finally the Gascon laughed, took the helmet from me, and re-moved the dent with three careful whangs against the stake.

'You know how,' he said. 'You just aren't strong enough.'

It's true. I'd watched a master armourer in Southwark take the dents out of a knight's helmet once, so I knew the technique. I just didn't realize that the simple motions required great strength and technique – there's a lesson there for swordsmen, if you like. The armourer made it look simple. Like the master archer, eh?

Since the cheap wine was free and he fed me, I sat in the Gascon's forge and repaired the liner, mending the places where the raw wool of the padding was leaking, washed it and hung it by the forge fire to dry. There truly are Christians in the world, and I mention him to

God every time I hear Mass. He and his good wife fed me a dozen times during the weeks we were in Bordeaux.

My point is that I got John's kit into better shape, and the master archer, Master Peter, saw it. That was good.

The cook was called Abelard the Deacon. The word in the company was that he'd been ordained a deacon as a young man, and they'd cast him from his order for gluttony. In truth, he wasn't fat like other cooks; he must have had some curse on him, for he ate and ate and never gained. He was tall and very strong, and I saw him fight and he was a killer. He was like a monster – no skill, but lots of strength. Sometimes, they are the most dangerous men.

He was also well read, and when he found that I had read some of the words of the great Aquinas, my status changed more than it would have if I could have arrayed myself in new armour. He became my protector against archers with a tendency to young men, and against men who simply like to haze the young, and against my true foes, the squires.

By the sweet saviour, they were my first enemies. I hated my uncle, but he was just a sad sinner, a miser and a rapist. The squires were my age, nobly born and very full of themselves. Their leader, Diccon Ufford, had made a campaign the year before with his knight, but the rest of them were as green as I was, and eager to improve their status by putting themselves above someone else. I was just about the only man they could be lord of, as the archers treated them with the scorn they richly deserved. To be fair, Diccon scarcely troubled me, but his lieutenant in all things was Richard Beauchamps, and he never tired of humiliating me.

As the cook's boy, it was my place to do whatever was asked of me, and I found that the squires devoted themselves to using all my time. My second night in Gascony, I was kicked awake to curry horses. The next night I cooked for my Lord and the captain of our retinue, Thomas de Vere, Earl of Oxford. I didn't try to play on our relation. Richard Beauchamps was the lord's squire; when I went to cut the beef, Richard took the knife from my hand and kicked me.

'That for your impudence, bastard!' he said. 'Carving is for gentles.'

I watched him for a moment – I was proud of my control – as he failed to carve the beef. My hands were shaking with anger, but I made myself take deep breaths.

'Then perhaps you'd like me to show you how to do it?' I said in my mother's best accent.

The Earl was watching us, and his squire couldn't really attack me in public, so he turned.

'You're dead,' he said. 'I'm going to beat you blue and make you beg me to stop.'

I smiled.

War.

Our war amused the archers. I'd love to say they all backed me, but they didn't. Most of them were twenty-five, or even older, and the affairs of boys were beneath them. Even John, who liked me and was truly grateful, then and later, for my work on his kit, still thought that any bruises I got from boys my own age were either deserved or part of growing up.

Try the organized hatred of six older boys.

When I carried a tray, I was tripped. When I curried a horse, dirt was poured on its back. When I cooked, hands would pour pepper and salt into my dishes. When I built a fire, people would piss on it.

The archers found it funny, in the way mistreating a mongrel dog can become funny.

I may have red hair and a temper, but I had never been the scapegoat, the Judas, before. I was usually top boy or close enough. I didn't have the right armour for the contest, and a bitter month passed while I grew some.

It wasn't the beatings. Richard beat me three times, I think. He lacked the pure evil to kill or maim me, and he wasn't as vicious as my uncle. But the endless hatred had an effect.

I never seemed able to get one of them alone, yet they quite regularly got me, three or four to one. The worst was when I was bathing. They took my only set of clothes and burned them. Then three of them beat me very thoroughly, leaving me bruised and naked by the river. Walking naked through a military camp is a good way to make yourself known to a great many men, let me tell you. I was the laughing stock of the camp for two days.

John found me clothes – too big to fit, dirty and full of lice.

I survived.

But I yearned to turn the tables, though I never seemed to manage it. I lay in wait for one of them and he never came to water his knight's horse, even though he'd done it three days in a row. I put salt in their food, and they either didn't notice or I hadn't used enough.

It was the cook who saved me. He liked to talk, so we talked, and after a few doses of Aquinas he started to protect me. Just in small ways.

'Two boys seem to be waiting under the eaves of the armoury tent,' he said one evening.

'A mysterious hand tried to salt the goose,' he mentioned the next day.

'I found a squire with no work to do, so I made him wash pots,' he grinned a week later.

At the same time, I had found something to love, and that was riding. I had never owned a horse. Indeed, I'd scarcely learned to ride, even while learning to joust – like many young men, it was enough to stay on through the course. I laugh now at what I thought was good riding, back as a boy in London.

Master Peter purchased me a small riding horse. I'll never know what the old archer saw in me, but he saw something – that horse cost him nine silver pennies of Gascony. I rode every day, every-where I could – I remember fetching six leather canteens full of water on horseback, once, to the vast amusement of the archers.

The truth is that, when I tell this tale, I make my life sound hard. The other boys annoyed me, and sometimes they hurt me, but I was also outside, riding, cooking, getting taught how to use a sword and a spear. The knights – men I worshipped the way the ancient men worshipped their gods – were not distant beings. They were right there with us, and every day I had a chance to speak to one or other of them.

My favourite, of course, was our own Earl of Oxford. He was a great lord, but he had the common touch. He spoke to the older archers as if they were comrades, not inferiors, and he ruffled my hair and called me 'Judas', which may sound harsh, but it was bet-ter than 'bare arse', which is what most of the men called me after the river incident. We were in his contingent; Peter was one of his sworn men, and we all wore the Oxford badge on our red and yel-low livery.

Like many boys, I was in a constant state of anxiety about my status. Technically I was a cook, not a soldier, and I was worried I would be left behind – either when the army marched or when the day of battle dawned. By blessed St George, what a pleasure it might be to be left behind for a battle! Bah. I lie. If you are a man-of-arms, it is in arms you must serve, and that was my choice. But fear of being left behind made me work very hard, both as a cook and as an apprentice soldier. I was big, even then, and I would walk out into the fields below the castle to cut thistles with my cheap sword, or to fence against a buckler held by my friend the cook.

One day – I think we'd been in France about two weeks, and the war horses were getting the sheen back in their coats after the crossing – I was cutting at the buckler, and Abelard was cutting at mine. This is a good training technique that every boy in London knows by the time he is nine years old, but I've never see it on the Continent. You cut at your companion's buckler and he, in turn, cuts at yours. The faster you go, the more like a real fight it can be, but relatively safe, unless your opponent is a fool or a madman. The point is that you *only* hit the opponent's shield.

We were swashing and buckling faster and faster, circling like men in a real fight. Abelard was two fingers taller than me and broader, but fast. He was trying to keep his buckler away from me, and I was trying to close the distance.

Suddenly there was the Earl of Oxford and half a dozen men-at-arms with hawks on their wrists. The Earl motioned to Master Abelard, who came and held his stirrup, and the earl dismounted.

'So, Master Judas,' he said. 'Those who live by the sword will die by the sword, or so it says in the Gospels.'

I bowed and stammered. I'd like to say that I held my head up and said something sensible or dashing, but the truth is that I stared at my bare feet – my dirty bare feet – and mumbled.

'He's very good, my lord.' Abelard didn't seem as tongue-tied as I was. It was also the first time anyone had told me I was good with a sword. I'd had suspicions, but I didn't *know*.

The Earl took Abelard's buckler and drew a riding sword from his saddle. 'Let's see,' he said.

I bowed and managed to stammer out that he did me too much honour – in French.

The Earl paused. 'That was nicely said. Are you gently born?'

I bowed. 'My father was a man-at-arms,' I said. 'My mother—' I must have blushed, because several of the men-at-arms laughed and one shook his head. 'No better than she needed to be, I suppose.' He laughed.

It must be hard to be bastard born. Luckily, I'm not, so I felt no resentment. And, praise to God, I was intelligent enough not to claim to be a distantly related de Vere then and there.

De Vere waved his sword. 'Show me some sport, young Judas.' He stepped in and cut almost straight up into the edge of my buckler. For a straight, simple blow, it was shrewd, powerful and deceptive all in one.

I made a simple overhand blow, and he pulled the buckler back the way boys do when they make the swashbuckle into a game. I stepped with my left foot and caught it as it moved.

Then I ducked away to the left, moving forward instead of back – another trick London apprentices use to deceive each other. Backing away is one way of fooling an opponent – closing suddenly is a better one.

He stepped back and cut from under his buckler on the left side, again catching my buckler perfectly with a strong, crisp blow.

We were close, almost body to body, so I sprang back and wind-milled my cheap sword, cutting the steel boss on Abelard's buckler with a *snack*. I pivoted, he pivoted, and he thrust – faster than a striking snake – and caught my buckler as I pulled it back. We were going quite fast by then, and if you are a swordsman, you will know that I had a complicated choice to make in half a heartbeat. We were close, and if I stepped forward and he did the same, I'd miss my blow. If I sidestepped and he stepped back, I'd miss my blow.

I was fast when I was young, so I stepped slightly off the line that we were moving on – circling a quarter step, you might call it – then passed forward fast and cut straight up – his blow thrown back at him.

Snick. A smart blow into the lower rim. I was quite proud of it, as he stepped forward too late, trying to get the buckler inside my blow. I had scored a real hit on a trained man. I slipped to the right with another turning step that John had taught me, pulled back the buckler, and the Earl's counter-cut—

Missed the buckler altogether and cut my left arm above the wrist.

At first all I felt was the cold, and the flat impact of the blow on my forearm. I laughed, because any hit to the body loses your companion the bout.

Then the pain hit. It was not a sharp pain, but rather a dull pain, and when I glanced down, I was terrified to see the amount of blood coming out of the cut—a long, straight cut, almost parallel to my arm, from just above the wrist to the elbow.

In hindsight, friends, I was the luckiest boy alive. The cut landed along the length of the bone, and the Earl, a trained man, pulled much of it, no doubt in horror. But at the time, all I saw and felt was the welling blood and the pain.

He was with me in a moment, his hand around my waist. 'Damn me – your pardon, boy.'

Abelard had his own doublet unlaced, and now he pulled his shirt over his head and wrapped my arm before I could see any more. The white linen turned red. I sat down. Men and horses moved around, and I had trouble breathing. I remember looking out to sea and wondering if I would die. Then my vision narrowed. My mouth began to taste of salt, as if I was going to vomit. One of the Earl's men-at-arms had a horn cup of wine, which he held to my lips. He was ten years older than me, round faced, with twinkling eyes.

'Drink this, lad,' he said.

I must have been dazed as I said something hot, like, 'I'm no lad! I'm William Gold!'

He smiled. 'I'm John,' he said. 'I meant no offence to such a puissant warrior.'

That's all I remember. If I passed out, which I doubt, it wasn't for long. It was my first wound, and I took it from Thomas de Vere, Earl of Oxford. Nothing better could have happened for my prospects, because he was a debonair, chivalrous knight, and by wounding me, he felt he was in my debt somehow. The world is full of men-at-arms who would have cut my arm and told me it was my own fault. In many ways, that wound was the foundation of my career. The joke is, it was so slight it didn't even leave a scar.

The life of the young is never a straightforward progression. So just after the Earl wounded me and his men-at-arms began to speak well of me, with immediate consequences for their squires, someone came to the army from London. I never knew who it was, but I think it was yet another squire from the Earl of Warwick's retinue. Whoever the bastard was, he spread the word that I had stolen a valuable dagger and been branded.

Well, you are all soldiers. There's nothing soldiers hate more than a thief – even though, if the truth be told, we're all thieves, even the most chivalrous among us, eh? We kill men and take their armour; we loot houses and take convoys; we steal on a scale no poor man could imagine.

Aye, but we despise a thief.

Consequently, the squires, after a week of forced respect, had a new reason to hate me. And they were loud. They harassed me morning and night. I was 'thief' at campfires and 'thief' in the horse lines. Men who had liked me stopped speaking to me, and men who had been indifferent cheered when three of the squires caught me and beat me.

I'd love to say that someone – the Earl, perhaps – came and saved me from that beating, but no one did.

Of course I fought back! I left every mark I could on those pop-injays, those pampered rich boys. I blackened their eyes and broke one blackguard's nose. But at odds of three to one, I was hard put to accomplish much, and sometimes, if they took me by surprise, I wouldn't even get to land a blow.

I had two cracked ribs, my nose was broken so often it lay almost flat and my left hand was swollen like a club. I couldn't be on my guard all the time, though I tried to be wary.

I went to Mass with John, where I knelt on the stone floor and said my beads and looked at the paintings. I knew more Latin than the priest, but he said a good piece about Jesus as a man-at-arms.

John rose from his knees. 'See you at camp,' he said.

'You won't stay?' I asked.

'I had a bellyful of this crap as a monk,' he replied. 'I've prayed enough for my entire life.'

I hadn't. The chapel was beautiful, decorated with the pillage of a generation of English raids and victories, I suppose, and it was the finest church I'd ever been inside to pray. I felt safe, and happy. After Mass, I went and said my confession – only the second time, I think, that I had made a private confession, but soldiers are honorary gentlemen, in many ways.

I was unwary walking out the door, and four of the squires were waiting for me. They pulled me down immediately – I didn't even land a blow – and Richard sat on my chest while another sat on my legs.

The bastard on my chest grinned and breathed his foul breath all over me. He was wearing Oxford's colours.

'Only criminals need to spend so much time in church,' he said. He bounced a little, but he didn't hurt me much – yet. Except, of course, that his bouncing moved my ribs.

This was going to be bad.

I cursed myself for a fool, letting my guard down. At the same time, I felt curiously absent. What kind of man attacks you just after you are shriven?

Best to get it over with.

'Is your breath so foul from sucking a pig's member?' I asked.

He turned so red I thought he might explode. He began to beat me – one fist and then the other, right to my unprotected face. There was nothing I could do: left, right, left, right.

I remember it well.

And then God sent me a miracle.

Like a mother cat picking up a kitten, the priest grabbed Richard by the neck and lifted him with one hand, then hit him so hard he broke Master Richard's jaw. I heard it go.

The other squires ran, but Richard just lay there and moaned.

The priest kicked him.

He screamed and moaned.

The priest looked at me. 'Go with God, my son,' he said.

It didn't raise my popularity with the squires. But that didn't matter as much as it might have, because we'd spent six weeks or more in Gascony, and suddenly the Prince was ready.

I'd seen him at a distance, with Sir John Chandos and other famous men, all instantly recognizable to a boy like me by their arms and their horses. For me, seeing Chandos was like seeing Jesus come to earth. But the Prince – by God, messieurs, the Prince was one of the best men I ever saw: tall, debonair and as full of *preux* as any man could be. Too few men of high station have the bearing and power to maintain their status in the eyes of the world, but the Prince looked just as he was – one of the most powerful lords in all the world, whether by strength of arms or strength of lands.

At any rate, the Prince did not ride out to visit the archers every day, so we seldom saw him, but at about the end of June, rumours began to fly that we were to march against the Count of Armagnac, because the French King and his army were busy in the far north, facing the famous Duke of Lancaster, our finest captain. Now, I could tell you that we didn't know anything about the Prince's plans, but I'd be a liar, because in an army of 5,000 men, in which 2,000 are men-at-arms, every man knew what the Prince intended, and his plans and stratagems were discussed round every campfire and in every inn. God help me I, too, criticized his plans. There is no critic louder than an ignorant fifteen-year-old making his first campaign.

I therefore knew that the King, that is, King Edward, had decided to knock the Count of Armagnac out of the war. The whoreson count had promised to become the King's man, but he had reneged, and we were going to make him pay – or so all the older men said. And certes, the Prince had hit Armagnac hard in the fall, so it seemed likely we'd march on Armagnac.

But then, as so often passes in war, nothing happened.

Aye, comrades. For weeks. We saw the ships sail in from England with more arrows and more livery coats – I finally got one of my own – and we practiced, and I cooked better meals. Some of the Gascon lords who had ridden in took their retinues and went raiding. I stopped bathing in the river to avoid being beaten or losing my new coat, which I had tailored to fit tight, like a knight's jupon.

And then we marched.

Chapter Two

When we marched, it was like a bolt of levin had flashed across the heavens and illuminated the landscape. Every man in Bordeaux – about 7,000 men – marched together, and we moved fast, heading north to Bergerac in the Dordogne. We were there before anyone could say where we were headed, and suddenly I learned a whole new set of lessons about finding firewood when 6,000 other men were doing the same; about finding a chicken, when 6,000 other men wanted one; about feeding my horse; about having time to sew; about finding a place to sleep. John was no help – he was as raw as I was myself. Abelard, on the other hand, was the consummate veteran, and he could spot a dry barn with a solid loft across six leagues of hills, predict it as being near the army's eventual halting place and ride there cross country to set his camp. Although Abelard held no rank above that of 'cook' with de Vere's retinue, he made himself indispensable by riding with the outriders, choosing a camp and arranging for the Earl's great pavilion and all the lesser tents. He worked hard and I rode after him, and found that I was riding double the distance the army travelled. I became Abelard's messenger boy, which suited me, as it meant I came in daily contact with the Earl and sometimes rode along with his men-at-arms or squires.

I have to laugh, even now. Listen – boys torment each other when there's nothing else to do and no Frenchmen to fight, but once we were on the march, that ill-feeling was mostly gone. You think I should have harboured a grudge? Perhaps. But to tell the truth, I was far more afraid that the Earl would leave me with the baggage then I was of the squires.

A few of them felt differently, though, as you'll hear.

And I admit that when I saw Richard riding with a bandage on his jaw like a nun's wimple, I mocked him.

At any rate, when we arrived at Bergerac after five days rapid marching, I slept for most of day, rose, ate Abelard's meal and slept again. It wasn't until our third day in Bergerac that I pulled my weight or worked, because I was so tired and awestruck by the cook's constitution. He was made of iron. He could ride all day and cook all night.

After our lightning fast ride across Gascony, we stopped and waited.

The waiting was brutal. And dull.

By then, I was wary all the time. And after sleeping a long time and working a day or two, I was aware of a certain watchfulness from the squires. I hadn't won them over. Most of the oldsters had something better to do than work on me, but the younger ones – and the fools, and Richard, who had had his jaw broke – weren't going to change their minds, and the oldsters weren't going to stop them. I could feel it. Abelard warned me – twice, in just so many words – that they meant me harm.

I took what precautions I could, but I couldn't hide for ever. We were still in Gascony, but I wore my sword all the time, and my jack when I could get away with it, and I did more work on horseback than any other boy my age.

Richard Beauchamp watched me like a hawk watched a rabbit.

I'd like to sound brave, but I was terrified, and the waiting made it worse. I was recovering from two broken ribs and a number of other, lesser injuries, and I was tired of pain. Pain wears you down – pain when you lie down hurts affects sleep, pain when you are awake affects your work – and lying on the ground makes everything worse.

The rapid march had seemed so decisive, and all the raw men like me thought it presaged a battle. We truly were fools – all the old archers of twenty-five said we might march all summer and merely burn a castle or two, but we were in a constant state of excitement. So every day that we awoke under the ancient, mouldering walls of Bergerac and had no orders was a day of torment. The speculation ran wild. We were going to await the King, from England. We were going to fight Armagnac. We would march home. The King of France was coming for us.

Nothing happened. And with the waiting came increased work, because foraging grew harder every day. Each day we had to ride farther to find wood, to 'buy' provisions from well-armed, well-warned peasants who hated us. Supposedly, we were *their* army, but ask a peasant who's just had all his winter meat stolen how he feels about his protectors.

It was the fourth or fifth day of waiting, and I was out with Abelard, looking for food. We came to a farmstead with a dozen outbuildings and we could hear screaming.

The peasant was dead. He'd been prosperous, and he was lying face down in his own yard with a spear through him.

Abelard's face grew hard. 'I mislike this,' he said. 'The Prince hangs men for this. Let's be away.'

Still he hesitated. If the peasant was dead, his whole farm – a very rich farm – was open to us.

You know how war is, messieurs?

I was learning very quickly.

Abelard dismounted in the yard, and I'll give him this, he went to see the peasant and tried his body, but the man was dead.

Peter went towards the nearest barn – a great stone barn that two men could have held against an army.

I went towards the sound of the screams.

Around the side of the house I saw the horses, and I knew them immediately. I recognized Richard Beauchamp's horse and I knew Tom Amble's, too. Both squires. The other horses were archers' rounceys like mine.

It has always been one of my virtues – or vices, whichever you like – that when I'm afraid I go forward. I saw their horses and I heard the screams, and I went forward.

One of the archers was raping a middle-aged woman.

She was screaming, and the other archer was mocking her.

The two squires weren't even watching. They were eating a ham, consuming it with the lust only a sixteen-year-old boy can bring to eating.

I stood frozen for perhaps as long as it took my heart to beat three times.

What is it that makes a knight?

I ran forward and I kicked the rapist – in the head. My feet were lightly shod, but I put him down.

The other archer was a Gascon – not a big man, but an old, canny one. He didn't waste any time. He drew his sword.

I whirled so I could see all three of them. 'So, Master Richard, this is your gentility? Killing our own peasants and raping their wives?'

39

Until I opened my mouth, I doubt the archers even knew I was English. They probably thought I was the son of the house, or some such.

Beauchamp swallowed a mouthful of ham. 'Look who it is? The Judas thief.' He laughed. 'Look, we have ham and a cook to make it for us – and no priest to come and save his worthless arse.'

I watched the Gascon archer. I was canny enough to know that he was the most dangerous of the lot of them.

Richard drew his sword.

Tom Amble was one of the oldest squires. He'd tripped me once or twice and had laughed when I was the butt end of a prank, but he'd never hurt me, and the look on his face betrayed his intense confusion. 'He's English,' he said, as if that made my person sacrosanct.

'Don't be a half-wit, Tom. If he blabs, we could swing for it.' Richard didn't seem unduly moved by the murder he was about to commit, and he wasn't about to charge me. In fact, he was circling quickly to get between me and the farm gate.

I retraced two steps until I had a wall at my back, then drew my sword.

Tom, bless him, just stood there.

The Gascon's eyes narrowed. 'We will have to get rid of the body,' he said, with Gascon practicality.

Then he started to edge to my right. As he passed the corner of the house he gave a little jump and went down. Just like that.

Abelard emerged from the shadow of the stone barn.

Richard Beauchamp went white. Abelard was a low-born man and not a man-at-arms, but everyone knew him and he had the ear of the Earl. Nor was he the kind of man to allow himself to be killed in a fight at a barn.

'Cover the poor woman,' Abelard said. 'Sweet Christ, masters, do none of you care a shit for your souls?' He smiled and took a step forward. He smiled because he didn't care a fig seed for his own soul. Or for women.

Amble went to throw his cloak over the woman, and Abelard waited until he'd done it, then placed a knife at his throat as he rose.

'Now, gentles,' he said.

The Gascon said, 'Fuck,' quite clearly in English. He could see how the whole thing was going wrong. He was a veteran and he didn't want to die in a farmyard, so he threw his sword down in the manure heap.

Amble was protesting his innocence.

Abelard the Deacon shrugged. 'Put up, or take what I have to give,' he said to Master Richard.

'You always seem to have these men to save you,' Richard said. 'The priest, the cook. One day, you won't have one of your lovers around.'

I stood away from the wall. I'd had a minute to compose my speech. 'We could just fight,' I said. 'Just you and me. With all these men watching. Or don't you want to face me unless other men knock me down first?'

Richard shrugged. 'You're a thief and a man-whore. I'm a gentleman. It makes me dirty even to touch you with my fists.'

I was trembling – with fear, shock, anger, who knows? I remember that I could smell the manure in the sun, and the roses; hear the sound of flies on the manure and the woman crying.

'I think you are just afraid to face me,' I said.

He shrugged again and turned to walk away.

Abelard cleared his throat. 'I have a suggestion,' he said. 'You come back and fight him, man to man.' He laughed. 'Or I just take this man under my knife to see the Prince.'

Richard stopped. 'You wouldn't.' He shook his head.

Abelard laughed. 'I'm tempted just to kill this one, to show you what life is like in France. Eh, *boy?*' He rotated the older squire on his shoulder and the young man screamed as his shoulder popped.

Richard Beauchamp frowned and sheathed his sword. 'And when I beat the Judas into a pulp?'

Abelard nodded. 'Then we're all done. You may go and I'll keep my mouth shut.' He rotated the other young man's shoulder and the man squealed. 'But you'd best hurry, if you want to save your friend's shoulder.'

Beauchamp looked at me and shed his swordbelt.

Then he shed his arming coat, and I shed mine.

Abelard let Amble go, and he crawled a few feet, lay by the barn and wretched up his last meal. He was a good fighter and he wasn't injured.

I would love to tell you of how well we fought and how I held him, but he almost had me at the outset. We went for counter holds, as wrestlers do, and in a flash he had my left arm, and he locked it and went to break it.

I didn't know the hold or the lock, and I was desperate, so instead of giving in under his grab, I slammed my right hand into his hated face, palm flat, and broke his nose. Then, because I was a moment from having my arm broken, my filthy fingernails searched for his eyes.

He let go my arm, slammed a short punch into my broken ribs, and we stumbled apart.

Remember that the priest had broken his jaw?

I pounced, despite the pain, stepped in close, took a blow on my shoulder and another on my cheek and punched over his arms into his jaw, using the advantage of my size. I broke it, and he stumbled and threw a clumsy right-handed punch to back me off.

I had fought other boys all my life.

I caught his right arm in my right hand at the wrist and pulled, jerking him off balance so that he stumbled half a step towards me, then I got my left hand up on his elbow and broke his arm with a snap.

He screamed like a cow giving birth, and I dragged him by his broken arm.

Abelard pulled me off him. I hit Beauchamp more than a few times after he was helpless. Now, I'm ashamed of that, but then ...

Then it was as sweet as a girl's kiss.

We rode back to the army, leaving a dead man and a desperately injured woman in a looted house.

That's the way it was.

We never mentioned what had happened in the yard again.

While I heard the truth said many times – that the Prince was waiting for word from Lancaster up in Brittany – I didn't believe it, because I didn't know enough about France to realize how close we were to the Duke and his army. Because the plan – in as much as the Prince had a plan – was that the Prince of Wales and the Duke of Lancaster would march towards each other, join forces and face the King of France, or, if he refused battle, devastate his lands.

Take it as you will, in early August, the Prince held a great council, and there he divided his army. He gave the Lord of Albret – a right bastard, and one of the hardest men and worst knights I've ever known, though I didn't know that then – about 2,000 men, most of the arrayed archers and some of the English men-at-arms and many Gascons. They were to hold Gascony against Armagnac and raid his demesne lands if they could.

The mounted men – the Prince would have no man who was not well-mounted – were to go with the Prince. Nothing was said about leaving cooks behind, or boys. A farrier looked at my little horse and pronounced him fit and ready for war, so I was going to war with my Prince.

It still makes me smile.

We marched the next day. We marched fast – faster, if anything, than we had on the way to Bergerac. I stuck by Abelard, because the looks I got from some of the squires were not just vengeful, but murderous, and we went north to Périgueux, a rich town, part of which was still French, but in territories we considered part of Gascony, and hence ours. We were not allowed to loot, and we paid hard silver for wine, which was growing harder, as no one had been paid for some time.

When we left Perigueux after a day of rest, we moved even faster. I was in the saddle all day, and I remember little except the morning, when I found I had fallen asleep by my horse without taking his saddle off. He was none too fond of me that day, and I felt bad – as bad as being beaten by squires.

We raced across south-western France, and it was all wonderful to me – steep hills, rich farms, often overgrown. A generation of farmers had been destroyed by a generation of war. You could hear wolves at night, and of course the plague had been through not ten years before.

Indeed, as I've heard peasants say a hundred times, you'd be hard put to decide which was worse if you were a Frenchman: the English or the plague.

We emerged from this near-wilderness at the great abbey of La Péruse, a few leagues from Limoges. I won't weary you with details, except to say that when we left Bordeaux I was a raw boy, and by Limoges I was a seasoned campaigner. I could find food and I could make a fire. I could help Abelard choose a campsite, based on local fresh water, wind protection, security and having a place to tether horses – there are a hundred factors that made one campsite better than another. Sometimes the pickings were slim and we all slept on rocks – 7,000 men is a great number, and if they have 15,000 horses, you have a fair number of bodies to feed, water and sleep.

At the abbey, the Prince held a ceremony I had never seen before. He unfurled his banner. It was a formal, chivalric declaration of war, and Sir John Chandos, his standard bearer, held it forth, snapping like three angry leopards over his head. The Prince made a speech about his rights and how just our campaign was.

I felt as if I was going to cry, I was so proud to be there, on horseback, with a sword at my side. Even as a cook's boy. In an army that murdered and raped peasants.

There was nothing chivalrous about what followed. We were now formally at war, in the domain of the King of France. We proceeded with banners unfurled, burning everything as we went. Abbeys, great houses and farms – all were sacked and burned.

It was stunning. I was, to be frank, horrified at first. I watched a dozen archers rape a pair of sisters and leave them weeping – later one of the men told me they were lucky not to have been killed. I saw children cut down for screaming too loudly; older men butchered by laughing Gascon brigands, and nuns stripped naked and sold to a pimp as whores.

Because that's what war is, friends, and everyone here knows what I'm saying.

It was an orgy. The land was rich and untouched, and old soldiers, archers who'd been at Crécy or Sluys, laughed and said they'd never seen the like. We took so much money as we went that when we were ordered to leave the farms and great houses of the Countess of Pembroke – an Englishwoman with holdings in France – we did. We went around them.

We spread across the country like a swarm of locusts, and with us went fire and sword, cutting and burning like a farmer clearing land. We ate what we liked, drank free wine, and forced the women to our will, killing the men. This was the land of the King of France, and the message we left was that he was too weak to protect his own.

Mind you, French peasants are no more foolish than English peasants, and most of them, when they had even a little warning, burned their crops, took their womenfolk and ran for the strong walled towns. But they left their sausages hanging from their roof beams, and we burned their cottages and made our meals from their hoarded savings of food, cooked on their carefully built homes.

When we took them by surprise, with our horses and rapid marching, we got everything.

I'd like to say that I neither stole nor burned, but the only sin from which I was free was rape, and that was only because of my sister.

A boy of fifteen does what the men he's with do. I took what I wanted, and that included Marie, a girl of my age or perhaps a little less. She'd been raped and hurt, and I took her in, carried her on my horse, cleaned her up and then used her myself.

The only difference I can offer is that I fed and kept her.

We were deep in the heart of France by this time. We were shadowed by French knights on horseback – in fact, several times the Earl of Oxford rode out to make them fight, but they slipped away like Turks. We were almost at the Loire – the famous Loire, a name even a boy like me knew – when we sacked a town for the first time.

Here's how we got in. I was far across the fields, looking for a spot to set up camp for the Earl, when I saw dust, which I knew signalled horsemen moving fast. By mid-morning, we learned from some of Warwick's men moving from our right towards the town that the Prince had ordered the town be stormed. I was determined to be there.

Abelard was less interested in the fighting. 'If we can be among the first into the town,' he said, 'we'll be rich.'

I liked the idea of that!

Don't imagine there was an order given or trumpets blared. It wasn't like that at all. We followed some of Warwick's men, and by noon we'd met up with our own Earl, abandoned any notion of camping to the north of the town, and instead were riding at a fast trot along the high road to Issoudun.

Let me note that while my wound and broken ribs had healed, I had no armour, no helmet and a cheap, badly made sword.

An hour after the sun was at its height, or perhaps two, our men started storming the town. They made ladders or stole them from farms, and tried them against the walls, but they were all too short. There was no order at all, and groups of men – ten or twelve strong – rode up to different points along the walls and had a go. The walls looked low, but close up they were too steep, recently refaced. The garrison was shit – too small, and cowardly. I could have held the place with fifty men today, but the French were on the defensive, and I'll wager the castellan didn't think we were serious. Later we heard the Count of Poitiers had stripped the garrison of all its best men for the field army.

We were serious, though.

Abelard and Master Peter met on the road, held a brief conference without the Earl, and suddenly we were galloping to the east, back out into the countryside. It made no sense to me, but as a new boy, nothing ever did, and I was wise enough to put my head down, my heels to my mount and follow them.

We tore down a narrow road, perhaps thirty of us, and ended up in a farmyard. Peter cursed, and we went through a gate and were moving across the fields; I could see the town wall a bowshot away to my left, and I realized what we were doing.

We rode hard. I remember that an archer fell from his horse in a lane, struck his head and was killed.

The rest of us left him and rode on. On and on, around the *faubourg* (the suburbs), then Abelard stiffened like a hunting dog, turned his horse's head and rode for the wall.

There was an apple tree growing in the shade of the town wall, and someone – lazy, or proud of his tree – had left it like a living ladder, right under the wall.

Now when someone has to climb an apple tree in broad daylight to see if the wall above it is occupied, guess who gets that duty?

I went, and so did my bitter enemy Tom Amble, as we were the smallest and lightest.

Abelard shifted my scabbard all the way round so my sword hung like a tail, out of my way for climbing – something any hardened man knows, but I didn't. Nevertheless, I was first up the tree, and I swayed a branch over to the wall and, without thinking too much about it, jumped.

I landed on the wall's catwalk, and it was then I discovered the wall was manned.

Everything seemed to slow to a crawl. Climbing the tree had been a lark – I was going to be first into the town, or perhaps Amble was. Even the jump – a jump that would have terrified me in London – seemed like an adventure. But once my feet were on the wall, it was too far to jump down and a dozen French sergeants were running at me, I had a great deal of time to consider my own mortality and foolishness – and to wonder where Amble had got to.

I drew my sword and got my buckler on my left fist.

Then I had a notion, and I put it into immediate effect. I retreated away from them, all the way to the next tower. That covered my back and caused all of them to pursue me down the catwalk, leaving the area by the apple tree empty.

Even as the first man – they were in no particular order – ran at me, and his sword slammed into my buckler – the first blow aimed at me in earnest during my whole career as a soldier – I saw Amble, hardly a close friend but in that moment the sweetest sight in all the world, leap onto the wall.

Then I was fighting for my life. For the first time.

It never crossed my mind to try and kill any of them. I fought purely defensively for long heartbeats. The wall was only really wide enough for two men, and my back was covered. And from the first, they were looking over their shoulders, because Abelard was the next man on the wall after Amble, and Master Peter followed.

I did well enough, if I may say so. After a long ten heartbeats or so, I chanced a counter-cut at the bolder of my two adversaries. I stepped back and avoided his blow easily, but suddenly I was in the fight, not just defending myself. Remember, I was big – bigger than these men.

I slammed my buckler into the smaller Frenchman's shield, and I probably broke his hand. It's not in the books, but it's a very effective blow, as any London boy knows.

He dropped his guard, and my back-cut caught him in the jaw.

Christ, how he screamed. I was appalled. He seemed to come apart under my blade.

The other man looked over his shoulder, then back at me. He wasn't being backed up by his mates – they were all throwing down their weapons, because Peter, the master archer, had put three feet of ash through one of them with his great war bow, and that was the end of them. My fellow flopped about a bit – I had severed most of his lower jaw.

I couldn't take my eyes off him. He screamed and tried to put his jaw back with his good hand.

Ever seen a kitten dying in the street? Abandoned by its mother, mewing and mewing its pitiful way to death? Why is that so heart-breaking, when a jawless man you've cut down yourself is just a wretched sight?

I didn't wait for help. I cut his throat, and only then discovered I'd bent my worthless sword.

That was all right, though, because now I had a dozen French swords to choose from.

And a town to sack.

We took so much coin out of that town that some of the profes-sional soldiers openly suggested we turn about and march home. I got almost a hundred ecus. For a boy who'd never had three silver coins, it was a staggering amount.

I was, by all accounts, the first man into the town. The Earl came and gave me his hand as a token of esteem. From that sack, I got two suits of clothes, a fine helmet and a French brigantine that was far better than John's. It fit, too. So when I clasped arms with the Earl, I looked like a man-at-arms for the first time.

Of course, I wasn't. I was a cook's boy. But in my mind, I was a great knight. I took several shifts and a fine kirtle for my whore, and she was pleasantly thankful to receive from me the looted goods of another French family, because that's how it was in France that summer. I had good shoes, handsome ones that fit, which I lifted off the corpse of a baker that Abelard killed in the door of his shop. I should have been warned by that incident. The man was protesting – and not very hard – as Abelard stripped him of white flour and fresh bread, so Abelard just cut him down rather than listen to him – if you take my meaning.

Anyway, I took his shoes.

The next day we rode hard, and then we sacked another town. Now men were dropping loot they'd taken earlier to carry better loot.

Peter, my master archer, gave me the best advice of my professional life at Vierzon. We'd just broken into the town – abandoned by the populace, who were cowering in the nearby royal fortress. I had a feather mattress on my back and I was eyeing an ivory inlaid chair I'd just dragged down from the second floor of a burgher's house.

Peter laughed. 'Listen to me, Judas,' he said.

Christ, I hated that name.

I paused. 'Yes, Master?'

'Coin. Only take coin. Best of all, gold. Nothing else is worth carrying.' He smiled.

I went back into the house and found a gold cross, a small gold cup and six more silver ecus. I left the rest.

Listen, some men have fine memories for fights. I myself can remember most of my best passages of arms, and I'll make the rest up if you keep the wine coming – hah! But I remember loot. I remember the Book of Hours I had at the taking of Sienna—

Ah, you fine gentlemen don't care about filthy loot.

But looting is what we do. That, and feats of arms. Listen. If you are born a rich man, you can perform your feats of arms on your family's money. But if you are born poor –and I started my career of arms with no more than the clothes on my back – war can enrich you. Let us not mince words.

At any rate, after Vierzon, we knew the French royal army was close, and we were racing for the crossings of the Loire. My hero, Sir John Chandos, and another captain, Sir James Audley, made a dash for the bridge at Aubigny and met with a detachment of French troops. They won the fight, but lost the race for the bridge. It was a great fight, or so I'm told. A passage of arms. But, militarily, it got us nothing.

The next day we turned east, heading for the coast and a rendez-vous with the Duke of Lancaster, or so we hoped, because the new rumour was that the King of France had 15,000 men.

The following day – perhaps two – we made good progress, then a brave French captain threw a garrison into a small castle right on our marching route, forcing us to take it. The man who commanded the enemy was a famous knight, Boucicault, and he had seventy more knights and 400 professional infantry, so we couldn't march around. Mind you, I didn't know that then, although I suppose I parroted the phrase. We couldn't leave them behind us because they'd have devastated our line of march and killed our stragglers and wounded, stopping us from robbing and burning.

They were the first organized opposition we'd met, and suddenly we became an army, rather than a horde of locusts. Within hours, every man was in the ranks with his own retinue, under the banner of his lord. The Prince formed us in a tight array, and we stormed the town – not in disorganized drabbles, the way we'd taken the last town, but in one overwhelming rush. The walls of Romorantin were in poor repair, and they fell at the first assault, but Boucicault, who wasn't much older than me and had been a fighting knight since he was fourteen, gathered his men into the citadel.

I cooked.

I mention this because I went up a ladder with Master Peter. I don't think I fought anyone, although I remember being afraid when the crossbow bolts started to hit men around me, and fear is very tiring. But after the assault, I got a good ivory, and then Abelard found me and ordered me to go get the fires lit.

Cooking on a hot day in the Loire Valley when insects fill the air, after storming a wall and looting, is truly miserable. And we failed to take the citadel, so that the men who came to eat the food I'd prepared – mutton, a whole pig and a pair of chickens for my lord de Vere – were surly. Several were wounded. The French were no cowards.

I was cursed for undercooked meat and for not having enough wine. Probably for having red hair, as well. Fatigue is the greatest cause of men's anger – fatigue and fear – and any captain knows that the two are the same.

That was a bad night. John came and ate – I'd saved the best for him, and he sneered at it. I even gave him my wine – I saw him as my mentor.

After he'd eaten, he pointed at Mary. 'Bring her here,' he said. 'I want a ride.'

I thought I must have misheard. 'What's that?' I asked.

'Give me your woman,' he said. 'She's too handsome for you. You're just a boy; she wants a man.'

Mary didn't speak any English, but she backed away. It had taken a week for her to start showing herself in camp at all.

The Gascon archer from the affair at the farmyard, a snaggle-tooth villain named Markus, grabbed her. He gave her a squeeze. 'Plenty here for all of us, boy,' he said.

I couldn't think.

I looked around for Abelard.

He wasn't there.

John walked over, grabbed her skirts and hiked them over her hips in one movement, exposing her.

It hit me then.

A few of you know what I mean. For those that don't, you have choices sometimes. Once you make them, they are made. If I let them rape her – fifteen or so men – that was a decision. If I didn't let them, that was another.

I'd like to say to a priest that I couldn't let her be hurt again, but that's not it at all.

The reason was that I wanted to be a knight, not a looter.

And the other reason was that she was mine, not theirs.

I turned, made my decision and acted. I wore my sword, even to cook – think about all the boys you've known. Of *course* I wore my sword to cook.

I didn't go for John. I went for Markus, who didn't expect me.

I drew it back and slammed the round-wheeled pommel into

Markus's mouth as hard as I could, which was pretty hard even then.

I made him spit at least four teeth.

He fell to his knees, and I kicked him as hard as I could.

I'd finished the sergeant in Vierzon. My uncle had left me pretty hard. Perhaps not hard enough to let a fourteen-year-old French whore get gang-raped to death, but hard enough for this.

Markus went down and was silent, and Mary got behind me.

John was looking at the point of my sword.

'Walk away,' I said.

And he did.

I was fifteen and he was twenty-five, and we were no longer friends. Nor was he my mentor any more.

And we both knew which one of us was the cock of the yard, and which one had backed down.

That was a bad night. The next day was worse. The Earl came and asked for volunteers to storm the keep. I volunteered and he turned me down. They went up the ladders three times and failed. We lost good men that day. Our archers swept the walls with their longbows, and the French – brave men, every one of them – came out just as our men reached the tops of the ladders, and threw rocks, shot crossbows and swept the walls clear with partisans and poleaxes.

Abelard was back from wherever he'd been. I told him the tale of the night before and he snorted.

'Listen, boy. These are *soldiers*. If you keep a pretty piece like that in camp ...' He shrugged. 'If you like her so much, let her go.' He looked away. 'If the Earl had taken you to the tower today, they'd have done her while you were gone. Eh *bien?*'

'She'll be done in ten steps if I let her go!' I protested.

He smiled a nasty smile. He looked away and started unloading the two mules he'd acquired, full of sausages and hams and bread. 'If we don't take that keep today,' he said, 'it'll be worse tonight. The boys don't exactly love you, Judas. Why are you making your life so difficult?'

That's not what I wanted Abelard to say, but the truth was that now that we were in France, he was like a different man – a much more dangerous, criminal man. Indeed, I had begun to think of France as a different world, like purgatory, or hell. The world of war.

Mind you, I was richer than I'd ever been, and I had a woman of my own as pretty as a picture of the Virgin, and a fine sword and a horse, so I wasn't complaining. Just trying to learn the rules. Trying to keep a little for myself.

But in some way that is not utterly base, I liked Mary for more than her slender body, her breasts, her soft stomach and what lay under it – or maybe I liked my image of myself as a knight too much. So after everyone snored, I woke her, stole one of Abelard's mules and led her out into the countryside. I got her clear of our picket posts and gave her the mule and a sharp knife.

I'd like to think she made it to Orléans and lives yet, a grandmother who says prayers for my soul. Or perhaps she curses me to hell every night. Perhaps she died a day later, taken by Gascons on the road.

Christ, I hope not. I pray for her still.

The next morning the Earl came and asked for volunteers to storm the tower. I'd been up late, but I volunteered.

He looked at me for as long as a calm man's heart beats three times, and then I knew he'd take me.

Abelard said, 'You're a fool.'

It was my second storming action. If storming Vierzon, with a small, badly led garrison was dangerous, storming Romorantin was insane. The donjon walls were forty-feet high, and every yard there was a French soldier or a French knight, in good, modern armour, carrying a crossbow or a bill.

The knights went up the ladders first. Say what you will about knights, and many hate us, we're not shy. The best-armoured, youngest men went up the ladders first. No one said aloud that we were only a feint. In fact, during the night the walls had been mined, and the Prince thought the mine would collapse one of the towers.

It didn't.

We had two siege towers of our own, full of the best archers in the army. Without them, the whole attempt would have been suicidal. Even so, with thirty ladders going up against thirty different points, and the flower of English archery sweeping the catwalk it was still horrible.

I was perhaps the fifteenth or twentieth man on my ladder. Other men carried it forward and put it up against the wall – it had massive supports, and was very difficult to overturn. We stood in a neat file behind the ladder, waiting for the word to go, while the crossbow bolts and rocks from the walls clanged off men's helmets or killed them stone dead.

I didn't know where to look. For the first time in my life, I thought of running away. One of the Earl's hobilars died at my feet, having received an unlucky bolt *down* through the crown of his kettle helmet. Blood came out of every opening in his body, and he thrashed like a bug on a pin. I raised my eyes and stepped back so as not to see him, and instead I saw an archer fall right off the siege tower behind me, and his head hit a rock in the road and split open like a melon. Bits of him decorated my brigantine.

Just beyond the corpse, I saw Richard Beauchamp, whose elbow couldn't yet be healed, Tom Amble and half a dozen of my former tormenters. Out here in the open at the base of the wall, we exchanged a glance that said it all.

Here, the only enemy was the wall.

Richard shrugged, dismissing me, and went back to watching the wall.

Back behind the siege towers stood the Earl, surrounded by his best men. They weren't hanging back. Far from it. They were waiting for a lodgement – for one of the ladders to score a success.

Then we heard a shout. I turned and saw the first knight on our ladder. He was about twenty-five, in fine armour, a heavy brigantine over good mail, with plate legs and arms and a basinet with a pig's snout, all shining steel from Italy, and over his red velvet brigantine he had a lady's gown. Probably his fiancée's. Such chivalric games were, and are, as much a part of war as raping French farm girls. He wore the gown to show his courage, to flaunt her beauty.

He ran to the ladder. I'd seen him before, but in that moment I realized that he was my de Vere cousin.

He ran to the foot of the ladder and past it.

He got *under* the ladder and began to climb the underside, hand over hand. In full armour. By God, he was strong, and noble. And fast.

It had never occurred to me until that moment to climb the underside of a ladder.

A man-at-arms a few men ahead of me ran to the underside and joined him, and before my head could take control, I was with them. He was, in that moment, my new hero. He was the man I wanted to be.

The first five rungs were easy.

The thing is that on the underside of a ladder, you cannot rest, you have to keep climbing, and in a brigantine and helmet, all your weight is in the wrong places. Everything hangs from your arms. Your legs don't take as much of your weight as they do on top of the ladder.

The strangest thing happened to me about ten rungs up. I suddenly wondered how the hell I was going to get over the wall at the top, since I was under the ladder. It almost panicked me. I couldn't imagine how I was going to do it, and I was now halfway up.

Down on the ground, men were starting up the front of the ladder.

A big stone came and plucked the first two men off, sending them crashing to the ground. That would have been me if I wasn't on the underside. Even as it was, the stone made the ladder bounce.

Another rung.

Another.

How was I going to get around the ladder to go up the wall?

Above me, my cousin, the knight in the lady's gown, and the other climber were faster than I. I watched the young knight.

God, he was good.

Just short of the base of the crenellations, he threw a leg out from behind the ladder, swarmed around it and vanished up it.

The hobilar followed him.

I was ten rungs behind. I didn't know whether they were alive or dead. I don't remember any sound, just the pure fear. The pain in the muscles of my arms. The way my smooth leather soles slipped on the rungs of the new ladder. The sheer distance to the ground.

I couldn't breathe.

And when I looked down, there was no one else on the ladder.

The ladder was resting on wooden hoardings – a sort of wooden catwalk that stuck out from the wall and allowed the enemy to shoot straight down at our assault parties. Most castles had hoardings stored in the donjons, waiting for this day. I was now level with the base of the hoardings – massive timbers that ran from the lower crenellations to the new wooden walls.

In front of me – remember, I was climbing backwards – our archers were visible on the siege towers, loosing onto the French-held wall. It gradually penetrated my head that a man was shouting at me.

He pointed.

I was running out of courage, so I did what you do when you are desperate: I attacked my fear. Remember, it is my blessing and my curse that I go forwards when I am afraid.

I threw one leg around the ladder, the way I'd seen the knight do, got my smooth sole on the outer side of the rung and started to change my weight.

Suddenly I felt the ladder begin to move.

Good Christ.

There was a French sergeant just above me, trying to throw the ladder down. He'd hooked it with some kind of pike, and he was pushing.

I don't remember how I got onto the wall, but I did. He was at my feet, dead, and I was standing on the wall. I must have climbed the last two rungs and jumped, and I still can't muster any recollection of the deed.

He fell on top of the hobilar.

But my heroic, well-armoured cousin had a longsword, four feet long, and he had swept an eight-foot space on the wall and was holding it. His eyes flicked over to me – even through his visor I could see their fierce glitter – and the moment he saw me, he stepped toward me and cut twice, fast as an adder, giving me a clear space. Then I was down on the wall and got my sword in my right hand and my buckler in my left.

Somewhere in the next minute, I took my first real wound. My legs were unarmoured, and someone got in a cut to my right shin. I never felt it. I got one man and threw him off the wall, and I kept Sir Edward's side safe for that minute. There was shouting – cheering – and suddenly the air around us was full of clothyard shafts.

In fact, Master Peter saw me go onto the catwalk, and only then saw that Sir Edward was alive. He shouted the news to one of the Earl's men-at-arms.

This is what it is to be a knight.

The Earl ran, in armour, at the head of his household to the base of our ladder, which men steadied and reset. Then they ran up the ladder – in eighty pounds of plate and mail.

The archers kept us alive. They *poured* arrows into the wall on either side of us, wasting precious shafts that we would need later in the campaign, but the French didn't fancy running that gauntlet just for a taste of Sir Edward's longsword. We were hard pressed, but never by more than two men at a time.

A minute is a long time under such conditions.

There are many forms of courage. We'd both taken wounds, and suddenly Sir Edward stumbled – a chance spear blow to the foot, it proved. He fell to one knee, and the French knight he was facing raised his sword to finish him – I was a heartbeat too far away – and the hobilar, already lying in a pool of his own blood, slammed his dagger hand into the French knight's groin from out of the pile of dead and wounded. The French hacked him to death, but he'd saved my cousin, who got back to his feet.

They prepared a rush.

And the Earl leaped in through the hoarding, his standard bearer right behind him, and speared a sergeant with his poleaxe, roaring his war cry.

I'm not ashamed to say I fell to my knees.

I couldn't believe it.

I almost died, because a Frenchmen couldn't believe it either, and instead of surrendering, he smashed his axe at me. I got my buckler up, pushed to my feet under his blow, and his haft smashed into my helmet. I was stunned, and I made the mistake of throwing my arm around him. He punched me three times as fast as a dog would bite, but even his steel gauntlet made no progress against my coat of plates. I tried to hook his leg.

I could smell his breath, and feel it on my face, because he had no visor.

He kneed me in the crotch.

The Earl's poleaxe slammed into the French knight's helmet.

Both of us fell to the ground, entangled.

It should have been over then, but it wasn't.

The Earl's men-at-arms came up the ladder and cleared the cat-walk, and in the time it takes a nun to say 'Ave Maria', we held two towers and fifty feet of wall. But then young Boucicault led a counter-attack.

I was still breathing like a bull who scents a cow. I had my helmet off, and I was crouching there, bleeding like a stuck pig and panting. One of the men-at-arms shouted, and John – the man who'd served me wine, and who I now saw to have three scallop shells on a black chevron as his arms – ran by, paused and said, 'Get up, William Gold.'

Good Christ. He knew my name.

I followed him. We ran along the wall, which is to say, I hobbled after him, and there were a dozen French knights in excellent harness fighting against the Earl and four of our knights. The catwalk was, as I said, only wide enough for two.

Boucicault was everywhere. I had seldom seen a man fight so well, and I watched him drive the Earl back, blow after blow, thrown so fast that the Earl had trouble getting in a counter-cut. He was bigger and faster than our Earl and, frankly, better.

Oxford fell back, and fell back again, until he was driven onto the hoardings of a small tower, where the flat area widened and all of us could join the fight. Now it was six men-at-arms – and one unhelmeted fifteen-year-old – against two French knights.

Boucicault didn't care. He leaped forward and hacked the Earl down with a great blow of his poleaxe, then stepped forward and blocked John's cut, occupying the space. Another French knight pressed in, and another – we were going to lose the tower.

John was suddenly toe-to-toe with Boucicault. He parried a blow of the poleaxe with his sword held in both hands, and then another, then he pushed in close to wrestle the French knight, and I took the opportunity to ring a heavy blow against the French knight's helmet. He staggered, and John got a hand under the Earl's armpit and dragged him out of the mêlée ...

Leaving me with the French knights.

That was my first fight with Boucicault. I had a good sword and we were the same size, but he was fully armoured and I didn't even have a helmet. He was dazed, and I had a leg wound.

He was trying to regain his balance and I cut at him two handed. He caught my blow high, kicked me between the legs and down I went.

That's what happens when you fight a knight.

You lose.

I rolled on the ground, trying to master my pain, and got my dagger off my hip and blocked an attempt to kill me from above – I had no idea who threw that blow – then I felt a strong hand under my armpits, and I was dragged bodily from the fight.

Behind me, Master Peter was setting the hoardings on fire. It had rained hard for a few days, but that had been a week ago, and now the wood was as dry as kindling. He'd smashed a railing to make splinters, and they caught, and that fire ran across the platforms like a living thing.

The French grabbed their gallant captain and backed away, and the Earl's man-at-arms carried me through the blaze.

In later years, men in Italy asked me why I stayed so utterly loyal. John Hawkwood saved my life – that day and fifty other times. He was a right bastard – the coldest man I ever met, and bound for hell if he doesn't rule it – but he was always good to me, and that day I would have died horribly had he not carried me out of the fire.

While I was failing to beat one of the best knights in France, Peter had decided, like the professional archer he was, that we weren't winning. He set the hoardings on fire to cover our retreat, and we retired from our dear-bought towers and climbed down the ladders, step by step.

The hoardings burned – first where we lit them, then it all caught, and then one of the tower roofs caught fire ...

And by nightfall, Boucicault had to surrender: his hall was burning over his head. We took him and all his knights and soldiers. We treated them well and ransomed the lot. In fact, we fed the lords a fine dinner that night, in the best traditions of chivalry. I helped cook it, despite two wounds and aching balls. Abelard didn't give a shit that I was injured, and said that if I volunteered for foolishness, I could pay the price. I hobbled about all evening in a daze, and went back to my empty blankets to lie down.

There was still light in the sky when a page came looking for me. By name. William Gold.

So I put my now stained livery coat and my best hose on over my filth, washed my face, and followed the page.

Two pavilions had been set side by side to make a great hall of canvas and linen. On the dais sat the Prince and Boucicault and the Earl of Oxford, as well as Sir John Chandos, Warwick, Stafford and the Captal de Buch, Jean de Grailly. The tables in the tent were full of men-at-arms and knights – there was John Hawkwood, well down on the left, and there was my cousin, Sir Edward, sitting just below the dais.

For a moment, it seemed to me I had been summoned to be knighted.

Well, laugh all you like. A boy can dream.

It was *almost* that good.

My enemy, Richard Beauchamp, had summoned me.

He looked like I felt. He had a black eye and two missing teeth, and he could barely talk.

'Gan'ye serf?' he asked.

When you have been at odds with a boy, it can take an effort of will to decide you are *not* at odds. It looked as if he was calling me a serf, but I was sober enough to see that he was hurt, and so it was pretty fucking unlikely that he'd summoned me for casual harassment. Nonetheless, I remember bridling.

Diccon, the senior squire, came by with a platter of roast beef. 'Well fought,' he said as he walked by. Casual. As if we'd always been friends.

Well.

Richard glared at me – or perhaps that was just how he looked in the fading red sunlight.

The page at my side said, 'I think Master Richard is asking if you could carve and serve. Sir.'

I wasn't being knighted.

But I waited on table with the squires, and I wasn't tripped. I carried a wine ewer and served the Prince with my own hands, and I ached with pride. I carved a goose under Diccon's eye. He nodded, satisfied, and went off to see to other things.

Boucicault drank, and the Prince drank, and Oxford drank. Long after dark, I was serving wine – still, to tell the truth, floating on air that I was serving my Prince with my own hands, which were none too clean. Despite the fact that my balls ached and I had pissed blood.

Boucicault looked up from his conversation.

He was the second French knight from the shop. The one who had been with de Charny the day I was arrested.

He grinned.

'I knew you would find a better profession,' he said in French.

The Prince glanced at me, and the Earl looked up. I wanted to burst into tears. Now it would all come out, and I'd be a thief all over again, I thought.

'You know my young Judas?' asked the Earl.

Boucicault raised his cup of wine to me. 'This young squire and I had a passage of arms today, did we not?' he said. 'And I remember him from a tourney in London. The *last* time I was a prisoner of you English.' Everyone laughed. God, I have hated that man in my time, but he spoke for me that day.

The Earl smiled at me. '*Par dieu*, young man. You fought in a tourney in London, and yet you are serving at my table?'

Other men laughed and that was the end of it. I went back to the sideboard, carved a morsel of kidney and put it neatly on a platter for a younger man to carry, and suddenly Richard was there. He took me by the elbow and led me out into the darkness.

Put a cup of wine in my hand.

We sat on a bench.

'Thief,' he said, pleasantly enough.

'Whoreson,' I replied, raising my cup to his.

Diccon came, and Geoffrey de Brantwood and Tom Amble and several other men I don't remember – all boys, then. We ate a quick meal of cast-off beef, and drank good wine. The pages waited on us.

'Why didn't you say you was a de Vere?' asked Diccon, fairly late in the meal.

I've thought of a hundred hot answers and a dozen cold ones, then and since, but I did the boy's thing, and it was the right thing. I shrugged and took another bite of beef.

We took Romorantin, and our march route was clear, but we didn't go far. Two days later we were before Tours. We wanted the bridges over the Loire, and the French wanted to hold the town, which was the biggest we'd tried yet. They got a garrison into it, led by their Marshal, Clermont, and the Count of Anjou.

The Prince put Lord Burghersh in charge of the assault.

It failed.

I cooked. We had fresh, virgin countryside to despoil, and I made a soup of sausages and leeks and some poor woman's carefully hoarded chicken broth. The soldiers gulped it down with fine wines from an abbey cellar.

I was serving my third kettle of the stuff – I liked good copper kettles, still do for that matter. I had paused to loot three matching pots from the ruins of an inn that morning. I made up the soups, cutting vegetables straight into the pots, while the assault went up the walls. I moved my stolen three-legged stool around the fire to avoid the smoke and to have a good view of the attack. The Captal's Gascons were brave, but the walls were high and the defenders were even more numerous than they had been at Romorantin. Burghersh was the Chancellor of England, and while he may have been a competent man-at-arms, he wasn't loved like Oxford, Stafford or the Prince, and that love can get a man one more rung up the ladder, one more push forward onto the wall.

At any rate, I was on my third big kettle of soup, and out of bread, when my cousin appeared out of the smoky, humid evening. He held out a wooden bowl and I filled it.

He sat – on my stool. Well, he was a knight.

He ate, I refilled his bowl, and he ate again. I found him the last – the very last – of the good French bread that Abelard had looted. He devoured it. I doubt he noticed that it was fine ground or white.

'You made all this?' he asked.

'Not the bread,' I admitted.

He laughed, but then his face grew solemn. 'You really are a cook,' he said. 'Lord Boucicault told me – privately – that you were taken in London as a thief.'

'Yes,' I admitted. I started an explanation, but he held up his hand.

'No one here cares,' he said. 'Listen, my squire is being sent back to Bordeaux. He broke both legs falling off a ladder.'

That's falling off a siege ladder, friends.

'I need a squire. And God has sent you to me.' Sir Edward spoke of God as if they were personal friends. Perhaps they were – he was a fine knight.

Abelard appeared out of the falling darkness. 'Are you taking my apprentice cook, Sir Edward?' he asked.

They exchanged a look, and I knew that Abelard had, somehow, made this happen for me.

We didn't take Tours.

What happened instead was not good. The King of France marched to Blois and crossed the Loire to our side. We heard about it from scouts about the hour of matins, and by the end of matins we were packing to move south, abandoning the siege of Tours, if one failed assault can be called a siege.

I didn't understand at the time – in fact, I was bitter that we were retreating – but Marshal Clermont had roughly our numbers inside Tours, and the King had twice our numbers and was coming up behind us. They held all the crossings over the Loire and cut us off from the Duke of Lancaster absolutely, so there was no way we could face them. Thus we turned south, abandoned most of our booty and ran for our lives.

I've heard it made to sound more glorious, but that's how it was. I lost two of my three copper kettles, but not one of my gold or silver coins, which should give you a fine idea of how accurate Master Peter's advice was.

In the suburbs of Tours, I did pick up a donkey. Talk about the miracles of God – a healthy donkey, wandering free, in the middle of a war. I loaded her as much as she could bear with Sir Edward's goods and a few of my own, and we ran south. As a former cook and a provident squire, I foraged food as we went.

We crossed two rivers in a single day.

River crossings are an army's nightmare, and the rivers were high for early autumn. The fords were about four horses wide and stony enough, but the slowness of the crossing made the whole army nervous and caused us to huddle up. By this time, the army had added a train of servants – French boys desperate for food – and whores – French girls desperate for food – and they huddled along with us.

At the second river, the Prince ordered them driven away from the army. This was military routine – we couldn't feed them any more and we were going to move fast. No one questioned it and yet, to me, it seemed the most brutal thing we'd done. We had, in effect, taken these people by force, to show that the King of France could not protect them. Now *we* could not protect them.

Bah, perhaps I should have been a monk. I was glad I'd sent Marie north, because I'd have died in my heart as a knight to drive her away from me with the flat of my sword, as I saw other men – even men wearing the spurs and golden belts – do.

At any rate, we crossed, and when the French appeared to harass our rearguard, Sir John Chandos and a few knights and a hundred archers drove the French right back north up the road.

You may note in this tale that the French always seem fearsome as individuals, but not nearly so *preux* in bodies. It is hard to say why. Man for man, their best knights were better than ours – not the Prince or Sir John Chandos, but most of the rest of ours. They feared our long bows, but I seldom saw a French knight with an arrow in him. I've heard dozens of stout yeoman who've never loosed a shaft in anger tell me that the bent stick won us our territories in France. Perhaps. I was always happy to have the archers close to hand, but fights are won sword to sword. And sword to sword, the French should have been our betters, but they never were.

We were usually fed, often paid, and most nights we got some sleep. The same men led us in the field and ate with us in camp. That wasn't the way with the French, and I think that eating, sleeping and getting paid are fundamental to war.

But then, I was a cook.

We halted at Montbazon, where the French cardinal Talleyrand met our army. He'd been to England, trying to negotiate peace for the Pope, but his bodyguard were all Frenchmen and greedy bastards to boot. Considering how intimately I later came to know part of the papal court, I wish I could tell you that I met Talleyrand, but I didn't. He was closeted with the French or hiding in his rooms.

We sent messengers and scouts west, looking for Lancaster. It was no secret that the Prince was desperate. To the north, the King of France marched to Tours and joined forces with his son, the Dauphin, then turned south after us with four times our number. We retired on Le Haye – that's a military way of saying we moved as fast as we could to get clear of the gathering French force, which wasn't just behind us, now: there were small bands of Frenchmen in every ford and behind every hedge. Abelard took a wound 'foraging'.

I remember this part well, because now I was waiting on tables every night with the commanders. I heard it all – every squire did. The Prince wasn't afraid, but he was deeply worried, and while he tried to watch his words, we all knew how important Lancaster's army – and his reputation and experience – were to us.

But the next morning, when I packed in darkness and left my favourite cup by the fire in my rush to get my knight on the road, the French were coming after us. As we marched out of the south of Le Haye, the French came in from the north. It was that close. Luckily, they missed us, and having marched all night, they halted for a rest, and it was noon before they knew how close we'd come.

We took Chatellerault without too much effort the next day, and the rumour was we'd hold it until relieved by Lancaster – it was a bridge town, and with it in our hands we could whistle at the French and wait for Lancaster to come down from the north. It was a lucky capture, and all agreed we were saved – indeed, that now we held the whip hand.

I curried horses. I had time to help Abelard. I made an early decision not to cut my ties with him or the company of archers. I was proud to be a squire, but I had no friends there. The squires had no love for me. While no one beat me or played tricks now, I had no friends among them. I seldom ate with them, and Richard and I were creeping back towards a fight. It was like a dance – and we were dancing towards a duel. We both knew it, and the other squires knew it, too. Since this was serious – sword in the guts serious – they didn't torment me. They just waited for me to be dead.

At any rate, I kept working with Abelard whenever I had time. We were in the same retinue, and now I knew everyone – not just Abelard and archer John, my former mentor, but John Hawkwood; Peter Trent, the master archer; Sir Edward Cressey, my master, and Thomas de Vere himself. As well as fifty other men – archers and men-at-arms and squires and servants.

Everything was fine, except that Lancaster didn't come. He couldn't. He was the best soldier England ever grew, but he couldn't get his army over the Loire. We waited three days for him, and there was more wine drunk at every dinner in the Prince's pavilion, and by the third night, tempers were flaring and Boucicault, who was still with us, used the term 'trapped' in a sentence.

That night, as I carved some questionable venison, a messenger came in and reported that the King of France was just east of us, at Chauvigny.

All conversation died.

The Prince was wearing black. He didn't always – that's just the sort of crap men say – but that night he wore black with his three white livery feathers embroidered in silk thread on his chest. He was the tallest man in the tent – or perhaps that's just how I remember him. He stood.

'Messieurs,' he said. 'If the King of France is really at Chauvigny,' he looked around. I swear his eyes came to rest on me. He spoke in French, of course. 'If he is at Chauvigny, then we have no choice. We must fight.'

By God, they rose and cheered him.

No one said, 'Christ, they outnumber us four to one.'

No one said, 'Christ, they've cut our retreat, and if we lose, we'll all be taken or killed.'

But certes, I confess that every one of us thought those things.

The next morning, we were up before the cocks. We all knew it would be a desperate battle, and the older men walked around steadying us. Master Peter came and put a hand on my shoulder and told me to fill every bottle I had with water, and that was the best advice I ever received. I had a big leather wine-sack and I filled it with watered wine; I filled four leather pottles with water, and a small cask. Then I loaded the donkey with all the vessels.

Then I got into my brigantine and my helmet. I buckled on my sword and helped my knight arm, which took almost an hour in the dark. I wonder if he was angry at me? I hadn't stowed all his harness well, there was rust on one greave and I got the elbows on wrong and had to take them off and do it again. All while John Hawkwood was bellowing for the Earl's men-at-arms to form.

My master never said a harsh word.

Bless his soul.

I saddled my horse, his war horse and his riding horse, then I fed and watered them. I was so flustered I had to take their bridles off to let them eat. I was doing everything out of order.

I felt the way you young men feel before a fight.

Terrified.

I followed Sir Edward up onto the walls, where we watched the ground to the south and west. As the sun crested the horizon, we could see the French already moving, their army a glittering snake in the hills to the south east. Between us was a range of low hills, heavily wooded, and two good roads (rare, in France), one on our side of the river and one on theirs, with the wooded ridge between them. Look here, friends. We're in Châtellerault. Here, at the top of the triangle. The King of France is here at Chauvigny, ten miles to the south and east, and Poitiers is at the other base of the triangle, ten miles to the south and west. See it? The King is marching on the highway from Chauvigny to Poitiers to cut our line of retreat.

I stood on the walls looking at the terrain while the Prince laid out his plan. He staked everything on the deep woods on the ridge between the river and the road. We could move in those woods, if we were careful and our scouts were good, and the King of France wouldn't know where we were. The Prince hoped to catch the King on his route of march – French armies are slow as honey. We'd cut his army in half and destroy it.

Or die trying.

We marched. For three miles we stayed in the open, on our side of the river. I think the Prince was still interested in avoiding battle, and I know that Talleyrand rode from the Prince to the King of France about the hour the bells rang for matins. At that time, we were west of the river, apparently running for the coast.

But as soon as Talleyrand left us, and his retinue of French knights were well out of sight, our screen of mounted archers found a good ford and we crossed the Clain River. We were all mounted, and we went up the bank and onto game trails in the woods.

The Prince's archers were brilliant at this sort of thing. They posted men at every major junction, even in the maze of trails – apparently, this is what they did when deer hunting with the Prince, when leading him to a prime animal. Our vanguard followed them, and as soon as the van came up to one guide, he'd mount and spur back ahead to rejoin his mates, so that we had a constantly moving chain of guides. The archers had two local men – poachers – they'd taken in the town and promised a fortune. I hope they got it, because they were good guides. One of Hawkwood's rules was always pay your spies, and always, always pay your guides.

When the sun was high in the sky, we were deep in the woods. I was with the Earl's men, and we were in the middle of the column, which was just one cart or two mounted men wide. Diccon, Richard and I took turns watching the baggage animals. We were sure we would fight at any moment, and we expected to emerge from the endless wood at every turn in the trail – on and on it went, and the green grew boring and frightening at the same time.

The carts slowed us. The Gascons under the Captal were our vanguard, because they spoke the language and a few of them knew the terrain, and they crept along behind the Prince's elite archers – crept, and yet outraced us in the main body, so that by an hour after noon we'd lost touch with the Captal's men altogether, which made the Prince curse and Burghersh wince. I know – I was right there, handing out watered wine.

That wood was waterless.

If Sir Edward had been annoyed with me in the early morning darkness, he was pleased with me at the lunch halt. Most of the knights had little water, whilst I could water my horse and his, and give watered wine to a dozen men.

We ate bread and cheese, our reins in our hands, and then we moved on. Even the Prince dismounted, now, to save the horses. Most of the knights took off their leg harnesses, to save weight and energy. Of course, under their leg harnesses they had only wool hose, so the brambles in the woods took their toll, as did the insects.

The sun began to sink in the sky, and it was clear, even to a fifteen-year-old squire, that we were not catching the French army.

Then we heard the cheers.

Sound carried oddly in the woods. We heard cheers in French, and the unmistakable sound of men fighting – swords and spears. On and on.

We tried to hurry.

Men started to push past the carts in the centre of the column, and there was no holding the Prince – he pushed ahead, and all the knights pushed ahead with him. I was on my turn with the pack animals. I wanted to go, but I didn't. I stayed and cursed the men from Warwick's division, who pushed past us and slowed us still further. The sounds of fighting intensified – the cheers grew to roars.

And then ended.

That was the most frustrating thing. There had been a great battle and I'd missed it – I was still in the deep woods with the insects and the baggage carts, just as I had feared all campaign.

That's it, messieurs. The Battle of Poitiers. I was with the baggage. Hah!

You know I wasn't.

And you know we didn't catch the King of France napping, either.

By the time we came up with the main body, it was almost dark, and our army was badly disorganized. The Gascons had caught the rearguard of the French Army and scattered it, capturing some nobles and killing a few hundred Frenchmen. But our Gascons and the Prince, who saw the last moments of the fight, had to retire in front of a French counter-attack, and they chose to retreat into the woods.

Most of us simply lay down where we were and slept.

We were tired, and the Gascons, who'd fought on horseback, were even more tired. The horses were blown, and so thirsty they called and called. There was no water in the woods, except a stream we'd passed several miles back.

Richard, Diccon and I went back to it. It was the first thing we'd ever done together. It wasn't an adventure – in fact, we came to the stream long before we expected, because we were moving at horse speed not cart speed. We let our horses drink, and we filled everything we had.

Then we went back to the army. After I took care of my knight and his friends, I gave John Hawkwood a full canteen, and Master Peter another. Then I found John – Monk John. He was staring wide-eyed at the night. I gave him a canteen and he drank it dry and embraced me.

'Sorry,' he said suddenly. 'By Christ, William, I don't know what came over me that night.'

We were all going to die, so it seemed a good time to restore friendships. He knelt and made his confession to me. By St Peter, he had some sins to confess. I made mine to him, and we were comrades again. I fed him some sausage and went back to the squires.

'Tomorrow I'll kill ten Frenchmen,' said Richard Beauchamp. He went on and on, describing what cuts he'd use. You know the kind of boy he was.

Diccon got to his feet. He was using tow with some fat and a bit of ash to make his helmet gleam. He wiped it with a cloth – he was a careful young man – and set it at his feet.

'Listen to me,' he said, and we did. 'I'm the only one of you who has done this. By tomorrow night, at least three of us will be dead.' There were only nine of us at the little fire. 'One of us will die foolishly – falling from his horse, perhaps.'

I thought of the archer I'd seen die when he fell from his horse outside Issoudun.

He looked around. 'One of us will die trying to be a hero, taking a foolish chance to get a rich ransom.' He smiled. 'I almost died that way, and John Hawkwood took a blow meant for me. Of course, he took the man for ransom, too.'

He said it with such flat confidence that we all believed him. This wasn't male posturing. Diccon had seen the real thing.

'And the third?' I asked.

Diccon shrugged. 'My best friend tried to face Geoffrey de Charny last year in Normandy,' he said.

I've said that de Charny was Lancelot come to earth. He was the best knight in the world. He carried the Oriflamme, the King of France's sacred banner. We all knew his arms, and we knew that in battle he was like some sort of moving siege engine. Men he touched, died. He had fought the Turks at Smyrna, and rescued the very cloth that touched the face of Christ. Not a word of a lie. He'd fought the heathen in Prussia. He'd fought in Italy, and had made all the great pilgrimages.

He was the best knight in the world.

Richard looked at Diccon in the flickering orange light. 'What happened?' he asked.

Diccon shut his eyes for a moment. 'He died,' Diccon said.

Richard could be a child – I think I've already shown that. Insensitive as only a rich boy can be, he said, 'How?'

Diccon whirled. 'He tried to match swords with de Charny. You want to know what happened? I was two arm's lengths away. Before I could reach him, de Charny cut at him three times – knocked him to earth, put a foot on his chest and rammed his sword point through his mouth.' Diccon said this in a shocking voice.

I was afraid that Diccon, who I respected a great deal, was about to burst into tears.

Hawkwood appeared out of the darkness. 'Shouldn't you boys be in your cloaks?' he asked. He looked at Diccon. 'Naught you could have done, Diccon.'

'He died.' Diccon was better in control now, but that voice wasn't far away.

'He died fighting the best knight in France – perhaps the world.' Hawkwood looked around. 'Go to sleep, you lot.'

I took a deep breath. 'What do we do, if that happens?' I asked. 'I had to fight Boucicault. He had mercy on me.'

Hawkwood smiled. 'So you know that, eh? You know he let you live.'

I nodded and swallowed.

Hawkwood nodded. 'When one of them is on the loose, you close up with your friends, form a hedgehog of steel and try to keep the monsters at bay until someone comes and gets you.'

'Someone like you?' I asked.

Hawkwood shook his head. 'Oh, no, boy. Not me. Perhaps your Sir Edward in a few years. The Prince. Sir John Chandos. Sir James Audley.' He smiled. 'Perhaps even you, Judas.' He laughed. 'If you survive tomorrow.'

Morning came. I slept. I can't say the same for everyone, but I had to be kicked awake, and my master was less than perfectly pleased.

I fetched water again and missed a lot of arguing among the higher orders. By St George, scared men are like a pack of old crows, and they squawked and squawked.

But when the Prince decided, we moved.

We marched south. The Prince intended to offer battle from a carefully scouted position – one we could only reach by, in effect, sneaking round behind the French camp. But the plan showed he was as canny as Lancaster ever was, because with good guides, good scouts and superb luck, we passed through Noailles at the break of day and set out banners on the hilltop just west of the town, clear of the damned woods. In one easy march, we rested on the flank of a river full of fresh water running free over rocks – I mention this because the moment we were in battle order, all the squires and servants were sent in shifts to water the horses and men. Better yet, we'd passed south of the French, and we no longer had them between us and Bordeaux. If we were defeated, or if we chose to slip away, we could simply outmarch them to the south.

We were saved.

And we knew it. It was a march of supreme daring, and we were too tired even to know the risk we were running. The Prince threw the dice, and won. We occupied the ground from Noailles to the River Moisson in the south, and to the woods of Noailles to our north, and the archers on the naked slopes started to dig trenches while the archers on the southern flank cut holes in the hedges through which to loose their shafts. It was like a little fortress. We halted, formed our ranks, went for water, and sat to eat our breakfasts while the bedraggled cardinal returned to beg the Prince for a truce. The Earl had just sent me to the Prince with a small keg of water – the prince's squires were fine gentlemen who didn't want to get their nice iron sabatons wet – when Talleyrand rode up.

'By the honour of our saviour and the Blessed Virgin Mary,' he invoked. 'Make peace while you can, my gracious lord.'

'Speak and be quick,' the Prince replied. He didn't even look at the cardinal – Talleyrand was at that time only slightly less powerful than the King of France. He might have been Pope. He certainly had more money than God. I doubt he was used to being told to speak and be quick.

I laughed.

Talleyrand glared at me.

The Prince was watching the crest of the hill to the north, which divided us from the King of France. Banners were starting to appear.

'Give me one hour to make peace, my gracious lord. In the name of Jesus Christ.' The Cardinal bowed.

The Prince turned from looking at the gathering French banners, the way a shipman might turn from watching a gathering storm. He nodded. 'One hour?' he asked, looking at me of all people.

'Just one,' Talleyrand said.

The Prince bowed. 'I will hear your proposals if the King of France will do,' he said.

Talleyrand took a cup of wine from my hand, drank it and put his hand on my head. 'God's blessing on you, child, even when you are rude to your betters.'

That's how I met the great Cardinal, of whom John Hawkwood said, 'He farts gold.'

After he rode away, the Prince took wine and water from me. He looked at my boots, which were wet from riding into the stream so many times. 'Good water?' he asked.

'Yes, my Prince.' Oh, how I remember those words. I was speaking to the Prince.

He nodded. 'The Cardinal may speak to his heart's content while we water our horses and have a bite,' he said. He looked past me to Burghersh. 'And then, my lords, we will pick up our banners and march – away.'

They nodded and smiled. Listen, my friends – we had loot and an intact army, and they outnumbered us four to one. While I served the Prince and his lords, I watched the far hill as they did, and we counted eighty-seven banners. King John of France had 12,000 knights. We had about 2,000 men-at-arms. Of belted knights, we had fewer than 800.

We had our archers, and they had a veritable horde of infantrymen, but their infantrymen, with the exception of the communal militias, weren't worth a donkey's watery piss.

After a few minutes, I went back to the Earl, who, with Warwick, was commanding on the left, near the marshes and the river. The insects were fierce, but the French were far away. We watched the Prince canter his beautiful black charger across the fields towards the Cardinal, who was sitting with his French knights under a banner of truce.

The Earl and Warwick already knew we were going to move. Men ate hurriedly, but suddenly the whole army – at least, all the men I knew – were in tearing good spirits. We'd marched around the French, and the Black Prince, bless him, was doing the right thing: turning his backside and slipping away. We weren't going to fight at all.

No one was more relieved than the same men and boys who'd been counting dead Frenchmen the night before, believe me. Sound familiar, messieurs?

Every man was standing by his fed and watered horse. Most men had at least a canteen full of water. We stood to our horses, ready to move.

The Prince cantered back across the fields. Men started cheering.

He was a fine sight, and we weren't going to fight.

We cheered, too, and he vanished into the centre of the army. An army of 6,000 men is a little less than a mile long, all formed in order, and he wasn't so very far away.

One of his squires galloped up to Warwick and bowed in the saddle.

Warwick laughed and waved to Oxford, who nodded and rode along the hillside to where I sat with his men-at-arms.

'Gentlemen,' he said. 'We will be leaving before the party.'

We all smiled, and the left wing of the army began to pick their way south, led by a dozen of the Prince's elite archers. All we needed was to get across the swamp.

The ground to our left was a damp swamp – deeper than it should have been in early autumn. I rode with the Earl, because he was using me as a mounted messenger. I was, at least in his eyes, a squire. Squires are generally accounted among the men-at-arms and not the servants. Or so I chose to account myself.

At any rate, I was near the head of the column as we marched off to the left. Marched is the wrong term. We slithered and slid down the steep ridge, then we squelched our way through the reeds and mud. We weren't moving very fast.

But I was nearly at the dry ground around the ford marked by the Prince's archers – I could see them – when there was a great shout behind me. It was a panicked shout. We were strung out across the hillside in a loose column, four men wide, all mounted. Ahead of me I could see our baggage carts, already crossing the ford. The Prince had this one in the bag – he'd sent our baggage ahead.

Down in the reeds, I could see the hillside behind me, but I couldn't see anything happening except the shouting of some of the men – mostly retinue archers – at the top of the ridge. They were pointing behind them.

'Go see,' the Earl said. I think he meant to send Beauchamp, but I had my horse turned out of the column and picking his way across the reeds before Beauchamp or Amble got the idea. In fact, I didn't go back along the column – the horses were chewing the trail to a morass – but laboured across the marsh a few paces, then rode straight up the ridge.

The moment my head was clear of the reeds, I saw it all.

The French had attacked. Fast and hard, and well led. Their chivalry were coming straight as an arrow across the low valley that separated the Prince's army from the ridge where Talleyrand had held his peace talk. They were mounted on armoured horses the size of dragons, and they made the earth shake, even from where I was.

Warwick was with the tail of our column and had seen the threat immediately. Whether by bad fortune or cunning plan, the French were attacking in two deep battles of cavalry, one aimed at the Prince, the other aimed at the gap where we'd left the line. So Warwick was dismounting his own retinue archers and all his men-at-arms to form a hasty line at the top of the ridge, slightly back to form a shallow 'L', with the Prince's battle to cover our now naked left flank.

It takes a half a cup of wine to explain, but I saw it in one glance.

I rode back down the ridge to the Earl, who had already picked his way clear of the morass. I reined in, but my horse fidgeted – curvets, bites.

'The French are attacking the ground we quit,' I said. 'My lord, Lord Warwick is forming a battle from the rear of our division. He will be hard pressed, and—'

The Earl was a young man, but old in war, and he didn't need any more of his fifteen-year-old squire's views. He raised his hand for silence and looked up the hill – he stood in his stirrups and looked at his column.

I watched him, and I watched John Hawkwood, who tugged his beard, reached down and loosened his sword in its scabbard.

The truth is, I was green as grass. It looked to me as if we were beaten, and I was on the edge of panic. But neither the young Earl nor the middle-aged professional seemed flustered. Rather, both of them wore the looks of men in a good game of chess – the Earl might have said 'good move' aloud.

My horse stopped fidgeting. You know why? Because I stopped fidgeting.

'On me,' the Earl shouted. He turned his horse's head and began picking his way along the marsh, not up the hill.

As it was – certainly by the Earl's intent – he had his picked men about him, but we were at the head of his elite archers, men who wore his livery. Men like Master Peter wore as much harness as a man-at-arms – Peter wore leg armour, a brigantine covered in red and yellow leather with rose-head rivets, a fine German basinet with a mail aventail. Most of his mates – the veteran archers – wore the same. The Earl had 120 of these men, and he had placed himself at their head when he called, 'Follow me.'

We rode. Riding through a swamp on a hot autumn day in armour is unpleasant, but I can't say I noticed.

The sound of cheers and war cries grew louder and louder.

As we emerged from the reeds, I could hear the French and feel the movement of their horses. I was shaking with fear and excitement. I thought we might have lost the battle by the time we got through the swamp, although when I went over it later, we rode only about 200 paces through the marsh.

Where we came out, at the base of the ridge, we were below the fighting. The French had crashed into Warwick's division at the hedge. The hedge saved us – nothing can stop a French knight with a lance on open ground, as I have reason to know – but even with the hedge, the first contact had pushed Lord Warwick and his men-at-arms back, and back again. His archers had shot their quivers empty – a good man can loose fifteen arrows in a minute. There was a handful of French men-at-arms or their horses lying like butterflies after a storm, dead and feathered, on the slope.

As soon as the head of our column was clear of the reeds, the master archers took over. The archer's pages – their servants – appeared out of the column and took their horses – one boy for each six horses. The archers walked forward about twenty paces. Their bows were ready strung. They all looked at Master Peter like musicians look at their conductor. He was watching the French chivalry on the ridge.

He had an arrow in his hand. He pointed it. 'Shoot for the rumps and backs,' he said. We'd come out of the reeds on the flank of the French, of course – and even in Milanese plate, man is *far* more vulnerable from the back then the front. I've seen a man shot through armour by a heavy bow, but not often.

Master Peter nocked his arrow. He didn't appear to aim. He drew and loosed.

His arrow vanished into the mêlée.

The hundred or so archers around him began to draw and loose, even as the first light-armed archers began to emerge from the marsh. The Earl sent them off further to the left, further around the flank of the French. I saw Monk John trot by, his eyes on the French. He gave his horse to a boy and sprinted along the dry ground, headed to the left.

The Earl's retinue of archers – 120 men, remember – *filled* the sky with arrows. The volume of their shafts was incredible. It's one thing to watch a few men at the butts on a hot Sunday after Mass; it's another thing entirely to watch a hundred men, every one of whom was probably his village champion. Their arrows were big and heavy – four or five to the pound, with the heads on. They cost a fortune.

They made a sound in the air like a woman beating pots when they struck.

The French at the top of the hill were scarcely annihilated. They were, as we later found, the picked men of 12,000 men-at-arms – the best armed and armoured – but their horses took a great many hits.

Even as I watched, a grey-bearded archer known as Gospel Mark shouted, 'Horse killers!' and drew from his quiver a misshapen thing like a child's drawing of an arrow. Some men emulated him. The big-headed arrows could knock down a horse. The fine bodkin-point arrows that were supplied by the government were better for penetrating chain and leather – if they were well tempered, which they were not always.

The French recoiled from the arrow storm. Then one of them turned his horse, and suddenly fifty of them – they looked to me like a thousand – angled their horses across the hill and came for us.

They had the hill behind them, and as soon as they put their horse's heads at us, instead of away from us, they stopped falling. The war bow isn't so powerful as to drive through the three or four layers a French knight wore in front.

Again, they made the earth shake.

The Earl walked back into the marsh until he was standing on a tussock, about thirty yards into the morass.

Master Peter turned and, leg armour and all, his veterans ran back, shouting, cursing and making the black mud fly.

The army servants – of whom, had things gone otherwise, I might have been accounted one – appeared as if by one of Merlin's spells and began to hand out sheaves of arrows. The veterans had already shot their quivers empty, and they couldn't go forward to retrieve their shafts.

Battles, my friends, are won and lost by brave men, but also by boys with sheaves of arrows, and the clerks who counted the arrows and made sure that the boys did their work. That was Bishop Burghersh. A mediocre man-at-arms, but a fine administrator. Because of him, and because of an order he'd issued fifteen minutes before, the boys came with the arrows, brought in a cart to the far side of the marsh. The boys were barefoot and quick.

The French knights crossed the open ground in about the time it takes to say a paternoster.

They came up to the edge of the marsh and kept coming. Many horses baulked at the reeds, because horses are smarter than men, sometimes. And the horses that baulked turned broadside to the archers.

Monk John and the lighter-armed archers were just now forming, still further to the left, so that the new French attack was once more caught in the flank by our heavy bows.

It was close, my friends. It was all a matter of heartbeats and inches.

The lead French knight put his head down, and shafts whanged off his helmet so hard that his whole body rocked. His lance caught one of Master Peter's archers and killed him, punching all the way through his body. The man screamed and blood shot from his mouth.

The French knight dropped his lance and drew his sword. He was about two horse-lengths from me, and once again I thought we had lost. I was still on my little riding horse, and I had my looted French sword in my hand. And I thought something like, Jesus Fuck, because the French bastard was a foot higher than me or more on a gigantic horse, and his sword was five-feet long.

He killed a second archer, even as Master Peter swung his bow and loosed at the knight, who was practically at the point of his arrow.

The arrow slammed into the man's chest armour and stuck, but the knight didn't seem affected. He didn't want to kill archers; he wanted to fight knights, and he saw the Earl and the Earl's standard, and he turned to go for them. Unfortunately, my horse and I sat between him and the Earl.

My horse was not a war horse.

His was.

His stallion bit my horse savagely in the neck and bore it down, and my little gelding collapsed, half reared, threw me into the muck of the marsh and ran, bleeding, from the stallion's bite.

So much for my first encounter at Poitiers.

I lay, half-stunned, in the mud – nice, soft mud, which, if you must be thrown, is the very nicest landing – and watched as the Frenchmen went sword to sword with John Hawkwood. John was still mounted – it is possible the French knight thought he was the Earl – and they both cut one handed. It was curious to lie and watch them above me, like birds in the sky – I had time to see things I'd never have seen if I'd been fighting. Neither guarded himself at all. They both cut hard, high, sweeping blows meant to stun or injure right through armour. One of those blows would have split an unarmoured man in half.

Slam, slam, bang.

Like an armourer's shop in Cheapside.

Another French knight appeared, and another, plunging into the marsh.

The Earl had sent his war horse to the rear. I don't know why Hawkwood hadn't, but the Earl shouted his war cry and appeared at Hawkwood's stirrup with a poleaxe. He thrust up, and caught the first French knight in the aventail at the base of the helmet, throwing him from the saddle.

Two more French knights joined the fight. Every one of them was going for the Earl, who was now obvious in his bright Italian plate armour and his red and yellow arms and coronet. Remember that he'd come across the marsh with his standard bearer and a few picked men, as well as his archers.

Sir Edward, my cousin, appeared by his side.

The French knights circled for the kill. They were close.

I levered myself to my feet. I won't say it was the bravest moment of my life. I'll only say that I didn't have to.

But I did.

I got to my feet and the world changed, and after that point I can only tell you what I remember.

First, about the time I got to my feet, the French knight the Earl had put down *bounced* to his. Christ, he was eager. Or angry.

And, once again, I was in his way.

This time, I didn't have an old gelding between my knees. I had my buckler off my hip and on my hand, and when he swung his sword, I didn't flinch, even though it was the longest sword I'd ever faced.

Fighting in mud is horrible, because everything is wrong. I wanted to close with him and get inside his absurdly long blade, but my legs were literally trapped. It was worse for him, though, in sabatons and leg armour, the mud just sort of ate you. I had on good high boots, and although one was full of water – the things you remember – I got one foot clear of the mud. He hit my buckler hard enough to dent the steel boss, and I lost my balance and was back where I started. We must have looked like antics.

I wasn't even afraid.

I finally got my left leg out of the mud and forward, and I cut. His blow cut the rim of my buckler and lightly cut my arm, while my blow rang on his helmet. A perfect cut.

Unfortunately, my blade snapped and he was unhurt, because he was wearing a fine helmet. The bastard.

Now I had a four-inch sword stump and a buckler against an armoured knight.

I'd love to tell you how I wrestled him to the ground and took him, but the truth is that one of the archers put a quarter-pounder arrow into his arse, and down he went.

I just stood there.

Alive.

He was trying to get up.

Then I took his sword. It was a magical thing – long, curiously heavy and yet marvellously light. He was face down in mud, and I stepped, hard, on the back of his helmet, and pushed his face down. His thigh and groin were pouring blood. I sat on his backplate, drew my dagger, and thrust it deep. Up. From the bottom, so to speak.

He died.

I took his steel gauntlets. Right there. With another man coming for me.

I got the right one on, and then I was using the longsword to parry, again and again, as a mounted Frenchmen – three bars gules on a field d'or – cut at me over and over as his horse pushed against me. The horse was desperate, locked in the mud's embrace. The French were churning it into the foam, and the horses were sinking further and further, but the first French knights had ridden in, and the sight of them encouraged more and more of them to try.

The blows rained down from over my head.

I can't remember what happened to three bars gules. That fight seemed to go on for ever, but it can't have been that long, because then I was standing by the Earl, thrusting my new longsword up at an eagle argent on a field azure, who had a war hammer and had just put John Hawkwood down with a blow to the helmet. After three failed thrusts, I changed tactics and thrust my sword into the horse, up from under the jaw, right into the brain, and the monster died instantly and fell.

The Earl's poleaxe cured the eagle knight of his attempt to get to his feet.

I bent over and sucked humid air. The world smelled of swamp and blood.

I straightened up, painfully aware that my cousin Edward and the Earl were only an arm's length away. My heroes. It took me three breaths to realize there was no one to fight.

No one.

In ten heartbeats, we went from desperate mêlée that might have won the battle for the King of France, to complete victory in our corner of the swamp. I've heard men say we won because the French couldn't get at the archers. Crap. We won because the French knights didn't want to kill archers; they wanted ransoms and chivalrous contests, so they all went for the Earl's banner. Had just three or four of those monsters gone off to kill archers ...

But they didn't. And Sir Edward and John Hawkwood, Sir Gareth Crawford, William Rose and I stopped them.

Heh.

The Earl started issuing orders. I did something absolutely brilliant for a raw soldier: I went and looked in the mud for the other steel gauntlet. They were a fine fit, and I knew what I wanted.

I wanted armour. I wanted to be able to go toe-to-toe with the French. I had learned a lot in one fight. I had learned that if you want to fight mounted, you need a good horse, and that if you want to fight on foot, you have to wear gauntlets.

See?

I got the second gauntlet out of the mud. It had a fancy engraved brass cuff, and that was just above the muck. I spent three or four very long minutes cleaning the muck out, and when I put it on my hand, the leather glove, a nice German chamois, was like slime, or the inside of a dead man's entrails.

I didn't care.

All over the edge of the marsh, archers were looting the dead or taking the wounded for ransoms. We'd cut down sixty of the richest men in France – just sixty, of 12,000 – but we broke the back of the French Marshal Audreham's attack. The great man himself was taken prisoner a few horse lengths from where I was cleaning a dead man's gauntlets, and brought to the Earl.

Again, being green, I thought we'd won.

But being halfway to canny, I looked around and saw that everyone older than me was either combing the ground for arrows or looting, and all of them looked like we weren't done.

I drew the right conclusion.

A page boy emerged from the mud and now-trampled reeds and handed me the reins of my gelding, who didn't even have the grace to look sorry. I thanked the boy – even then thinking that might have been me, holding the horses – and walked my horse to the edge of the marsh, where Oxford was drinking water from a cup and looking up the ridge to where the rest of the English Army was straightening itself out. The bulk of the French knights had fallen on Warwick and the old Earl of Salisbury. They'd all failed, although they'd probably come closest against us.

But by our saviour, the plain – from the top of the next ridge, where Cardinal Talleyrand had held his peace conference, all the way to the place where the Noailles Road crossed the Poitiers Road – was full of French soldiers.

For a moment I couldn't breathe, and I'm pretty sure every Englishman there felt the same.

How could there be so much armour in one place?

It was as if the fields of Noailles had grown a crop of iron and steel.

The French chivalry had dismounted.

And now they were coming.

They were in six great divisions, with banners prominently displayed. I knew a few. In the centre of the rear was the great red blot that was the Oriflamme, the sacred banner of St Denis and France. Under it would be Geoffrey de Charny, the best knight in the world, and the King of France.

I could see the Dauphin's banner in the front. I was too green to know who the others were, but every great lord in France was present – I hadn't known there were that many knights in the world – and they started up the valley at the Prince and Salisbury.

The Earl of Oxford ordered his archers forward to the edge of the firm ground. We wouldn't be taken by surprise again – armoured men on foot can be fast, but not as fast as horsemen. Our archers formed neater ranks, and boys and camp servants brought up more sheaves of arrows as we began to loose them into the flank of the French advance.

The French flinched away.

The Earl turned to me. 'Judas!' he said. 'Go to the Prince and tell me what he desires. Tell him how we fare here.'

I nodded. I was by my horse. Richard was nowhere to be seen, and all the Earl's noble squires were, as it proved, struggling to come up from the baggage.

I rode back along the base of the ridge to keep clear of the French, then up the hill, into the Forest of Noailles at the back of our army, and along our ridge to the middle of our line, where I could see the Prince's banner. The ride only took me as long as it takes to read a Gospel reading, maybe a little longer, but when I left the Earl, the French were far away, suffering under our shafts, and by the time I reached the standard ...

The fighting had started.

What I hadn't known, because I was with the Earl, was that at the top of the ridge, the whole face of the English army was protected by a trio of hedges, with two great gaps. The gaps were about forty men wide.

The whole of the Battle of Poitiers was played out in those gaps.

Only about a hundred men at a time could fight. It was like some kind of terrible tourney, because a thousand English men-at-arms duelled eight times their number of French men-at-arms, but both sides were able to rotate men out of the line. The fighting was fierce and protracted in a way I've seldom seen.

In fact, I'll say that I think the hand-to-hand fight at Poitiers was the worst I ever saw. The French sent their very best, and the English wouldn't give a foot.

When I rode to the standard, the Dauphin's division had crashed into Salisbury's at the right-hand gap, and the fighting sounded like a riot, with pots and pans as participants. The French roared, 'St Denis!' and the English roared, 'George and England!'

The Prince stood by his banner with his war horse. Around him stood Chandos and the Captal and twenty other commanders and great lords. They were watching.

Chandos spotted me and called, 'Messenger from Oxford, my lord.'

I slid from my horse and knelt. 'The Earl of Oxford sends his respectful greetings, my lord. We are behind the right flank of the French advance, holding the line of the marsh. We have defeated one party and captured the Marshal d'Audreham. The Earl desires to hear what my lord wishes.'

The Prince smiled at me. 'That was nicely put. Have you fought?'

'Yes, my Prince.' Now that made me glow.

He smiled. Then he started walking. He walked to the hedge, and archers got out of his way. Fifty knights followed him.

The archers had hacked an opening in the hedge too narrow to crawl through, and the other side of the hedge was crawling with Frenchmen, but it gave a view, like the crenellation on a castle curtain wall. The hedges themselves were twice the height of a man, and as thick as a road is wide.

He looked out over the swarm of French knights who filled the hillside, though in no particular order.

'Where is the Earl of Oxford?' the Prince asked me.

I pointed down the ride and well off to the left. 'My Prince, you can just see the leftmost tail of our division – the light-armed men and some Welsh – see?'

The Welsh were men of Cheshire, in green and white parti-colour that blended into the marsh reeds all too well.

'*Par dieu* – that far? So the French are behind us, too?' he said.

The Captal leaned in to us. 'The hill is nearly round, n'est pas? So of course the Earl is almost behind us, and yet on the flank of the French.'

The Prince nodded. 'Anything the Earl can do to prick the flank of the French assault will help relieve the pressure on Salisbury and Warwick,' he said. 'Go with God, boy.'

To be sure, I sat my horse for three long breaths, watching the shocking havoc of the two mêlées at the gaps. Blood actually flew – it rose like a hideous mist off the stour.

Then I rode down the ridge and through the marsh, back to the Earl.

By the time I returned – perhaps half an hour after I'd left – our archers were utterly spent of shafts. Let me be frank, they had hit many men, and every hit from a heavy arrow wears a man, saps his courage, reminds him of his mortality and the weight of his sins. But the archers hadn't slain more than two or three hundred, for all the weight of their shafts had darkened the sun.

On the other hand, the whole French right wing had flinched, perhaps unconsciously, away from us. And as the morning wore into afternoon, the archers who had no place to loose their shafts up on the ridge – blocked by the hedge or by the mêlées – came in twenties and hundreds down to us on the flank, pouring their murderous barbs on the flank of the French again, galling them like spur rowels and pushing them a little further. And as our archers gained this ground, so the Earl moved his banner forward, so that by the time the sun was high in the sky, the Earl's banner was more than a hundred paces clear of the marsh. The result – I had no idea of this at the time, but I understand it now – was to take almost all the pressure off Warwick's men.

In the centre, the flower of the English knighthood stood chest to chest with the French chivalry. Neither side gave. From our newest position, I could see it all, and they were all intermixed, a great, writhing steel millipede.

About that time, Burghersh released the last reserves of arrows. Our archers were spread along the whole line of the Moisson, as far as the marsh protruded into the French lines, and there was no particular order. Our men would go forward to within range of the French and launch two or three shafts with great care, and return, discussing their shots. It was like watching a village archery contest. The French had all their archers – mostly crossbowmen – with their last division under the King of France's hand, and they didn't loose a shaft at us.

But when we received about a hundred sheaves of arrows, just at nones, Master Peter gathered his men and gave them ten arrows apiece. He had a brief exchange with the Earl, and the Earl sent me for the rest of the squires, who were busy watering horses. With the squires and all the men-at-arms, we had perhaps a hundred armoured men.

With the best of the archers, we were perhaps 300, arrayed as we used to say 'en haye', like a plow, with the cutting edge, the men-at-arms in the centre, and the archers on either flank. We went forward boldly, the Earl with his standard, carried now by John Hawkwood, who had a bandage on his head.

The Earl halted us less than a hundred paces from the flank of the French main battle, and the archers didn't loose at random. Instead, for the first time, they loosed in great volleys to the orders of the master archers, so that all the shafts fell together. The range was short.

'Nock!' called Master Peter.

'Draw!'

'Loose!'

You could hear the bodkins strike.

Men screamed.

'Nock!' roared Peter.

'Draw!'

'Loose!'

The Dauphin's division was broken in two volleys. It was like watching a herd of horses panic, or a flock of sheep – first a few men died, then others began to shuffle back – then the next flight struck and more men fell, and there was screaming everywhere, and then Master Peter called 'Nock', like the Archangel Gabriel's trumpet, and they knew the wrath was coming upon them again.

Flesh can only take so much, even nobly armoured flesh.

In Italy, they say the Dauphin was the first to run. I was there.

It's true.

I'm not sure what to think of him. He was my age, wearing the best armour on the field, surrounded by superb knights, men of true worth and high reputation. At that point in the fight, I had faced four or five men for perhaps ten minutes, and to be fair, the Dauphin stood in the stour for almost two hours. I have no idea how much fighting he did.

But I'll tell you this for nothing. I don't know one English man-at-arms, nor one Gascon, even a lying bastard like the Bourc Camus, who claims to have swaggered swords with the Dauphin. Maybe his father's men hurried him out of danger when we moved against their flank. Or perhaps he's the cowardly bastard everyone says he is. But he was the first to go. I saw him. Golden lilies powdering a field azure.

When he edged out of the mêlée, many knights came with him, and more followed, and suddenly, all the Frenchmen on the left, facing Warwick, were retreating. After more than an hour of stalemate, they fell back down the hill in surly disorder – not a rout, just a retreat. They still outnumbered us, and the Count of Anjou – we saw his banner – gathered half a thousand men and came at us on the flank.

The archers emptied their quivers and we fell back, all the way to the marsh. The archers scampered away from the French knights, who must have been exhausted. But not too exhausted to have a go at the Earl.

84

Anjou himself ran at our line, and the men-at-arms with him charged us hard. We'd been backpedalling, and we had to halt about fifty paces from the protection of the marsh, or be cut down running.

I was in the second rank, about five men from the Earl. I used my new sword over my cousin's head. He fought with a sword and buckler, and I used my longsword as a spear, with my left hand halfway along the blade, thrusting over his shoulder or under his right armpit. I don't think I killed anyone, but neither was I hit, nor was Sir Edward. We held, and held – Christ, how did they do this for an hour? Then Edward knocked a man flat with a backhanded blow, and the man waved weakly and cried, 'Me rendre!'

Fair enough. The Earl pushed forward, but Anjou had pulled back and was reforming his conroy – his company. I pushed forward past my cousin, who was accepting the surrender and ransom of his noble adversary. There was a knot of Frenchmen still fighting – one had hacked the Earl's banner pole in half. Hawkwood put his pommel in the man's face – almost no one had a visor in those days – and the man fell back.

I cut hard with my new sword. The second man was just turning to face me, and my first cut – a rising cut – knocked his sword aside, and my descending cut was very strong. Strong and, by luck, perfect. He had a quilted linen aventail, and my blade went past his guard, through his aventail and beheaded him.

Blood gouted from his neck.

Men around me cheered.

And the other Frenchman fell to his knees and made himself my prisoner.

Friends, I think I laughed aloud. Grown men thumped me on the back.

Anjou's company backed away.

Once again, I thought the battle was over.

And once again, I was wrong.

At the top of the Cardinal's ridge – well, that's what I called it all day – we saw the lilies of France and the flaming red silk of the Oriflamme. Even while I received a guerdon – my first – a token of my captive's surrender, the King started down the ridge towards us. He had about 3,000 men, the cream of his army. His men were fresh, and they walked quickly down the hill.

Our archers loosed their next-to-last shafts at point-blank range, and knocked over a few men.

Warwick's archers, and Salisbury's, loosed whatever they had left. But archers, even master archers, tire, and we were nearly out of arrows. The density of the French meant they'd trampled the ground into which we'd shot all day, and when some of the younger men, like Monk John, ran forward to retrieve shafts, they came back with very few, because the rest were broken.

The French King's Italian crossbowmen went up the hill first. About 200 of them broke off to face us under their master archer. I heard his voice yelling orders, and they wheeled off like old Romans. They were good.

Unfortunately, you cannot move forward with a pavise and a spanned crossbow. So having faced off against us, they had to halt and span. I think they thought our veterans were shot dry.

Master Peter was a canny devil. Every one of his archers had three shafts under his right foot, where they couldn't be seen.

They loosed them.

Just like that, the Italians were gone. They ran. The English shafts punched right through their great pavises. I saw it happen in Italy, too, and it broke their morale. I doubt we killed ten of them, because they had good armour, but as soon as they took hits, they ran. They were mercenaries, not patriots.

And, thank God, we didn't have to stand their return volley.

Then the King's division was past us, walking quickly up the hill, with ten great banners and the Oriflamme in the centre. From where I stood, I could see de Charny's arms – at this distance, his arms appeared to be three red dots on gleaming white.

The greatest knight in the world.

I was watching when the royal messenger came to the Earl. I didn't hear a word through my helmet, but I knew what he was asking. He was asking that the Earl send every man-at-arms who could walk to the top of the hill, to try and hold the King of France and the best knight in the world. Sir Edward was already trotting, in full armour, up the hill, going the long way round Warwick's archers.

He was my hero – and my knight. What could I do but follow?

By the sweet saviour, I was tired. There is a special fatigue – some of you will know it – when some parts hurt, and other parts are so far gone that it seems they might just refuse their service to the rest of the body. I had no leg armour, and still my left thigh muscles were exhausted. I was more hobbling than running. Sir Edward drew ahead of me as he reached Warwick's men, and then he turned in behind them and I lost him.

The King reached the top of the hill, and his division slammed into the Prince. Even as I hobbled along, I saw the centre of the English line stagger back from the hedge for the first time, losing five paces in as many breaths of air. Fresh, expert fighters in the very best armour money could buy, facing tired men who had braved two attacks that day, and who were usually none too well armoured to start with.

I started to run, and be damned to my left leg. John Hawkwood caught me up and I was determined not to let an old man like him pass me. Other men-at-arms from Oxford and Warwick's division pounded along with us – about sixty men-at-arms in all, and only three or four belted knights among us, I swear.

The English centre gave another step or two. A handful of French knights spilled around the edge of the mêlée and began hacking at the end of the English line. All the English men-at-arms who could stand were committed in the centre, and the French still outnumbered us – even with their third line alone.

But they didn't outnumber our archers.

John Hawkwood started calling, 'On me! On me!' as he ran. Perhaps he meant to raise the spirits of the men fighting, but to the archers of Warwick's division, with no foes in front of them, his call meant something different.

Friends, in the main, archers don't go toe-to-toe with men-at-arms. There are excellent reasons, and the greatest is that no good archer wears iron gauntlets or arm armour – you cannot wear an arm harness and shoot a bow well. Yet in a mêlée, your hands and arms are the likeliest to draw a blow – even a sloppy, amateurish blow.

But—

But this was for everything. All of us knew it. Every Englishman – and every Welshman, Irishman, Scotsman, Gascon and man of Artois and Brittany – in our army knew that we'd stopped two French attacks, and that if we stopped this one …

Well. If we didn't, we'd lose and be dead.

The archers began to cheer, 'God and St George!'

George and England.

George and England!

Par dieu, gentles, I can still hear it – because when 6,000 men pick up a cheer, it is loud. It is a weapon of its own. It grew louder, and men broke ranks and charged into the flanks of the French line or ran down the hill to envelop them. It wasn't planned.

It was devastating.

Even then, the French knights were, in fact, the best fighters in the world. And I was far enough behind to watch what happened to one group of archers who separated themselves from the pack and ran behind the French line. Then Marshal Clermont, with perhaps five other knights, turned on them like lions on hyenas, and they died. I knew Clermont by his arms – trust me, war was a business to me even then, and where other boys spent the summer learning Latin verbs or how to plough, I knew which coat of arms was worth a ransom, and who was the most dangerous to face, and Clermont scored well in both lines.

His sword was like a living thing. He stepped out, cut, and an English archer folded over his spilling guts. He blocked a second cut from another man, stepped in under it and rammed his pommel into the man's unguarded face. Then he stepped through him, rotating his sword so that he cut the man's throat and thrust from low into the guts of the third – so hard that he batted the man's buckler aside.

That's why archers don't fight knights.

I followed Sir Edward, then, and he ran to the Prince's banner in the centre. As I ran up, utterly winded, my left leg afire with pain and exhaustion, the Prince was pointing off to the right with a gauntleted hand, and he was grinning. At his hip, mounted, was the Captal de Buch – a young man, but another famous fighter, and a Gascon. Even as I stopped and tried *not* to heave my guts out in front of the flower of English chivalry, the Captal slammed his visor down and raised his sword. There was a cheer. He had about fifty men-at-arms and another hundred mounted archers – the kind of archers who wear leg armour and ride heavy horses. They rode off to the right in a cloud of late summer dust and a rumble of hooves.

The English line gave another few feet.

I straightened up, and there was the Prince, smiling at Sir Edward and John Hawkwood and another Gascon, Seguin de Badefol, who was later the captain paramount of all the mercenary companies in France, but that day was just another penniless Gascon adventurer – he had a dozen men-at-arms with him, in bad armour. I fit right in with them.

The Prince looked us over. 'Gentlemen,' he said, 'with the grace of God and your aid, I will now win this battle.'

We all bowed. It's odd to tell that in the midst of a stricken field we bowed, but he was the very Prince of chivalry, that day. We bowed like dirty, dusty courtiers, and then we formed a tight array, and followed the Prince into the very centre of the English line.

Thirty men-at-arms. In a battle of thousands and tens of thousands, it shouldn't have been enough.

We didn't crash into the French. In fact, I found myself behind a knot of men, too far from the mêlée to fight, but close enough to feel the desperation. I didn't know what to do. A veteran would have known to wait his moment and then push in, relieving a tired man, but I'd never been in a close press before.

But luck stayed with me. I was behind an English knight – Sir John Blaunkminster – he thanked me later, and we were friends, so I know his name. At any rate, he took a blow to the side of his helmet from a poleaxe and stumbled back. His stumble took him past me, and I caught the French knight's poleaxe on my new sword – Good Christ he was strong – and I was fighting.

I was fighting just to stay alive and not give ground, but the French were desperate, ruthless and very good, and before I'd breathed a hundred times, I had two dagger wounds – it was that close, and many of the French were letting go their shortened spears and poleaxes and using heavy rondel daggers. And wrestling.

I lost my sword. I don't even remember being disarmed. Perhaps my hands couldn't hold it any more. At any rate, I took a hard blow to the head, which rocked me. I chose to stumble forward, not back, and got my opponent around the waist. He pounded the back of my head with his sword pommel, and I bore him back into the crush and down hill, then suddenly he tripped and went down. He was slippery with blood – his limbs were armoured and mine were not, so *any* blow he threw hurt me. Armour is a weapon.

But I was on top.

I tried to open his visor, but his armoured hands were as fast as mine.

I remembered my dagger and went for it. By this time I was straddling his chest like a child on his father, slamming my armoured left fist into his visor over and over. Because if I let him have a second, I was done for.

My right hand found my dagger.

My fist closed.

I drew it and slammed it into his visor.

The third downward thrust did the trick, but I'll wager I stabbed him ten more times.

That's a fight I'll take to my grave.

The problem with a mêlée is that in the moment after you kill an opponent, you sag, and you are very vulnerable in your moment of triumph. I sagged.

An armoured foot caught me in the shoulder and kicked me off my victim. I fell on my back. I've no idea who kicked me, but it hurt, and I was slow getting up, and when I did, men were cheering all around me.

The French were giving way.

There were archers all around the rear of their division, and we were pushing them back down the hill. I saw Sir Edward in the press, and I saw the French backing down the hill, closing in around their King. Men-at-arms near me simply sank to their knees, or sat like chastened dogs.

But Sir Edward was pressing down the hill with the Prince. The Prince was shouting orders, his faceplate up, and even as he shouted, Sir James Audley began to gather volunteers from the victors – men with horses nearby.

My horse was not good, and he was far away behind the hill, so I followed Sir Edward down the hill. He was hunting a good ransom.

We had won. Men were still fighting, but the French were starting to fall apart. Their first retreat had been disciplined, but now the Earl of Oxford's archers were shooting a few hoarded shafts into their backs, and then throwing down their bows, picking up their bucklers and charging into the rear of the French line. The French flinched away like a wounded animal.

It must have occurred to every man on that battlefield at the same time that we could ...

... take the King of France.

What do you think the King of France is worth as a ransom?

Friends, in the moment of victory – may you all live to know it – everything falls sway: fatigue, wounds, everything. You are a fresh man. While your enemies are suddenly full of self-doubt and fear. This is when men die.

Sir Edward headed for the lilies and the Oriflamme. I was twenty paces behind him. All around us, men were still fighting – I saw a

French squire stagger, trip on his own intestines, fall, rise and try to stagger on. I saw a knight with a dagger wedged under his armpit still fighting, and another with three English archers on him, holding him down and trying to finish him while he fought back with fists and feet. But I ran past all these, because Sir Edward was my knight.

And he was going where I'd have gone anyway.

Some of the Frenchmen were falling to their knees and asking for quarter. Others were suddenly killing Englishmen – running a few steps and then turning to swing their heavy swords.

Sir Edward was just ten strides ahead.

We were under the Lilies of France. I could just see the King, with twenty men-at-arms around him. We were perhaps five paces from the Oriflamme. Ah, gentlemen, what a fine company you might have formed from the killers who were circling the King of France like sharks around a dying porpoise? There was the Bourc Camus, the evilest knight I ever knew, but a deadly killer; there was John Hawkwood, and Sir John Blaunkminster and Dennis de Moirbeke and Bernard de Troyes; there was John Norbury and Seguin de Badefol. I've heard about 600 men claim they were in that fight, and half of them claim to have taken the King. They're lying.

I was *there*.

There, too, were all the squires from Oxford's division – Richard Beauchamps and Diccon Ufford and the rest. They'd come the short way, into the rear of the French. But they'd missed the honour we gained following the Prince at the top of the hill, when the day was lost and won.

Still, there we all were around the King and his son and perhaps thirty desperate French knights.

And Geoffrey de Charny.

Sir Edward plunged in like a young knight bent on errantry, and he led the squires forward to the man who held the Oriflamme. De Charny was so deadly, and so renowned, that there was empty space around him.

Men were curiously hesitant to strike the King of France or his young son. The fighting had an odd flavour, almost a tournament air, except that they were beyond desperation and we were very, very tired.

Sir Edward put himself at our head and led us forward.

De Charny was not a small man, but nor was he one of the giants who tower over a battlefield, a head taller than other men. He wore a plain steel harness and a red wool cote over it, and he wore a single star on his helmet for the Order of the Star. When he saw Sir Edward, he raised his spear, saluted Sir Edward, and stepped out of the huddle of men protecting the King—

And Sir Edward was dead.

He took the French knight's spear just under his aventail, through the neck. De Charny was so fast that I don't think Sir Edward ever knew to parry.

De Charny pulled the blade free of my knight's neck like the tongue of an adder wagging and reversed his grip, then he struck down, hard, through Richard Beauchamp's guard as if his heavy spear were a sword, and then the spear point glided into Beauchamp's eye and out again as the great knight turned his cut into a thrust in mid-motion. As Beauchamp fell off his spear, he reversed it again and felled Diccon with a simple staff-blow to the temple, delivered with crushing force.

The next squire to face him was Harry Dearpoint, and he was already panicked, and didn't set himself to fight before he had the point in under his arm to the lung.

We were saved by the Bourc Camus. He threw himself on de Charny, pinning the man's arms. But de Charny flipped the Gascon right over his body and slammed him – in armour – to earth. Camus leaped to his feet, apparently unhurt, and faced the lion, but a blow from the staff broke his nose and he was down.

The Bourc gave me time to gather myself. I was standing like a fool with only a heavy dagger, and de Charny stepped over the Bourc Camus.

I tackled him. It had worked on my last opponent, but my last opponent hadn't been Geoffrey de Charny. I got my arms around him, but he kneed me in the gut with a steel-clad knee, turned me and raked my arms with his spurs. I was trying to hold on, trying to dig my rondel into his side, but he was wearing a complex and very expensive coat of plates and my dagger wouldn't bite. Then other men were by me. I had his waist with one arm – something had gone wrong with my left – as I slid down into a well of pain. Then I was on the ground, but luck – fortune? The will of God? – put his ankle in my hand. I got his spur and pulled as hard as I could, and somewhere miles above me, a Gascon pushed at him with a poleaxe ...

... and he fell.

I'm told that when we brought him down, there were eight of us on him. One – Tancreville, one of the Prince's squires – was dying from de Charny's dagger in his bowels, but he had the French knight's other leg.

I still had my dagger. I was being pushed into the mud, and another man was standing on my hip. The pain was nothing to the pressure. I got the tip of my dagger in behind his leg armour and pushed.

To be honest, I think I gave him his death wound, but Seguin de Badefol and John Hawkwood both claim the same thing. Or they did until they died.

I'll tell you this, though.

He faced at least fifteen men-at-arms at once, and killed six, wounded five more and died fighting. I never saw his like.

But even while I lay in the mud – dry dust mixed with blood – with a broken left arm, two punctures in my left leg, and a bump on my scalp the side of a goose's egg, I said to myself that *that* was the knight I wanted to be.

Christ, he was good.

God have mercy on his soul, for he lived the life of which we dream, and died better than any man I've ever seen.

I went in and out of consciousness. Thank God, I wasn't badly wounded, but I had an accumulation of cuts, scrapes, breaks and bruises that lasted me for weeks. I lay by de Charny for over an hour. A few paces away, King John of France was captured. I lay there while the very flower of French chivalry were cut down, killed or taken prisoner by a few hundred Englishmen and Gascons. The archers were loose now, killing or taking men prisoner, and many a tavern and inn house from London to Durham was built on the proceeds of that hour.

The Prince received the King of France as his prisoner, and treated him as a chivalrous man would treat a King, bowing low and giving him the best of everything. And the Prince knighted a dozen men at the top of the hill. He knighted John Hawkwood, although there are some who dispute it. He might have knighted me, but I was lying in the mud, and no one was collecting the English wounded yet, because everyone was so tired.

It was thirst, of all things, that drove me to my feet. But I was in some sort of fever dream, and I stumbled about a few paces.

Men were looting de Charny's corpse, and suddenly that seemed unseemly to me. I drove them off, like a lion clearing vultures off a corpse, and they – Gascon brigands, every one – reviled me, but fled.

Fuck them. He deserved better than to be stripped naked and left to rot.

In the end, I sat down hard, and I was looking into his face. Was he still alive, even then? I don't think so.

But he told me things anyway.

You laugh.

A battlefield is the strangest place, friends. So many men have died that the ties that bind this world and the next are frayed, and the other world is close. God send you never lie all night with a desperate wound and no water, listening to the four-footed wolves feed on bodies while the two-footed kind take gold and slit throats.

He told me, 'He is worth most who does the most.'

Eventually, I took his sabatons, his spurs and his dagger, which was clutched in his right hand.

That's how it was.

And then John Hawkwood found me. I was halfway from de Charny's cooling corpse to the river, lying face down in the dust. Sir John never told me why he found me – I assume he was looting. There's something there, like a passion play: that Sir John Hawkwood was knighted by the Prince on the battlefield, and went straight back to picking corpses for gold.

Of course, I had, too.

He gave me water and helped me to camp. Water restored me to a dramatic degree, and the other world fell away, although as we crossed the field, me supported on his mail-clad arm, I thought that Sir Edward was leaning on one elbow waving to me, while Richard Beauchamp cursed me, and I wept.

The Earl of Oxford came and sat with me later. He congratulated me on my courage, and told me that my prisoner was still safe and was still mine.

'Sir Edward is dead,' I blurted.

A shadow crossed his face. 'Ah,' he said. 'I didn't know.'

'De Charny killed him.' I must have sounded strange. 'With one blow.'

Oxford met my eyes and put a hand on my arm. 'Yes,' he agreed.

'One blow!' I said, my voice rising. 'He never even got his guard up!'

Oxford leaned forward. 'Yes,' he said sadly. 'Sometimes it is like that.'

'He was a fine knight!' I said. I remember that I said that, because then I burst into tears.

Oxford sat with me for a long time. He was a good lord.

Later, about dark, Hawkwood came back. 'If you got yourself a full harness, I'm sure the Earl would have you as a man-at-arms,' he said. Ever the businessman, Sir John.

'I can't afford a harness,' I said, or something equally foolish.

He laughed. His hands were brown with dried blood, and I saw that he had a small pile of iron gauntlets – the most saleable item of armour – on the ground by his tent. 'It's free,' he said, waving at the field. 'I confess that the process of trying pieces on can be ... wearing. Come on, Judas. I'll see you right.'

He held my hand while a pair of archers splinted my left arm after straightening it, then he led me back onto the darkening battlefield. We didn't have the time other men had, and many of the choice bodies had been picked clean already, but the corpse of Walter de Brienne was found by the heralds just as we passed into the area the locals now call the Champs de Mars. He'd been lying at the bottom of a pile of bodies, including a horse.

As soon as Hawkwood saw him, he called to Master Peter, who was busy stripping purses, and a dozen of our archers, including Monk John.

'I'll pay cash for that corpse,' he said. 'Intact.'

They rolled the horse off Walter de Brienne in no time, and six men pulled him out of the pile. He was in head-to-toe plate, the very latest. And he was my size – a big man. Sir John had seen that immediately.

His beautiful breast and backplate would never fit me, because he was old and overweight, but his legs and arms fit well enough. I was going to spurn his helmet as he'd vomited blood into it.

'Are you a blushing virgin?' Hawkwood said. 'This is a brothel, miss, and this is a man's prick.' He shoved the helmet at me. It was far, far better than mine, with a magnificent aventail of fine mail, but the man's blood and bile was all over it. I turned and heaved, and John laughed.

Monk John stripped de Brienne's arm harnesses and stacked them and the upper and lower legs like firewood beside me. I was trying to recover, and he slapped me on the back.

'I owe you, laddy. Here's the payment. You'll be a man-at-arms. Who knew, when you were a little thief at the door of the Abbott?' John laughed. 'You'll be a gent. Remember us little archers, eh?'

I got to my feet, and the archers made a game of it. 'We're building a knight,' they said, laughing. They ran all over the field, squandering their spirit like drunkards – indeed, we were all drunk on victory and fatigue. I got a new-fangled Italian steel frontplate, and a magnificent blue velvet-covered brigantine, and a pair of fine hardened-steel shoulder rondels in the Italian style and several pairs of gauntlets.

'They like you,' Hawkwood said. He was sitting by me in the dark as Abelard came and dropped a chain hauberk in my lap. The links were superb – almost white in the moonlight. 'They like to see one of their own go ahead,' he added.

They did, too, because while we sat there, men came and embraced Sir John and complimented him on his knighthood. And men brought us wine. Abelard drank deep. 'I'm waiting to hear some praise for that shirt,' he said.

Hawkwood spotted a hole. 'Didn't help the last owner,' he said.

Abelard grunted. 'I carried that fucking mail across the field,' he said. He grinned at me. 'The Duke de Bourbon,' he chortled. 'Never say I didn't do anything for you, Judas.'

And that was the Battle of Poitiers.

Paris 1357–59

Paris? Paris was ... astonishing. Horrible. And damned confusing. When the French tried to rid themselves of their King. Oh, I was there.

After Poitiers, nothing went as we expected. I spent enough time with the Earl of Oxford and the Prince after the battle to know what *they* expected, and I was present – carving meat – when Sir Neil Loring came to Bordeaux from King Edward of England. He told us that all we had to do was hold the King of France and wait for all France to fall in our laps like ripe fruit.

But it didn't happen.

What happened was much worse – for France and for us.

First, Paris declared itself to be the government. Ah, *mes frères*, that's purest crap, but it's true nonetheless. Before Poitiers, there were quite a few Frenchmen – nobles, merchants, peasants and churchmen – who thought King Jean was anything but 'the good', and after the battle, such voices were loudest, and instead of ransoming him, they as much as declared they could govern better without him.

Truth be told, he'd failed them. He'd never beat us in the field, and now he'd failed, lost and been captured. With him went, well, the government, eh? Dead or captured. His cowardly son, the Dauphin, slipped away and tried to govern, but Paris wasn't having it, and when the parliament was summoned, they voted no money for ransoming the King of France and damned little for war.

Perhaps you remember, messieurs? Or do they tell a different story in Hainault? I'm damned sure the French tell a nicer story now. Not one about how they ate each other while we nibbled at the edges.

Paris ended in the hands of a mercer, who made himself the

tyrant. He was named Etienne Marcel and, after a lot of blood and words, he emerged as the leader of a party. Charles of Navarre – you must know that name. I'm no follower of his, by the Virgin. Navarre was the son-in-law of the King of France and, despite that, the most treacherous, conniving bastard France ever produced. He was also the head of a party, even when in prison for treason, where King John had put him. He was put there because he and his brother gave us, the English, much of Normandy. When King John was taken at Poitiers, Charles of Navarre – still in prison, mind you – began to talk, and people began to listen.

I had a friend, a French knight – you'll hear more about him – who used to say that Charles of Navarre was so poisonous he left a trail of slime wherever he crawled. Ha! Be your own judge.

Navarre's brother, Philippe, wasn't in prison, and he signed a treaty with King Edward, and the war moved out of Gascony and up north to Brittany and Normandy. Navarre handed over the keys to Normandy, will he, nil he, and every free companion – every man not bound by a feudal oath or retinue pay – picked up his harness, borrowed money from the Italians and headed north, where the ransoms were rich.

I was in love with being a gentleman, which I was, of sorts. In the big, rambling, tumbledown archbishop's palace in Bordeaux, the Prince kept great state, and I was one of many squires who attended on him personally. I was loosely attached to the Earl of Oxford, who, himself, went back and forth between England and Gascony freely. No one provided me wages, so I had to scrounge in a distinctly ungentlemanly way to maintain myself in a tiny garret room under the eaves of a private house. But it was dry and warm.

Bordeaux became a rich town overnight, both as the Prince's seat of government in Gascony, as the entrepôt for the sale of all that loot, as the banking centre handling the ransoms of half of France's nobility and, of course, as the centre of the English wine trade. There was a great deal of money moving about the town, and it was annoying to be poor. At the same time, the town was full of refugees and peasants, displaced from their homes by the war, and they were fleeced like sheep, and sometimes bought and sold like them, too.

Well, I can make a thousand excuses.

It started innocently enough – my landlord raised the rent of my tiny room, and I was in the street with too much armour and too little cash. Then and there I considered following Sir John to

Normandy. He was taking his leave of the Earl of Oxford to go with Seguin de Badefol and Petit Mechin to see what ransoms they could gain in the north. But it was autumn, and I had released my own capture on parole to collect the gold for his ransom: 450 ducats. A Genoese offered me 100 ducats flat on the ransom – in cash. I was sorely tempted, as I wasn't eating very often or well, and the high point of my week was waiting on the Prince's table after Mass on Sundays and feast days, because with the other squires I could eat the pickings, which were richer than most food I could buy. I am not ashamed to say that sometimes I would fill a leather bag with food – roast peacock, roast beef, messes of rice with saffron – anything that the cooks would let me take.

The same evening that Sir John offered to take me to Normandy as a man-at-arms, he invited me to dinner at an inn called the Three Foxes. It's still there.

I loved that place – my first castle. It was built where two streets emptied into a square, and the inn itself was laid out in a triangle, which narrowed as the two streets converged. It had some glass windows in brilliantly mullioned panels, and beautifully carved woodwork – carved, I'm given to understand, by an artist who could not pay his tab.

I had no duties that day, so after a contemplative walk across the river, where spitting over the edge of the bridge was considered a proper gentlemanly pursuit, I assure you, I searched my empty purse – a habit – and was properly amazed to find a half a silver bit wedged under the rivet that held the strap on the outside of the flap. I stood there like a fool, staring at the value of a night's lodging.

A girl of perhaps my own age, if one is generous, approached along the bridge, dragging her sister, who was a year younger. Both were pretty, in a plain, wholesome French way, and dressed in smocks that did them no justice.

'Suck your cock, messire?' said the older girl. She smiled prettily. In fact, for a prostitute, she was the most cheerful creature I'd met with. 'My sister's a virgin. You can have her for…' She paused, my little merchant. 'A gold ecu.' She looked at me expectantly.

I must pause to mention that apparently I looked like a lord. I confess that I spent my loot – and I had some – from Poitiers on clothes and whores and their clothes – and some wine. I did not, for example, travel home to see my sister, or send her money. I thought I'd send her money when the ransom came in. I agonized about it, and as the weeks dragged on, I grew despondent. And despondent *men sin*. When you feel you are bad – well then.

'An ecu for your sister's ecu?' I asked. I thought I was quite witty. *Par dieu*, possibly that's the only reason I still remember this episode, *mes amis*.

She shrugged, unimpressed. 'Well?' she asked.

'If I had any silver at all, I would buy the both of you dinner,' I said. It was my turn to shrug. I held up my half of a silver penny. 'This is all the cash I have, sister.'

She grinned. 'It would buy all three of us dinner,' she allowed.

'I have a dinner engagement with some gentlemen,' I admitted. She frowned.

While we were flirting over money, there was an altercation at the south end of the bridge. I thought it was merely traffic, as the narrow streets of Bordeaux were never built for the traffic the English brought, but it was worse. It was a crowd. A mob.

Mobs formed quickly. The war and the Black Death had robbed us all of any pretence of common morality. We fornicated, and God did not care much. We killed each other – you know, eh? The two go wonderfully well together. Sin and sin. Murder and fornication. If you wish to understand my peers, know this: we were killers because of the Black Death.

The mob was made up of poor men, and they had a Jew. And some sort of African – black as pitch.

I'll be honest, I want to tell the truth, messires. Had it just been a Jew, I might have let him die. I'd like to think I might have tried to save him, because Our Lady was a Jew, and Jews, despite what the Dominicans say, are people just like you or me, and if you deny it, I will cheerfully prove my assertion on your body with that sword right there. No takers? The ecumenical conference is over, gentles.

But the black man – I'd seen him at the palace. He was a big, pleasant fellow called Richard Musard, and men called him 'The Black Squire'. Like me, he lived in the half-world, neither lord nor peasant. Men said he'd been a slave.

Either way, he was one of mine – whatever mine were.

The two men were tied to heavy wooden boards. I assume they were to be burned.

The two girls froze.

'Get behind me,' I said as kindly as I could. See, I went to hell from kindness!

Bah, don't believe it.

At any rate, I handed the older girl my silver penny. 'Run and eat,' I said. 'Meet me at the Three Foxes after evensong and you can work off the meal.'

She smiled. 'Pleasant enough, messire.' She took her sister by the hand, kirtled up her skirts and ran.

The crowd started up the span of the bridge.

I drew my sword. It's worth noting that I wore my beautiful long-sword all the time. And as a squire in royal service – even unpaid – I had every right to wear it. All the time.

When I drew it, I put myself above the crowd.

A knight carries justice in his scabbard.

'Halt,' I yelled. My adolescent voice was against me. My shout was more like a squeak.

The sword was loud enough, though.

The men at the front shuffled to a stop, while the men behind pressed them forward.

'Halt!' I shouted again. I pointed at the black man. 'That man is a royal squire, and you will all die if you do not let him go.'

There were seventy or eighty men, a handful of hags, and more people gathering every minute.

I doubt they heard me. When you confront a crowd, you need to act quickly and decisively, and you must speak the same way.

'Fuck your royals and their fucking taxes,' roared one emaciated farmer at the front. He was almost speechless with rage and some-thing else – something a crowd brings to men.

I cut him down. I knew how to use my point to open a man's guts, and I was too fast for him. He fell to his knees on the bridge, looking at his intestines.

And I put my sword's point into the chest of the next man in the crowd. 'Want to die?' I asked.

The farmer whimpered once and died at my feet. I killed him to quiet the crowd. No other reason. Just so you understand.

The fellow pressing against my sword spat in my face, so I cut him in the neck, and he pitched forward, spouting blood.

Now they flinched back from me.

I walked towards them. I had the upper hand and, like any other bully, I revelled in it. They backed away, crouching like the *canaille* they were, and then they began to run like whipped dogs.

I cut Musard off his log, and gave him my rondel in case they came again, then I cut the Jew free.

He hugged himself a few times, pulled his beard and, of all things, smiled.

Smiled.

He bowed. 'Suleyman Bashid, at your service,' he said, bowing, with a hand on his heart.

Good Christ – he lent money to the Prince. The crowd had been about to kill one of the Prince's tax farmers and one of his servants.

Musard was as pale as old ashes, and he shook for a moment. Hell, I shook for a moment. Then he embraced me, and he was a big man.

'By the lord our God, I thought this son of Israel and I were dead men, and that as barbarously as could be done.' He was shaking.

'Let's get you away,' I said.

'Suleyman was due at the palace before vespers,' Musard said.

I walked them back across the bridge, and right to the ruined brick gates to the palace courtyard, where a pair of belted knights sat in a shelter with fifteen men-at-arms day and night – the Prince's guard, all in black with white ostrich plumes on their chests. I aspired to be one of them some day. Sir John derided them and said that real men-at-arms spent their days fighting, not watching the Prince eat.

Sir John Blankford received Musard and Bashid, paid me a thousand compliments and gave me a rag to wipe my sword clean. I still had it in my hand. I had rather hoped the Jew might reward me with something a little harder than his handshake, but I was to be disappointed. So I bowed to the knights and made my way back across the bridge, watching the corners and alleys carefully. I'd killed enough men by then to know that the two I'd just put in the mud had brothers, sons and cousins who might want me dead.

I made the Three Foxes in time, and Seguin de Badefol was sitting with Sir John, one of the younger Albrets, and Bertucat, known to everyone as the Bourc Camus.

Sir John rose to his feet and took my hand. The Gascons all grinned.

'It's the little cook,' barked the Bourc. His eyes glittered. 'What are you making for us tonight?'

When you are sixteen, such jibes seem to have real meaning, real intent to harm. In fact, with that mad bastard, I suspect he did intend harm, but I was too on edge.

I sat on a stool and sent the boy for a piece of tow and some oil.

Sir John ordered a pitcher of wine, a joint of beef and some bread and gravy. Two women, as hard in their way as the bread was in its way, came to serve our table. The Gascons fondled them – they appeared to appreciate the rough wooing with equal enthusiasm, which is to say none at all.

I felt uncomfortable.

They were all good men-at-arms, but I felt I was with criminals, not men of birth who sought glory and honour. I knew these men. I knew the Prince and his men.

I was no fool, messieurs. Sir John Chandos had the luxury of being courteous because he had manors and peasants to maintain him, and royal favour, and Sir John Hawkwood had his sword. It made them different men. But I aspired then, as I aspire now, to the status of knighthood, like de Charny.

Sir John waited until I'd eaten – I confess I ate a great deal – then leaned across the table. 'Your health, my young friend.'

I drank with him, then I proposed the healths of other men. The Bourc sat up.

'But why am I last?' he asked. His eyes, as I say, glittered.

I'd had enough of his shit, even if he was the top sword in Gascony. 'Last?' I asked him.

'You propose the healths of other men before me,' he said.

'You lie,' I insisted. 'I had no intention of toasting your health at all.'

Every head turned.

And Seguin de Badefol, who was a great lord and no one's bastard, roared a great laugh, kicked his longsword from under the table with his left leg and slapped me on the back.

The Bourc was on his feet

Seguin shook his head. 'No, Bertucat. I forbid it. He's a boy, and a brave boy, and you only got what you had coming.' He looked at me. 'So, what of it, messieur? Will you come with us to Normandy?'

I intended to go with them. What did I have to hold me in Bordeaux? Poverty? The Prince? He scarcely knew my name.

'What will we do in Normandy? Will we take service with a lord?' I asked.

The four of them looked at each other, as wolves look around their circle when they discuss dismembering a flock of sheep, I imagine.

'We will serve the King of England, of course,' Seguin said. He twirled his moustache, which tapered to needle points. 'But we will *be* the lords. We will be companions, and sign articles to form a Company of Adventure, as they do in Italy and Greece. We will take ransoms and share the profits; we will take castles and sell them to the King of England.'

'And if he doesn't want them, we will sell them back to the owners!' said Albret – the younger one.

Sir John nodded. 'A little scouting to find the weak lords and weak holdings, and then, in two or three weeks of work, we storm a dozen of them, sell the ransoms, put the screws to the peasants for protection, then sell the castle and move on.' He reached out and took the lace point that tied my somewhat threadbare jupon. It had once been gilt bronze and the replacement was waxed leather. 'A man can make a hundred Venetian ducats a month.'

'Easily,' Seguin de Badefol said.

'A virgin like this won't make a fart,' Camus said. 'Listen, cook's boy. The fastest way to make silver is to take convents of nuns. Rape them all with your soldiers – rape a girl ten times and she's a willing whore. You know why nuns make better whores, boy? Because they won't kill themselves. They believe in God.' Camus stared at me.

'You speak like a horse shits, Gascon. God will punish you for suggesting such a course – no man would actually do as you suggest.' My hand was on my sword, and my blade was four inches clear of the scabbard.

He laughed. 'God is a lie, boy. There is only Satan, and I am his disciple.'

'Shut up, Bertucat. You're drunk.' Sir John sounded merely weary, not disgusted.

'I don't like the little cook and I want him to stay here,' said the Bourc. 'But I need someone to rape the little choirboys. There's men who will pay for that, too.'

Sir John put his hand on my arm. I had started to rise from my chair.

Camus leaned back and his eyes rested on mine. He was tall – taller than me – with black eyes. He was handsome, with high cheekbones. He had a bone in one ear instead of an earring – the bone of a woman, everyone said, but no one said which bone or whose it was.

'Stop staring at me, catamite. I do not like your eyes.' His, which were deceptively gentle, bored into mine.

'No man tells me where I may look or not look. Much less a man who advocates the raping of nuns.' I was on my feet.

'I'll kill you when Seguin is not here to stop me, little cook's boy,' he said. 'I break things I do not like. I do not like you.'

I looked at him. My hands were shaking, but his mad gaze was no madder than my uncle's. In fact, there was something similar about them, and my hate boiled over.

'Let's go,' I said.

Sir John grabbed my hand. 'Not like this, boy. He'll gut you. Let him go, Bertucat.'

'Fuck that,' I said with all the bravado of my sixteen years. I got to my feet and walked outside into the yard, turned and drew my sword.

The Bourc emerged from the inn, grinned and drew.

Sir John was behind him. It was dark in the courtyard, but there were torches.

He came at me while I was still thinking we might abuse each other with words, and I just managed to turn his first strike, which was as fast as an adder's tongue and as strong as a smith's hammer stroke. I fell back a pace and he cut at me again – one, two, to either side of my head.

I raised my sword to parry the two head cuts – each block took my hands higher. With a snort of pure contempt, he punched with his left hand at the pommel of my sword, flinging my arms over my head. I lost my balance, and he kicked me between the legs. I fell forward on the ground, puking from the pain.

Sir John roared, 'No!'

Camus laughed and he kicked me again, in the back, so I fell forward in the mud. Then he stabbed his sword deep into my arse – once, and twice.

'Butt Boy,' he mocked.

I wished he'd killed me.

I tried to get to my feet. I was weeping, and rage, fear and humiliation warred for possession of my soul. Blood trickled down the backs of my thighs.

He laughed. 'I'll have your sword, Butt Boy,' he said.

I wasn't going to give it to him. I don't know what he expected, but he clearly thought the fight was over and he grabbed at the sword.

I flicked it at him, one handed, a weak, false-edge rising cut fuelled only by fear and hate.

I caught the base of his left hand and cut off a finger.

He dropped his sword. '*Merde!*' he roared in Gascon French.

I raised my sword to kill him. I was absolutely going to kill him, unarmed.

Sir John Hawkwood saved my life and my career. He had already picked up a piece of firewood, intending, he told me later, to stop Bertucat Camus from killing me. Instead, he hit me on the head from behind.

I fell to the ground unconscious.

When I came to, I was in the Three Foxes, in a room paid for by Sir John. And my two little whores were waiting on me hand and foot.

Over the next month or so, Richard Musard and I became fast friends, and we took over the running of the Three Foxes. It proved, after the fact, that the Gascons had 'protected' the place until they left it, charging the landlord protection money and running a string of prostitutes under the eaves. It's good for an innkeeper to have a good sword on his payroll – a soldier can often talk other soldiers out of doing damage or fighting, and a really good sword discourages violence.

I lay in bed for three days, and Richard visited twice. The two girls – named Marie and Anne, in the best tradition of Gascony – worked the inn, and no one stopped them, of course, because the inn's strong arm had just ridden north to Normandy.

I'll make this brief – you all want to hear about Paris and Brignais. I want you to know what our lives were like in the companies, and this is all part of that. So, in short, by the time my wounds healed, I had fifteen girls, and the Black Squire and I ran the inn. The innkeeper was a big man, but not a brave one, and he was used to being bullied by a much more evil bastard than me. Musard terrified him, with his black skin.

As to the girls, I am not proud of being a pimp, but there are ways and ways. Even then, I wasn't willing to pimp directly. In fact, Marie did all the work, and all Richard and I did was glare at the customers and collect the coins.

Sometimes a girl would come and say she'd had a problem.

The first time was the worst, but it made life easier for us. Anne was working on her back and the man she'd taken started to hit her with his fists. She screamed. Marie came for me, but I was already moving. I went into that room – a room barely big enough to fuck – and there's a man my size, stinking of wine, his hose and braes off, his hairy arse bare, pummelling this small girl—

Good Christ.

I caught one of his hands the way I'd learned from Abelard, in a dagger lock. Look here – punch at me, see? I catch your hand like this – *eh bien*? – I could make you scream like a woman giving birth.

So I trapped his hand under my dagger blade and twisted, and he came off the girl. He followed me down the steep steps to the courtyard, bellowing curses and bile all the way.

I put his left hand on the chopping block in the inn yard and drove my rondel dagger through it. I left him there, nailed to the block, until Anne came, kicked him a few times, raised her skirts and pissed on him.

Afterwards, she kissed me and called me her true knight.

Aye, the paragon of chivalry and protector of women.

Here's the funny thing, though. I took good care of Geoffrey de Charny's rondel dagger, but I must have left the man pinned to the chopping block too long. Because when I took the dagger free, the whoreson's blood had left a stain on the steel, and I couldn't polish it out.

Ah, I have shocked you, messieurs. Let us discuss this like gentlemen.

Running an inn was hardly to be reconciled with the life of a knight, you might think, and yet, what men-at-arms do in the field is rape and murder. We kill each other and we kill peasants. We burn farms and we take loot – even in Italy, and twice as much when fighting pagans or saracens.

I went to a hard school that summer of Poitiers. And when I was done, I had learned how to kill and how to survive. I thought I was a fine sword, a good lance and a gentleman. I confess to you that what I knew of chivalry might have fit inside one of the illuminated letters monks use at the beginning of a gospel – just one. I wanted to be worth more. I wanted to fight, and be *preux*. That's what I knew.

Of chivalry's finer feelings, I knew next to nothing. In fact, I was worse than that. I heard the old troubadour songs about courtly love, honour and loyalty, and I thought them lies.

I did fear the law and the loss of respect. I knew full well that if the Prince ever heard of any of this, I'd have been out in an instant. But thanks be to God, our clients were discreet. We gathered girls, and they came to us, for no better reason than that neither Richard nor I beat our girls – Christ, men are animals. I was an animal. I rutted with every girl in my stable. I was their lord and master.

I confess, I ate well, dressed well and, twice a week, I waited at table on my Prince. I remember one evening, he stopped in a corridor where I was enjoying a cup of his wine with two of his squires. I was wearing a good black linen jupon, carefully embroidered with crosses, and matching wool hose, and I had a silk coat over the whole in a fine red-brown. It was my best, and my shoes matched, and I had de Charny's dagger in my belt.

The Prince stopped and I made my obeisance.

'You have done well for yourself, Master Gold,' he said. I flushed, because he knew my name. 'Has your prisoner paid his ransom?'

'No, my Prince.' I tried to smile, to make it a joke. 'Some ... money from rents, your Grace.'

He laughed. 'Ah, you have rents?' he said, and I could see I'd just climbed in his estimation. 'I am remiss, Master Gold. Are you John or William?'

'William, your Grace.' I bowed again.

'I remember you from Poitiers, and elsewhere,' he said. 'I seem to remember you as a cook.' He laughed.

'I was a cook,' I admitted. 'My mother was a de Vere and my father served as a man-at-arms, but ...'

He nodded absently. 'Yes, of course.' His eyes scanned the crowd of courtiers, who were pressing in, wondering who I was. Sir John Chandos stepped up closer to the Prince and took my hand.

Sir John Chandos, shaking my hand.

'I remember you at Poitiers,' he said. 'You were there when de Charny fell.'

'I have his dagger,' I said. I didn't mention that I'd just used the paragon of chivalry's dagger to pin a bad client to a chopping block so my whores could punish him. That seemed like a bad idea.

The Prince smiled at me. 'You fought well,' he said. 'Men like you, with the help of God, gave me that victory.'

He turned away and I was aglow. For a moment I forgot that I was a pimp. I was a great man-at-arms, a soldier in the retinue of the finest prince in Christendom, the best lance in the west.

Sir John Chandos waited until the Prince swept on down the corridor. 'You were a cook,' he said pleasantly. 'And now you seem on the road to being a knight.'

No one was more pleased to hear it than me. I had waited tables in the archbishop's palace for almost a year, and suddenly my service was remembered.

I went home, floating on a cloud of knightly valour, and ordered Marie to wash herself and decline clients. I ordered wine and we had a fine night.

Towards morning, she kissed me. 'Am I allowed to tell you that I like you, protector?'

I rolled on top of her and tickled her. We were very young to be so hard, and neither one of us was as hard as we pretended.

Sometimes, we had a fine time.

Spring came, in the year of our lord 1358. Sir John sent me a letter for the Prince, which seemed to me an odd conceit, but I read his covering letter, blushing at his praise of me. He had more than eighty lances, and he had fought his way across Brittany – not, as it proved, Normandy.

I read enough of his letter to the Prince – pardon me, gentles, but the only seal was on his letter to me – to know that he had seized castles for the King of Navarre and was offering them, unofficially, to our Prince.

I gave his letter into Sir John Chandos's hands, and he looked at me very thoughtfully and gave me five golden ducats for the delivery – a great deal of money.

It wasn't many days after, when I stood in my room at the inn – a fine room – dressing for court. I was not wealthy enough to have a male servant, but Marie generally saw to my appearance with the practicality of a farm girl. I remember she wanted to go to Mass, and wanted me to come – she wanted us to go to Mass together. I was not an enemy to God like the Bourc, but neither was I a hypocrite, and I didn't relish facing God with a purse stuffed full of coins from whores.

Killing men is so much nobler, now, isn't it? And look at that young cock – afraid to face God while aglow with praise from his worldly Prince, and still breathing hard from a fine morning ride with his whore. How many men live in a man?

At any rate, I was half dressed, in my hose and braes and a shirt and sleeveless doublet when there was a commotion in the inn's yard.

I threw open the windows and looked out.

There were half-a dozen men on bad horses in the yard.

Richard Musard had his sword drawn.

You could tell at a glance that these were hard men, and that the talking part was over.

Listen, I had learned a dozen lessons from the Bourc Camus. I'd worked on my swordsmanship and my jousting all winter, because I was never going to allow myself to be so easily bested again. And I'd learned that when the talking is over, you fight. In fact, you can save a great deal of trouble if you start fighting while the other bastard is still talking.

The Three Foxes had a slate roof and lead drains. I was out the windows of my room, over the balcony and onto the stable roof before I'd really thought it through. I *knew* what to do.

'It's my inn now,' said the leader. He was English, tall and broad like an archer. 'You kept it warm for me. Now run along and play, Blackie.'

The other five men chuckled. They were hairy, about ten years older than me, with grey at their temples, flat purses and a lot of spring mud on their boots. They weren't archers, though. Archers always have bows.

They were brigands. Mercenaries, or worse.

Richard didn't budge. 'Whose man are you?' he asked.

'I'm my own man, Blackie. And I won't ask again. Walk away.' He reached for his sword.

I felt he'd asked one too many times. After the Bourc, I'd learned a great deal about who was dangerous and who was merely tough.

I jumped onto his back from the stable roof. De Charny's dagger went into the top of his head and he was dead before I had control of his horse. I wheeled the horse and dumped his body in the yard.

I backed the terrified horse – no horse likes the smell of blood – until I was at Richard's side.

'That took you too long,' he said pleasantly enough. 'I didn't think I could kill them all myself.'

Oh, how I loved him. I never saw him lose his nerve – then or later.

'Marie was dressing me,' I said, as if the other five weren't even there. 'I was busy.'

The five men were disconcerted to say the least.

I raised my bloody dagger. 'Get you gone,' I said. 'Or I'll kill the lot of you. This is Bordeaux, not the marches. We don't allow broken men here.'

The closest man to me met my eye, and I knew in a moment that he was the most dangerous of the lot. He didn't care. His eyes were vague, empty.

I addressed him directly. 'I'm the Earl of Oxford's man,' I said. 'Get you gone.'

He looked down at his former leader, now leaking into the already foul mud of the inn yard. 'Fuck me,' he muttered and turned his horse.

The last man of the five was not as hard and looked as if he would weep.

'*Par dieu,* messire! Have pity! We are Englishmen no worse than you!'

The fellow next to him was, one could see, the castle lawyer of the group. Seeing me hesitate – I'm death in a fight, but soft as a snail inside, as all the girls knew – he leaned forward.

'It's all a misunderstanding, messire. We need work.' He smiled. I'm sure he meant it to be ingratiating, or reassuring, but his ugly breath and worse teeth were enough to cause grave offence.

'And you meant to take my inn to have your work,' I said.

'We could help you run your inn,' he said.

Marie leaned over the balcony. 'Like fuck, messire! I don't need five new rams poking at my ewes. *Eh bien?*'

I summoned Christophe, the inn's lord. 'Messire, would you do me a favour and feed these men? And give them a place to sleep tonight?' I asked.

He shrugged. He was making a fair amount of silver these days, as I took less out of him than the Gascons had. 'For you? Anything, messire.'

'What in the name of all the apostles are you doing?' Richard asked me.

I shrugged. I didn't know myself. In fact, in my heart I knew I'd done the wrong thing, and that they'd catch me sleeping, kill me and take my girls.

But they were English, and the empty-eyed man had been at Poitiers. I knew him immediately as one of Master Peter's men. So I waited for the other five to pass me, and I held him back.

'I know you,' he said slowly. He fingered his dirty beard. 'Why?'

'Why what?'

'Why let us stay?' he asked slowly.

I had thought he was slow, or stupid, or had received an injury, but now I realized he wasn't English. He was from the north. York, or even further.

'You were at Poitiers,' I said.

'Heh,' he said, and smiled. 'Samuel Bibbo,' he said, extending his hand. 'An' you too, eh?'

We shook.

I promise you that wouldn't have ended well, but then, everything happened quickly. It was that evening at court that Sir John Chandos took me aside.

'Master Gold,' he said. 'You have something of a mixed reputation. A fine blade, men say. And as brave as a lion.'

I could hear the 'but', so I didn't let the praise go to my head.

'Brave men are as common as lice here in Gascony. The Prince is here to govern, and not to loot his own lands.' Chandos was a man I never wanted to cross – he was distant, careful and very slow to anger. He was always courteous, even to those he detested. 'The Prince needs men who are brave and loyal and *thoughtful*.' He sat back. 'You are very young – and I think you had a misunderstanding with the law in London.'

I nodded, chilled to the bone. Was I about to be dismissed from the Prince's court? I could feel it.

But Sir John Chandos was much more subtle than that. Instead, he let the threat of my colourful past stay on the table between us, so to speak. 'Some men say you are cunning. One man – Sir John Hawkwood – says you are wise beyond your years. I understand you can read.'

'Yes, my lord,' I answered.

'Like a clerk?' he asked. He put a document in front of me. It was a draft, full of blots and misspellings. It was in Latin. A grant of lands to a Gascon lord.

I read a sentence of the mediocre Latin aloud. 'It is a land grant,' I said.

Sir John steepled his fingers. He rocked back and forth slowly. 'Very good,' he said. 'Do you seek to serve the Prince?' he asked.

'Yes,' I said. I was surprised at my own vehemence.

He looked at me. His eyes didn't move, and I suspect I fidgeted. I had a great deal about which to be nervous. Many secrets that could be used against me.

'We will see. I will try you, and see what metal there is in your body. Come, Master Gold. You will have your future with the Prince's household in your own hands. I have a man for you to meet.'

We walked along one of the bishop's endless corridors to a small solar – like a closet with a fireplace, set in the wainscotting. There was a young man with an older man's forked beard sitting on a low stool. He had ink stains on his right hand and a touch of ink at the corner of his mouth – a touch that added to the perpetual sneer he wore.

'Master Chaucer,' Sir John said. 'This is William Gold, Esquire. He serves us sometimes. Master Gold, this is Geoffrey Chaucer, a page of Prince Lionel's wife's household, and with us at this time to do the Prince a service or two. I have a mind to send the two of you on an errand together.'

'I am mere clay to accompany your Gold,' Chaucer said. He looked at me. 'Best send him on his own.'

His intent was uncivil, but he smirked and bowed.

Sir John Chandos was so unused to any form of cheek that he continued, assuming Chaucer had been respectful. 'In light of the letter you brought from Sir John Hawkwood, the Prince would like an answer taken straight away. And perhaps, ahem, a further message for Paris.'

Chaucer looked at me. 'He doesn't have a clue what you are talking about, Sir John,' he said. He smiled at me in a patronizing manner.

Sir John glared at him, having caught the tone. 'Keep a civil tongue, young Chaucer.' He looked at me. 'This is all about the government of the Prince's realm,' Sir John said. 'Can you keep your mouth shut?' asked the old knight. Well, he was old to me, even if he was reputed to be one of the top fighting men in the world.

I bowed. Let's be frank, *compères*, never ask a man if he can keep a secret. Who will say no, eh?

'Give me your solemn word,' he said.

I knelt. 'I swear to keep your secret, my lord,' I said.

'On his brothel, he swears it,' Chaucer said.

'What's that?' Sir John asked.

Chaucer smiled. He looked like a ferret when he smiled. 'Nothing, my lord.'

Sir John looked at me, clearly off balance. Chaucer had the habit of putting you off balance. He was that kind of boy.

'The King of France has negotiated a peace with our King Edward,' he said portentously.

Now, in truth, this was mighty news. It struck me in ten ways. First that my employment was going to end, and I hadn't even worn all my harness yet. In fact, all my looted armour was in pawn with the Italians – why redeem it when there was wine to be drunk – but now the war was going to end.

At another level, it meant there was some hope of getting my prisoner's ransom paid, which would give me the money to—

Good Christ, what was I going to do?

The war had, at that point, dragged on for twenty years. France was bankrupt; England was better off, but the grumblings I heard from new drafts were that, despite recent victories, parliament wasn't voting the King any more money to fight.

It was like a lightning bolt. King John had shipped out of Bordeaux earlier that year, taking his growing retinue of fellow prisoners and servants, as well as all of the bloody Count of Armagnac's silver plate. I only mention that as I was there when it arrived, and I directed its polishing – my goldsmith skills weren't completely wasted – and King John thanked me.

Well, I think it's funny.

Where was I?

Oh!

Peace.

Sir John allowed me to digest this information. 'If you were to take a return letter to Sir John Hawkwood, the Prince would esteem it a favour,' he said.

'He means that now we're to have peace, you'll be wanting a job at court,' Chaucer quipped.

'Of course I'll go,' I said, privately agreeing with the annoying boy's assessment.

Sir John nodded. 'You'll need an escort,' he said.

'I have a small retinue,' I said. The arrogance of the seventeen-year-old knows no bounds. 'And I'd esteem it a favour if I might have Richard Musard.'

Sir John fingered his beard. 'A retinue?' He smiled. 'How many men and how armed?' He looked at me. 'I seem to remember you as a cook, lad, not a great noble.'

I glared, preemptively, at Chaucer. 'My lord, I have an archer and four men-at-arms available for pay.'

He nodded approvingly. 'Muster them for me this evening in the courtyard with your horses and arms. You will be paid. I'd prefer it you would leave immediately.'

I walked out of the palace floating on air – I was to have my own indenture for four weeks' service as a direct contractor. It wasn't just the money. Very well, it *was* the money, but it was also honour. For the rest of my life, I would be able to say that I mustered a retinue for the Prince of Wales.

I ditched Chaucer at the gate – I didn't like him – and ran to the inn.

I ignored the castle lawyer – Christopher, as he proved to be called. 'Where's Sam?' I asked Marie.

'Riding Helene.' She smirked. 'He paid.'

Richard made a motion with his hand to his dagger. It was rude, and it conveyed a great deal of information. Sam hadn't wanted to pay, but he had paid.

'Gentleman, a knight is with Petit Claire,' Marie went on. She held up a solid gold Venetian ducat.

'By Saint George, he can take her home for that.' I grinned at my leman, who grinned back. 'And keep her.' Claire was by far and away our most beautiful girl; she was also a vicious, willful bully who probably needed a whipping from me. She got them from Marie instead – Marie insisted on being the only voice of discipline.

I think she liked it.

I walked over to Richard. 'We have a contract – a retinue contract – from the Prince. To take a message to Sir John Hawkwood in Brittany.' I grinned. 'Four weeks full pay.'

Whores and inns fell away. Richard bounced to his feet. '*Ventre Saint Gris!*' he swore. 'My harness!'

'And mine. Send the inn's boy to fetch them. Send one of the girls to the market for two wicker baskets. Send round to Rolf the armourer for two apprentices to bring it all up to fighting condition.'

Marie looked at me. 'You will spend all our money,' she said.

I rolled my eyes. 'This is what it's for, my sweet.'

'For war? We lie on our backs and fuck strangers so you can make war?' she spat at me.

'Yes,' I said, and went about getting horses.

Richard and I didn't have horses. Owning a horse in Bordeaux was fiendishly expensive. After Poitiers, I owned a fine golden war horse for a few weeks, but his stall and manger cost me more than I spent on my garret and my food, so he went to the first rich knight who offered.

Now I needed a riding horse *and* a war horse, and the pleasure of it was that I was buying in a depressed market. The Prince hadn't fought a campaign all year, and he was about to leave for England; there was no word of any fighting, and knights going with the Prince were selling out. Word of the peace was probably alive among the horse and arms merchants – they always know these things first.

Richard and I issued our orders to servants and girls and went to the horse market under the walls. On second Sundays it was a proper market. The rest of the time it was a dozen dealers with a hundred horses, some of them right hard bargains.

To my immense delight – I felt God was on my side – my golden warhorse was standing in the lines, looking a little dejected. I walked up to the bastard we all called Jamais, because it was the word he used most often, and pointed at my former horse.

'That horse looks familiar,' I said. 'Where'd you get him?'

I sounded not like a customer, but like a man looking for a stolen horse.

Jamais shrugged. 'I forget,' he said.

There you go, then.

'What will you take for him?' I asked.

'Fifty florins.' The florin was a Florentine gold coin, the standard coin of all France, let me add.

I had six florins. I had a lot of other coins, too, and some un-minted silver and gold, but I only had six florins. 'Give me that in Livre Tournois?'

He spat. 'A thousand. But I won't take French coins. Fucking Paris has devalued them all. Again.'

I had a great many French coins. 'What?' I asked.

He spat again. 'The so-called Council of Eighty has ordered all the coins withdrawn. They plan to clip them, adulterate the silver and re-issue them at a profit because the fucking peasants won't pay their fucking taxes. They are reducing the value of the coins by a quarter and charging a fee for the privilege. Got me, squire?'

I did. I'd heard about it, but I hadn't understood. Now I knew why every customer all spring had paid in French silver. Parisian, especially.

Yes, our horse dealers had to be masters of international finance. So, apparently, did young men who ran brothels.

Richard was looking at horses, and he chose a fine dark bay, big and heavy. Like Richard, in fact. We both chose good riding horses.

'I'll let you have the lot for a hundred and fifty florins,' Jamais said.

Richard grunted. 'Seventy,' he said.

'By the sweet lord who gave his life for our sins, messieurs *les gentilshommes*, have a little mercy on an old horse thief.' He had his dirty black wool cap clutched to his breast, as if he were a piteous spectacle while he gouged us for Italian gold we didn't have.

Richard smiled. 'Jamais, this is us. Richard and Will, penniless squires. We *sell* horses. We don't buy horses. Now we have a contract with the Prince and we need to be mounted.'

Jamais leaned forward. 'War?' he asked eagerly.

I shook my head. 'Courier.'

Jamais spat. Again. 'Fucking peace. We'll all be vagabonds. A hundred.'

That sounded fine to me. I'm poor at bargaining – I didn't have a hundred, or even ten, but a hundred sounded like a bargain, as the knight who purchased my golden stallion had given me a hundred florins for him.

Richard shrugged. 'Seventy-five.'

'Fuck your mother!' Jamais swore. 'Kill me and take them, whore-master!'

We all laughed. Richard looked away. 'Eighty.'

Jamais stared off into the heavens. 'Next, you'll be asking for credit,' he said. As Richard began to comment, he held up a hand. 'And you'll ride off into France and die, and I'm out all my money. So yes, eighty. In gold.'

We spat in our hands and shook, and then Richard and I hoisted our bags and went off to the Italians.

The Riccardi were Lucchese bankers, and they had an office in Poitiers. But they'd been mostly ruined by the war, so we banked – if our constant pawning of armour and looted jewels could be called banking – with the Genoese house of Bardi. So we went there. We thumped our bags of French and English silver on the counters, and boys – banking apprentices – started counting the coins.

'An armourer's boy came for your armours, messires,' said the master of the house, Raimondo. He bowed, as if we were really knights. I suspect we were all exactly the same to him. Whores and bankers – everyone is the same to them. And doctors, I suppose.

I nodded.

'I thank you for such prompt repayment of your pledges,' he said.

Richard glared at me.

Right, by taking our coin to the Genoese, we put ourselves in their hands. Now they'd take their cut first. And they'd handed all the gear over covered in rust, and mice had chewed our straps.

Christ, I hate bankers.

I noted they took all of our Italian coins, then all of our English coins, to cover the pawn of the armour. But that left a gleaming pile, and now they had six apprentices counting. Twenty girls earn a great deal of coin. And we hadn't hit the inn for the protection money owed.

Maestro Raimondo fondled his golden beard and watched as the pile grew smaller and the stacks of French coins, gold and silver, grew. He shook his head. 'French coin is virtually worthless,' he said. 'The Council of Eighty and the Provost of Paris have declared that the Dauphin's latest coining scheme is illegal, so just now, there *is* no legal coinage.' He made a clucking noise, as if all this was beyond his control. 'I can give you, hmm, sixty florins for the lot.'

Unlike Jamais, he wouldn't budge.

The most annoying thing is that he was making a huge – usurious – profit, and he knew it, but he didn't care whether we took his offer or not. What was worse, he would loan the French silver at par – at true value.

Sometime in the long process of counting, Master Chaucer appeared to negotiate a bill on London, and with him was a senior notary of the Prince's household, a fox-faced man named Michael Hoo; sometimes a customer of Marie's, and known to me. I introduced young Chaucer to Richard. Richard liked him immediately – there's no accounting for these things – and they talked nineteen to the dozen. Chaucer had never met an African and was asking Richard about his childhood, and Richard was delighted to have an audience.

I'd never even asked, so I felt a fool. Chaucer's special talent.

While we stood there at the counter of the Italian bank, I learned that Richard had been born a Christian, in the far-away Kingdom of Prester John; that his father was noble and his mother less so; that he'd been taken as a boy by the Sultan of Cairo, who was, apparently, perpetually at war with the King of Aethiopia. It was a stirring tale, and Master Chaucer drank it in – intrigue in the Aethiopian court, the great knights of the realm, the fights with the Sultan.

Musard could tell a tale, too. He was just to the point of holding forth about the style of soft armour in Aethiopia, and the qualities of horses, when Maestro Raimondo returned to the counter from his clerks. He beckoned to me. 'Even after recounting, I'm afraid I can do nothing for you. I have no need for French coin. Master Hoo? I believe you are next?'

Hoo smiled at me. 'Sir John Chandos can probably change your money,' he said.

I looked at him. 'Really?'

Master Hoo shrugged. 'I have reason to know, the Prince runs his household in Livre Tournois. I'm sure he'll give you a better rate.'

Chaucer smiled at Richard. 'My pater's a wine merchant, so we follow money markets. The fluctuation in France is ... temporary. As soon as King John pays his ransom, the markets will recover.'

Raimondo looked at the young page. 'You have the mind of a banker!' he pronounced.

'Perish the thought,' Chaucer said. 'I'm sure you meant that as a compliment, but ... Christ, how disgusting. Still ...'

Raimondo spread his hands. 'Do you gentlemen know something about King John's ransom?' he asked.

Chaucer grinned. 'Yes, Maestro, but nothing I can share. Master William, if you collect your coins and pay the counting fee, we can go to the Prince.'

Master Hoo, the notary, leaned over the counter and whispered a few words to the banker.

Maestro Raimondo smiled. 'Ah, perhaps I am over-hasty. I think, given news of the ransom of the King of France, I might manage eighty florins.'

Richard nodded. 'A blessing on you, sir.'

Chaucer looked at Master Hoo and the notary shook his head. Chaucer grinned. 'You're being fleeced like a sheep. Come, the Prince will give you a hundred and twenty. Do your whores keep you so rich you can burn forty florins?'

Up until then, our whores and the court had been well separated. Chaucer threatened that. Men like Hoo never talked, but Chaucer talked all the time.

Nevertheless, he was a boy, and I underestimated him.

Everyone did.

Maestro Raimondo bowed. 'Perhaps. Perhaps I could manage a hundred florins and no counting fee as a favour to such fine military gentlemen.'

'Baaaa!' Chaucer intoned derisively. 'Baaa! Baaa!'

But we took it.

Later that afternoon, my shirts were patched and ironed, my trousseau was packed, my armour was clean and rust free, and in some cases newly riveted, with clean leather straps. If I listened carefully, I could hear the sound of the master armourer – a friend from my earliest days – putting new links into my haubergeon. We had a small cart, riding horses, food, wine ...

Sam and I sat at a table.

'Hadn't planned to go out again so soon,' he said.

I wasn't born yesterday. Very well, I was seventeen – I *had* been born yesterday – but I knew this gambit. 'Double pay as an archer,' I said. 'Twelve pence a day, and a *regard* of a florin in gold.' I leaned forward. 'Half that for the rest of them – and I pay it to you.'

Sam fingered his moustache. 'I knew I liked you.' His smile was false, but we didn't know each other yet, and he was an ancient man – twice my age.

I put the florin in gold on the table, and slowly added the other four. My archer was called Sam Bibbo. His men – first the castle lawyer, the mouthy and rather foul Christopher Shippen; then the youngest and least experienced, a former valet named Rob of Boston; another proper archer (shows how observant I am, not) John Hughes, whose father was a yeoman from the Lakes in the north of England, and Peter of Bramford, a cordwainer's son, who'd followed his trade with the army to Poitiers and fallen into bad company – or so he said.

Of the four, I reckoned Sam a deadly man and a good archer, and I was right enough. I marked Christopher as useless, and I was dead wrong. I marked John as a fool, and I was right, but he made a fine servant; and rated Peter as a useful man, and I was far from the target.

However, once bought, they stayed bought. It might all have gone very differently, from the first, but *par dieu*, it did not. I think on it now. My reputation and my career started with these men.

Had they been false – *eh bien*, messieurs. It is as God wills it to be, eh?

Sam closed his hand over the money. 'We serve the Prince?' he asked. Even hard men, in those days, longed for the security and authority of direct service.

'Yes,' I said.

He shook his head. 'Deal.'

In my seventeen-year-old imagination, I expected a thorough examination of our horses and armour, a detailed evaluation, perhaps some criticism. We were polished and washed, and all four of Sam's men – my men, now – had linen tapes in red woven in their horse's manes by the girls.

I was proud as Lucifer. Probably prouder.

We made a fine show. Richard and I had good harness, if you ignored the fact that both of us wore a looted patchwork of armour where no two pieces went together. On mine, for example, I had fancy leather strapping with fine metalwork, but every strap was a different colour. Nothing to worry you in a fight, but any professional would look at my harness and know what a patchwork it was – I was an ill-made knight, and no mistake.

Richard was a little better, as his harness had been given him by the Prince, and all his leather was at least one colour – a boring brown, but it matched. None of it had been made for him, but the quality was good.

Our horses were excellent, though, and our men looked professional. Sir John Chandos came out on horseback, rode round them once, nodded to the clerk and grinned.

'I know that bastard,' he said, pointing at Sam.

Sam grinned. 'I know you, too, sir.'

Sir John looked at me. 'You're lucky to have a man that experienced. Listen to him. He knows things. Understand me, sir?'

I nodded.

'I am far easier in my mind knowing that you have him. Sam, this little mission matters, mind me? And see the boys make it back.' He grinned.

Why did I find a good archer wandering lose as a criminal? Because God didn't want me to spend my life in a brothel, friends. I have no other explanation.

The clerk drew up a letter of indenture, offering us all double pay – Richard and I were to be paid as knights, the rest as lesser men-at-arms, and Sam and John Hughes as archers. The rates were excellent. Of course, we all knew that it generally took the Prince's household a little more than a year to clear accounts, so we wouldn't be paid by Christmastide, but it was honorable pay, and all the moneylenders would give coin against it.

Chaucer followed us back to the inn on a rouncey. He had a sword, with rust on the hilt, and a pannier full of food and clothes. His horse wasn't bad. Ahead of him, on a better horse, rode Master Hoo, in tall leather boots and wearing a woollen coat trimmed in fur and a hat worth as much as my sword. Master Hoo chose a girl, paid, smiled at me and paused on the stairs.

'Early start, young sir?' he asked.

I nodded.

He pursed his lips, then smiled at the girl and led her away.

Chaucer looked around the Three Foxes, examined the girls, then looked at me. Nervously.

'I, er, want one,' – he was not the pushy merchant's son of earlier – 'of the girls.'

I just looked at him.

'What, er, do I do?' he asked.

I let the silence lengthen. I'd taken a fair amount of shite from the boy, and I thought I should let him stew.

But Marie, damn her, liked the look of him – all sensitive and intelligent, I suppose. 'Which lass do you fancy, my master?'

He bowed to her. 'I . . .' he stammered.

She sent him upstairs with one of the older girls and strict orders to take her time and be polite.

Women.

Mind you, he paid cash.

When he was gone, I sat with Richard. He was sewing a small tear in the sleeve of his jupon, and his girl – Anne-Marie, I think, but they were all Anne or Marie – watched his minuscule sewing and laughed.

'That was quite a tale,' I said. As the only black man in Bordeaux, he was well known, and because he was black, some people thought he was a spawn of Satan, while others assumed he was a paynim. Some of the girls wouldn't lie with him. That sort of treatment could make a right hard bastard, but he was far better bred than I in many ways; he was very well spoken and he wouldn't cheat at any game. Not even to win money. He was a prankster when he was young, though, and he did like a tall tale.

Anyway, he grinned at me. Our eyes met.

'You made it all up,' I said.

He nodded.

'Well, you had me going,' I said. 'Where are you really from?'

He frowned. 'Not sure,' he admitted. 'My mother said she was from Aethiopia. And that she was born a Christian.'

I nodded. Richard was indisputably Christian. He went to Mass often, and went to church at least once a day, sometimes three times. I went to church less than once a week, and hated the way every word in the Gospels seemed carefully written to remind me of how far I was from grace.

'Where did you grow up?' I asked.

'At the court of Granada, in Spain,' Richard said. He shrugged. There was a long pause. 'I was a slave.'

The words cost him something.

But they cemented something, too. I remember that I looked away a moment, because it was a horrible thing to admit. And then I looked back, into his deep-brown eyes. 'Well, if we do this well enough, you'll be a knight,' I said.

Anne Marie heard my leman calling her, and got up and walked to the common room.

'I was an apprentice in London,' I said. 'If we become knights—'

He laughed bitterly. 'They'll never make either one of us knights.'

In the morning, there were many kisses and farewells, but we were on the road north before the sun was high. We moved fast, made small camps and saw virtually no one. Brigands weren't likely to pick on us as we wore too much armour, and carried a small banneret displaying the Prince's colours. Once we cleared Gascony, the marches were empty. There was a French garrison at Marmande; and Nadaillac and the town of Gourdon were held by a brigand-lord who fought both sides. Such men were becoming more common, and we skirted his hold, camped well up his valley, then Richard and I stripped to our arming clothes and went back at night and climbed the hill above his castle to take a look. Chandos had told Richard that the Prince was considering storming Nadaillac, and we felt that a little scouting might get us included in the expedition.

It was a strong place, set on a hilltop like a woman's breast. The sides were steep, and a single road wound to the summit. But we watched six men water some horses, and two women haul pails on yokes, and came to the conclusion that the water inside the place wasn't good as they all used the water from a spring halfway down the hill. It seemed worth knowing.

After Nadaillac, we had no further adventures until we were almost to the Loire. We rode along familiar roads and paths, discussing the campaign of Poitiers, pointing out to each other the places we'd fought, the towns we'd stormed – acting like pompous young pricks, in other words. Sam smiled at us from time to time and chose the camp sites.

We had a safe conduct signed by the King of France. This puzzled me, and puzzled Richard, since we were, as far as we knew, going to arrange the transfer of French castles held by Sir John Hawkwood to English control. By Christ, we were virgins in the ways of Kings and Princes. Master Hoo rode almost entirely silent. Young Chaucer spoke to him more than to the rest of us, and I sussed out that Chaucer was the older man's apprentice.

As we entered Tours, I was nervous as a maid on her wedding night, riding under the portcullis. A single capture would beggar me, and I couldn't afford even a small ransom. I was wearing my fortune, in armour and clothes and horses, and it seemed insane to ride openly into France.

But we did, and after the castellan looked at our documents, he wrinkled his nose. 'Signed by the King,' he said, and kissed the parchment. 'Only twenty days ago. Did you gentlemen see him?'

Chaucer bowed. 'I had that honour, monsieur. At a tournament in Westminster, not two weeks ago.'

The castellan, who had ignored Chaucer as a servant, now looked down his nose at the boy. 'Really?'

'Yes, monsieur. I give you my word. I received this and other safe-conducts into my own hand. Indeed,' he smiled winningly, 'I wrote them out.'

The castellan leaned forward, called for wine and treated us with more consideration. After we'd been served wine, he asked, as if by chance, 'Is it peace, gentlemen?'

I looked away. The dissimulation of a seventeen-year-old is not something on which to depend. He grinned and Chaucer grinned back.

'Please, my lord. You didn't hear it from us.' He bowed.

He had a way with him, that imp of Satan. Master Hoo glared at him, but said nothing.

The castellan poured more wine. 'Ordinarily, I hate the English,' he said, 'but tonight, I will make an exception. To peace!'

We drank to peace.

I made the avert sign under the table.

North of Tours, there was war everywhere, and we rode through a wasteland of burned farms, ruined crops, weed-choked fields and rotting corpses. Some of them were very small.

'Ah, chivalry!' Chaucer spat when we found a mother and three children dead at a crossroads.

'Leave off, by St Mary, you foul-mouthed clerk!' I said. 'You talk of what you do not know. This is not chivalry, but foul murder.'

'Oh, aye, keeping maidens as whores in a brothel – that's chivalry,' he said.

'Not a maiden among 'em,' Richard said. 'Leave off, Geoffrey. It's our trade.'

'That's just my meaning,' Chaucer said. 'Take it at its best, your chivalry is nothing but strong men running a brothel. You protect the weak in return for exploiting them. When they mislike you, you kill them. When they are in the way, you kill them. When you need to punish another knight, you kill his weak people. Pimps and whores!'

I was stung. 'The life of arms is a life of honour,' I said. 'Without men of arms—'

'Murder, rape and thievery is not a trade,' he said. 'Dress it up in pretty armour and fine silk, it's still crime.'

I punched him so hard he fell off his horse.

'I didn't kill these children,' I said. In truth, the sight sickened me, and in my heart I suspected he was right – and hated him the more for it.

He sat in the horse manure on the road, rubbing his jaw. 'Fuck you,' he said.

Richard reached down a hand.

'Fuck him. He hit me!' Chaucer said. 'Aren't you going to say anything?'

Sam watched impassively.

Christopher watched the hills around us.

Master Hoo whistled between his teeth. I realized he was laughing.

Richard smiled. 'Sure, I'll say something, master page. You had that coming. Watch your mouth.' He reached down his hand again. 'Care to get back on your horse?'

Chaucer didn't speak again that day.

I don't regret the blow. I understood his point – then and now. Remember, good sir, that we were children, all of us. Angry, violent children.

We had passes and *sauvegardes* to the Lieutenant of Brittany. His name was William Latimer, and he was no one's idea of a paragon of chivalry, but that's not part of my story. He and all his troops were with Lancaster before the walls of Rennes, and we rode in through the heaviest rain I'd ever seen. The siege was months old even then, and not likely to succeed – the walls were bad, but the French holding them were the best that France still had in the field.

Master Hoo had an audience with the Duke of Lancaster, and Chaucer saw some clerks he knew, and the news was the same: Sir John Hawkwood and his routiers were not in the field with the Duke's army, where they were supposed to be. They were up country, serving under Sir James Pipe, who was supposed to be Lancaster's lieutenant in Normandy. In despite of King Edward's orders, Pipe and a dozen sub-contractors were seizing French garrison towns in Normandy, not towns turned over by supporters of Charles and Philippe of Navarre, but towns held by royal garrisons of the King of France.

Whatever Master Hoo said to my lord of Lancaster, he didn't like it, and he made that clear in a hundred ways. We were all very glad to see the last of that camp.

As we rode north and east from Rennes, we entered what I can only describe as the world of war. If there had been burned fields and dead children in southern Brittany, Normandy was hell come to earth. Villages were blackened rubble. Whole forests had been burned to black sticks. In one field, I still remember an entire herd of sheep had been massacred, with the shepherd, his wife and their bairn all dead among their sheep. Not one sheep had had its hide lifted and no meat had been taken. They were blown up with gas – ten days dead, or more, bloated and horrible.

Chaucer looked at it all and said very little. But from time to time, he'd smile at me.

Sam Bibbo looked at it and spat. 'Vermin,' he said.

He didn't speak a great deal, so I was interested. I rode up next to him. 'You were a bandit,' I said.

He looked at me and made a smacking noise, like a man blowing a kiss at his sister. He flushed red, and I thought I'd gone very wrong.

But then he looked at the ground. 'Taking armed folk to ransom,' he shrugged. 'It ain't pretty, but it ain't the same as this, is it. Eh?'

It was late October by the time we found Hawkwood. He was holding Le Neubourg, a prosperous and very strategic town at the crossroads of southern Normandy. He had a dozen lances under him, and he'd laid the whole country around under his obedience, collecting *patis* far and wide – that's a sort of informal tax that English garrisons collected from French peasants. Like protection money, only a little more feudal.

Anyway, he gave us a royal welcome.

I dismounted in the yard of the citadel, and John of Boston held my horse.

The gate guards sent for Hawkwood, and he came down, booted and spurred, to meet me. We embraced like old companions. I introduced him to Richard and to Master Chaucer, who was, for once, on his best behaviour, and to Master Hoo.

Hoo had been silent – ill, in fact – since Rennes. But now he fairly bounced with enthusiasm. 'We have an answer to your query, Sir Knight,' he said.

'That was speedy,' Hawkwood said.

'From which you might deduce the Prince's interest,' Master Hoo said.

I looked at Richard. I thought we were the principals. Master Hoo smiled at me. 'You can go – your work is done,' he said, as if dismissing a servant.

I'd ridden across half of France, but it had never really occurred to me *why* we'd brought the notary and the page. They both spoke beautiful French, and Chaucer was good at buying things and making the locals like him – he had beautiful manners when he bothered, and I was learning a great deal of courtly behaviour from him, to be honest – but I'd assumed he was along for experience with us, the professionals.

Until that moment, when John Hawkwood squeezed my shoulder. 'We'll talk later,' he said.

Leaving me and Richard standing in the courtyard with our men.

I glared at young Chaucer's back, as he followed the Prince's notary into the keep. 'It's as if we were carters, and having gotten the wagon to market, the merchants no longer need us,' I spat.

'I think you got it in one,' Richard said. 'Let's get a cup of wine.'

A day later, Hawkwood found me in the local wine shop and sat down. He nodded to Richard and to Sam, who was drinking with us.

'Are you gentlemen at leisure to do a little fighting?' he asked. 'There's a French knight troubling my garrisons and I plan to ambush him. I could use a few more swords.'

Sam shrugged. I remember grinning.

'What's with the secrecy?' I asked. 'Where's Master Hoo and his boy?'

'In the keep, where I can protect them,' Hawkwood said. 'This is Normandy, not London. I assume you lads can protect yourselves. Master Hoo is too valuable to risk outside the keep.' He fingered his beard. 'Mounted and ready to fight at sunset, after vespers.'

'Harness?' Richard asked.

Hawkwood shrugged. 'If you want to stay alive,' he said. 'Unless that black skin is charmed?'.

Richard flushed.

An ambush – a mounted ambush – is complex to lay and complex to use, and deadly dull to wait in. Mounted men need to be well hidden by deep brush or trees, but they need to be able to ride out of their covers with ease. The ideal ambush is deep, old woods with little underbrush. France has a plentiful supply of deep, old woods, because the nobility has the peasants cowed and forces them to accept private hunting woods. They dot the landscape, and sometimes the roads run through them.

We rode for two hours, in near total darkness, with a dozen scouts ahead of us on light horses. Sam, I'll note, went out with the prickers.

A little before midnight, we met another band. Hawkwood clasped hands with the leader, and we rode in among them in the soft moonlight. Their captain was Sir Robert Knolles, a famous knight. He had a forked black beard – that's about all I could say about him in the dark.

Together we made about fifty men-at-arms and another fifty archers. We headed north.

'If we catch him, we string him up,' Knolles said. He was speaking of the French knight we were out to ambush.

Hawkwood shrugged.

'No one will ransom him. In fact, there *is* no one to ransom him. The French have collapsed. The whole country is a bunch of grapes, ripe for us to pluck.' Knolles barked a laugh. 'Are we agreed?'

Hawkwood was watching one of his prickers, a vague form in the moonlight. 'Sir Robert, we seem to have arrived. If you and your men will take the left side of the road, we'll take the right.'

Sir Robert nodded. 'Helmet!' he called out. A pageboy brought him his heavy basinet. He looked old to me. And wicked.

We filed off into the woods. Sam came and helped Richard and me to get our horses under cover.

'Should we dismount?' I asked.

Sam grinned in the moonlight. He was missing a few teeth, and his smile was no maiden's joy. 'I would,' he said. 'Why be the first man into a fight?'

Where we were placed, we couldn't see the road, or the moon, or even the sky. It was so dark that when I let go my reins to turn and piss, I almost lost my horse. When Richard needed to piss, I held his reins.

By these tiny steps does a man go from being a raw recruit to a veteran – such as knowing how to tie your hose and braes so you can piss while wearing armour. I showed a young man last year at Chioggia.

No shame to being new-minted. Often, the new-minted coin has better gold.

The waiting went on and on, and we moved too much and our horses nickered and other men snored – yes, someone went to sleep, but it wasn't one of mine. At some point, I realized it was lighter than it had been.

I felt as if someone had poured sand behind my eyeballs.

And then I heard an owl hoot twice – the signal – and everything happened very fast.

There was a crashing sound to my left front. I got my sabatonned left foot in the stirrup of my tall, golden horse, and then he moved, damn him, with me bouncing along off the ground.

There's good things about wearing armour. One is that if your horse bounces you through deep brush, all that happens is that you get pine-needles in your visor. I slammed a tree, ripped through a thicket, then I got my right foot over the saddle. I saw something move ahead of me and reached for my sword, all while trying to tuck my right foot into my stirrup. I got it, and stood in my stirrups – that's how you ride a war saddle – and got my sword out of my scabbard.

My horse burst out of the trees into a clearing.

There was another man moving ahead of me on a horse as big as mine. His horse was black and his armour glittered in the moonlight. His helmet had an impossibly tall peak. He saw me, and turned his horse and spurred at me.

But of course the clearing wasn't a clearing. It was a bog.

He went down so suddenly I thought he'd been sucked into the earth. There was a tiny rivulet running down the middle of the boggy meadow – tiny, but three feet under the level of the grass – and his poor horse stepped in it and he was thrown.

He was on his feet in a moment. I was sure he wasn't one of ours, and I swung down at him and my sword hit his helmet solidly.

Against a good helmet, you can swing all day and not accomplish much. On the other hand, most men don't like being hit on the head.

Goldie was a fine animal, and he backed on command and half-reared, and I cut again at the Frenchman – at least, I hoped he was a Frenchman. I connected again, this time atop his shoulder.

He stumbled and Goldie kicked him. I heard his hoof strike, a hollow sound against the French knight's breastplate. He had one of the new ones – just two pieces – and it didn't cave in.

He was knocked flat.

I backed Goldie.

The injured horse screamed.

I could hear fighting, sword on sword, very close by.

The French knight wasn't moving, so I slid down from my saddle. I ran to the French knight as he tried to get to his feet, and slammed my pommel into his helmet. Down he went again, and this time I sat on him.

I opened his faceplate.

He glared at me. 'Bah!' he said. 'God is against me. I am taken.'

'Are you worth anything?' I asked.

It is hard to shrug while an armoured man sits on you, especially when you are in a swamp. But he wriggled. 'Not a hundred florins,' he said. 'Perhaps fifty? I am du Guesclin. You know the name?'

I didn't, so I shook my head.

'Would you do me the service of killing my horse?' Du Guesclin said. 'He was a fine horse. Christ only knows how I will replace him.'

Richard appeared while I cut the horse's throat – somewhat ineptly as I was splashed in blood. My harness was already a squire's nightmare – bogs and armour are not friends, and my sabatons collected the most remarkable amount of stinking mud.

He laughed, and then he saw the French knight.

'You lucky bastard!' Richard said.

'I'll split the ransom with you,' I said sportingly.

Richard slapped me on the back. 'I'll do the same.' He stripped his right gauntlet and held out his hand to the Frenchman. 'Richard Musard,' he said.

'Bertrand du Guesclin,' said the Frenchman.

Richard looked at me and shook his head. 'I think we're supposed to hang him,' he said. 'He's the French brigand Sir Robert is hunting.'

'Is that Sir Robert Knolles?' Du Guesclin asked. He laughed. 'That rapist is calling me a brigand? I live here. This is my country.'

Sam appeared out of the darkness. The sky was almost light, and he looked at the French knight and shrugged.

'That's him, right enough.' He looked at me. 'What do you plan to do, my lord?'

I don't think Sam Bibbo had ever called me 'my lord' before.

'If you gentlemen will release me, I'll pay my ransom wherever you want it sent,' du Guesclin said.

'If you don't inform Sir John ...' Sam made a face. 'He'll know. Sooner or later.'

I sent Richard to find Sir John. I moved my prisoner across the meadow, hobbled Goldie and ate a sausage. I shared half with du Guesclin, and gave him some wine. He was my King John. He was a real knight, and I waited on him the way I thought he deserved. This was the chivalry for which I yearned.

He handed me back the leather bottle of wine. 'You are a cut above the routiers,' he said. 'Could I try one more time to entice you to let me go? I will pay – and I'm not worth any more. Your Sir John will kill me.'

I shook my head. 'No he won't,' I said confidently.

Half an hour passed, and then a party of horsemen came into my meadow from the north. Richard dismounted to cross the brook, and Sir John and three of his men-at-arms rode around the perimeter.

He dismounted and bowed. 'Messire du Guesclin. I have long wanted to meet you.'

Du Guesclin smiled bravely. 'Sir John Hawkwood. I cannot say I feel the same about you, messire.' Nonetheless, he took Sir John's hand.

Sir John turned to me. 'You took him?'

I nodded.

Sir John nodded. 'William, you have just made your reputation.' He looked at me – not old man to young, but man to man. 'What do you intend?' he asked.

Everyone was quiet. I felt very much out of place. The sand was back behind my eyes. I was aware, in some dark part of my head, that I hadn't taken this man fairly – it was simply that his horse had stumbled in the dark.

'He's offered a hundred florins ransom and I've accepted. I intended to let him go. Saving your Grace.'

Sir John laughed. 'Christ, I have Galahad serving in my convoy. But yes, William. You have my grace.' He nodded to me. He turned back to du Guesclin. 'Yesterday, I'd have strung you up from the nearest tree, messire. But ... things change. May I take you aside and whisper in your ear?'

Du Guesclin tensed – I think he expected to be taken aside and killed – but his sense of his own dignity overcame his desire to live, and he bowed. 'I put my trust in you, sir,' he said.

I put a gauntleted hand on Sir John's steel-clad arm. 'I'd take it amiss if he was to die here,' I said.

Sir John gave me a cold glance. 'Galahad,' he spat, and beckoned to du Guesclin, who followed Sir John into the woods.

They were gone for far longer than I expected or liked. I was walking across the meadow, my thighs burning with fatigue and my head swimming, when I saw the sun dazzle off Sir John's steel arms.

Du Guesclin was with him, and not face down in the forest.

When they emerged, du Guesclin nodded to Sir John.

Richard bowed. He ordered John Brampton to dismount and share Christopher's horse, and gave the boy's horse to the French knight.

Du Guesclin embraced us both. 'I thank God I was taken by two such gentle knights,' he said.

'Two such great fools,' Sam muttered.

'The Inn of the Three Foxes,' Richard said. 'At Bordeaux.'

Du Guesclin mounted, got the feel of the little horse and smiled. 'I'll pay by the end of the day,' he promised us.

And he trotted his horse away.

Sir John rode with me on the long road back to his keep. 'You have become a canny man-at-arms,' he said. 'But that might have gone badly for all of us. It might have been better if you'd put your whittle into his eye, eh?' He looked at me. 'You heard Sir Robert say we were to kill him.'

'I didn't hear you agree,' I said. 'And to the best of my knowledge, my lord, we are not at war with France. Indeed, Master Hoo is carrying the word of the truce far and wide, is he not?'

Hawkwood looked at me, as if seeing me for the first time. 'So, there is something inside that head besides empty chivalry. You know that, eh? Do you know what else Master Hoo is saying?' he asked.

I shook my head.

'Thank God, then. Listen, my young friend. Things change. Kings change. Their policy changes. Kings are the most inconstant creatures – more so than young maidens.' He laughed.

'But you are a routier – you serve your own ends, and not the King's,' I said.

Sir John stroked his beard. We rode on a ways, and he played with the length of his stirrup for a while. He spoke to one of his scouts. I assumed we were done when he turned to me.

'I serve the King as surely as if I wore his livery and served under his banner,' Sir John said. 'Routier, my arse.'

It is odd what can sting a man.

That night, I dined with Sir John and his men-at-arms in the great hall of his keep. Master Hoo was there, and young Chaucer waited on the table. I worried he might piss in my wine.

I was pleased to be allowed to dine with the knights. Richard and I sat quietly. Nothing was said of the capture of du Guesclin. Nor of peace.

In fact, they were all planning to march on Paris. It sounds absurd, but a few hundred Englishmen were planning to take Paris. Hawkwood was in on the enterprise, and so was Sir Robert Knolles and Sir James Pipe – all the King's officers in Normandy, in fact.

I found myself sitting by Master Hoo late in the evening. I leaned over, emboldened by wine. 'How can they attack Paris?' I asked. 'We've made peace with France?'

Master Hoo looked at me over his nose and grunted.

He was almost too drunk to talk.

I admit I was shocked.

Chaucer leaned over, sloshed wine into his master's cup and sneered at me. 'Paris isn't currently held by the King of France or his son, either,' he said. 'Paris has declared itself . . .' he seemed at a loss for words.

'*Communes*,' Master Hoo enunciated clearly. 'Paris and Amiens and the northern cities.' He nodded gravely. It would have been more impressive if his cap hadn't slipped further down his head at every nod.

'So Sir John and the other bandits plan to plunder the Isle de France while no one can protect it,' Chaucer said. 'King John will return to find he is king of a graveyard full of corpses.'

'Which will suit our master perfectly,' Master Hoo allowed.

Lads, until that moment, I had imagined there were two kingdoms, France and England. I had thought that in France, a bad king ruled a hard nobility who abused hordes of ignorant peasants, while in England, a good king and a fine parliament ruled benignly over good men and true. Laugh all you like. I thought that our king went to make war in France by right, and to protect England from the deprivations of France. And did so openly and honestly, making war justly.

Following Sir John and listening to Master Hoo was undermining these assumptions as surely as a good engineer undermines the walls of a town.

So I turned to Sir John – full of indignation as only a young man can be – and I couldn't contain myself.

'You are destroying France?' I asked. 'For the King?'

He laughed. 'Destroy? France is ten times the size of England.' He shrugged. 'But France will never threaten England again, that I can guarantee you.' He grabbed my shoulder suddenly. He was a little drunk and very strong. 'Come!' he said, and he started to climb the tower's stairs, which coiled like a worm up one flank of the keep. Up and up we climbed, the stairs turning so tightly that a misstep could send an unwary man crashing to the bottom.

My calves were burning by the time we emerged on the castle's roof. There were four men on duty – Sir John was a very careful captain. He led me to the edge of the roof and pointed east, towards Paris.

As far as the eye could see, there was fire.

All the way up the Seine valley, towns and hamlets burned.

'Do you not think the silken girdle that binds all of France is parted this night?' he said and laughed. 'Listen, virgin. Every man of blood in England is here this autumn. We'll take ten thousand ransoms, we'll burn their fields, we'll throw down their churches, we'll unbind peasant from lord. There's no one to stop us. By the time King John returns from his tournaments and festivals in England, he'll have a merry time finding his own ransom.'

It was ... horrifying, and yet so bold. So much fire. Like the twinkling of all the stars in the heavens.

'But surely the King is against this—'

'Judas,' Hawkwood smiled. 'William, the King, *ordered* this.'

At last I understood, or thought I did. 'Ah!' I said. 'And Master Hoo has come to order it to end.'

Hawkwood shook his head. 'I'm drunk, or I wouldn't say so much,' he said. He looked at me from under his brows. 'But I want you to understand, lad. Master Hoo has come to order us to work faster. And to turn over the towns we take to *his* officers, and not those of the King of Navarre, as per the treaty.' He shrugged. 'That's why I sent the letter to you.' He sat with his back against the wall. 'That, and it seemed a pity that you waste your youth in Bordeaux when there's a fortune to be made here.'

'The Prince is paying me double wage for guarding Master Hoo,' I said.

'How's the Three Foxes?' he asked.

I smiled. 'It does very well.'

Sir John nodded out over the ruins of France. 'Imagine, then, that there was another inn that rivalled yours – indeed, that it was ten times the size and the girls were more beautiful, more skilled at love, the inn was better, the rooms cleaner. And imagine how many men they could employ to harass your inn. Imagine that you came to blows; imagine that by good fortune, you won a fight with the other inn. Would you walk away, letting bygones be bygones?'

I frowned. 'As soon as they rally, they'll come and burn me out,' I said.

Sir John nodded. 'And so, once you have them backing away, you *stay at it.* Until the other inn is burned to the ground and yours is the only one standing. Eh?'

Two days later, I declined Hawkwood's offer of employment. I was a retinued man-at-arms, and I couldn't be forsworn.

He embraced me. 'When you want to be rich, come and fight with me,' he said.

And we rode away.

Sam set us on the road for Rennes, and we rode about three hours, then Master Hoo came alongside me.

'Now that we are free of Sir John's spies,' he said, 'I'd like you to turn our party toward Paris.'

'Paris?' I said, dumbfounded.

'Paris,' said the notary.

We made good time up the Seine. Sam was alert all the time, and he put us on our guard. We ran across an English band on the second day, but they passed us as soon as we hailed them in English.

The fourth day, and we were riding hard. We were just west of Maule, and suddenly Sam pointed, and we saw smoke and movement across the valley, and the sparkle of the autumn sun on armour.

We made what preparations we could. We had letters of passage from both sides, but the routiers were seldom interested in letters, so we put arrows to bows, loosened our swords in their scabbards and donned our helmets.

Sam tried to take us around whatever was happening in the valley, but there were no road signs and no directions, so we rode along the edge of the valley for almost a mile, only to run into a web of hedges and stiles. Sam dismounted and crossed a hedge, and came back.

'No way through,' he said. 'Perhaps we should wait for darkness?'

In four weeks of travelling, it was the hardest decision I'd had to make yet. I looked at Richard.

Richard nodded. 'Darkness might be good,' he opined.

Master Hoo shook his head. 'Time is of the essence,' he said. 'I've been too long on the road already.'

He turned his horse's head and began to ride back the way we'd come, forcing our hands.

An hour later we were spotted by a pair of brigands, and we saw them run around a barn and up a slope, calling as they went.

'That tears it,' said Sam.

We began to trot. I led the way, and we dashed along the valley floor, the Seine sparkling on our left hand. The road cut in, away from the river, and we cantered along it.

There was a village on fire to the south, and another just to the west on a stream, and a religious house at the bottom of the stream's valley. I could see that the road crossed the stream at a ford below the religious house.

And I saw armed men mounting horses in the religious house's yard.

Even as I watched, armed men emerged from the abbey's gate, riding to cut us off from the ford.

'Ride for it!' Sam called.

We went to the gallop. I didn't like the way Master Chaucer rode – he seemed to bounce like a sack of turnips – so I turned to shout to him, and there was the Bourc Camus, fifty feet behind Chaucer and riding a jet-black horse like a fiend of hell. He yelled and Chaucer turned to look, but the horse interpreted his change of weight as indecision and threw him.

Just for a moment, I thought of leaving him.

But I was on retainer to the Prince to protect him, so I pulled up, turned Goldie's head, and readied my lance.

I had no idea if the Bourc Camus was a fine jouster, but I knew damned well that I was not. I was a better rider than I had been the last time I'd had to fight on horseback, but the tiltyard hadn't been a big part of my training.

I decided to kill his horse. It's not done, in jousting, but this seemed different.

Camus flipped his visor down and brought his lance into line about ten strides out.

My lance wasn't a heavy one, but I misjudged my strike. My lance came down, and instead of hitting his horse, my lance struck his lance – perhaps he raised it to guard himself – and both spear points went down into the earth. We both had to let go our spears or we'd have unhorsed ourselves.

Master Chaucer flung himself out from under our hooves.

Goldie spun under me, and Camus was struggling to draw his sword. I got mine out first and I cut at his arm.

'*Merde!*' he shouted.

I cocked my arm and cut again.

It's very hard to hurt a fully armoured man with a sword, even a heavy longsword.

There's a way to do it. I just didn't know how yet.

Camus got his blade free and cut at me.

I ducked and cut, blind, even as more of his men-at-arms came down the road. He hit me in the head and his blow twisted the basinet on my head, making everything harder. I cut again, desperation and panic fuelling my blows, as his second blow hit my helmet.

My blow caught something soft and cut through it.

There was a pause in the rain of blows, and I managed to get my visor up and my hand on the beak of my helmet, then with one tug I reseated the helmet on my head.

Richard, bless him, had blown through Camus's retainers at full gallop, unhorsing one with his lance – he was clearly a better jouster than I – and riding clear.

Camus was fifty paces away, trying to control his war horse with only his legs. I'd cut his reins and his hands.

Richard waved at me.

I got Goldie under me, backed him a few steps, and found Chaucer cowering by the stone wall to my left. I extended my left hand, and he took it like a drowning man – I hauled him up behind me.

Richard crashed into the men-at-arms again, but they didn't have much armour and weren't eager for a second encounter. Even as he closed, a single arrow from across the ford buzzed by like a huge wasp and buried itself in one horse's withers, and that was the end of the fight. Richard came out of the dust, sword high – I turned and followed him, and we trotted across the ford in a fine spray of water.

Sam and John Hughes had their bows in their hands on the far side. Master Hoo was farther up the bank with Christopher and Peter. Rob had caught Chaucer's horse and was ludicrously proud of himself.

Camus got control of his horse and rode down to the ford as we got Chaucer mounted.

'Shoot him?' John asked me.

'Only if he tries to cross,' Richard said.

Camus had his visor up. Visored basinets weren't all that common back then, but all the Gascons had them. I think they spread them.

'Ah,' he yelled at me. 'The Butt Boy.'

'You ride beautifully,' I called. 'Is it a Gascon style?'

'I'll have your head on a spear, Butt Boy!' he yelled.

'If your horse comes another step, my archer will drop you in the water,' I said. 'I have a warrant and a safe passage from the Prince of Wales, and you are in defiance of him.'

'Fuck your Prince,' he said, and forced his horse into the water. 'We are the masters here now.'

Sam loosed.

The arrow went into the horse's head just below where the mane emerged between the ears, and the horse dropped in the river as if poleaxed. An expensive horse, too.

Men piled into the shallow ford to pull the Bourc clear of the water.

'Let's ride,' I said. I slapped Sam Bibbo on the shoulder and he grinned.

'I'll pay you double for that,' I said.

'Putting that evil bastard in the water was my treat,' Bibbo said.

An hour later, we found four nuns and a priest at a crossroads.

Richard rode up to the priest. 'Can we be of service!' he asked.

One of the nuns began to scream.

She screamed and screamed.

Another nun began to beat at Richard with her fists. Considering she was about five feet high and he was a fully armoured knight on a war horse, you can see why this sticks in my memory. She meant him harm. She didn't care what harm she took in return.

Richard backed his horse away. 'Sweet Jesu,' he said. 'Leave off, *ma soeur*. I've done you no harm.'

'All of you,' she shrieked. 'All of you! I'll kill you all, you hell-spawn!'

The priest just shook his head. 'Ride on,' he said. 'And do us no harm, I beg.'

The nun stood in the road behind us. 'May Satan rape you! May demons rip out your eyes! May he grind your flesh with a mill – rip you with red-hot pincers! May you take the plague!' she shrieked. 'Boil in oil! May worms eat your eyes, you shit-eating English!'

We rode a little faster, as if her curses carried weight.

Chaucer watched me. I felt his eyes on me, and I looked away from the nuns and at him. 'What?' I asked.

He shrugged. 'Hawkwood's men, or Knolles', or Camus' or one of the other captain's men raped them all. Good fun. Very chivalrous, no doubt.' He nodded. 'Perhaps they had it coming.'

'Camus' men are Gascons, not Englishmen,' I said.

Chaucer nodded. 'That makes it different, I'm sure,' he said.

She was still screaming. She was too far away for her words to carry, but the shrill tone was like a witch, I thought.

I leaned towards him and he flinched.

'Richard and I saved your life,' I said.

Chaucer shrugged. 'My ransom, I expect.' He smiled his annoying, superior smile. 'Camus wouldn't kill me. He'd just sell me to the Prince.'

I got control of myself and rode away. Richard rode with me.

'Let me hit him, next time,' he said. He grinned. 'By God, William, that was a good fight.'

It was our first one together, as brothers-in-arms, so to speak.

The next day, we made contact with Sir James Pipe's men, and Master Hoo gave them some sort of password, and we were taken to the Lieutenant of Normandy. Bah – perhaps he was made Lieutenant of Normandy later. I can't remember.

Sir James held the convent of Poissy. From the walls, we could see Paris on the horizon.

He had fewer than 500 men, and he was waiting for Knolles and Hawkwood. He met with Master Hoo for half an hour, and Hoo emerged looking grey. I'd just seen to the horses – by then I was resigned to being a sort of military servant, and I'd admitted to myself that Hoo was the one in charge of the expedition. Richard and I got the convent's servants to curry our horses. Given what we'd seen on the road, the convent made me ... anxious.

There wasn't a nun to be seen, and all I could think of was the Bourc Camus' assertion that nuns made good whores.

By the blessed virgin, this courier duty was giving me heartache.

At any rate, the horses were fed and clean for the first time in six days, and most of the men were already asleep. Chaucer was lying across a saddle, out cold.

We were tired.

'We need to ride. Immediately,' Hoo said.

I just looked at him. But he was not given to dramatics, and he hardly ever spoke.

'It is ...' he shrugged. 'I can't say. But we must go. Now.'

As I say, I'd realized he was the true commander of our enterprise, so I hauled our tired horses out of the stables, kicked the men awake – I didn't kick John Hughes or Sam Bibbo, by the by. That would have been foolish.

Richard shook his head. 'What the fuck?' he asked.

Chaucer got to his feet. 'You curried my horse!' he said to Richard.

Richard shrugged. 'William curried your horse, you ingrate.'

Chaucer looked at me as if waiting for the trick. He probably was.

Richard raised an eyebrow. 'Why don't you repay him by finding out why the hell your master needs us to ride right now?'

Chaucer nodded. 'I'll try,' he said.

Of course, while he tried, I had to saddle his mare. I looked at Goldie and shook my head. I'd been on him for two solid days and he needed rest, so I saddled my riding horse.

We were out the gate with three hours of late autumn light left.

'Paris?' I asked Master Hoo.

He nodded.

'Messire, may I ask how dangerous this is?' We were moving briskly.

Hoo shrugged. 'In truth, lad, I have no idea. Everything just went to hell.' He looked at me. 'You and your friend have done a fine job of keeping us alive so far. You are luck's own child. Let's pray you haven't burned it all.' He stopped for a moment. 'I have good credit with the Prince. I swear to you that if you get me to Paris, I'll see you well.'

'Can I ask what all this is about?' I tried.

'No,' he said.

'Sweet Jesus,' I muttered, or something equally blasphemous.

We reached St Cloud by the simple expedient of riding all night and not giving way to the temptation to hide. There was fire all around us, but very few people, and the roads were clear. I have seen this many times – if you move fast on a good road it's very hard for an enemy to ambush you, and in many cases, no one will lay an ambush on a highway.

Luck? Good strategy? Whichever way you take it, we entered St Cloud as the sun rose, in heavy winter rain. There were guards on the gate, in hoods of crimson and royal blue – the colours of Paris. Their weapons were ill-kept and they had the indefinable air of incompetence that marks the militiaman.

Master Hoo spat. 'Fuck me,' he said bitterly. He glanced at me. 'Be very, very calm, messire. This is not—'

He had no more time to speak, because we were surrounded by the militia at the gate.

They read Master Hoo's *sauvegarde* over and over, until I became convinced that none of them could read. My hands were numb, the gloves of my steel gauntlets were soaked through and bitter cold, and rain was running down the middle of my back between my shoulder blades, having soaked through my best three-quarter cloak about two in the morning.

The 'captain' of the gate was younger than I was and very full of his own importance.

Master Hoo looked bored.

I began to grow angry. I was cold and wet, and I at least wanted into the warmth of the guard room, but none of the Paris militiamen seemed inclined to offer us so much as a cup of small beer.

'May we come in and get warm?' I asked.

The man nearest me snarled. He had a partisan – a spear with heavy side lugs. He raised it and made to place it against my throat.

I caught it in my left hand. I was still mounted, and without thinking I gave my riding horse the command to back, and he backed, dragging the Frenchman off his feet. He let go his weapon.

Quite a few crossbows were suddenly levelled at me.

'Your English friends are burning their way across France,' the captain said. 'We hesitate a little to let you into our city? Eh?' he asked.

'Your man tried to poke me with a spear,' I said. I extended the spear to the captain. 'Then he seems to have dropped it.'

'Fucking aristo,' spat the man whose weapon I'd taken. 'Let's just kill them all.'

'Why are you here?' the captain suddenly asked John Hughes.

The Cumbrian looked blankly at him.

Now, I happen to know that John had been in France ten years, and spoke good, if Gascon, French. But he glared sullenly at the French captain, and the captain went from man to man. 'Why are you here?' he finally asked me.

I shrugged. 'To escort that man,' I said. I waved at Hoo. Let him fight his own battles.

'Your *sauvegarde* is signed by the King of France,' the captain said. 'The King is a prisoner in England and no longer the head of our state. Your safe conduct is worthless.'

'Let's kill them all,' said my friend, who had his spear back.

'Shut up, Guillaume,' said the captain. I saw this as a positive sign.

Master Hoo shrugged. 'I have …' he paused. Getting words out of Master Hoo was like pulling the teeth of a healthy man, and I think he was guessing what he should say. 'I have certain information – for the consideration of the government.'

'What information?' asked the captain. 'What part of the government? Don't ask me to believe that King Edward of England will treat with the Provost of Paris.'

'Is the Provost of Paris now the head of government?' Master Hoo asked.

I looked at Chaucer.

There were about twenty Paris militiamen on the gate. The more I looked at them, the more I thought we could take them. But we'd need to have a little surprise.

So I stopped looking to Chaucer for information and started catching Richard's eye.

'Perhaps,' said the captain.

Master Hoo reached into his pouch. 'I have a letter for Master Etienne Marcel,' he said.

The captain reached for it.

Hoo held it out of his reach – we were all still mounted, remember. 'For Master Marcel himself,' he said.

The captain rolled his eyes. 'Very well – why didn't you say? I'll send an escort – the Bois de Boulogne is full of Navarrese renegades and Englishmen. And fucking Gascons.' He smiled grimly.

An hour later, we were escorted over the Seine on the St Cloud bridge.

The Paris militiamen weren't very good, and they didn't ride particularly well, but they were enthusiastic, and from them, in an hour, we learned that the Dauphin was a virtual prisoner who signed whatever the Provost and the Bishop of Laon, Robert Le Coq, told him to sign.

I saw Master Hoo take note, and I was ready when he caught my eye.

'Eh, messire!' I called. 'Your girth is slipping.'

All the Parisians were happy for a break, for all that we were deep in the woods of the Bois de Boulogne and supposedly surrounded by broken men. In fact, it was pouring sheets of cold rain from a lead-roof sky and I assumed we were safe – no self-respecting Gascon criminal would go abroad on such a day.

Men dismounted, and I went to Master's Hoo's horse and played with his saddle.

'Can you take our escort?' he asked.

'Yes,' I said.

He nodded. 'Do it,' he said.

I went straight to Richard. 'Hoo says we have to kill the escort. Right now.'

Richard looked around.

Someone in the escort understood English. Or, just possibly, they'd been told to kill us in the woods.

Their leader was a journeyman butcher, a big brute with a huge falchion – a sword like a meat axe.

He shouted, 'Paris! St Denis!' and killed Master Hoo with one contemptuous swing of his enormous weapon.

Hoo never even called out. He slumped and fell, blood from his almost-severed neck pumping onto the muddy woods road.

Richard had his sword in his hand immediately and cut down the Parisian nearest him.

I was a horse length from the butcher, who was obviously the most dangerous man in the party. I drew and touched Goldie's sides to send my sword into his back.

But, of course, I wasn't on my war horse.

I was on my riding horse, who shied.

The big bastard was on me in one turn of his horse.

I didn't, honestly, think I could parry that meat-cleaver with my longsword, but a few moments later I was still alive, and his sword had passed harmlessly down the length of mine, like water running off a roof. He was open. I cut at him.

He had a kettle hat on, and my blow caught the brim and slammed it down into his mouth. He couldn't see and it must have hurt.

He swung wildly and killed my horse.

Par dieu! I was in armour, or I wouldn't be here to tell this, because another of the militiamen put his spear into the middle of my back, but my backplates and mail held. My poor palfrey fell forward onto its front feet and slumped to the ground, and I managed to get my feet under me.

I thought the butcher was huge before, now he was eight feet above me, and his weapon crashed down. I got a piece of it on my sword, but the rest blew through my guard and, thanks to God, slipped down my pointed helmet, slamming into the top of my shoulder. It bit through my pauldron, stopped on my mail, and left me a bruise that lasted weeks, but I wasn't dead. That's what armour's for.

I backed off the road into the trees, dragging my two opponents after me. I had no idea what was happening – rain on a helmet drowns most of the clues your ears give as to where anyone is – and there were horses and men moving everywhere.

In London, when we practised two and three on one, I had learned that the best way is to take the easy boy first, and then take your time with the tougher boy. The bastard with the spear was terrified – doing his duty, but scared spitless, and he was just prodding at me.

He prodded with the spear while the butcher was getting control of his horse, and I got the shaft in my left hand and cut along it with the sword, so that thumbs and fingers sprayed. He was out of the fight.

I had taken too long, though – I could feel the butcher coming at me in the rain, and I let myself fall to the ground in a clanking pile, as his blade parted the air over my head. I took too long getting up, and he had his horse turned.

He came at me, his horse giving a little half-rear. But it wasn't a war horse, and when I shouted, it shied – he cut too early, and I let the blow go and slammed my sword into him.

He rode by and turned his horse.

Armour. It goes both ways. He was in chain from his knee to the crown of his head, with leather pieces buckled over and a heavy coat of plates.

There's something terrible about giving your best blow and having it fail. I had hit him hard – twice.

He came at me again.

I spiked his horse in the muzzle with my point and stepped out of the way.

His horse screamed and reared.

Lightning crashed, and a levin bolt blew across the sky so brightly that, for a moment, I couldn't see anything.

I stumbled back and crashed into a tree just as a second tree came down, apparently struck by the lightning.

I looked left and right. Despite the cold rain and winter wind, I was sweating like a horse and choking for breath – and I'd lost my opponent. I flung my visor up and turned through a circle.

The rain was crashing down now, and I couldn't see the next tree.

There was thunder all around me, and I couldn't tell, through my helmet, what was fighting and what was nature.

I bent forward and breathed, water running down my nose and over my face.

Something gave him away. I raised my sword before I even raised my head and his blow fell on my outstretched blade, near my hands, and skittered along the blade – sparks flew as his edge bit at mine.

As soon as his blade was clear of my body, I used the force of his blow to turn my sword, as I had on horseback, but since he kept throwing the same overhand blow, I was getting practice at turning it back against him, and my counter strike – this time I ignored his head and armoured torso. I cut into his arms just above his heavy leather gauntlets, below the cuffs of his chain shirt. He had some protection, but whatever it was, it didn't stop me from breaking both of his arms. He screamed and stumbled back, and I reversed my weapon, holding it as I had at Poitiers, like a two-handed pick, and I drove it into his face.

Three or four times.

Later in life, I learned to be a competent swordsman, praise God. But in the Bois de Boulogne, in the pouring rain, I learned that the point, not the edge, is what rules in a fight between armoured men.

When I was sure he was dead, I stumbled out onto the road.

All of our men were gathered around Master Hoo.

He was still dead.

Chaucer was shaking his head.

The rain poured down.

'What a fucking waste,' Chaucer said. His voice broke. Perhaps he wept – who could tell?

Richard looked as tired as I felt. 'You put that big fuck down?' he asked.

I smiled. 'No thanks to you.'

'I was a little busy,' he said.

I was proud. Du Guesclin had fallen over a brook, and it took ten of us to bring down de Charny, but the Paris Butcher, while no knight, was all mine. I'm a different man now than I was then, but that was a fair fight, and more than fair.

He banged his helmet against mine. 'Well struck!' he said. 'I got two,' he added.

Chaucer turned to me. 'While you two crow over your murders,' he said, 'my master is dead.'

Sam was holding his cloak over his head. Like most veterans, now that the fighting was over, he was just trying to stay dry. He never mentioned how many men he'd put down, if any, but he looked at Hoo and shook his head. He pointed north and east. 'St Denis is that way,' he said. 'If we leave the road, we might get clear.'

Chaucer slapped my breastplate to get my attention. 'Are you abandoning the enterprise, messire?' he asked.

'What enterprise?' I asked. 'Only Master Hoo knew what the hell we were doing here. If he knew himself.'

The rain poured down.

Chaucer reached down and took the heavy leather scrip that Hoo always wore under his short cloak. He made heavy work of getting the scrip off Hoo's corpse.

'We should bury him,' I said.

Richard nodded.

Christopher shook his head. 'Jesus *fuck!* Are you two children mad? Wood? We're in the heart of France! Every man is agin' us! Can we just get the fuck out of here?'

Chaucer took Hoo's cloak.

'Take his boots,' Sam commented. 'Those are good boots.'

Chaucer hesitated.

Sam looked at me, but I was too tired and too rattled by the fight to understand his look.

John Hughes coughed. 'Take his boots or I'll take 'em myself, yunker.'

'Monastery,' I said.

Richard understood immediately. 'We can do that,' he said. 'Put him over his horse.'

Chaucer looked at us as if we had multiple heads. 'We may have the fate of two kingdoms in our hands,' he said. 'He's carrying a copy of the draft treaty for the Dauphin. Master Hoo told me it's essential to King Edward that the Dauphin ratify the treaty.'

The rain poured down.

'Why? For the love of God? By the virgin, Chaucer ...' I shook my head. 'Is this one of your stories? Why is the Dauphin's treaty so important?'

'Because the treaty gives us half of France,' Chaucer said.

'Christ,' Richard said. 'By the Virgin.'

'Which half?' asked Sam.

No one laughed.

'So why the rush?' I asked.

Chaucer looked at me a long time.

The rain fell.

I was being judged by a sixteen-year-old inkpot, the son of a rich wine merchant.

'You don't have the need to know,' Chaucer said quietly.

Sam sighed. It was audible over the rain. 'Because Sir James Pipe told Master Hoo that Charles of Navarre escaped from prison four days ago,' he said. 'He's headed for Paris, and if he gets to the Dauphin first, the treaty is cooked. Right, Master Chaucer?'

Chaucer glowered at him. If anger were fire, Chaucer might have kept us all warm.

'Yes,' he spat.

I looked at Richard. 'Why couldn't I know that?' I asked.

Richard shrugged.

'Can we get the fuck out of here?' asked Christopher.

'How can we get to the Dauphin?' I asked Chaucer.

Sam spat. 'You boys are mad,' he said. 'Wood. Solid wood. I don't know how Master Hoo planned to penetrate Paris, but he was good at this part. The crowd there would rip us apart.'

Boys was the right word. Chaucer was sixteen, and Richard and I were a year older.

Sometimes, mad boys do things.

'Where's the Dauphin?' I asked Sam. 'Do you know?'

Sam nodded. 'The dead men said he was in the Louvre.'

'Where's that?' I asked.

Sam blew out his cheeks in exasperation.

'We'll see it as soon as we ride out of the woods,' Chaucer said. He looked at me. He was no coward. I admit that. That is to say, he was scared of a great many things, like any man, but he could control his fear and act ... like a brave man.

'Does it have its own gate?' I asked.

Sam sighed. 'Yes. Listen, gentles. Recall what Sir John Chandos said – to listen to me? This adventure is at an end. You are brave. We fought well. We cannot fight our way into Paris.'

'I can ride up to the porter of the Louvre and we'll be with the Dauphin before vespers,' Chaucer shouted.

Richard looked at Bibbo. 'We have to try, Sam,' he said.

'Well,' Sam said. He looked at Hoo's body. 'There is a small monastery house just past the wood on the right. I lodged there in forty-eight.' He looked at me. 'We can take Master Hoo that far. Leave coin for a Mass or two. I'd ... like to see him fair.'

I nodded.

Sam looked at Chaucer. 'And then we'll see,' he said.

'We can do this,' Chaucer said. He might have seemed brave, but he really sounded desperate.

Sam shook his head. 'I'll come along,' he said. 'If only to see what the hell you do when you die.'

If the monks found anything remarkable about a party of Englishman riding abroad on the Isle de France, they didn't say a thing. They didn't seem afraid – the day porter opened the gate, and let us in. We gave him Master Hoo's corpse, and explained that he'd been murdered by brigands. Apparently that sounded likely.

We left the monk ten gold florins for candles and a Mass. It was past noon when we left, and only as we went back into the rain on our tired horses did I see how *big* Paris was. Paris was, and is, about ten times the size of London.

Nevertheless, we could see the Louvre looming over the fields and shanties. We were on the right side of the river. All we had to do was ride six miles through the largest city in Europe. Being boys who believed we could save the world, we had to try.

And Sam Bibbo humoured us.

We came up under the walls of the Louvre almost unchallenged. That is to say, a number of men in red and blue hoods yelled at us. We rode on, and they ignored us, because it was pouring rain. No one is brave in a downpour. At least, no one dry is brave. If you are already wet, it's different.

Chaucer had never been to Paris, but he'd heard a great deal about it, and read books. Sam *had* been to Paris, as an archer in a retinue during the long truce. But he didn't know how to get into the Louvre.

Really, we were fools.

But God smiles on fools and lovers. Doubly on men who are both, and I have always been a good lover of women. So we rode up to the Louvre, and there was a sort of shanty town running back away from the ditch. I felt at home, because it's like that around the Tower, too, but this was worse, and bigger.

Christopher had the idea of asking. We were trying to be secretive, but he got fed up and asked a whore who was standing in the cold rain as if that was her job. She had a soaking red dress and looked to be twelve.

She didn't seem to be afraid of us, which, to be frank, I found odd.

'Can you take us to the Louvre? To the gate where they admit visitors?' Chaucer asked her.

She shrugged. 'I suppose,' she said. 'I might.'

Richard held up a gold florin. Lo, the mighty knights will achieve their quest, but only if they have a florin.

Gower never wrote a romance like this, and neither did Chaucer, although he might have. Hah! That makes me laugh.

We gave her ten days' wages in gold, and she took us around a corner of nasty tenements and up what I'd have taken for an alley, except that it ended in a wicket gate with a half door and a very elegant small portcullis.

It was closed.

'Oh!' she said. Now she was frightened. 'Ne'er seen it closed before.'

It had been a long day. The sun was setting somewhere far beyond the clouds, and the rain was falling as if God had elected to cleanse the earth again. I knew that if we rode away, we'd never get this close again. I *knew* how lucky we were to have reached the wicket of the Louvre.

'Blessed St Michael,' I said aloud. I drew my sword, rode to the great wooden half door behind the portcullis and started pounding on the gate with my pommel.

Richard joined me.

Chaucer pulled his hood tighter around his face. 'We're all going to die,' he said.

Sam laughed aloud. 'You think *they're* mad?' He laughed into the rain. 'We're *following* them.'

Far off, Notre Dame rung the half hour.

Chaucer was cold. His lips were blue. He wasn't as well dressed as we – armour may look cold, but it blocks the wind, and good plate will keep the clothes under it dry. Or perhaps it would be better to say, warm and damp in a cold, clammy way. Mind you, my cloak had soaked through a full day ago, so my warmth was a relative thing.

Still, Chaucer's mind was working. 'She isn't used to this being closed,' he said aloud, and his teeth chattered. 'The Dauphin thinks that Charles of Navarre is in Paris.' He shook his head. 'It's not fuck-ing *fair*.'

Richard looked down the alley. There were a dozen people watching us. So much for secrecy.

'Write a note.' Richard grabbed Chaucer's arm. 'Say we're on a special errand from the King. Say anything. Write a note.'

Chaucer shook him off. 'In a downpour?'

Richard laughed. 'We can fight in the rain. You can write in the rain.'

In the end, he could, although it took Sam holding his huge Scot's wool cloak over the notary while he scribbled. As we waited for the ink to dry on the scrap of parchment, Geoffrey told us *why* he had a scrap of parchment ...

Richard looked at Sam. 'Now you shoot it over the wall.'

Sam was completely still for a moment. Then he nodded. 'Of course I do.'

We tied the note to a shaft, and covered it with a bit of silk from the lining of my arming jack. This all took time, and it was getting dark.

Then we held the cloak for him, while he bent his bow and strung it. He took the shaft and, in one swift movement, he bent the bow and sent the shaft into the air.

The twenty or so people watching all said, 'Oooh,' together.

'Good Christ,' muttered Chaucer. 'Shall we ask the whore if she has a place for all of us to sleep?'

'With our horses and armour?' Richard asked. 'No thanks.' But he smiled at her.

She smiled at him. Women who could see past his dark skin always liked him.

Suddenly the wicket gate opened.

There was a big man – older, but a fighter, you could see. He was in armour, with a heavy pole-hammer in his fists, and there were ten men like him at his back.

The portcullis stayed down.

'Who are you? State your names and styles.'

Chaucer was too cold.

Richard looked at me.

'I'm William Gold. I'm a gentleman of ...' Christ, what was I getting us into? 'Of the Earl of Oxford's retinue. I have escorted this worthy man.' That for Chaucer, and he never thanked me. 'From Bordeaux. He has a copy of the King of France's agreement with the King of England. Messires, we are cold and hungry, and we have fought brigands and Paris militia, and we would very much appreciate it if you would let us in.'

Chaucer glared at me, so apparently I'd said too much.

But the older man in armour nodded brusquely and removed his helmet. 'I'm Robert de Clermont,' he said.

Didn't mean a thing to me, but his sergeants were opening the portcullis.

An hour later, still damp and cold, Richard, Geoffrey and I were standing before the Dauphin. King Charles V as he later was.

He was young – about my own age. His brother Philippe was even younger, and stood by him, playing with the hilt of his dagger. He looked like a saint: pale, dark-haired, with translucent skin, a long face and a noble brow.

His hands never stopped moving. He should have been a tailor, not a King. His eyes never met mine, but darted around the room. I understood that the Paris Commune played him a merry dance and treated him badly, that he was riding a bad horse as best he could. But I also thought that he'd lost Poitiers for France by leaving the field.

We bowed very deeply. He looked us over carefully.

'But you are just boys?' he said – rather spontaneously, I think.

Chaucer had fortified himself with two cups of hippocras and he smiled. 'No younger than your Grace,' he said with a fine bow.

The Dauphin nodded and looked at his brother, then at the Marshal of Normandy, Robert de Clermont.

Chaucer bowed again, was suffered to approach and handed the Dauphin a heavy scroll.

'The draft of the treaty,' he said. 'My ... I was sent to ask for your approval.'

'Who sent you?' the Dauphin asked. He might suffer from battlefield anxiety, but he was as sharp as a new knife.

'My lord, the King, your father,' Chaucer said boldly.

'You met him?' the Dauphin asked.

'Yes,' Chaucer said.

'In person?' the Dauphin asked.

'Yes, your Grace,' Chaucer replied. 'I copied out our safe conduct as his express direction.'

I nodded in secret approval. When lying, it's best to stay close to the truth.

The Dauphin nodded.

Chaucer bowed again. 'My lord, if I may?'

'Speak, sir,' said the Dauphin.

'Your Grace knows that the King of Navarre has escaped from prison?' Chaucer said.

The Dauphin pursed his lips.

'Yes,' he said.

'We wanted to reach you before ... the King of Navarre.' Chaucer sounded unsure of himself for the first time.

'Why?' The Dauphin asked.

Chaucer stood as if dumbfounded.

'Why?' he asked again. 'Do you imagine I have any freedom of action? I might have, but Charles of Navarre will rob me of that. What does my father imagine I'm doing here. Governing? I am not completely in control of the gates of this building. I do what I'm told. When I don't, the Provost has some of my friends beaten. Or killed. And this agreement ... is worthless. Because there are no funds to pay my father's ransom – because the Provost of Paris is the law, and not I.'

Chaucer's mouth moved like that of a fish out of water.

'When Charles of Navarre comes – I've already signed his safe conduct – I will sign whatever he orders me to sign. He will give me orders in his own name, and in the name of his ally, the King of England. Whom you gentlemen claim to represent. As if the King of England is suddenly solicitous for the health of France. A murderer might stab a victim a few times and then hold his hand and ask after his health, eh?' The Dauphin was halfway off his chair now.

He turned to the Marshal of Normandy. 'See to it these men are fed – and outside the walls before Charles arrives in the morning.' He laughed. 'With his English army.'

He rose from his chair, walked to the fireplace and threw the whole treaty – seals and all – in the fire. When he laughed, he sounded a little mad.

We were escorted out. Politely.

We were fed. Well enough.

A very efficient house staff – this was the property of the King of France, and he had the very best domestic servants in the world, I think – dried our clothes.

It didn't matter. Because we left in the dark, into a steady rain.

*

Sam led the way. He knew where he was going, give or take a few miles. The ground was soaked and our horses were not recuperated after only six hours rest. Young Bob was all but crying with fatigue, and the rest of us weren't much better.

But we made it away from the walls of Paris. As we rode north, across the fields and on small farm roads, we saw Navarre's patchwork army marching down the main road from St Denis. I saw his colours on his banner at the head of his army. And I saw Sir James Pipe's banner.

Chaucer reined in.

Sir James Pipe passed within a few hundred paces of us.

'We'll have a clear road to Normandy,' Sam said. 'These gentry have cleared it for us.'

I saw the Bourc Camus' colours, black and white. And de Badefol's. And Hawkwood's.

I just sat there, dumbfounded. 'Are we on the wrong side?' I asked.

Chaucer breathed in and out a few times, like a dying man. When he spoke, his voice was gasping. 'I ... how? We talked about it. He said the treaty was everything. That we had to reach the Dauphin.' He looked at me.

For the first and perhaps only time, I felt bad for him. He'd been really brave, resourceful, loyal and capable. By my standards, he'd proved himself.

Richard shrugged. 'I don't think we're all going to be made Knights of the Garter this time,' he said.

A crowd was pouring out of Paris, cheering Charles of Navarre. Now Paris had three masters: the Provost, the Dauphin and Charles of Navarre.

I met Richard's eye. 'We cocked this up,' I said.

He shrugged. 'We did what we were ordered to do,' he said.

'That's our story,' I agreed. 'Let's stick to it.'

That was hard. The feeling of failure. The feeling that somehow we were on the wrong side.

I remember looking at my little pennon with the Prince's white feather in white on a black field. I wasn't sure I should still be displaying it openly.

But I had days riding across the devastated landscape of the Isle de France and the Seine valley to contemplate just how we'd got the whole thing so wrong.

Every night, at small fires that didn't really warm us, we shared looted wine and chewed it over again and again.

I had begun to harbour a suspicion that we – that is, Master Hoo – had been used. The fourth night on the road, we were camped in a corner of a burned-out stone barn. It had enough of the upper floor left intact to provide a feeling of dryness – mostly false, but with a fire of dry timber from what had once been the house, we did well enough.

I was trying to work some oil into the straps on my sabatons. The straps under the feet were about to give, and that required an armourer to pull the rivets. Rich men pointed the sabatons to their shoes, but that meant having a steady supply of shoes that fit just right.

Richard was sewing.

Chaucer was staring into the fire.

Sam was asleep, as were the other men. We were young and raw, so we sat and talked. They were older and knew how desperate our situation was, so they slept.

'May I have your beeswax?' Richard asked.

I tossed him my housewife – a small fabric pocket that held my horn needlecase, my silver thimble, my beeswax and my sewing knife. Every soldier has one.

He missed his catch and it went *splot* into the muddy water at the edge of the fire.

I shot to my feet. 'By all the saints, you useless mongrel! All my thread wet! And my pins ruined! Give me that—'

'I meant no offence …' He looked very hurt. Richard had been treated worse than me as a boy and he didn't stand up well to harsh words. Blows, yes – he was brave as a paladin – but words …

'Leave off,' Chaucer said. 'Your foul temper is your least attractive trait, on a long list of them.'

'You're a canting hypocrite, and your lying story landed us in this state—' I barked.

'You can't kill everything you don't like, bully-boy,' Chaucer said. 'I never lied—'

'Yon story about the treaty – Master Hoo never said such a word! Or if he did, he didn't say it to you!' I shouted.

Chaucer deflated. 'Never said it to me – aye. That's the truth. But I heard him say it to Sir John Hawkwood.'

'Leave off, Will. You do have a foul temper and we don't need it just now,' Richard added.

'And some of us are trying to sleep, *gentle* knights,' said Christopher.

'Ah, my friends. Tempers flaring?'

I whirled. My sword was on my bed-roll; his sword was at my nose.

Bertrand du Guesclin, of course.

'My turn to be host, I think?' he exclaimed.

He had twenty men-at-arms with him, emerging out of the rain.

I saw Sam Bibbo strike Christopher sharply, and the two of them rolled out from under the wooden floor into the rain and were gone.

Du Guesclin never even saw them go.

I sighed. 'God's curse is on me,' I said.

Du Guesclin smiled. 'What do you think you are worth to ransom?'

We spent Christmas with the French knight. He was growing more famous every day, so Frenchmen were flocking to his banner. As yet he had no office – in fact, part of his problem was that there was no government to give him an office – but in Normandy he was the French commander.

We slept warm, in wattle huts in the woods.

We were spoiled of all our armour. And our horses.

'Just a loan,' he quipped. 'I know full well you didn't strip me, but France's need is great.' He smiled. He wasn't a cruel bastard, but he did lord it over us.

He must have gone on a long raid – a *chevuachée* – but he came back after a week, and he had a great hart, a boar and other meat, so we had a proper Christmas feast. He let us hunt, and Richard and I managed two brace of hares – we fed the camp for a day and a night.

The wine flowed. And talk turned to feats of arms and the war, as it was bound to do. It took du Guesclin a fortnight to ask us why we were abroad in France – with so many routiers riding, he took us for another such party until some chance remark of Chaucer's got his attention – it was Candelmas night, I think. We'd just heard Mass from du Guesclin's priest, a big fellow with a weight of muscle that belied a quick head. Unlike most priests, this one – Père Joseph – read Latin well, and knew his gospels and his Aquinas. He hated Englishmen, but we got on well enough, and he taught me the new beads I'd only seen monks use: prayer beads. I'd all but stopped praying until I was taken. I owe Père Joseph for that. With him, I started saying the paternoster and the Ave Maria like a son of the church.

But that bores you, I'm sure.

At any rate, we were seated around a great open fire. It was Candelmas eve, we'd all taken Communion, and we were sitting together like comrades – he had six other English knights, a dozen prosperous archers and ten of his own men gathered around a bonfire, like an open-air round table.

He turned to Chaucer. 'What treaty is this you had?' he asked.

I missed whatever had led up to this, but at the word treaty, all fell silent.

Chaucer bit his lip and looked at me.

'If there ever was a secret,' I said, 'it scarcely matters now.'

Du Guesclin's eyes locked on mine. 'What treaty?' he asked.

'King John signed a treaty with King Edward at Windsor – in August.' I shrugged. 'Master Chaucer was there – he can tell it full. We had orders—' suddenly I had that feeling again that I was in over my head. The worst of it was that I *liked* du Guesclin. Better than I liked Robert Knolles or the Bourc Camus.

'Yes?' du Guesclin asked.

'To take a copy to the Dauphin,' I said.

The Frenchmen present all became quiet. The Englishman closest to me was a man-at-arms from the north, James Wright. I saw him again in Italy. He made a face as if he'd eaten something bad. 'The Dauphin? He is the enemy, surely?'

Du Guesclin leaned forward. He put a skewer of deer meat across two big stones, moved his riding boots a little to see they were toasted, and held out a silver beaker for a villain to refill. 'You never made it?' he asked.

Richard laughed bitterly. 'We made it. An hour before Charles of Navarre rolled into Paris.' He shrugged. 'Your Dauphin burned the treaty.'

Du Guesclin narrowed his eyes. 'You were on a diplomatic errand?'

I nodded.

'You took a little time off to fight me?' he asked. Aside, in his broad Norman French – to an Englishman, the language of lawyers! – he said to his friends, 'He captured me – the ambush at La Foret.' He made a motion as if to say 'that story I've told you'.

It was my turn to laugh. 'John Hawkwood made me. When he asks me to ride, I ride.'

Several of the French men nodded in approval. One said, 'That's how it is,' and nodded emphatically.

Du Guesclin rubbed his beard with his left hand and sipped wine. 'Really, then, I should release you all.'

Richard nodded. 'Yes!' he said.

Du Guesclin looked off into the dark.

'Perhaps you could decide that the lot of us were worth a hundred florins,' I said.

'Hah! I've already paid you,' he said.

'I'll just send it back,' I said. I could tell we were winning this round.

He sighed. 'So many gold florins slipping through my fingers.'

'You lucky bastard!' Jamie Wright said. 'Well done!'

The next night, we watched snow fall. Du Guesclin restored Goldie to me – an act of true friendship, and one I treasure. My horse and arms were his by right. No one in Normandy in those days made quibbles about diplomatic missions and *sauvegardes*. We were lucky – had one of the other French routiers taken us, we'd have been dead or bled for silver.

The way we'd have done if we took them.

Du Guesclin had an iron stool; it folded, and he sat on it like a King. 'Tell me of the Dauphin,' he said. 'Our commander, de Clermont—'

I was sitting on carefully broken-up firewood, and I was more sprawled than sitting. 'The Marshal of Normandy,' I said. 'I met him in Paris. We almost exchanged blows.'

'That would have been honour for you,' he said. 'He is a great knight, and a most puissant man-at-arms.'

'Hmm,' I said. 'He had a pole-hammer and I had a horse.'

Du Guesclin laughed. 'I like you. For an Englishman, you are not so very bad.' He leaned forward. 'Tell me of the Dauphin.'

I shrugged.

'Many in Normandy would have me support Charles of Navarre,' du Guesclin said. 'Men say he's reached an accord with the Dauphin.' He shrugged. 'I'm a country boy. I don't pretend to understand what is happening in Paris.'

'Nor I,' I said. 'Bertrand, it's not my place to tell you how to run your country.'

'The more so as you've done your part to pull it to pieces, eh?' he asked.

I nodded.

'But nonetheless.' He laughed.

'Well ...' I remember sitting, not sure what to say, when Chaucer joined us, bringing me wine – he wasn't always an arse. I made space for him on the wood pile, and he shared the wine.

'Bertrand wants to know what's happening in Paris,' I said.

Chaucer shook his head and rolled his eyes. 'I think that might count as comforting the enemy.'

I took a swallow of wine and spat it in the snow, where it showed like new blood. 'Who exactly *is* the enemy?' I asked.

Chaucer met my eye and nodded. 'Sometimes, even you have a point,' he said. He turned to du Guesclin. 'Paris is rent by factions, and anything I tell you is probably already changed, but there are at least four factions. The Dauphin's party – men who consider themselves the government.'

'But they are not the government,' du Guesclin said. 'The King is the government.'

Chaucer waved his arms. 'Just so, *mon vieux*. The second faction is the King's party, men who served the King – many of them were at Poitiers and are now prisoners – some released or ransomed, some who escaped from that field. They consider themselves the government, and the Dauphin to be either a tool of the enemy or a dupe.'

'Yes!' du Guesclin said.

'The third faction is that of the Paris Commune. It, itself, is split into two factions, one led by the Mercer, Etienne Marcel, who seems to want to be the Tyrant of Paris – he and Robert Le Coq and the Council of Eighty intend to rule France, I guess, by assembly and election.'

Du Guesclin shook his head. 'I have heard all this, of course, but never put this way. Surely this Parisian grocer has little power.'

'Twenty thousand men, an army and many professional soldiers,' I said. 'Your Marshal told me he had hired a professional knight to train the militia – Pierre de Villiers.'

Du Guesclin nodded. 'I know that name. He is from here.'

'The other Parisian faction is less tied to the assembly. It is led by the richest merchants, who want a complete reform of the laws and the coinage, and who accuse the King of gross mismanagement,' I said. Chaucer cast me one of his few approving looks.

'And into this mess rides Charles of Navarre,' Chaucer said.

'That imp of hell,' du Guesclin said. 'He leaves a trail of slime wherever he goes, like some foul snail.'

I laughed. 'I wish you'd speak your mind,' I said. 'Stop sitting in resentful silence.'

Even Chaucer laughed.

Du Guesclin shook his head. 'He tried to buy me when he escaped.' He glared at the fire. He really wasn't much older than we. 'Now his army is full of Englishmen. And yet he prates about saving France. He would be all things to all men, but he has no honour.'

Chaucer sat back. He had Master Hoo's boots on, I noted. 'Honour,' he said dismissively. 'How can you two – knights – prate of honour? You saw the raped nuns on the road, William. What honour is there?'

Du Guesclin shook his head. 'There is honour everywhere! Almost every day, I fight. Every child in Normandy knows my name.' He spoke with complete satisfaction. 'I've faced the very flower of England and Gascony – and in the main, I have won.' He bowed in his seat to me. 'Sometimes, fortune has been against me. I rape no nuns; I fight my King's enemies. There is honour everywhere.'

'Master Chaucer is quick to see the flaws in chivalry and slow to see the glory,' I said.

Chaucer grunted. 'This from a man who runs a brothel to pay for his horses.'

To be honest, I had forgotten the brothel. Just for a few days, at the clearing in the woods of Normandy, I had prayed with a priest, practised my sword cuts with Jamie Wright and felt like a knight.

'Who will protect the weak, if not the men-at-arms?' I asked.

'Sweet Jesu, William! How can you even ask that? Who in the name of God oppresses the weak? It's only you men-at-arms. If you all died of a plague tomorrow, every peasant in France and England would only cheer.' Chaucer drank more wine.

Du Guesclin narrowed one eye and raised an eyebrow – it was a look he had, when he was thinking. 'But surely this is what the "hoods" in Paris say?'

Chaucer looked at his hands. 'Perhaps,' he admitted.

Du Guesclin shook his head. 'Foolishness. What would you prefer? A tyranny of *money*? Look at Italy! Men are bought and sold by merchants. Men-at-arms are at least men who crave public renown and fame, who are strong and well-trained and enobled by the thousand penances of war and pain. Are there bad men among us? *Bien sur*! But by St Denis, there are bad priests and bad Popes, and no one says that Christ should be dismissed! Is Paris so well-directed? What I hear is a tale of greed and crime, of women oppressed, of churches despoiled for their silver by the crowds.'

Chaucer looked surly.

'What of the Turks?' I asked.

Du Guesclin looked at me.

'Surely it is noble to fight the Turks – who threaten all of Christendom?'

Chaucer spat. 'Go fight them then.'

'Perhaps I will yet,' I said.

Du Guesclin laughed. 'You two must be a pleasure to ride with, *hein*?'

Du Guesclin had another problem, which was that suddenly all of the King of England's officers in Normandy had become the captains of Charles of Navarre. Du Guesclin wasn't at war with Charles of Navarre – it complicated his operations, and our release as well. I sent word to the Three Foxes – a letter copied fair by Master Chaucer – asking that one hundred florins be paid to du Guesclin's agent, who proved to be our Genoese banker.

Du Guesclin pointed this out to Chaucer. 'You think it is the men-at-arms who make war,' he said. 'Ask who takes the gold from both sides.'

I spent January learning to use a lance. Du Guesclin was a fine lance, and he was surprised I was so bad at using the weapon. He had a quintain in the woods, and when the ground was frozen hard, I rode at it every day. Jamie Wright hooted at my poor horsemanship, and Richard winced when I was struck by the sack of turnips on the back of the swinging arm. Almost a week into my training, I cocked it up so badly that I managed to fall onto frozen, bumpy ground.

Du Guesclin stood over me and shook his head. 'By St Lo,' he said. 'One hears this story, but never actually sees it.'

All around the clearing, men were laughing.

Jean de Flery and Michel de Carriere, two of his most trusted men, were laughing so hard that they sat in the snow.

De Carriere looked at me and pointed, unable to speak. He wheezed and finally looked at his friend. 'How is it these men are driving us out of Normandy?' he asked.

Richard, who was quite competent with the lance, rode a course, slammed his point into the shield so that splinters flew and trotted up to the laughing pair. 'It's the long bow,' he said. 'It's faster than the lance.'

Well, that shut them up, but it killed the bonhomie of the clearing for a day.

I was black from the bottom of my arse to the top after that fall. It didn't heal for two weeks, and every time I bathed, they all laughed *again*.

Candlemas came, and we heard Mass again – it was more churching than I had had in years – then du Guesclin got word that our ransom had been paid.

'I have Sir James' ransom as well. And letters from the King of Navarre.'

We had dinner, and all the French knights were silent. It was not a festive occasion.

It can be hard with men who are both friends and enemies, but who speak a different language. I wasn't sure about their silence – it might have been the season, with Lent about to start, or it might have been the war.

We didn't want to ask. In truth, although I've glossed over and made light of it, we were prisoners, and from time to time, an angry Frenchman would propose killing the lot of us. It's happened. We were eager to go. It was so close that we all feared some last-minute difficulty.

The tension at dinner that night was like the heavy air near the sea in mid-summer.

After a few sallies that failed, I turned to my host. 'What troubles you, my lord?' I asked boldly.

Chaucer stepped on my foot. But I thought then, and still do, that some things are best met head on.

Du Guesclin made a face. 'In this, I will hope that you can share our anger. Michel wants me to be silent – he thinks that to tell you this will be to tell a secret, yes?' He looked at de Carriere, who glared at him.

'The person of the Dauphin was seized by Etienne Marcel three days ago. They took him prisoner and killed Marshal Clermont and every other servant of the King that they could find in Paris.' Du Guesclin pursed his lips.

'And the King of Navarre condones it!' shouted de Carriere – he was usually a pleasant, if silent, man, as young as we ourselves, but he had drunk deep, and his anger was as deep as his draughts.

Chaucer spoke carefully. 'This is what we ... sought to prevent.'

'So you say,' de Carriere said.

Du Guesclin shook his head. 'If you English dismember France,' he said, 'what will be left? Who will till and work the land? Who will pray? Have you English thought on what will happen if France collapses into anarchy?'

There was, in decency, no answer we could make.

The next day, wearing our own armour and riding our own horses, we rode away. We rode into Normandy, where there was no royal administration to be found. The siege of Rennes was over, and the men who'd participated in it were all serving in the King of Navarre's armies.

We rode south through lands that were already showing signs of recovery. It was early March and the men were tilling. Women leaned on stone walls and watched us ride by.

This part of southern Brittany had never been a theatre of war, but now it was English, as English as Gascony. And when we reached Gascony, it looked prosperous. Spring was peeking out of every sunny morning; birds sang.

We reached Bordeaux late in March. Lent was almost out. The air was clear, the girls were pretty and we sang as we rode the last few miles.

The Three Foxes looked about the same, except that there was a table in the front of the yard, and at it sat Christopher Shippen and John Hughes, playing dice. I bridled, but Marie threw herself into my arms, and Sam Bibbo came down the stairs – was it her door that had opened?

He clasped my hand, and we had to tell our stories ten times as wine was served and all the girls had a holiday. Ah, I had sworn a hundred times to give her up, cease my fornications and send the girls away.

That good change did not last out my Marie sitting on my lap and telling over our accounts. Taxing me with having run risks and been captured.

I put de Charny's dagger on the oaken chest by our bed, looked at it and thought hard thoughts.

But that didn't keep me out of the bed.

The Prince was in England for a tournament, and so was Sir John Chandos. The Prince's Lieutenant for Gascony was Sir John Cheverston, and he was reported to be marching up the Dordogne valley. Richard and I rested a day, gathered our retinue and rode north after him.

Fortune is a fickle mistress.

After months of hardship and failure, we arrived at the siege of Nadaillac, young Chaucer in tow, in time to present Sir John Cheverston with our damp and somewhat moth-eaten array of *sauvegardes*.

He was a hard man, with a greying forked beard and heavy moustache, a broad forehead and a ferocious temper. His steward warned us before we were taken to this tent that he was in a mood.

'How long were you two scamps on the road?' he asked. 'Chandos must have been scraping the barrel when he chose to send you. Where's Master Hoo? He's been sore missed by the Prince.'

'Dead,' I said. 'Killed by the militia in Paris.'

Sir John's squire helped him get his aventail over his head, and his stained arming cap emerged. 'Where in the nine hells were you two, that he was killed?'

'Fighting,' I said.

He looked at us and shook his head. 'And you were captured,' he said in disgust.

'Yes, my lord,' I answered humbly.

'Am I allowed to know exactly *why* two such very young scallywags and a rogue of a notary were sent to Paris?' he asked.

'We thought you might tell us?' I said quietly.

Cheverston spat and took a cup of wine from his squire. 'I'm of half a mind to send you back,' he said. 'The Prince ordered me to acquire a safe-conduct from the French so that I could clear the bandits from the Dordogne, but he didn't leave me orders as to where I should get such a document.' He sighed. 'You boys have had a hard winter – its in your faces – and I suppose you expect to be paid?'

What do you say to that?

We stood silently. With our caps in our hands.

Richard leaned forward. 'May we ... stay on for the siege?' he asked.

Cheverston shrugged. 'If I'm paying your wages, you might as well be of some help. I don't suppose you know anything about the Chateau of Nadaillac?

Richard and I spoke out at about the same time. 'We scouted it last autumn,' we said in unison, like monks chanting.

We showed him the spring on the hillside.

It took me six months to accomplish nothing for my own reputation. It took one evening for me to make it.

Richard and I took ten men-at-arms and a dozen archers in light harness, and we worked our way up the hillside in the dark. There was very little cover, and we made noise, but the siege had gone on for weeks and the garrison was lax – they expected Sir John to buy them out soon enough, and the fighting had been sporadic, to say the least, as the men inside were mostly the same kind of Gascon routiers who made up most of Sir John's army.

Let me tell you about lying all night on sandy soil. It's dull. Every noise is an enemy; every rock digs into you, despite your harness. I wore my brigantine and my arm harness, and no legs, sabatons or breastplate. I couldn't be comfortable.

Sam Bibbo snored behind me.

The stars crept across the sky.

When you go out to lay an ambush, you go out full of the soundness of your plan and the excellence of your men. By the time the moon has crept halfway across the sky, the plan seems like lunacy and the men with you a paltry force to face the destined counter-ambush, or far too large and noisy for the task. The enemy is never coming.

What I remember best was the tricks my eyes played on me and the plans I *hadn't* made. Somehow I'd forgotten to tell everyone under what circumstances we'd retreat. I lay there and worried as my stomach roiled, and I farted too much.

Ah! Command. Everyone desires it. But once you have it, it's a fool's game, and you are always better off having some other man, who you tell yourself is brilliant, *preux*, daring and sure – let him make the decisions.

A night ambush is for a monster of self-assurance.

I kept thinking that the sun was rising, that it was lighter. I have no explanation for this, except that as I rolled over to start telling men to withdraw – this happened at least twice – I realized that it was still black as pitch, even with moonlight.

When I heard the clink of metal on stone, I assumed it was from one of us.

Then a boot scraping, and then metal.

Sabatons. A knight in full harness, walking on the road.

I raised my head.

In the moonlight, they were like a procession of the dead – twenty men at least, in harness, coming down the road.

Was it a sortie?

But they had another half a dozen men with yokes.

They'd come for water.

So much for my night of worries.

I had chosen a spot below the road, with a clear view. My archers were all to my right, so they had unobstructed shooting, and my men-at-arms were on both sides of the road but a little lower down.

I waited, my heart beating so hard that I could watch my brigantine's plates move in the moonlight.

The last man passed me.

I stood up. 'St George and England!' I roared.

We killed or took them all.

It wasn't a great feat of arms, but all the famous names were off fighting in the north with Navarre, and so Richard and I made our names. I took the Captain, Philippe de Monfer – he was the man in sabatons – sword to sword. He hacked at me overhand – most men do, to be frank – but in two years I had learned a few things about the longsword. I held mine in two hands – one hand on the hilt and one almost at the point – caught his first great blow over my head, threw my blade around his neck and threw him to the ground, using my sword as a lever. He went down with a crash, and Sam stripped him of weapons while I stood on his sword arm and fought off his squire. The squire had an axe. I cut at his hands until I broke his fingers. He gave himself up.

Richard took four men. He was getting better, too.

The rest threw down their weapons. These were routiers, not great knights. They weren't worth much – in fact, Cheverston hanged a few of them – but we made a fair amount on our ransoms.

That was all in the future, though. The taking of Nadaillac was an event, as much for the French as for us, because the 'captain' had preyed on both sides. Cheverston had a writ from the Black Prince to clean out every nest of robbers in the Dordogne, and with the fame of our deed behind us, Sir John sent us, as he had threatened, back into France to get him the permission he needed to make war against the brigands who preyed on both sides. He also gave me letters to Charles of Navarre, two of the King of France's officers and the Dauphin.

He read them over very carefully after a scribe had copied them fair. 'Listen, Master Gold. None of us really knows who is governing France these days. We do not want to break the truce, but we do not want to offend the wrong ... hmm. The wrong government. If you can, get me a *sauvegarde* from all three: the Dauphin, the King of Navarre and the King's lieutenant. Understand?'

I think I smiled. 'All too well, my lord,' I said.

'Sir John Chandos says you have a good head on your shoulders,' he nodded. 'Governing is not all about swords, eh? Get this done for the Prince and I'll see you are rewarded.' He looked at me. 'I'd have sent Master Chaucer on this mission, but he, mmm, is not available.'

I bowed gratefully.

A letter had come to the army from England and ordered Chaucer home for a wedding. I wasn't that sorry to see him go, but Richard was. We gave him a fine dinner, and so did Marie, as he passed through Bordeaux.

We rode north in spring. Our horses and gear were the worse for wear after almost ten months' constant campaign, but we had just made our fortunes and we were cheerful. We sang. We told stories. That's when we missed Chaucer the most, of course – he was an endless fund of stories, and that's *before* he went to Italy.

We repeated our earlier route to Tours. The same royal officer passed us, with the same courtesy – this is one of the reasons the same men are used as couriers again and again. Once you are known, passing borders and gates is much easier.

North of Tours, we stayed within France and rode on to Paris. We passed north through a sullen country, full of furtive people. Bibbo was on his guard. I'd learned my lesson from du Guesclin, and now we went into our cloaks as soon as we'd eaten, and we kept watch all night. My page, Rob, was growing into a man, and had a good sword from Nadaillac; the rest of them were solid enough. We were used to each other's ways – we could halt and, in an hour, the food was cooked, the fire out, the horses curried, fed and picketed, the blanket rolls laid on fresh-cut bracken of whatever type the area allowed, whether plundered straw or pine boughs. The taking of Nadaillac had improved our kit by four small tents, simple wedges of white linen that went up easily and stowed flat in wicker panniers. We often used them to roof over other structures, byres and barns and roofless hovels, but they were better than a sky full of rain, even by themselves.

By day, very little moved across the country. We never saw a wagon or a cart. Sam and John took to riding with their bows strung and over their shoulders, because despite the spring sun, there was an air of thunder over the whole country.

Twice we passed manor houses with smoke coming from the chimneys, but they weren't interested in having us, so we rode on.

Forty miles south of Paris, at Etampes, we found the town taken and full of an English garrison. They claimed to be holding the town for the King of Navarre, but they gave us lodging, let us refill the feed bags for our horses and baggage animals, and we got wine and news.

The news was that the Dauphin had escaped from Pairs and was raising an army.

Word was that he was at Meaux, on the far side of the Seine. That set us a fine problem as we didn't relish entering Paris, especially Paris controlled by Etienne Marcel and his red and blue hoods. Word was they were killing every aristocrat they could find.

The English held the lower Seine, but it was a hundred *dangerous* miles round Paris to the English-held crossings.

We discussed trying our luck.

But the captain of Etampes told us that the Isle de France was 'the very cockpit of war', so we elected to go south around Paris. We decided to go straight to the King of Navarre.

I wanted to see the trail of slime, I guess.

We rode north first. We weren't following a rational route, but rather jumping from English-held manor to English-held castle. It was interesting to talk to the captains – all new men, as far as I could tell, many as young as me, and some – you may laugh to hear me say this – the sweepings of English prisons. Hard men were pouring into France from England. They were here for plunder and nothing else. Most had only the vaguest idea of what side they supported in the French civil war.

Most of the lesser men thought they were fighting for England. Even more of them thought of France as an enemy country to be mined of silver.

To be frank, none of that bothered me unduly, but it was starting to trouble Richard. Twenty leagues west of Paris, we almost had to fight for our lives when Richard accused a tiny garrison – just six men, all drunk as lords – of being 'thieves and rapists'. Unsurprisingly, free-born Englishmen, even when they *are* thieves and rapists, resent the term.

Not that criminal behaviour was limited to Englishmen. The Gascons were unbelievably bad, and the Breton and Norman French were, if anything, worse. The whole countryside from Rennes east to Meaux had become a carpet of fire and smoke, and a generation of prosperous Frenchmen watched their carefully horded surplus destroyed in two hideous summers.

It is my observation that beaten men do not revolt. Beaten men lie under the lash and abandon hope.

But men who have had hope, men who have seen a way out of grinding poverty and injustice, men who have the wherewithal to own weapons and use them, they revolt.

Our party was camping in a small hunting lodge – ruined, of course – in a patch of woods close enough to Paris that we could see the haze of smoke Paris cast into the air. Sam said that from the rooftrees he could see spires.

We were there, of course, because Richard had made the 'garrison' of the local manor house so angry.

During the middle watch of morning, I was shaken awake by Rob, my page.

'Fighting, Master Will.'

I was up and out of my cloak. I climbed the old ladder to the roof – or rather the remnants of the roof.

The manor house was on fire. Someone like du Guesclin had just taken out an English garrison less than a mile away.

'To arms,' I said.

Rob woke everyone. John and Sam came up, stringing their bows, both still naked from the waist down and looking like frowzled satyrs.

The screams started almost immediately. Richard was arming, but he kept looking up at me – he wanted to 'do something'. A man was being killed very slowly, perhaps two men.

In the summer of 1358, raids were mostly a matter of a few men – twenty men-at-arms was a big force. Charles of Navarre's 'army' never mustered more than a thousand men, and the Dauphin had about the same. I say this to justify our actions as we therefore assumed that our party would be roughly the size of any enemy we encountered.

Perhaps we should have been warned by the screams.

It took us an hour to arm everyone and pack the camp in the dark. We left a very scared Rob with six pack horses and all our spare gear, and the rest of us struck out cross country, which is difficult at night, and it took us *another* half an hour to cross the half-mile of farmland that separated us from the manor house.

The two voices kept screaming.

On and on.

You don't think a man can scream that way for long.

He can.

There was the first light in the sky – the so-called false dawn – when we emerged from the hedgerows to a small, ditched farm road hard by the manor house.

It was *crammed* with men. Armed men. Perhaps 200 men, perhaps 500.

'Back!' I roared. The hedges must have blocked the sound.

They were as shocked as we.

In a glance, I saw the fields around the manor teaming with men, most of them in jacks, or mail, with helmets, but some in smocks, with farm implements. The manor house was burning, and there were two men crucified like our saviour on roof beams, being roasted alive.

I was backing Goldie.

For once, the mad man was Sam. He had his bow strung, and suddenly it was in his hand. He nocked an arrow, and loosed. Nocked again – now the crowd had seen us, and there were shouts, a growing wave of shouts.

He loosed again.

I realized he was killing the men on the crosses.

He feathered one man in mail who was running at us, and then I had to cut down into a crowd, because I'd waited too long and they were coming out of the field to my right.

Goldie was a war horse, and he knew his business. I gave him the touch of the spurs that told him to clear me a space, and his iron-shod hooves went into action like four immensely strong knights wielding maces. He whirled and I hung on. I hit one carl – he had a jack and a skullcap, and my blade bounced off his skullcap, but he went down like a slaughtered pig anyway.

And then I started clearing them off Sam Bibbo, who was trying to put men down with his bowstave. He'd tried to keep loosing arrows, and he, too, had missed the tide of men coming out of the fields.

I couldn't leave him.

His horse panicked. There were too many men with too many agricultural implements in the dark, and the rouncey reared.

One of our assailants put a pitchfork into the animal, and she screamed and threw Sam – he flew a good horse's length and hit the ground hard enough to make a noise.

If you want a good idea of your fighting skills, try fighting an endless tide of men in the dark for possession of the unconscious body of a friend.

You want me to talk to you of chivalry and knighthood?

I did not run and leave my friend.

I didn't know just where he was, but I gave Goldie the spurs again and we leaped forward; he shot out hooves in all directions, and I cut and thrust into the mob. It seemed to go on for ever, but in fact took less time than saying three paternosters, according to Richard.

Who, thanks be to Christ, now appeared, also fully armed and also on a warhorse.

The two of us cleared the space of a small Parish churchyard. And John Hughes, bless him, came up, dismounted between us, and found Sam. Sam's horse was down and dead. So were ten other men, or more.

We put Sam over John's saddle, John held my stirrup leather and we rode off into the darkness.

We picked up Rob and our pack animals, and moved from cover to cover all day. We could see the roads full of men – armed men.

Sam was unconscious, and for the first time, Richard and I realized how much we relied on the old archer. We both kept wanting to ask him things.

Like, 'Who the fuck are those men?'

Richard watched them from a tree. He was still in all his harness. 'If the Dauphin has this many men, why hasn't he driven us back to Calais?' he asked.

I watched them too. 'They look like Paris militia,' I said. 'But they are twenty miles from Paris and there isn't a hood to be seen.'

'No cavalry; no knights.' Richard shook his head.

We climbed a low, wooded ridge and followed it for a few miles.

At evening, we halted. We had no idea where we were. We had moved across France by asking our way – there were no signs and the roads were appalling. Usually Sam knew the way, and when he was wrong, we didn't comment.

Now, on our own, all ways appeared the same.

However, after a restless night – Richard and I never took off our harnesses – we woke to a beautiful spring day. In the distance, we could see a church tower. The bell was ringing. It was unreal.

Richard and I left the rest with Sam, who seemed better – his colour had improved and he was muttering, whilst his eyes were moving beneath the lids. We cantered along the paths towards the steeple we could see.

There was a town. It wasn't a big town, but prosperous enough.

It was, in fact, a village of the dead.

They had died a while before – perhaps the October or November of 1357. There were corpses in the door yards, and corpses in the streets. The women mostly still had their hair, and some of the people wore the remnants of clothes. There were children.

The bell continued to ring.

I rode to the tower.

Richard reined in, and then started to back his bay. 'Are you mad?' he asked. I want no more of this. They look like they could rise in the dance macabre!'

'I want a look from the tower,' I said.

The truth is that the sights of that town are with me yet, but I needed some sense of where I was, and I knew I'd get that in the tower.

I dismounted at the church door and left Goldie with Richard. I'd never seen him so jumpy.

I assumed that the wind was ringing the bell.

Wrong.

It was a young man. At least, I guess he had been a man. Someone had flayed all the skin from one side of his face, very neatly, and it had scabbed over, while the other side of his face sagged.

I think I gave a shout. I may even have shrieked like a maiden.

He put his hands over his head. He had no thumbs. They'd been severed and healed.

He had one eye.

I think you lads are getting the message.

It took me twenty breaths to get over the shock. I've never seen a man so disfigured and yet alive, and the wonder of it was that he was so terrifying – he, who could not have hurt a small child. The wreck of a man – why is the wreckage so full of fear? Is it just that we all of us fear death? Christ, I fear *that* death – unmanned. Made hideous. The Lord be with him.

I was tempted to kill him. Yes, I was.

Instead, I walked around him, as if he might do *me* harm, and climbed the bell tower.

In the room above the bell pulls, I found a corpse. Not so old. Bloated. A woman. And the thing below me began to bellow like a bull.

I was paying a high price for a look from a church tower, I can tell you. There's more wounds than those you take from swords. The dead woman – his mother? His sister? – and the monster himself – they people my dreams, some nights.

Who was he?

Who was she?

I climbed.

In the belfry were half a dozen men, strung up in the rafters like sausages being kept for winter.

Richard says I roared my war cry. Bless him, I think he lies. I think I burst into tears, but I truly don't remember.

I do remember looking out from between the rotting legs of one poor bastard and seeing Paris, and in another direction, the Seine, clear as the shoe'd foot that had fallen away from the corpse by the eastern arch.

I fled. I'd like to say I cut the men down and saw them buried, but I fled. I almost fell down one of the ladders, and I tried not to look at the bloated corpse of the woman, and would have passed the wreck of a man, but he was on his knees.

'Kill me,' he said. His lips were ruined and it was difficult to understand him, but he was obvious enough. 'Why not kill me? Why leave me alive? Kill me!'

I backed away from him.

'Kill me!' he shrieked. 'Was I not good enough to be killed?'

I fled.

I vaulted onto my horse, and Richard and I rode through the

streets so fast our horses' hooves threw sparks, and we didn't stop until we were in our little rock fall camp.

'Sam's awake!' John called. 'St Michael, you two look like you've seen ghosts.'

We moved north cautiously. The bell was ringing again, but we avoided the town and came down out of the low hills onto the flat by the river. To the east, we could see men – perhaps thousands of men – on the road.

'Who killed them?' Richard asked. He was almost grey under his dark skin. 'Who would do that?

I shrugged. We both knew that any of the bands hunting the Isle de France might have massacred a town – French, Gascon, English.

It had happened six months earlier.

We rode on.

Sam was off his head – awake, but raving, calling out to men who weren't there – and in the mid-afternoon, John started puking his guts out.

Rob's armpits had swelling in them. He had a high fever and he fell from his horse, which was the first I knew he was sick.

Christopher spat and backed his horse away from Rob, who was lying in the road where he'd fallen from his horse.

'Plague,' he said.

Peter – silent, morose Peter – turned his horse, threw his cloak over his head, and rode away. I could hear the sound of his hoof beats for a long time in the early summer evening. He galloped.

Christopher dismounted under a spreading oak tree that was a thousand years old. 'I'll find a camp site and I'll make a fire, but I won't tend him and I won't breathe the same air. The miasma.'

I was already touching the boy. Besides, I'd spent a day with the corpses of my parents, and the Plague, which had hit London again and again, had never troubled me or my sister. We were hardened, like good steel. Or perhaps just pickled.

Richard dismounted. 'I thought it was that town,' he said. 'I've had trouble breathing. All. Day.'

Then I became afraid. Plague isn't an enemy you can fight, and who it touches, it kills. Not five in a hundred walk away.

In a way, I was lucky, because there was so much to do.

Christopher was as good as his word. He found a camp site 200 paces off the road, where four oaks made a clearing by the stream that ran down to the Seine. He got the tents up, saving one for himself, which he set at the top of a small rise, about fifty feet away.

We set to gathering firewood. We only had one axe, but with the peasants cleared out of the surrounding country, there was a staggering amount of good oak just lying on the ground. We collected ten armloads or so, and broke it up in a forked tree – quicker than using an axe. I put our two pots on, full of water.

'I'll get some food,' Christopher said. 'Listen, cap'n – I want to help. I just don't want to die.'

I managed a leaderly smile. 'You didn't just ride off, and that's something.'

He nodded at Sam, who was muttering in a tent. 'He's got it, too. Bet ya.'

I hadn't even considered that.

Christopher rode off to forage, and left me alone with three very sick men. I hoped he'd come back. Richard struggled against the sickness for a few hours, then suddenly he was in the heart of it, silent, sweating, with swellings on his groin and armpits as big as eggs. Bibbo was slower, but he was raving. He thrashed, and I considered tying him down. But I got a tisane of herbs into both of them.

I could do nothing with Rob. He was burning hot, dry as a bone, and had trouble swallowing, and before Christopher returned, Rob was dead. I wrapped him in his cloak and carried him a hundred paces or so into the woods.

Believe it or don't, but tending them was so hard on me that burying Rob was like a rest. I dug – the soil was good, even in the trees. France is so rich – why can't they govern themselves?

Heh. Mayhap we help with that.

I didn't put him deep, but I was a good three hours at it. When I came back from the woods, Christopher was kneeling by the fire. He had four hares, each on a separate green stick, and a pot of warmed wine. It was a hot day.

'The boy's dead?' he asked.

'I buried him,' I said. With those words, I realized that Richard, Sam, and John were doomed as well.

'Let's eat,' he said. 'Roads are full of French. No cavalry. I almost got caught – had to lie up.' He shook his head. 'This is all fucked up, you know that, right?' His voice cracked a little.

'We'll make it,' I said.

He looked at me. He was older than me, and for all his carping, he was a steady man. But just then, he needed me to tell him that everything was going to be all right.

'We have food. There's two of us, so we can keep watch. We can't be more than a day from the English garrison at Poissy. Tomorrow I'll send you—'

He just shook his head. 'I'm not going back out there alone,' he said. 'The roads are covered in men and women. Peasants. Everywhere. I lay up in a little wood a mile north of here, listened to a man give a speech.' He looked at me. 'It's a rebellion. They're going to kill all the English and all the gentry.' He shrugged. 'I think they got Peter. I think they strung him up and opened his guts by the road. But I didn't stop to be sure.'

'We'll need to take turns on watch,' I said.

'Why?' He asked. 'I mean, you and me, we can take what, five of the bastards? Better to die.' He shook his head. 'Like the end of the world. Maybe it is. Mayhap—'

I reached over and flicked the end of his nose.

'Eh!' he bridled. 'No call for that!'

'We're not dead yet. Nor are our companions. Let's do our best.' Christ, I sounded pompous, even to me.

That was a long night. Christopher made his apologies and withdrew to his little fortress on the hill.

I sat by the fire with de Charny's dagger and some tow, some lard and some powdered pumice. I meant to get the stain out of the blade. I knew I'd be up all night, and my head was doing some strange things.

Richard fouled himself and had to be cleaned. I suppose I could have left him. In fact, I thought about leaving him in his own dung. By the Virgin, I even thought of getting Goldie and riding away.

Instead, I cleaned him and dripped some warm rabbit broth into him.

John awoke and demanded food. He looked like a monster in the glow of the fire, his eyes wild, his long hair everywhere. I gave him a joint of hare and some broth – he vomited bile and sat suddenly, then rolled over and threw up everything he'd just eaten, before falling forward into it.

I cleaned him.

Sam sat up and looked at me. In a perfectly normal voice, he said, 'I have the Plague, don't I?'

I got up and went to him. Christopher had set the tents up like awnings, with one side lifted on poles, so the air could pass through easily and I could go from man to man. I could see them all from the fire. I went and knelt by him. 'I think so,' I admitted.

He shook his head. 'I's salted. Had it as a young'n. Ain't right.'

That put the chill of pure fear into me.

'You had a bad fall—' I said.

But he was gone again, his eyes closed, his breathing coarse, like a man snoring.

John staggered to his feet – I assume with some notion of going somewhere to be sick – and vomited all over himself, then fell headlong across the fire. The burning coals galvanized him, and he leaped to his feet again before collapsing.

I poured water over him, but not until I'd found embers in the pitch darkness and put them together carefully, found bark and made up the fire again, adding twigs and small bits of oak.

Thank God it wasn't raining. Thank *God*.

I thought of Master Peter. Hiring me because I could start a fire.

'What happened?' asked Christopher out of the darkness.

'John fell in the fire,' I said.

Christopher came into the edge of the firelight. 'Need ... help?' he asked.

'John just threw up all over himself and then fell in the fire. Sam's raving. Richard may be dead. I haven't been to sleep—' My voice was wild.

I tried to get control of myself.

Christopher grunted. 'I'll clean John,' he said.

'He has the Plague,' I said.

Christopher came into the firelight and sat on his heels. 'Maybe not,' he said.

'What do you mean?' I asked.

He shrugged. 'Sam doesn't have a pustule on him, does he?'

I hadn't checked in hours, but I looked – high and low, so to speak – while Christopher held a lit taper.

'None,' I said. 'And he said he was salted.'

'There you go, then.' He looked at John. 'John's got something bad, but it's in his guts.'

'Rob died of Plague,' I said. 'I know what Plague looks like.'

He shrugged. 'I'll take my chance,' he said.

There are many forms of courage.

When the sun rose, Christopher was on a pallet of ferns. He was hot all over and had swellings in his armpits. He lay there, saying 'fuck' over and over, then he was silent.

The shattering work came to an end. I made them as clean as I could. I burned what they had been wearing.

About noon, a dozen armed peasants came. I heard them, but I didn't have the energy to get into my harness, so I walked to my bedroll – still roped tight – picked up my beautiful longsword and drew it.

They came down the forest trail. The leader had a good brigantine and a fine helmet. In fact, he had Peter's helmet.

The men behind him had a wide variety of arms and equipment, but the last fellow wore the red and blue hood of the Paris Commune.

'Stop where you are,' I said. In French, of course.

The leader paused.

'We have Plague,' I said.

They all froze.

'Fucking Englishman is just saying that,' spat the third man in the line.

'Want to come look?' I said. I think my voice and my fatigue must have carried conviction.

'May you all die of it,' said the leader.

Then they walked away – quickly.

I drank the rest of the broth and ate the cold rabbit. Then I went to my bedroll and took out the cheese and sausage I had there and ate it all. I didn't feel sick, which was a miracle.

Then I drank the wine I had. It wasn't enough.

I cleaned them all and tried to give them a little white wine that Richard had.

Then I sat by the fire, polishing Sir Geoffrey's dagger. When I couldn't face that any more, I said my beads. The beads made a tiny, regular noise as I told them, almost like a weaver's shuttle moving against the loom.

I prayed a long time. I lost myself in it.

I came out because Sam was asking for water. I had filled all the leather bottles, so I took him one and he drank deep. 'Fever broke,' he whispered. 'Sweet saviour, I'm weak.' His eyes met mine. 'I want to make my confession,' he whispered.

'I'm no priest,' I said.

A tiny smile flickered around his eyes. 'Just go and fetch one for me, sir?' he said.

I heard his confession. Like most of us, he'd gone through the commandments pretty thoroughly.

That's between him and God.

The thing that did me a world of good is that as he spoke, his voice got stronger. I left him for a few minutes to hold Richard's hand, and when I came back, he was up on one elbow.

'Master William, I think I may stay in the vale of sin,' he announced.

I wanted to kiss him.

In the morning, he was able to move around. He helped clean John and Christopher.

About noon, Christopher died.

I just sat by the fire for a while. 'Is it the Plague? What the hell is this?' I asked.

Sam just shook his head. 'Soldiers get sick,' he said. 'I didn't have the Plague, but Chris did. Look at him.'

He stank.

I carried him, wrapped in his cloak, and buried him by Rob. Something had tried to dig Rob up, but failed.

I spent time putting Chris just as deep.

You know how long it takes to dig a hole for a man?

I stopped twice to go back and check on the others. Sam was better each time, and by the third evening he was boiling water, setting out tapers and cleaning the camp.

On the third morning, Richard was better. John ate and didn't throw it up.

We were two more days there.

I hadn't lost a man in months of campaigning, and in four days I lost Peter, Rob and Chris.

We were thin when we rode on. Goldie had lost weight, but we now had enough horses – sad, but brutally necessary.

We rode along the Seine, riding as hard as my recuperating men could handle, and came to Poissy by evening. They made a long chalk of letting us in the gates, but in the end we satisfied them that we weren't carrying Plague and that we were English. I put Richard and John into the charge of the nuns, and rode off with a potboy from the hospital as my page, and Sam, armed to the teeth, to find

Charles of Navarre. The garrison was petrified by the peasants' attacks – easy pillage had turned into hard duty. They weren't even looking over the walls.

We crossed the river and rode north and east. Charles wasn't hard to find – he was stringing up every peasant he found on the roads – and the trees laden with rotten fruit, sometimes fifty or a hundred in a row, are another of the beautiful memories I carry of that summer.

The second day, we found his army. Almost the first banner I saw was du Guesclin's; near it was Sir John Hawkwood's, and some other unlikely comrades – a Bourbon, a minor Ribercourt, a Scottish mercenary called Sir Robert Scot and Sir James Pipe. I didn't know most of the knights, but their arms were all French, although I saw the black and white eagles of the Bourc Camus and gave his tents a wide birth.

Navarre's army was just settling for the day. They were very well-organized – as they should have been, with a thousand professional soldiers from both sides as the core of the force. Navarre had almost the whole chivalry of the north under his banner. The Jacquerie had terrified the first estate, and the men of war were not amused.

Sir John Hawkwood received me like a prodigal son – the more so when I told him of my errand for Sir John Cheverston.

He smiled his thin-lipped smile and raised a silver cup, almost certainly the spoil of a church. 'Here's to a fine feat of arms, young William. I knew you had the makings of a knight.'

I shrugged and possibly even blushed. This praise was delivered in public, in front of forty men.

'It was nothing – we took them by surprise.' I shrugged.

Du Guesclin pushed through the crowd to me. 'Were they armed? Awake?' he asked.

I grinned. 'Very much so, Sir Knight.'

He laughed. 'Then the contest was fair. And before the eyes of half a thousand English knights, a fair deed of arms.'

He warmed my blood. I dismounted, gave my horse to my pot-boy and embraced du Guesclin. 'What brings you here, messire? I have seen the trail of slime – or rather, the human fruit in the trees.'

Du Guesclin shrugged. 'The *canaille* make war on us all – rape maidens, kill nobly born children. They are the common enemy, and my lord the Dauphin,' he shrugged, 'is not in the field.'

'The Dauphin has found it more politic to leave us to fight the

Jacques while he cowers in his mighty fortress.' Hawkwood's contempt was absolute.

'I saw them on the way here. They wiped out an English garrison on the south of the river – burned two men alive on crosses.' I shrugged. 'I've seen our men do as much to them.'

Hawkwood nodded. 'As have I. But if we let them feel their power – they'll overturn the world order.'

Du Guesclin spat. 'You have brought this on us, messire. So many good knights are dead—'

Hawkwood laughed. 'Ah, messire, you are better born than I – a mere English yeoman. You should know better than that. The Jacques are out for your blood because you have failed to defend them. I heard a tale a month back – pardon me, it does no credit to a French knight. A deputation of wealthy peasants came to a lord not far from here. My men had just burned their barns. They went to their lord and asked him if he would go and fight – with my men.' Hawkwood smiled a grim smile. 'He explained that he stood no chance at all of defeating a hundred Englishmen with just he and his son.'

Du Guesclin, his friend de Carriere and a dozen other French knights all nodded along.

'And the leader of the peasants said, "We don't care whether you win or lose, my lord. As we owe you our tillage whether it rains or the sun shines, so you owe us your very best effort in our defence, whether you win or lose. For this is the obligation of l'homme armé to the men who till the soil.' Hawkwood looked around.

The French knights were silent.

'And the lord said, "But we will fail. And die."' Hawkwood laughed. 'And the leader of the peasants said, "Then go die, my lord. That is all we ask."'

Du Guesclin was angry. His shoulders were tense under his blue jupon and I could see the muscles in his neck. 'This does not justify the wholesale murder of my class,' he said.

Hawkwood shrugged. 'To the Jacques, it does. You have failed them.'

Du Guesclin turned on his heel. 'We do not need to stay and listen to this.' He walked away, taking a mass of Frenchmen with him. A few paces away, he whirled. 'If you love them so much, why not fight for them? Eh? Why fight with us?'

'You're paying,' Hawkwood laughed. 'You're paying me and a

thousand other Englishmen to kill the peasants who pay the taxes that maintain you.'

Du Guesclin didn't turn around. He walked away and his men followed him.

I winced.

'That was impolitic,' I hesitated. 'I like him.'

Hawkwood grimaced as if he'd been hit. 'Do you ever look at the blood, the dead peasants, the wrecked villages, the burned barns, and wonder what it's all for?' he asked.

I looked at the ground. 'All the time,' I admitted.

Hawkwood nodded. His jaw jutted slowly, as it did when he was moved by great emotion. 'It's our living, and never forget that. They are amateurs. They are not like us.' He shook his head. 'But sometimes ... I think it is all worthwhile if we destroy them. As individuals, many are fine men, but as a whole ...' He shook his head.

'But you are fighting for them,' I said.

He looked at me as if I was mad. 'They're paying, lad. Take care of yourself first.' He waved and shrugged. His shrug dismissed the suffering of France.

I had letters to the King of Navarre, so I went to his great pavilion and spent an hour cooling my heels on a bench with a dozen Gascons, all waiting for an audience. The King of Navarre's star was climbing – his Spanish officers were haughty as cardinals, and a mere 'English adventurer', as I heard myself called, was unlikely to impress anyone, most especially as I declined to offer a bribe to the boy who tracked 'appointments'.

After an hour, I saw a man in black and white parti-colour approaching. I wanted to vanish, but I wasn't about to give up my place on the bench. It was the Bourc Camus, trailing men-at-arms, and he came to the bench. Two of his men seized it and dumped us all on the ground.

While he was laughing, I put my fist in his face.

Gascons fear nothing, it is true, and I wasn't going to cow a dozen Gascons with a dagger, but neither was I capable of backing down. So I drew de Charny's dagger and snapped the flat pommel into one miscreant's jaw.

The rest of them took me seriously, so they formed a rough circle.

'Eh, messire,' said one gap-toothed rogue. 'You will pay now.'

'The King of Navarre sends to ask why this unseemly disturbance?' said a man with an arrogant lisp to his French. He was as tall as I am, with broad shoulders and the belly most men get in middle age, but he was so big he commanded immediate respect. He looked at me.

Camus bounced to his feet. 'This English bastard tried to steal my place,' he said with a winning smile.

My heart was beating sixteen to the dozen, but I forced a smile, too. 'Pardon me, messire, but I believe you, not I, are the bastard,' I said.

Camus went white.

You know that *bourc* means bastard, eh? I'm sure a herald knows such things.

Camus' hand went to his dagger.

I turned to the big man as if the Bourc didn't exist. 'Is it nothing to the King that I am here from the King of England's Lieutenant in Gascony? I am not on some idle errand, messire.' I looked at Camus, implying he *was* on an idle errand.

'By Christ's passion, you are a dead man,' Camus said, and he came at me, dagger high.

I stopped his blow with my left wrist, the way every English boy learns, and the Navarrese men-at-arms parted us.

Suddenly Charles of Navarre was there.

He was of middling height, very handsome, with curling dark hair, a fine beard, sparkling dark eyes and a warmth that I usually associate with the most beautiful and clever women. He almost always wore a smile, and he had a way of fixing his gaze on you that made you feel you were the most important person in the world. Sadly, he also had a way of giving in to fits of childish temper that dispelled the illusion that he was a great man and left the observer with the feeling that the King of Navarre was less than he might be.

He had immense presence, though, and all the men immediately fell silent.

'Gentlemen,' he said softly, and turned his smile on each of us in turn, like a ray of sun on a cloudy day. 'Friends, we are embarked on a high and dangerous *empris*, and many beautiful ladies, and many innocents, depend utterly on our good faith, our brave hearts and our strong arms. Is it right that any of you indulge in a private quarrel when so many depend on us against a rising tide of chaos?'

I bowed.

Camus whispered, 'He cannot save you, little boy.'

I ignored Camus. 'Your Grace, I have letters from the Lieutenant of Gascony. To whom shall I pass them?'

Navarre looked at me with very little interest. He gave a slight shrug – he was assessing the impact of his pretty speech on the crowd. The big Spaniard gave a small nod, and I stepped over to him, bowed and handed him the two scrolls of parchment that were addressed to the King of Navarre, whose domains, may I add, touched on Gascony in several places.

'Martin Enriquez de Laccarra,' he said, offering his hand to clasp. 'I am the King's gonfalonier. You are the English squire – Gold. There's a Gold and a Black, yes?'

I had heard of him, of course, the captain of the Navarrese in Normandy. The Prince spoke highly of him as a knight. I was flattered that he shook my hand. 'Black is my friend Richard,' I said. 'He is recovering from a sickness at Poissy.'

'You two make good fame together – very proper,' Enriquez said. 'In brief, what does Sir John Cheverston want?'

'He asks safe conducts for all his men, so he can exterminate the brigands in the high valleys, north and south. Even going over borders, if required.' I explained about his army and the quest set him by our Prince.

King Charles passed me, going back to his pavilion. He paused in the curtained doorway, where, I think, he thought none could see him. He held up his right cuff, where I saw that he had a small mirror set in the cloth, and he used it to look at himself.

My friends, I've never seen a *woman*, even in the East, with a mirror attached to her clothes. Good God.

Enriquez saw what I saw, and effected not to notice.

'You have a quarrel with the Bourc Camus,' he asked quietly.

'I do,' I admitted. 'None of my making.'

He shrugged. 'My Prince has forbidden all forms of joust or duel until the peasants are crushed,' he said. He smiled pleasantly enough, but something of his manner reminded me of Hawkwood, or Chandos. 'I mean to see his will enforced.'

I bowed. 'I will obey,' I said.

'Excellent,' he said. 'I predict the King will sign your safe conducts as soon as I can catch his attention.'

Sam, John and I slept in Hawkwood's camp in borrowed blankets.

The next day, servants brought us a breakfast of wine and stale bread with good soft cheese, then a French priest said Mass. Two Gascons tripped me and a third tried to kick me in the groin while I was down, but Sam broke one of the bastard's fingers, quick as that.

Afterwards, Sir John surrounded me with his own men. His chief officer was John Thornbury, a solid man from the Midlands, a few years my senior and a head shorter, but already a famous fighter.

'Camus hates you,' he said, and I admitted this was true.

He laughed. 'We'll see you right, Will Gold.' He spat. 'Fucking Gascons, eh?'

I found myself quite popular with the English. I wasn't used to popularity, but my recent feat of arms and my 'official' status acting for Sir John Cheverston gave me a name in an army full of famous men.

I liked it.

Reputation is everything – any boy knows as much. To enter a strange camp and discover that a thousand men know your name is a heady drink for a boy of seventeen.

At any rate, we were on the road after sunrise, and a little after midday we reached Mello, a small town twenty miles north of Paris, where, army rumour said, the leader of the rebels lived.

We made camp, observed at a distance by half a hundred cavalrymen. Sir John took us out from the camp, riding hard, to drive the enemy off, and we chased them north and east almost two miles, and saw their camp – a well-dug-in position on a round-crested ridge with steep sides. We sat our horses at the base of the slope, letting the animals breathe, while we looked up at the palisade at the top.

'That's steep,' I said.

Sir John stroked his beard.

John Thornbury whistled. 'They look pretty good,' he said.

I started and pointed. Just above us, in a watch-port, were a dozen well-armed men in red and blue hoods.

Sir John looked at them under his hand. 'Paris militia,' he said.

'But … the King of Navarre is the master of the Paris militia!' I said.

Sir John shrugged and smiled his small smile. 'Today, he has chosen to be the brother-in-law of the King of France,' he said. 'Another day, he may choose to pose as the defender of Paris.'

We rode well to the north, in a great circle, looking for a hill that would overlook the peasant army, but we didn't find one.

That night, men in our camp said their confessions and saw to their armour. The veterans went to sleep, and the new men – among whom I include most of the French knights – stayed awake all night bragging about their prowess.

Morning dawned and we all armed ourselves. An army of men-at-arms putting on their harness is like a nest of ants when a horse kicks it up: all at sixes and sevens, and I thought all morning that if the peasants had the sense to attack us at dawn, they might have won a great victory.

As it was ...

When we were fully armed, we learned that the King of Navarre had arranged a parley with the leader of the peasants, a local man named Guillaulme Cale. Martin Enriquez drew us up in three battles, with one mounted battle and two dismounted; I went with Sir John Hawkwood in the mounted battle. Bertrand du Guesclin was six horses to my left.

We stood by our chargers on a beautiful June morning and watched Guillaulme Cale ride down the steep hill from his nearly impregnable position. He rode across the fields between his camp and ours, with just two men, both of whom looked like knights, to my great surprise.

I expected the King of Navarre to ride out to meet him, like the Prince at Poitiers with King John, but there were no cardinals here, and no rules. About fifty paces from our front lines, Enriquez and a dozen Navarrese men-at-arms closed around Cale and threw him from his horse. They bound him.

He was about twenty paces from me, and I heard him call out, 'Is this your *courtoise*, monsieur the King?'

Charles was on foot, with a poleaxe. He was deep in conversation with one of the French knights, and he didn't turn his head. Cale was dragged past him, kicking and demanding justice, and taken to the rear in our camp.

'You gave me a safe conduct, you liar! Caitiff! God will punish you!' cried the peasant leader.

He was beaten into silence.

All this was done in full view of the peasants on the hill. Many had come down the hill to see the parley, and more had come pouring out of their fortified camp at word that their leader was taken.

Enriquez trotted his charger across our front. He waved to Sir Robert Scot, who commanded the mounted men.

Scot closed his visor.

We all followed suit.

Next to me, Sir John said, 'Through them – and straight up the hill before they can form. Or we'll have a hard fight.' He pointed at the crowd at the base of the hill.

We started forward to the sound of a trumpet. We went forward at a walk, harness jingling. The very harmony of Mars – the sound of horses and armour.

I had a borrowed lance, and I blessed du Guesclin for his patient hours of training me. I'd have been terrified of using a lance in a crowd this dense, but now I felt confident. Indeed, riding in a cavalry charge is the closest a mere man can feel to God's angels. The power is immense. The *feeling* of power is . . . like what priests prate of.

And riding through badly armed, poorly disciplined peasants is a special, evil pleasure. They stood in arms against us. They were our enemies, I had no doubt of that. I owed them for Peter.

But they were poor devils, for all that. The better armed men stayed together in clumps, and we ignored them and smashed through the men who turned to flee. It's always that way when cavalry rides down infantry.

I've heard men brag about how many Jacques they killed that day. I'll save my bragging for more worthy foes. I killed my share.

We rode over them, and up their long hill – diagonally to save our horses. Two hundred good spearmen could have held us all day on that slope, but after smashing the front line – if you can call it a line – we rode unopposed up the ridge and fell upon their camp, and the whole peasant army broke and ran for their lives.

And died.

Down on the plain, the better armed men reformed in our wake and met the whole of the King's battle, all the dismounted knights, English and French, who went through them like the scythe cuts the wheat.

The lucky ones died there.

The unlucky ones were taken.

Their camp was full of women, and they died hard. None of them surrendered, that I remember. They knew what was in store for them.

Every child in that camp was spitted on a sword.

I have seen every horror war can offer, but here was something I didn't expect: the worst atrocities weren't done by us. The English did their part in the battle, and most of them rode or walked back to camp.

It was the local French knights who killed the children.

The worst was Camus. He tried to coral a group of women and coax them to surrender, and when they fought, he promised them horrible deaths and made sure his promises were carried out. I was dismounted – Goldie had taken a spear point in his breast and I was seeing to my horse – when he ordered his men to kill them all.

I didn't want to hear any more, so I got my armoured leg over my saddle.

'Leave one!' he shouted. 'Flay her face and leave her alive to tell others not to defy me!'

Sam Bibbo grabbed my reins from me and rode down the hill – I couldn't stop him.

At the base of the hill, Sam put a hand on my shoulder. 'You're a nice lad,' he said. 'Soft, in some ways. That's what happens – yon. Worse when a town is stormed.'

I gritted my teeth. 'Camus is a worm. A serpent. A demon from hell.' I thought of the man with half his face flayed away, and I knew who had massacred that town.

Sam shrugged. 'That's as maybe. You may do as thee list – after I take you to camp. You cannot rescue them.' He waved at a dozen wounded men – our whole tale of casualties. 'Poor John took an arrow in the leg – bad luck. I'll see him well bedded.'

I followed him.

I felt like scum.

It wasn't that I could have done anything.

It was only that, like the French lord in Hawkwood's story, I could have died.

The pursuit of the Jacques went on for a day and a night, and whole villages were wiped out – every human creature killed – for ten miles around our camp. The celebrations started immediately, with terrified, peasant-born servants offering us wine and bread made by men and women whose blood was now fertilizing the earth.

I didn't sleep well. John Hawkwood did, though. I know, as he shared his tent with me.

Thanks to his good offices, my safe conducts were signed by King Charles. Since we were less than a day's ride from the Dauphin's castle at Meaux, I collected my goods, thanked Sir John and made to leave.

Sir John rode with me until we were a mile or so from camp. He pointed to a group of riders shadowing us.

'Bertucat means to kill you,' he said.

'I'd be pleased to meet him any time,' I said. 'When it is one to one, and not twenty of his against three of mine.'

Hawkwood nodded. 'Twenty to three is more the Bourc's speed. Can you take him?'

I nodded.

Hawkwood nodded back. 'I think so, too. If I can arrange it, I'll send word. It would do great things for your renown. And I'd like to see him wiped away, like a stain on the earth.'

'I should be back in a day or two,' I said.

Hawkwood embraced me and we were away.

Meaux is a mighty town, with the fortress of Marche on the opposite bank, and walls as high as ten men. It rises straight out of an island in the river, and has two bridges with wicket gates on each.

I thought – indeed, we all thought – that the rebellion was broken. So Sam and I rode along roads peopled only by the dead – mostly men cut down from behind as they fled, by the flower of French chivalry.

We passed south of Clermont, and the bodies dwindled away to none, then we came across a party of tired knights. They were all local men, knights of the Beauvais, and they saluted us as we passed.

'We had a sharp fight this morning, messires,' one called out. 'The curs are not yet beaten.'

I wanted no part of them, so I rode on.

But as we saw Meaux rising out of the valley in the distance – you can see it from eight miles away – we began to see the size of the army laying siege to it.

An army the size of the one we'd just faced, or larger.

I had the wildest notion – what if every peasant in the world had risen against their lords? What if this was the end of the world? I've heard that in monasteries during the Plague, men died believing the whole of the human race had been destroyed, and looking at the host gathered against the walls of Meaux, I wondered the same.

We turned our weary horses north. I changed from my riding horse to Goldie and loosened my sword in its scabbard.

'We should go back,' Sam said.

That meant riding half the night, in the dark, on narrow, unmarked French lanes.

'No,' I said. We rode on down to the river Marne.

'We'll be killed,' Sam said. 'I'll offer odds on it.'

'I'll take that wager,' I said.

The ferry was open.

I'll not belabour the point, but imagine what the ferryman was like. He cared nothing for death or rebellion. He'd never heard of Guillaulme Cale. He demanded an exorbitant fee, then he took us over the river to the north bank. The peasant army was on the south.

I felt vindicated and Sam laughed. 'I'll be happy to pay,' he said.

At nightfall, we approached the royal castle of Marche from the north. We were challenged by a party of horsemen in sight of the gate, and when I said I was a messenger for the Lieutenant of Gascony, one of the men-at-arms approached.

'What's your name, sir?' he asked. I knew him immediately.

He was Jean de Grailly, the Captal de Buch. I'd seen him lead the charge at Poitiers.

I raised my visor. 'William Gold,' I said. 'I was at Poitiers, my lord.'

I was embraced and taken home to the castle, to dinner.

The Dauphin wasn't at Marche. He was away in Burgundy, raising an army to fight Charles of Navarre. As it proved, he needn't have bothered, but when he went, he had no way of knowing.

In the meantime, Etienne Marcel had sent an army of Parisian militia to snatch the Dauphin at his headquarters, at Meaux. And the Mayor of the town opened the gates to the Parisians.

The Parisians joined hands with the Jacques.

Wait, lads. I know you want to hear about the battles, but there's a delicious irony to all this. Charles of Navarre was making himself a hero to the nobility of France in crushing the Jacques. The Dauphin was ruining his standing as the 'first noble' by ignoring the rising.

But – at least wherever I was – the Jacques were allied with Marcel's communal troops, and they were acting for the King of Navarre. God knows, the attempt to seize the Dauphin at Meaux was all for King Charles.

I've known a lot of treason and seen many men change sides – benidictee, in Italy it was our daily bread – but Charles of Navarre was the only King I ever saw abandon a winning cause, and betray it to the enemy, when he had been leading it. I won't say the Jacques thought they were fighting for King Charles.

They were just poor fools led by the nose.

Which didn't make them any the less dangerous. They had thousands of men packed around Meaux, and inside the town – a rich town. They held the walls and the citadel, and they were building engines to batter at Marche. They were desperate – all the survivors of Mello fled to them, so they knew what was coming. They were determined to take Marche and use the Dauphin – or at least his wife and children – as hostages.

I had ridden into this trap like a fool – I had lorded it over Sam when we crossed at the ferry.

When he saw what we had at Marche – a party of military pilgrims returning from fighting in Prussia, led by the Captal and the famous Count of Foix, and the lord of the castle, the Sieur de Hangst and his conroy – we had perhaps sixty knights. Sam Bibbo was a fifth of all the English archers – the rest were in the Captal's tail – and we had another twenty crossbowmen, and when he saw what we'd joined, he looked at me and laughed.

'I may not pay you yet,' he said.

Perhaps a hundred armed men, plus twenty male servants. The Princess had thirty women – all the daughters and wives of great nobles of France – and another fifty female servants, as well as a small horde of noble children. As I say, when Sam saw what we'd ridden into, he laughed in my face.

'All safe now, eh, sir?' he asked.

'Who nursed you when you were sick?' I asked. 'Who rescued you when you fell from your horse and hit your head?'

'And why was I there in the first place, I wonder?' he asked.

'We're not dead yet,' I said.

'Not for lack of trying,' he insisted.

The trouble was, we weren't provisioned to stand a siege. The other problem was, we had too many hot-headed young knights and too many noble girls.

Women complicate everything.

I hadn't been in that castle an hour when a pair of young women, wearing, may I add, clothes more daring than anything my girls in Bordeaux ever wore, confronted me on the stairs.

'What is *your* name and style, messire?' asked the taller of the two. She wore a flowered silk gown that clung to her hips and bound under her breasts. Her hair was down – a style I'd hardly ever seen, because women in military camps keep their hair under caps for all sorts of reasons.

I noted that her surcoat – also silk – had buttons on the side, under her arms, and that the gown was so tight the cloth puckered at the buttons and left gaps between.

Where you could see flesh.

Gentles, I don't think I'd seen a woman who was alive and hearty in a month. That noble sprig was perhaps seventeen – my own age – and her womanliness burned like fire from between those close-bound buttons, so that I almost felt I could *smell* her, like a stallion smells a mare.

I was abashed. I don't think I'd ever had cause to speak to a noble girl. On the other hand, I had learned the knack that women were, for the most part, women, and much the same as men. So, with about the same effort it took me to force a smile at the Bourc, I pushed one across my teeth at this apparition of Venus. 'William Gold,' I said.

'Hmm,' she said. 'Never heard of you. Nonetheless, should you not be in your armour, messire? Perhaps doing some deed of arms, and not here in the castle, safe with the women? Eh?'

Had I been thirty years of age and a little more experienced, I'd have made an elegant answer – mentioned my prowess in riding to their rescue across half of France, for example.

Instead, I blushed, and stammered something about fatigue.

'Fie! Sir Knight, we are a castle of maidens against an army of dogs. Get to the walls! And let us hear no more of your being tired.' She and her companion, a pert, blonde thing a foot shorter in royal-blue wool with silken flowers in her hair and sleeves so long they trailed on the steps, pushed past me and vanished down the stairs.

'You get to that,' Sam said. 'I'll have a nap.'

In fact, the castle was full to bursting with beautiful women. The nuns were beautiful, the Dauphine herself was beautiful, and she surrounded herself with the prettiest – and richest – women in France.

I had no armour against them, and nor did any other man. Even grown knights who should have known better, like Jean de Grailly and the Count of Foix – a subtle bastard if every there was one – were unable to stop them from directing our defence. Young knights armed themselves, mounted their chargers and rode out across the fortified bridges, looking for a deed of arms.

Several were killed, dragged down and hacked to death, and the only thing that saved the rest of us was that we wanted our deeds of arms to be visible to the audience on the tall towers, and most of the peasants and Parisian militia were too quick-witted to linger under our walls.

It was a great time of vows, in my youth, and men would make vows without a thought. Amazing vows. I made a few myself, and suffered with some eye patches and the like. It was the vows that killed us in the castle of Marche – the vows and the lack of supplies. It was a great fortress, but the peasants had caught it unprepared. So while the young men swore not to bathe until they'd killed ten peasants, and other such pretty things, we had two days' fodder for the horses and four days' food at half rations. And 100 men against 10,000.

And a small army of nubile beauties determined to see us act out the *chansons de geste* under the walls.

War is never what you expect it to be. Sometimes, it is like theatre – like a passion play. Sometimes it is like the Black Plague – all death and horror.

Sometimes it has an element of humour.

I rose late the second morning. I think, now, that I had a touch of fever, and I was only just recovering. I'd been riding and fighting, and I'd missed a great deal of sleep. So my first morning at Marche, Sam let me stay abed – in a real bed, raised off the floor, in a small solar. I remember it had crude armorial frescoes on the walls and I thought it was a palace.

I awoke when Perkin, my English potboy from Poissy, brought me hippocras. He'd arranged for my two shirts to be washed, and all my caps, and they were dry and crisply ironed.

I felt like hugging him. That made me think of Rob, dead and buried in the damp soil of the Seine Valley.

Younger than me.

'A party of gentlemen has just gone out to fight,' he said. 'Some of the older knights tried to stop them.' He shrugged.

He brought me a basin of clean, hot water, and he'd borrowed me a razor. Considering I'd barely talked to him, he was bidding fair to be the best servant I'd ever had. Rob struggled to curry my horse, bless the boy, whereas Perkin seemed at home with the whole routine.

'Whose razor?" I asked.

'Milord de Grailly,' he said proudly. 'Eh, sir, mind the steel – it'll rust if you look at it.' This from a wizened lump of twelve years, half my size.

'You sound like a Londoner, imp.' I grinned.

'So do you, sir.' He produced a clean, dry linen towel. 'Sit on the stool, sir, and I'll make you trim for the ladies. Of whom there are a great many, and like the flowers of the fucking field. Begging your pardon.'

I laughed.

'Don't laugh, sir, or I'll nick you – just when I have your shirt clean.' He tried the razor on me and clucked like a hen. 'Sit tight.'

Suddenly he vanished. There was some talk, and he came in followed by a man of twenty in a fine pair of boots and a stained leather jupon. Perkin had a strop in his hand.

'I'm not letting it out of my sight,' said the young man, then he stopped. 'Pardon, my lord.'

'Think nothing of it. Come in and share my hippocras.' I motioned to the other stool. My solar was the size of a lady's closet, you have to imagine.

He was my own age – smaller, but his hands looked as hard as mine. 'Squire?' I asked.

He grinned. 'To Milord de Grailly,' he said. 'One of six,' he added. 'My da is one of his great friends.' He grinned. 'Tom Folville.'

I considered that this was exactly the kind of sprig of nobility who had tormented me during my first campaign. On the other hand ...

Perkin touched up the razor and handed the squire the strop. 'Nice kit,' he said.

'You know how to use that thing,' the squire said. 'By the saints, Perkin, will you teach me?'

'Mayhap after the peasants kill us all,' Perkin nodded, 'I'll have time.' He grinned.

If you haven't guessed that Perkin was as great a find as Sam, well, think again. He had that gift of making people like him. Lords and commons, men and women. He wasn't big or handsome. He was brave enough in a pinch, but he was not a doughty man.

Well, you'll hear more of him.

He shaved me, all the while telling me the state of the food in the castle and how little fodder was left for the horses. He didn't tell it like gossip – he noted where he'd heard each titbit and what validity he attributed to the teller.

I hadn't been shaved neatly in so long I'd become used to looking like some wild hermit in the tales of Arthur. It felt odd to have most of my beard gone. He put beeswax into my moustache.

'Ladies about,' he said with a twinkle.

'How'd you come to be a potboy in Poissy?' I asked.

He shrugged. 'My knight died,' he said. 'You came along, eh? And you needed me.' He smiled.

That was that.

'You are from London, though,' I said.

'Temple Bar,' he said proudly. 'Apprentice tailor.' He shrugged.

'I was to be a goldsmith,' I said suddenly.

He grinned. 'Good,' he said. 'I aim to be a famous knight, meself.'

Well, well.

Groomed and clean, wearing clean clothes and with all the lice out of my arming coat, I went down into the hall. There were no women to be seen. I ate some bread and cheese, and walked across the hall to where the curtain wall steps rose into the smoky heights of the rafters. Since no one challenged me, I climbed the steps and walked out onto the wall.

There I found twenty young women on the wall, watching a fight on the bridge.

Most of them had their hands to their mouths.

One had already fainted.

I leaned out over the wall and saw why.

A dozen young knights – on foot – were trying to hold the main bridge over the river. Two were down.

'Where are the other knights?' I snapped at the nearest girl. 'Where is the Captal?'

My pretty friend from the day before, still wearing her 'gates of hell', pointed down the north wall. 'They have gone across country!' she shouted.

Sometimes, folly is so rampant it's hard to credit. But the party from Prussia had elected to probe north and find food, and in the absence of any professional soldiers, a dozen young sprigs had vowed to hold the bridge all day.

I watched for ten breaths.

'Christ almighty,' I said aloud.

My pretty friend put her hand on my chest. A very, very affecting gesture.

'Will you – save them?' she asked me.

Her eyes were a beautiful hazel-brown. She had a snub nose, and a dress that showed little glimpses of her naked flanks. She was tall, and better born than me, and she was, in effect, asking me to go die for her.

'Yes,' I said into her eyes.

I armed as fast as I ever had in my life. I had Perkin to help, and Jean de Grailly's squire. Tom Folville got my arms on me, laced them to my hauberk and stood back.

'I could come with you,' he said.

I thought about it. To be honest, I thought that if he came with me, it might lessen the glory, but there were an awful lot of militia on the bridge, and only the eight knights.

'Will you run when I say run, and retreat when I say retreat?' I asked.

He nodded, his eyes huge.

I wondered suddenly if he had been hoping that I would say no.

'Ever fought before? For real?' I asked.

'Every day, in Prussia,' he said.

That was reassuring. I had my legs laced and Perkin was closing the straps. 'Get in your harness,' I said.

He vanished. Perkin finished the buckles on my legs and got my breast and back – opened them on the hinges and closed them again and began buckling me in. 'This doesn't really fit you,' he said.

'What?' I asked. I'd worn that harness for more than a year.

'It's too big. Too much play at the hips.' He slapped my back and the backplate moved. 'Made for a fatter man. Can't be helped. Hold out your hands.'

He put my gauntlets on, raised my helmet, slipped the aventail over my head and seated the cloth liner with two practiced jerks, one front, one back.

I took my longsword and walked, clanking softly, down the hall and down the steps to the main hall, then out into the bright June sun. There were four crossbowman on the bridge gate. I turned and looked up at the battlement, and there they were: twenty beautiful women.

Well.

Tom came at a run – high boots, a good brigantine, plate arms, and an open-faced basinet. Let me remind you that most men wore them open-faced back then.

'Stay with me and keep men off my back,' I said. 'You're too lightly armed to step into them. Understand me?'

He nodded soberly.

Perkin appeared with a pottery cup of . . . water. 'Drink,' he said.

Sam came across the courtyard in his shirtsleeves and hose. His hair was unbound, and he had his bow and a big quiver of arrows. He shook his head. 'Lost your wits, lad?' he asked.

I raised my visor. 'I won't be long,' I said.

'By St George,' he began, but a fluttering handkerchief caught his eye. 'Good Christ,' he said. 'Women.'

Perkin collected the cup, refilled it and handed it to Tom.

Sam tossed his hair. 'If I kill ten men, you think I'll get one of they?'

Perkin smiled.

I shook my head. 'No,' I said.

'Well,' he said, 'professionally speaking, yon's a fine audience. Just don't die.'

I nodded again.

The sergeants on the gate got it open. Suddenly, there was a great deal of screaming from the ladies on the wall.

I thought it was for me, so I pranced my way out onto the bridge like, well, like a young man performing for young women. This was just like a London square, except that I had a lot more armour.

The rights and wrongs of it meant nothing to me, in case you wonder.

But as soon as I was clear of the gate, I saw what they were screaming about. Two of the young knights were down.

I ran.

Running in plate legs is – not as hard as it sounds, but it requires some practice. Legs are soft. Steel is not soft. Everything has to fit, or the top of your greave pounds into the top of your instep, or the back of your greave slams into your ankle, or your knee gets clamped in the main plates of the articulation . . .

Really, there's a lot to go wrong.

I ran.

It was about fifty paces to where the two knights were down.

They were in full harness, but the nearer of the two had a Jacques on his chest and another towering over him with an axe.

I didn't save him.

Sam did. His first arrow spitted the lad on the knight's chest the way a butcher spikes a carcass.

The axe man swung, and buried his axe in the Jacques who'd just swallowed Sam's arrow. Bad luck.

The axe man could see me coming. He couldn't take his eyes off me. He got his axe up over his shoulder and stepped back for room to swing.

I cut off his hands. Maybe not 'off', but I didn't stop to check.

Then I knocked him flat as his limbs pumped blood onto the cobbles of the bridge.

The man behind him got my pommel in his face. I caught the tip of my sword in my left hand and started using the whole weapon like a two-handed dagger. I ignored blocks and attacks – that's what you do in armour, when your opponents have no armour. Anything an untrained man can throw one-handed can be ignored.

Maybe not always, but in a crisis.

Some of them had staves and many had spears. A few had axes or pole-hammers. Of all those, the spears are the most dangerous if well-used. Spear blows I had to turn. But some got through. Early on, one came in and hit my faceplate, raised it a fraction and went in under the plate, slicing along my cheek and punching in between my head and the helmet liner.

I killed the bastard.

I was sure I was dead. I had a spear sticking out of my helmet.

It fell out.

There was some blood, but I didn't seem to be dead.

I made it to the second downed man. Another of the young knights had straddled him and was holding his ground.

I stepped up next to him and roared, 'Form a line!'

I took a breath, knocked a spear aside with a flick of my blade, turned my whole body – one thing you can't do well in harness is turn your head – and shouted, 'Tom, kill everyone *behind* us!'

Then I faced front, made a sweeping two-handed parry and started clearing space. I made wide, sweeping two-handed cuts, and the unarmoured men stepped back.

One of the young French knights stepped up on my left.

Something hit my leg, caught in the butterfly on my right knee, and suddenly my leg was bleeding. I stepped back onto something squishy.

Tom had a man in red and blue up against the bridge railing, and another was crouched over the clothyard shaft in his guts, the red blood running between his fingers. He was praying to the Virgin.

A fourth knight joined our impromptu line, and we filled the bridge.

In front of me, a big sergeant in good mail raised a huge, spiked club – what the Flemings call a 'Guden Tag'. He called, 'They are only four! We can—'

One of Sam's arrows buzzed over my head like a huge wasp and struck him, and dust came off his mail and coat. He looked at the arrow and I thought, You never think it will be you.

'At them!' I called, and the four of us charged.

They gave way.

We killed a few. I was already tiring. Armour makes you almost invulnerable, and it's really very comfortable, but when you fight on foot in armour, you spend your strength like a drunkard in a brothel. And I had not yet learned to save my strength.

Nevertheless, we cleared the bridge all the way to the chapel at the far end – the Meaux bank.

A crossbow bolt hit my breastplate like a punch in the gut and I staggered.

The man next to me took one in his vambrace, and it deformed the metal and broke his arm.

'Back!' I shouted. Christ, why hadn't they just pelted us with crossbows from the first?

The whole thing was insane.

'We can't retreat,' said the man at my right. 'Ladies are watching.'

'We cleared the bridge, messieurs. They will have to deem that enough chivalry for one morning. I bid you retreat, messieurs.'

I suited action to word.

Another bolt struck, and this one whanged off my helmet.

The man on my right took a bolt in his thigh, right through his cuisse, which, on examination, proved to be boiled leather over iron splints.

He gave a squawk and fell, and the Jacques came for us in a wave.

Paternoster, qui est in caelis.

We were in a lot of trouble.

The knight with the broken arm had already walked back. He

was halfway across the bridge, and he was the smartest of the lot.

As the knight on my right went down, he stumbled into me, and by habit I let go my sword with my left hand – I had my right on the hilt and my left near the point – and caught him. I had him from behind and my luck was holding, so I began to back across the bridge, dragging the young scapegrace.

The Jacques wanted him, though, and they bayed like dogs as they ran after us and started stabbing with their spears. These weren't peasants with pitchforks, but prosperous men in hauberk who probably served in the *Arriere-ban*. But, to be honest, they were mostly stabbing at the man I was dragging, so I kept backing.

The man on my left turned and ran. I won't say he didn't choose wisely; I'll just say that he left me.

I backed another few paces, and Tom ripped into the men on my left like a harrow cutting spring earth,and bounced away like a boy playing ball. He was light on his feet. I had time to admire him.

I made another few steps. There were blows to my feet and blows to the back of my legs, chest and arms. A hail of blows.

Every step became harder. Oddly, it wasn't the weight of my armour, although that was something, nor the pain of my left leg harness, which was killing me – I didn't know till later that a chance blow had cut my thigh strap – it was the weight of the French knight, all on one arm. A body is an unwieldy thing at the best of times, and an armoured body is heavy, floppy and very smooth. And I couldn't quite get my arm all the way around him.

Tom bought me a moment's respite.

I decided that I had to change grips. I tried to hoist the wounded, or dead, man on my hip, and I lost him and he fell.

He screamed, because he fell on the crossbow bolt, which was firmly wedged in his leg.

On a positive note, he was alive.

There were a dozen adversaries *right there*. In a fight, one thing can lead to another as firmly and logically as one note leads you to sing the next at Mass. I parried a spear-thrust, a half-sword parry that turned my body to the side, left leg forward. A spear shaft slammed into my left side, knocking me off balance, but I stepped with it and snapped a cut up from below. Then I hit something and the spear-men fell away – I swept my sword up over my head and flicked it from side to side, the way a man with a scythe cuts grain.

I thrust one poor bastard though the body, and my sword stuck fast. I took a blow, staggered and got the tip free, rolled my wrist in a little windmill and drew blood.

Tom finished a man I'd wounded, then killed his partner.

I couldn't breathe. I'd reached a point of fatigue where I couldn't raise my arms.

I looked back.

Sam was on the bridge. He had four arrows in the fingers of his bow hand, and he ran at us.

The Jacques nearest me flinched away.

I got a deep lungful of air, bent over and passed my sword blade under the French knight's arms, so I had him from behind, pinned against me, with the blade in front like a deadly embrace. He slumped forward and the blade bent.

If it broke, we were done.

I began to shuffle back as fast as I could go.

Sam's first arrow picked up the man closest to me and spun him around like a heavy punch.

As I stumbled back, Sam leaped up on a bridge stanchion for a clear shot, balanced a moment and loosed into the next Jacques, who fell noisily. I gained another three paces.

Tom blocked a spear thrust.

Sam feathered a third man.

He had one more arrow, and he showed it to the Jacques. He flicked them two fingers and they cursed and growled, then he drew his great bow all the way to his ear and held it there, in their faces. Tom spiked the boldest fellow in the knee, and we gained five more shuffling paces.

The castle's crossbowmen loosed a volley, all together – six or seven bolts that felled the front rank of the men on the bridge in a spray of blood – and we were in the gate.

My French knight was alive.

I wasn't sure I was, and I sat in the dirt and bled for what seemed to me a long time.

Perkin appeared. He handed me a cup of water and I drained it, then another and another. He began to unbuckle things.

My hazel-eyed Venus appeared. I was sitting on a barrel in the yard with Perkin under my arm, unlacing my left arm harness while I drank water with my right hand. She curtseyed.

'You were brilliant,' she said. 'The Dauphine sends you this as a token of her esteem, messire.'

I couldn't take my eyes off her. I don't think I'd ever wanted a woman as much.

She had an embroidered riband in her hand, and she was, I think, a little put out that I wasn't leaping to my feet. She leaned down.

I smiled at her. 'My lady, I beg your pardon, but I'm not at my best,' I said.

'You could unlace his right shoulder,' Perkin said.

'Oh!' said my beautiful visitor. She took the cup from my right hand and drew off the gauntlet. She smiled at me and draped my right arm over her shoulder as Perkin had my left.

'There's blood—' I said.

'Christ on the cross,' Perkin muttered. 'Why didn't you say?'

But my chivalrous lady reached in and unlaced the right harness at the groin – her eyes flicked to mine – and then she unbuckled the straps inside the thigh – one, two – and brought her hand away covered in blood.

She smiled at me and licked at the blood on her fingers.

I swear to you.

'I love a brave man,' she said.

By our sweet and gentle saviour, I was ready to be transported to heaven in that instant – or to kill every Jacques in the town.

Or to have her on the straw.

She wiped her bloody hand on her fine gown and got to the buckles on the greaves. She and Perkin took the whole right leg off in one pull.

There was a *lot* of blood in my hose.

And then I was gone.

I awoke when the hot iron touched the back of my leg. I wanted to scream, but there was something nasty clenched between my teeth.

My first thought was, Sweet Christ, I've lost my leg. And it was my last.

I wasn't out long. A barber was rubbing ointment over the whole wound, and it hurt as if all the demons of hell had decided to torment my right knee.

Then he pasted honey over the ointment. He looked at me. 'It's really nothing,' he said. 'Happens to horses all the time – get a wound right on a blood vessel. Easy physic, if I get to it in time.' He held out his hand and Perkin handed him a length of fine white linen, which he began to wrap around the wound.

Perkin leaned me forward and looked into my eyes. 'You in your right mind?' he asked.

'No,' I said.

He smiled and handed me a cup of mint tisane with honey. 'Drink this. Here, chew on these,' he said. He handed me two wizened red things like dried flowers. They had a wonderful taste.

'Chew. Chew more. Now spit,' he said, holding out his hand.

I obeyed.

'Now drink the rest of the cup,' he said.

The surgeon tied off the cloth. 'Change it twice a day. Tell me if the flesh gets proud.' He smiled. 'Horses don't get gangrene,' he said, then he bowed and withdrew.

'What was that stuff?' I asked.

'Drink it *all*,' he said.

I complied.

He took the cup. 'Good night, m'lord.'

It always made me feel funny when men addressed me as 'my lord', as I was lord of nothing but a horse, a sword and some armour.

I lay back, wondering what the sharp-tasting drug had been.

There was a very quiet knock and my chivalrous friend opened the door. She smiled sweetly and slipped in, carrying a wax taper in a stick. 'The Dauphine says one of us must sit with you all night,' she said.

She had on a plain working woman's kirtle with an apron.

'I'm sorry that I bled on your lovely gown,' I said.

She smiled. 'I will wear it at court. My dear man, there is no better adornment. I will say, 'Oh, that's the blood of William Gold, who saved the Duke de Bourbon on the Bridge of Meaux. I was helping him with his armour.'

There was another knock, and she went to the door and took a covered cup.

'Here,' she said. 'It's honeyed milk with a little spice. My father used to take it when ... he was hurt.' She smiled.

I had seen rings on the fingers of the hand holding the cup.

'Am I being served by all the Dauphine's ladies?' I asked.

'Two at a time,' she said.

'Am I so dangerous?' I asked.

'I imagine that you are quite fearsome to your enemies, messire,' she said. For the first time since the courtyard, she let her eyes meet mine. 'But as I have a high heart of my own, I believe that I can meet you in an encounter – alone. I felt that two of us might put you … at a disadvantage.'

'Ah, mademoiselle, I'm afraid I am no match for you, and you alone have me at a grave disadvantage,' I said. I'd listened to a romance or two. The girls at the Three Foxes used to read them aloud, those as could read. And players would recite them. The Provençal ones and the Italians were the best.

She settled gracefully on the edge of my bed. 'Drink from our cup,' she said.

'Does the cup come with a kiss of friendship?' I asked.

She leaned over, almost bored, and kissed me lightly on the lips. I caught her – my hand against her back – and kissed her harder.

I'm not sure what I expected from a high-born girl. But I didn't expect her mouth to melt open under mine, and for her to lean into me and breathe into my mouth.

Later, she said, 'Did you expect me, then?'

I denied it, and she jumped off the bed and hit me lightly. 'Liar!' she said. 'I'm too predictable. A light of love.'

'My sweet and beautiful friend, I had no expectation but of an uncomfortable night with a nasty wound.' I smiled at her – winningly, I hope.

She frowned. 'And yet you chewed a clove. I can taste it in your mouth.'

'Medicine,' I said.

'Only for foul breath,' she said, but she laughed. 'Perhaps our horse doctor uses it.'

'Please come back,' I said, patting my narrow bedstead.

'No, messire. Too many such kisses and a girl may find herself with an unwanted swelling about the waist.' She smiled. 'Do you think my blood is any less hot than yours?'

I knew the answer to that.

'I do hope that you stay on watch all night,' I said, 'because I'm not sure my strength is up to two or three or four of you.'

'Fie!' she said, swatting me. 'That was ungentle.'

'Benidictee! You may tax me, and I may not tax you back.' I was getting the pace of her conversation.

She smiled. 'Precisely, messire. I am to be adored, not to be teased.'

'I could, perhaps, adore you more effectively if I knew your name.' I smiled.

She nodded. 'I am Emile de Clermont.'

I put my hand on hers without thinking about it. 'Your father was the Marshal of Normandy?'

She dropped her eyes. 'Yes.'

'I met him. At Paris. With the Dauphin.'

'You did?'

'Last autumn. I was acting as courier for the Prince of Wales. Your father came to the gate of the Louvre, fully armed. We—' I smiled. 'We almost fought. *Par dieu*, we were so cold and wet.' I smiled at her. 'Clermonts must be destined to rescue me.'

I was prattling on in this manner when I realized that she was crying. Like my touch to her hand, her tears were not in the game. She was truly crying.

'They killed him,' she said. 'By My lady the Virgin, the *canaille* killed him. And two days ago, I saw my mother's castle burn. Christ – I want to be braver than this.' She stood up. 'I'm sorry, Master Gold, you are a better man than I thought. Let go my hand.'

Instead, I pulled. I didn't pull hard.

In a fight, you can learn everything – everything – from an opponent at the moment when your swords meet. The contact of the two blades is so intimate that a more experienced swordsman can read intentions, skills and weaknesses in one quick beat of a man's heart.

How much more, then, can a boy or girl learn from the touch of a hand?

She didn't want to go.

She came into my arms and turned her head away.

I wiped her tears with my free hand and then licked my fingers.

'That's not funny!' she said. 'You are mocking me.'

'Perhaps,' I admitted. 'You are afraid.'

'So? I'm a weak woman. Women are afraid of everything. So I'm told.' She was pulling away.

'I was afraid today,' I said. She relaxed.

'You'd have been some sort of a monster if you hadn't been, I think,' she said.

'So I can be afraid, and you cannot?' I asked.

She began to relax against me. 'If I just lie here,' she said, 'will you – not entice me to do as I would rather do?'

'Depends,' I said.

'On what?' she asked.

'On whether you lie on my right knee or not,' I said.

Much later, she said, 'You were an *apprentice goldsmith?*'

'Why so shocked? I can kill your enemies *and* repair your jewels.'

She laughed and then burst into tears. 'You are very much not what I expected an English knight to be.'

I had enough experience of women to know not to explore every comment.

She had a bad dream and gave a low scream.

I woke her up.

'They're going to kill us all,' she said.

'Not unless they get better armour and some siege machines,' I said. Will, the bold, bluff English squire, that was me.

Suddenly she was kissing me.

I'd been the most honorable of men for long, dark, pain-filled hours, and suddenly, in heartbeats, her kirtle was gone and we were ... far beyond what might have been agreed, if such a thing could be discussed.

She hoisted my shirt.

'Sweet Emile,' I said.

'Psst,' she said. 'I will be dead in two days.'

I pulled her shift over her head. 'You will not, on my honour.'

She laughed, the way I have learned women laugh when you utterly fail to understand them.

And there was no sleep after that.

She dressed, kissed me and went out just as the stars dimmed. The blonde girl in the blue wool dress came in directly and looked at me with a fiercely disapproving glare.

My knee hurt like fire. I was in a castle out of food, under siege by a sea of enemies who intended our destruction.

I couldn't have been happier.

My disapproving blonde friend sat primly, as far across the solar as she could manage.

I chivalrously went to sleep.

The older knights returned at first light, and I was awakened by the clatter of their hooves on the bridge.

In the second hour after matins, Jean de Grailly came. He praised me, I praised his squire Tom, and he explained that they'd brought in very little food.

'We think we'll mount every man-at-arms in the castle and sortie,' he said. 'Perhaps cut our way through the canaille. The Count of Foix believes we can lift the siege. The Dauphin is just two days north of us, and the King of Navarre is a day's march away.' He paused. 'The Dauphine says she would rather die than be rescued by the King of Navarre.'

'My lord, I can understand that sentiment,' I said.

De Grailly laughed. 'And I, too! Can you ride?'

I tested the leg. 'If I was helped onto my horse,' I suggested.

'Excellent. You are a man after my own heart. I might even mistake monsieur for a Gascon.' He grinned. 'I will send your squire to arm you in the second hour after midday.'

'In that case, my lord, I'll eat,' I said.

'I trust you slept well,' he asked me, and I swear his eyes sparkled.

'As much as I needed,' I agreed.

He grinned. 'Very like a Gascon.'

Perkin was my next visitor. 'How was my lord's night?' he asked.

'Are you mocking me, you rogue?' I asked.

'Mmm. On balance, yes, my lord, I think I *am* mocking you.' He put a wet towel and a bowl of steaming water on a stool. 'I believe you can wash yourself, messire? And may I mention that messire has a certain perfumed smell to him that, unless messire has been visited by angels, might have come from a certain lady?'

'Perkin, did you give me cloves for my breath?' I asked.

'By our sweet saviour, m'lord, someone had to. You might have killed her, else.' He didn't smile. 'I think that m'lord's left leg harness is badly damaged and doesn't fit worth spit anyway.'

I had to admit he was right. I'd worn it all over France, but not in a fight – and it didn't fit. It was two inches too short – the greaves caught on the sabatons and I had bruises on both insteps. Fine for riding – hopeless for fighting on foot.

'First, I think I prefer Master Gold to M'lord.' I met his eye.

He frowned. 'I'll consider it. Do you have the ready silver to purchase leg armour?'

I shook my head. 'You have our purse, Perkin. What's in it?'

He took it off his belt and opened it. 'A little more than forty livre tournois. Not enough to buy anything but food on the road.'

'Can the armourer fix the strap on the cuisse?' I asked.

'Already fixed,' he said. He really was the best squire and servant any knight ever had. He unrolled the bandage on my knee, sniffed the wound and then began to re-bandage it. It hurt like all the sins of all the sinners in hell, and I groaned. I might even have squeaked.

'She's married,' he said.

I was too busy being in pain. This cut took several heartbeats to register.

'Her husband had his arm broken in the fighting. Rumour has it they detest each other, but I thought you needed to know.' He leaned close. 'He knows where she spent the night. She made a point of making sure he knows.'

Par dieu, messieurs. This was my introduction to the lives of the rich and titled. It didn't matter. I'd already given her my heart. That brave, yet terrified girl.

Why didn't you tell me? I thought. I was in a state of mortal sin. I was about to fight, and possibly die, in a state of mortal sin.

Just for a moment I thought of her, and her kirtle going over her head, and I thought ... Oh well. An eternity in hell.

I smiled. Friends, I still do. Do you really think God sends you to hell for the disport of two willing friends? I think the priests clip us too close, and I am reckoned a pious man for a man-at-arms. But I was younger then, and the whole thing preyed on my mind.

About midday, Tom came and, with Perkin, he began to arm me. And when I had my cursed leg harnesses on – the bases of the greaves already cutting into yesterday's bruises – Emile slipped in the door. She looked angry. Her chin was high, she was slightly flushed.

'Monsieur,' she said, and put a cup on the table with a click.

'Madame,' I said with a slight emphasis. But I smiled at her. I confess to you, gentlemen, as I have confessed to a hundred priests, that the sight of a woman like that is usually far more to me on the edge of death than all the promises of all the Popes in history.

Her eyes dropped. At the door, she flicked her eyes up at me. I was there, as she hoped. She paused in the door while a man might count three. She smiled and licked her fingers. And was gone.

Lying on the table under the cup was a triangle of pinky-red linen.

I picked it up and put it in my doublet next to my heart. Please note that I did *not* wear it outside my armour. There's fools and fools.

I did wear the Dauphine's favour from the day before, however. I had Perkin attach it to the peak of my basinet.

Tom had to help me down the stairs. My knee had stiffened and I couldn't make it do its duty, so it was tiring quickly. Tom got me out to the courtyard, where Perkin had Goldie and a pair of stools. They got me up on the tallest stool, and then, with some pushing, they got my bad knee over the saddle, so I was on.

I was the first knight mounted, but the Captal came out, approached, took my hand and then looked carefully at my knee.

'You really might be a Gascon. How are you?' he asked.

'Fine,' I said.

He laughed, and Tom started to arm him at the stable door. By now the captain of the castle and all the older men were arming, and a number of the younger knights. When the Captal was mounted, Tom went to help the Count of Foix, who had two squires of his own and a dozen knights in his train. His equipment was the most magnificent I'd yet seen, and he appeared to be going to a tournament, not a mortal fight. He had a panache in his helmet of peacock and ostrich; he wore a silk coat over his magnificent brigantine which was studded with golden nails.

You get the picture.

When he was armed and mounted, he rode over to me and raised his visor. 'I understand Madame the Princess gave you that yesterday,' he said conversationally.

I bowed in my saddle. 'My lord is correct.'

He nodded. 'Do you really think you are the best man among all these worthy and noble gentlemen?'

His intention was to be rude. He was tense and what the French call 'disobliging'.

I bowed again. 'My lord, after Madame the Princess was kind enough to grant it to me, I thought it would be rude not to wear it.'

'It looks like a brag, to me. But you are young, and English, and probably don't understand such things.' He shrugged – no easy feat in armour – and turned his horse away.

I was too young to answer the bastard as he deserved. I just sat there, my knee hurting, thinking about what I'd do to him if I ever had the chance.

Fast, dashing talk is hard. You have to practice. You have to read – the romances are full of *bon mots* to shoot at your opponents. I vowed to read more. I sat on Goldie, stared at his back and stewed.

It was as hot as the hell I was destined to visit with my soul steeped in the mortal sin of adultery. Sweat soaked my cap and my helmet liner, and trickled down my back under my arming coat and shirt. Knights came one and two at a time into the yard and armed, and the appearance of each was a little event – ladies cheered; men shook hands.

It was my first chance to see the French – from inside, so to speak. They were, and are, great knights, but there is an element of performance to everything. Each knight had to be seen and admired; had to arm publicly and hear the plaudits of the ladies. Meanwhile I sat and sweated as my knee burned like sin.

Until Emile entered the courtyard. I was watching the French knights, trying to imagine which one was her husband. There was a murmur – I turned my head and there she was, dressed in her gown, with my blood on it. She paused by one French knight's horse and curtsied, back straight, eyes down. Then she danced among the horses, crossed the yard – the English and Gascons were all together, and the French were all together, and a few feet separated us like a wall – and paused under Goldie's nose. She curtsied.

What could I do? Spurn her? I grinned. 'Madame,' I said.

'I … we … put all our faith in you,' she said distinctly.

There was a murmur of outrage from the French.

I drew my sword and saluted her. 'I will try to be …' I began, and then I thought of a line from the Alexander Romance. My mother used to read it to me when I was little – the monks had a copy which I'd used to learn French. I waved my sword. 'Only death, madame, will prevent my return. Victorious.'

She flushed and smiled. A French lady at the edge of the yard clapped her hands together.

The Captal grunted. 'Excellent, my big English mastiff. When we've killed all the Jacques, we can fight the French.' But he grinned wolfishly at me. 'Never mind them, stay close to me, or the Sire de Bourbon will have you off your horse in the mêlée.' He shot a glance at one of the French knights. 'Her husband's brother. Eh?'

We were *not* a band of brothers. Somewhat shamefacedly, I put my sword away, and emotion made me shove it home in the scabbard a little too hard.

The captain of the castle arranged us in ranks, and we shuffled about the yard, forming a dense column. The enemy was already formed on the far bank, their flanks anchored on stone buildings either side of the bridge entrance, and they had crossbowmen in the houses.

De Grailly had half a dozen professional archers, and Sam was with them in the bridge-gate tower. That was all the support we were going to have.

Let me add that the Jacques were fools to come out and fight at all. Much less to pack in like lemmings at the entrance to the main bridge.

The main gate opened.

I was in the third rank, behind the Captal's shoulder, with Tom – the last man mounted – at my right hand. The Count of Foix was in the front rank, with the captain of the castle and the Duke de Bourbon. They were there from *social* precedence, although, to be fair, they also had the very best and latest armour.

The Captal was far and away the most famous knight – and the best, I think. As a mere Gascon, however, he was in the second rank.

The French. Well might you all shake your heads.

We walked out the gate. As soon as we were on the bridge, the head of the column began to move faster – it was a tricky manoeuvre, getting the column to a charge on the bridge without crashing into the enemy in dribs and drabs.

Just as I passed into the brilliant sunshine beyond the bridge gate, the first flight of English arrows hit the Jacques and men fell.

The Duke de Bourbon put his spurs to his horse. The captain's horse shied, and the Captal pressed past him – I stayed with him, and we galloped down the narrow path, barely three horses wide. I was struggling to get my lance into its rest when I felt a change, and my left rein hung slack. One of the French knights had cut it as I rode past.

By St Thomas, gentleman, try riding with a lance and no control of your horse on a bridge just five ells wide! I was saved by the closeness of the press – Goldie had nowhere to go but forward, and I grabbed the curving cantle of my war saddle with my left hand, jamming my shield against my left thigh and losing the reassuring cover of its shadow against the crossbows. I put my head down, and rose slightly in my stirrups as Bertrand du Guesclin had taught me.

Some poor bastard in the front rank took my lance in the chest and died instantly. My lance tore a great hole in him, then snapped, and I bounced back against the rear of my saddle and snapped forward again as the lance broke. Goldie, maddened by the blood, the gallop and the waiting, crashed into the press, kicking and biting, and I had no control over the damned horse, who was going like a demon from hell. I reached for my sword as Goldie did a curvet that almost unseated me, but I got my right hand on my hilt and pulled – the sword stuck fast.

Good Christ, that was a terrible moment. A crossbow bolt struck my visor and tore it off its hinge, so it hung from the right, bouncing against my head and face. What was worse, the forcible removal of my visor showed me that Goldie had carried me past the Jacques and I was all by myself, with men all around me, reaching for my harness – a bill slammed into my right foot, and the sabaton held, but the weight of the blow hurt my ankle.

I fell back against my cantle, and Goldie caught the change in weight, bless him, reared and kicked.

I got my right hand back on my sword hilt and pulled.

The belt moved on my hips and the sword stayed scabbarded.

Not that I stopped to make choices, but I couldn't dismount – I was surrounded by foes – and I couldn't control my horse, either.

And I had no weapon.

My right knee throbbed like some devil's torment. And some of the knights on my own side were trying to kill me.

I got Goldie to rear again and kick. As he came down on his forefeet, I pinned my scabbard with my left hand, shield and all, and pulled at the hilt with my right, with all the power of desperation.

A spear point caught me from behind and threw me forward over my horse's neck, which of course made Goldie bolt forward.

Finally the sword came loose in my hand. I sat back, hard, to try and slow my mount. Now I was deep in the ranks of the Jacques – I cut, more from habit than from a feeling of combat, and they scattered.

Another bolt struck the top of my left shoulder and it felt as if a giant had punched me. But if you must be hit by a heavy missile, the top of the shoulder is the place – overlapping metal plates lie over chain, and under the base of the helmet's aventail, there are three or more layers of steel. It's the very best armoured part of the body.

I had a bruise for two weeks, and I still almost lost my seat. I rocked back and forth, trying to find an opponent, every sway in the saddle forcing me to grip with my knees.

Behind me, there was a roar, a panicked shriek, and suddenly the whole mob of Jacques was in flight.

I attribute it to divine intervention. I didn't break them, and neither did the Captal, or Tom, who, it proved, was close behind me. We shattered their ranks, but they were ten to one against us, and they had crossbowmen on the roofs. Sooner or later, they could have killed every one of us, but they didn't. Instead, they succumbed to fear and broke.

And the dashing French knights hunted them through the streets.

I took my time gaining control of Goldie, who was mad with battle-rage. I had one rein, and that was not enough, so we rode deeper and deeper into the town, and eventually, without intending to, I emerged at the land gate on the south side, with Tom at my shoulder. There was no guard at the gate.

'If we hold the gate,' I called. I remember how tired I was. 'If we hold the gate, they can't escape.'

He dismounted, caught Goldie's bridle, and I got off – and fell to the ground. My right knee didn't want to take my weight.

Tom dragged me clear of the gate and some fugitives ran past us.

'Tom, run for it,' I said. It was clear I couldn't fight, and he wasn't going to live long, trying to hold two horses and cover me, too.

He shook his head. 'If I repair your bridle, can you fight?' he asked.

'Just prop me up and go,' I said.

So I spent the rest of the fight leaning on a water barrel in the gateway, with Goldie's bridle in my hand, helping to hold me up. Tom rode for the Captal, who came soon enough. I don't remember much after that, except that I watched the French knights hunt the Jacques through the town and through the countryside. I didn't see anything like it again until Cremona – that's another story – but I knelt there on one knee and wondered how men who called themselves knights could hate their own peasants with such ferocity.

I wanted to be a knight, but I was beginning to think that in the process, I might have to change what knighthood was.

I was in the castle of Meaux for five days. I had six wounds – Jean de Viladi swears to them, and who am I to complain? I was much doted on by the ladies, and one lady in particular. I worried I'd be poisoned, but the Captal assured me that this was not the French way.

As far as the ladies were concerned, I'd ridden into the Jacques, first of all the knights, and cut my way through. I hope the irony of this wasn't lost on the man who cut my reins. The bastard.

For two nights – two beautiful, sin-filled nights – Emile came to my room, but on the third night, she came with another woman, who would not leave, and on the fourth night, she didn't come at all. Instead, the Princess came.

I tried to bow, and she came to my bedside and smiled somewhat hesitantly. She put a hand on my hand. 'Monsieur,' she said. 'My husband will return tomorrow from Burgundy, and with him comes a great army to smash this rebellion – and take Paris, too.' She smiled bravely. 'I will leave it to him to reward you as you deserve for coming to our defence,' she said. She smiled, then frowned and looked around the room, as if for support.

I knew some of the language of chivalry. 'I need no reward but your thanks, my lady,' I said. 'I hope that you feel I did justice to your favour?'

She flushed. 'Monsieur, I was very foolish to give you such a thing, and I must ask for its return.' She had the good grace to look ashamed.

Well, to have a favour revoked is ... not a good thing.

'Send Perkin for it. It is attached to my helmet,' I said. 'I'm sorry if I ... disappointed you.' Really, what could I say? English squires don't chat with Princesses, much less task them.

She looked at me under her lashes – not flirtatiously, but more questioningly. 'Ah, Monsieur, you were never disappointing. But this has become a matter too elevated for me. Or you.' She leaned forward slightly. 'A certain person is leaving – with her husband. She wishes to send her ... farewell. Yes? And I cannot be seen to favour you. I'm sorry. My honour is engaged.' She leaned back.

'Please tell the certain person ...' I said.

She turned her head away. 'Monsieur, you cannot imagine I would carry messages between you.'

By the head of St John! I had imagined that very thing. She inclined her head graciously, and as I couldn't bow, I took her hand.

She allowed it, and I felt something hard in my hand. She nodded and left the room.

I had a ring – a very beautiful ring in gold and enamel.

I was still shaking my head when the Captal entered with Perkin. 'Can you ride?' he asked.

I nodded.

He pursed his lips. 'I'm on my way to the King of Navarre. I think I'd best take you with me. There's a nasty little rumour making the rounds in this castle. It might cost you your neck.'

I looked away. 'I'd be honoured to travel with you, my lord,' I said. 'But I was sent by the Lieutenant of Gascony to get a safe conduct signed by the Dauphin, and I fear it is my duty to wait on him.'

The Captal nodded. 'Let me have it,' he said. 'I'll see that it is signed today – they owe you that – but I promise you, my young faux Gascon, that if you sleep alone here, you won't wake up.'

I must have flushed. I know I straightened up in bed and said, 'But she's gone, and her stinking husband with her!'

The Captal shook his head. 'My young scapegrace, no one cares about the state of your amours with the lady in question. The *Dauphin* has been told that you, ahem, slept with his *wife*.' He shrugged. 'These things happen. It will all blow over in a few years.'

We travelled south to Paris across a landscape dotted with peasants and Parisians swinging from trees. In some places, we passed manor houses burned to the ground – at one road junction, I saw two Parisian 'hoods' swinging in the wind, rotting away, and just a few yards further down the road, a young nobleman's corpse was being pecked by ravens – the corpse, you understand, was a few days older, and had yet to be cut down.

The roads of the Beauvais were packed with refugees, and the refugees were themselves from different sides. There were noble refugees, clinging to their few remained valuables or hollow-eyed with torment – some noble women with their children, looking as if they had endured more than they could bear. And peasant women, in much the same state, but with fewer possessions. And then peasants with their men folk – these the victims of the English and Navarrese – the more routine depredations of our professional looters.

But the French nobles – the remnants of Charles of Navarre's army, and the great army the Dauphin was bringing from Burgundy – saw all concentrations of refugees as potential gatherings of Jacques and tended to attack them without too much investigation.

Perhaps it was the fever of my wounds – the ongoing pain in my knee scared me – or the weight of my sins.

Perhaps it was the children. There were dead children everywhere. Christ, even now ...

We rode, tight lipped and silent. I wanted to be done with the whole thing, and for the first time in three years, I considered going back to smithing. Knighthood didn't look very noble in the June of 1358. Can deeds of arms be measured against raped women?

Can bravery in battle and loyalty to your lord be weighed against murdered children? Were we supposed to protect these people or not?

I didn't even notice where we were going until I could see Paris. I only remember the dead and the blank-eyed, then waking in a stinking pile of straw in a barn outside St Cloud. There was sheep-dip in the straw – it was all I could get.

Well, that and Richard Musard, who threw his arms around me as soon as I dismounted. 'Did you get the *sauvegardes*?' he asked, ever practical.

I nodded weakly.

'We'll be famous!' he said. Richard had a great deal more confidence in the honour of Princes than I did just then.

'Have you got John?' asked Sam.

Richard nodded. 'I brought him here on a cart; he's finally on the mend. The wound festered . . .'

Sam nodded. 'I want to see him.'

I wanted to see him, too. The trip had bound us together.

'When did you get to St Cloud?' I asked.

Richard shrugged. 'As soon as I healed up, we were on the road. Sir John Hawkwood has taken good care of me.'

St Cloud, the very gateway to Paris, had an English garrison, and Sir James Pipe was the captain of it. The King of Navarre was rallying an army – to liberate Paris, or so he said.

After we visited John Hughes, we put our camp gear with his and made up beds of dirty straw. Sir John Hawkwood himself brought me wine, and news, and Perkin sat on a barrel end, repairing my kit. He found me a pair of leather and splint legs – pretty enough, but heavy and clumsy compared to my beautiful steel pair that didn't quite fit. With the help of a mercenary armourer, he was fitting the legs to me, while I lay on my dirty straw, getting bitten by insects and considering an end to my career of war.

I wanted to be interested in Sir John's news, and I finally asked, 'If the King of Navarre is making himself captain of Paris, why the hell did he smash the Jacques? Surely they were on the same side?'

Hawkwood looked away. It was evening, there was a fire burning in the barnyard and Sir John's twenty or so lances were cooking their food or watching their servants cook. The fire backlit his face and made his expression hard to read.

'I'm not sure whether my employer knows from day to day what he's doing,' he admitted. 'But unlike all the other sides, he pays regularly.'

'How many sides? The Navarrese, the English, the Dauphin, the Parisians, the Jacques – have I left anyone out?' I asked.

Hawkwood continued to watch the women by the fire. 'Well, there's the Holy Roman Emperor and the Pope – and the King of France, in England.' He shrugged. 'I'm not really jesting – the Pope and the Emperor have their fingers in this dough. The Pope is supposedly working to raise the King's ransom.'

You have to remember that back then, the Pope was a Frenchman who lived in Avignon, not an Italian in Rome. Eh?

'But when Charles of Navarre smashed the Jacques,' I insisted, 'he was attacking his own power base.'

'Worse,' Sir John said. 'He was helping the Dauphin recruit – even though I understand the Dauphin found it prudent to spend the time in Burgundy, leaving his wife to face the Jacques. *Eh bien?*'

Perkin coughed in his hand, and arranged my rolled-up riding cloak as a pillow so I could sit. Then he elevated my right knee, which was less swollen.

Hawkwood laughed. 'A pox on your coughing, you rogue. I've heard the story and I'm as curious as the next varlet. Did you cuckold the Dauphin?'

'No!' I said with, I confess, a little too much spirit.

Sir John smirked. 'Of course not. But every French knight is looking for you. I promise you, lad, it's going to be rough on you. Word is she came to your room to thank you and you, ahem, took advantage of her.'

'I was never alone with her,' I hissed.

'Course you weren't.' Sir John grinned. 'Well, it's one conquest the French can't take back, eh?' He got to his feet and said, 'I was going to ask you and Sam to join me as a lance – the money is the best it's ever been – but I think Paris might be a little hot for you this year. Best you go back to Gascony.'

I all but ground my teeth in frustration. I thought of the knight with the broken arm on the bridge – I'd never seen his face, the bastard, but he was her husband. I'd saved his life, and he'd done this: poisoned the well against me – with words.

My beautiful deed of arms, ruined by malicious gossip.

For the first time, I began to hate the French.

*

I left the suburbs of Paris a day later, with my knee almost a normal size and my fever abating. I didn't wear harness for a day, but the woods were full of desperate men, and our second day south of the bridge, Sam put an arrow in a lout by the roadside, and we stopped by the cooling corpse so I could put on the whole harness.

It wasn't very pretty any more.

My breast and back had a dozen creases and a deep pit in the front where I'd taken the bolt on the bridge of Meaux. There was rust darkening the bottom of every crease – the best squire in the world can't get into the bottom of a crease every day. My left shoulder piece was badly deformed by another crossbow bolt. My helmet had two dozen cuts and nicks, each with a corresponding dent. My beautiful leg armours were gone, replaced by leather and splint – done by an enthusiastic amateur, and they were a livid blue-purple that didn't match any other part of my harness. My arm harnesses were still beautiful, although somewhat hacked about. The brazen edging on the elbows had several deep cuts.

My gauntlets were a book in which you could read every missed parry and botched cover of my last ten months.

I walked with a limp and I leaned too far to the right when I rode.

But two armoured men and an armed archer seemed enough to keep the roads empty. We passed the village of the dead – we didn't go through. The bell tower was silent.

We didn't mention our own dead, but we both knew we'd lost men. I won't say their shades came to our fires, but I will say that I thought about them a great deal, especially Rob, whose death seemed the most unfair.

There were flowers in fields that should have been tilled, and many, many scavengers in the air and on the ground, peasants who moved silently from field to field, slithering like animals – mere movement, and feral movement at that, along the hedgerows.

A day north of Tours, we saw a party approaching – half a dozen knights and men-at-arms, with a closed box being carried by two mules, and a cart, and a dozen mounted crossbowmen. We watched them carefully, but I knew the arms – the flag was that of Jehan le Maingre, whom I had last seen being taken prisoner before Poitiers.

We were the smaller party, and we had only a small flag of truce, which Perkin bore on his spear below the arms of the Prince of Wales. I was minded to ride around them, but Richard was sure we'd get a good reception from such a famous knight, and he rode across the fields to them with Perkin at his side.

My heart hammered in my chest. I was afraid that at any moment they'd kill him. I had lost any faith I'd ever had in chivalry. I trusted my friends and no one else. I had even been a trifle uneasy with Sir John Hawkwood.

At any rate, Richard came back quickly, and I could see from his riding that something was wrong. Perkin stuck to him like glue.

Richard reined in. 'It's Le Maingre,' he said. 'He demands to fight you. He says it is a matter of honour – a private quarrel – and so, despite his state as a prisoner, he can fight. Or so he says.'

'He's still a prisoner of the Prince,' Perkin said. 'And you, sir, are wounded. You cannot fight him.'

I shook my head. 'What the hell? Why does Jehan le Maingre want to fight me?'

Across the fallow field, 200 paces distant, a shining figure detached from the column and started toward us. His horse's hooves raised puffs of dust from the field. He was moving quite fast. He had a lance.

If anger can be read in the way a man rides – and it can – this was rage.

'By the passion of Jesus,' I swore and seized a lance from Sam. Sam's face was a study in disinterest and he said just one word.

'Don't,' he said.

But I was tired of Frenchmen and their rules and gossip, so I took my lance – a sharp lance, the type we use in war – and rode at Le Maingre.

My knee wasn't bad. I got myself straight on my horse, and I got the lance down and into my lance rest without shaming myself. I steadied the lance and aimed it at the crest of his helmet as I'd been taught, leaned a little forward and touched Goldie with my spurs.

All in all, it was probably the best run with a lance I'd ever had. I got it all together, and my lance point was on target—

He smashed me to the ground. I bounced. If I hadn't had a steel breastplate, I'd have been dead. As it was, my once-beautiful breastplate took a tremendous dent – he hit just a few fingers width from the crossbow bolt – and broke some ribs.

I was knocked unconscious. Which is just as well, because le Maingre informed Richard Musard that if I'd been conscious, he'd have killed me.

He took Goldie – that was his right by the law of arms as he'd bested me in single combat – and rode away.

Young men recover quickly. I did – I was up the next day and riding a plug, while Richard, looking like a lord, rode his magnificent bay. Every man on the road assumed I was his squire.

My pride took longer to heal. I had put some thought into leaving the life of arms, but now I wanted revenge.

The difficult part was that I wasn't sure just who I wanted to take my revenge *against*.

It was clear to me that chivalry was a closed company. That the men who lived inside it – at least the French – would use any means, no matter how dishonorable, to exclude outsiders.

And to be fair, it was equally clear to me that we English used the language of chivalry as a cloak of convenience under which to conduct ruthless war for profit.

Nothing makes a young man angrier than the discovery that he is not valued, not respected, and that his best efforts are wasted. Wait, I lie. The thing that most angers a young man is the confusion of discovering that the philosophy he allows to govern his actions is a nested set of lies.

I glowered at every man on the road – I wanted a fight every day, to prove to myself that I wasn't a loser. Not a fool. Christ, the *ease* with which le Maingre had put me in the dirt. I really didn't understand, then, how great was the divide between the competent man-at-arms and the trained man-at-arms.

I hid from my various moral dilemmas – adulterer, murderer, false knight – if that was possible, and instead concerned myself with my worldly repute. All I could think about as we entered Gascony and rode south along the good roads through the unburned farms was that I'd been made to look a fool. That I had failed. I had no worth, no *preux*. And that somewhere in the north, Emile would be told by her smirking husband that I'd been taught manners by a French lord, who'd dropped me in a field like the goldsmith's apprentice I was.

So much for giving up a life of arms.

Richard more than stood by me. Richard probably saved me from hell.

Every night, we sat at campfires, me with broken ribs and more badly damaged than my scarred and rusting armour. Richard lived in a simpler world. His gentle Jesus was closer, his Virgin Mary was always there for him. He didn't doubt knighthood; he merely found many men wanting.

Pardon – he didn't say any of those things, right out.

But when we were close to Bordeuax, he handed me a cup of wine. 'Remember, what you said? When I said I was a slave? And you said you had been a London apprentice?'

'What does that have to do with it?' I asked. I was entirely surly.

'You said that some day, we'd be knights.' Musard stared out at the stars for a little while. 'Did you think it would be easy?' He leaned forward. 'They don't want us, William. They want to keep it all for themselves. The power, the riches, the pretty girls. Even the honour. Honour is like money, William. There's not really enough of it for everyone. If you'd saved – I don't know, if you'd saved Sir John Chandos on the bridge – he's rich enough in honour to let you have some. But this French lord? He isn't going to let you have any.'

I nodded. 'That's what I'm saying!' I spat.

Richard sat back and crossed his legs. 'If you were a black man who'd come to all this from Spain, you'd have thicker skin, brother. Do you believe in God?'

'Of course! What do you take me for, some heretic?' I snapped.

'No. But listen.' He spoke slowly, as if speaking to a child. Which, that night, I was. 'Do you believe in priests? In the Mass?' he asked.

I nodded. 'Of course. Where's this going?'

'Yet some priests are foul bastards, lecherous and vile. The Pope is a Frenchman who may be our enemy. That Talleyrand, a cardinal of the church, is hardly living in poverty. People say he's the richest man in the world.' Musard shrugged. 'Bad priests don't touch the truth of our saviour. Bad knights don't touch the truth of chivalry.'

I was angry, and I wanted to stay angry, but his words went home.

We rode into Bordeaux just before the gate was closed the next day, and I had begun to feel a little better. England would save me. I allowed myself to think about my sister. To think that my outstanding ransom from Poitiers might be paid. That and the pay from a year in the saddle for the Prince.

I began to see another life.

We rode in, an hour before sunset, just after the feast of the birth of St John the Baptist. The guards at the gate stopped us, despite our arms.

One of the gate guards was a northern retinue archer. He knew

Sam, and he beckoned to him and they exchanged words. Sam came back to us and shook his head.

'I know you gentlemen won't do as I ask, but I aim to ask anyway. I'd like the four of us to ride away, now. Just turn your horses and ride.' Sam shrugged. 'The Three Foxes is no longer ours.'

I grew hot. I wanted a fight. 'I'll kill all of them!' I said.

Sam put a hand on my bridle. 'No. Things have changed, here. That's what Harry was telling me. The Prince is back, and there's good law here. And the Prince's men-at-arms do not run brothels.' He looked at the two of us. 'The Prince knows.'

'Fucking Chaucer,' said Richard. His lips were tight.

Sam shrugged.

'But we have the safe guards!' I said.

Sam raised an eyebrow. 'If Sir John Cheverston ever really wanted them, he still does. He's in the field. I propose we go and take him the *sauvegardes* – and send them via Perkin. See if we can collect our pay without being arrested.'

Richard whistled. 'Arrested!'

The word was like a bolt of levin going to my heart.

Sam nodded. 'I'm guessing that they intend to declare you out-laws and degrade you from the rank of squires.'

Richard sat silently on his horse.

I thought about the French. 'To hell with them,' I said.

Richard met my eye. He was crying. 'God damn them all to hell,' he said. It was the first time I'd ever heard him speak openly against the Prince, whom he loved.

Two days later we fell in with the Captal and headed to his own estates in the south. Richard poured his heart out to the Gascon lord while I just sat on my horse and hated everyone.

By the time Richard was done telling our tale, we were sitting on stools around a fire – the Captal had a pavilion and had invited us to dine with him, which was lucky, as we were penniless as well as friendless.

He rubbed his chin and watched the fire. 'You two wastrels ran the Three Foxes?' he asked. He grinned. 'You sound very Gascon to me. Have I said this before? Listen, the Prince will not forgive such a thing. No shadow must touch his honour – he sees himself as the greatest knight in the world, the very pinnacle of chivalry.' De Grailly made a face. 'In truth, I think perhaps he is, and it is a very difficult rank to hold. Men gossip. You must not only be a great knight, but you must keep men from hating you for it.' De Grailly watched the fire. 'May I loan you two a little silver? I would not recommend that you visit Sir John Cheverston. He won't want to arrest you, but he will. He is the Prince's man, and whatever he thinks privately, he will degrade you.'

For the first time in years, I thought of my branding as a thief. Of how men who knew perfectly well I was innocent stood by and watched. I sat by the fire and hated. Now there would be no money. Nothing for my sister. Nothing for me.

But to tell the truth, messieurs, it sat easier on me than on Richard. I'd had my doubts about princes. I had tasted the bile before. Richard, despite slavery, believed that if he served loyally, he would be rewarded, and he took it very hard.

Richard shook his head. 'It's not fair,' he said, with the tone of every young man who makes this discovery. 'We have spent a year – your pardon, my lord – but a year in the saddle for the Prince.'

Jean de Grailly shook his head. 'You did run a brothel,' he said. 'Save your protests! I'm not against you. Listen, if you don't ride to Sir John Cheverston, he can't arrest you and you won't be degraded. I'll see to this, I give you my word. Give me your *sauvegardes* and I'll pass them to Sir John. I have influence with the Prince. In time ...'

'By God, we don't have time!' I said. 'We beggared ourselves to make this trip. What are we to do, my lord?'

De Grailly spread his hands. 'I say you remind me of Gascons,' he said. 'Go be Gascons. Join the companies.'

The companies. The men who raped and murdered for money. Like organized brigands or pirates under a false flag.

'Seguin de Badefol is recruiting,' De Grailly said. 'I can give you lads a letter.'

Richard spat. 'I will be the Black squire indeed,' he said. 'God's curse on them all.'

Brignais, 1362

Taken by surprise, and frightened by the terrible cries, the French lost heart, and although they ran for their arms, the companies already pressed so hard upon them that they gave them no time to arm themselves. An army which included so many barons and valiant knights thus had the misfortune to be routed and put to flight, and many were killed and wounded. Those who were able to mount their horses and don their armour nearly all fell into the hands of that vassal of the King of France, Petit Meschin. So great were the ransoms and the booty that all the Companions became rich. Their victory made them so confident and daring that the court of the Pope of Rome, which had experience of being fleeced by the companies, feared that it would see them arrive in Avignon.

Villani, *Istorie*

Aye, messieurs, I was at Brignais, although there were damned few English left with the routiers by then. It was a fine fight, and a rich day for most of us.

Richard and I had ridden away from Bordeaux in the late winter of 1358. Sam Bibbo thought for three days about leaving us – he said he was done fighting – but in the end he came, and John Hughes came with him. Perkin had nowhere else to go, but he made no secret of his dissatisfaction at my being reduced to what he called, with some accuracy, *banditry*. By then, Charles of Navarre had tried, and failed, to make himself King of France. He would continue trying for some years, but by the summer of 1358, the banner of Navarre was nothing but a flag of convenience for every brigand, bandit and rapist from the Loire to Provence. Sir John Hawkwood was there, in the Auxerre, and so was Sir Robert Knolles and Jean de Grailly and the Bourc Camus and a great many other professional men-at-arms.

Richard didn't want to go to Sir John Hawkwood. It was never stated between us, but I think we both felt that if we were going to be bandits, we'd be bandits where John Hawkwood couldn't see us. Auxerre was big, and we were small men.

Those were the days in which the companies formed. The first 'Great Company' was that of the archpriest, Arnaud de Cervole. He grouped many of the Breton and Gascon mercenaries into one mass of killers in 1358 and tried to take Marseille. Richard and I were there. We failed, but we made some gold, covered our debts and drank a great deal. Jamais sold me a new war horse, who was never a patch on Goldie. He was a big brute and I called him Alexander. Mostly he liked to bite other horses and make trouble; he didn't know the hundred fighting tricks that Goldie had known, and he was brutal to ride in a joust as he'd flinch from the spear point.

Not that I did a lot of jousting in those years. We rode, but seldom fought. When we did fight, it was to raid and counter-raid – a war of ambush and nerves, of convoys on roads and sudden descents.

In 1359, we went north with Sir Robert Knolles. There was a rumour that the King's peace was falling apart and that the King would make a campaign in person. By one of the ironies of the profession of arms, my captain from the year before was now my adversary; we faced the archpriest as we skirmished among the ruined crops and devastated country of the upper Loire Valley. He was as incompetent facing us as he had been leading us, and Knolles took us to good booty.

It was brutal. Mostly we plundered peasants. We'd form a company of adventure – a group of men who made an oath about sharing plunder and standing by each other – these agreements were usually made between wolves at inns. The better captains employed spies to watch the roads and to visit towns that might have a weak wall or an undefended gate. The less professional, or simply temporary, companies were formed for a single 'adventure' based on the whim of the most famous 'knight'. Oh, my friends, the language of chivalry was maintained at all times. We fought a 'passage of arms' with the desperate defenders of small towns, and then we 'took them by storm' in a 'feat of arms' that left a lot of peasants dead and their wives and daughters raped and sold. When we took a town, we plundered it down to the plate on the altars and the coins in old women's money-boxes. Only after we'd sacked a town for a few days would we rally the surviving principal citizens and inform them of the *patis* they owed us – sometimes with individual ransoms for the richer men. If we chose to stay, we charged tolls on the road and exacted taxes from the same peasants we'd brutalized in the sack, and when the French sent an army against us, we faded away, split into small parties and ran for the safety of Gascony or Normandy, where we met up again – to plan the next raid.

Richard and I served with Knolles in the hope of being reinstated with the Prince's household. We were never formally humiliated, but my reputation was very dark – a pimp, a thief and perhaps an unchivalrous lover. I led a lance, and Richard led another, but neither of us was trusted with a command, and as the campaign wore on, it seemed less and less likely that Knolles intended to unite with the King's army landing at Calais, than that he was plundering France for his own benefit. I ended up in the garrison of Champlay in the Auxerre, bored, mildly prosperous and no closer to serving my Prince or cleansing my reputation, and every town from which I exacted *patis* made me dream of the ringing bell and the village of the dead.

I drank a lot.

I had found one way to salve my conscience. The Italian bankers followed us like vultures and wolves, and I put my money into their books and began to purchase my sister's elevation. I wrote a letter on her behalf.

It was late in 1359 – September or October.

I sat on a well-built oak stool that had once belonged to a prosperous peasant, and I penned the letter by the light of his burning farm. I wrote to the prior of the commandery at Clerkenwell. I styled myself 'William Gold, Squire' and requested that the money go to a religious dowry for my sister.

I paid in almost everything I took. My sister probably needed 1,000 ducats. After I paid my lance and fed my horse and paid Perkin, I had perhaps forty ducats a month – for a life of utmost violence. But I paid it out, and every payment seemed to make me a little less black. I began to go to Mass for the first time in years.

And I began to look for ways to be a knight. Amidst the moral sewer that was war in the Auxerre.

In late October, our little garrison stormed a nearby manor house held by one of the Dauphin's supporters. It was a fair bit of fighting. I was the first man into the house, through a shutter I caved in with my poleaxe, and Richard came in on my heels.

We penned all the women – high born and low – in the chapel, and protected them until all of our own men were gone. It was the beginning of something.

Richard and I didn't talk of it, but when our eyes met ...

We knew.

About the same time, the King was landing at Calais, and with him was the Prince of Wales and the Duke of Clarence, Lionel and all the best English captains. Richard and I sat in a mercenary garrison and writhed with anger. We drank. It is a tribute to our friendship that we didn't go for each other.

Richard and I were not captains of the town, by any means – that job went to a rising star in the companies, a Scotsman named Sir Walter Leslie – but we were captains of smaller companies, and if men thought us hard, that was all to the good. We staked out the

Angel, the best inn left standing in the Auxerre, which had thirty girls and six good cooks. It was a fine inn, three storeys of whitewashed plaster and heavy dark beams, with good red wine and terrible ale.

Have I told you that inns are to soldiers as paradise is to priests?

My enemy, the Bourc Camus, held the next castle-town for Knolles. He raided the countryside that belonged to my town, as if we were enemies. Even among criminals and murderers, he was a byword for evil. He struck the weak whenever he could, and his special provenance was taking women and turning them into whores, whom he sold to traders like chattels.

My friends, we were hard men. We did many bad things, and our sins piled up like gold in a money-changer's booth, but the Bourc was a different kind of evil. He pleasured himself in the abject humiliation of the weak.

We had a skirmish at night – we caught his retinue raiding our sheepfolds, and we drove them off. I tried to get to him, but my horse was too shy of the dark and wouldn't cross a wall. The Bourc escaped, but we rounded up half a dozen of his brigands – peasant boys he'd turned into spearmen.

Of the six we cut off, three fought to the death.

Listen. In our kind of war, no one fights to the death except the peasants on whom we preyed. I confess that if one of the French lords were to capture men like this, they'd be hanged – not for nothing were they called brigands – but between ourselves, we'd sell them back. We had our own infantry by then: Gascon mountaineers. They carried small bucklers and a pair of wicked javelins, and they could fight in any terrain.

These boys were different. They weren't Gascons at all; they were locals. There were men and women in Champlay who knew them, yet they were fighting devils.

The other three had to be beaten to the ground with spear-staves. It's not that they were particularly good fighters, merely that they kept fighting.

When we tried to talk to them, they sat like sullen animals and said nothing. Even when John used a little rough persuasion.

I'd never seen the look those peasant boys had, except on broken men going to be hanged in London. Their eyes were dead somehow, and yet they burned with hate.

Three days later, the Captain of Champlay (as he called himself) had a parley with the Bourc at a stone bridge. The bastard sat on his horse with his black and white banner, and most of his followers in his own motley. He had two of the Albret bastards in their father's arms, and a couple of Englishmen, but all the rest of his 'knights' wore his colours.

I sat on my bad war horse and watched him through my lowered visor. Neither my commander, Sir Walter Leslie, my friend Richard, nor I, trusted the Bourc a whit.

As Sir Walter parleyed with him, I watched his knights. They had miserable armour and one was mounted on a plough horse. The ones with open-faced helmet looked shockingly young.

Sir Walter released our three captives, and they stood, abject, by our servants. Finally, one of the archers pressed them forward at spear point, and they walked, like condemned men, across to the middle of the span.

The Bourc looked down at them. 'You surrendered?' he asked, laughing.

All three flinched.

'Please, my lord, we were beaten to the ground,' one boy whined. They were the first words I'd heard him speak, even when John Hughes broke one of his fingers.

The Bourc drew his sword and killed the boy with a single snap of his wrist.

The other two didn't run. They just stood in the centre of the span until the Bourc's sword took their souls.

Then he looked at Sir Walter. 'Don't bother bringing me any more trash,' he said. He turned his horse and his eye caught mine.

He laughed. 'Hello, Butt Boy.'

I was growing up. I didn't flush or stammer. I rode forward and raised my visor. 'Wounds all healed?' I asked. 'Or shall I kick your arse again to remind you which of us—'

He snarled. He had a sword in his hand, still dripping from the cold murder of three brigands, and he swung at me. Under a flag of truce.

Sir Walter raised his hand, even as the Bourc's blow missed me by a finger's breadth as I leaned back in the saddle. Our archers sprung forward, arrows to bows, and the Bourc raised his sword. He laughed. 'You're a dead man,' he said.

'I've heard all this before,' I said. 'And here I am.'

Richard had my bridle.

I pushed my big horse forward. The deaths of the boys penetrated my armour of vice. Many things did that autumn. Why? Because they were like me, those boys? Because I was not utterly lost to sin?

'You are a coward and a caitiff, Camus, and I challenge you. I will prove on your body that you are nothing but a terror to boys and virgins.'

My words hit him like a flight of heavy arrows. Hah! I was growing up.

He turned. 'Easy to challenge me when you have all these war bows at your back, Butt Boy.' He spat. 'Someday I'll catch you alone and use you like a woman.'

'Does that thought excite you?' Richard called out.

The Bourc froze and his face grew as red as new blood.

We laughed.

'Dead! Both of you! I will destroy your souls and send you to an eternity in the abyss!' he hissed and rode away, and his retinue fell in behind him.

The peasants called him 'the demon'.

I rode back into our little town as filled with emotion as if I had just fought a battle, and Richard and I laughed and embraced over it. A war of words, yes. But we won. There comes a point in every man's life – perhaps in every woman's, too – where you learn how to turn the words of your adversary. To fight word to word, like sword to sword. Some never learn. Some become word-bullies.

A few days later a party of Bretons tried to kill us and take the inn. Richard took a nasty wound in the thigh, and I might have died if Sam hadn't put arrows into three men. They attacked without warning, but by then I slept with a dagger in my hand, and when I slept alone, I wore mail. There were loaded and cocked crossbows in three places about the inn, and we were wary when we went out.

We killed them all. Four of them were, as I say, Breton mercenaries, but the other two were young boys of twelve or thirteen.

I had been to Mass the day before – I was learning to pray again. I stood there with the blood of a twelve-year-old boy dripping down my longsword to form a puddle on the tiled floor and I prayed. Good Christ, how I prayed.

I prayed that there might *be a God*. That's all I could manage.

I tell you true, monsieur. It took less than a week for God to answer.

Richard and I were sitting in the inn. In fact, we were discussing leaving Knolles and running for the coast – to see if the Prince, or Prince Lionel, would take us.

'We have nothing to lose,' Richard said.

'They might hang us, or publicly degrade us,' I argued.

Richard spread his hands, which were long-fingered and delicate compared to mine. 'If I stay here much longer,' he said, 'I will be nothing but a criminal. A felon.' He looked away.

We had probably had far too much to drink already when a party came in – probably the last party to get through the gate that day. There was a priest, a pair of monks and two nuns. The girls had a go at them because the church provided us with some ready customers, but the nuns didn't even unveil and the monks were silent.

At some point I became suspicious of them, and I ordered Helen, one of the older girls, to see if the nuns were women at all. She took them a flagon of wine, leaned over the table and put a hand on a nun's gown. The nun gave a very nun-like screech and backed into a corner.

Better safe than sorry, thought I, and gave Helen a moulin of silver for her trouble.

The priest ordered wine for all of them and they kept to themselves. He was a nondescript man in a brown gown that reached to the ground – what we used to call a long gown – but under the gown, he wore boots with spurs, like a knight. That made me suspicious.

The two nuns made me suspicious, too. As soon as they relaxed a little, they were too loud, too free, and they gave the man orders. Something about them wasn't right.

After they had eaten, the priest asked Helen to speak to the innkeeper, and she sent for me. I went over to the table with Richard at my back. He was limping. I was ready to draw, my blade oiled and loosened in my scabbard.

The nuns sensed my alarmed hostility and became silent. More, the younger one cowered against the back of their snug. The monks glared with that mixture of fear and anger that characterizes the man with no fighting skills.

The priest, on the other hand, appeared very calm. He indicated empty places. 'Please,' he said, 'join us and share a cup of wine.'

I sat, and Richard watched my back. That's how it was.

'I need to get to Avignon,' he said carefully. His eyes flicked up to Richard. 'You may sit. I confess that I have several weapons, but none of them to hand.' He smiled.

I turned in time to see Richard return the smile.

I nodded. It was possible he really was going to Avignon. It didn't add up, but it was possible. And the man himself looked familiar. The hood on his gown made his face difficult to see and read, and he wore a white linen cap, like a scholar – or a soldier, except that his was a clean, sparkling white despite days on the road.

'Whom do I pay?' he asked. 'For passage?'

I glanced at Richard. 'You want an escort?' I asked.

He nodded. 'I had six men-at-arms and a dozen crossbowmen,' he said. 'I've lost all of them. I need to get to Avignon. With both of my brothers and both sisters. Intact.' He nodded. 'Alive.'

Again, he seemed familiar to me. But I couldn't place him, and I didn't know any priests, so I stopped staring at him and turned to Richard.

Richard sat. 'I'm willing to discuss it,' he said. 'Messire.'

Richard and I still wanted to be great knights. We were more eager to do good deeds than farm boys safe at home. We had a great deal of sin to expiate.

'It would be a bold adventure,' I said.

But Richard shook his head. 'Auxerre is packed with brigands,' he said. 'You are foolish to come this way.'

The priest shrugged. 'I go where the good Lord sends me,' he said. 'I was with the convoy—'

'What convoy?' Richard asked.

'The cardinals who went to make the peace treaty. We were with them on the road – they are too slow. And too rich.' The priest smiled. 'Everything about the church that I despise in that convoy. Arrogance. Worldly power. Pomp and display. Wanton sin.' He shrugged. 'My sisters are safer in an inn run by professional killers.' He met my eyes. 'I know you,' he said. 'I ask for your help.'

His eyes were not soft. Damn, I knew him from somewhere. His words – *I know you* – struck me like sword blows. He knew my kind? Or he knew me, personally?

I smiled, the way you smile when you think you may have to fight. 'How far behind you is this convoy?' I asked.

He shrugged. 'I will not be the agent of its destruction,' he said, and I swear he knew exactly what he'd just revealed.

'You are English,' I said.

He nodded. 'I am a servant of God,' he said. 'Will you help us?' He flipped back the hood on his gown. 'Will you help us, William Gold?'

His face had a scar from the corner of his mouth to one eye. And a new scar – he was wearing a clean cap to cover a bandage.

I knew him then. He was the Hospitaller knight I'd met when I was about to flee London.

Richard was still hesitant. I wasn't. I had prayed, and this was what God offered me.

'I'll take you past the worst of it,' I said. 'I'll get you clear of the Auxerre.'

The priest – my eyes went to his right hand, and on it burned a ring – a red jewel with an eight-pointed cross, and the ring was on a hand with the swollen knuckles and scarred fingers of a swordsman. He wasn't just a priest. But I knew that now.

He nodded. 'God bless you,' he said. 'I am Fra Peter.'

That's what comes of praying.

Richard was adamant. 'You go,' he said. 'I'm going to take the convoy.'

We looked at each other for a moment, having switched roles too dramatically not to notice the change. Richard was going to raise a company of adventure to sack a church convoy, and I was going to escort nuns.

'Why?' I asked.

Richard shrugged. 'The church has always been against the Prince,' he said. 'And they're rich. They're blood suckers, William. We can be rich.'

'Come with me,' I said.

Richard shook his head and wouldn't meet my eye. 'I misdoubt we can do both. Your man asked for you.'

I took his shoulder in my right hand. 'Richard, we talk about being better men ...'

Richard looked away, and then back into my eyes. 'You go do what's right for your sister,' he said. 'And so will I. I'll split whatever I take with you. If you want to turn the money down, fine, but this is our chance to be free of this crap. This endless shit.'

I thought about it for half an hour. Then went and found him at a table with two of the Hainaulters we preferred, because they had no ties to the Gascons. 'A word, Richard,' I said.

Musard rose and followed me.

'Better if I attack the convoy and you escort the nuns?' I asked.

Musard shook his head. 'No.' He smiled. 'But a damn courteous offer, brother.'

He didn't call me brother often. Nor embrace – he didn't like to be touched – but he threw his arms around me then.

We bought them a half-dozen Hainaulters for sixty florins – men we'd been with all summer, and knew. We made ten gold florins on the deal, and felt we'd done a good deed, as, in fact, we had.

I promised to lead them across the Bourc's territory. I thought I could do it, and leave Richard to prepare a small army for us. A Company of Adventure. The cardinal's convoy was crawling across France, and we wanted a piece of it. I thought I could be back before Richard marched. Richard did not.

But the priest – the knight, and I was sure he was a knight – needed me. And I was going to oblige him if it killed me.

It almost did.

The nuns were noblewomen – English noblewomen. They were, I think, in shock at the loss of their servants, who had been murdered. And as I heard their story, told in fits and starts, I realized that they seemed wrong, as nuns, because they were not demure. They were, both of them, women used to command. Shock, horror and violence only left them angry. Neither would tell me why they were crossing war-torn France.

The knight was from the Priory of St John at Clerkenwell, near London. That's where I'd seen him. He was a brother-knight of the Order of the Hospital. The same order that protected my sister.

God had spoken, indeed.

Still, I wondered what he was doing escorting two nuns and two monks across war-torn France. The nuns held him in high esteem and the monks leaped to obey him.

The man had not said anything, but it appeared, from what the monks said, that he had single handedly held off six routiers in an ambush that had killed their men-at-arms. I was used to men who bragged all day – bragged about the women they bedded, bragged about knife fights in taverns – yet this man didn't even show his weapons. He seldom smiled, and he never, that I saw, displayed temper. He was courteous to every soul he met, ready with a blessing, and he never cursed or blasphemed.

He was like a paladin from the chansons.

I worked very hard to please him.

We left the Angel an hour before first light. My Hainaulters were good men with good armour, and I took Sam Bibbo and John Hughes to scout and keep me alive. After the nuns were mounted, I led Fra Peter aside.

'My lord,' I began, and he put a steel-clad hand on my arm.

'Fra!' he said. 'Brother. I am not a party to human lordship.' Those words might have been said with false humility, but instead, they were said with something like humour. As if he found his own views amusing.

I bowed in the saddle. 'My, er, Fra. We have to cross territory held by a man – a man whom even the brigands hold to be evil. I intend to take you north—'

'We came from the north,' he said quietly.

I nodded. 'Yes, my lord. That is, Fra Peter. But there is, from here, but one road south, and the Bourc Camus lies astride it, with armed men on every river crossing. We need to go east along the great river first, and then we can pass through the eastern fringes of his territory with less risk.'

He had a short beard, and he ran his fingers through it and pursed his lips. 'Good,' he said.

'Fra, if the Bourc attacks us in force ...' I turned and looked at the two women. 'None of us should allow ourselves to be captured.'

'That is in God's hands, not mine,' he said. 'We must do our best. Beyond that – *Inshallah.*' He smiled, his dark eyes far away.

'He is a horrible, brutal man,' I insisted.

'When you say, "man", you include the horrible and the brutal,' Fra Peter said. 'We all bear the mark of sin.' He looked at me, and I felt myself judged. 'Will you ask about your sister, or have you forgotten her?' he asked suddenly.

Sweet Jesu, I'd been with them for half a day and a night and I hadn't asked. 'How ... how is she?'

Fra Peter smiled. It was a slow smile, full of grace, and it lit his face. 'She is a remarkable woman,' he said. 'Blessed by God.' He looked at me with his hard, soldier's eyes, and I was judged again.

He was starting to make me angry, pious bastard.

I led us north at a rapid pace. We turned along the lower Marne and crossed the river that marked the Bourc's boundary about eight leagues from his precious bridge.

The knight of the Order came and rode next to me. 'Tell me more about this Bourc,' he said.

'The Bourc Camus,' I said. 'He makes children into killers. He openly proclaims himself to be Satan's son come to earth. He brags of it.' I met the knight's eye. 'Nothing would please him more than to take a pair of nuns.'

The knight nodded. 'He won't take them,' he said. 'I chose you for a reason.'

Those words sat with me all day, I can tell you.

That night, under an autumn moon, and with a hard frost burning like white fire along the ground, I kept them moving. The English nuns were fine horsewomen, and too brave to grumble, but the monks were not. Despite which, we trotted across barren, burned fields with the cold orb of the moon high in the sky above us.

Sometime after the moon set, we saw movement to our right, in the high ground, where there were two fires. But I caught no sounds and saw no glint of reflected light, so we rode on in silence punctuated only by the rattle of armour and the jingle of horse harness.

I was very afraid, and I saw my fear as a penance and I revelled in it.

I have known drunkards who have stopped drinking and thieves who have stopped stealing. I've listened to their stories in convents and monastaries, and we all share this. You do not know what the bottom is until you have started to climb out of it.

It was a long dark night, and I didn't lose my nerve, even when the first crossbow bolt snapped across the frozen air in front of Alexander.

Two years of petty war had taught me that, in a small party, the only possible response to ambush is to attack the ambush. I'm sure that this habit would eventually have seen me dead, but as a doctrine, it was as good as anything produced by the scholars at the University of Paris.

I flipped the visor on my basinet down and put spurs to Alexander. I got my lance couched, identified a crossbowman kneeling in the ditch by the road and went for him.

He decided he could get his weapon spanned. He was brave and determined, and so were his fellows – four more brigands in black and white. They were in the ditch on a long curve, so that they had 300 paces of clear shot.

I had almost 200 paces to ride, and my brute of a horse wasn't very fast.

The Hospitaller knight was coming up on my shield side. I couldn't see the Hainaulters and had to hope they were covering the nuns and monks, because ambushes usually had two parts.

One of the crossbowmen got spanned. He hesitated a moment, his eyes wild, his head jerking back and forth between me and the Hospitaller. I was in armour, however poor, while the Hospitaller was in a long brown gown.

The boy shot the brown gown.

He *missed*.

Fra Peter struck the four of them the way a hammer strikes an anvil. In two breaths, he had landed blows on each of them and they lay in their blood. His horse kicked in two directions.

I reined in, my sword unbloodied.

The Hospitaller dismounted. He knelt by each corpse and prayed. The third man moved and the knight pinned him gently and opened his clothes, after checking and shriving the fourth.

'He's alive,' Fra Peter said and began to explore the man's wounds.

The man. The boy. The brigand was perhaps fifteen.

I watched him carefully – the boy – and when he went for the basilard at his belt, I stepped ungently on his hand.

Fra Peter looked at the hand, took the dagger and shook his head.

'You may as well just kill him,' I said. 'He won't talk. He's old enough that he's been one of the Bourc's killers for two or three years.'

'He has a soul, and free will,' Fra Peter said. 'As do you.'

He was bandaged, tied and then tied to a saddle. I stood in angry silence. I was intelligent enough to know that Fra Peter had just equated me with one of the Bourc's child-brigands.

A day's ride saw us south of the Bourc's territory. At each halt, the knight fed the boy and paid him no more heed. He took him away to defecate and brought him back, red with shame.

He was *good*, but he was also a clever, dangerous man. I saw what he was doing to the boy. He gave the boy nothing. The boy had nowhere to perform. No torture to resist. No statement to ignore. The knight's complete disinterest was very clever.

We camped that night by a rushing torrent that was, thankfully, only ten paces wide. I crossed with John Hughes and we built a good fire and dried our clothes, then built a pair of brush shelters facing the fire, and hiding most of it, a tactic we'd learned from the bloody Gascons. By the time the main party rode up, we had hot water in kettles and Sam Bibbo was already high on the ridge above us, signalling the all-clear with a mirror.

Fra Peter dismounted, and very carefully picketed and curried his horse. His war sword, which he mostly carried on his saddle and not on his belt, was more than four feet long. I hadn't seen many swords as long or as sharp. The point was elongated, like a cook's skewer, and fatter at the point – reinforced for piercing armour. He allowed me to examine it with an amused raise of the eyebrows.

I emulated him and curried my brute of a gelding. I seldom did – horses had become mere tools since Goldie – but I was under his spell, and even as I resented him, I sought his favour.

Sam came in in the last of the light, by which time my Hainaulters and I had woven a hordle – a fence of brush – to block the wind and hide the fire from prying eyes to the north. Then we gathered round the fire and got warm. The nuns served wine – I was surprised – and the Hainaulters, who were for the most part men as hard as me, all muttered their thanks and searched their memories for the manners they should show to noble women. And nuns.

Fra Peter walked away from the fire.

'Where are you going?' I asked. 'The Bourc's men may be out there and we need to set a watch.'

Fra Peter nodded. 'Of course. I will be happy to take a turn. In the meantime, I intend to kneel. And pray. You are welcome to join me.'

I must have flushed.

He put a hand on my arm. 'It is easy to resist change,' he said. 'It is easy to wall God out of your heart. But I sense that you want something more than life as a killer. What do you think about, when you contemplate your life? What do you want – beyond gold?'

I couldn't meet his eye. 'I want to be a knight,' I said. 'But I am not sure what that means.'

He nodded. 'Come and pray. Let me show you how.'

'I know how to pray,' I shot back. 'And you? *Brother*? When you killed those three men today, were you *holier*?'

He led me two more steps away from the fire. 'I am not holy,' he said. 'Listen, boy. And I call you boy, because that is what you are. Listen, *boy*. When we take our vows, they ask us, would we take the cross if we knew that in killing, we risk hell? So that other, weaker men and women might achieve salvation?' His dark eyes cut me like blades. 'If I risk hell, killing the enemies of the church, what are you?'

'Damned!' I spat, like the angry boy he called me. 'I don't care.'

He shrugged. 'It is the ultimate defence, is it not? Indifference.' He shrugged again. And smiled. 'Listen, William. Will you allow me to teach you to pray?'

'*Paternoster, qui es in Caelis, santificatur . . .*' I began.

He laughed. 'That isn't prayer,' he said. 'That's repetition.'

Despite my anger – the kind of anger young men achieve mostly through understanding their own shortcomings – he had me. I was curious. I wanted his regard.

I wanted to change, too.

'Can you see pictures in your head, William?' he asked me.

I suppose I shrugged. 'What kind of pictures?' I asked.

'Can you see your sister?' he asked. 'Look into the darkness and close your eyes. See your sister.'

'This is praying?' I asked.

'Do you see your sister?' he asked.

'Yes,' I admitted. Truth to tell, I was horrified by how hazy my visual memory of my sister was.

'What is your favourite scene in the Bible, William?' he asked.

'Epiphany,' I said. 'The gifts of the magi.'

'Splendid,' he said with real satisfaction. His pleasure relaxed me. 'Can you imagine the blessed Virgin?' he asked.

I discovered, to my horror, that the blessed Virgin bore a striking resemblence to Emile.

'See her, in a lowly stable, surrounded by animals, William. With the newborn Christ child on her knee.' He was speaking quietly. I was simply obeying. As he imagined the scene for me, I obediently filled in the details.

'Now, can you see the magi? The three kings?' he asked.

I added them.

'And their retinues. They are, after all, kings.' There was gentle humour in his voice.

I added men rapidly: Sir John Chandos, sitting on his horse, and Sam Bibbo, on his. Sir John Hawkwood and Bertrand du Guesclin. It was an odd, mixed set of retinues, and my three kings looked very much like the Black Prince, the Dauphin and Charles of Navarre.

'Now put yourself there, William,' he said.

And there I was. With snow on the ground, and a bite in the air, and the rattle of horse-tack and the feel of fur at my throat. The virgin's crown and halo were a glow of gold past my Prince's shoulder, and my horse fidgeted.

'Can you see the Christ child?' Fra Peter asked.

I could not. I tried to push forward, but all the men in front of me – all the better knights – blocked my view. I realized that I was far at the back, and that I had a wall of famous men between me and the Christ child.

I made to dismount ...

... And Fra Peter was holding me up. I was swaying in the darkness, my eyes unfocused and his arm was around my waist.

'So,' he said. His teeth showed in the new moonlight. 'You are your sister's brother.'

'That is prayer?' I asked.

He blinked. 'To those who can achieve it,' he said. 'You will leave us in the morning?'

'I must,' I said. But I was wondering if I shouldn't simply ride away and follow Fra Peter.

'You should sleep,' he said.

Indeed, I was so shaken I couldn't think.

'Try,' he said. 'Try the prayer, when you can. I will be in Avignon for a long time. Come and see me there.'

'And my sister?' I asked.

'Needs her dowry. But in truth, young master, your sister is better at seeing to her needs than you are to yours. You should visit her.' He shrugged. 'Will you accept my blessing?' he asked.

I bowed my head.

When he had pronounced his benison, he said, 'You intend to attack the convoy.'

'Yes,' I said. 'No. Now I don't know.'

He nodded. 'Go with God,' he said. 'See where he takes you.'

The next morning he rode away, with his noble nuns, his two angry monks, his boy-soldier prisoner and six fully armed Hainaulters. I watched them until they were gone at the base of the valley.

'I liked him,' Sam said.

'Me too,' I allowed.

I thought about it all, silently, for the fifteen leagues of the ride back across the Bourc's territory. Sam and John rode by me. We were as cautious as men crossing enemy territory in broad daylight can be.

The ground was frozen, and we cut across fields, through hedge-rows and over old stone fences, but often we had to go on the road.

We saw no black and white.

I came to the Bourc's bridge from behind – from the Bourc's side. Sam and I scouted it carefully, hearts hammering in our chests.

There were four men in a blind of branches, upwind of the bridge. Two were asleep and two awake. We were above and behind them, and Sam crept forward from cover to cover. I watched him from above as he went – an hour to move fifty paces.

I thought I was going to throw up. The tension was not my kind of tension. I prefer to be in the thick of it. I loved Sam Bibbo, and at another level, I'd saved him from the Plague, or whatever the hell he'd had, and he represented ... something. Something good.

I didn't want him to die.

It was an education in stalking, watching him cover ground. Twice, *I lost him*, despite staring right at him from fifty paces away.

Finally, he rose to his feet with a slow inevitability. He had his bow in his hand, string, and four arrows in his fingers.

He drew and loosed so fast I scarcely followed the first shaft. I saw him draw the second to his ear, but I didn't see him loose it, because I was on my feet and running for the Bourc's men.

I might have saved my strength.

They had two crossbows cocked and ready, and neither of them ever left the blind, where they were pointed at the road. The four went down in five shafts. One died in his sleep.

When we went back to the road, John pointed mutely at the hillside behind us. He had a shaft in his own hand and he used it to point to a place on the hillside where a tree was dead.

Bibbo winced.

'What?' I asked.

John Hughes sucked in his cheeks and spat. 'There's a watch post to cover the rear of the one you heroes just stalked,' he said. 'It's empty or we'd all be dead.'

We walked up the hill and looked at it. It had a hut, a pair of watch posts with woven branches and screens of brush, a firepit and the corpses of a young girl and a young boy.

'Christ,' Bibbo said. 'I missed all this?' He shook his head.

'Let's get out of here,' John said. The corpses spooked him more than our poor scouting.

I followed some tracks outside and came to another clearing, this one with hoof prints.

I shook my head. I went back and put my hand on the ashes of the firepit.

'They were just here.' I scratched under my chin in thought, and Jesus my saviour vanished. 'They've gone for the convoy, with every man they have,' I said.

Bibbo nodded. 'That's it,' he agreed.

'Let's ride,' I said.

Hughes paused. 'Give me two Ave Marias,' he said, and disappeared into the woods.

I knew he was gone to fire the huts and the corpses. I was tempted to stop him, because it would warn the Bourc, but I also realized that if the Bourc turned back from his attack on the convoy, Richard would be safe.

We made the gate of our town alive and untouched, and I got to the inn to find that Richard had marched.

I got a nag for a riding horse, to spare my war horse, such as he was, the brute. Sam and John followed me as we rode at day's end with three horses apiece, searching east along the valley for the convoy and our friends.

Perkin was at the inn. He said that Richard had gathered almost sixty men – thirty lances, almost two dozen Gascon spearmen, and a pair of English archers who belonged to Sir Robert Knolles but didn't have anything better to do. Sixty men should have been easy to find.

We rode hard until the moon set, and then made a cold camp. A camp on the edge of November in the Auxerre highlands is cold indeed. No fire, no warmth except your horse. And it is brutal on horses, even horses like ours. We drank wine and rubbed our steeds down – even the nags.

An hour after the last horse was picketed, there was a noise. We jumped up to the maddened chaos of our horses and saw wolves. They were gone before we could kill one.

Sam shook his head. 'I'm going to watch,' he said. 'I ain't sleeping anyway.'

John and I pressed as close as we could. I slept for an hour, I think.

Sam woke us. He dismounted and gave his horse to Perkin, who had disobeyed me and started a very small fire and heated wine. God praise such a man.

Sam pulled the saddle off his poor hack. He set it on the ground, threw his three-quarter cloak over it and sat back with a groan.

'Well?' I asked.

'The Bourc's men are out there. I spotted them down by the river – black and white banners.' He shrugged. 'That's one device I know in the dark, eh? I'm guessing he's going to stop the convoy and charge them a toll.'

'Any idea where?' I asked.

'No,' he said. 'But John needs to get going and keep an eye on Camus.' He nodded at Perkin, who handed him a beaker of hot wine. 'Benidictee, lad. Master Gold, this is my last fight. I mean to do my part, but when we divide the spoil, I'm done.'

What could I say?

Sam Bibbo was a more famous man than me. He'd been at all the fights. He'd been down and up – famous, a criminal, a royal archer. He didn't need to follow the likes of me, but his presence meant that other men took me seriously.

'I'll miss you, Sam,' I said.

He nodded, looking into the fire. 'John Hughes will stay, won't you, lad?' he asked.

Hughes, already rolling his cloak on his saddle, grunted.

'He likes the life,' Sam said.

'Bollocks to you, Sam Bibbo,' Hughes called softly.

Bibbo ignored him. 'My bones hurt every morn, and my back – by the saviour, Will, I'd rather spend a night in the saddle than a night lying out on the ground.' He looked at me. 'And the Bourc – when men like that come to the fore, it's bad. I served with Chandos and the Prince. Remember the man you killed in the tavern? He liked to hurt people. I should never have fallen in with him, either.'

I nodded, the way young men do when older men talk about pain. It's the same way boys nod when men talk about sex. I had no idea what pains he meant.

Of course, now I do, eh?

But I was cut by his words. 'Are you comparing me to the Bourc?' I asked.

He shrugged. 'I was glad you helped yon priest,' he said. 'You're ten times the man the Bourc is. But will you be in ten years of this?'

We rose while there was still mist in the streambeds and we rode hard. John was gone before first light, off to watch the Bourc's banners, and Sam, Perkin and I rode north and west, looking to find Richard.

But the Black Squire had moved at first light, too.

Bibbo sat on his horse, looking at the tramped ground and drowned fire, and cursed. 'I should ha' just ridden in and told him.' He shook his head. 'But, Plague take me, I wasn't *sure*, and I didn't want a spear in my gizzard in the dark.'

'Nothing for it,' I said, and changed horses. So did Sam and Perkin. We rode into the fog.

An hour after the fog began to lighten, we heard movement – quite a lot of movement. The brilliant fog was so thick that we couldn't see much beyond our horse's noses, and dripping wet. I reined in, and Sam rode forward.

He came back and shook his head. 'Unbelievable they've made it as far as they have,' he said. 'There's gold tack on some of the *mules*. It's two fucking *cardinals. Twenty men-at-arms*. He shook his head.

'The three of us aren't likely to take them. We need to find Richard,' I said. My nerves were getting to me. The fog, the Bourc, the church convoy. .

I could see the disaster coming. Even Sam's determination to leave.

I dismounted from my horse in the dripping fog, knelt on the wet grass and prayed.

And then I rose and took three deep breaths. In my head, just as I could *see*, however dimly, the virgin Mary, so I could see the lay of this valley, with its broad flats at the base, its sharp angle halfway to the town of Guye, and the road along the flat. I could *see* the hedges along the heights, and the stone walls that crisscrossed the ruined fields.

If it was me, I'd hit the column where the Bourc was. At the narrowing of the flats.

If I was Richard, I'd be on the other side of the ridge, waiting for the fog to clear so that my Gascons and archers would be effective.

Bless Fra Peter. Looking at things inside my head is a habit I received from him, for good or ill.

'I believe that the Black squire is on the other side of the ridge, above the fog, shadowing the convoy,' I said.

Bibbo nodded. 'Good,' he said. 'Yes!' he added with a little more excitement. 'I see sense in that. We ha'n't crossed their tracks – that much I'd swear to.'

'On me,' I said, and mounted with an effort. My hips didn't love a night on cold ground, even at the age of nineteen.

We rode carefully. The fog carried noise oddly – snatches of Avignon gossip, the shrill voice of a man who clearly thought himself in charge, an angry imprecation and a squeaky wagon wheel.

Then, as suddenly as the parting of a curtain, we rode clear of the fog. We moved as swiftly up the ridge as we could. Sam was ahead of me – he came to a gap in the hedge and stopped.

So did my heart.

Then he waved, and a broad smile crossed his face.

And in fifty paces, I was with Richard. He grinned and pounded my armoured back.

'They're right below us!' he said. 'What?'

'The Bourc is just to the south, at the Narrows,' I said. 'With half a hundred men, or more.'

Richard paused.

'We found one of his camps deserted. His whole area is deserted. Even the castle he holds for Knolles is empty. He's after the convoy.'

Richard looked at me.

Richard Musard and I have fought over most of the things men fight over – women, loyalty, even money – but in some ways, we were two men with but a single will. He looked at the fog.

'The Bourc will hit the convoy whatever we do,' I said.

He smiled, and his smile spread until it covered his whole face.

'And then – we *save* them.' Richard shook his head. 'Kill the Bourc, save the bishop—'

'Sam says it is a cardinal,' I put in.

Richard laughed aloud. 'By God. By God. We'll be knights in a week!'

I agreed. It all seemed like God's will.

We had sixty men. We put all of them behind the ridge that lines the edge of the Seine, above the road, and we moved fast – at a canter – along the ridge top to our new position, which depended on my sense of the ground. I sent Sam and half a dozen of our Gascon bidets down into the valley to watch for John Hughes, while keeping a weather eye on Camus and the convoy.

As I've said before, waiting in ambush is one of the hardest things a soldier does. The waiting always seems to go on for ever. There's lots of room for doubt – in fact, it's a rare ambush where I don't decide I've made an awful error.

But the two cardinals and their convoy moved across Auxerre with the reckless assurance of a drunken soldier who has just been paid. They were as brazen as an old whore, and just as well-defended.

John Hughes appeared out of the mist before we heard the convoy. He laid it all out for us – twenty men-at-arms, the number of mules, where the two great men were – in some detail. He added that there were seventy mules, ten horses and six wagons.

'Have you seen Sam?' I asked.

'He's watching the Bourc,' Hughes said. 'Bastard is moving along the valley.'

Tricky.

'He wants you to let the Bourc hit the cardinals first,' Hughes added.

Richard grunted. 'We couldn't stop him anyway.' Richard looked at me. 'Two cardinals? This will make us famous,' he said.

I suppose I shrugged.

He shook his head. 'I don't like fighting for the church.'

'Sit here if you don't want to come,' I said. 'But I mean to have a piece of the Bourc.'

'For that, I'll join you,' he said.

We moved along the ridge top, out of the mist and with good visibility for leagues. We moved carefully, watching and listening for the cardinal's train at the bottom of the valley.

The mist burned off about an hour after a working man would have gone to his fields, if there had been anyone left to till the fields of the Auxerre, which there was not. As soon as the mist became transparent, the Bourc struck, his men-at-arms crashing through the riverside brush, panicking the pack animals and killing several of the papal men-at-arms in their first charge.

I brought my men up to the ridgeline and formed them. Men were still coming up and I needed every straggler. We sent our Gascon javelin men down the gullies. They moved like the cattle-thieves they were, silent and almost invisible.

I saw the Bourc's banner advance, and advance again. His men ripped into the pack animals, killing many of them outright. They opened every load, destroying manuscripts and textiles, chopping things like chalices and icons into pieces for the precious metal.

A month before, I might have done the same. But watching it was – different. And I hated the Bourc.

As the sun rose toward nones, my men reached their positions. The looters were like vultures and raven on a kill – gorging, with no notion of danger.

I looked at Richard, and he smiled and slammed down his visor.

We both raised our hands.

Our men-at-arms came forward at a canter. The bidets rose as one from their ambush and threw their darts at the horses of the Bourc's men-at-arms, and my four English archers – all four of them at widely different points, standing in good cover with their arrows laid out before them – began to rain shafts on Camus' troopers.

I hadn't made a detailed plan of attack, but Richard and I knew our business; the archers were veterans of a hundred fights and as many hunts, and the Gascons, as far as I could tell, made war for sport.

Which meant, unfortunately, that the enemy Gascons knew what to do when ambushed.

The Bourc didn't hesitate. His banner dipped once, and his men dropped the loot in their hands or scooped one more chalice into the leather bags they all carried, then they were charging down the road, low on their horses, with the lesser armed men behind. There were three or four horses down, and the javelin men were gathering in clumps to finish the dismounted riders or take them for ransom. The longbow arrows continued to reap horses. At least one shaft – probably one of Sam's – caught a poorer man-at-arms in the unarmoured back and plucked him from the saddle.

Richard led our men-at-arms at his men-at-arms. I was already half a league off to the right, behind the fight as it developed below me, but I pressed my brute of a horse to a heavy gallop and rumbled along through a meadow of drying flowers that had recently been a monastery's largest ploughed field. The Bourc was an evil bastard and I suspected he'd have another force. Perkin and I were all the reserve I had.

Camus saw Richard and turned towards him and his men followed. The two bands of men-at-arms were nearly equal in size, but Richard had the hill behind him. I thought it was all going well until a troop of horsemen in armour emerged from the road to the south. They were as far behind me as I was behind the fight. I stood in my stirrups, annoying my horse by trying to gallop while looking back over my cantle.

There they were, confirming my fears.

Gascons or Navaresse. A reserve – a blocking force behind the convoy, in case any of the rich priests tried to run.

It's quite hard to count from the back of a galloping horse, but my impression was that there were as many armoured men coming up behind me as were ahead of me.

Gascons. They have no compunction about killing each other.

I knew where one of the archers was and I was going to pass his lair, so I rode down the meadow to the low stone wall and put my horse at it – not out of any desire to show my riding, but because I had no time to find a gate.

He tried to baulk.

I pricked him with both spurs. I wasn't losing the Bourc this time.

He rose like an old cat and his hooves struck the wall – a wall no higher than my knees. We were over, and I was on the road. I knew arrows had come from here. I pulled on my reins and saw an apiary – abandoned, of course. 'John!' I roared.

It wasn't John it was Sam. He appeared from the trees.

'More men – behind me on the road. Slow them!' I called. I had a moment's hesitation – it was Sam's last fight and I was ordering him to cover our rear.

He waved and went back to the trees.

I got my horse back to a massive canter and headed north along the riverbank.

The fight on the hillside was about 200 heartbeats old by the time I rode around the woods – a mêlée that was already spreading across the hillside. The Bourc's men were holding – I assumed they were so bold because they knew they had reinforcements coming.

And a fortune in gold hanging in bags from their saddles.

I put my horse's head at the Bourc's banner and lowered my lance. Getting the lance into the rest was no longer the struggle it had been for me in the early days. Nobly born boys did this from age eight or nine, and I hadn't started until fifteen or sixteen, but I was improving. I got my lance down, flipped my visor down with my left hand and tried to line my lance point up with the Bourc's banner-bearer. I couldn't find the bastard himself.

It is hard to see from inside a basinet. Until I closed my visor, I had some appreciation of the battlefield. Once I closed it, I could see one opponent. There's a lesson there somewhere.

The strictest interpretation of the rules of war would have said I should have shouted or announced myself, as I was riding into the Gascons from behind, but I made a different choice. I hit the banner-bearer in the middle of his back and probably killed him instantly – my lance broke under his weight as he went off his mount – and the Bourc's black and white standard went down.

There was an immediate reaction.

I got my longsword out of the scabbard and looked again for the Bourc. He was nowhere to be seen. I could see Richard, locked in mounted combat with one of the Albret bastards, and I could see several coats of arms I knew, but most of the Bourc's men wore his black and white, and any of them could have been the man himself.

The fight came to me. I felt the thunder of my opponent's approach in time to duck, almost to my horse's neck, and his sword cut just touched my helmet – I had a glimpse of his black and white cote, and then I was sawing at the reins left handed, trying to get around. My brute of a horse didn't like my idea and was, in fact, turning the opposite way, so that my opponent got a free cut at my back. I swear I felt the blow before it hit – I knew where it was and I knew there was nothing I could do to stop it, and all because I had a poor horse.

He cut when he should have stabbed, so my backplate took the blow low, near the kidney – I pissed blood for days – and he must have taken a bit off the high back of my saddle, then I was around and our horses were flank to flank. I got my blade up and caught his – our cross guards locked. He had no visor, and I backhanded him in the face with my left gauntlet. Blood sprayed, and he fell back – his sword fell away from mine, and I stabbed twice, in rapid succession, as he tried to back his horse. My first stab caught his helmet and slid off, but the second went into his cheek and through the roof of his mouth, and he was done.

Then I was in the thick of a mounted mêlée. I'd never been in one before. Blows fell on my head and shoulders – my head was snapped around by a heavy blow, and I was shoved forward over the front of my saddle. I had just enough courage and spirit to snap back with my sword – short stabs with the point. I buried my blade in a horse's unprotected neck, and horse and rider fell, and I thought, Jesu, I've put three of them down! Where is everyone?'

I leaned back against my saddle – my back shrieked in pain and I got my blade over my head and caught a mace coming in. My new opponent pressed, and I hammered him with the pommel of my sword – he drove the butt of his mace into my throat, and I got my left hand onto his visor and forced it up. I lost the visor.

We both fell from our horses together. I assume the two horses separated, leaving their human cargoes to fall, but before I even felt my brute's change of weight, I was down and lost my sword.

He didn't lose his mace, he swung it at me.

I got my dagger free – got it in both hands and parried.

See? De Charny's dagger. I knew you gentlemen would want to see it. Three sided-solid steel, forged from a single piece. I've stopped a poleaxe with this; I've used it as a crow-bar in a burning building. It's not so much a blade as a bar of steel with a point.

I got it in both hands, and he swung and I stopped the mace, then I got his wrist in my own left hand. He let go with his right and slammed me in the head, rocking me back, then he was trying to get atop me, but I had his right arm, now, in my left. He tried to pound at me with his left hand – my visor saved me and the dagger started searching his armour for a weak point. I rammed it up under his arm and his mail held – my point skidded off the cuisse protecting the top of his thigh.

He was still trying to get on top of me, to pin my arms with his knees. His steel-clad limbs looking for anything soft – between my legs, under my arms.

But I had his right arm, and my left hand made it to his neck – a basic wrestling lock that any English boy knows.

I rolled him and broke his arm.

He sagged immediately. The pain must have been like the kick of a mule, and I had him off me while he screamed. I knelt on his broken arm and pushed his visor up, and . . .

. . . It was the Bourc.

I won't say it was the finest moment of my young life – it doesn't quite rival Emile pulling her kirtle over her head – but by Christ it was good.

In retrospect, I should have killed him. But – here's the irony – I had begun to see myself, as it were, reflected in this evil man. He was beaten and wounded. Screaming in pain.

I didn't kill him.

Sometimes, the most moral decisions are the ones that cause everyone the most pain. Fra Peter taught me that, later.

I put him over his horse – what a struggle that was, and only Perkin's appearance, like the miracle machine in a passion play, saved me from dumping him on the ground as a bad job. Perkin got under him and pushed, then roped him to his fancy saddle. I managed to get back into my own saddle – some horses don't run away when you want them to.

Richard had just taken the older Albret boy.

Gaillard de la Motte – a good man, but at the time I barely knew him – was killing Camus' men who'd been dismounted. He rode over, waving a lance head covered in gore. 'They're not gentlemen,' he said, as if shocked. 'They're peasant boys dressed up like knights.'

So am I, I thought. Though I wasn't precisely a peasant, I still felt some sympathy for those boys.

Who were dying. Every one. My men were offering them no quarter, and now the survivors of the cardinal's men-at-arms were rallying and joining us, and *they* weren't offering quarter either.

I got my men-at-arms together by raising the Bourc's black and white banner and waving it. Richard roared his war cry, 'The Black Squire, the Black Squire!' Until we had a dozen mounted men, then we went back down the road. We left our squires and valets to plunder the enemy and find the gold.

We met the second force near the apiary. They had horses down, and they'd stopped to cover their wounded against the archers.

We blew right through them like falcons through a flock of song-birds, and they scattered. The fighting spread across the hillside, and then it was over – I don't think I went sword to sword with a single man.

I was focused on Sam Bibbo, who was standing in the road, loosing shaft after shaft at the Bourc's men-at-arms as if he was in some personal Crécy or Poitiers. I positioned my horse just behind him, sword in hand. I was sure – as sure as I'd ever been – that he would die, and I was determined to keep him alive. I even prayed.

I'm guessing that God had a chuckle at our expense. Sam didn't die. By the time the day was another hour older, we had a small fortune in gold, a dozen men-at-arms to ransom and only one man dead: a Gascon knight.

Late in the fight, as my Gascon mountaineers charged into the back of the mêlée on the hillside and started killing horses, I found that we'd migrated far enough west that we were in among the convoy. As de la Motte, his Hainaulters and our Gascons began to eliminate the last resistance, I found myself facing a cardinal. He had a long, ascetic face and a princely air, somewhat marred by a shrill voice.

'Child of Belial! Thou creature of hell!' he spat at me. 'To rob the church! What is thy name, creature, that I may curse thee to the base of the pit of hell?'

I reined in and raised my visor. 'Eminence,' I said. 'I believe our timely appearance has—'

'Curse you and your kind!' he screamed.

He was the Cardinal of Périgueux – Tallyrand. The most powerful man in Avignon. I met him again, as you'll hear if you keep my cup filled.

He was not afraid. By God, he should have been, but his sense of his own power was absolute, and I could not get through to him. He began to say aloud the words of the sentence of excommunication.

'My lord!' I screamed. *'We saved you.'*

He struck me with the sceptre in his hand.

Richard Musard took my reins and hauled my horse around. 'I do not think we'll be made knights this day,' he said quietly. 'They think we're the Bourc's men.' He thrust out his jaw – something he only did when he was angry.

Our men were lusty and loud as we turned our horses toward Champlay.

We rode back to Champlay and handed all our prisoners to Sir Walter. If I had considered handing the looted gold back to the church – and I did consider it – those thoughts were wiped away.

I remember that night, too. There are few treats as fine as feasting after victory. I tied the Bourc to a chair and then piled the gold coins – English leopards, French ecu, Italian florins and ducats – on the table. We had twenty-seven men-at-arms, four English archers and twenty Gascon mountaineers. We counted the archers as full shares and the Gascon spearmen as half shares, and everyone was satisfied. Some of the Gascons felt we might have done better to take the princes of the church and hold them for ransom, but such things weren't done. Not yet. Not by us.

Richard and I drew double shares, as it was our *aventur*. I made 240 florins in cash, with a lot of gold bits, an ivory crucifix, a nice set of black onyx beads and a small reliquary, somewhat knocked about. I won that over dice that night.

Richard had taken the elder Albret bastard. We kept him, and the Bourc, as they were worth money, and we kept their horses and armour. I sold the Bourc's horse for a hundred Florins the next day, and my own horse for thirty – make your own judgements on their merits – and I spent the whole sum on a single horse, another golden-tawny horse, rising sixteen hands, with clean legs and a pretty head. He wasn't Goldie, but he was calm and smart, and I called him Jack. I was done giving horses romantic names. I liked Jack. Best of all, Jack liked me.

Young Albret, our prisoner, announced when I returned from a ride over the fields that he didn't want to go back to serving Camus. His voice trembled when he said it.

Richard called me over. Albret was seated between Sam and John, and he was panting like a man who'd fought in the lists an hour. His eyes were full of tears.

'You won't believe this!' Richard said.

Camus was conscious, and he sat at a table, tied to the chair. He watched us like a snake.

Albret pointed at him. 'Take him away. He says he is Satan come to earth!'

Camus grinned.

Sam went and hoisted his arm behind him – his broken arm – and hauled him upstairs. He locked the Bourc in a room and left him with two black eyes and a broken right hand. I hadn't been there to hear what the other men heard, but I gather it was pretty bad.

The Bourc caught boys young and made them monsters, like him. He had boys rape their sisters. He had them fight each other – to the death.

He kept the survivors and made them his own.

The Albret boy was terrified of him, and believed that he really was a servant of Satan come to earth.

Sam returned, sickened. 'I shouldn't have done that,' he said. 'He makes me sick.'

Later in the morning, Sir Walter came and took the Bourc away. He was an important man in some circles, and too important for men-at-arms like us to string him up.

In our inn yard, he turned to me – two black eyes, broken arm, broken hand – and smiled. 'Don't let me catch you,' he said. 'You know nothing of what I can do to a man. You are weak. I am strong.' He laughed. 'You can't even kill me.'

He was still laughing when he went out the gate.

By my reckoning, I could have saved almost a thousand people by ramming this dagger into his eye.

Sam took his time in leaving us. He stayed for a while because of a girl, and then he stayed because we launched a series of raids on the broken remnants of the Bourc's band – of course, Knolles' men weren't supposed to make war on each other, but that was France in 1359. We took their territory and made it ours, collected their *patis* from the handful of surviving peasants, and blessed St John, they were a beaten and pitiful lot. One dark night in November, we crept up on the Bourc's town of Malicorne. We'd built scaling ladders that we could assemble on the spot, and we put them to the wall and stormed the place.

There were about a dozen of his 'children' and some other broken men. We put them to the sword and felt better about ourselves. He now held nothing – he would return from his captivity, or wherever he was, to nothing.

I took my ready money to the Italian vultures and paid it toward my sister's dowry. Maestro Giancarlo was kind enough – and he was much less of a bastard than the others – to point out that I was more than halfway to my goal.

Beyond the Auxerre, the world was moving around us. King Edward landed with a magnificent army and sat down to besiege Reims, which had somehow staved off the Earl of Lancaster in the year after Poitiers. The King of Navarre met with the Dauphin and surrendered to him. To this day, no one knows why. There's those that say he felt he could hurt the cause of the Dauphin more from inside the government, and there's those that say the bastard was so steeped in betrayal that he betrayed himself. But while Navarre took himself out of the war, his captains continued to fight in his name, even after he ordered them to cease – like Knolles and his brother Phillip – and the Bourc, who we heard was free and raising another force in Gascony. We never had a mouton for him – Sir Robert Knolles ruled that our capture of the bastard was against the laws of war.

As I've said, I should have killed him.

The King of England moved towards Paris in three great columns. The Captain of Troissy, one of Sir Robert's most trusted men, Nicholas Tamworth, arrived at Chantay to raise a field force for an *aventur* in Burgundy. He promised fresh fields and untouched country.

He stayed in our inn, drank our wine and slept with our girls. He was a careful planner, and he sent a dozen men north into Burgundy to find a castle that was strong enough to be held, and vulnerable enough to be taken by escalade, without a siege.

He flattered us, me and Richard, a great deal. And he offered to make us corporals – commanders of a dozen lances.

Messieurs, I want you to understand. Richard and I, we wanted something better. We had *tried* to do something well, to act from conviction. And the cardinal branded us felons and published our names at Avignon as traitors to Mother Church. My name! In a scroll against the 'criminals who serve Satan'! While the Bourc went free!

By our saviour, messieurs, we had some dark days. Tamworth seemed to offer us salvation. We'd been feasting him for two days when Geoffrey Chaucer rode through the inn yard, dismounted and yelled for wine.

We didn't kill him. Firstly, we'd shared too many hard times, and second, it was clear from his beautiful boots and his fine cote that he was a man of some importance – and Tamworth treated him like a lord.

Richard spat with indignation. 'He serves the King! While we fight for scraps!'

As it proved, he served Prince Lionel of Clarence, and we had hundreds of gold florins in bags at our Italian bank. But we both attributed our fall from the Prince's grace to Chaucer, and he did nothing to dispel our anger. In fact, he pranced about our inn, demanding clean linen and sneering at everything – the girls, the wine, the cleanliness.

He sat with Tamworth for two hours, drawing on the table in wine, and then he slept a few hours, mounted a girl and tossed a few coins to one of the boys. He tried to avoid me, but I caught him in the barn. He was saddling his horse.

'Don't touch me,' he said. 'I'm a royal messenger.'

I leaned against the stall. 'Richard was your friend,' I said. 'I don't mind you treating me like a leper. But Richard?'

He had the good grace to look abashed, but he kept saddling his horse. 'What was I to do?' he asked. 'Lie for you? The Prince's sénéchal – one of your regular customers, may I add – blabbed, and you were done.'

I grabbed his shoulder.

He cringed away and drew his dagger. 'I know what men like you do,' he said. 'I hate all of you. By God, if you touch me, I'll see to it the Prince has you quartered.'

'I'm not going to hurt you,' I said. 'I want to know why you burned us. What have we done to hurt you?'

He spat. 'You make me feel dirty,' he said.

'This from a fucking spy?' I asked.

'Spy?' he asked.

'Didn't you just bring Tamworth his orders from the King?' I asked.

He was pulling his horse out of the stall by the bridle. 'Not your place to ask,' he said.

'Perhaps I don't have the need to know?' I asked.

'Why don't you go kill some peasants?' he said.

'For the King?' I asked. 'Or Good Prince Lionel?'

He mounted. 'Keep your foul mouth shut,' he spat, and rode out our gate.

The Constable of France picked him up a few hours later and ransomed him. I had nothing to do with it.

We went into Burgundy. We had sixty men-at-arms and as many archers, and Sam was still with us. We had regular lances by then, as I remember, so Sam was my archer and Perkin was my page. He was sixteen now, and still very small, but I had him in a good haubergeon, a fine steel helmet from Milan and steel gloves. He still seemed to know everything.

Richard had his own fighting page – more like a squire – named Gwillam, a Welch boy who'd come with the Cheshire men and somehow washed up with us. And we had a pair of Irish horse-boys, too – also the flotsam of the King's army. They were Seamus and Kenneth, and they were big, they could ride anything, and they loved to fight – like Gascons, really.

As corporals, we each had a dozen lances – that is, a dozen men-at-arms, a dozen archers and a dozen armed pages or varlets. Each lance shared a fire and a tent. It was becoming a system – the boys entered as servants, grew to be armed pages and then graduated to be men-at-arms. The archers were getting thinner on the ground

– there were never really that many of them, and by the winter of '59, all the good ones were serving the King. All but Sam and John and a few hundred more like them. While we'd held Chantay against the Constable, Knolles had pushed south in Provence and been defeated – aye, it was a complicated year – and most of his good men deserted him.

I'm off my tale. We rode east and north into Burgundy, and we stormed the castle of Courcelles, which our archers had carefully scouted. It was deep inside Burgundy, and perfectly sighted to base raids. We took it in one assault – I was the first man on my ladder, and that was terrifying. I took a dose of hot sand all down my back, and it burned away all the leather straps on my old breast and back, but I got up the ladder, sent one Burgundian to the devil and the rest threw down their weapons.

Over the next three days we spread out like a plague. We took manor houses and small castles by storm, at night, killed the inhabitants and stripped the houses. We moved so fast that the locals couldn't organize a defence, and twice we caught the local baron's forces on the road, trying to intercept us, and beat them up. The second time, we took him prisoner – that's the Count of Semur. I sent him along to the Prince of Wales, whose column was nearest to us, with my compliments. I did it with every sign of chivalry, and I know the count found me a good captor as he said as much.

And then one of the Prince's squires rode in under a flag of truce and ordered Tamworth to cease making war in Burgundy under the pain of the Prince's displeasure. King Edward met with the Burgundians at Dijon – an hour away from us, may I add – and they paid him 200,000 moutons for a three-year truce.

We didn't see one mouton of it, and we'd done all the fighting. And messieurs, in case you've missed the point, this was royal war, not brigandage. Everything Tamworth did, he did on direct orders from King Edward. We were soldiers, not brigands – until the King disowned us.

To add to our ire, the Burgundians granted Courcelles – the castle I'd stormed – to Nicholas Tamworth. He kept a few men to hold it, but dismissed the rest of us.

And to crown it all, the Prince of Wales released my prisoner, the Count of Semur. Perhaps it suited his policy, but he stated to his council that the count had been taken 'by bandits, and not in a regular episode of war'.

As the last straw, the squire who came to order us to desist also informed me, and Richard, that we should not return to court or to England.

As a soldier, my fortunes had never looked better. Tamworth praised me to the skies, and said my exile from the Prince was all politics and that he'd 'look into it', but the continuing exile stuck in my craw. Twice in one autumn, I had performed a good feat of arms and been punished for it.

But even then, I might have stayed the course. I might have lasted out the exile.

Richard came into the house we shared and spat on the floor – something he never did. He collapsed onto a stool, stripped his helmet and aventail off his head before his Welshman could help, and hurled it at the walls so hard it broke the plaster and left a broad patch of willow lathe.

'God's curse on all of them,' he said.

Perkin handed him a cup of wine.

He looked at it for a while.

I put a hand on his shoulder. 'Don't fret, brother,' I said. 'Tamworth will see us right.'

He looked at me, and he didn't look like himself. He had bright colour in his dark cheeks, and his eyes sparkled as if he was mad. His eyes were wide like a young girl's.

'Nothing will see this right,' he spat.

'We've lived through all this before,' I said. 'We're good men-at-arms and they'll bring us back.'

'The Prince of Wales has just accepted the homage of the Bourc Camus,' he said. 'The Bourc is to be his liege man for Gascony and command part of his army.' Richard's eyes met mine. 'Think it through, *brother.*'

I was pleased when my men chose to come with me. When I went south to find Seguin de Badefol, I took with me ten men-at-arms, including de la Motte, and ten archers and pages, and Richard did just as well. We were moving up in the world – our own twisted world. Mind you, my armour was a patchwork of rust and old leather, and every fight had left its mark – my leg armour was more dirt and horse sweat than leather and iron. My fine basinet was brown.

The King of England moved away from Burgundy with his great army and settled down to the siege of Paris. The end was coming

– we all knew it. The Dauphin couldn't hold Paris for long, and Paris had already survived the Plague, the Commune, Etienne Marcel and the King of Navarre. There were no reserves in Paris.

Then the weather struck. King Edward had campaigned through the winter, and the weather had been merciful; his 'allies' in the companies had isolated Paris and Burgundy from the rest of France for the critical time. Even though he'd failed at Reims, he now had Paris under his hand, and he had, in one day of negotiations, knocked Burgundy out of the war.

All England needed was three weeks of decent weather.

Instead, we had three weeks that reminded everyone of the passages in the Bible about the flood that cleansed the earth and floated the ark. The English army was tired, and despite the King's political victories, men weren't getting rich and the army was too big to feed itself. When they sat down to the siege of Paris, they were sitting on land that the English and Navarrese companies, the Jacques and the French themselves had devastated for four years. If Paris had no reserves, the Isle de France was a desert.

Seguin de Badefol had offered to take our lances, and he was three days ride from Paris – he had a contract to serve directly under the Prince as Prince of Gascony, and he offered us good rates. We caught up with the Prince's forces at Gallardon. I saluted de Badefol – we'd been together several times – and bowed to Jean de Grailly, who promised to represent both of us to the Prince.

By my hope of heaven, I swear that the sky was blue. We could just see the towers of Paris, then a black cloud swept in from the north like the hand of God, and in the time it takes a swift man to run a league, it was dark as late afternoon and driving rain fell, and a great wind blew. The road turned instantly to mud and the carts stuck. Then the rain turned to hail, the temperature fell and things froze. Horses died. Men were soaked through their jupons, the heavy garments holding the freezing water against their skin, and night fell.

The King's army wasn't shattered. English armies had supply trains and remounts, fletchers and armourers – they could, and did, bring food all the way from England – but men and horses died that night, and carts were lost. Men called it 'Black Monday' for a generation. Most of us who were there say that Black Monday cost the King Paris, and thus France.

De Badefol's men didn't have regular supplies, so we had to forage, and as the rain fell and our horses starved, we had to go farther and farther into the countryside – up to forty miles from Paris – to forage. The Dauphin had come up with a strategy to avoid facing us and only raid our supplies – du Guesclin's strategy, whether it was he who mouthed it or not – and we faced fighting every day as we foraged in the rain.

It was announced that the King was sending representatives to Chartres to arrange a peace.

At the time, I was almost at the borders of Normandy, trying to find enough grain to feed 200 horses for a few days. France was so badly scarred that it had begun to appear that there simply wasn't any grain.

I was sitting on Jack at a crossroads. My archers were all searching the village to the south of us, combing the cellars, literally, for a trap door holding a treasure of grain. And to the north, most of my men-at-arms were plunging their lances into a series of sodden hayricks, looking for anything, or anyone, who could lead us to food. The rain poured down like God's tears for our sins, and the road under Jack's forefeet was as soft as mush.

I had sentries out in each cardinal direction – mounted men at the corners of fields. One was Perkin.

He sounded the alarm, blowing a small horn, and then bolted towards me.

I stood in my stirrups and turned Jack. It was hard to see in the rain, but something seemed to be moving across the fields to the north, and also behind me, to the south.

Richard was laying siege to Paris and I hadn't seen him in days. This raid was all mine, and something was wrong.

I had to assume that the force behind me was French.

I rallied my men-at-arms, who reached me first. I formed them in a tight knot on the road and pointed at de la Motte. 'Cut your way through them, make a hole for the archers and keep going.'

'What are you doing?' he asked me.

I pointed at our two Hainaulters and the younger bastard of Albret, who had stuck with my force since the fall. They all had excellent armour and were good men-at-arms.

'We'll be the rearguard. Go!' I shouted.

Hainaulters are solid men. Antoine and Marcus shrugged, wiped the water off their faces and put on their gauntlets. With Perkin, who was the best mounted page, we had five men-at-arms. We rode along behind the main force, watching the body of French come down from the north like a hammer on an anvil.

Sam led the archers out of the village and joined de la Motte on the road. He waved at me and I waved back.

The force from the north was now close enough to count. There were forty of them.

Marcus whistled between his teeth.

'Please tell me you are not going to fight all of them,' he said in his clipped, Germanic way.

I watched as de la Motte's men-at-arms slammed into the force to the south of us. I saw Sam wave his arms, and I saw my archers ride off into the fields, mud and all.

'My lord,' Marcus said.

The Frenchmen behind us were forming for a fight.

Perkin looked at me.

I shrugged. 'We're going to charge them,' I said. 'If we fight well, we can push through and run for it. If not, friends … well, I'll see you in hell.'

Marcus laughed. 'We could just throw down our arms,' he said. But he had his visor down.

We lowered our lances and charged.

I had the best horse, so I was in front. My adversary – I knew him immediately – also had the best horse. Jehan le Maingre. Boucicault.

I knew his coat armour when we were still forty horse lengths apart. I set myself and got two deep breaths.

As our lances crossed, his dipped slightly and slapped mine to the ground – his lance point caught me in the centre of the breastplate, just above my bridle arm, and slammed me back against my cantle. I lost my lance, but not my seat, and passed him.

By St George, he was a good lance.

Jack baulked at the dense mass of the French. Being a very different horse from Alexander, he turned and jumped the stone wall that lined the road, and as I was still trying to recover my seat from the lance strike, I came off.

My arse hit the wall and my shoulder hit the ground – I went upside down over the wall, and pain lanced through me. Still, I got to my feet, sword in hand, in the mud of the field.

I could just about stand. The pain in my lower back and hips was as intense as anything I'd ever known.

Bertrand du Guesclin rode up to the wall on the other side. I raised my sword in salute and he raised his visor. 'If you'll come back to the wall of your own free will, I'll knock a hundred florins off your ransom,' he said, grinning.

'I don't think I can climb the wall,' I admitted. 'But I yield to you.' I took a few steps in the mud and fell, and that's all I remember.

I returned to my wits in Reims. I'd been hurt badly – I had the black bruises to prove it – and I'd caught something in the cursed rain. But Perkin stayed by me and nursed me, and I lived. I missed about thirty days.

My ransom was set at 200 florins, which seemed to me unfair. It was a large sum, and I had no estates to pay it. But Boucicault explained to me that it was based on the damage I'd done to the French, which I suppose was flattering, in a way.

I was surprised to find the very noble Jehan le Maingre was willing to speak to me, but he sat on my bedside and laughed. He even laughed ruefully.

'De Charny thought you had something, and he was never wrong,' Boucicault said. He made a face. 'In '58, men said you'd raped my cousin, the Dauphine.' He shook his head. 'I almost killed you, but now I find that she rather likes you, and you helped defend her castle – bah. I'll never kill a man for a rumour again. In fact, I owe you an apology.'

'Which didn't keep you from unhorsing me,' I said, still smarting from the ease of his strike.

He held his arms wide. 'That is war. I am a better knight than you, that is all.' He saw me writhe and smiled. Jehan le Maingre set an international standard for arrogance. But he was handsome, slim, extremely rich, a fine musician and a brilliant soldier. He and du Guesclin vied to be the 'best lance in France'. I, on the other hand, was a penniless Englishman, a self-taught man-at-arms, and who was I to resent him?

'Indeed, you are lucky that your service to my cousin is so well known,' he said. 'The Dauphin ordered us to kill every routier taken in arms.' He smiled – a very expressive smile that admitted he was no hypocrite and didn't see routiers as very different from other kinds of soldiers. 'Du Guesclin reminded him that you served him at Meaux, and he included you in his cartel. My old friend the Captal is covering your ransom. You have friends.' He smiled. 'Really, du Guesclin should have charged more for you.'

I will confess to you that this sign that some men accepted me as a knight – as a man-at-arms – made it worth being captured.

He paused in the doorway. 'By the way,' he said, 'The Vicomtesse d'Herblay is in Reims. She sends her regards.'

The name meant nothing to me. 'I am not acquainted with the vicomtesse,' I said, trying for my very best Norman French accent.

He looked down his long nose at me. 'I think you are mistaken,' he said. 'If I were to mention that her baptismal name was Emile . . .' he added.

'*Par dieu!*' I said, all but springing from my bed.

'I have not told her that I met you as an apprentice in a shop.' He smiled.

Ha! I told her myself.

At some point I had stopped wearing her favour. There's something particularly grim about wearing a woman's favour while you threaten peasants and bully women into revealing where they hide their grain. I wondered where it was. Packed with my spare shirts? I had a leather bag of clean, dry linen shirts, and it lived with my good doublet, my two best pairs of matched hose without holes, and some bits of jewellery – in the wagon of a Genoese banker who rode with the Captal. He held all my ready money, too.

The next day, du Guesclin visited me. He was coming to be thought a great man amongst the French, which suited me – the more especially as he introduced me, at my bedside, to a room full of Norman and Breton knights.

'William Gold, gentlemen. He took me in '57 and was quite the gentleman about it; he helped save the Dauphine at the Bridge of Meaux – you know the story?'

'By God, sir, did you save the Duke de Bourbon?' asked a sprig.

'*Par Dieu*, monsieur, I may have. I was busy, you understand,' I drawled. Being a man of reknown – even a little reknown – was vastly more pleasurable than being thought a brigand, liar, thief or rapist.

I received a certain amount of hero worship, and I felt much better.

The worship of good men is itself anodyne, messieurs.

After they left, I wondered why it was that I was more popular with my enemies than with my own people.

A day or two passed. I hadn't read a book in years, but my host, the French King's lieutenant of Reims, had a library of over twenty books, and all of them were about chivalry. I had never seen a book about chivalry – I used to read a little Aristotle, but mostly Aquinas, psalms and sermons. I read a poem by John Gower once, and enjoyed it, although I'm pretty sure he wrote it against men like me.

I knew there *were* books on chivalry. I knew that the great de Charny wrote a list of questions for the Order of the Star, and I knew that the stories of Sir Lancelot, for example, were written down. But I had never read anything like Master Llull's book of chivalry, and I devoured it. I read it through, and then read it through again.

When du Guesclin came, I asked him about the book. He shrugged. 'I was never much of a reader,' he admitted. 'But my father's master-of-arms says he was some sort of Spaniard – that he was a knight, and fought the Moors, and then became a hermit, and then a priest.'

'He thinks that knights are chosen, by God, to protect the people.' I looked down the page. 'He thinks there ought to be schools to train boys to be knights.' I looked at du Guesclin and he smiled.

'Anyone can be a knight,' he said. 'Surely we've seen that in the last ten years. Give a peasant a good horse and a harness and a few year's of training, and if he has a good heart and a set of balls, he can fight. You and I both know this.'

I gnawed my lip. 'But ... isn't there more to being a knight than having courage and a harness?'

Du Guesclin shrugged. 'No.' He smiled wryly at me. 'Well, perhaps there is more. A good sword is a help.'

A voice from the doorway said, 'Fie on you, Monsieur du Guesclin! I thought better of you, sir.'

Now, in France, as in England, when you are sick (if you are lucky and have rich friends) you are put in a closed bed, a bed with heavy hangings, many pillows and a pair of feather mattresses over a roped frame. You can't see anyone beyond the hangings. This means that women may visit you so long as they don't enter the hangings, so to speak.

That was Emile's voice. I'd hoped, but how on earth could a noblewoman visit a routier without comment?

'If any peasant with spirit can be a knight, why is this war so vicious?' she asked. 'Isn't it true that when we let any lad be a knight, they murder and rob at will, drunk on the power of their arms, whereas true knights have discipline and restraint?'

Du Guesclin was inside the hangings with me. His eyes met mine and he shrugged. 'Madame may have the right of it,' he said, 'but when I need to go up a hill into a shower of English arrows, I care little about the ability my lads have to show restraint, and only that they have the spirit to face the arrow storm.'

Emile's voice hardened. 'And when you've beaten the English and they all go home? What then?'

Du Guesclin shook his head. 'Not a problem for me, Madame. I am the merest fighting man.' He rose from my bed.

I grabbed his hand. 'May I write a letter to Richard Musard? I asked.

He shook his head. 'The Black Squire has gone away south to Avignon on a mission. The Captal sent a squire – Thomas, an Englishman – with an offer to pay your ransom, which,' he smiled, 'I may have done you the disservice of accepting. He left before you returned to consciousness.'

'I'd like some clothes and things,' I admitted.

'I'm sure you have friends in Reims who might arrange to dress you,' said du Guesclin. 'I must go. I'll visit tomorrow. Do you know that the peace is signed? The King is to return to France at midsummer. The war is over.'

The words chilled my blood. I was a soldier. I was in the twilight between being a man-at-arms, a squire or a knight – a recognized member of the community, a ranking gentleman. A knight would never need to feed himself, whilst a starving man-at-arms was called a brigand.

The war was ending just as I was making my name.

But I had no more time to consider the destruction of my fortunes, because Emile said, 'Do you, too, believe any man can be a knight?'

'I have to hope so,' I admitted, 'because I'm rather like any man myself. If only high birth makes a knight, I will never make the grade. And yet, my lady, I agree with you this far. I have recently seen what happens when boys are broken in spirit and trained to war like dogs to the chase, and it is truly horrible. Certes, if a man is to be a knight, he must know something of the rules and customs of being a knight – of chivalry – or he is a mere killer.' I paused and opened my curtain a touch. 'I missed you,' I said.

She was pregnant – well along, in a flowing kirtle that empha-sized the pregnancy rather than hiding it. The whole kirtle was silk, figured in swans, her husband's badge. Her kirtle and over gown were worth about twice my war horse's value.

I cannot tell you which shocked me more, her preganancy, or the slavish adoration inplied in the heraldic dress – a gown that emphasized her condition and her master. That stressed that she was *property*. Like a retainer, or a man-at-arms.

All my thoughts must have been on my face.

She laughed, the nasty little laugh she used to hurt herself.

'There, you see me as I am,' she said. 'Fat as a hog, blotchy-faced and ugly.' She hung her head in mock contrition, then glared at me, eye to eye like an adversary, daring me to speak. 'If you'd kept the curtain closed, you need not have known.'

'You are just as beautiful pregnant as not,' I said. It wasn't quite true, but really, one doesn't have to be bred to court to know what to say to a pregnant woman. 'And I am yours, body and soul, whether you are beautiful as heaven or come to me with leprosy.'

Her smile.

But my sense of honour was as sharp – and double edged – as hers. 'I can't say that I've brought your favour much honour.' I hadn't realized how bitter I was until I heard myself whining like a baby. 'Killing peasants,' I heard myself saying. 'Burning towns.'

We watched each other for some heartbeats.

Both of us armed with the weapons to do the other hurt.

She nodded and looked away. Bright – even brittle – she said, 'Monsieur du Guesclin says that you require clothes. I took the liberty of sending for a tailor on your behalf.' She smiled then.

I was holding the hangings open to watch her, and now she rose – still graceful as a dancer. 'As you are a cripple and I am a hog,' she said, 'I don't think that the gossips of the world will be troubled if I open your curtains and this window and give you some air. I know that the best doctors are against it, but then, my midwife says all man-doctors are fools.'

I just sat back and smiled like a fool – and worried that I was un-washed and unshaven. 'You will have to send the tailor back home,' I said. 'My ransom and the purchase of a new horse will wipe out what I've saved.'

She leaned in and brushed my lips with hers, as fast and controlled as a master swordsman. Then backed to her stool. 'That's as close to an embrace as I'll dare,' she said, matter of factly. 'I'm watched. This baby is very important to my husband.' Her eyes flicked to the door and she smiled. 'But I'm more than rich enough to satisfy my fancy. And I fancy getting you some clothes that don't look quite so, mmm, manly.' She had my doublet in her hands, having picked it off the back of the chair. It was almost unrecognizable to me, it was so clean and well-repaired by the servants of the chateau, but she looked at it as if it was covered in bugs.

'Did you ... make it yourself?' she asked wickedly.

In those days, a doublet was a small garment. Not the sleeved cote of today, but a sleeveless vest, usually two layers of linen (hence 'doublet' or doubled linen) whose sole purpose was to hold up the hose – hose were separate then. *Par dieu!* Messieurs may remember how we dressed when I was young. At any rate, the hose were pointed, tied with laces to the doublet, which was worn over the shirt and under the cote, or jupon. While I owned a couple of nice cotes and gowns, they were in my baggage. I wore armour, all day, every day, and I didn't need to wear a gown with it. In winter, sometimes one put a gown over the armour.

Ah! While we're on the details of costume, I'll add that sometimes I wore a quilted jupon over my doublet to protect my skin from my mail. That was a truly horrible garment. It smelled so bad that it attracted dogs. I saw that it was gone. Horrible as it was, it fit me and my mismatched harness perfectly.

And as a final note, the doublet took especial stress as it also served to hold up my leg armour – don't imagine nice white armour, but leather and splint contraptions with plate knees that weighed too much and tore the fibre of my doublet from the constant stress.

Why have I shared all this?

At that moment, I hadn't owned clean, dry, fashionable clothes in years. Or rather, I owned them; I just never wore them. I was dirty and my seams split all the time, and when I slept with a woman, I usually begged her to work on my clothes while she stayed with me. My shirts were all sewn by whores and camp-followers.

So when Emile asked me if I made it myself, I probably flushed.

'Allow me to dress you,' Emile said gently. 'You saved my life.'

'Your husband ...' I said quietly.

'You saved my husband's life, very publicly. The Dauphine approves of you. The nasty rumour, which, I confess, I believe was spread by my husband, has died away. Pregnancy has given me,'

– she smiled, and the fire in her eyes would have burned a monk – 'power. 'Let me do this.'

'As a service for an old friend?' I asked. She wore his colours: she was his woman now. So spoke the angry boy we all have in our hearts.

She opened my small window – really, little more than an arrow slit. The air of spring wafted in. I could smell ... growth. I must have inhaled a great gout of air, because Emile laughed.

'I will give my thanks to God that you are on the road to recovery,' she said. 'Du Guesclin despaired of you in your fever. You know I came then?' she asked, somewhat hesitantly.

'No,' I said. The angry boy was silent.

'Boucicault doesn't approve of me,' she said. 'He never has,' she added. 'Prig. Prude. Sanctimonious hypocrite.'

I must have looked surprised.

She looked away. 'I wasn't ... a virgin when I was wed, somewhat hastily, to my husband. If I'd been a servant girl, I'd have been turned out of doors.'

I laughed lightly. In London, among merchants and artificers, this sort of occurrence was so commonplace that I'm not sure I can remember a girl who was wed without a bulge under her gown.

Emile choked, 'I thought of killing myself,' as if that was a matter-of-fact statement, a commonplace.

'It is not so great a sin,' I said. Odd to take the husband's side. 'It is really of no moment if your husband-to-be is a trifle ardent in paying his attentions—'

She looked at me, and I wasn't sure what her face was saying – anger? Indifference? Daring my comment? 'Not my husband, dear.' She turned and looked out the window. 'I was not a good girl.'

Why on earth do people tell each other these things?

She was trying to hurt herself. Not me.

It sat there, between us.

Perhaps to a real nobleman, this would have been crushing, a proof that she was a soiled flower, a worthless, honourless trull. There was something in her voice that told me she was, in fact, daring me to be appalled.

But I was a child of London and war, and all my other women were real whores. To me, she was the essence of – perhaps not modesty, but womanly dignity. Pregnancy sat lightly on her, and added ... maturity, perhaps, without detracting from allure. Oh, no.

The allure was shouting at me, despite her folded hands and the anger on her face.

Perhaps it takes a many-times betrayed man of war to recognize a woman who has come a hard road, and is looking—

I shrugged. 'So?' I said. 'I'm sorry, Emile, are you trying to tell me you are of no worth? Because I know your worth. I care nothing for your other lovers.'

She turned her head. Her face was in shadow, backlit by the spring sun. 'How many do you think I had?' she asked.

There's a moment in a certain kind of fight where you think you are winning, and then, without warning, you lose control of something – perhaps your opponent's left hand – and there is a particular feeling as you realize you have lost it, and you know the blow is coming. And there's nothing you can do to stop the blow.

I cared *nothing* for how many lovers she'd had as a young girl – Holy Virgin, no one counted my score – but her face and her posture said that this was … vital. Essential. And I had lost control of the trend of the conversation.

Except she wasn't trying to hurt me. She was trying to hurt herself, of course.

'You had enough lovers to tarnish your reputation and harm your opinion of yourself,' I said. 'But not enough to affect my opinion of you.' I leaned forward, regardless of the pain. 'I know who you really are. I know who you were in the siege. That is all there is, to me.'

Her eyes widened. Leaping from the chair she sat in, Emile leaned over my bed and kissed me. 'You are a true knight,' she breathed. 'I will treasure that.' But she was gone before my left arm could pin her. 'The tailor is a present from me. If you love me, don't spurn him.' She pulled a ring off her finger. 'The Dauphine gave you a ring. Where did it go?'

I sighed. 'I pawned it,' I admitted.

'Holy Mary mother of God, you had a love token from the Dauphine and you *pawned* it?' She shook her head.

I shrugged. 'Horses eat a lot,' I said.

'Will you promise not to pawn this one?' she asked. 'On your word as a knight?'

'Does it come with a kiss?' I asked. I shrugged. 'I am scarcely a knight.'

She waved a hand in dismissal, as if my hopes and fears on that subject were of no consequence.

'Emile, you see me a captive, taken in arms by a good knight. You knew me in the siege as a rescuer, a man from a grail romance.' Was I spurred by her recital of her past lovers? I'd never said this much to Richard. 'I'm no knight. I ride with routiers and collect *patis* from peasants and sometimes I rob the church.'

She set her jaw. 'That is not who you really are,' she said. Her eyes locked with mine, and they were as hard as diamonds. 'We do what we must, eh, monsieur? But that need not be the sum of who we are.' She pulled the ring from her finger and reached it out.

I tried to snatch her hand. She pulled it away.

'If you aren't faster than that, you'll never beat Jehan le Maingre for me.' She had avoided another attempt by my left arm to pin her to the bed. 'I will visit again. Don't get well too soon.' She smiled and extended the ring again.

I held out my hand, and she placed it gently on my finger. 'Be my knight,' she said.

It is uncomfortable when you meet another person's eyes for too long. It is as if you have no secrets left.

I cannot say how long we were like that.

It was long.

Like a fool, I broke it. 'You are beautiful,' I said. 'Pregnancy makes you ...' I tried to find a word for her.

'Fat,' she said. '*A demain, m'amour.*'

My ransom didn't appear from the Captal. The tailor came every day for three days, measuring, cutting and showing me fabrics at my bedside. The truth is that I agreed to everything he suggested. If I had any taste of my own, it was mostly direct emulation of older men I had admired: Sir John Cheverston, Sir John Chandos, Jean de Grailly and, most especially, my sometime mentor and nemesis, Jehan le Maingre, whose slim good looks seemed to mock my large build and bright-red hair. I told the tailor, in some detail, what I liked on each of these men.

He was a patient man. He heard me out and asked some questions about styles. After two days, he pursed his lips and said, 'Scarlet and black.'

'What about them?'

'Those will be your colours. Your, mmm, patroness has suggested that I design arms for you, as well. Gules and sable.' He fingered his beard. 'I have a little scarlet broadcloth – a very little, dyed before the war. Black is expensive, but everyone wears it. Your hair, coming out of a sable cap, will be ...' he smiled. 'You will be wanting a new arming coat,' he said.

I agreed.

He nodded. 'Two cotes, two doublets, two gowns, one with fur, six shirts, six braes, six black hose and six red hose. A hood hat. The short gown, trimmed in sable, and a second gown plain. Two pairs of shoes and a pair of boots.' He smiled. 'A pair of wicker panniers and a leather male, or trunk. A full cloak and a half cloak. Six linen caps.' He looked up from his wax tablet. 'Anything else?'

'Gloves?' I asked hopefully. I loved gloves. They protect your hands in brush, or in a street fight.

'Gloves, for monsieur. My god-brother can make them. Chamois or deerskin?' His stylus poised over the wax.

I had no idea what the difference was. 'One each?' I asked.

Judging from his face that was a foolish answer, but that's what I got.

In between visits from the tailor, I read about chivalry. My host had de Charny's questions, and I read them. Some of them made little sense to me – his refined sense of what might constitute right and wrong in the taking of a man's horse and arms in a tournament were beyond my experience – and he didn't seem to ask the questions to which I wanted answers. How many peasants can you torment for their grain before you cease to be a knight? Must you fight, regardless of the odds against you? When is surrender still 'worthy'?

But other questions fascinated me.

And Vegetius might have been a captain of routiers. Some of his advice bore no relationship to war as I knew it, but his views on ambush and the chance of battle seemed solid enough. And scouting. *Par Dieu*, monsieur, the old Romans knew about scouts and spies, eh?

My host, the Captain of Reims, Gaucher de Chatillon, appeared at my bedside the next morning, dressed in immaculate green and gold. Three days closeted with a tailor had caused me to examine clothing. I still do.

He bowed at the doorway. 'Monsieur, please accept my apologies for not attending you before. My lord the Marshal has told me how you helped to defend our cousin the Dauphine, and all French gentlemen owe you a debt of gratitude.' He bowed again. 'I am also given to understand that you preserved my friend the Duke de Bourbon in the face of the foe, and the Comte d'Herblay.'

It is very difficult to bow from a bed, but I tried.

'Your lordship does me too much honour,' I protested.

'Faugh,' he coughed. 'I do not. But I am here with the pleasant duty of telling you that your ransom is paid and you are a free man. Indeed, I can go further and suggest that we travel together, as I am going to the King of England's tournament and passage of arms at Calais, in honour of the peace, and I thought you might care to come. Peace may be in the air with spring.' He coughed in his hand. 'But the roads are still full of brigands.'

He handed me a scroll. I opened it to find a letter from the Captal.

'I didn't bring a man to read it for you,' the Captain said with a bow. 'I gather monsieur is a voracious reader, as I'm given to understand he is galloping through my small library.'

'*Ma fois*, my lord! I had no idea there were so many fine books about chivalry!' I said, or something equally passionate.

The Captal had arranged for me to fight on the Prince's English team, if I was recovered.

I all but leaped from my bed. This was recognition – forgiveness – perhaps a permanent appointment, all at the tip of my sword.

A spike of pain rose from my right arm to the middle of my chest, and I gasped.

De Chatillon caught me as I stumbled. 'I took a bad wound in '57,' he said. 'It took me months to recover. Muscles forget their duty in bed.'

The French had treated me as a gentleman – in fact, as an aristocrat – so I couldn't very well tell this famous knight that I needed the tournament at Calais as my chance to prove myself. Or perhaps I was just too proud.

'I'll be ready to ride,' I said. 'When?'

He smiled. 'So eager,' he said. 'I won't be at leisure until Monday next.'

So I had five days to be in shape to ride.

Du Guesclin came to tell me I was free. I undervalued you,' he said ruefully. 'Five hundred florins would have been a better price.'

'At least I pay,' I said, more nastily then I had intended.

When he asked, I told him about the knight I'd taken at Poitiers, who had never paid.

Du Guesclin tugged his beard. 'This disappoints me,' he said. 'I don't know the gentleman, but I will endeavour to find him.' He came and sat on my bed. 'Your horse and arms are safe,' he said. 'A certain person paid me a small *patis* to release them. I shouldn't charge for your arms at all – really, my friend, you need a new harness.'

'Alas, I would have to capture two or three worthy gentlemen to have the cost of a harness,' I said. 'Rather than enjoying your hospitality.'

'It would seem unpatriotic if I wished you good luck,' du Guesclin said, but he grinned. 'Will you fight at Calais?'

'If I'm healed enough. It means ... everything to me.' I wasn't afraid to admit this to du Guesclin. He *knew* me.

'May I ... loan you some armour that I'm almost positive will fit?' He looked away to hide a smile. 'I have a fair amount. Captures and the like.'

As a brag, it was clever.

'I can't wear your captured English armour at Calais, you rogue!' I laughed.

He made a very Norman shrug. 'Armour has no name,' he said. 'And I have a nice cuirass from Italy – with a lance rest.'

'Well ...' I had tears in my eyes. Life hadn't prepared me for people to be so kind. To be frank, I was suspicious, but I couldn't imagine a reason for du Guesclin to humiliate me.

On Friday, between eating salt fish and trying to swat the pell with my sword, I was visited by the tailor.

Four young boys carried my panniers up the stairs to my tower and laid them on my floor, and he spent more than an hour showing me the ins and outs of my wardrobe. I had everything he'd written on his tablet, and more – a dozen black scarves, neatly folded; a new purse on a new belt with a hook for de Charny's dagger, in red and black; a sable hat with a scarlet feather. Two pairs of gloves, one red and one chamois coloured. The malle had a razor and a small horn box for soap, and a sewing kit with hanks of red and black linen thread for maintaining all my finery, and needles, and white linen thread for shirts. There were hose and matching garters in red and black leather with fine buckles.

He insisted that I try every garment. Meanwhile he and his boys sat on my floor, despite his own fine clothes, and re-tailored the lining of my red and sable coat; adjusted the fit of all my hose, the four of them stitching back seams at the speed of running mice. Finally, they all worked on my arming coat, parti-colour in red and black. It came in panels of heavily quilted wool fustian, and they constructed it before my eyes, chatting away merrily.

I felt a pang of longing for my master's shop. I tried to sit and help, and the master shook his head.

So I watched, and chatted, and marvelled that all these riches were to be mine.

I am only repeating last Sunday's sermon to say that the outer man often reflects the inner man. At Reims, I did some good for Emile and began to learn a little about chivalry – and in return Emile clothed me. Indeed, she set my taste for life – *par dieu*, gentlemen, I still wear those colours, as you can see.

I attended Mass on Sunday dressed in my new clothes. No one commented on them, but for a day, I was as fine as Jehan le Maingre and I outshone du Guesclin, who glanced at me at the holy-water basin and said, 'To look at us, monsieur, men would think you took me. I knew I charged you too little.' But he winked, and I couldn't take offence.

I wore Emile's ring, as well.

My hip hurt, but I could ride and walk and swing a sword.

Emile came to see me after Mass. I had made it to Mass and back under my own power.

She had two women and a man with her, and I heard her laugh from the base of my stairs. She came in like a breath of spring, and even as I bowed, carefully showing a fine length of sable fur trim, she laughed again.

'By the Virgin, sir, I heard that you were so eager to be gone from us that you leaped from the bed on hearing there was to be a tournament at Calais.' She had on a high head-dress that made her look like a Turk – or at least, how I imagined a Turk back then. The scarf fluttered in front of her eyes when she curtseyed.

I blushed and stammered.

She smiled at my confusion. 'Here are some friends of mine,' she said. 'This is my sister, the Vicomtesse de Chartres. You remember my friend Isabelle from the castle at Meaux?'

'How could I forget so old a friend,' I said.

The small blonde woman frowned, and snapped me a quick and rather empty courtesy. 'Monsieur,' she muttered.

'And the foremost musician of our age,' she said. 'My friend Guillaume.'

He raised his eyebrows slightly, gently turning away the flattery. 'I love music, and I serve it, but there are better men then I and better women, too, in every convent and monastic house.' He smiled. 'My lady thought it might please you to hear some music.'

What could I say? I had hoped that she would contrive to visit me privily, and I had imagined ... well, I had imagined things.

Love is jealous. Here I was, with her, and yet already bitter. Why had she brought all these people?

The man called Guillaume was dressed far more richly than I, and I put him down as a popinjay. He played the lute and sang so well that I dismissed him. The three women talked among themselves, and I sulked.

Youth. Wasted on the young.

Thankfully for everyone, my host appeared with du Guesclin. Du Guesclin had two boys with armour. Chatillon bowed to me and then to the musician.

'Ah, monsieur!' he said.

The musician rose and bowed with an irony that moved him up in my estimation.

'Our musician was knighted by the King,' Chatillon said with a wry smile. 'Now he is Monsieur de Machaut.'

'So our worthy captain *forced* me to bear arms and fight you English in the siege,' Machaut said.

Now I was interested. 'How did you find it?' I asked.

Machault shrugged. 'Terrifying,' he admitted. 'I am not bred to it like your gentlemen.'

'Monsieur Machaut is too modest,' du Guesclin said. 'He stood in the gate for an hour, crossing swords with the flower of English chivalry. He honoured his name and the act of his knighting.'

Machaut laughed. 'I was beaten to the ground by three men wearing Clarence's colours, and then I lay under their feet, trying not to be killed or taken for ransom.' He was competely at ease – unafraid, in this company, to own up to his failure as a man-at-arms.'

Suddenly, I saw a great deal in him to admire. 'We are all terrified, are we not, messieurs,' I said. 'Not once the fighting starts, but before, yes?'

'Faugh!' said Chattilon. 'I wouldn't admit to such a thing. For myself, I know no fear. I sometimes shake with eagerness to be at the foe.' He bowed to the ladies. 'Sometimes I shake so hard in my eagerness that my knees strike together.'

Du Guesclin nodded his approval. 'It is in facing the fear that we are brave, not the absence of fear,' he said.

Machaut caught a louse in his collar and killed it between his nails. 'Yes – well. I fought three times, and it was harder to make myself go forward each time.'

My eye met du Guesclin's and we both knew what we knew.

It gets harder to go forward.

For all the seriousness of the conversation, I had a new appreciation of Machaut's quality, and now I listened more attentively to his music. In some way, he reminded me of Chaucer. He was witty and widely read. Every time he mentioned a writer – he sang us a poem by the great Italian, Dante, and then he said the words in French – I was determined to read *everything* they'd written.

I was determined to learn to ride better, to read more, to learn to fight better and to joust constantly. What I needed was enough money to live like a gentleman. A gentleman could do all these things.

My little room was crowded with all these people and my panniers of clothes and armour, and Chatillon graciously allowed us to move to his wife's solar, which was the next level in the tower and a much larger room. I was the last out my door, and Emile was just ahead of me – she rested her hand on mine in the doorsill, leaned back as if to speak and put her lips on mine.

I have met Catherine of Sienna, the living saint. She said that God came to her like colour to a blind man. In the minute she said as much, all I could imagine was that kiss of Emile's.

She moved away, and I was left unable to breathe.

The rest of the afternoon slipped away – idyllic. I tried to touch her again, but there was no chance and too many eyes. I told a few tales, and du Guesclin recounted how I took him in the darkness, and Chatillon told some tales from the sieges. Machaut sang us a lay of Lancelot, and another of Sir Tristan.

When the ladies rose to leave, du Guesclin's eyes met mine.

'Next time I find myself questioning the value of chivalry,' he said, 'perhaps I will think of this afternoon.' He glanced at Machaut. 'He surprised you, yes? He surprised all of us. He was really very brave.'

'I can see that,' I said.

As Emile made ready to depart, I took her hand and bowed. 'I owe you a great deal,' I said to her hand.

'*Ma fois*, my dear,' she said. 'It was a pleasure, and doubly so to see you so fine, and with men of your own caliber. This is where you belong. I wanted you to taste this.' She leaned forward. 'Come back to me, my Lancelot. I shan't always be fat as a hog.'

Her hand squeezed mine, caressing the ring.

'I will come back,' I said. 'On the sanctity of the cross I swear it.'

She smiled, and then she was gone.

We rode north and west across Normandy to Calais. The company was excellent – Chatillon was years my senior, but a gentler man, a better knight, I don't think I ever met. He reminded me of Chandos – indeed, they were peers. His household were men of his own stamp, and du Guesclin and I were fast friends by the end of the ransom time.

When we came to Calais, after much sorting of safe conducts and the like, we found that the peace talks, far from being over, were still going strong, with the King of England and the King of France locked in a fight over the precedence of their renunciations. The King of England had to renounce his claim to the throne of France, and the King of France had to renounce his claim to the parts of France being ceded by treaty to England. Neither man relished the prospect. Half a thousand churchmen seemed to gather around them like vultures and ravens at a battlefield.

The first night in Calais, I found a note from Emile inside my chamois gloves. I read it a dozen times. I still have it, and I'll be damned if I share it with you, but she did mention in an appendage that she was looking into the ransom of my prisoner from Poitiers.

Somehow, that little detail brought home to me that we would meet again.

I was three days in Calais before I could arrange a meeting, through Tom, with the Captal. I attended him at breakfast – he had a whole inn, while I lived under the eaves of a cottage.

'The Prince will receive you,' he said. 'Now that you are ransomed, I'll try and get you in today. Tomorrow at the latest.'

Sure enough, I attended the Black Prince that very evening.

I bowed my very best bow. The Prince was having a dinner for many of the French knights he'd taken at Poitiers, and the Captal arranged that I be invited. I sat with du Guesclin, who had most definitely *not* been taken at Poitiers.

Chaucer was there. I found it hard to hold on to my dislike of him, and I greeted him warmly. He, however, kept his distance.

Sadly for me, the Prince's reception was about the same. Sir John Chandos took me by the arm, the Captal stood by me, and I made my best bow to the Prince as Sir John said, 'My lord, here is Master Gold, who has done your Grace and his father good service in Gascony since we last heard of him.'

'We heard of him quite recently, and under circumstances most entirely creditable to a squire,' the Prince said. He glanced at me. 'I am told that Master Gold was falsely accused by a man. To the *great* detriment of his repute,' he said, somewhat acerbically. 'The enmity of a peer of France is not timely, Master Gold. Sir John Chandos has been unstinting in your praise. Sir Robert Knolles states that you are the best man of your companions.'

My Prince had never spoken to me so long, or so fairly, and I was almost unable to move.

'And Monsieur de Chatillon and Monsieur de Guesclin are your *ardent* admirers.' The Prince leaned a little closer. Not for nothing was he called the black Prince. He was at the edge of anger, and his scowl was dark. The Captal cleared his throat. 'Your Grace,' he said chidingly.

'John, I cannot have him,' the Prince said very distinctly.

I flushed.

'Sir John did not let go my hand. 'Your Grace,' he began.

'I detest to be made to appear ungracious to my vassals.' He took my hand. 'Master Gold, you deserve better by me, but while you hold the determined dislike of a peer of France, I cannot have you by my side in a tournament that has enough political difficulties to start a new war.' His brow clouded over as fast as an April day in London. 'John – enough. Master Gold, whatever passed between you and a Princess of the royal house of France, the rumour that sticks to you precludes your direct employment by the crown of England. And you have the reputation of a brigand and a routier.'

I stood perfectly still, trying to make the words go away.

'Perhaps in a year or two, something can be done. In the meantime, I imagine that Sir John will provide you with work.' He inclined his head.

I bowed. Should I have barked? Spat? Damned him for an ungrateful Prince?

Perhaps I should have asked, 'Who gives us our orders?'

But I bowed deeply and withdrew.

. The Captal clamped my arm in his and pulled me, literally, through a curtain. I knew where I was – this was the side-table where the squires and cooks prepared meats for table.

The Captal looked at me – that look, again; the one that said he was sorry for the injustice of it – but he was going about his business.

Sir John Chandos put a hand on my shoulder. 'I'm sorry, lad. I thought, after du Guesclin spoke up for you, that you were made.' He gave a little sniff. 'I'll send you word. You'd best go.'

Tom appeared from the torchlight and took my arm.

I found it hard to see.

I was crying.

I was living in a tent – I couldn't afford an inn in Calais. I went to my tent, and Perkin, who had already heard the news through the endless network of servants, handed me a cup of wine.

Before I could be drunk, du Guesclin appeared. He came straight in through the flap and caught me sobbing.

Monsieur, have you ever been offered all you want? And then had it taken away?

When I left Emile, it was to fight in the lists as a gentleman beside my Prince, wearing her favour. Win or lose, I would have been made. If the Prince didn't place me in his retinue, with steady, honorable pay, then some great lord would have done so. Perhaps even Oxford or Lancaster.

In an hour, because of an ugly rumour started by a man whose life I once saved, that was gone. And yet, while I wallowed in it, I also saw that like Sir Gawain, I was the author of my own failure. I lay with Emile, and earned the pettish hatred of this man, who in that hour, I hated more than I hated the Bourc.

Du Guesclin came into my tent. Perkin poured him wine.

'I'm sorry, my lord. I am unmanned.' I was helpless to talk.

Du Guesclin shrugged. 'They are all much alike, Princes,' he said, and drank some wine. 'Mine thinks I'm a routier, too.'

In the end, we played chess. I'd like to say we spoke of love, or chivalry, but instead, he offered to sell me a good horse at a reasonable price.

I was moving a piece, and my glance fell on Emile's ring.

'Would you take a letter – to a friend?' I asked.

Du Guesclin's eyes went to my ring. 'You ask a great deal,' he said, and grinned. '*Par dieu*, monsieur, if it were not for the great love I bear you, I might try to know your sweet friend the better myself.' He leaned back. 'I will take you her letter. And any other you send me.'

I leaped to my feet. 'By Christ, monsieur, you are a true friend.'

Du Guesclin shook his head. 'For an English routier, you are a good man.'

I warmed my hands on the brazier and wrote Emile a note.

Madame,

The writer of this missive wishes you every felicity, every comfort in your delivery and every hope for . . . I paused. Women – young women – died like flowers in childbirth. What I wanted to wish her was *life*. I stared at my small square of parchment – where did Perkin find these things? *. . . every hope for a speedy recovery for mother and child.*

A sudden chill prevents the writer from paying his devotions in person. Be assured, my sweet friend, that the writer will think of no other until . . .

Until what? Until I earned so much notoriety that I was just another routier? A hired killer? A collector of *patis*? What other end-game was there?

By God, I was determined to find one.

. . . Until your devoted servant is able to come to your side.

I finished it.

Du Guesclin held out his hand. 'Let me see it before you seal it,' he said gruffly. 'If I'm to carry my death warrant—'

'Is d'Herblay so dangerous?' I asked.

'He represents a certain . . . kind.' Du Guesclin shrugged. 'He has money, and the ear of the Dauphin.'

As I finished folding my note, I heard a stir. I had a moment of hope that it might be Sir John Chandos, coming to tell me that all was forgiven? At some level, I wondered that the Prince hadn't even mentioned our original transgression, the Three Foxes. Forgotten? I put wax on it and jammed my seal into the wax.

As if summoned in a passion play, Master Chaucer poked his head into my tent.

'Pax?' he asked. He was parchment white – afraid of me, and little wonder. The beeswax candles and the oil lamps together couldn't give him a ruddy glow, he was so pale.

'Monsieur du Guesclin?' I said with a bow. 'Master Chaucer, an English squire. Who you may recall.'

The two men eyed each other warily.

Du Guesclin palmed my note, sealed and folded a dozen times.

He bowed. 'I must go prepare for the lists,' he said. 'I remain sorry that I will not face you there.'

'Monsieur may be satisfied that in the fullness of time, we will meet on some field or other,' I said.

We embraced. Chaucer watched us like a falcon, and when du Guesclin was gone, he shook his head.

'But you'll gut each other with poleaxes,' he said.

'Have you met Guillaume de Machaut?' I asked.

Chaucer paused. 'Yes,' he admitted, as if I'd dragged it from him. For once in our relationship, I had him off guard.

'I met him at Reims. He impressed me deeply. And I thought of you.' I shrugged.

Chaucer was dressed to ride, in a short wool gown and tall boots. 'Sir John Chandos is sending me to Hawkwood,' he said. 'He said that you would escort me.'

He turned to face me and our eyes met.

'The Prince employs Hawkwood, then? Unofficially?' I asked.

He looked away. 'Not my damned business to answer.'

'I'm just a routier?' I put in again.

Chaucer bit his lip. 'You know the score as well as I do.' He turned away, his nerves showing. 'Damn it, Gold! I didn't rat you out to the Prince in the first place! In fact, I tried to make it better.'

I shrugged. 'There's a lot of dirty water under that particular bridge,' I assured him. 'I'll escort you. I assume that Sir John Chandos expects me to take service with Hawkwood?' I paused. 'Even in peacetime?'

Chaucer set his face. 'It's a dirty business, Gold, and no mistake.'

My name was struck from the rolls of the lists at Calais. I collected my borrowed armour and the clothes my love had bought me, and I rode east, looking for Sir John Hawkwood. I had Chaucer at my side, and Perkin, and I picked up almost a dozen English archers in Calais. They knew which way the winds were blowing. The King was selling his garrisons in France to the King of France, and when that happened there'd be no employment for archers at all.

The end of the war was forcing change, and some of those changes were hard on the professional soldiers. The King of France had to hand over more than a hundred castles to the King of England, but the King of England had to hand another sixty to the King of France. The problem both men faced is that of these almost 200 castles, routiers and brigands held two-thirds of them. They sat in all the vital castles and towns, collecting *patis* and fighting each other, looting the countryside and taking what they wanted. Some of them flew the flag of France, some the flag of England, and some of Navarre. The treaty included them, but no one had asked their opinion.

Sir John Hawkwood had a company in his own name, operating from a pair of castles in the Auvergne country in the very centre of France. They flew the flag of Navarre, and they served no interest but their own.

Sir John welcomed me with open arms. He spoke for two hours with Master Chaucer, who rode away again. Then he inspected my English archers and embraced me as warmly as du Guesclin had.

'About time, lad. I'll make your fortune,' he said.

And that was my new goal. A fortune. And the settlement of a certain dispute with the Comte d'Herblay.

Richard Musard returned to Sir John in late September. He'd gone to Avignon with an English knight on an official embassage – and returned to Calais to find that he, too, was officially repudiated by the Prince. The Captal told him where to find me, and despite our shared anger, we were delighted to be reunited. We drank a great deal and he admired my clothes, which were still well-preserved at that point. There was very little fighting that summer. Everyone was waiting, on edge, to see what the King of England would do. Whether peace would be signed.

Richard had John Hughes with him, and I had Perkin – the last remnants of our former lances. The rest of the men had melted away – most of the Hainaulters had gone to other companies, and Marcus, who could write, sent to us inviting us to join the German Albert Sterz in pillaging the north of France, but Sir John offered us steady employment and a home. Besides, most of his men-at-arms were English, and men like John Thornbury and Thomas Leslie kept the company well-ordered, if not prosperous. De la Motte joined us from a Gascon company, with news of the Bourc Camus, who was rising in favour with the Prince.

One of the developments of that autumn was that the money-lenders slowed their flow of cash to us to a trickle. It was clear that peace was to be signed. We were not going to get wages from anyone. Some of the men left for Brittany, the last active theatre not covered by the treaty.

There were rumours that we might get employment in Spain, or Italy. There was a papal order that all routiers prepare to go on crusade.

So with no credit, I had to bear the expenses of a war horse, two pack horses, a squire, four archers and my own food. Perkin had had a war horse, which he lost when he was taken outside Reims. As my status fell, his did, as well.

In the autumn of 1360, it looked as if I was to have *nothing*. Richard complained of my temper, and Perkin tended to watch me out of the corner of his eye – I had hit him several times.

I was glad that Emile was not there to see me. I folded my red and black finery away and went back to my old clothes and my old ways. I even prepared a letter – a letter full of self pity, I promise you – to tell her to forget me, as I was nothing but a bandit.

In late autumn, a man came with a retinue. He bore no arms, but I knew him. Chaucer. And John Hughes knew the archers.

'King's men,' he said smugly, in his Cumbrian accent. 'Bodyguard archers.' He pointed them out. 'Sam was one of 'em, for a while. Paid by the King, or the Prince. The best.'

I thought that Chaucer would stay, but he was ahorse in our yard again in the time it took me to lace my doublet. I ran down in my hose and Hawkwood caught me at the base of the stairs.

'Better hurry, Master Gold,' he said. 'Your friend isn't staying.'

It was cold. Steam rose off the horses, and their nostrils vented smoke like dragons.

Richard had one of Chaucer's hands in his when I went out.

'I'm for London,' Chaucer said. 'I'm done with playing courier.' He smiled his old, sly smile. 'I've found something better.'

'I'm glad someone has,' I said. 'Can I trouble you to take a letter to my sister?'

He looked at his archers, who shrugged.

'I could do wi' a cup o' cheer,' said the big bastard by Chaucer's right side. He swung a leg over.

I ran into my corner of the common room, where most of the men-at-arms slept, and I wrote Mary a letter – a long letter.

I told her most of the truth – of what I was and who I served. I told her that I had paid a little less than two thirds of her dowry, and that the rest might have to wait, as I was short on war. I smiled when I wrote that. I smiled to think of her.

I folded it, sealed it and addressed it care of Clerkenwell.

Then gave it to Chaucer. He finished a jack of wine and poured more into his flask. 'Clerkenwell?' he asked, looking at the address. 'Damn, Gold, you make me feel as if I was home already.'

'Will you be back?' I asked.

He looked at Richard, and then at me. 'Not unless I have no other choice.' He looked both ways. 'What they are doing now ...?' He shook his head.

'If you see my sister, will you write to me?' I asked.

Chaucer smiled. 'You kept me alive a few times,' he admitted. 'I'll write you about your sister.'

We bowed to each other, and he embraced Richard. Not me.

Then he rode away.

It was two days after Chaucer came and went that Sir John summoned us to the great hall, and we sat at trestle tables.

He came out in a gown, like a lord. 'Fear not,' he announced. 'We have employ.'

Richard shouted, 'Where?' into the cheers.

Sir John laughed. 'Provence,' he said, and Richard frowned.

A great deal happened in a few weeks and I may not get the order of events the right way round, but the way I remember it, the first thing that happened was that Richard came to the room we shared. The word room is far too grandiose and makes one imagine a closed bed and a fine chimney, when what we had was the slates of the roof at the level of our necks so we had to stoop all the time, no window, and a space a little smaller than a soldier's tent, which we shared with our armour, our spare saddlery, our clothes, and a woman or two with her own basket of goods.

I was sitting on my spare saddle, sewing a patch on my beautiful arming coat and thinking bitterly of Emile.

Richard arrived, not by the door, but by the smoke hole, which was an easier way into our little loft if one was superbly muscled. He lit a cresset.

'You are sewing in the dark, brother,' he said.

I snorted.

'I think it's time that someone told you that you have become a churl and a barbarian,' he said cheerfully. 'Cheer up. The world is not as dark as you seem to think.'

'Sod off,' I said. 'I assume you got the miller's daughter to lie in the leaves.'

Richard shook his head. 'Nothing of the kind, brother. I went to visit our banker and arrange for a little loan.'

I kept my head down and continued sewing. My stomach turned over, though. I could face a dozen French knights, but the banker – good Christ how I hate bankers.

'He informed me that we had a credit – if I may use the term *we* in the broadest sense – of two hundred and fifty florins.' Richard grinned.

'You *are* fucking with me,' I said.

'Not in the least, and may I add that I find this distrust injurious? Seriously, brother, you have been an arse and a half the last month. I've wonder what ails you.'

'You were turned away by the Prince just as I was,' I said.

'Nor do I intend to live for ever as a routier but, brother, here we are, and we have enjoyed this life ere this. Have we not?'

I growled.

Richard pressed on, 'So I must speculate that there was, or is, something more – something you lack that makes you such a snark.'

I turned on him, ready to put him on the floor for his presumption. I'd had enough of his shit, and I could tell he was mocking me the while.

Then I saw that he was holding a scroll, sealed with a swan.

'And I asked myself, who is the Viscomtesse d'Herblay?' he continued, stiff-arming me and holding the scroll as far from me as he could manage. 'And will a letter from the lady help you or make you worse?'

'You bastard!' I shouted, and the two whores in the next smoke hole pounded on the wattle partition between our rooms.'

'Untrue!' Richard said. 'I'm no bastard.' He and I were well-matched in a hundred mock fights and a few real ones, and I couldn't get the scroll from him.

'Give me your word to cheer up!' he shouted.

'I swear!' I promised.

Christ, I loved that man.

He gave me the scroll. Two months old, but most welcome nonetheless.

She had found my capture, and used her social wiles to force him to pay me his ransom. And she wrote, 'Whatever your foolish Prince may think, you remain for me a true and gentle knight.'

Whatever my boil of loathing, she lanced it. With money and soft words.

'Ah,' said Richard. 'You and this countess are friends?'

'We were at Meaux together,' I said.

'Ah, she helped you hold the bridge?' he said. 'Or perhaps she is a nun?'

I looked at him, and he desisted. Real friendship is knowing when to stick the needle in, and when to leave off. Richard – perhaps because he'd been a slave – was always very tender with me when I was down.

'She found my French knight and made him pay his ransom!' I said.

Richard smiled. 'I gather that this cures whatever has been ailing you,' he said.

I went to the bankers that day and paid a hundred florins on my sister's dowry.

I think it was a few days later and Richard and I were eating a good meal in a good inn, which is why I think I must have gotten my long-lost ransom, when he told me of his trip to Avignon.

'The Pope is a Frenchman,' he said, which I acknowledged. All Popes were French, in my experience. I poured him some more good wine.

'So the King – our King – sent to him to ask if he'd help raise the King of France's ransom. To which the Holy Father agreed. After a great deal of negotiation.' Richard shrugged. 'One of the things our embassy guaranteed in the King of England's name is that no English or Navarrese companies would attack Provence. So I ask myself why a royal messenger guarded by royal archers has come to Sir John.'

'And now we march on Provence,' I added in. 'I can see through a brick wall in time,' I added, one of John Hughes' best expressions.

'You can?' asked Richard. He'd taken the rest of my archers, or rather, we shared them so that we had the biggest lances – the largest number of men. They were all gathered around, because we made the archers loose shafts every Sunday, and we rode at tilt or swaggered swords – anything to keep the edge on.

Amory, the youngest of my new archers, a Staffordshire man with no home to go to with peace, sat cross-legged, making bowstrings. He looked up.

'Well, sirs, mayhap I cannot see through the wall. What's it mean?'

Richard and I glanced at each other. He gave a slight nod, as if to say, You say it.

'Good King Edward and his son – you're all loyal to them, eh?' I began.

The King himself would have been heartened by the response – the grunts and smiles from ten hard men.

'If we went back to England, how would he get us back here to fight?'

Amory took the question seriously, rather than rhetorically. 'On ships?' he asked. 'I come on a ship.'

Jack Sumner laughed, but I speared him with a glance. 'Right you are, Amory. But that ship costs money, and arraying you in Staffordshire costs money and, who knows? Even an imp of Satan like yourself might go home and find a wife and decline to serve his Prince.'

Men laughed.

'As long as we have employment in France,' I said, 'we are here, ready to hand. And by fighting here, we make France weaker.'

Amory grinned. 'Aye!' he said.

'But Provence? An' the Pope?' asked Jack Sumner. 'The Pope's gathering the King o' France's ransom.'

'And if he never pays it?' Richard asked.

'Sweet virgin,' Amory said. 'We keep France.'

I shrugged. 'We keep France, and we keep the Pope's money, and the King of France is a broken shutter, banging against an empty barn.'

The archers grinned. Easy money. And service to the crown.

It didn't sound like glory, a better repute and a fortune to me. Nor did I hate the French so much.

When we speculated to Sir John, he told us to keep our views to ourselves.

And the last incident I remember before we marched was the brothers – the Ashleys, Hugh and Steven, who joined us that week. They were a pair of Englishmen, both knights, both well born and both attainted in England. Sir Hugh was attainted for multiple murders, and he was quite proud of them. He'd killed men who, as he said, 'Got in his way,' in his home county in the north of England.

They were big men and they, literally, threw their weight around. They'd never fought in France, but both had fought against the Scots, and against the French at Winchelsea.

They were determined to make names for themselves in France and get pardons, which had certainly worked before. But the end of the war and the Treaty of Brétigny, as it was being called, were flies in their very personal ointment.

I think it was a day or two after Richard and I talked of Avignon – again, I can place it because I was sitting comfortably on a well-lit settle in the common room of an inn, drinking good wine and not swill – that Sir Hugh came in and stood by the fire – it was late autumn – and cut me off from my light.

I was sewing. What do you think soldiers do in their spare time?

'I'm sewing,' I said.

'Proper in a young maid like yourself,' Sir Hugh said.

'You are in my light,' I said.

'My light now,' he said.

I sighed, because I'd had two days to prepare for this. Sir Hugh was no bigger than me. No smaller, either.

I put three stitches through my lining to seal it off, bit my thread and put my needle in its case.

'I'd rather beat the piss out of you outside,' I said loudly. 'But if you insist, I'll do it right here.'

Every head turned.

'And I thought you was just a blushing virgin,' Sir Hugh said, and his right hand shot out.

He was a good fighter, but he couldn't school me, and he barked his shin on the bench early in our bout and I got him on one knee and banged his head on the chimney despite the heat.

He roared like a bull and tried to throw me off. His left hand slammed into my temple and I saw stars, then my right punched him in the forehead and snapped his head back against the chimney, again, and down he went.

I didn't kick him when he was in the rushes, and he turned and threw up, then got slowly to his feet, holding one hand between us. 'Fair enough, sprig,' he said. 'Sew all you like.'

'Thanks,' I responded.

I won't say we were friends after that. He and his brother were hard men, and they were happy to take things that weren't offered. But after that fight, they let us alone.

We then we marched south, for Provence, with almost forty lances in our company, and on the road we merged with other companions, until there were thousands of us. The Bascot de Mauléon told me later that there were 10,000 of us that winter, headed for Provence. Perhaps.

We didn't celebrate Christmas. I missed it – I love Christmas. But Christmas means a church that isn't burned, a priest who hasn't been killed and an abundance of bread and sweets and meat. And children. There's no Christmas without children.

In 1360, in southern Auvergne, as we came down the passes, we had 10,000 professional soldiers and another 8,000 desperate men and women. We had war horses and armour and weapons, baggage carts, banners, the glitter of spear points like a thousand stars, the weight of mail like lost love tugging at your heart, the stirring song of serried companies singing.

But we didn't have an abundance of anything except rain, and we had no children and no priests.

I did get a present for Yule. Richard called me down to the yard, where a royal messenger was riding away with his bodyguard archers. He tossed me a silk envelope and I opened it.

Master William Gold,

I have reached London, by the grace of our lord, and found your sister with ease. I have enclosed a few words in her own hand. I send my assurance she is well-housed and well-considered, although her house for the most part keeps silence, and I only saw her for as long as it took to push your letter through a grate. Hers arrived a day later, and now, I hope my friends in the Prince's household will see it to you.

Send my best regard to Richard Musard, with my deepest wish that both of you may find a way clear of France. London is better.

Your servant,

Inside, a single parchment sheet folded very small.

Dear Brother,

Fra Peter told me that you lived, and indeed thrived, as it were, in service of our Prince. And bless you, the sisters are very kind to me, and treat me as if I was a novice and not a serving woman. The

*Commander has twice stopped me to tell me you sent money for my
dowry. Good brother, no woman ever had better.*

*Let me say also that the Plague came here again, but I am salted,
as you are, so I went out to the sick, and the good lord worked
through me. I am very happy here.*

*Be safe. And may the Grace of our Lord Jesus Christ and the
fellowship of the Holy Ghost be with you always.*

I wept.

For me, the battle of Brignais started under the walls of Pont-Saint-
Esprit. It was a day or two after Christmas, and we had marched
south with the speed that only routiers could march – thirty and
forty miles a day, despite rain and snow. We were hard men, and
we could move quickly. We didn't have servants to shave us, and
farriers to look after our mounts. We went unshaven, and when a
horse threw a shoe, we left him behind – and stole another.

We outran news of our coming.

Pont-Saint-Esprit was a bridge town on the Rhône, just twenty
miles north of Avignon. Sir John Hawkwood said that Seguin de
Badefol had spies in the town, and that we could take it by escalade,
despite it being one of the strongest fortified bridge towns in all of
France. Except, of course, that Pont-Saint-Esprit isn't in France. It's
in Provence.

At any rate, the whole host pillaged Roquemaure and Codolet, in
both cases we took the inhabitants by surprise, and we took everything.

Sir John came to us that night, and proposed that if we took a
path over the mountains, with guides he trusted, we could take the
richest prize – a whole city.

By then, I knew Sir John well enough to know when he was
hiding something. He whipped his men into a fury at the thought of
a whole town – a rich town – to take. He sounded disinterested in
the ransoms and the money, and I smelled a rat, but I had no idea
the scale of the rat I was taking on. Richard felt the same, and he
tugged his beard and stared at the first stars.

'What do you think this is about?' he said.

We'd both seen the royal messenger. But we didn't know anything, and that rankled.

Richard and I led the English vanguard. We climbed the steep pass, and at the top, we found piles of brushwood that Hawkwood had paid peasants to drag there. We made huge fires, and warmed ourselves, and then, at about the first hour of the morning, we went down the mountain on the other side.

The moonlight was pale and cold. The moon was full.

We assembled our ladders in the ditch, and detachments of archers stood directing us, like men unsorting a jam of wagons in Cheapside. I moved to the head of a ladder by right, and when Hawkwood gave the word, up I went. First man on a ladder, into a town with a heavy garrison.

I don't remember a single fight from the storming. The garrison was unready and easily terrified. Most of the citizens surrendered abjectly, but the fifty richest families barricaded themselves in a church that had a strong stone tower in the north of the city. They took their jewels and their daughters, barricaded the doors, and swore they'd hold the church until rescued by the papal army, which was just twenty miles away.

Hawkwood came in on horseback, by a gate we'd opened after we butchered its defenders, and he rode to the church with twenty men-at-arms, looked at it and gave it over as a bad job. He swept through the town like a blade through butter, and I could see from the way his mounted company moved that they were looking for something.

By nones the next day, the Bourc Camus arrived with another company. Richard and I avoided his black and white clad men. Houses were burned, but Hawkwood's archers kept the mercenaries under control, and he began to negotiate a ransom for the whole town with several of the town's magnates, who he already had in hand.

The papal army didn't move.

It was the second day after the storming when the situation exploded. Richard and I were counting our winnings; we'd taken over a house, and if we roughed up the inhabitants, I swear to you we were the gentlest tenants in that place. We had coins and some gold objects, and Richard had acquired a squire named Robert and a pair of servants, two likely French lads named Belier and Arnaud. John had found himself another senior archer as a companion, Ned Candleman, and we had another eight archers. So we had mouths to feed and the loot had to be shared. We were already planning to start our own company, even then.

John Thornbury appeared in the street, shouting for us. I remember going to the window, my brigantine unbuckled – my armour was in a sorry state by then – and all I could think was that the papal army was going to attack us.

I leaned out into the street. 'What ails you, John?' I asked.

He was looking north. 'Gather your lance. There's going to be trouble with the Gascons.'

Nothing would please me better. A fight with Camus?

Richard and I had our men together and moving before you could say five paternosters. We pounded through the narrow streets and terrified locals cowered in doorways or slammed their doors shut.

We were late to the party.

We came to the square in front of the church, and it took me a moment to determine what was happening, because I came expecting a fight, not a massacre.

The Bourc had grown bored of laying siege to the church, so he offered them their lives and freedom in exchange for surrender – if they gave up the church and left the town, he'd let them take everything they could carry. It was a common enough solution to strongly held houses in the countryside.

Remember that these were the fifty richest and most noble families in the town. Remember, too, that Hawkwood was looking for something. The truth is, he'd encouraged Camus to get the little siege over with. Whatever Hawkwood was trying to find, it had become obvious that it was in the church.

As we came up to the square, the oath had been sworn, the Bible kissed, and the great nail-studded oak doors of the church were opening.

The Bourc Camus sat on his great black war horse in the middle of the square in front of the church, watching as the doors to the nave were thrown back. About forty men stood there, with their swords in their scabbards. Behind them cowered a hundred women. Most of the men and women were richly dressed, and all of them had bundles, like peasants.

The men began to file out the cathedral doors, led by a priest with a cross.

Camus spat on the ground in sheer disgust.

I was watching Hawkwood. He was looking at the newly surrendered refugees the way a man buying a horse watches the horse – eyes narrowed, nostrils flared. He touched his horse with his spurs and rode past Camus into the square. 'Which of you,' he said, 'is Pierre Scatisse?'

The man at the head of the column was a nobleman. You could tell – straight back, unbowed head, angry eyes. A young woman clutched his arm. She glared at Hawkwood with the same look of contempt as her father.

The man stopped. 'By what right do you ask anything of us?' asked the man. 'And where is our escort?'

'Which of you is Pierre Scatisse?' asked Hawkwood again.

The little column began to shuffle past him.

'By God!' he shouted. 'Produce Monsieur Scatisse or take the consequences!'

The nobleman stopped. 'None of us is Monsieur Scatisse,' he said. 'I live here. I would know.'

Hawkwood trembled with frustration. I could see his anger, and it transmitted to his horse, who began to fret. Later – much later – I learned that Scatisse was the man who was taking a convoy with the Pope's contribution to the French King's ransom.

And he wasn't there.

Camus laughed. He rode his horse along the column, his horse's hooves ringing on the square's cobblestones in the cold air. He passed the nobleman, drew his sword and cut down at the priest, severing the man's cross and cutting into his neck.

'Kill them all,' he called.

The nobleman whirled, drawing his sword. He cut down the first brigand to come for him, and the second, but Camus towered above him, hammered through his guard and split his head.

Every mercenary in the square fell on those folk. Except two.

The men were killed.

The women were raped.

The nobleman's daughter took her father's sword, stood over his corpse and fought. She didn't last long before a pair of Gascons threw her down and took her.

And that was the end of me.

I gather that I stood there for a long moment, watching the massacre unfold, neither helping nor harming. I have no memory of that time.

But when the two Gascons threw the girl down, something snapped.

I killed them.

I don't remember it.

But I remember Camus. He was sitting on his horse, watching the rape and murder like Satan, with a gleam of savage satisfaction. This was his world. This was all he wanted of it – that men humiliate each other; that men suffer degradation whether they are victims or criminals.

I rammed my longsword's point into the soft back of his thigh before he even knew I was there, and then I slammed an armoured fist into his hip and hammered him out of the saddle. His head hit the pavement with a hollow sound, like an empty gourd, and I raised my blade—

And John Thornbury took my sword arm from behind.

Both of the Ashleys had my arms, and Richard Musard stood between me and my prey. Camus lay on the stones and his eyes wouldn't focus. Behind him, the French girl who'd used the sword tried to cover herself. She was bleeding and weeping.

Sir John planted himself in front of me. 'William,' he said, as if I was a fool. 'What am I going to do with you? This is no place for a private quarrel.' He spoke to me as if I was a small child.

'Sir John, we *swore* to protect these people. To escort them to Avignon. We *swore!*' I think I was sobbing. The French girl got a dagger from her father's corpse.

Sir John shook his head. 'You don't know what this is about, lad. It's not on your head. Now, be a good lad, take your men and walk away.'

John Hughes saw what the girl was about, bless him. She put the dagger to her throat, but before she could do it, he had the dagger. She raked her nails across his face, and he slugged her hard enough to put her down.

Then he picked her up and threw her across his shoulder, and we left the square.

The next day, John Thornbury brought me thirty day's pay and told me that I had to go. He sat at my table, had a cup of French cider and apologized for Sir John.

I knew what was coming. It had been happening my whole life.

'Sir John asks that you go away until the Bourc is somewhat calmer,' he said. 'We need the Bourc's men, and his allies.' He shrugged. 'He's a monster, and that's the saviour's own truth, but we can't be too picky just now.'

I drew a deep breath and said nothing.

He went on, as embarrassed men do, speaking to hide silence. 'If we'd found the ransom money here,' he began.

'What's that?' asked Richard.

Thornbury looked at both of us, his eyes narrow, then he looked away. 'It doesn't matter any more,' he said.

But Richard started to stand up. 'You mean all of this was about the King of France's ransom,' he said quietly.

Thornbury got to his feet. 'Come back in a few days,' he said. 'Send Perkin or Robert to make sure of your welcome.'

We were all on our feet.

'You mean to say,' said Richard, 'that the King of England, having made a treaty with the King of France based on his ransom, tipped you off to come and steal that ransom? So he could abrogate the treaty?'

'And beggar France?' I put in.

Thornbury spat. 'You two children need to go to school. This is the world. We're not knights of spotless renkown. We're soldiers. We kill and maim. That's what we do. If the King orders us to do something and it will make us all rich, who are we to question it? We should have picked up 400,000 florins when we took this town. Think of that, you two pious fucks – 400,000 florins. Your share would have been between 400 and 800 florins each. Enough to buy all the French girls in the world. Buy masses, if you want. Buy an indulgence from the Pope, if that's what your pretty little conscience needs.' He glared at Richard. 'Don't come back until you've mastered your tender soul, Monsieur. It'll get you killed. Until you do, you are not welcome in this company.'

He pushed past me and left.

I stood there, breathing hard, then I looked at Richard. He was nearly red, he was so furious. 'I will never come back,' he shouted at John Thornbury. 'Tell Sir John Hawkwood that I spit on him.

'I doubt he cares,' Thornbury shouted back.

I suppose we should have been worried that the Gascons would attack us, or that Hawkwood would take some revenge, but it didn't happen like that. We collected our loot and summoned our people – Ned and John; Perkin and Robert; Arnaud and Belier; Amory and Jack and the other six. And the girl, whose name I didn't know, who stared in stony silence. She'd eat and dress herself, but she hadn't said one word since she came along with us.

'Friends,' I said, 'Richard and I have been dismissed from Sir John's company. We are not short on money and we can continue wages.' My confident speech petered out – I had no idea where I was going or why, so I guess I frowned.

Richard nodded. 'If you come with us, there could be some hard times,' he said.

Arnaud laughed aloud. 'Hard times?' he asked. He shook his head. 'I've eaten more in the last month than in the last five years.'

Belier said nothing, but I saw his eyes on the woman. Even stone-faced and silent, she was pretty. More than pretty.

'Leave her alone,' I said.

John Hughes nodded. 'What do you reckon, gentles?' he asked. 'Take service with another lord? Petit Mechin has a company – and I hear he hates Camus like we do.'

In that moment, I loved John Hughes. The words 'hates Camus like we do', that moment of solidarity, rang like a clarion and was engraved on my heart.

'Where's Mechin?' I asked. 'Or Seguin de Badefol?'

Richard shook his head. 'I think we should leave this life.'

Even in the circumstances, I remember being stunned. 'And do what?' I asked.

He shook his head. 'I don't know,' he admitted. 'I only know that if I don't walk away soon, this will be the sum of who I am.'

I heard Emile, then: *But that need not be the sum of who we are.*

They all came with us, and we rode out of the gates of Pont-Saint-Esprit on the first day of the new year, 1361.

You want to hear about Brignais, so I'll spare you the whole tale of my next year. We rode with de Badefol, and we came in sight of the Mediterranean, and swept like a horde of locusts along the Côte d'Azur until, by August, we came to Narbonne. The woman we'd taken – did we save her? I'm still not sure – rode with us. She didn't speak, and nor did she lie with any of us. When an archer tried, I hit him.

She also didn't bathe or brush her hair or behave like a woman, and after a few weeks, her presence was a burden on every campfire. We didn't even know her name, so we called her Milady.

We took some small towns, but in general, the Narbonnais and their cousins in the Rouergue were ready for us. Their towns were strong and well-garrisoned, and we were always short of food and fodder, so we could never sit down to lay siege to so much as a forti-fied house without feeling hunger. We moved fast, trying to repeat the victories of the fifties, when companies of English and Gascon freebooters had surprised towns all over France, but the easy pick-ings were gone, and by a process of elimination of the weakest, only the strong remained.

The knights and militia of Carcassonne and Toulouse knew their business – perhaps having Gascons as neighbours had made them hard. They shadowed us night and day, struck our camps, killed our sentries, stole our horses and murdered our sick and wounded. Not that they had it all their own way. When we caught a party of them, the tables were turned, and if a man of Carcassonne wasn't worth a ransom and we took him in arms, we hanged him from a tree.

One day in May – already hot, under a magnificent blue sky – we fought four Provençal knights at a ford. We'd found a dovecote in which to camp, and they'd seen our smoke and come at us – four mounted knights and a dozen of their own routiers with spears and helmets.

It was a bitter little fight, with no quarter asked or given. I dropped one of their knights in the ford with my lance, and Richard got another, then we were fighting for our lives. Ned and John made all the difference, and as we fought on, they stood on the bank and slowly killed their way through our opponents, unhorsing the mounted men and killing the unarmoured footmen.

Finally, the last knight and half a dozen footmen broke and ran.

We killed them.

I rode the knight down, caught him and beat him from the saddle with my sword. Richard put his sword through a gap in the man's coat of plates while he writhed on the ground, but he never requested our mercy. Then we chased the footmen.

All of them.

It took us some time, and when we returned to the ford, John and Ned were stripping the corpses with Arnaud and Belier. A slim young man was just lacing his hose on the river bank. I didn't know him, but Ned didn't seem to pay him any heed.

Provençal's were good fighters, but their equipment was anti-quated – mail shirts and leather reinforcement. The smallest of them had a nice pair of steel greaves, which I admired, but my legs were about a foot too long for them. John Hughes took them and, as I watched, he gave them to the young man.

The fellow looked up at John and smiled.

I had never seen her smile, but I knew immediately that it was Milady. I was still mounted and I rode over.

She looked up at me. She didn't appear afraid. She said, 'I know how to fight.' She said it as if we'd had a hundred conversations.

I was dumbfounded. 'You washed your hair,' I said.

'It was filthy,' she said. 'I cut a lot of it off.'

'Leave her be,' said John in a low voice.

'I'm going to be a man, now, if you don't mind,' she said.

Later, in Italy, we had twenty women in harness. We were famous for it, and the Italian men-at-arms shat themselves to think they were fighting women – and losing. But in the summer of 1361, there weren't a lot of women fighting in armour in the world. I thought about it.

'That's fine,' I said.

John Hughes gave me a small, approving nod.

Milady took a place in our little company as if born to it. She could fight and she could forage. She was small, but her riding was a far sight better than mine or even Richard's, and her use of the lance was as pretty as ... as she might have been.

The next night, when Richard produced his dice box, she joined in.

I still have no idea what happened. It was as if she lost her soul, and then, one day, she found it – or another soul, the soul of a harder person. A man.

No. Not a man, as you'll hear.

Her name was Janet. And in the complex cross-currents around us, as dangerous as the currents in a river when boys are swimming, the fact that she kept a woman's name said something.

She changed our people.

The very first day she recovered her voice, we were sharing the loot from the dead Provençal knights, and Milady – we continued to call her that – looked at me.

'Just give me the fucking money,' Jack Sumner said for the third time to young Amory, who apparently owed him gambling debts.

Milady looked at me and frowned. 'I will not have swearing,' she said. 'Not among my lord's retainers.'

Jack looked abashed. He mumbled and apologized.

I reached for my share of the money.

'You should have a man to carry your purse,' she said to me. 'It is

302

ignoble for you to handle this money yourself. You practice largesse – you give to the poor, you host others in your hall. You pay no attention to money. That is the way of being a knight. Let another man watch it for you.' Her mad eyes bored into mine. 'When did you last give money to the poor?'

Perkin bowed to her. 'Milady, I am Master William's squire, and I will carry his purse.'

She sniffed. 'See that it is done.'

Perkin beamed at her.

We mounted up and rode, heading north to rejoin the main 'army' of routiers. We called ourselves the Grand Company, and we had a good few men-at-arms.

As we rode through the sunshine, Milady began to sing. She was a southerner, an Occitan, and she sang the old songs. Her French – it wasn't really all French – was hard to understand, but *par dieu*, she sang *comme une ange*, like an angel. She sang the songs of courtly love, and songs of war. She sang of Richard Coeur de Lion, and she sang of a peasant girl on a hillside refusing the love of a knight.

She held us spellbound.

That night – the first night of her speaking – we *paid* for a sheep from two terrified young peasants, butchered it and ate it in the shepherd's stone cot, which was open on one side, where we built a roaring fire. The sheep we did in parts, not whole, and we had wine. Then Richard produced a deck of cards – the new cards that all the routiers spoke of. I hadn't seen them. Some men said they came from the east – from India, even.

The cards Richard had were like the ones the Dominicans used to teach the catechism, except that the religious symbols had been replaced by those of venery – stags, ducks, spears and hawks. They were beautiful – hand-painted on fine parchemnt and pasted like artworks on fine paste board. Richard had taken them off a merchant we'd despoiled in the taking of Pont-Saint-Esprit.

Milady pounced on them like a young girl on a silk ribbon. 'Do you play?' she asked. 'Piquet?' She smiled. 'I promise that I will deal gently with you, messieurs. My father taught me to play.'

At the words 'my father' her whole body gave a convulsive shudder. Then she pasted a smile on her face. 'No matter. Let me teach you, *eh bien?*'

I remember that I leaned forward. 'Would you rather dice, my lady?'

And she shook her head. 'Dice are all very well, but a gentleman plays cards.'

I wanted to humour her – even then. 'For high stakes?' I asked.

'A true knight never counts the cost, my lord,' she said. 'He wagers whatever he will, and if he loses, why, he pays. Rich or poor, a true knight never counts his coins like a merchant.'

Richard laughed. 'This is why merchants own more and more of the world!' he said. 'And why Italian bankers defeat French knights.'

She frowned. 'No, sir. Whatever amount of coin they amass, they are men of no worth. Only those who put their bodies in peril can be accounted *preux*. Those who will not risk death can have no *preux*.' She smiled at me. 'Surely I need not tell you this, monsieur.'

She smiled at me, and at Richard.

I sat back. 'What of us? We take coin to fight.'

She shrugged. 'Bah! A gentleman must feed his horses and his servants. Only a fool ... my father ...' She paused and a shade passed over her face. 'My father says only a fool or the Pope can expect a man to fight for nothing.'

I liked her nonsense. 'And can a base-born man enoble himself by a life of arms?' I asked.

She smiled. It was the pure smile of a maiden – lips slightly parted, eyes bright. 'Of course!' she maintained. 'Who but a malcontent or caitiff would say else?'

Richard was grinning like a fool, or a big, happy dog. 'Jesus,' he said aloud.

'And I will thank you not to take the lord's name in vain,' Milady said. 'A knight is at all times respectful of his lord's passion. A knight, by the pain of his armour and the labour of his wars, suffers with our lord every day.'

I think I swallowed. Hard.

But we drank, we played cards, and all the silver from my purse went into Milady's. She giggled. 'I will need my own squire,' she allowed. Her eyes fixed on Amory. 'You – you have a gentle way with you. Do you fancy being my squire?'

The snap of her words brought the boy to a position of deference and he leaped to do her bidding.

I think we all did.

The next few days were spent moving fast. We stared down a pair of knights at a river crossing and convinced them to move aside.

We saw a strong force coming on the road an hour later, and we judiciously moved into the high hills south of Narbonne, with the sheep and the wolves. I don't remember much of those days, except that we were enjoying her company so much we scarcely noticed that we were suddenly the focus of a papal hunt for malcontents. There were twenty papal men-at-arms chasing us, and another twenty mounted corssbowmen, and we were riding through deadly country, where a sudden rockfall could kill your horse. But again, Milady knew the area, and again, she knew how to move through it.

'We hunted here,' she said with a brittle smile, because hunting reminded her of her father, which reminded her of Pont-Saint-Esprit. I could follow her thought, and I was careful not to mention anything to do with that place. Richard was not so quick, and I had to kick him a few times.

There are few things as fatiguing as commanding men – and women – in flight, and doing so while attempting to control their tempers and their emotions. Richard couldn't take his eyes off Janet, despite some admonitions from me. Amory was in the same state – not so much love as helpless adoration. John Hughes looked at her with a fatherly, protective air, which made him surly with me. And so on.

It wore on my temper, and when the load slipped on Jack Sumner's mule, I lost my temper.

'Get your head out of your arse and see to that animal!' I shouted. 'By the mother that bore you and god's Grace, I should leave you to be taken. And the papal knights will string your useless corpse up by the roadside unshriven!'

Sumner *had* hovered by the pre-dawn breakfast fire instead of taking care with his packing. I'd noted it.

He didn't quite meet my eyes and his face was working.

I could feel her coming. I could hear the horse picking its way along the hillside.

I thought I knew what she was going to say, and I was ready to have it out with her. Her presence was focusing our men on the wrong things.

She rode up next to me without so much as jostling my horse on the narrow track. Among her other abilities, she rode like a centaur in one of her romances.

'Well?' she said, imperiously, to Sumner.

He looked at her.

She raised an eyebrow. 'You have justifiably angered your lord,' she said.

Sumner stammered. Sumner was a tough bastard who'd have knifed his own mother to get a fresh horse, but he stammered.

She cocked an eyebrow at me and turned her horse's head. I trotted up our column in a state of shock. I'd expected her to take his side, which, in retrospect, was foolish of me. She *always* deferred to my command.

At the head of the column, she motioned to Richard to fall back – he'd been riding with her – and when we had the privacy afforded by rapid movement on a narrow track, she said, 'A knight does not lose his temper.'

'Then I'm no knight,' I said, spoiling for a fight.

She looked at me. 'You are a knight. And if you seek the rank, and achieve it, it is on your shoulders to support it. A knight is in control of his temper – always. This is the essence of courtesy, and courtesy is at the heart of knighthood.'

I thought of Chatillon, and du Guesclin, and Sir John Chandos. And even Hawkwood.

I had never seen Sir John Hawkwood lose his temper. Then I considered Boucicault.

I winced.

She smiled. 'If you wish to command others, you must always show that you are in command of yourself. This my father taught me.' Her eyes met mine – too wide, too open, too bright.

'Perhaps I'm just a common churl who kills men for money,' I spat.

Her mad eyes met mine. 'You saved me,' she said in a low voice.

I couldn't hold her eyes. There was something burning there and I had to look away.

I also remember another evening – we'd outrun our pursuit and found a stream coming out of the high hills towards Spain, so we washed off the dust and dirt, and in some cases blood, of five days of moving fast. She bathed with us – like the man she'd made herself – sometimes.

I refused to let myself look at her body, but I was aware of it.

And afterwards, we lay around the pool. All the men had put shirts on – that was the effect she had – so she put on a shirt.

That's not what makes the moment memorable, nor was the

flask of Gascon wine that was going around. Amory and Ned were in the rocks above us, on watch. John Hughes, moving carefully, climbed up to them with wine.

'I could teach you to ride better,' she said. She lay between Richard and me, and it was hard to tell which of us she addressed.

'What is wrong with my riding?' Richard asked. He raised his head.

She smiled at the blue sky. 'You are not in command of your horse, and he knows it.'

Richard sat up. 'Really?'

'Yes,' she said. She turned her head and smiled at me. Her teeth were much whiter than a peasant girl's. 'And you are no better. If I didn't know better, I'd say that you were afraid of horses. Did you learn late?'

Par dieu, mes gentils! I sat up and found myself nose to nose with Richard.

She laughed.

I think that Richard had only known prostitutes and camp women. He was tough as nails, gentle and true, but he was a fool with women, and he never had a chance. My Lady had all the skills of the nobility – all the skills, to be frank, that Richard and I lacked. While we rode, she would chat, or even discourse. It was as if, having been silent for two months, she had to make up for lost time.

I liked her a great deal.

Richard was hit with a poleaxe.

In a matter of days, our lives changed and changed again. We caught up with the Grand Company, and as we rode past Narbonne and turned north into the Rouergue, Richard changed, too. One night, he saw his love to bed – not a sign, by the by, that his feelings were returned – and came to sit with me at the fire.

'This is no life for a lady,' he said.

I guess I'm an insensitive brute. I thought it was a fine life for her. Emile had given me some notion of what a well-born girl had to look forward to – and worse if she'd been publicly shamed like Milady. A convent? At best? Whereas with us, she was safe as houses. She seemed to me to be blooming like a summer flower in high heat.

So I shrugged. 'She looks fine to me,' I said. 'Better every day.'

'When I was in Avignon,' he said, 'I met a man – a great lord. The Count of Savoy.'

'The Green Count?' I asked. He was a great noble *and* a famous knight. One of the few great men who still risked his body in the field. I was picking up Milady's language.

Richard nodded. 'I could take service with him.'

'He has a great name,' I agreed, 'but I doubt he'd accept Milady as a lance.'

'Oh, as to that,' he said dismissively. 'She doesn't need to continue that charade. I'll provide for her.'

That didn't sound like what I saw every day, but on the other hand, I was more interested in a little loot, and in where my captain intended to spend the winter. The loot was because I had just two payments left on my sister's dowry. When it was paid, I was a free lance. And spending the winter? I was determined to ride to Emile. Time spent close to Milady Janet had convinced me I needed Emile.

A rumour had come that Sir John Hawkwood and some of the other companies had gone over the mountains to Italy after cutting a deal with the Pope. The rumour came from one of the Florentine bankers who rode with us, and when he'd told me the rumour, he handed over two letters – one from Sir John Hawkwood, requesting that I rejoin his company for the spring campaign, and one – a small, well-wrapped package – from Bertrand du Guesclin. He thanked me for the return of the borrowed armour – the fine breast and backplates he'd loaned me for the tilt at Calais – and he enclosed a note from 'a friend'.

Monsieur my heart,

I hear from our mutual friends that you are alive, still brave and still in the field. My thoughts turn to you often, even while I sit at my high window and spin. In the spring I will bear my lord another child – but these are the petty concerns of a young matron, and I pray that wherever you are, you spare a thought for one who thinks of you each day.

I enclose something that I hope you will treasure for my sake, and for your own.

And she signed it, the little fool: 'Emile d'Herblay'.

I sat on my horse with an army flowing around me, and a great rage rose in me because she was pregant, again. Because I was not with her. Because, in fact, she went on with her life, doing as a wife must, and I went on with my life, doing as a mercenary must.

We weren't just an army of mercenaries. To understand the years of the sixties, you have to understand that we weren't an army or a nation, but we had aspects of both. Badefol's version of the Great Company had about 8,000 professional soldiers, but another 12,000 men, women and children – desperate people, yes, but some merely looking for a better life or tired of oppression and tyranny. We had, in one vast army, men who had been Jacques, women who had fled brutal husbands, children who fled hateful parents; men who had been Flemish burghers, men who aspired to be English knights. It was not an army of looters and rapists, although we committed those crimes with increasing frequency.

It was also a very young army. I was about to be twenty-one, and I was older than most of the women and quite a few of the men. I had been at war for five years – some of the men-at-arms had been at war for twenty, but most were on their second or third campaign.

At any rate, we attracted a surprising number of women. We had women who had been nobles, like Milady, and women who had been merchant's wives, and women who had been peasants, serfs, nuns, whores – the whole morality of our moving tribe was shockingly at odds with the morality of the towns. We had very few rules.

Of course, we lived by the sword, and we died like lemmings. Our women died of exposure, childbirth and famine; our children were thin beggars, and our men fed their horses before they fed the women and children. I'm not moved to argue that there was anything particularly noble about our army of mercenaries, except to say that, for a great many men and women, it was the closest thing to *power* they ever achieved. Odd, because many of our people were refugees from other bastards just like us. I'd read Aristotle and Aquinas, by then. So I would sit with my back against my saddle, some nights, and contemplate such things.

Emile's cursed note came with a package. It proved to be a book. It was, in fact, Sir Ramon Llull's book of chivalry. It was a beautiful thing, with gilt capitals and four magnificent, painted miniatures – one of two knights jousting, and one of a hermit talking to a knight.

That night, I sat with my back to my saddle and flipped through the pages of the book. And out of nowhere, my eyes filled with tears and I wept.

Janet came. She picked up the book and laughed aloud. '*Par dieu*, this is a fine book!' she said.

She ignored my tears, read a passage aloud, then put the book back down and returned to the fire.

In mid-September, Richard, too, received a letter. He and I rode to Arles with our lances, and no one troubled us on the road. We weren't allowed in the town – towns were very wary of us – but Richard got a tailor to come out and fit him for some new clothes. We also sold an armourer a lot of cast-off stuff – mostly mail – and he fit Richard with a better coat of plates and matching arms, so that Richard looked less of a routier and more of a gentleman.

My take as a man-at-arms about equalled the daily cost of maintaining an archer, a squire and a page. I didn't have the money to care if my armour was brown with rust, nor could I afford to care if my straps matched, or whether my rivet heads were decorated. I just cared that it all fit, didn't weigh too much and lasted well in the rain. By that fall, I had two different leg harnesses, two different arms, a coat of plates that had once been very beautiful but was now a uniform black with sweat and rot, and I was on my fifth war horse, a heavy animal that had once, I suspect, been a cart horse and never really been properly broken. But I made the second to last payment for my sister's dowry.

The bankers were still with us, so somewhere I had two suits of good clothes and a fine cloak, but really, what would I use them for?

I digress. On to Brignais.

We returned from Arles to find a papal officer in our camp. He was recruiting for the Pope's army in Italy, and for the crusade that had been preached. Our rambling, unsanitary morass of a camp covered three hillsides, and it was several days before I found myself looking at him.

He wore a simple brown wool habit, like a Franciscan, over spurred boots. By his side hung a fine sword in a red leather scabbard. He was tanned so darkly he might have been Richard Musard's brother, and he had a long, very white scar that ran from his left temple to the corner of his mouth on the right. It showed even through his magnificent moustache which was as berry-brown as his gown, but white where the scar crossed it.

I'd seen him before, of course. In England. And I'd helped him take a party south through the chaos of '58. I bowed. 'Fra Peter,' I said. 'What news of my sister, my lord?'

He smiled. 'The blessings of the Lord be with you, my son,' he said. 'Your sister will be a light of the church.'

'And with you, father,' I responded automatically.

'Brother,' he corrected gently. 'I am but a brother-knight. I have taken my vows, but I am not a priest.'

How do you make small talk with people like that?

'I fear it has been some time since I confessed my sins,' I said weakly, hoping he had a flash of humour.

He shrugged. 'I can't help you, as I'm not a priest.' He raised an eyebrow. 'And as you are excommunicate.'

'I ... what?' I choked. Oh, I know men who take the prospect of eternal damnation lightly. I am not one of them. 'What?'

'After the events of Pont-Saint-Esprit, the Holy Father excommunicated every routier in Provence.' My knight Hospitaller shrugged. 'Would you like to know more of how your sister fares?'

I must have smiled. 'Yes, my lord.'

'Yes, Fra Peter!' he barked.

I laughed, because I admired him so, and I'd made him bark. 'Yes, Fra Peter,' I answered like a dutiful schoolboy.

'She thrives. She works hard, but she is devoted to Christ and to St John, and well-beloved of the sisters. It is her dearest wish to be allowed to join the order.' He tilted his head slightly to one side. 'I have arranged to have our Holy Father issue her an exemption from the article that requires a certain patent of nobility.'

I hadn't considered the patents of nobility. A lump formed in my throat. 'I have paid her dowry,' I said.

He nodded. 'I hoped I would find you. I take my vow of poverty seriously – I have nothing. The order requires the full payment of the dowry for a new sister. I expect that you have some money, as you are a ... mm ... a *professional* man-at-arms.'

I laughed. 'You want me, a penniless mercenary, to give money to the church?' I held my temper in check. I had been practising, since Milady put the matter to me so clearly. 'Fra Peter, I have given almost every ducat to your order for more than a year.'

His eyes never left mine. 'You must do as you think best,' he said carefully. 'But if you can complete her dowry while I have the document for her patents ...' he shrugged and looked away. 'I'm sorry, Master Gold. But not every member of my order feels as I do about your sister's pedigree.'

I have no idea why that set me off. I have never been proud of my birth – nor ashamed. My parents were wed, which is more than some can say, and my pater served good King Edward as a man-at-arms. That was as gentle as a man needed to be, I felt.

Perhaps it was because I had so much admiration for Fra Peter, but his words, ill-chosen or not – perhaps I was just touchy – seemed to cut me.

'My sister's pedigree is as good as any woman's in England,' I spat.

His eyes met mine and I regretted my outburst. So, like any young man, I threw oil on the fire.

'And anyway, aren't you supposed to be recruiting us for the Pope's war in Italy?' I asked with all the heavy sarcasm a twenty-year-old can muster.

He stepped closer to me. 'Yes,' he said. 'Are you interested?'

'Do I have to donate my time?' I asked.

He looked at me. His eyes didn't express hurt or disappointment. More … amusement. 'Do you still seek to be a knight?' he asked. 'Or do you imagine that you have reached that estate already?'

That was the closest he had come to an insult, and as cuts go, it was deep and true.

Once again I was looking at the toes of my boots. 'No,' I confessed.

'No,' he agreed.

That night, Richard came and announced that he was taking Milady and riding away to join the Green Count. Well, he'd never hidden it, and I knew what he planned.

I must say, he looked very fine in green and sable – the Black Squire, in all truth. His armour looked good, his horse gleamed and his clothing was clean and neat. He had new shirts and new braes that almost shone white.

I was very sad that he was leaving me. I think that just then, I hated Milady for coming between us, but her conquest of him had been so sudden and so complete that I knew the cause was hopeless.

Let me be clear. I don't think she meant to conquer him. She was simply, singly, and fully herself.

We had a fine night. We sat by a fire and drank, and we talked. If I have time, I might tell you half the things we said. Some were antic, and come were deadly serious. Milady sat with us, and John Hughes, Ned, Amory and Jack. Men I knew came by to say goodbye to Richard – all the remaining English and Scots knights who hadn't gone to Italy, and there were a few: Walter Leslie and Bill Feldon were there, and a dozen more who made their names that summer or the next, or died trying.

But as conversations will go around a fire, a moment came when Milady had me all to herself. She was expert at arranging things like that. She was sitting with her back to John Hughes, and she suddenly leaned over to me. 'Come with us,' she said.

I was damned sure that was not what Richard had in mind. 'Perhaps when I get a good ransom,' I said.

She smiled. 'You will.'

I shrugged.

'What do you want it for? This ransom?' she asked.

I looked into her mad eyes. They were still too wide and they still sparkled too much. 'I love a lady,' I said.

She nodded. 'That is as it should be.'

'Winning her will require ... some money,' I said.

Janet laughed and sat back. 'My father said ...' she began, and the old shadow fell across her face.

'Never mind,' I said.

Janet shook her head, hard – too hard – and leaned forward. 'He said, "Never count the money and never count the odds."' Her eyes met mine.

And I thought, Why is she going with Richard?

'What do you want, Janet?' I asked. We were close enough to kiss. I didn't *want* Milady, but there is something – when you can feel the warmth of another person's face – something beyond intimacy.

She pursed her lips. 'I want to be a knight,' she said. 'It is all I've ever wanted. My father had no son.'

So. And so.

Sometime after the North Star began to go down, the Hospitaller came. We made him welcome – anyone could see he was a great knight.

'Wine, brother?' I asked.

He nodded. 'I never say no to wine,' he said, and he drank a fair amount. He hindered our conversation for a little while, but he was so mild a man that after a time we went back to our own ways. And in truth, Milady had mended our manners with nothing but gentle derision.

Eventually, I raised a cup of Burgundy to Richard. 'I will miss you. My best friend.'

Richard was drunk. He came and put his arms around me and

rested his forehead against mine. 'I want to be a *knight*, he said. 'Not a fucking killer for hire.' He took a deep and somewhat drunken breath. 'You should, too. You're too good for this shit.'

'Yes,' I said. I wasn't worthy. But at least I knew it.

As I left his embrace, I saw the Hospitaller watching me.

I lay under a cloak, looking at the stars, and listened to Richard and Milady make love. Or rather, I listened to him make love. It's a common enough set of camp sounds, and I wager I've made them as much as any man, and yet, almost painful to listen to, especially when you lie alone with only the darkest of thoughts. I thought of us all – me, Richard, Milady and Fra Peter. Three of us wanted to be knights. Half the men in our camp wanted to be knights.

I knew the words. I knew Sir Ramon's book almost by heart.

When Janet left Richard's blankets, I heard her movement and I got up. It was early autumn, and I found Milady sitting by the fire. She smiled at me and relieved me from some shadowy apprehensions. I'm not sure what I feared – for him or for her – but her smile seemed relaxed.

'I don't think I'll be a good wife,' she said. 'Don't sell my armour, eh, *mon amie*?'

'Of course you will be,' I said.

She shrugged. 'Promise!'

I nodded, built up the fire and went back to my cloak.

The next morning, with a hangover of epic proportions, I watched them ride away. His squire, the welsh boy – now a man – went with him. Her squire, Amory, and her archer – my friend John Hughes – stayed with me.

'I'm not welcome,' Hughes said.

I sat down with him as he stared at the fire.

'He wants her to be a wife,' Hughes said. 'It won't work. But Master Musard said if I went with them, I'd put her in mind of her harness and her horse.'

I forced a smile. 'John, I promise that if I go to get married, I'll take you along.'

He looked up. 'You'd better,' he said. 'She made us better men. Can we stick to what she taught?'

'Yes,' I said, and I meant it.

I left John Hughes to watch my kit, and I went to the Genoese. I extracted my small balance, and I had him write me a letter of credit. I sold him all my nice clothes, and every other item I owned, everything Emile had bought me, except the armour I wore every day, and her favour, and Llull's book, which I left with him – my sole deposit.

Then I took my money to the Hospitaller. He was praying, and I had to wait for him. Eventually his mild eyes crossed mine, and he rose smoothly to his feet and tucked his prayer beads into his sword belt.

'William?' he said. I swear he knew exactly what I'd done.

'One hundred and seventy florins,' I said. 'Every copper I possess. I kept five florins back to pay for fodder for my horses.'

I handed him the letter of credit. He read it and fingered his beard. 'I share your views of Mother Church,' he said. 'Many men do.' He rolled the letter and tucked it into his purse. 'My order is very rich. We also spend a great deal on the poor, on arms against the infidel, on nursing and on food. But none of that matters. What matters to you is that you have taken this money by force, and now it will go to benefit your sister.' Again, his eyes locked on mine. 'You are better than this life around you,' he said.

I was looking at the tips of my toes. 'No, brother,' I said. 'I'm not.'

He put his hand on my head and blessed me. 'My God thinks you are better,' he said. 'He made you in his image, not to rob and murder, but to protect the weak and defend the defenceless.'

Rudely, I shrugged off his benison with all the desperate cynicism of a twenty-one-year-old. 'You have all my money,' I said. 'You can keep the blessings. Besides,' I said, with a dark joy. 'I'm an excommunicate, remember?'

I walked away.

Youth is truly wasted on the young.

Later that morning, I took my riding horse and rode out into the country. I was looking for a fight.

Instead, just outside of camp, I found a small crowd of peasants. They were mostly women, and they were looting a corpse.

I knew one of the women; she had sewed for me and her name was Alison. She was bent over the corpse, her breasts showing under her kirtle, her hands bloody. She was taking the rings off the man's fingers.

She grinned at me. It was a scary grin, but I think she meant it to be comely. I dismounted, dropped my reins – my former cart horse didn't have the spirit to walk away – and knelt. The women scattered, except Alison – women gave men-at-arms a wide compass, unless they were drunk or liquorish. And for good reason.

He was one of ours, a Gascon. In fact, he was one of the Bascon de Moulet's men, a corporal. He had good wool hose and clean linen braes – not so clean now that he'd voided his bowels into them.

He had one puncture wound under his jaw. Somewhat idly, I pushed my eating skewer into it, and it went right up into his brain. I cleaned my skewer on his shirt, and yes, I ate with it that night.

Later, I took Alison back to my blankets and we made the beast with two backs – about six times. In daylight. I had been fiercely loyal to Emile for a long time, but word of her second pregnancy gave me the excuse I craved to behave badly. Alison was wild, and not altogether of our world; her eyes glittered in an odd way. On the other hand, she had hair as red as mine and no inhibition that I encountered, and if I wanted to lose myself in a body, her body was made for me.

When we were tired, or sore, I watched her play with my clothes. She knelt, naked, on my blankets, and she tied every set of points on my doublet. She arranged everything, almost like I had the clothes on.

I was admiring her, and wondering why she had to fuss endlessly, when she said, 'Who killed him?'

If you are a man, a naked man on an early fall day, lying with a naked woman, it's not murder that comes to mind. More especially, if you are a killer, and murder is done every day. 'Foot pads?' I said, running a finger over her hip. 'A brigand?' I added, meaning it as a joke.

'I knew him,' she said.

'So did I,' I added.

'No, I lay with him,' she added, without shame. Alison wasn't much on shame. 'He was kind the way you are. Why don't you have points all the same colour?'

Her changes of subject were always too much for me. 'Who cares?' In truth, I had leather laces on a third of my points, and four or five different colours of wool and silk cord, and some linen. Half my 'points' no longer had their metal tips. I looked like a rag-picker's child.

'I care,' she said. 'I almost didn't come with you. You look ... lopsided. Uneven.' She ran her hand over my stomach. 'Naked, you look right. Animals are never lopsided. That's why they look right.'

Mad as a drunken monk.

'When an animal *is* lopsided – when a cow loses a horn – other animals worry about her and stay away.' She looked at me. 'One of my breasts is larger than the other. I'm lopsided.' She smiled. 'That's all right. I'm getting used to it. I must go.' She pulled her kirtle over her head. She didn't kiss me; she just walked away, hips swaying. If one of her breasts was larger than the other, it didn't show in clothes.

I stayed with Seguin de Badefol until November, then we signed an agreement with the Lieutenant of Languedoc and collected a small ransom. De Badefol kept most of the money and left us.

The Great Company began to break up.

John Hughes, Perkin and I sat around a small campfire. It was raining, but we were old campaigners – we had a set of other men's cloaks and blankets rigged to make a pretty fair shelter, and we had a good fire and some stolen wine.

Hughes sat on his blanket roll, sewing a pair of hose. Patching, probably. We looked like jesters in suits of motley. 'John Hawkwood is on his way back,' he said. 'He was fighting for Montferrat in Italy, now he's coming back this way.' He looked up. 'That's what the bankers say.'

For John Hughes, that was a long speech.

'You want me to go back to Hawkwood,' I said. 'He sent me a letter.'

'We all know,' said Perkin.

Hughes met my eye. 'Yes,' he said. 'We'll be brigands in a month at this rate, preying on travellers.' He shrugged. 'I've done it. I'm a soldier. The line may be thin, but I know which side I want to be on.' He looked at the fire. 'And there's Perkin and Amory and the rest. You agree?'

The other men looked up.

'If we don't show them something better, what will they become?' Hughes said.

I grunted and thought, What have I already become?

'Let's go find Hawkwood,' I said.

Out trip across northern Provence was perilously close to brigandage. My carthorse developed something grim and died, suddenly, on a rainy December day – and we waylaid a small convoy of church-men, took their money and their horses, and rode on. They had six men-at-arms and a dozen crossbowmen. We took an insane risk, and it paid off: the crossbowmen all ran and the men-at-arms were worthless.

As a side comment, routiers had a saying in those days that if a man-at-arms was worth a shit, he was with us. And only the cowards and the worthless men were on the other side.

It had some truth in it, or perhaps it's just the lies men tell to justify themselves when they kill. In this case, the priest leading the column sat on a magnificent war horse and cursed his own defenders for being faithless cravens. I noted that he had nothing but a clean shirt, his Franciscan habit and his horse. I ordered him off the horse, and he dismounted with the strangest smile. I looked in his script and his bags. He had two clean shirts, a fine silk rope belt and a rope of coral beads around his waist. His horse had the plainest saddle, and his malle proved to hold two books of sermons and an unilluminated gospel. Every other priest in the convoy wore wool and silk and car-ried gold and silver, but this man, the leader, had nothing.

I'll be honest. I almost killed him, simply for having nothing. But I didn't. The rain was pouring down and he stood unshivering in the road – I took my own heavy cloak off my cantel and put it around his shoulders.

He raised his hand and blessed me.

We left him alive, and warmer.

We were chased by a French royal force for three days. If they'd taken us, they'd have hanged us at the roadside as brigands and highwaymen. And I suppose we were. But we eluded them and slipped north to Chalons, where we found Sir John Creswell. I knew him a little, and he knew of me, and here I was with three lances, short only a man-at-arms, and he hired us on the spot. He and his men were rich – they'd forced the Green Count himself to pay a huge ransom. I heard that Richard, my Richard, had saved the Green Count from capture and been richly rewarded.

I was glad for Richard. And I was damned glad I'd given the good priest my cloak, even when I was wet through.

Well. It's good when a friend makes good. You have to be pretty low to curse another man's good fortune.

And I tried not to curse, tried not to blaspheme. I fought to con-trol my temper, to give to the poor.

But I swallowed a great deal of cursing that month. Another Christmas came and went, and I didn't celebrate it. I rode out on patrols, collecting *patis* from peasants who hated me, beating a few of them for insolence or for hiding grain I needed for my mounts. I was good at all this, and I didn't think of Emile, or of Geoffrey de Charny or Ramon Llull or the Hospitaller. I thought of my sister once or twice. She was safe, and I hoped that she would pray for me. I imagined her becoming a full sister. In my head, it was a knighting ceremony.

I envied the others, because all the other men-at-arms were rich, and had fine armour and good horses, while I looked like one of the mounted brigands we'd mocked in the days after Poitiers.

However, I was good at my work and known to be so, and just after Christmas, Creswell made me a corporal. In those days, a corporal was a man-at-arms who led many lances, often thirty or forty. Forty lances can be more than a hundred men.

My promotion raised a lot of hackles. Sir Hugh Ashley – an actual belted knight – had moved from Hawkwood to Creswell in the mountains, expecting promotion, and he made it clear that he felt I was a poor choice.

In truth, I was a late-comer to his company, and Creswell was busy adding men while he had the money to pay them – he said he planned to take us back east to Brittany to fight in the war there. I had to recruit my own men, but I found some, and I had ten lances. I borrowed money from a Jew – his rates were far kinder than the Genoese, whatever the church may say – and bought myself a good coat of plates and some repairs to my arms and legs. I got myself a new saddle for the first time in three years. When you command other men, looks matter.

I missed Richard. I missed having a man as good as I am myself, to trust. Perkin was solid, and John Hughes was worth his weight in minted gold coin, but Richard ... By Christ, I missed him. Because Richard was my friend, and friendship is more than trust and shared experience.

Our new Great Company was commanded by Petit Meschin – have I mentioned him before? Terrible bastard – a fine fighter, but cut from the same cloth as the Bourc Camus. The jest of it was that he was a Frenchman, not a Gascon or a German or an Italian. He was actually a vassal of the King of France, and he'd spent the Poitiers campaign fighting against us as a loyal servant of the French crown. But in the late winter of 1362, he rallied the little companies that Seguin de Badefol had largely abandoned in Languedoc and led them north, towards Burgundy. All told, we had almost 16,000 fighting men. Most of them were Gascons, but we had Germans, Hainaulters, Italians, Bretons, Scots, Irishmen, Frenchmen and a handful of Englishmen, which has its own dark comedy, because after Brignais, most men thought of our army as English.

In fact, there were just three English companies there – Creswell's, Hawkwood's and Leslie's – although Sir Robert Birkhead was there, too. He had a company, but all his men were Gascons. Of course, Hawkwood already had Italians and Germans, and there were a handful of Englishmen in the Gascon companies.

But by then, most of us had been together at least two years. We were no longer a mass of brigands and robbers assembled to loot. We were like a moving nation, with our own customs and own laws, and we had a certain spirit that's hard to describe. We had contempt – deep contempt – for the fighting abilities of the enemy. And the enemy was anyone richer than we. Or weaker. Even our long tail of peasants and camp-followers had begun to develop a spirit.

In late winter, we pounced on the Auvergne by rapid marches. We joined forces with Peter of Savoy – another bastard son – to take towns on the Rhône, while the King of France scrambled to raise armies ahead of us and behind us. My old captain the archpriest, Arnaud de Cervole, was put in charge of raising a mercenary army to fight us, but of course, all the best men were with us, and the King of France didn't offer enough money.

Jean de Bourbon, who I had rescued on the Bridge of Meaux, was appointed commander of a second French army. I imagined that Emile's husband, the Count d'Herblay, would be with him. Indeed, their estates were in Burgundy.

When I sketched this out on the frozen ground, I became very keen for the new campaign.

But instead of sweeping a victorious, vengeful horde into Burgundy, the vice began to close on us in early March. We'd heard that there was another Great Company operating in the south – the Spaniards – and that they would occupy the King of France's field army, but they accomplished nothing and made a truce, so a third French army was freed to contain us from the south.

Creswell got sick. We were all sick that winter, because we were out in the open with no fires all day in rain, snow and mud – it never ended, and as the noose of steel closed around our necks, we had to move faster and faster to avoid getting hanged. At any rate, Sir John Creswell summoned me to his pavilion – a grandiose name for a simple square tent with a wattle-and-daub chimney laid up to allow for a fire – and ordered me to take command.

I had never commanded anything but a handful of lances, and as the rain fell and the roads, such as they were, were churned into ever deeper mud, I had to coax several hundred men and their lemans and servants to rise with the sun, harness their carts, pack their goods and move. When all our lances were together, we had almost 300 lances in Sir John Creswell's company, and as we marched north and west, the other corporals joined us, and my job became more difficult – twice. First, simply because I had more men to command. Second, because none of the other corporals thought I was the right choice to command.

I suppose it was difficult, but I can't remember being as happy since I was in the Prince's service. I rode up and down, put my shoulder to a camp-follower's cartwheel, dragged donkeys out of the thick black soup that filled the holes in the road, and generally led ... by example.

Every day, I practiced the lessons that Milady had taught.

Courtesy – even to a prostitute with a stubborn mule.

Largesse – to peasants burned out by their own knights.

Loyalty – to Sir John Creswell, too sick to take command, and to my own people.

Courage – the physical kind never came hard, but as that March wore on, a true Lent of the soul, the skies never once let us see the sun, and I had to be everywhere – cheerful, and sure.

High up the Rhône, I rode across country with a pair of men-at-arms – good men who later followed me many years, John Courtney and William Grice. I knew them from better days and they came with me willingly enough. I needed to find the other companies we were supposed to make a rendezvous with, and plan our next move. We'd lost touch with Petit Mechin in the mountains, and I only knew the whereabouts of Peter of Savoy.

I found him sitting on his horse in the watery March sunshine with Sir John Hawkwood and John Thornbury. They were wearing their arms, like noblemen, and Sir John had his own arms on a banner held by a man-at-arms, and I remember thinking, By God, he's done well for himself.

I didn't ride very fast. I wasn't sure what reception I'd get, and I wasn't sure whose actions had been the right ones. But a fair distance away, Sir John raised a gauntleted hand and gave me a salute, and when I rode up, he clasped my hand and embraced me as if I was the prodigal son. Thornbury was more reserved, but he clasped my hand warmly enough.

'I hear you are running Creswell's company,' Sir John said.

'Trying, Sir John,' I admitted.

Sir John nodded. 'I know you have it,' he said simply. 'I'm sorry we had a difference of opinion,' he added.

I think I burst into smiles. Until I saw black and white colours coming down the road.

It's strange what can set a man off. I think I would have apologized to Sir John then and there – from his point of view I'd broken discipline, and I understood that better now that I was doing a little commanding of my own – but one sight of Camus and I was angry, ruffled and unrepentant.

Sir John's eyes went where mine had been and he put a hand on my reins.

'He's not worth the stinking carcass of a rotting dog,' Sir John said. 'Don't rise to him.'

Our eyes locked.

What he was saying, for those of you too young to understand, was that if I crossed the Bourc in public again, Sir John would have to back him, and I'd lose my command. Or be dead. And that Sir John understood this to be unfair.

This injustice is woven into the story of my life. Like Nan's da, the alderman. He thought it was unfair, too. Even when he told me to never enter his house again.

Perhaps I'd grown a little, or perhaps I was so in love with command that it steadied me. Perhaps all those lessons on knighthood were finally getting a grip on my stubborn heart. Camus rode up to join us with Peter of Savoy, and he turned his mad eyes to mine. 'The Butt Boy,' he said.

I just sat my horse and bowed to Peter of Savoy. 'I'm here for Sir John Creswell,' I said. I explained that we had lost touch with Petit Mechin, and they all nodded, even Camus.

Savoy shrugged. 'Marshal Audreham is close behind us,' he said. 'We must take a couple of towns and win ourselves a crossing of the Rhône, or we are well and truly fucked.'

Sir John nodded. To me, he said, 'I believe I may have been mistaken in coming back from Tuscany.' He smiled. 'You have to see Tuscany to believe it. Impossibly rich. Beautiful.' He smiled. 'And full of little, foolish men who want to hire us to fight for them.' Just for a moment he looked like Renaud the Fox.

'*Eh bien*, Sir Jean. We are not in Tuscany, but right here, facing the might of France.' The Bourc was wearing the kind of armour I dreamed of owning – Milanese white armour. Probably made for him. His eyes met mine again and he said, quite evenly, 'Soon, I will kill you.' He smiled. 'I will humiliate you and then kill you, so men will mock you for ever after you are dead.'

I turned to Sir John. 'Is this how knights talk to each other?' I asked.

'I mean it,' hissed the Bourc.

I shrugged. 'Horse or foot. Any time, any weapon. To the death. I'll make my challenge public, so that if you have me murdered, every man-at-arms in the army will know you for what you are.' I straightened my back and met his eyes.

Blessed Virgin. Later, in Italy, I read how the Goddess Athena, who the old men believed in before Christ came, used to whisper in the ears of heroes, sending 'winged words' to help them. I didn't hear any words, and yet, the words came to me as if from God, and they struck him like the hammer blows of a poleaxe. I'm proud to say that I delivered my words in a tone of banter.

Peter of Savoy laughed. 'Fight Camus when we're clear of the French, eh, Gold?'

I nodded. 'Yes, my lord.' I said it crisply and loud.

And men – these knights of ill-reknown – laughed. Not at me, but at Camus.

We dismounted at an old roadside auberge – gutted, ruined, rebuilt, burned again and now roofed by a daring sutler with an old red and black striped pavilion. He'd collected stools and benches from the local town and made a decent sitting area that was snug. So snug, in fact, it was hard to breathe.

As the leaders of three companies, we got a table and stools of our own. We drank small beer and Sir John made our plan. We had about 900 lances and we had to assume that Petit Mechin was on the other side of the ridge behind us, with the French right behind him.

'Lyons,' Sir John said. 'If we take Lyons, they'll have to pay us to leave. We'll be rich. Best of all, we'll be safe.'

Peter of Savoy shook his head. 'We'll never get into Lyons,' he said. 'Last spring they raised the wall. It has a *bailli*, two thousand men and two out-castles.' Even as he spoke, he was drawing – in beer, of course – the course of the river. He put filberts down. 'Rive-de-Gier and Brignais. And here's Le Puy.' He sighed. 'I can't see taking Lyons by escalade.'

Sir John thought.

Peter of Savoy grunted. 'We have no choice. Needs must when the devil drives.'

Camus sat slumped.

'William Gold and I will take Brignais and Rive-de-Gier,' Sir John Hawkwood said. 'By escalade. You two wait six hours and try Lyon. If the garrison is alert, light the suburbs afire and retreat on us.'

None of us disagreed. We had the more difficult task, and yet I was well satisfied. I finished my small beer and rode away into the watery sunshine.

I was filled with confidence as we rode cross-country, and then, as I came down on my own convoy, I watched the line of carts and wondered why they were tailing along behind instead of protected in the middle of the column.

I got my horse to a heavy trot, and rolled down the hill, headed for the front of the column, the priest's excellent war horse labouring in the heavy mud of the unploughed fields.

At the front, there were half a dozen horsemen, arguing. There was Sir Hugh and Richard Cressy, two other corporals and John Hughes. Hughes was as red as a beet. There was a dead man lying under the horse's hooves.

I knew immediately that Sir Hugh had usurped command in my half-day absence, and that he'd made some error that caused the others to come after him. I could see it all in their postures and those of their horses. I put my gauntlets on and made sure my sword was loose in my scabbard.

They roared at each other like stallions fighting over a mare, and I rode up behind Sir Hugh without being noticed.

'Gentlemen?' I said, as I pushed my horse in behind his. I wasn't too gentle.

Cressy didn't really know me. He was a good man-at-arms, as big as a small house and cautious. He was barely capable of being a corporal and lacked even the most rudimentary organizational skills.

He also lacked both courtesy and self-control. Although even at twenty-two, I was learning that courtesy – the very foundation of knighthood – was all about self-control.

I mention this because, alone among the corporals, he'd never suggested, by word or deed, that he thought he'd be a better acting captain that I was. His eyes met mine. 'This idiot,' he said, pointing at Sir Hugh.

Sir Hugh tried to wheel his horse. He didn't like having me behind him, and he was afraid of what I might do.

'He took the wrong fucking turn and killed our guide!' Cressy said.

'He betrayed us!' Sir Hugh said. 'I made no error!'

He had his horse around, now, and he was glaring at me with a hand on his sword.

John Hughes, who was the informal captain of the archers, just shook his head. 'He grabbed command from Cressy and fucked it away,' he said. 'Order of march changed, down the wrong road, all so he can grab some market town that isn't where he thought it was.'

I looked at him. I didn't think anyone would back him – if he'd had skills like that, he'd have been a corporal. 'I'm surprised any of you obeyed him,' I said.

Hughes spat. 'He *said* he had orders from Sir John Creswell,' he said.

'Well, Sir Hugh? I asked. An hour with Sir John Hawkwood and I was emulating his careful, clipped speech and mannerisms.

Sir Hugh glared at me. 'I, sir, am a belted knight, a landed man, a servant of the King. I should be in command here. These men obey me as their natural superior.'

I nodded. 'Prepare yourself,' I said. 'We're going to fight right here. If you unhorse me, you can try and command the company, but in truth, Sir Hugh, you couldn't command a sack of meal in a mill. If I unhorse you, I expect nothing but silent obedience from you. We have an adventure ahead of us, and I, for one, don't have any more time to waste on you.'

'With pleasure, *boy*, he said. He gathered his reins and drew his sword. 'Butt Boy!'

I put that away for later. The Bourc's insult in Sir Hugh's mouth?

He came for me without the formality of choosing ground or seizing a lance. He held up his sword, high above his head, and cut at me – one, two, three times. He wanted to close and grapple, and he pushed in as close as his horse could manage.

My horse – the horse I'd stolen from a priest – proved to have more fight than I'd imagined. He side-stepped and bit Sir Hugh's mount savagely, ripping off a piece of the other horse's nose and scattering blood.

Sir Hugh's horse stumbled and half-reared, and I got my sword in both hands and thrust Sir Hugh cleanly through the aventail. My sword went in just where the collarbone met the breastbone. I'll be honest, I didn't care if I killed him, because he was large and dangerous and I needed to get on with my part in Sir John's plan.

My two-handed thrust penetrated his chain aventail and stuck in bone, but the whole force went into his breastbone, and he lost his seat and fell to the ground. The fight was over.

To add insult to injury, my horse kicked him when he tried to rise. Compared to the kick of a stallion, my little poke was a pinprick.

I ignored the man under the hooves of my horse. 'Gentlemen,' I said. 'We are going to try a bold adventure – to seize the walls of Brignais this very night.'

Ah. *Preux*. yes, I had *preux*. Courtesy, loyalty, largesse, courage and *preux*.

Four hours later, we left our warm fires of the previous light and mounted our horses. Our pages carried our ladders. We rode along the web of roads, following John Hughes and Ned, who had scouted the route, and we assembled our ladders in the ditch without being challenged.

I had about ninety men. I'd left the rest in camp, under Cressy.

'Fast as you can, *mes amis!*' That was my first battlefield speech.

We went up the ladders, and instead of being first, I waited with Courtney and Grice and six other men-at-arms with good harness and good fighting reputations. We were the reserve.

We didn't even have to fight. We utterly surprised the garrison, and took the place while most of them were locked into their guard rooms from the outside. As soon as we had the gate tower in our hands, I sent Courtney for the rest of the company.

We stripped the garrison to their braes, and threw them out into the night, then built up the fires and gorged on their stores. We moved into their guardrooms and barracks and stables.

A day later, Sir John Creswell came and took the reins away from me. His news was grim – Sir John had taken Rive-de-Gire, but the Bourc and Savoy had failed with Lyon and failed even to fire the suburbs. The main French army, with the archpriest and the Lord of Tancraville, was closing in on us from the north.

He was coldly polite to me, and the only thing he said was, 'Hawkwood says you've run the company better than I do myself.'

Well, messieurs. I'm sure Sir John meant it as praise, although it is possible he meant it to sting Creswell. Hawkwood wasn't called 'The Fox' for nothing.

The second day after we stormed the place, Creswell sent me to find Petit Mechin with six lances. Every man he sent with me was one of my friends – men, squires and archers. With the countryside crawling with French troops, it was an insane risk to take. In fact, like David with Bathsheba's husband Uriah, he was sending me out to die. He knew it, and I knew it, and worst of all, when he ordered me out, Sir Hugh stood at his shoulder, his right shoulder a mass of linen bandages, and smiled at me. He had what he wanted.

We left before dawn, and I led my band away from Brignais and headed directly north; they didn't question me. I'd had time to think, by then, and what I decided was that Camus was in league with Sir Hugh. I know that sounds insane, but command in an army of criminals and mercenaries isn't about chivalry. Or gentility.

No, that's wrong. The qualities of chivalry had given me a good reputation. The men would follow me. I was just. I was well-spoken and temperate. It was my supposed peers who disdained chivalry and justice.

So we went north until the sun began to rise, and then, when we could see Arnaud de Cervole's outriders, I led my men into a stream bed, and rode along it until I'd crossed most of the archpriest's front. Twice we stopped and stood, knee deep in icy water, holding our horse's heads, but they were terrible scouts and we really needn't have worked so hard.

When we emerged from the stream, we were between the expanding crescent of his scouts and the main French army. We swept west, riding slowly and carefully from copse to copse, raising no dust. Four times that long late winter's day, I came in sight of the main French host. I counted banners and whistled, then groaned. Jacques de Bourbon, Count of La Marche; Jean de Melun, Count of Tancraville; Jean de Noyers, Count of Joigny, and Gerard de Thurey, the Marshal of Burgundy, were all arms I knew and banners I could read. And, of course, there was the Count d'Herblay, in azur and or checky – I saw him immediately. I counted thirty-nine banners and had the whole of an apple down to the core while watching them from under a tree. I estimated they had more than 6,000 men-at-arms and another 4,000 armoured infantry.

This scout of mine is accounted one of my finest deeds of arms, but in all sober truth, I ran little risk. Cervole was a poor commander, and besides, Bourbon owed me his life, and if I'd been taken, I'd have made them release me, or so I told myself.

At dark, I slipped Cervole's forward pickets and rode due west. I assumed that if the archpriest was marching towards a target, that target must be Petit Mechin. But I overestimated the archpriest's scouting, and by dawn the next day, I still hadn't found Petit Mechin, or even his outriders or foragers.

The sun was high in the sky when we turned back south, because we could see – well, John Hughes and I thought we could see – a smudge of dust on the far horizon.

Hughes and I sat just below the edge of a ridge line, so we couldn't be seen silhouetted against the bright sky.

'Should we just ride clear?' I asked him.

Hughes had an apple, too. He chewed, groaned, then took another bite. 'You'd know better than me,' he said.

We moved fast, despite fatigue, fear and horses near done – that was a long day, and a hard one, with our goal moving almost as swiftly as we did ourselves, so that every time we descended a small ridge, we lost all sight of them and our spirits went lower than our horse's bellies.

After nones we found foragers stripping a stone barn, and they were from Badefol's company – that cheered me again, because despite the fact that he'd run off taking all our money the autumn before, he was a good leader and a brave man, and we were in a tight spot. In effect, he came out of retirement in Gascony when he heard how badly we'd fared.

At last light, I rode in among his company from the north, and his lieutenant John Amory took me to the great man himself, where he sat on a camp stool, listening to a man recite the Chanson of Alexander. De Badefol was an old-fashioned man, but he rose and grinned.

'Looking for work?' he asked.

'I come from Sir John Creswell,' I said. 'And I've seen Bourbon's army.'

Instantly, his banter went away. He took my shoulder. 'Come, we must find Mechin,' he said.

We walked up the hill a little further. I wanted a fire and some of the wine – I swear I could smell wine a mile away in those days – but we walked over the rocky ground to the great captain's pavilion, set with his banner high on the hillside.

I had to explain everything that had happened for a week since we'd lost him in the hills.

Mechin, as you may have heard, was not a big man. He was quite small, and he had the temper we always pretend Frenchmen have. He burned like a torch, for all that his hair was grey and his beard as white as mine is now, but he shared with John Hawkwood the kind of intelligence that allows a man to think his way out of a trap, or through a contract, or into a great marriage alliance.

About the time that I said I'd taken Brignais, he bounced out of his seat. '*Par dieu!*' he said. 'Then we have a crossing of the Rhône, yes?'

I had to demur. 'Brignais doesn't have its own bridge,' I began.

'We can put across a bridge of boats,' he said.

'Like Great Alexander!' said Seguin de Badefol. He was obviously delighted to be emulating the great conqueror.

Mechin all but bounced up and down. 'We will pass over the bridge and *pft* – we're gone.'

I took a little while to describe the archpriest's army. Forgive my digression – now I know that Tancraville was commander, but given my bias for professional men-at-arms, I took it for granted that Cervole, for all his failings, would have the command. More fool I!

I told my story, and my count of banners, and Mechin winced. 'By God, gentles,' he said, 'we do not want to face these armies together.'

Badefol had scouted the army of Marshal Audreham to the south, and he reported fifty-four banners and two marshals of France. Now it was my turn to wince. Three to one – perhaps as much as five to one.

We faced three armies: Audreham, the archpriest and Tancraville. Each of them was larger and better armed than our own. Worst of all, they took us seriously, and they moved with minimum baggage and no women, so that they moved faster than our 'nation of thieves'.

'Where's Hawkwood?' Mechin asked.

I laid out the world around us as best I could: beans for the castles, grains of barley for our forces and peas for the enemy. I put in Lyons and Brignais and everything I could remember.

Badefol slapped my shoulder. 'You discourse about war like a priest talks theology' he said. 'Better, because you aren't full of shit!'

Well, you have to take flattery where you get it, I suppose.

Mechin looked at my little illustration and nodded, fingering his moustache. 'Let us turn further south,' he said. 'Let us turn towards the good Marshal Audreham.'

Badefol nodded, satisfied. I was many years and social levels their junior, but I was temporarily one of them, and I dared greatly and asked, 'Why?'

Petit Mechin grinned. 'You have a head on your shoulders and no mistake, young man, and your illustration on the table does me as much good as a painting of Christ does a poor sinner. So listen to me. If you have to fight two men in an alley, what do you do?'

I stammered. 'Run?' I murmured.

Mechin laughed. He had a woman's laugh, high and wild, but genuine and happy, not mad like Camus. I liked him immensely for such short acquaintance.

'No, young man. Or rather, certainly, but if your back is to the wall and you must fight them both?'

Sometimes, being questioned freezes the head – you just stare at your interrogator and wonder. This was not my finest hour.

Badefol got it. 'You feint a thrust at one to buy a moment's peace and run the other bastard through,' he said.

'I can see you've fought in some alleys,' Mechin said.

I was humbled. But they laughed and slapped my back, and someone finally put a cup of wine into my hands.

The next day we marched south along a high ridge line. I took my six lances and we rode out far ahead of the army with most of Badefol's company, and after nones we came in sight of Audreham's advance guard.

We had our orders.

We attacked. We had sixty lances all told, and they had twice as many, and we met them in a ford, and drove them from it. We had about twenty English and Flemish long bow men, and they dismounted and ran to the streamside and began to loose shaft after shaft into the southerners. I saw a dozen enemy lances head upstream.

'Follow me!' I called, and led my men: Grice and Courtney, Perkin Smallwood and Robert Grandice, de la Motte – he'd just rejoined me – and a few others. Ah, messieurs, I should remember their names and styles, for they were good men of arms, every one, and that was a feat of arms for any book. We rode west through broken country for a quarter of a league or less and there they were, breasting the stream.

Our opponents chose a terrible crossing, took a risk and paid. We caught them in the water and gaffed them like spawning fish with our spears. I captured a young knight – I was disappointed when he proved too small for his beautiful new harness to fit me. It fit Perkin, though, and he took it and wore it. I sent the young man home on parole to get me a thousand Florins, a price he named himself.

An afternoon's fighting, I didn't lose a man and I made a thousand florins. It's a tale of its own how I came to be paid, but *par dieu*, gentlemen. With a dozen men-at-arms and ten archers, I held a mile of streamside against 300 knights.

Another thing, the horse I'd stolen from the priest was magnificently trained. Every day I rode him, I learned another trick he could do – there were hand commands, knee commands and spur commands. I would discover them by mistake, but after three weeks on this magnificent animal, I spent time with him, riding around a field and trying different combinations. I suspected he had voice commands – he was a very intelligent animal, for a horse – and he fought brilliantly at the ford, backing under me and changing direction as soon as he felt a shift in my weight.

As soon was we'd beaten them and seen their backs, we rode back north to find de Badefol, who sat twirling his moustache like Satan's lieutenant – he was an evil-looking man, and no mistake. He grinned and nodded when he saw our prisoners and haul of armour.

'If you weren't such a giant, you'd be easier to arm!' he called.

In truth, after that skirmish I was the worst-armed man in our band, and it rankled. We were fighting in winter and had no servants – everything I owned was brown and orange, and my clothes were all besmottered with rust.

And yet, 1,000 gold Florins, even in expectation, seemed to cure all my woes. And I was proud of my feat, and prouder still that I'd behaved with steady courtesy to the young knight I'd taken. I hadn't had to despoil a peasant or burn a house in weeks.

As soon as we were sure we'd driven them from the field, we

turned tail and ran ourselves, all the way back to Mechin, who was waiting six miles up the valley with the rest of the Great Company, at the crossroads to Lyon.

He already knew from our outriders, and before we reached him, the army was marching north. By chance, I was the first officer to reach the little man, and he hugged me. 'The ill-made knight triumphs!' he said, and other men laughed.

Well, I hated the name, but when you are a mass of rusty brown, you know what you're being teased for.

We marched north. At the edge of night, there was a stir at the front of the column and I was afraid we were fighting. I assumed that the archpriest had stolen a march and surprised us.

I had my gauntlets on, and Perkin was slipping my helmet over my head when John Thornbury reined in by my horse.

'Not an attack, then,' I said.

He shook his head. 'We burned the castle at Rive-de-Gier and ran,' he said. 'The whole royal army of France appeared from over the river. Brignais is under siege.'

I thought of my beans and peas and barley. Brignais under siege threatened everything. 'Does Mechin know?' I asked.

Thornbury nodded. 'I'm to fetch de Badefol. Sir John's with the little Frenchman now.'

I followed him. No one asked me, and I certainly didn't have enough lances to count as a captain, but he didn't say me nay. I'm glad I went.

When I came in with Thornbury and de Badefol, Sir John Hawkwood was sitting across a two-board table from Petit Mechin in the ruins of an abbey hall. The army was halted outside on the road, and the word was we were moving all night. A pair of whores were satisfying a line of clients outside the burned-out hall, and a small boy was collecting coins from the men in the line.

Life in the field. I want you to see this – the best soldiers in France were planning their battle to the accompaniment of the grunts of twenty customers.

Very well. You want Brignais. The end of the companies. The death of the Nation of Thieves.

Mechin was picking his teeth when I came in. He had both Albret's at the table, Camus, of course, Sir John Hawkwood, Leslie, Birkhead, Naudin de Bagerin and another half a dozen captains. He looked at me and smiled.

'Heh,' he laughed. 'You all know the news?'

I think we all nodded.

'Worse than Poitiers, and no mistake,' Sir John said.

Mechin smiled. 'I didn't come out so well at Poitiers,' he said. 'And you did, you dog of an Englishman.'

Sir John smiled.

'Listen,' Mechin went on. 'Creswell is in Brignais with half a thousand men. Even if we could leave him, our ill-made knight and his friends have all too efficiently fixed Marshal Audreham in place astride the road south. The archpriest has the north road to Lyons.' He shrugged. 'We have no choice. We are trapped like a badger in his earth.'

'Fight?' asked de Badefol.

'Fight,' said Sir John, with professional distaste.

'Fight,' said Mechin, and his eyes sparkled.

We marched all night.

Mechin made the plan, and it was a good plan. He divided the army into two parts. All the lesser men-at-arms – the brigands and the routiers and the men with bad horses – went with Mechin himself. They marched straight at Brignais. Two hours before dawn, they dismounted, formed in close order and marched to the top of the high ridge that towers over the castle of Brignais and emerged into the open, spear tips sparkling. Then Mechin sent a herald, as if he was the King of France himself, to the Count of Tancraville, inviting him to try the issue in combat. Listen, I'm not proud of what I did as a routier at times. I was just learning what it might mean to be a knight, to have honour, to be just. But I'm proud of that moment – an army of little men and squires challenging France's very best men-at-arms. With a certain joy.

The Count of Tancraville accepted Mechin's challenge to battle. He took the time to arm his men, and he knighted his son and a dozen other rich young men. He formed his army in three great battles – the first led by the archpriest, the second he led in person, and the third led by Jacques de Bourbon.

The archpriest begged Tancraville to wait until the sun burned off the morning mist. And he insisted that attacking Mechin up the hill would lose him knights he didn't need to lose.

Most of the archpriest's men were routiers like me, and the Count of Tancraville replied, with stunning honesty, that he didn't care if the archpriest's whole command was killed.

I wasn't there for any of this. I agree that my account isn't the same as that rascal Villani's, or others you may have heard, but by the Virgin, messieurs, I knew a thousand men who were there, and neither of those fellows was within a hundred miles of the spot. I wasn't there, because I was with Seguin de Badefol and John Hawkwood, riding like the devil.

We went south, again, in the darkness, along the left side of the same great ridge that had been on our right the day before. We were all well-mounted, and we'd left all the riff-raff – even our own riff-raff – behind.

Perhaps the greatest jest of Brignais is that the peasants helped us. Never forget the Jacques, friends. French peasants hate their masters, who screw them for silver the way a laundress twists cloth. Someday, mark my words, Messieurs, some day the Jaques will have their way. Their hate can suffocate you, though. So great that they would help us – the routiers – defeat their own aristocrats, who claimed to be their defenders. Twenty local men led us south and then east over the next ridge. At midnight, with no moon, we were climbing the ridge with our reins in our hands, on foot, our spurs clanking with every step. But first light found us coming upon Brignais from the south, and if the French knew we were there, they didn't give a hint of it.

We came up about the time a man eats his bread and drinks his small beer after his first prayers. We dismounted again and stood by our horse's heads in a deep fold in the ground, and we couldn't see a thing.

John Thornbury came by and ordered us, on pain of death, not to enter the woods in front of us to look at the enemy.

An hour later, when we could clearly hear fighting, Sir John Hawkwood came in person. In my small battle – Seguin de Badefol's division – we had 600 men-at-arms. There were four of these divisions.

Petit Mechin had all the archers, crossbowmen and spearmen.

Sir John reined in two horse lengths from where I sat. Harness is heavy, so most of us were sitting in the wet grass.

'Messieurs!' he called. Some dozen men were already mounting – there's always some excited bastard who moves before he's ready. It was their horses that pay the toll.

'Mechin has beaten the archpriest – held the ridge and driven de Cervole down the hill with heavy loss.' He held his hand for silence. 'Twice. Now the Count de Tancraville's banners are moving forward.' He grinned. 'By the time I'm done speaking, Tancraville will be past our position and well up the ridge.' He looked back and forth. 'In two hours, we will all be very rich, or very dead. It's at the points of your lances, messieurs. Fight hard, and France is ours.' His smile didn't crack when he said, 'Fail, and we'll all hang like criminals.'

I think that's when I realized that we had no priests among us. Listen, friends, no man likes to imagine himself to be the villain, eh? But we were all excommunicate, by the Pope himself, and we didn't even say prayers as we formed. That got me in the gut. It made my insides roil.

Perhaps for comfort, I dismounted, reached into my purse, took out Emile's favour and pinned it to my aventail. I knelt in the wet grass and thought of being the lowliest man-at-arms following the Three Kings.

We mounted, and filed off from the right, passing in long files through the wood to our front; the manoeuvre seemed to take for ever. In fact, it took longer than de Badefol intended, and the hammer of Tancraville's attack fell fully on the spearmen and archers.

And they held. That wasn't the plan, and I know damn well from John Hughes that they were cursing us by then, thinking themselves abandoned, or that we had lost our way in the darkness. The plan was risky – too complex – and we were late.

I remember emerging into the full light of a moist March day. The sky was full of water, and while it wasn't raining, the cold wind that blew from the north was damp.

The French host was laid out below us like a carpet of eastern stuff – all colours and glitter, in patterns made by the more uniformed conroys of the great nobles. By the gentle Jesus, they looked like the mightiest host in the history of Christendom, with more banners than I'd seen at Poitiers, all in one great mass, pressing into our poor footmen.

In once glance, I saw Tancraville's banner. And pressed close behind it, Bourbon's banner, and close to it, my friend the Count d'Herblay's. And just downhill from that, the banner of the Marshal of Savoy.

All packed into the bowl of open ground at my feet. There was nothing between us but a gentle slope of grassland that rolled from the edge of the forest all the way down to the castle of Brignais, a little more than two leagues away.

De Badefol was tense, and even Sir John was nervous. It was plain as the nose on your face that we were late, and waiting for the next 300 men-at-arms to trickle out of the forest was killing us, the more especially as our surprise was over. As soon as we emerged, the game was up – the French commanders saw us and began to wheel the third battle to face us. Bourbon, with the Burgundian lords and the Savoyards.

Christ, it was close.

They were badly ordered, and had already been ordered forward into the slowly folding footmen at the top of the next hill.

Our men were losing. Step by step, the foot were driven back. The shafts no longer flew fast from our archers, and any veteran of Poitiers could tell that our archers were too few.

I was among the first of the men to emerge from the wood; the rest of our men-at-arms seemed to be picking their way with ludicrous slowness, so that I despaired.

I watched the left flank spears – Gascons – fold. They had stout hearts, but more and more of the fresh French knights got into their ranks and cut them down. They didn't run; they just seemed to collapse like a tent with its ropes cut.

Now the enemy had their third division formed. They were eager to be at us, and so on they came.

On the far flank, the archpriest rallied his mercenaries for one more charge into our archers. You'd think, the way the archpriest's men had been sacrificed, that they might have changed sides. But they didn't. Damn them.

Seguin de Badefol sat on his war horse, watching men emerge from the woods behind us. He watched us and watched the Bourbon division. I could read his mind. At some point, we would have to act – or retreat and abandon Mechin.

That point was close.

Sir John Hawkwood had all his men in line. They were mounted, lances up, ready to ride. He trotted over to me.

'William, if this goes like a sow's belly, follow me out. We'll get clear or surrender to someone I know.' He gave me a friendly nod. 'There's better pickings than this in Lombardy.'

I nodded, but I had already pretty much settled on dying. A ransom would break me. I had nothing.

In fact, I was tired to death. I had spent everything – my soul, if you like – the last few weeks. To see it all lost ...

Men were shifting.

When the field is lost, and all about you quail, that is where you find out who you are.

I rode out ahead of my section of the line and pushed up my visor. '*Par dieu*, friends!' I called. 'We have nothing to worry about.' I pointed my lance, one-handed, at the French chivalry. 'There's enough ransoms there for every man here! Stop squabbling.'

When I returned to my rank, John Thornbury slapped me on the back, and other men grinned.

Seguin made his decision. He raised his lance, held it over his head – no mean feat – and called out.

'To hell!' he shouted.

In terms of pre-battle speeches, it was the best I've ever heard. We knew we were beaten. We knew where we were going. He didn't pour honey on it.

We had about 2,000 men-at-arms when we started down the long hill at a walk. The wet wind had become a rain. I was to the right of the centre and had become aware that d'Herblay was opposite me. My last conscious thought was not about strategy or tactics, honour or chivalry, or even ransoms and wealth, but whether Emile would thank me for making her a widow.

I shouted with the rest, and we fell down the hill like an avalanche of steel and horse flesh.

I aimed my priest's horse at d'Herblay.

We came together at the speed of two galloping horses. It had taken two days to get to this point, and then the battle ran faster and faster – like a runaway cart on a downslope, suddenly there was no controlling it. No predicting its course.

I don't remember the moment of impact. I remember the long charge – the rain, the sound of 2,000 horses rumbling down a hill. The feeling of a wonderful horse under me. The knowledge that, for once, my lance-point was on target, steady and easy.

It was ... beautiful.

And then I was through their line, my lance shattered in my hand, and I was drawing my sword while a pair of coustilliers – lesser men – tried to pound me from the saddle with spears.

I couldn't see any of my men – Perkin generally stayed at my shoulder, but the only man I could see was Seguin de Badefol, and he was surrounded.

I cut my way to him. He must have had ten knights on him.

Here's what happened.

One man was in Burgundian colours; he was closest to me. I came on him from behind, and in one swing of my war sword I dropped him – concussed, dead, or merely smart enough to drop the ground, he was out of my fight. The next fellow in green and gold whirled in his saddle, but he had to stretch across his body to reach me, and I spiked him in the armpit with my point two handed, and he was gone. So was his squire, who tried to reach me. I killed his horse as mine danced under me – forward, back, a half-rear, a lashing forefoot. Why a country priest had been riding a prince's war horse was beyond me.

Seguin and I ought to have died right there, but I fought better than I'd ever fought before, and my nameless, stolen horse powered me from opponent to opponent.

So instead . . .

John Thornbury erupted from the back of the mêlée and slammed into the man-at-arms, hammering Seguin with a mace. Blood flew like the rain, and the man seemed to jump off his horse.

The Burgundians melted away. It was shocking how fast they vanished, and I was slow to react. I was, in fact, so sure we were all about to be killed that I was hunching my shoulders, breathing like a bull, ready to fight to my very last ounce of strength.

Then I saw one of Camus' black and white villains grab the reins of a knight in Bourbon's arms, and I realized that we were *not* losing. When routiers take the time to take ransoms, it means we're winning.

Companions, it was like the sun bursting into full flower over the battlefield. I was a dead man . . .

. . . and then I was not.

I stood in my stirrups and had a look. I had time – no one near me was fighting. To my left, up the ridge, there were still men fighting against Mechin and our footmen. But in front of us, the northern levies of the King of France were melting like snow in the desert, or throwing themselves off their horses and begging to be ransomed.

To my right, I saw Jacques de Bourbon. I'd saved his life once, and I determined to have him. He had two sons by him, and either of them was worth a fortune. But in the time it took me to ride ten horse lengths, they were already ringed with men like me, so I carried on, angling my horse to my right, downhill.

I caught a knight's reins without having to try – he cut himself free from the rear of the crush and there I was. I took his reins and he begged my aid. He opened his visor and gave me a gauntlet.

'Ride with me, monsieur, and I will protect you,' I said.

Twenty horse lengths further on, I found myself among Hawk-wood's men. We were all intermixed, but I was watching for Savoyards, and there they were. Sir John took the Marshal of Savoy under my nose.

There was still a knot of men fighting. One had green and black arms, and I cantered at him. At lance-length, I rose in my stirrups – he was hammering Sir Robert Birkhead – dropped my sword and leaped at him, right out of my stirrups, arms spread. I hit him, wrapped him in my arms and carried him out of his saddle to the ground.

We hit hard. He broke his arm and I wrenched my left shoulder.

Nonetheless, he tried to rise. I put a hand on his elbow, opened my visor and said, 'Yield, brother.'

Broken arm and all, he barked a laugh.

We were lying under a tangle of horse's legs and hooves, and it seemed comfortable to be out of the fight. He was in pain, but he grabbed my hand. 'Christ,' he said. 'I never thought we'd lose. Milady is in the camp.'

Rape and murder. That camp was about to become hell on earth.

'Save her, William,' he begged, and passed out. Damn him.

Men made their fortunes in the fight. Mercenaries retired from arms and went to live on rich manors.

The French army, on the brink of victory – or past it, if you ask me – suddenly collapsed. Mechin's desperate footmen held past all expectation, then surged forward down the hill to complete the rout. Within an hour, we were in their camp.

I had taken two more knights, so that I appeared to be leading my own conroy. I had lost Perkin and Robert and de la Motte, but I wasn't worried. They'd find me. I had one goal in mind from the moment Richard spoke. I rode into the Savoyard camp and rode my war horse up and down the tented streets, calling, 'Milady! Janet!'

The rout of their army was behind me and all around me, and

archers and Gascon spearmen were pouring down the hill. The more able women were already running, and a few had horses.

'Milady!' I screamed.

It was an odd moment, for me. I was trying to save someone. It was suddenly very, very important to me.

'Milady!' I roared. I turned to the knights I'd captured. 'Gentlemen, will you support me in an attempt to save a lady?'

The Burgundian knight flushed. 'But of course, monsieur!'

The other Savoyard didn't answer.

We spread out. The edge of the wave of murder was just washing against the tents at the southern edge of the camp, and the screams had begun. Why hadn't the other women run? They had children; they had things they valued too much; they wanted to wait for their men. Or they couldn't believe they'd lost.

I couldn't find her. Simple calling wasn't working, for whatever reason. I decided to reason it out. The Green Count himself wasn't in the field, but Richard was. On the battlefield, he'd been near the Marshal of Savoy. I found the Marshal's arms on a tent off to my left and rode to it.

One street away, two Gascon spearmen were taking turns stabbing a priest. They roared and he screamed.

Hell.

I rode off to the right. Two tents past the marshal's pavilion was a long, low tent of simple white linen, but the third tent in had a green pole striped black. I rode for it.

A woman screamed.

A man came out of the tent clutching his side. As I watched, he fell to his knees, blood flooding under his brigantine.

I heard the woman scream again and I was sure it was Milady.

Still mounted, I used my sword to cut through the side of the tent.

He had her hair. She had a wicked, long dagger, but he was wrenching her back and forth by the hair while using his other hand to raise her kirtle. He was laughing at her efforts to kill him.

I put the point of my sword into his laugh.

I reached down, caught her and boosted her across my saddle. In the same motion, I stripped the long dagger out of her hand.

'Milady!' I shouted at her. I couldn't slap her – in gauntlets, you can kill a person with a slap – I just backed my horse through the slit.

My Burgundian had his sword across his saddle-bow and was covering me. The other knight I'd taken was nowhere to be seen. He'd ridden away.

I wonder what de Charny would have said about the situation. Eh, messieurs?

We rode north to get free of the looters. In fact, we made a great loop – almost five leagues – to stay well free of anyone who could hurt us, and by the time we capped the ridge Milady knew who I was. She was shaken. In fact, she was silent.

But as I set her down by my old wreck of a tent, she smiled. 'I'm going to be a man again, if that's all right,' she said, very quietly. 'I want to be a knight,' she said.

I nodded. 'Me, too,' I said.

There's a particular exhaustion that smashes you down after a day of fighting in harness. It's not just fatigue – the mind can only handle so much violence, in my experience. Add the stress of leadership, the quest for a woman who is about to be hurt, and hurt badly, and the likelihood of defeat ...

After Brignais, I lay down on my pallet in my squalid tent and went to sleep, still wearing all my harness. Other men seized ransoms or pursued the beaten French. I was asleep.

I came to with that confusion that comes with fatigue, sleep and darkness. Night was falling and our camp was in a state of near riot.

Milady was shaking me. 'Hello?' she said, over and over, with a certain brittle cheerfulness.

I didn't know who she was or where I was for long heartbeats. I thought for some reason that I was in the Castle of Meaux, with Emile.

Perkin cured my confusion by leaning into the tent. 'Sir? he asked. 'I have all your prisoners, but it's getting pretty bad out here.'

It was, too. Never, even in storming a town, did I see a lawless riot like the night after Brignais. The men were exhausted and elevated at the same time. Men of low birth, men who had, until a few months earlier, tilled the earth, suddenly had captured lords worth the value of a hundred farms or more.

Men were killing each other for their prisoners, or gambling a dozen fortunes away at dice, while friends gathered around them with weapons drawn. A young woman – whore or not, she was young and pretty – came past us dressed only in a kirtle, and she had two French knights on a rope. I have no idea how she came to have them, but they were her prisoners.

Armoured as I still was, it was all I could do to get to my feet, and my muscles protested – the skin at my hips where the weight of my awful coat of plates rested was rubbed raw, and under my arms, at the top of the muscles that rest where a woman has breasts, it hurt like the lash of a whip every time I raised my arm.

Stooping to exit the tent required an act of will.

Perkin had Richard Musard and my brave Burgundian, whose name I didn't know, and two more knights. They were stripped to their arming clothes, and they were sitting at a small fire.

Musard was lying on a pallet. The Burgundian had a drawn sword in his hand.

I leaned over Richard, who winced. 'You broke my fucking arm,' he said.

'I could have spent the time capturing someone worth money,' I said.

Richard managed a small smile. 'I'm worth a ransom, Will. Never doubt it.'

I shrugged. 'Listen, brother, there is no ransom between us. I'm sorry about your arm, but when the coast is clear, you are free to go.'

'How like a trained ape he is, your black man,' said a familiar voice. 'I don't suppose you'll do the same favour for me? I'm almost family, am I not?'

Firelight and muzzy-headedness didn't help. It took me a moment to know him.

'You don't remember me? Oh, you knew my wife so much better, I think.' His sneer was palpable, like a blow.

'The Count d'Herblay,' I croaked, with a bow.

'I won't rise,' he said.

Perhaps foolishly, I looked at Perkin. 'Whose capture is he?' I asked.

'Yours, sir,' he said. 'You put him down, man and horse together. I reined in to take him before the other jackals had him.' He grinned.

I grinned back. But then all of d'Herblays' barbs made sense.

I ignored him. I was sad, and afraid, that he knew too much and would punish Emile. And I wanted to kill him. I very much wanted to kill him.

My Burgundian bowed. 'You let me keep my sword,' he said,

'and your squire chose to allow me to help him defend us against—'
he coughed delicately into his fist, 'marauders.'

'Your brothers and sisters in arms,' said the Count d'Herblay. 'I
didn't know that there were so many criminals in the world. And
whores to service them.' He nodded with apparent amicability at
Milady as she emerged from the tent.

'Better men-at-arms than you, it would appear,' I said. He made
me angry very easily. Why not? He had what I most wanted in the
world, and he didn't seem to place any value on her. But then I
thought of everything Milady had taught me – and other men. I
thought of how well it had worked, to show *nothing* to the Bourc. So
I showed d'Herblay nothing, either. Nothing but courtesy.

He shrugged. 'Any thug can swing a sword or wield a lance,'
he said. 'That's all knights are, thugs in fancy dress. You and your
companions prove it.'

The Burgundian whirled on him. 'Do not allow despair and defeat
to rob you of your honour, monsieur. These gentlemen have taken
us today. That is the fortune of war, which may turn in our favour
another day. Fortune does not rob chivalry of its power.'

'Chivalry is a myth for ignorant little men,' d'Herblay said with a
superior air. 'To gull the small-minded into fighting.' He looked at
me. 'Or to excuse the tyranny of raw force.'

I bowed to my Burgundian. 'William Gold,' I said.

'Ah!' he said. 'I know of you. You don't appear so very like Satan
as you are described, monsieur. However, you will want my name
and style, and I'm afraid I will prove a disappointment. I am merely
a squire, Anglic de Grimard, and I doubt I'm worth 500 florins.
Indeed, even that would beggar me.'

D'Herblay laughed nastily. 'Why, then, you should have stayed
home!' he said. You are like a man who wagers on a game of dice
and then announces he has no money to pay.'

De Grimard whirled on him. 'I obeyed the summons of my lord,'
he said.

D'Herblay shrugged. 'The more fool you,' he said.

You can imagine that by this time I wished with all my heart that
I'd killed the noble bastard ten times, but that was who he was: an
endless drip of caustic commentary. It is a commonplace to say that
such people hate themselves most of all – it doesn't really help to
know it.

I'll add that all around us that night, men were being murdered for no better reason than that they were not worth a ransom. I could have killed him. My life might have been very different if I *had* killed him.

I never thought of it, though. He was Emile's husband. I'd saved his life at the Bridge of Meaux, and I wasn't going to ruin that now.

The last knight was really John Hughes' capture – a knight from Tancraville's retinue, A member of the Rohan lineage named Jean de Meung. He rose and bowed.

'I am most pleased to find that I am the prisoner of a gentleman,' he said, a little stiffly.

'Don't believe it!' said d'Herblay. 'He's a branded thief, a traitor to his sworn lord and an excommunicate.' He smiled at me. 'Aren't you, my dear?'

At any rate, men came out of the darkness – twice in the next fire-lit hour – and tried to take my captives. They were all Gascons, and they were ... wanton. Feral.

One group we chased away with a display of arms – we faced them down like you face down a pack of wild dogs, with shouts and gestures, and they slunk away.

The second group did the same, but again, like feral dogs, they turned at the edge of the firelight and threw themselves on us. They had little armour and a wretched array of weapons. I don't even know if they were Gascon routiers or merely desperate men who had joined for plunder. They attacked us by firelight and we killed them. Richard held a dagger and did his best; de Grimard and I fought back to back at one point; de Meung stood by the Count d'Herblay and put men down with a great two-handed axe. John Hughes emerged from the darkness with Ned Candleman and Jack Sumner and our two servants,both of whom had good mail shirts and pole-arms. They were all drunk, but they were all alive, and after they came back to us, our little camp was secure and our prisoners could stop defending themselves.

Sometime after midnight, the tumult died away. Perkin helped me disarm, and we rolled dice for watches. I drew the very last watch before cock-crow – the best watch of all – and I fell onto my pallet and darkness came down.

The morning after Brignais was the beginning of the end of the Great Company. Who would have predicted that victory would destroy as effectively as defeat? We smashed the remaining armed power of France and took a fortune in ransoms, but we were not really an army. We had no King. We served no legitimate authority. We were under ban of excommunication. We didn't really have a single commander, or if we did, Petit Mechin was interested in money and glory, not in, for example, making himself the King of France. We'd won a victory that, in a proper war, would have ended in a major concession of territory, but we were routiers, and we held no ground.

The truth was that by the morning after Brignais, most of the footmen were already hungry. We'd picked the district clean before the battle happened. There wasn't enough forage for the horses. There wasn't enough food for the men. The Army of Thieves, as the French called us, had 20,000 human mouths to feed, and we didn't have a supply train. We lived like animals, from day to day.

Not that our victory was useless. After all, had we lost, we'd all have been executed – our captives were remarkably truthful about that. And we had a great many captives – most of the high and middle nobility of Northern France, and a few from the south as well.

Hawkwood immediately formed a company for the purpose of getting our ransoms paid. He enlisted two Genoese bankers and Petit Mechin, who, as a Frenchman, knew what men were worth and where they lived. I joined his company immediately and handed over the Count d'Herblay and the Frenchman, de Meung. Camus, who had taken a dozen ransoms, also joined the enterprise, and I spent a morning – a damp, dull morning – standing too close to the mad bastard while he glowered at me.

Twice I saw him talking to d'Herblay.

That should have troubled me, but I was having difficulty – exhaustion, combat and too much wine had left me less than half a man. My body ached, my head ached and my spirit hurt. I became disgusted with the whole proceeding – an essential part of the management of war, but a tedious and bureaucratic one, whereby each prisoner was entered into the accounts of the enterprise with his home and his potential value, and negotiations began as to his ability to pay. A single man-at-arms couldn't hope to force a noble prisoner to pay a ransom, although sometimes we could resort to the courts – the very courts of the defeated country. I do not jest – Richard Musard sued a French lord in the court of Paris and won, for cheating on his ransom! But by then, Richard had the support of the Green Count and all his 'interest' in Paris. A small man like me had nothing. We needed to band together and purchase the interest of the great banks. Messieurs, have I said how much I hate banks? They made such a profit from all our fighting.

Hawkwood stopped me at the slanted door of the Genoese pavilion. 'I'm off to Italy in a week,' he said. 'Thornbury and I all but deserted our company to come here.' He smiled – one of his rare, genuine smiles; not the smile of the fox, but the smile of the friend. 'I'd like to recruit you, William. Italy is rich and the contracts are regular. It is not banditry.' His face registered some emotion: disgust? He was a hard man to read. 'You deserve better than this,' he said.

I assumed he meant my clothes. In truth, I looked like a rag-picker.

I don't remember what I said. I probably shrugged; I may even have blushed.

Sir John put an arm around my shoulder. 'D'Herblay is worth three or four thousand Florins,' he said. 'Perhaps more. Meung is worth eight hundred. For that much, you can purchase a fine harness, a couple of good mounts and raise the service of a dozen more men-at-arms.' He hugged me tight. 'It's business, William. Come to Italy and make your fortune. If you still want it, in Italy you can be a knight. But don't come a pauper. Come with a dozen lances and you'll make your way.'

I embraced him. He told me that the rendezvous was at Romangnano, in Savoy.

'Savoy?' I asked.

He nodded. 'We're making war on the Green Count,' he said. 'Well, in the spring, anyway.'

I went and wandered the camp. I think that I wanted a woman, but I couldn't find one. What I found was exhausted chaos, in-fighting and desertion. Many of the Gascon lords were already packing – the Albrets were among the first to go. They had a fortune in ransoms, and they didn't need to form a league with the Italian bankers to get their money.

I was drawn by a man and a woman's voices shouting, and as I came closer, I realized it was Richard and Janet. I ran the last few steps to find that he had her arms, and she was dressed in my clothes – my worst arming cote, with laced-on sleeves, over a shirt of very dubious origins. He was trying to pull at her arms, and even as I rounded the pavilion behind mine, she snap-kicked him in the groin. He blocked the kick with his knee, and she, with breathtaking fluidity, predicted his defence and threw him over her hip – on his broken arm. He fell with his broken arm flapping like a wing, and I confess that I ran to his side, not hers.

'His fucking arm is broken!' I shouted at her.

She spat. 'He treats me like a *woman*.'

Richard was writhing on the ground. The pain must have been incredible. 'I'm trying to get her to pack!' he spat.

'I'm not leaving!' she shouted. 'I will not go back to being a lap-dog!'

'Perkin!' I roared. The poor lad ran up, my dented basinet in one hand and a rag of kirtle smeared with ash in the other. It was almost funny – trying to polish that old basinet was a little like trying to make a real knight of me.

'Sir?' he asked.

'Perkin, get me a surgeon,' I said. I turned to Milady. 'We're all leaving,' I said. 'There is no more Great Company. Petit Mechin is going to Burgundy. Sir John Creswell has said he's going to Brittany.' I forced myself to smile for her. In fact, she looked like a vicious shrew when she was angry: eyes narrow set, cheeks hard with rage and stubbornness.

She glared like a cat at Richard and then gave me the false smile women use when they are angry. 'Where are *you* going?' she asked.

John Hughes had been sharpening his long knife, and he stopped. Ned Candlewood was engaged in his usual off-duty pursuit: drinking hard at a bottle of wine. He put the glass bottle carefully on the ground. The brothers Arnaud and Belier – now fully armed and no longer servants – stopped fighting over a good basket and turned to look at me. Jack Sumner and Amory – no longer young Amory, either – stopped playing dice.

For good or ill, I was the captain of my own little band.

I propped Richard up against one of the ash-splint baskets that held my harness – when I had a good harness. 'Richard? Would you care to come to Lombardy?' I asked. 'Sir John made me an offer. He wants me to use my money from the ransoms to raise a dozen lances to fight in Italy.'

'Oh,' Milady said. Her exhalation had some of the sound of a woman in the release of love. 'Oh, Italy.'

Richard's face darkened with blood. 'I will *never* fight for that bastard again,' he said. 'I have a lord – the Count of Savoy. He will pay our ransom, and we will return to his court and *fight* John Hawkwood and his lawless brigands, thieves and rapists.'

I squatted down by him. 'Richard, I'm not ransoming you. You are free to go. I told you so.' I put a hand on his shoulder.

He shook it off. 'You have seduced her!' he spat.

For too damn long, I had no idea what he meant. I said something stupid, like, 'What?'

Milady said, 'Don't be a fool, Richard.' She said it with a certain bored lassitude.

Finally I understood. 'No, by the saviour, Richard. There's nothing between me and Janet.'

'Why does she want to go to Italy? Why is she *against* going to the Count's court?' he spat. 'I have bought her all the pretty dresses a woman could want.'

Now, before you say he's a fool, remember that we were all twenty years old or so, and our blood was hot. He loved her.

'I don't want your fucking prison!' she hissed. 'Why do you want a wife who has to have three cups of wine to spread her legs? Go find a nice, *normal* girl and leave me alone!'

This to an audience of a dozen.

Richard turned to me. 'You bastard,' he said. 'You ... you ... *fuck!* I'll kill you when I'm able.'

His hate was palpable. I was young enough to imagine that it would fade. 'Richard!' I said. 'Get a grip, man! I haven't touched her, and I won't.'

He *spat* at me. 'Thief!' he said. '*False Knight!*'

I shook my head in disgust. As I say, I didn't really believe his anger would last. He was wounded, a prisoner, and his woman was giving him a lot of crap.

His woman. Heh, there speaks ignorance. He may have been her man, but she, I think, was never his. At some level, I think she hated him.

When you command – when you put yourself above others, to lead them – you learn a great deal. Some of the lessons are harder than diamonds. Some cut like blades. People have many motivations, and damaged people never show you the things they hold most dear.

The next day, or perhaps two – we lay in a state of exhaustion for a long time – the Genoese established all the ransoms and agreed on a schedule of payments that satisfied us all. Well, not all, as you'll hear.

I had d'Herblay at my fire that afternoon. It was April, cold and wet. He didn't have many clothes, and he was obviously suffering, so I offered him a cloak.

'Why don't I just live in your cast-offs?' he asked bitterly. 'On your fucking charity.' He narrowed his eyes. 'Five *thousand* florins!' He spat. 'I'll have to sell estates, you little thief.'

I wasn't as raw as I'd been two nights earlier. 'If you can't afford it, perhaps you should have stayed home,' I said, with Fra Peter's calm voice.

'You *do* know she's dead?' he said. It was a strange turn in the conversation. I lacked the experience of men like d'Herblay to know how desperately he wanted to hurt me. I was used to men who used violence to settle hatred. D'Herblay used words.

At any rate, he watched my face like a lover. I took too long to understand. I'd taken several blows to the head at Brignais, and I must have been slow. I swallowed.

'Dead?' I asked.

'In childbirth,' d'Herblay said, with obvious relish. 'Dead. A corpse. Stinking in the ground.' He laughed, perhaps a little wild.

I sat as if my sinews had been cut.

You don't know what you take for granted, until it is taken from you. I suppose I always imagined I'd win her in the end. Or perhaps I made an effort not to think about her in those terms at all.

I also realized that I had been walking around for three days with her favour – torn from her favourite dress – pinned to my aventail. In front of her husband.

By the sweet and gentle saviour of mankind, I can be a fool.

Oh, but the height of my folly was yet to come.

I've heard men say that loss gives way to anger, and others that most of us deny loss – I heard a very good sermon on that at Clerkenwell one Easter. But the loss of Emile hit me like a longsword to the helmet, and I reeled from moment to moment as if I could not get the ground to be steady under my feet.

I went to a meeting with fifty other men-at-arms where Petit Mechin told us how the ransoms would be apportioned and how the money would work. It wasn't complicated.

'A week hence, we'll send convoys of prisoners to the relevant royal lieutenants,' Mechin said, as if this was an everyday matter. 'They will sign for the prisoners and present us with receipts, and we will pass those receipts to the bankers, who will pay us, and collect the ransoms at their leisure.' He shrugged. 'No doubt they will make an enormous profit but, messieurs, the only alternative is that we go and attempt to collect each ransom ourselves. The truth is that we have no one with whom we can negotiate.' He gave a lopsided smile and twirled a moustache. 'The government of France has effectively ceased to exist.'

To give you an idea of the scale of the rapaciousness of the Italian banks, my two ransoms totalled a little less than 6,000 gold florins. Under the scheme proposed by Mechin, I was to receive, in actual currency, about 500 florins, and letters of credit equal to another 1,000.

A superb recompense for a few hours of fighting, you might say, but assuming Messieurs Bardi made good on the ransoms, they would have another 3,500 florins merely for handling the paperwork.

At the meeting, I noted that Sir Hugh Ashley stood with the Bourc Camus. I remarked it, and I remarked it when I found the Count d'Herblay wrapped in a new cloak, sipping wine from a good horn cup at my fire, and talking to a very young man in black and white livery.

I remarked it, but it didn't penetrate the moral concussion I had received from the anger of my closest friend and the death of my love. Know this, messieurs, I was courteous to other women – I even lay with one or two – but I never, ever forgot Emile in those days. She *was* my chivalry. I worried that I had not heard from her, but I never forgot her for more than an hour.

The next day, Sir John Hawkwood passed my camp. His lances were ready to march, his baggage carts loaded, and he himself was dressed like a popinjay, in a fine long gown over a short jupon of golden silk, with a great bag-hat on his head. He looked like a wealthy merchant.

By contrast, I didn't even have a change of clothes, because Milady was wearing my spares.

He didn't dismount, but clasped my hand. 'Sir John Creswell asked for you to be a deputy,' he said. 'I assume he did it in a bid to hold you here, but I like anything that raises you in men's estimation.'

It was hard not to be flattered by that. I looked up at him, tried to smile and remembered that Emile was dead.

'What's wrong, lad?' he asked.

The problem ...

Companions, the problem between me and Sir John was that while he saved my life and built my career, he was never a man you'd tell about love or death. His mind was a thing of cogs and gears, not flesh and blood. He was loyal, though; he was always a good friend to me.

But if I had told him about Emile, he would have given me that look he saved for men far gone with drink, or professing a desire to die in the field, or other failings. I once knew him to say that the only difference he could discern between women was the quality of their banter. I *saw* him kill a nun in Italy to prevent two men-at-arms from fighting over her.

He was not the man to share my sorrow.

So I shrugged. 'A deputy?' I asked, feigning interest.

'You take the convoy to Auvergne,' he said. 'With Camus.'

I must have shuddered.

He shook his head. 'Drop your foolish feud before it kills you,' he said. 'Think of him as a bad horse that must be ridden. Get through the ride to Auvergne and come to Italy.' He grinned. 'Remember, some of those prisoners are mine!'

It was almost two weeks before my convoy was ready to ride, and I stayed clear of Camus, but we had problems every day, because my men and his had to struggle over the same ground to find forage and fodder. The army was breaking up, faster every day, and there was less and less authority. Sir John Creswell held Brignais, and he didn't even let the rest of us in the gates. He was afraid that another routier captain would take it from him – that sort of behavior was the order of the day.

Truly, there is very little honour among thieves.

The women were gone, and that made more trouble, because Milady was the last woman in the camp except a pair of old whores who had nowhere to go. Richard would not speak to me. Neither would he leave without her.

I lived in a fog of emotion, and I was surrounded by more of it – John Hughes said he'd rather have gone to hell than spend another night in that camp. It was like that.

There was a lot going on around me, and I was mostly deaf to it.

It was on a Sunday that we mounted, gathered our prisoners and rode west over the ridges for Auxerre.

351

We didn't have to go so far. The other prisoner convoys had left earlier, and there was some attempt to keep them apart so that the royal lieutenants couldn't conspire against us, but ours was held in camp – Sir John Creswell seemed to be the reason, and I was vaguely angry. I say vaguely, because I was so unaware. Milady rode at my side, dressed in looted armour, and I wore my harness; so did all my men and all Camus' men. Sir Hugh rode with us, and he was all honey to me. I thought nothing of it, even when he drank with the Count d'Herblay all three nights on the road.

It was mid-April when we rode down a long ridge to the cross-roads, where the road to Gascony crosses the road to Paris and the Road to Provence – a crossroads in Auxerre that every routier of that time must have known like an old friend. It was pissing with rain, and we came down the ridge just about nones – not that Auxerre had a working set of bells to announce the hour. We routiers had seen to that.

Ahead, we could see fifty men-at-arms sitting in sodden splendour on the road, watery red, blue and gold.

At the same time that we came down the ridge to the east of the crossroads, there was another party – a dozen wagons and twenty horsemen – coming down the far ridge towards us. I knew a moment of fear until I saw their colours.

They were churchmen, with a heavy escort of men-at-arms.

I ignored them. I rode up our column to the Bourc, and nodded as politely as I could manage. 'How do we handle this?' I asked.

He smiled. It was a horrible smile, one full of knowledge. So might Satan have smiled at Eve in the garden. 'Any way you like,' he said, with real amusement.

I knew right there that something was wrong. I knew he *wanted* me to know something was wrong.

At some further level, I didn't care. I think I knew then that I was betrayed, and I was prepared to let it happen. Why not? Emile was dead.

'Who is the lieutenant of Auxerre?' I asked, staring into the rain.

Camus barked a mad laugh. 'Does it matter?' he asked. 'I have a safe conduct.'

It was true.

We rode down the ridge.

The Lieutenant of Auxerre was my old friend and enemy,

Boucicault. Seeing him cheered me, and I rode up to him with my hands bare of gauntlets and offered my hand to him.

He let his horse shy slightly, widening the distance between us. The distaste on his face was palpable.

'My lord, I have the prisoners for exchange,' I said into the silence.

'I am required to ask for your letters patent and your safe conduct,' he said.

This was the sort of tedious bureaucracy that ruled our lives – the French seemed more hag-ridden with it than anyone else, but I hadn't been to Italy yet.

I reined my horse to one side, writhing at the humiliation of having my hand refused by Jehan le Maingre.

I was in harness, with my dented basinet on my head – Christ, I remember thinking how marvellous Boucicault appeared in shining blue and gold harness, with all his points tipped in real gold, all his harness leather in matching blue, his eagles worked in enamel on his shoulder rondels.

My eye caught movement and I saw Richard take Milady's bridle, and for the first time in two days I thought, Why is Richard here?

Milady screamed, 'William! It's a trap!'

In that moment, I saw it.

I saw Sir Hugh flip his visor down.

I saw the uncontrollable smile spread over d'Herblay's face.

I saw Richard strike Milady, and I saw her fall back, and he took her.

I saw Camus, convulsed with laughter.

I saw Boucicault turn on me. He didn't smile or frown. He said, 'William Gold, I arrest you in the name of the King of France as an infamous bandit.'

As I say, I saw it. Creswell had held me back until Sir John was gone so that he could take my name off the safe conduct.

Like the blow that puts you down, I never saw it coming.

I think, if things had been different, I'd have fought better. If I'd thought Emile was alive. If Richard hadn't betrayed me.

Instead, my realization of the betrayal was all at a distance, and if Camus hadn't laughed so heartily, I might have let them take me without a fight. But his derision – and his long-repeated promise of the humiliations he would heap on me and my corpse – caused me to back my horse. Two French knights tried to get my reins, and one got my steel-clad elbow in his teeth. I eluded the other by luck – I half ducked and his armoured fist brushed the top of my basinet and carried on; he lost a stirrup and I put the toe of a sabaton into his horse's side. The horse reared, he was down and I was a free man.

Things were happening over in our convoy. I got my longsword clear of the scabbard and half-reared my horse, looking for an opening.

Jehan le Maingre nodded heavily. 'He's mine,' he called to his men-at-arms.' He flicked me a salute with his sword and flipped down his visor.

Jehan le Maingre was, in that moment, the knight I wanted to be. Confident. Brave. And courteous. He saluted me, man-at-arms to man-at-arms.

I sat on my stolen horse with my rusty armour and put my spurs in, unwilling to go easy.

It is a tribute to what chivalry really is, even on that day, that no one interfered. They let us go at each other. Camus's mad laugh rang in my ears.

Boucicault's sword swept up, two handed. He was a fine horseman, and he guided his stallion with his knees, pointing its head for my midriff. I raised my sword one handed to guard my head on the left side.

His horse crashed into mine as his blow fell like a bolt from Jove in the heavens, and it was so sudden and so hard that it went through my guard and struck me on the helmet. My horse turned away from his, and his second blow, fast as an adder, hit my left shoulder. I couldn't get my arm up high enough to parry his blows – my leather and splint arm-harnesses didn't fit well enough. He hit me a third time, and I responded by snapping a blow behind me.

I missed.

I got my horse around as he hit me in the head – again.

I was reeling now, but I gritted my teeth and gathered my horse under me for one final effort. The nobly born bastard was beating me. I wasn't used to being beaten.

I caught his next blow, and our blades ran down, hilt to hilt. I powered my blade over his, rotated the point, wagering everything on getting my point into his neck or his faceplate.

I caught his faceplate. I ripped a gouge across it, and his pommel caught me in my visor and punched me off balance, then his back cut to my head knocked me from the saddle.

When I hit, I hurt. When I say hurt, I think, in that moment, something *died*.

So I didn't twitch when the sergeants came and took me.

I didn't move when they cut the spurs from my heels, and I didn't shout or fuss.

In fact, I noted with a sort of detached satisfaction when Richard Musard rode away, because he had Ned Candleman, John Hughes, Perkin and Robert Langland with him. He had our two French boys and Amory Carpenter and Jack Sumner. Camus said something. Richard Musard shouted back, Sir Hugh rode his horse in between them, and all my people rode away. I'm happy to say that John Hughes and Perkin never took their eyes from me all the way up the ridge until they passed out of sight.

Then the French put a noose on the tree.

Camus wrote out, 'William Gold – Thief' on parchment. He rode up. 'To hang around your neck,' he said, with a smile. 'Don't fear, Butt Boy. When you are dead, I'll take your body and make leather of your skin.' He laughed. 'Maybe I'll have you stuffed.' He smiled. 'I wanted this moment to tell you that I did this. Me. I bested you, merely by using my head. I undertook to make your friends – your own captain, Sir John Creswell, and your friend Richard – betray you. I hope you like it. I hope that you see you are utterly defeated, and I am victorious. You are nothing – worm dung.' His voice burbled and rather ruined the effect of his own superiority.

He leaned over. 'I'll have the woman, as well,' he said, grinning. 'And eventually, the black squire. In this world of shit, destroying you and your friends is the greatest satisfaction I can have.' He laughed. 'All of you will be my slaves in hell!'

I'd like to say that he didn't scare me, but a royal sergeant was preparing my noose and I was excommunicate. I was going straight to hell, and for excellent reasons.

Camus, the very tool of Satan, was grinning at me. I was about to die.

'Tell my master, hello,' he said. He turned and rode away.

Boucicault rode up. I noted he had a crease in his beautiful helmet and another on his right pauldron. 'I'd like to give you a priest,' he said. 'If I didn't have express orders to the contrary, William, I'd save you just to spite Camus. For my part, I'm sorry. I'm doing my duty.' He glanced at Camus. 'I promise you that in time, I'll make that one pay.'

I couldn't bow as my hands were tied behind me, and I could barely stay in my saddle because the sergeants had cut my stirrups. But I nodded. 'If you get him,' I said. I managed a shrug. 'He's evil.'

Boucicault made a face. 'All of you are about the same, to me.' He looked around, clearly hesitant to get on with it. 'But de Charny said you had it – had the makings of a knight. This ... is the wrong end for you.'

I wanted to beg. I really did. I wanted to say that I'd start again, that I wouldn't be lured by easy money and fighting, that I'd try to learn all the rules and please my Prince and ...

Hah. I was too proud. Add to my sins, too stupid and arrogant to beg for life from a man who, however much I may sometimes have loathed him, was not happy with hanging me.

'You know what I hate?' he said in a low voice.

Camus yelled, 'Get on with it!'

Boucicault ignored him. 'You know what I hate?' he asked. 'I hate that d'Herblay, whose worthless arse you saved at the Bridge of Meaux, actually helped contrive this.'

I shrugged again. It was all getting far away, somehow.

Emile was gone, and so was Richard. I had lived a worthless, sinful life. You know what I said to Boucicault, there in the rain, with the noose around my neck?

I said, 'I forgive you, Monsieur le Maingre.' I nodded and drew myself erect.

Listen, you wretches. I'm very proud of this part.

I said, 'I'm going to pray a paternoster. When I'm done – maybe even a word or two before ...' I shrugged.

He bowed. 'You should have been a knight,' he said.

I started my prayer.

'Paternoster, que est in caelus ...'

It is remarkable how we can think about many things at once.

The prayer was genuine. I had led a worthless life, and my soul was condemned to hell, but I truly repented, and my understanding was that my repentance was good for something. Even from a worthless murderer like me.

But at the same time, it was curious how long I'd taken to say the first line – it was as if time slowed. I had time to think about several things, about the taste of Emile's skin in my mouth ...

Santificeteur nomen tuum ...

About the feeling of the charge of 2,000 lances ...

Adveniat regnum tuum ...

About the moment when the gates closed on the Bridge of Meaux and I had saved Jacques de Bourbon ...

About serving the Prince at table ...

Fiat voluntas tua ...

About meeting de Charny in the shop ...

Sicut in cael, et in terra ...

About putting my dagger in him at Poitiers ...

About my sister, and my uncle ...

Panem nostrum cotiadianum da nobis hodie ...

About Nan, my first woman ...

Et dimitte nobis debita nostra ...

Meeting Richard; the Inn of the Three Foxes ...

Sicut et nos dimittimus debitoribus nostris ...

The Abbott, my sister, Emile, Richard, Sir John, de Charny, Sir John Chandos ...

Et ne nos inducas in tentationem ...

Almost at the end.

The convoy of churchmen had arrived. I could hear them – the creaking of the carts, the hooves.

'Stop!' said a loud, harsh voice.

I opened my eyes, Hoping against hope. Why not?

I saw the Franciscan whose horse I was riding.

His heavy blue eyes met mine. 'That is my horse,' he said.

Camus laughed. 'When he's dead, you can have it back.'

The Franciscan looked at Camus, and I swear the servant of Satan flinched. 'It is my horse, and I will talk to this man,' he said, riding up to me.

He was a poor rider. You could see that.

In a moment of about-to-die insight, I guessed my wonderful horse had been given to him by a rich patron, precisely *because* he rode so badly.

His eyes weren't mad, but they had something of the same quality as Camus'. This was not a man who saw things in shades of gray. 'Have you confessed?' he asked me.

I shook my head. 'Nay, father, I'm excommunicate,' I said.

He smiled and his face lit. 'It happens,' he said, 'that I have a special power conferred by the Holy Father to shrive such as you,' he said.

'I'm sorry I stole your horse,' I admitted.

'Is that the sum of your confession?' he said with a surprisingly gentle smile. 'Perhaps your good cloak was a fair exchange. I never needed a war horse.'

'Father, I've led a hard life, and my sins are about as black as they can be.' I didn't shrug. It was for everything – me, this priest and my soul.

'Are you in a hurry to die, then?' he asked.

Can you imagine a man who makes you smile when you have a halter around your neck?

I bowed my head. 'Bless me, Father, for I have sinned grievously, and I can't even remember when I last made a full confession.'

'Better,' he said.

I heard hoofs – clip clop. A damn big horse.

But I kept my eyes down. I began my confession. I won't bore you with it, messieurs. You've heard the meat of it, anyway.

The Bourc Camus shouted, 'Hang him – push the priest off. By Satan! Must I wait all day?'

'Silence,' ordered Boucicault.

'Fuck you,' said Camus. 'I knew I should have put the sword to him when I had the chance. I will not be gainsayed.'

'I don't believe you were done confessing,' said the priest.

But I had to look.

Camus drew his sword.

Boucicault drew his sword.

The black and white men-at-arms outnumbered the French at this point, but I don't think Camus could have taken Boucicault.

It didn't matter, because one of the men-at-arms from the religious column, dressed in the long black riding cloak of the Hospitallers, trotted up the road. He didn't even have a sword in his hand. He reined in between the French and Camus.

'Gentlemen,' he said firmly, as if they were his children.

Boucicault breathed deeply. 'Sir Knight,' he said and sheathed his sword.

Camus laughed. 'Out of my way,' he said, and he slammed his blade two-handed at the black-cloaked knight.

It wasn't magic. I saw what he did. When you are on the edge of death, you see things.

His right hand collected the cloak and intercepted the blow. It must have hurt, but he showed no sign, and his right hand ran up the blade and seized it near the point, while his left hand, travelling with the speed of a thought, seized the hilt. He leaned forward and his horse lunged powerfully – it must have been trained to do just that – and he used Camus' sword against him like a staff, getting the point right under his chin.

Using the Gascon's own sword as a lever, he threw him from the saddle. Camus hit the ground and didn't move.

The Hospitaller nodded to Boucicault. 'My lord is taking this man's confession,' he said. For the first time, I think, he actually looked at me.

It was, of course, my acquaintance. How many Hospitallers did I know? How many were riding the roads of France that spring?

Two black and whites came and took their master.

Boucicault bowed. 'May I leave this in the hands of the church?' he asked. 'I mislike the murder of this man, even given the life he's led.'

The priest nodded. He had the accent of a Provençal – of a peasant, in fact. He nodded. 'I take responsibility,' he said. 'Body and soul.'

Boucicault nodded at me. I swear he might have winked.

Had he kept us waiting there all that time, waiting for the priest? I won't ever know.

But I think he did.

The Hospitaller walked his horse to me.

I swear, all he did was look into my eyes. 'Pierre?' he asked the priest.

'I am only a few months into this young man's life,' he said. 'I would despair, except that he is but the product of Satan's will in our time.'

The Hospitaller tugged at his beard. His eyes never left mine. 'Look at his cap,' he said.

By happenstance – in an attempt to dress myself better, I suppose – I was wearing my best arming cap. The one my sister had made, with the cross of the Order of St John on the crown.

'Tell me what you want more than anything,' he said suddenly.

There are times when, despite inclination, all we can do is tell the truth.

'I want to be a great knight,' I said.

'More than you want to live?' he asked. 'More than you want to save your soul?' he asked.

Now that I had said it, I wondered at myself.

I burst into tears and said, 'Yes.'

There I sat, a halter around my neck, on a stolen horse in rusted armour, weeping my fool heart out.

For me, that's the end of Brignais.

Italy 1362–1364

It is our custom to rob, sack and pillage whoever resists. Our income is derived from the funds of the provinces we invade; he who values his life pays for peace and quiet from us at a steep price.

Konrad von Landau, German Mercenary Captain

We're almost there, messieurs.

Italy.

I didn't get there by any direct road.

Before they took the halter from around my neck, Sir Peter – the Hospitaller – made me swear.

He made me swear to obey the law of arms. And to obey him.

And Father Pierre Thomas made me swear to go on crusade, when and where he commanded me.

Of course I agreed. I was about to die. It is something, when they offer you everything you want, and the punishment is the reward. And then ...

And then Father Pierre Thomas took the halter from around my neck. 'Be reborn into the life of Christ,' he said. His gentle smile was there, as if he saw humour in his own comment.

Sir Peter – fra Peter, as I was to find was proper – shook his head about my armour. He cut it away from me. He didn't even unbuckle the straps; he cut them.

One piece at a time fell off me to lie under the tree. A pair of mis-matched splint greaves; a right cuisse in faded blue and copper, and a vibrant crimson cuisse in leather, studded with iron and brass in alternating rows of rivet heads. I fancied that cuisse, and it fit well. He cut the straps.

A heavy coat of plates – sixty or seventy in all, raw from the hammer and covered in leather on both sides, well-riveted in brass a long time ago, with a dozen tears, rents and weapon-wounds, some lovingly closed with expert stitches; some barely holding with old thongs or badly placed threads, or bound in wire. I would guess five or six men had worn that armour. It wept rust.

It made a noise as it fell to earth – an almost-human protest.

Arm harnesses – matched, but very poor. Badly made, garish, ill-fitting.

And my poor helmet. It was the last thing I had left of a finer harness – covered in dents, but lovingly maintained by my squire. The chain aventail shone and rippled, and the turban I'd wound around it to hide the worst damage ...

Clank.

I had a chainmail haubergeon. I'd had it since Poitiers. Perkin had kept it clean and it was a uniform, well-oiled brown. Fra Peter examined it.

'It's one thing to symbolize rebirth,' he said. 'And another to be a damn fool. Get the mail off and we'll oil it for you.'

His squire came forward. He was not English but Spanish, Juan di Ceval. I had never met a Spaniard – even in the odd glow of 'not-death', I was curious to meet him. He came and collected my mail. He also unlaced my aventail from my old basinet. He took them both and rolled them in hides that were themselves so oily they shone in the sun.

Sir Peter looked me over. 'You stink,' he said. 'It's not just sin. Do you really live this way?'

I was not in the mood to make excuses, but this stung. 'I'm a soldier,' I said.

Sir Peter raised an eyebrow. 'Young man, I have fought in the East for fifteen years.' I wore my armour for three weeks at a stretch, during the siege of Smyrna. I am used to living in the open and fighting in all weathers. You are dirty because you choose not to practice the discipline that would allow you to be clean.'

I said nothing, which indicates, I think, that I was not an utter fool.

They stripped me to my skin. Father Pierre Thomas walked me to the stream beyond the crossroads and watched while I bathed with Fra Peter's soap. Fra Peter brought me his razor. I had never owned a razor as fine as his – he even had a small bronze mirror in an ivory case.

He smiled, as if reading my thoughts. 'I have a weakness for nice things,' he said. He shrugged. 'I am a man, not a saint.'

I sat naked on a saddle, and he and his squire shaved my beard. It was odd, as if time was suspended. No other traffic came down the road. Birds sang. The sun came out for the first time in days. I shivered, warmed and shivered again.

Father Pierre Thomas opened his panniers and produced a pair of braes and a shirt. They were very fine, the cuffs lovingly worked.

He blushed. 'People ... give me things.' He shook his head in wonderment.

Sir Peter nodded. 'Because you are a living saint.'

Pierre glared at him. 'Please stop saying that,' he asked politely. 'I am a sinful mortal like everyone else.'

Sir Peter nodded, his head tilted to one side like a puppy's. 'Like everyone else, except that you cure the sick and bring happiness wherever you go.'

Father Pierre Thomas shrugged his shoulders. 'I do not mean to show impatience,' he said, 'but while the saving of this young man's immortal soul is worthy, we are due in Avignon.'

Sir Peter nodded. I put the clean shirt and braes over my clean skin. Fra Peter handed me a pair of brown hose, my own boots and a long brown robe.

The brown robe had the eight pointed cross on the right breast.

'I'm not worthy to wear this,' I said.

'None of us is,' Fra Peter said.

Juan picked my spurs up from the road. He and Fra Peter re-strapped them in two minutes, from leather they had in a basket on a donkey. I was surprised.

I walked the stolen horse over to Father Pierre Thomas, now fully dressed. 'Father?' I asked quietly as he was looking out over the valley.

There was a great deal to see in that valley, if you were newly reborn. The sun shone on fifty fields choked with weeds; at the southern edge stood a stone keep, fire-blackened, the near wall cracked; closer to hand, a small ring of village huts had been burned, and their thatched roofs had fallen in, so that they appeared as black cups on the green board of the earth. And just off the road, where Father Pierre Thomas's eyes went, was a church. Its destruction was too new to warrant the name 'ruined'. It had been burned. A human skull lay on the lintel.

He sighed. 'Yes, my son?'

'Your horse,' I said, holding out the reins.

He smiled. 'A beautiful horse,' he said. 'Do you know that I am the papal legate for the east?'

I had no idea. I thought he was a village curate.

He laughed. 'I am the least warlike of men, nor do I think that fire and sword are the weapons to convert Islam. Look what they do here.' He shrugged. 'But the Count of Toulouse, my father's lord,' he smiled again, 'gave me this war horse. Because in his notion of the world, I would need such a beast to fight the infidel.' He patted the horse's nose, which, to be honest, I would have hesitated to do.

He looked at the horse. And at me. 'Men like Fra Peter reassure me that not all violence is towards destruction. That some men must fight to cauterize the wounds that Satan makes on the earth.' He shrugged. 'I do not need a war horse. But you will.'

He leaned forward and breathed into my horse's nostrils. 'I was born a serf. My father is still a serf,' he said. 'We helped raise this horse. I know the dam and the sire. As there are horses, raised by hand with love for man's purpose to fight well, so may there be men, trained with love, to fight well for God's purpose.'

I asked no questions. It really was as if I'd died. I simply rode away with them and headed south. We rode through the ruptured landscape, and I was forced, through eyes just opened, to see what the last six years of war had done to the richest province in France.

Ah! You don't want to hear about it? Eh?

War destroys, my friends. Sometimes, the builder must knock down the old foundations to build anew, but otherwise, we call a man who knocks down a house an arsonist, or worse. Eh?

We'd raped France a hundred times by then. We rode along roads choked with fallen branches and weeds. We rode through villages without a single roof, and we passed fifty churches whose stones were cracked and burned, like the teeth of a charred corpse. We saw vacant-eyed people on the roads. Some wore ragged finery. Had they been gentry, brigands or peasants?

You couldn't tell. They all had the same empty eyes.

Once we were into Provence, the roads improved, and so did the scenery. The towns were walled, and most of them had destroyed their suburbs and walled up all their gates but one, which made entering and exiting a laborious process.

One of the curious aspects of donning a Hospitaller robe is that suddenly I was admitted to these towns without further question. I was served cheerfully at tables by young men and women who would have cringed to see me, or fled at the rumour of my approach.

Some days passed in a haze. It was, truly, as if I had been reborn. I'll pass over that now.

We were south of Pont-Saint-Esprit, in country I'd never seen. I think it must have been our last night before Avignon. Fra Peter, Juan and I were to sleep on the floor of the common room of an auberge just inside the gate of the town – a small place, really just a house, recently converted to an inn by a young man and his wife, eager to benefit from the increase in trade from pilgrims travelling south. We had a leek soup that was delicious, and then Fra Peter sat back, unbuckled his sword and leaned it against the wall. He waved to the good wife, who appeared delighted to serve us.

'My lord?' she asked.

Fra Peter nodded. 'How's the wine hereabouts?' he asked.

She nodded, eyes wide and serious. 'My father has his own vines,' she said. 'Our wine is very good. A cardinal told me so.'

'Well,' Fra Peter said. He barked his odd laugh. 'He'd know. Pour us a pitcher and bring us some cups.'

She curtsied and reappeared with wine.

I hadn't had wine since I was hanged. I drank off my first cup rather quickly, and I looked up to find the squire and the knight watching me. Fra Peter was smiling.

'Our Lord loved good wine, too,' he said. 'Never forget the Feast of Canaan.'

Juan drank his with relish. The pitcher was vast and deep, good red clay and nicely glazed. We poured our second cups.

'You can't wear my habit in Avignon,' Fra Peter said. 'Nor is it my intent to make you a brother knight. I can't see it.' He smiled down into his cup. 'But that may just be my own arrogance.'

I said nothing. I confess I felt some disappointment. Odd, as vows of chastity and poverty would not have suited me at any time.

'But you have sworn to accompany Father Pierre Thomas on crusade.' He looked at me. 'I wonder if you would wear the red habit.'

Juan smiled. 'As I do,' he said.

I had never seen Juan wear any habit at all. I said as much, and they both laughed.

'Donats,' they said together, and then Juan returned to his usual silence. Fra Peter nodded. 'Young men of noble birth pay a large sum to the order to be trained. They owe some service later, and are called 'Donats'. In battle, they wear a red habit.'

I sighed. 'I have no money,' I said.

'Ah,' said Sir Peter. 'I believe that in fact you have some thousands of gold ducats due you.' He drank more wine. 'Money you have from taking ransoms in battle.' He swallowed. 'Better, at least, than money looted from peasants paying *patis* to keep their daughters from being raped.'

'I have never raped,' I said hotly.

He nodded. 'Father Pierre Thomas would say that every woman you took, because she had no other choice, was rape.' He sighed. 'Father Pierre Thomas is a saint, and I am not. So I'll confine myself to the reality of the man-at-arms. Few women can protect themelves. Will you protect them?'

'I will,' I said.

He nodded. 'Have some more wine,' he said.

The next day we reached Avignon. I'm a Londoner, and to me, London defines what a city should be, but Avignon was a fine city. A little hag-ridden with priests, I confess, and more whores than all of Southwark ten times over, which says something about the state of the church, no doubt, but they were pretty and well-paid, and the churchmen were, for the most part, well-educated and clean. The palaces were magnificent, and the streets were well laid out, narrow but comparatively clean. There were influences that I learned later were Arab or Saracen – for instance, some of the streets had trees trained to run up the shop walls and cover the street from rain or sun.

You could buy anything in Avignon: a beautiful woman, a fine musical instrument, magnificent armour, a horse, the death of a cardinal. You could buy most of those things in London, but they were more expensive and harder to find.

My new-found Christian idealism received some near-mortal wounds. In Avignon, you could sit in a tavern drinking fine wine and watch a monk fondle a child too young to be in school while a priest and a nun embraced in a closed booth. Discussions of philosophy and theology could result in daggers drawn – and used. The Cardinals plotted for power and exercised what they had with a naked purpose that was at least more discreet among merchants and nobles in London and Paris.

That said, though, the new Pope, Urban V, was widely reputed to be the best man to hold the throne of St Peter in two generations, and he was advocating crusade on the one hand and church-wide reform on the other.

We were a week in Avignon before Father Pierre Thomas received an audience. To my shock, I was taken along – clean and clothed decently, in well-tailored dull-red hose and a matching cote with a short brown gown. There were apprentices in London who dressed better, but it was a world with a certain reversal of worldly fashion, and my clothes carefully proclaimed my status as a man-at-arms bound to a churchman. I had neither sword nor dagger. I missed de Charny's dagger. Its loss was more real to me than the loss of armour. Like Emile's favour, it had always been the physical embodiment of my chivalric desire.

The papal palace was both new and recently redecorated, and the paintings were as magnificent as the fabric in the hangings. I have always particularly loved gold leaf – the richness of gold, the way it looks over other colours, over leather, over wood. The papal palace at Avignon was a riot of gold leaf – there was more of the stuff than I'd ever seen before in one place in my life. The choir screen in the great cathedral was one solid mass of gold leaf, and the audience hall was decorated with two magnificent frescos, one on either wall. My memory is that one was the worthies of the church, including, of course, the last four popes, and that the other wall was the resurrection of Christ. Later, in Italy, I saw many better frescos, but that afternoon in late spring in Avignon, I had seen a few painted murals in England, but never the richness, the glow, the vitality, the gold leaf, of the frescos of Avignon. I gaped like a fish.

In fact, apparently I missed the whole of Father Pierre Thomas's formal introduction. I did note that he was a bishop, not a mere priest, as well as being the papal legate to the east. His precedence in the papal palace was very high. I had had no idea. Bishops, in my experience, wore crowns and mitres and garments of gold and had magnificent rings on their fat fingers.

At any rate, the papal nuncio answered the Bishop's greeting. Father Pierre Thomas – I always think of him that way – knelt and kissed the Pope's slipper and then his ring. The Pope then rose and embraced Father Pierre Thomas .

I must form loyalties very quickly as, in my head, I was already his man. I was – transported is not too strong a word – to find that the man I served was embraced by the Pope.

The audience took most of the day. Urban had been elected after Father Pierre Thomas left for the east, and Pierre had raced from distant Candia back all the way to Paris to try and enlist King John of France for the crusade – and to try to get the Pope's approval to use the Great Company as a tool against the infidel.

I didn't know that at the time.

At any rate, I stood behind Fra Peter and flexed my knees. Wool is all very well, but May in Provence is like high summer in London, and there was sweat running down my back. I tried to catch Juan's eyes – we were of an age, and he was the only man in the party who watched the pretty girls sway their hips and who licked his lips when the wine was served – but he was not interested in a whispered conversation in the papal palace.

My attention kept going to the frescos.

At some point, I looked up and saw the ceiling.

I heard several of the Pope's attendants laugh. I continued to watch the ceiling. There were stars in gold leaf on a deep blue – I'd seen work this good in London – but also the devil and his legions, who looked strangely like men I knew, and God and his angels, who appeared to me to be led by the Count of Savoy and Richard Musard.

I may have laughed.

Christ sat enthroned between the hosts, and he judged men and women. Some were taken to hell under Satan's feet, and others went in raptures towards heaven. Not all of the figures were clear, and some were not very well painted, but I remember particularly a woman – something in her expression reminded me of Emile, and she was poised. Christ's pointing finger showed that eternal joy was her lot, but her face conveyed the doubt she'd had, the sins she'd feared.

Juan drove his finger into my ribs with the force you only use on friends. My head snapped down and I reached to snatch his hand, but he was too fast.

'Hssss!' he said, or words to that effect.

I looked around.

Father Pierre Thomas's heavy gaze rested on mine.

Later, near the end of our interview, we were moved forward, and one by one we bowed and kissed the hem of the Pope's robe. Juan was enraptured. Fra Peter was detached. I was willing enough.

The Pope touched his crozier to my back as I prostrated myself. 'Ah,' he said. 'Young man, I take it you love paintings.'

My tongue seemed stuck to the roof of my mouth.

Father Pierre Thomas leaned forward. 'A soldier, your Holiness.'

'Your bodyguard?' the Pope asked. The weight of his crozier on my shoulder was like the weight of a lead pipe.

Father Pierre Thomas laughed. I wager not many men laugh in papal audiences. 'I have no bodyguard,' he said. 'I am one poor sinner, and my death will merely martyr one more Christian.'

The Pope's crozier was removed, and he leaned forward. He, too, had eyes like Father Pierre Thomas. Gentle, and yet I reckon he'd run his abbey with a rod of iron. As I raised my head, he took my chin in his hand. 'What kind of soldier?' he asked.

'I was a routier,' I croaked. It was more than a statement; it was like confession – all my sins in one word.

He nodded. 'I thought as much. What did you see in my paintings, young man?'

A woman who reminded me of Emile.

I remained silent.

'Redemption, let us hope,' the Pope said. His attention went to another man, and I was free.

It was in Avignon that I first trained with Fra Peter.

I had watched him train many years ago, in the courtyard of Clerkenwell, while I sat with my sister. I knew now that he'd merely been accustoming himself to a new war horse.

The Knights of Saint John had a preceptory – a house, almost a palace – in Avignon, and another to the south, overlooking the sea near Marseille. The preceptory was filled to overflowing, not with knights, but with princes of the church and great secular noblemen. However, the preceptory was also the command post for the papal army, which had at that time just been placed under the command of another Hospitaller knight, Sir Juan di Heredia, a name of great renown. In fact, my friend the donat squire was his nephew. Just to show you how small the world of arms is, it was Sir Juan – or Fra Juan – who had pursued us in the days just after the attack on Pont-Saint-Esprit, when Janet came to her senses.

I met him on the first day we were in town, and he never looked at me. But a week later, when I stood stripped to my shirt and hose, lifting stones in the yard, he stopped, a dozen men at his heels, and smiled at me. His eyes roved the yard of the palace for a moment and settled on Fra Peter, who was standing at a pell, breathing hard. He'd hit the pell so many times I'd lost count.

'Is this red-headed barbarian yours, Pierre?' he called.

Fra Peter crossed the yard, wiping his face on his shirt. It was already hot in Provence. Ah, the sun of Provence. 'Oh, aye, he's mine.'

Sir Juan nodded. 'Good size.'

Fra Peter grunted.

'Can he fight? Sir Juan asked.

Fra Peter. 'Of course he can fight. He won't win, but he'll always fight.'

I must have flushed. Sir Juan paused. 'You think you can win a fight with a knight of the order?' he asked me.

I bowed. 'Absolutely not,' I said, 'my lord.'

Sir Juan coughed and waved. 'Looks to me like he's on the path to wisdom,' he said, and led his entourage to their horses.

That day was odd for me, because, absent a few days at the Three Foxes, I had never trained, purposely, since I had swaggered my sword against a partner's buckler in London. I had fought – quite a bit – but the notion of lifting stones for strength, or practising balance on a beam, or vaulting over a wooden horse – I'd never done any such.

It takes time to learn exercises, and most young men resist them, annoyed or embarrassed or impatient. I was instantly in love. Exercise made a certain sense to me, and I could feel every stone I lifted, and how it related to the rest of my body.

When we went to the pell, Fra Peter made us fight the pell in a different way than we practised in England and Gascony. We didn't just swing at the pell; we fought it. Juan would circle the pell like it was a genuine opponent, circling and stabbing, circling and cutting, parrying blows so well-imagined I felt I could watch them develop.

When I had my turn, the two of them stood silently, watching me hit the pell. I had a borrowed sword, and I felt the hilt was too short, but I cut until woodchips flew, and I stabbed repeatedly at a knot in the wood until I hit it.

A young man of seventeen or eighteen crossed from the lodging house of the preceptory and came to lean against the railings of the barricade that surrounded the pell. He and Fra Peter exchanged greetings. His French had the same heavy accent I'd heard from many mercenaries: southern German.

I went and attacked the pell again. More chips flew.

The young man on the barricade laughed.

That punctured my new piety and the focus I was growing to go with it. I whirled, furious.

He shook his head. 'Ignore me,' he said.

'Would you care to show me what is so funny?' I asked through my teeth.

He shrugged, an expressive, Italianate shrug. 'I'm not sure even I could tell you what you do.' He leaned back. 'But I promise you it's funny.'

'Come in here and we will laugh together,' I said.

I confess that I expected Fra Peter to interfere, but he did not. Juan opened the barricade, and the new boy stepped in. Juan solemnly handed each of us a wooden sword – we call them wasters in England. You can kill a man with a waster.

My adversary took up a ludicrous posture – legs apart, body rotated, sword cocked back so far that it came around his head and pointed at me. He looked like a mime or an acrobat mimicking a swordsman.

By this time in my life I had fought a lot of men. One thing I knew, and respected, was the authority with which he adopted his ludicrous pose. He snapped into it, and then he was still.

Mime or not, he was absolutely confident.

I held my sword in the centre of my body and edged towards him cautiously.

He stepped forward and his blow rolled off his shoulder as his hips uncoiled.

Juan poured water on my head. 'Don't worry,' he said. 'He does that to everyone.'

My head rang for a day, and I didn't fight or exercise for three days. I mostly sat in my bed – an actual bed – in our inn, a fine hostel owned by the Knights of Saint John, who owned every building on the street outside their own gate, just as they did in London.

Then Fra Peter sent me on an errand to the commanderie by Marseille, which took me a week – it shouldn't have, but the *bailli* there assumed I was really a donat, and sent me off on an errand to Carcassonne. From there I had a message to carry for Narbonne, and then back to Avignon. I was stiff as a board when I got off my horse in the yard of a stable in Avignon. I carried my message to Sir Juan di Heredia, and he opened my sealed satchel and read several missives. Eventually he looked up at me. 'Get some rest,' he said. 'I gather you've had a busy week.'

Fra Peter was sitting with the German boy who had split my head in the common room of our hostel. 'What took you so long?' he asked, and I knew in a moment that he knew all about my trip already.

'The *bailli* sent me to Carcassonne,' I said. My eyes slid off his to look at the German.

Sir Peter nodded. 'The *bailli* was told to try you.' He raised one eyebrow. 'You thought we'd just trust you?'

I guess I *had* thought they'd just trust me.

The German smiled and rose from his bench. He bowed. 'I wish to apologize,' he said. 'My blow ... was not properly controlled. I hurt you.' He made a motion with his hand. 'It was a compliment, if you like.'

'A compliment?' I asked. By Christ, the German kid was annoying.

'You were *almost* too fast for my blow,' he said. 'So I traded speed for ... control. I should not have. I'm sorry.' He was stiff and formal, and Fra Peter permitted himself a very slight smile.

I was aware I had passed some sort of test with Fra Peter, and the joy of it gave me the grace to bow. 'No one has ever apologized for hurting me, that I can remember,' I said, but I took his hand. 'Now will you tell me what was so funny?'

He raised an eyebrow and looked at Fra Peter, who nodded.

'Well,' he said, and shrugged. 'You have never been taught how to use a sword.'

I bridled, let me tell you, messieurs. 'I've been using a sword since before you were born,' I said.

He shrugged. 'Do you know how to read?' he asked with the warmth of a youth.

'Yes,' I said. Few men like me could read and I was quite proud of it. 'Latin, French, and even a little English.'

He nodded, his point made. 'So you've been reading as long as you've used a sword?'

'Longer,' I agreed.

'You are aware that there are other men who read with more facility than you?' he asked, leaning forward. 'Faster, more accurately, more ... what word is it? More holding of knowledge?'

'Yes,' I said.

'And you can ride?' he asked.

'Yes,' I answered.

'Not really,' Fra Peter said.

That was two slurs on my fighting skills.

'Ah!' said the German. Actually, by this time I suspected he was Italian and not German at all. Germans have a different kind of arrogance. 'So you know how to ride, but you are not much of a rider?'

'I have many failings,' I snapped. 'Where are we going with this?'

He shrugged again and looked even more Italian. 'You have used the sword all your life, but because no one has ever taught you to use it, you have never *learned to learn*, and thus, you grow no better. I would go further. At some point – perhaps in a monastery – you studied the sword with the buckler.' He stroked his stringy beard. 'You have a developed *imbrocatta* and two interesting wrist cuts – inside and outside rolls of the wrist. These were taught to you. You practice them. Almost every other guard and cut you reason from first principles every time, like a small boy attempting to debate Aquinas.'

Unless a man is either very, very good or utterly lost, there come to him moments where things are revealed, and we know them immediately to be true. I have had this happen in various ways. I have heard something I knew to be true, but ignored it for years, and I have heard things that changed my life immediately. When the Italian said I had learned sword and buckler – that I had two wrist cuts and a thrust – that was true. Damn it, Thomas Courtney taught me those wrist cuts in a London square in the year '50 or so.

But in that set of sentences, I was convinced. He'd hit me, and I hadn't blocked his simple attack, and now that I thought of it, in a cascade of swordsmanlike considerations, his blow was very like the one Boucicault had used on me – twice. His words made sense.

'Teach me!' I said.

He shook his head, his face pained – really pained. 'I am just a student,' he said. 'I have so much to learn. There are men in Swabia who teach this art – another man in Thuringia. One in Naples, I hear.'

Fra Peter shook his head. 'Well, well, it is a day for me to eat crow. William, I imagined you'd take your horse and ride for Burgundy, and look, you came back to me, and now you really are my problem. And I sat here to keep you from attempting to murder our Friulian visitor, and instead, you ask him to teach you.' He put a hand on my shoulder. 'I'm delighted that you have shown yourself a better man than I expected.' He rose and threw some coins on the table. 'The House of Bardi has a table of accounting in the main exchange in the street of Goldsmiths,' he said. 'If you wish to take the next step, Sir Juan and I have set your donation at one thousand florins. Think of it as the ransom of your soul.'

It stung, the way he said it. But he paused by the door. 'By the way, your sister is now a full sister or our order.' He smiled, a sort of lopsided smile. 'So perhaps saving Golds has become an *empris* – something our whole order is required for. Listen, William, I urge you to pay the donation. One of the things most missing in your life is a structure for your actions. Join us, and we will train you.'

I rose. 'You will have me?'

He laughed. 'Don't imagine we're choosy,' he said. 'We're far more desperate than that.'

The Italian accompanied me to the street of goldsmiths. 'I suppose I could teach you a few things,' he said. 'How to stand. How to move. A few postures.'

A year before, I'd have spurned him. Learn swordsmanship from a boy? But my eyes were open, and the mould of my life was broken. I had to start again. No reason not to start again as a swordsman.

The street of goldsmiths was three times the size of the similar confluence in London, and so richly adorned that to walk down the street was to see a greater display of crozier heads, inlaid swords, episcopal rings, copes, vestments, chalices and jewels than you would see on display in any palace in Europe.

At the south end of the street, there were twenty tables set up in a small square. There were a variety of hard men on display – some in mail, some in leather, some in coats of plates, all with large and very obvious weapons. On the tables were enough coins to ransom the King of France – well, perhaps not, but on those tables were at least 50,000 florins. You could change a Saracen coin for new minted Italian gold. You could change French debased coins for pure Flemish coins. And so on.

'Messire, can you point me to the table of the Bardi?' I asked a man who looked English. He proved to be a Dane, but his English was good and he had his mercenary walk me to the Bardi, half the street away.

I waited for a pair of Paris merchants on their way to the fairs to change their money, then I offered a slip of parchment from my purse. In truth, I was nervous – I expected a great deal of delay, and perhaps outright refusal. I think that in my head, I tied Richard's and Sir John Creswell's betrayal to the whole prisoner ransom scheme – I think I expected further abuse.

I was stunned when my local Bardi representative – Doffo, a

senior man, more used to being an ambassador of Florence than a table banker – leaned across the table, took the slip of parchment from his nephew, read it, tapped his teeth with a gold pencil and looked at me.

'You are William Gold, the English knight?' he asked. He sounded respectful.

I probably simpered. 'Yes, messire, I am he.'

He tugged his beard. 'I heard you were dead,' he said. He raised an eyebrow. What he meant was, prove you are who you say.

'I had some troubles, it is true,' I said, 'but I was ... rescued by Fra Peter Mortimer. Of the Hospitallers.'

'Eh?' he asked. 'Will Fra Peter vouch for you, young man?'

My Friulian leaned across the counter. 'I will vouch for him, Messire Bardi. You know me.'

Of course. There could only be so many Italians in Avignon.

The pencil tapped again. 'I will, of course, guarantee your money, messire. My memory is that you are an old customer, although we have never met. But – I apologize for the inconvenience – your share has been claimed.'

I had expected as much, but his gracious manner had given me hope. 'Ah,' I said.

He shook his head. 'No, no. Fear not. You are palpably alive – even your red hair testifies for you.' He looked up at me. 'May I offer an interest-free loan until we work this out? How much do you need?

'A thousand florins,' I said. 'Make that one thousand and one hundred.'

'By Saint Jerome,' he said. 'Are you buying a bank?'

'I am becoming a donat of the Order of Saint John,' I said proudly.

He brightened. 'Ah!' he said. 'This small fortune goes to the church?'

I nodded.

He offered his hand. 'Done. A mere matter of notation then.'

Let me explain, if you do not know the banks and the church.

The better Italian banks took in specie – gold and silver – by collecting the papal tithes and other religious taxes and monies of account. They farmed these moneys: took them in and made a small profit.

Actually, an enormous profit, over time.

Imagine collecting the tithes from the entire Christian world, less only the schismatics of the east.

The money that they lent and brokered was that money. They didn't actually move the money – the bags of silver collected in England largely sat in London. Can you see it? There's a vault in a basement. It's full of money. It is the Pope's money, and he spends it in Italy. The Bardi use money collected in Italy to pay the Pope's debts there. It's all on paper. The money in England may go to pay for churches, or to reward nuns or feed the poor, but the rest – nine marks out of every ten – is used to loan out at interest. It engenders more silver as surely as girl horses and boy horses make more horses, except that the money never gets sick.

Over time, the effect has been to move the money slowly but surely to Italy. That's not because of the Pope, rather because of the merchants and the banks. Once in a while, you see a specie train, guarded by a small army, taking gold over the Alps. You never see it go the other way.

Does this put you to sleep, messieurs? You are fools, then. For bankers, war is not about fighting. War is about gold.

At any rate, what my new friend Doffo was saying was that handing me 1,100 gold florins would have been a heavy risk, but writing me a note to the Hospitallers saying that I'd paid 1,000 to them actually cost him nothing in the short run, and he had plenty of time to check my story and put the screws to—

Ah. That thought reminded me . . .

'Who collected?' I asked.

'Sir John Creswell is marked as your captain,' he said. 'I believe he collected.' He shrugged. He shrugged because 1,100 florins – more gold than most peasants would earn in their whole lives and the lives of their children – was not enough to seriously concern him.

Bankers.

He wrote me a receipt, and his spotty nephew counted me 100 florins. I signed. He signed. He sealed.

'Check back,' he said. 'We have means to collect from Sir Creswell.' He snorted. 'When I have seen to that, I will happily pay you the balance.'

We shook hands and I walked away.

Messieurs, you want to hear about the fighting in Italy. So I will not dwell on the summer of the year of our lord 1362, except to say that it was among the hardest, and perhaps happiest, of my life.

England and France were at peace, and the Pope was attempting to organize a crusade against the Turks. I'll speak plainly about the Turks later – I fought them many times over many years, as you will hear. They may be infidels, but they are fine soldiers, wonderful archers, men with a strong sense of honour, and all of them ride better than me.

Hah!

But at that time, the Turks had just taken two Christian cities in Europe, and it was the scandal of the world: Adrianople and Gallipoli. They were just names to me – I had no idea how well I'd come to know them later.

But although neither King Edward of England nor King John of France had committed to a crusade, it seemed possible, even likely, that they'd both go. That sort of negotiation was the reason Father Pierre Thomas was a legate, which, by the way, is an ancient Roman military rank. Well, I enjoy knowing such things!

So in high summer, Fra Peter, Juan and I carried letters from Father Pierre Thomas and the Pope to the King, all the way across France to Calais.

Before we left, I trained every day with Messire dei Liberi, the Friulian lad.

He reduced swordsmanship the way I had seen Cumbrians and Cornishmen reduce wrestling, to a set of postures called gardes. Some of the gardes I had heard or, or seen used, in London and Bordeaux. The Guard of the Woman is much the same everywhere, although different men use it differently.

But the Friulian had something – I think it was anatomy. He said he'd studied a year at Bologna – even in England, we know Bologna is the best medical school in the world. But he had theories of how the body moved, and how best to put strength and speed into your sword. Many were profound. A few were nonsense.

Here is where he was different from the many charlatans I have seen teaching boys to use their weapons: when you showed him that a theory or posture was nonsense, he grinned and dropped it from his repertoire.

Let me tell you a secret. Every master-of-arms knows this secret. I can impart it to you, but none of you will be able to learn from it. I'll try anyway.

You can teach a man *how* to use a sword, but you cannot teach him to use it. The knowing how is not the same as the use. An untrained yokel – me, for example – can defeat a superbly trained man for many reasons. The Italians roll their eyes and say *fortuna*. The French, more piously, say, *Deus Veult!*' The English say, 'The luck of the devil'.

There is more to battle than training, armour, conditioning and good horses.

Because there are so many imponderables to a fight, many men who teach the way of the sword are charlatans. Or they are good swordsmen, but they add all sorts of falsity to their teaching.

Mercenaries like me may be bad men, full of sin, but we can spot this sort of chaff in an instant. Unlike many students, we have been in fights. Many fights. We have a simple rule – if you want to teach us about our profession, you must first prove you are better – not once, but many times.

So, it is not that I had never met a man who claimed to teach the way of the lance and sword before I met young Fiore. But I will say he was the first I ever met, and one of the few, who was utterly honest, almost ruthless, in his approach. He treated fighting as Aquinas treated religion. With logic and deep understanding of the most basic parts: the body, the sword, armour.

I remember one afternoon finding him in an armourer's – really, a finisher who took pieces from a smith and prepared them for sale, with straps, coverings and fancy brass.

'Have you seen the new Milanese stuff?' Fiore asked me.

Imagine an eighteen-year-old sitting in an armourer's shop, flexing shoulder armours. Picking up spaulders and testing the limits of their flexibility.

Of course, I had, however briefly, owned some Milanese armour. I said, 'Yes. I had a breast and backplate for a year.'

'Ah!' he said. 'How did they affect your ability to cut across your body?'

I couldn't remember, but I had a feeling it had limited my cut.

'Ah!' he said, and smiled. 'Let us go play in the yard.'

In late spring, he announced that he was going to Nuremberg, in High Germany, to study with a sword master there. I was envious, but we embraced. I was leaving for England.

He was in the same sort of anomalous position as me. He was travelling about, fighting in tournaments and carrying messages for money. He did small duties for the Knights, and they gave him permission to use their preceptories as hostels. Something to do with his father.

'I need to fight,' he said.

I laughed. We were fighting every day, by then.

'No – in battle,' he said seriously. 'It must be very different from duels and chivalric encounters.'

We'd had this discussion a dozen times, so I shrugged.

'Come on crusade with me,' I said.

He grinned. 'Of course, I must,' he said. 'I have already sworn it. I will be back in a few months.'

We embraced again, and he rode for Germany with a bag of letters for the banks. Meanwhile, I rode for England.

That was a happy trip.

First, I was formally made a donat in Avignon. I knelt all night at an altar, swore my devotion to the Knights, swore to obey and serve, and was given a red surcoat with a white cross, which I confess I wore every day for some months, I was so proud.

The ceremony was well attended. I was not a knight but a squire, in the eyes of the order, so I received silver spurs and the demand that I obey all knights. I thought of Sir John Hawkwood. After the ceremony and the vigil, I was bleary-eyed with lack of sleep, and Juan took me out to eat in a fancy inn with a gilded ceiling somewhat dulled by the fire in the hearth and greatly enhanced by half a dozen very attractive young women bringing the wine.

We had lamb.

After we ate, Fra Peter came and sat. I was pleased, in some remote, human way, to see that he watched the prettiest girl, a dark haired woman with an elfin nose and a smile that would stop your heart, who seemed determined to lean over my table for as long as it might take me to see to her naval.

I misdoubt but that Fra Peter was younger than fifty – perhaps younger than forty – but it pleased me to see that he watched her the way he watched a fight.

Why do other men's failings please us?

Never mind. He tore his eyes away. By God she knew the effect she was having, and she minced away from us with a backward glance and a quarter of a smile – so well done, my friends, that I'm still talking of it, ain't I?

It's like the perfect sword cut. You don't forget it, once you see it done.

He tore his eyes away and blushed. He met my eye.

'You have done well, William,' he said. He reached into his brown robe and produced – de Charny's dagger. 'I return this to you,' he said. 'I suspect that you'll want it, as we're going to England and you look naked without a weapon.'

Then he rose and embraced me. So did Juan.

'Tomorrow,' he said, 'we will go to the armourer and have you fitted for a decent harness. I'll draw some munitions stuff for the trip. And you'll want a sword,' he added.

We drank. After some time – talking of arms, fighting and horses – he stood up. 'I'll leave you, gentles. I'm too old for this place.' He managed a smile at Dark Hair, and she smiled back at him, damn her.

Juan and I had a second cup of wine. And a third, and perhaps a fourth.

We talked of everything: the world and the crusade. I stood up. 'I'm for bed,' I said.

Juan agreed, and we walked home on a clear summer evening. I left him at the door of our lodging and went to the outdoor jakes.

Then I went back to the inn.

Before the bells in the cathedral tolled for Matins, Dark Hair and I had repaired to her tiny bed in the eaves, hard by the pallets of a dozen other girls. She held my hand while she negotiated with them in rapid Provençal, and held out her free hand.

'Give me a few moutons to pay them,' she said, and flushed. I could feel it in the half-dark. 'Ah, monsieur, I'm no whore, but a poor girl, and these are my friends who will lose a little sleep.'

I gave her a gold florin.

She bit it.

Another girl, as pretty in another way, watched this transaction and giggled. 'For a florin, we could all stay and help,' she said, but her friends led her away.

As it turned out, we didn't need any help. Her neck was warm and salty, and her mouth was deep and tasted of cloves and cinnamon.

I saw Anne a dozen times before we left for Calais, and she welcomed me eagerly enough that I think, despite my florins, she liked me. I've known a hundred women like her – somewhere in the misty half-world between whoredom and 'honest' labour. We slipped out to walk the river and went out in a boat, and we ate fish in a riverside tavern, and we ...

Never mind. It wasn't love, but it was pleasant.

The last night, I told her I was going and she kissed me and said, 'A girl likes a soldier ever so much better than a priest.'

The ride across France was like a chivalric *empris*. We camped almost every night because there were no inns; we rode armed all the time, and I had to practice the discipline my knight spoke of so often, washing what I could every day, changing linen without taking off my rented armour. As he had said, it wasn't that hard. I learned every day – learned what many squires are taught by their knights, but no one had ever taught me.

I learned to wash my own clothes, and to dry them on the rump of the pack horse.

It wasn't all learning. I taught *them* to cook. The three of us cooked in strict rotation, and their initial attempts were laughable for men who had lived in the field all their lives. But their cooking was of a piece with my swordsmanship – they'd never been taught better. I bought pepper, saffron and good honey and I showed them where, even in the ruin of France, one could pluck a few herbs from the foundations of a burned cottage.

I won't bore you with what effect Richard's betrayal had on me, except that I was not as quick to love Juan as I might have been. And while I loved Fra Peter – and I did – I yet contrived to keep a little distance between us.

The trip, and the dinner, however, eroded my intentions. We had no other companions and we became very close.

I was learning so much, so fast, that I don't remember much of the scenery. I learned that I had never learned to properly care for a horse, because I had never been a real squire. When you are out in the rough for weeks, and it rains is cold, you must work very hard so that your great brute of a war horse is not made lame for life, or dies of a fever.

I learned how to start a fire – better, faster and from all sorts of things. Fra Peter could make fire with a stone and the pommel of his sword – it was like watching a priest perform a miracle.

I learned to cook a few new dishes from Anne, in Avignon, and I taught them as well. The one I liked best was the Provençal dish I had eaten so often in Avignon – cassoulet.

I learned to be a better scout, for a campsite, or an army.

And every day, I learned to ride better. I learned to saddle and unsaddle, tack and untack, faster and more gently. To clean and maintain all my equipment and Fra Peter's.

Every day, we practised with our swords, often cutting the inno-cent vegetation. This allowed Fra Peter to discourse on how to cut or thrust, and then to further discourse on how to clean and sharpen.

You might have thought that, as a professional man-at-arms, I'd have resented this.

Perhaps Fiore and I aren't so different. When Boucicault dropped me in the road, I learned a bitter lesson.

I wasn't anywhere near as good as I thought I was.

Messieurs, Sir Jesus had the right of it – those of us who live by the sword will die by the sword. To us, the only thing more danger-ous than our enemies is our own complacency.

I wasn't too far gone to learn. I was twenty-one, and I'd just started to grow.

Calais. A fine town, growing every year. By the saviour, it is still growing. I reckon the town fathers don't want King Richard to renew the war: they make their profit from being England's door into France.

I thought it was the end of our journey, but after a meeting with a papal officer, we took ship for England.

I was overjoyed.

We landed twice, but our little ship carried us up out of the chop of the Channel and all the way to London. We landed across the river because of some trouble – I can't remember what it was. Our horses came up out of the hold, and it was a day before they were anything like recovered. Fra Peter went ahead to the priory at Clerkenwell, and Juan and I stayed with the horses.

When they were alert and well fed, we rode them over the bridge, and I had the immense pleasure of wearing my donat's coat into London.

Juan was the perfect companion – happy to be pleased. We rode west through the streets, and I showed him the tower, the churches, the Cheaping, the goldsmiths.

I was enthusiastic about my city, and yet I was all too aware that it was small next to Paris and dirty next to Avignon.

My sister was no longer at Clerkenwell, but had moved to the sis-ter's convent in the country. Despite that, our arrival at Clerkenwell had a sort of homecoming air to it, and we were welcomed by the prior in person and fed in the great hall. I felt as if I was a member of this great order.

The hall and barracks were packed. The order had been recruiting for the crusade, and they had twenty donats, mostly veteran men-at-arms. It made me proud to be one of them.

We stayed a week. There was nothing for Juan and I to do except watch the more attractive scullery maids, exercise in the yard and swagger about the streets of London, which we did with the attentiveness and belligerence of young men. London had had a generation of swaggering young men, fresh from victories in France and Flanders, and we were tolerated or ignored.

The beer was good.

By the third day, I was torn between conflicting desires, the strangest of which was to leave before something – some nameless fear – came to pass. I think I feared arrest. It is hard to say.

But I had nightmares two nights, and I dreamed of the Plague – I think it was the first time, but scarcely the last.

I woke the fourth morning, in the quiet certainty that I had to go and see my uncle. It is difficult to explain even now – I feared and hated him, and meant him harm, yet I had to visit.

I rose, walked down to the Thames and swam, and helped two boys from the Priory to water horses. Then I went back to my cell and washed and put on clean clothes. I left my war horse and my donat's coat, and I walked, dressed like a modestly prosperous apprentice or journeyman, through the streets to my uncle's house, wearing dull colours and a hood.

As I neared it, my heart beat harder and harder, and my breathing grew shallower. I was afraid.

The door was shut, which it should never have been on a day of work.

I stood looking at it for a while.

I knocked, and there was no answer.

I was … relieved.

I walked up the conduit to Nan's house. I had been told never to visit her again, but on the other hand, she had probably been my closest friend.

The shield of the Order was a powerful one. I couldn't imagine being shown the door by an Alderman of London. Not if he wanted to be buried in a church.

I didn't call at the shop door, but went to the garden wall, as I had used to when we were courting. I think that I hoped she would lean out from her window – I know I looked at it.

Suddenly she appeared.

I think my heart stopped.

She was not the most beautiful woman I'd ever seen – not after France – but beauty is a wonderful thing, and when you decide on beauty, it never fades. Nan was ... herself. And my heart soared to see her.

The look on her face was priceless. She looked at me as a man, judged me worthy of a second look and gave the slightest smile, not really flirtatious but a firm acknowledgement of me, my upright carriage and my muscles (women look at these things even when they don't think they do) and then – remember, I had a hood and she couldn't see my hair – something gave me away. Her eyes became fuller and deeper and her regard solidified, then she leaped to her feet, leaned out the widow, shouted, 'William!' and vanished.

I could hear her running down the twisting chimney stairs.

The garden gate flew open and there was her mother, who grinned. An excellent sign.

'Look what the cat dragged in,' cackled her mother. 'William Gold, you haven't been hanged. How fares it with thee?' And she put her arms around me and kissed me on each cheek.

I confess that I found the phrase 'haven't been hanged' a little too close to the bone, but I laughed, and then Nan slammed into me. She'd added flesh since fourteen, and she was hardly light – her hug was as hard as a man's – but despite some gains, I picked her up and twirled her around her father's garden.

'Stop that, William! I weigh ten stone, now, and you'll hurt your back.' She laughed. 'I'm an old married lady with two daughters.'

Her mother put a hand on my shoulder. 'Come into the kitchen and tell us your adventures,' she said.

So I did.

An hour on, with two cups of candian wine in me, I met Nan's da, who came in wearing enough finery to be abroad in Avignon or Paris – wool hose in his guild's colours, and a jupon with a long velvet gown over it, all trimmed in fur. For July in England, it was a bit much, and he started stripping off before he noticed me.

'William Gold?' he asked, and before I could fear his reaction, he was pumping my hand. 'We heard you was at Poitiers with the Prince,' he said.

They had?

'Your sister wrote to us,' Nan said, eyes cast down but smiling widely. 'And again last autumn, to say you'd paid her way to be a full sister. That's how we knew you were...' she looked up. 'Prosperous.'

'A sister of the Order!' the Alderman said. 'You must bathe in gold, young William. How fare ye? Are you ... a scholar?'

I laughed. 'I'm a soldier, master. I serve a knight of the Order, myself. I'm a lay brother.' I shrugged. 'The ladies have already heard all my stories.'

Which is to say, I'd left out the horror, the love-making and the dirt, and told the war stories in which I seemed a hero rather than those in which I seemed a fool. Like most young men at home after war.

Master Richard rose and embraced me. 'Be free of my house,' he said graciously. 'Not that my wife and daughter haven't made you so already, I have no doubt.'

I asked what I'd waited all that time to ask. 'How ... is my uncle?'

Master Richard made a face like a man whose drunk bad milk. 'He still has his mark, and he does some business,' Master Richard said. 'Your aunt died.'

Nan's mother spat. 'He killed her.'

Nan looked away.

Master Richard spread his hands. 'You don't know that,' he said softly.

I heard other news – how Tom Courtney was a full member of the guild, one of the youngest ever; how my sister and two other sisters had come during an outbreak of the Plague and were held to have worked miracles, and how Nan's husband, a mercer, had fought at Winchelsea when the French came, and now was an enthusiastic member of the London bands – the militia.

'He'll be home in a day,' Nan said. 'I pray you like him.'

I smiled at all of them. 'I'm sure that I will,' I said.

They invited me to sup and I bowed. 'I have a friend,' I said. 'My fellow donat, a Spanish gentleman. I would esteem it a favour if I might bring him.

That was easily done. There's no merchant in London who doesn't like having a Spanish aristocrat at his table.

Before returning to the priory, I walked up the hill to the abbey. There was Brother Bartholomew, who gave me a great embrace, and, to my shock, there was 'monk' John, last seen on a battlefield. He, too, gave me an embrace.

We looked at each other warily.

He shrugged. 'It wasn't the life for me,' he said. 'I'm not sure I'm meant for God, neither, but the food's good.' His eyes were far away. 'I'm not ... it wasn't ...' he met my gaze and his was troubled. 'You know what a life it was.'

I laughed – not a laugh of fun, but a laugh that understood. 'John, I'm a lay brother of the Order of Saint John.'

His own roar of laughter probably said more about us and our lives than any speech, but he hugged me more warmly than before.

They took me to the old Abbott, who was no longer serving, but mostly sat in the cloister and read.

For a long moment, I feared he wouldn't know me.

'I'm Will Gold, Father,' I said.

'I know,' he said. His hands, old as bones, came up and clasped mine. 'God love us, child, you came back.'

Dinner with Nan was a delight. We shared a cup of wine while Juan entertained her parents with stories of Spain.

We met by chance in the passage by the stairs – me going to the jakes and she returning from the pantry. She leaned over and kissed me very hard, then shifted herself down the passage, as light on her feet as ever.

Later, at the door, her mother bussed me on each cheek and said, 'Now you come back when you are in London, but not so often that you make Nan see stars. You hear me, Will Gold? Your manners are pretty and your friend's a gentleman born; see you act one, too. Do I have to speak more clearly, young man?'

Nan sputtered. 'Mother!'

'Mother nothing, girl. I'm flesh and blood like you. I have eyes.' She glared at us and then smiled. 'Be off with you. I'll go inside – for as long as it takes me to say a paternoster for you.'

I kissed Nan – the sort of kiss that lingers between what might be considered friendship and what might be considered lechery. She smiled at the ground, twined her fingers with me briefly and went back inside.

I decided I didn't really want to meet her husband.

Juan and I walked through the darkening streets to the priory. He looked at me in the light of some cressets and said, 'They are good, worthy people.'

I nodded, suddenly devastated to realize what I might have had.

The way I tell this, it may seem to you that I was almost hanged for my misdeeds, and then I was rescued, and like the conversion of Saul on the road to Damascus, my life of sin was over. But I tell you, gentles, my heart varied between black and white, hope and despair. If you have comitted sins – bad sins, not the venal ones the priests rant about – and you spend time with good people, whether people like Fra Peter or people like Nan's mother,you *have* to look at yourself. These good people are mirrors, and unless you are a liar and a caitiff, you *see*. Every day I saw. Some days – many days, if I wasn't given exercise and hard work, like a troublesome colt – I considered slinking away.

Every day.

Bah! Never mind. But I tell this like it was ordained, and the truth is that I was still unsure. Still ready to bolt.

The next day I went to the Bardi factor in London and drew a little money. I bought the Abbott a pair of reading glasses – the Venetians made them. I'd seen them in France, and in Avignon everyone had them.

I bought Nan a brooch of pearls. I walked to the gate at sunset and pinned it to a ribbon, which I hung on the latch. Then I knocked and walked away.

Our last day in England, Juan and I rode the horses out to Southwark and prepared them for the ship, then I rented a hack and rode to the nunnery to visit my sister.

As a donat, I was allowed to meet her in the parlour, and she was so happy to see me, so happy that, in her eyes, I'd turned to God, that mostly all she did was cry. And yet, to my delight, when her eyes were dry, I saw that she had become one of those tough-minded nuns who gets things done. We fell into each other's arms. I have seldom sobbed tears while grinning like a loon, but there I was.

She told me a few of her adventures – this brought on by my remembering Nan and her mother to her – and she grinned like a man.

'Aye, the Plague, brother,' she said. 'My foe and Satan's tool.' She tossed her shoulders back. 'I don't understand the ways of men, and war, and yet, when I understand that there is Plague among the whores in Southwark, and my sisters and I pack to go to their aid, I feel something, and I wonder if it is the same thing you feel when you hear the trumpets.'

Courage comes in a number of forms. Going to a place with Plague – of your own free will?

But to gain a little benison in her eyes, I told her of the days when Sam and all my men had Plague, and Richard, too.

'And you tended them?' she asked.

'What else could I do?' I answered.

She kissed me. 'God loves you, William Gold.' She grinned, and for a moment she had a little imp in the corner of her mouth, as she sometimes did when we were children. 'And so do I. Listen, brother, you paid my bride price, and I can never repay you, but I pray for you each day. And I fear you need it. You live with war. It is all around you, and a man who stands on a dunghill gets shit on his feet.'

She put a hand on my arm – I'd started to hear her swear.

'I live more in the world than most married women,' she said. 'I try to heal the sick, with God's help, and I see the shit every day.' She paused. 'Need you go back to war, brother?'

I had thought all these things, so I looked at the polished floor and said, 'I'm a soldier, sister. I hope to be a knight.'

She hugged me tight. 'Go with God, then. Write to me sometimes, when you aren't too busy.'

I was the one who wept, then. To see her ... solid. Not just solid in her faith, but with humour, toughness and understanding. And love. She was better than me.

But it had all been for something. After I saw her, I think I saw myself differently. Again, it was no road to Damascus, but I think it was a road, and I could follow it to knighthood.

England had two more surprises in store for me.

Fra Peter was called to the tower to speak to the Chancellor of England – probably about the crusade – and Juan and I were left cooling our heels in Southwark for two additional days. Where ships called and where whores leaned out from inn balconies and called suggestions after you.

'Hello, Red! You could be riding me in comfort on a feather bed before the bell rings?' I remember that, because the lass was big enough to ride.

They could make me blush. It wasn't like France or Avignon. Whores in London have rights, and they are ... English.

At any rate, we tried hard not to commit various sins, although our attempts at abstinence were not cloistered, and we tempted ourselves constantly, all but patrolling the main thoroughfare. Ah, youth.

At any rate, we stopped to drink in the King's Head. It was full of royal household men coming back from a royal hunting trip and debating money matters. There were two dozen royal archers and some squires.

I saw Sam Bibbo in the same moment he saw me.

And over his shoulder I saw Geoffrey Chaucer.

Chaucer was a royal squire, or like enough. He sneered at me from a distance, but I could tell that he was interested to see me there, and eventually – the inn wasn't that big – we came together. I was chatting to Bibbo.

I smiled at Chaucer, showing all my teeth. He'd helped with my sister after all, so I was prepared to let bygones go by.

He didn't offer a hand. 'You're back,' he said.

'And away again,' I allowed.

He looked at Juan, who was a quick study and had picked up my hesitation.

Juan bowed, gloved hand to his chest.

Chaucer returned his bow. 'Spanish?' he asked.

Juan smiled. 'I am from Castile,' he said.

Chaucer smiled. 'Ah, it is warmer there, signor. And the towns are beautiful and the people the most courteous in the world.'

'You know Castile?' Juan asked, delighted.

'I know that water can be more precious than wine, there,' Chaucer said. Then he turned back to me. 'We heard you were dead,' he said. 'Betrayed to your death by Richard Musard.'

I shrugged. The world of soldiers and arms isn't that big.

'Musard stabbed you in the back?' he asked. 'I'm surprised. I thought better of him. Even if you are a far cry from a gentil and perfect knight, you were his best comrade.'

This man always spoke faster than I. He made my head spin, asked hard questions and danced away like a swordsman demonstrating his skills. I wasn't sure myself what I thought of Richard's betrayal, but in that moment I found that I wasn't ready to be shot of him. I took a deep breath. I said. 'Richard was a friend.' I met Chaucer's eyes. 'There was a woman involved.'

Chaucer barked his laugh. He had grown – he was no longer a wiry boy but a man. 'A woman? Between you and Musard? By the saviour, monsieur, there was a time when I thought the two of you closer than men and women.' He laughed his nasty courtier's laugh, but then he looked at me and shook his head. 'Your pardon, Gold. My mouth runs before me, sometimes.'

'You haven't changed,' I said. 'But *par dieu*, Master Chaucer, it is the first time I have ever heard you admit it.'

Juan looked at me and then at Master Chaucer, as if gauging the likelihood of violence. I took a step back. 'Never mind, Master Chaucer. Perhaps I have only myself to blame, at that. I'm going back to Avignon with Fra Peter.'

'Mortimer?' Chaucer nodded. 'I understand he's going to Italy.'

'Italy?' I was thunderstruck.

'Italy?' Juan said, obviously delighted.

'Italy?' asked Sam Bibbo. He'd listened to every word without comment.

Sam Bibbo told me that evening he'd like to go to Italy. He said it would take him a week to tie up his affairs and leave the royal guard, so we sailed for Calais without him, but by the time we'd arranged to travel with an English pack train bound for the fair at Champagne, he arrived, with two horses, his weapons and armour.

Our first night on the road, after I'd introduced him to Fra Peter, we sat on our saddles, both of us sewing. I might have stepped back five years.

'Why?' I asked. 'You were royal archer?'

He shrugged. 'I took a wife,' he said. 'She died in childbirth. All my friends are dead, or in the companies. I don't have a trade.' His steady eyes met mine in the firelight. 'Three weeks ago, we drove stags and hinds for the King and his court, and a dozen ambassadors. Thirty hours in the saddle and on foot, moving animals; guiding nobles decked out like merchants to their shooting stands; or frightening the beasts along the woods. Driving 'em to their deaths.' He looked at the fire. 'Half the lads hadn't been at Poitiers or any other fight. Archers are yeoman's sons, now, or better. It's not the way it was.' He looked away. 'Like as not it's all in my head. Mayhap I was away too long.' He sewed a dozen stitches and looked up. 'No one to talk to, neither. Neighbours all think I'm some sort of freak. Or a dangerous killer.'

That was a hell of a long speech for Sam Bibbo.

The next night, he said, 'You taken religion, young William?'

I sat back. Had I?

He went on, 'I mean to join one of the companies. If you are going to Avignon with the Knight, we'll part at some point.' He was embarrassed. He made a face. 'Rather go with you.'

I leaned back. 'Sir John Hawkwood invited me to join him,' he said. 'He told me to raise ten lances.' I shook my head. 'But I'm bound for the crusade, Sam. And I will not be foresworn.'

Sam tugged at his grey beard. 'Huh,' he said, and that was it for a day or two.

The ride back to Avignon was harder than the ride north, for a dozen reasons. The countryside seemed more dangerous – we were attacked east of Paris by men so desperate and skinny they seemed like another species. We had to trade watches at night. Sam was a vital addition, and I could see him and Fra Peter growing, if not closer, at least to some sort of arrangement.

We were in the Auxerre, less than a day's travel from the tree where I'd almost been hanged, when Sam spoke up while we sat chewing rabbit.

'Sir Knight, a bird in England told me you was bound for Italy. Is it true?' he asked.

Juan sat up straight.

'Perhaps,' Fra Peter said slowly. He looked at his wooden bowl.

'Why would a Knight of St John be in Italy?' I asked. To me, it sounded like walking into a Southwark brothel – a little too much temptation.

'Italy is ... at the centre.' Fra Peter shrugged. 'Of a number of things.'

Juan hardly ever spoke up. He was often silent, his lively eyes darting about, and when I had him alone, sometimes he'd boil over with questions, asking me ten or twenty things at once. But that night, his curiosity – and his pent-up desire to fight, like any normal boy – burst forth.

'What things?' he asked. 'Why? Why Italy? Because of Rome? The war with Milan?'

It was as if he had just discovered the power of speech. We were all silent after his outburst, and then we all laughed, even Fra Peter.

'Where do I begin?' he asked. 'I suppose it is about history, and about money.'

'Money?' asked the Spaniard. 'How can a crusade be about money?'

More laughter. Is anything more amusing than a seventeen-year-old?

Fra Peter sighed. 'Do you know what it is to be a Knight of St John?' he asked quietly. 'We are supposed to heal the sick and fight to defend the Holy Sepulchre, but Jerusalem was lost before I was born and I've never even worked in the hospital.' He glanced at Juan and rocked his head from side to side. 'I may be for Italy, yes. King Edward asked me to take a message to your Hawkwood. He made it clear that in doing this, I would be helping the cause of the crusade.'

He sat back and looked up. The stars were just coming out.

'At the same time, the Pope, head of the church, is also a worldly seigneur with temporal power and temporal lands that must be defended, in Provence and in Italy. The Pope is at war with Milan. The routiers prey on the Pope, and the Pope seeks to send them to fight Milan and the infidel. The Pope ordered me and my brothers to spearhead this effort.' He shrugged. 'The Pope has an army, and the commander of that army is another of my brothers, who needs more knights to support his efforts to cleanse Provence of the routiers by force of arms. And in the east, more of us hold the island of Rhodes, and there we fight the Turks. Except that we don't always fight them – sometimes we temporize or negotiate. Does Christ care whether you make a pilgrimage to Jerusalem through Christian lands or Moslem lands, so long as you go?' He shrugged. 'I have heard Venetians say that the sultans rule Jerusalem better than the Franks ever did.'

'And the money?' Juan went on.

'Do you know what it costs to maintain Smyrna and Rhodes? Perhaps a hundred thousand florins a year, to maintain four hundred knights and six galleys. A crusade? If we want to have ten thousand men for a year,' – he laughed – 'three hundred thousand florins of gold, and that's before we feed a man or a horse, or ship them to the Holy Land.'

Juan stared, eyes wide. 'Holy Mother of God,' he said. 'Is there so much money in the world?'

Sam nodded. 'So, you'll go to Italy after you visit Avignon,' he said.

Fra Peter spread his hands to the fire. The first hint of autumn was in the air. 'Master Bibbo,' he said, 'I can't predict where I will go next any better than a leaf on the wind. A year ago I thought that we were about to see the greatest crusade since good King Richard marched, but now, I'm sorry to say, I can't guess when the King of England will go, or even send his son.' He frowned. 'I'm maudlin. So I'll confess to you that I'm not convinced that a great crusade would be the best way to deal with the infidel. But to *fail* to have a crusade would itself be a blow.' He lay back. 'Enough lessons. When I am on the road, like this, eating rabbits under the stars . . .' His eyes met mine. 'It's not a bad life.' He lay, looking at the wheel of heaven. 'I'll likely go to Savoy first. And then Italy. You'll like Italy.'

Bibbo groused about our pace, but he stayed with us until Avignon. Messire Doffo Bardi was gone back to Florence, but his suddenly self-important nephew informed me that I had a balance of 855 florins, a small fortune. As we had come all the way south with some English and Dutch merchants, I went to the book market, bought a small and fairly undecorated copy of Galen, the old Roman doctor, with some receipts in Greek, and sent it to my sister in the care of the English merchants, with a note for her and another for Nan.

The harness I had ordered in the spring was complete.

I was so excited by this that somehow it took me three days to go and see it.

Young Fiore had been back from Nuremberg for two weeks when we came.

'I fought a duel!' he said by way of a greeting.

I laughed. I hadn't fought anyone in five months. Well, I had played at sword and buckler in London with Juan, more for old times' sake than anything. Juan and I had adjusted the English game to our longswords, and we would take turns cutting and thrusting at a buckler held by the other.

It turned out that the German master in Nuremberg had been less than enthusiastic about having a foreign pupil who was critical of each thing he taught; they'd fought, and Fiore had left him bleeding and had to flee the wrath of his students.

'They should thank me,' Fiore said with the sort of arrogance that always marked him.

'Perhaps they loved the man,' I said.

He grimaced. 'He may have been a fine man,' Fiore said, 'but he was the merest inventor of tricks, as a swordsman.' He rolled his eyes. 'And so many pious mouthings and mysterious sayings.' He drank wine, and his eyes met mine. 'A charlatan.'

'You learned nothing from him? I asked.

'Oh, as to that,' Fiore grinned. 'I learned a number of things.' He narrowed his eyes. 'He had a theory – he divided all fighting into two parts.' He shrugged. 'I will never think of a fight in quite the same way again.'

Juan leaned over and poured more wine. 'Then, pardon me, Fiore, but he was no charlatan.'

Fiore sat back, ignored a magnificent pair of breasts passing at eye level and shook his head. 'He knew a great deal,' he said dismissively, 'but he couldn't sort his knowledge from his ignorance. Like a priest who preaches the true word of God and heresy by turns.'

Juan raised an eyebrow, turned to watch the beautiful girl pass off into the rough crowd of servants and soldiers by the wine barrels, and looked at me with one eyebrow faintly raised.

I agreed with Juan. I agreed about the girl, agreed about Fiore's failure to react to the girl, agreed about Fiore's arrogance.

All that in a glance.

But here's the thing. Fiore was the real thing. Fiore is to fighting what a Dominican is to religion.

The armour fit well. Some of it was perfect, and some could have used another fitting before I left. The helmet was fine; the breast and backplates were Milanese work, altered to fit me. The arms were perfect, and the legs were a little large. But the whole sparkled in the sun, and I felt like a new man. I had not been so well armed since the morning after Poitiers.

I paid in gold florins.

I don't know how long we were in Avignon – it was such a pleasant time, and such time passes swiftly. Juan, Fiore and I were inseparable, and we went to church, prayed, drank, played chess, rode about the countryside, practiced at arms, and debated the world. Fiore was a well-read man, and my trip to the book market for my sister had reawakened my spark. I bought a gloss on Aquinas and a small copy of Cicero's letters in Latin – a new discovery from the ancient world that somehow seemed exciting to me, and the more I read, the more I wanted.

Fra Peter was busy all the time, and once his horse was curried and fed, Juan and I had no other tasks. I had money, and I spent it.

I think my favourite memory is waking in a cottage under the walls – a pretty place I'd heard of from a priest in the curia and rented for a few days. I woke with Anne under my hip, and we made love, then I lay with my head on her tummy and read Cicero to her.

'Are you going to be a priest?' she asked, and laughed.

Juan had a girl, as well, and the two of them, Anne, myself and Fiore went for a picnic in the late summer hills. Fiore never seemed to have a girl. Nor did he have a boy – he was above such things. He was a priest of the sword.

Very well! I'm boring you by remembering that some times were good times. Ingrates! I'll go back to war and death.

At some point – a week or two after we returned – Fra Peter had us to dinner at the preceptory, in the hall. The invitation seemed to extend to all the donats – there were forty of us by then – and to the mercenary men-at-arms who had been serving the order in the papal army. Serving the order directly, that is, paid by the prior.

We received the Prior of Avignon's thanks for our services – in the field and, specifically, on the embassage to England, which was more thanks than I ever received from the Prince of Wales. Let me tell you this of the Order. It could be venal, and it could be petty, and *par dieu*, it could bog itself down in petty politics and bureaucracy, but men were praised by their leaders and rewarded at every chapter meeting and every evening at prayer. This instant reward of even minor virtue taught me a great deal, and soothed my soul, as well. A man may change – and be rewarded for that change.

But the Order also existed in the world of sin and death.

Over wine, Fra Peter told us that he would be going to Italy, and that the crusade was delayed at least a year, and perhaps two.

'I feared this,' he said. 'The King of Cyprus is on his way. He should be the leader of the crusade – he knows the enemy and the conditions – but the Pope has offered the command to the King of France. And there is more corruption involved than you'd find in the corpse of a week-old Plague victim. The crown of France and its dependents have an old claim to the crown of Cyprus . . .' Here Fra Peter showed more anger than I'd ever seen in him. 'Talleyrand is using his influence to block the true King of Cyprus from coming here – to keep Father Pierre Thomas from exercising his authority.' He sat back suddenly. 'Merely in an attempt to get his own family some land grants in the east. In truth, young masters, it is not the Turks who will defeat Christendom. We will defeat ourselves – through greed.

Routiers and cardinals. They deserve each other.' He shrugged. 'But I am not being a good knight. My lord, Father Pierre Thomas, will be going across the Alps to speak to the Count of Savoy, and I am to escort him.' He looked at Juan, and then at me. 'The Pope has great hopes that the Green Count will go on crusade.'

While I understand now what was at stake, at the time I was twenty-one years old and the shock of near death and betrayal had worn off. I had some new ideas of knighthood – and I had better armour.

I wanted some adventure.

The idea that the crusade was delayed for as much as two years dismayed me utterly. 'What are we supposed to do?' I asked.

Fra Peter was looking at the table. The Prior fingered his beard and looked elsewhere. The other knights present, including di Heredia, smiled silently into their wine.

The truth was evident at that table. The knights had been building up their strength – adding brother knights, donats and mercenary men-at-arms. Those men had stood the Pope in good stead when the routiers threatened Avignon, but now, with the Pope waffling on the idea of the crusade, the order was going to cut its losses. Men-at-arms were easy to find. Even donats – volunteers – cost money.

Di Heredia looked down the table at me. 'You gentlemen are to be released from your obligation until the crusade becomes ...' he looked apologetic. 'Ahem. More ... likely.' He looked wistful. 'And thus the Order loses the best fighting men I've had under me in many years.'

The Prior leaned forward down the table. 'Of course, you are all sworn to the crusade. When Father Pierre Thomas summons you, we expect you to come!'

Juan and I murmured with the other donats and men-at-arms.

I might have revolted. I was not so tied to my new life that having the Order spit me forth might have caused me to go back to my former life. I have seen it happen to other men.

I lay in my bed the next morning – not lifting stones, not wearing my new harness – but thinking to myself, like a routier, that the church had cozened me of 1,000 ducats and was now letting me go.

When Fra Peter knocked on the door of my little cell, I sprang up. I knew his footsteps. I flung back the oak door, and he was there – plain brown gown, eight-pointed cross and a smile.

'Master Gold,' he said. 'You and Juan are to stay on and help me escort Father Pierre Thomas to Savoy, and if required, beyond.'

'To Italy!' I said.

He raised one eyebrow. 'Perhaps,' he said.

In fact, it was typical of the complete chaos of the time that having just released almost 100 excellent men-at-arms that they had paid and trained for two years, the Priory of Avignon now needed to hire a dozen men-at-arms on short notice.

Fra Peter wasted a day chasing down a pair of our Germans who were, we heard, just a day's ride away.

That afternoon, after I'd cleaned and oiled my new harness, which was in no need of care at all, I went to find Juan and we went out into the sunshine. I needed money – that's what I remember.

Instead, I found Sam Bibbo with a pair of mounted men in patchwork harness. I remember thinking, Is that what I looked like? They were under guard by four papal officers, and they were riding very slowly.

Sam waved, spoke to the guardsmen and came up the street to me. In a moment, I was embracing John Courtney and William Grice. They were headed for Italy, but had come south from Pont-Saint-Esprit because they'd heard I was alive. At the gate – where they'd have been disarmed – they heard there was escort work at the Temple, and they gathered their city escort and came looking for me. I hadn't seen them since the morning of Brignais, or a day before.

They were two men-at-arms among six travelling together. They'd fought in Brittany and in Burgundy, and they wanted better work.

William Grice met my eye. 'It's hell,' he said. 'Sweet Christ, Will Gold, you look like St Michael.'

'Please do not blaspheme,' Juan said.

Grice put a hand on his sword hilt and looked at me.

'This isn't hell,' I said. 'We don't swear.'

Courtney laughed. 'He *is* St Michael.'

That evening, after some wine and some stories, I sat down with Fra Peter. 'I've found four men-at-arms interested in taking service in Italy,' I said.

He nodded. 'Your own men.' he said. 'Your other life.'

'I ... still want to be a knight. A real knight.' I found the words difficult to say. 'I know these men. Hard men, but true.'

He drew a breath and let it out slowly, then turned to face me. 'Very well. My Germans have already gone – over the mountains to join Sterz in Italy. I'll hire your routiers.'

We left Avignon under Fra Peter's command. We were a fine company – John Courtney and William Grice, de la Motte, Fiore, young Juan, Sam Bibbo and I. I paid careful attention to how Fra Peter led these men, who had been my men. Unlike Juan, he didn't seem to dwell on details, like swearing. Instead, he led by example, repairing his own tack and cooking. When William Grice proved to have a nasty abcess on an old wound, Fra Peter took us to an inn and spent two days there, draining it, filling it with honey and draining it again. He was an expert physician, but then, most members of the Hospital were.

Courtney muttered about being in the company of saints for a few days, and finally desisted. He made a great show of buying a whore in the inn, but this was wasted on Fra Peter.

Then Father Pierre Thomas joined us, and there was no more blasphemy. I had scarcely seen Father Pierre Thomas since my first days in Avignon. He had drawn another escort and ridden into Burgundy, trying to raise funds for his crusade. Now he went to Savoy on the same mission. He ate with us every night, whether we stopped in inns or hostels or made camp in the woods.

As the high ground east of Avignon rose towards Italy into the true Piedmont, we found fewer houses, and those we saw, we distrusted. The companies had been here, and they had despoiled both sides of the main market road for a league or more. Farms were burned, and towns gutted.

But the companies were not alone at fault. There were huge Plague cemeteries. Churches collapsed from lack of care. The third night, we camped in deep woods on the flank of a great ridge, and the air had the cold bite that portended winter. I was the scout, and I found a spring on the hillside with a ruined chapel above it. We used a pavilion roof and blankets from our pack mules to roof what had been a Mary chapel, and we were snug and warm when the freezing rain struck. It seemed blasphemous to light a fire by an altar, but the church was stripped to the walls, and only the remnants of some brightly coloured frescos suggested the place had ever known human hands.

I had been on scouting duty, which relieved me of camp chores, so I sat down with an oily linen rag and began to clean my harness.

Fra Peter sat heavily by me. 'Good camp,' he said. 'Well chosen.'

I caught Will Grice's eye. He smiled. But he saw me polishing away at my corselet and he laid his own out on the floor, got some ash on a piece of rag and began to hit the worst spots. 'Easier on a nice bit of stone floor, eh?' he asked me. He glanced at Fra Peter. 'He treats you like a squire.'

'I am a squire,' I said. I remember that, because it settled something.

When I had my blade oiled – a day in the rain will work through the best scabbard in Christendom – I looked at the fire and found that our living saint, the papal legate to the east, was cooking.

I shot to my feet.

He pointed a wooden spoon at me. 'Leave me be,' he said. 'I was a peasant boy cooking with my mother before I was the Pope's friend.'

He made a beautiful bean soup. I have to say, he needed no cooking lessons from me.

That night, he told us all something of his life – how he had been born to serfs, how his parish priest had sent him to be educated by the Franciscans, and how he had risen in the Order, gone to the University at Paris, and become the voice of reform in the church, although he didn't put it that way.

He was so easy to talk to, that Juan spoke up. 'Father?' he asked. 'Is it right that the church has so much wealth?'

Every head turned. Grice and Courtney, playing dice, ceased. Sam Bibbo put down the bowstring he was making.

Father Pierre Thomas shrugged. 'There is no easy answer,' he said. 'Our church is composed entirely of sinners – do you know that?' He laughed. 'Not a single sinless man amongst us since Jesus. Men are venal and greedy. Proud. In fact, men commit sins every day, and men of the church are no different. But the sins do not make the words of Christ less important.' He rocked his head back and forth. 'I have avoided your question – your true question – like a true man of law. Here it is, then. The church needs money, because the church must have money to face Islam, to save Constantinople, to feed the poor, to guide and protect pilgrims, and to build hospitals, schools and orphanages. It needs this money. But I do not say that the church uses the money this way.' He looked away. 'And that should make every Christian angry.'

The next day, Grice dismounted to get something out of his

horse's hoof. We were on a narrow trail, going almost straight up, or so it seemed to me. I was the last man, covering the rear against bandits.

Grice looked back at me and waved. When I came up, I expected some teasing. Instead, he said, 'Never met one like him. The priest.'

I nodded.

'If they was like him, the world would be a better place,' Grice continued.

'He saved my life,' I said.

Grice nodded, as if something complex had been explained. 'Ah!' he said.

We practised every day the weather allowed. I remember Fiore unhorsing me with one of his infernal tricks in a meadow so high that it seemed I'd fall to my death. Instead, I just hurt my hip and cursed the Friulian for two days while it healed. But I was a better lance and a better blade, and I could now hit Fiore occasionally. More than that, I could go a long time not being hit myself. We practised odd things, too – one man against two or three, on horse and foot. Cuts with sharp swords; covers and parries. Facing a lance with a sword.

Sometimes we were merely playing. It's something I have seen with troubadours and musicians. They will simply *play* an instrument, making odd sounds, slapping the sound board or thrumming the strings to see what new thing they can find. Thanks to Fiore, I saw weapons in a new way.

De la Motte took to the whole thing immediately, grinning as Fiore hit him in the head without any apparent effort. He grunted.

'Perhaps we could be a travelling sword school,' he said. 'I'll be the fool who makes the crowd laugh and throw pennies.'

Perhaps I tell this badly. It was a fine trip.

The Green Count was holding his court at Turin. He had a fine castle there and we were expected. I had had days to consider what it would be like to see Richard Musard. Days to consider his betrayal, or simply his inaction. Days to think what he must have thought of me.

The last night, in another ruined chapel, I knelt before Father Pierre Thomas and said my confession. When we were done, I placed my hands in his. 'Father, I need your ... advice,' I said.

He smiled. 'I know absolutely nothing of how to use a sword.'

His delivery was perfect, and we both laughed. 'But I am at your service, my son. What advice?'

'You will, I think, remember how you found me?' I asked.

He smiled. 'A sinner. About to go to hell unshriven.'

I nodded. It was succinct and damningly accurate. 'Yes, Father,' I said. 'Do you remember what led me to that place?'

'A life of violence?' he said gently.

'Yes, Father. But ...' I began to tell him of Richard Musard.

He raised a hand. 'You love this man?' he asked.

I paused for perhaps ten beats of my heart. 'Yes, Father. He is – was – my closest friend.'

Father Pierre Thomas shrugged. Around us was the ancient chapel. Above Father Pierre Thomas's head, an image of the lamb flickered in the firelight, and the Archangel Michael's sword seemed to move. 'Then that is all there is,' he said. 'What are this man's sins to you? You see to your own. He betrayed you? Perhaps, and perhaps not, but our Lord was quite firm on what you should do: turn the other cheek.'

I hesitated.

Father Pierre Thomas laughed. 'It is sometimes as if we have two religions; two versions of Christianity. One for the knights and one for the rest of us. Listen, my son. There is but one way. Jesus did not tell me to turn the other cheek and you to fight.'

I confess I smiled, too.

He was a good priest, but I'm not sure he would have done well commanding routiers. And yet ... sometimes I wonder if he might not have converted them all. He was not like other men.

We arrived at Turin. The Green Count was one of the richest nobles in Christendom, and we were escorted by his uniformed sergeants to an inn and housed like kings. The inn itself was prettier than many great houses in England, despite the mountains and the vast, grim fortress and the bad roads. We had blue ceilings, gilt stars, frescos and coats of arms everywhere.

And baths. *Par dieu*, there were bath houses, with vats of piping hot water, pools of icy cold water and giggling girls in thin linen shifts with towels. I tell you, messieurs, that the infidel promise their warriors a paradise populated by virgins, which has never seemed so attractive to me. But a paradise full of bath houses ...

At any rate, we were clean, and as neat as an army of loaned servants could make us. The Court of Savoy kept great ceremony, and the Count was as eager for us to appear magnificent as we were ourselves – all of us except Father Piere, who didn't seem interested in any of it.

Still, I went and waited on him as his own squire when he put on his bishop's robes, and before my eyes, the son of a peasant turned into a great lord of the church. Only the slight twinkle in his eye revealed that he held some secret amusement at his rank. I was learning about irony from Cicero – still in my baggage with Ramon Llull. I think that Father Pierre viewed his own promotion to legate with irony.

I was resplendent in my red surcoat over spotless armour. By chance, my white cross on my red surcoat was the same device the Savoyards wore. Fra Peter wore his white cross on black.

We filled the courtyard of the inn, seeing to last-minute buckles; William Grice's swordbelt had broken, so there I was, my breath steaming in the cold winter air, snow falling and my fingers red, sewing like mad despite my finery and my harness. Grice was mortified – first, to be so shabby, and second, to be holding everyone up.

The Green Count's escort arrived.

And, of course, it was commanded by Richard Musard.

I knew him instantly. I'd thought it through ten times since confessing, but I didn't do any of the things I had so carefully planned, because I had a needle in my mouth and an awl in my hand.

I met his eye. He had a basinet on, but his visor was strapped up. He wore a beautiful harness and his surcoat had a coat of arms. He wore a fancy silver collar over the surcoat. His dark skin contrasted beautifully with his steel-silver helmet. He looked like a military saint in a painting.

His eye went right over me – about six times. I tried to watch him while I sewed Grice's sword belt, and I suspect I both cursed *and* blasphemed, but I got the belt patched and began to replace my heavy needle in my precious needle case.

And there he was. His horse's head was in my chest.

I looked up and grinned. 'Hello, Richard,' I said.

I'd say fifty emotions passed over his face. His eyes widened.

He turned his horse when one of his men-at-arms called, 'Sir Richard!' and he rode away. He flicked a backward glance at me and I got to see that he had golden spurs.

I breathed carefully and tested my new-found resolutions about ... everything.

'Mount up,' I said.

It was a difficult evening. The Green Count himself – Amadeus of Savoy – was the soul of courtesy to Father Pierre Thomas, but he ignored the rest of us as if we didn't exist. There were fine ladies and gallant gentlemen. Fiore's instruction had not included dancing, and I was only a squire, so I watched. I served Fra Peter at table, and was content.

It may seem odd that a man who had commanded, who had led men in battle, could stand at the side of the hall and carve roast swan, but there it is.

About midnight, we all trooped out of the Great Hall to hear Mass. There was snow falling and it was very cold. Fra Peter was given high precedence – after all, the Order was pre-eminent in the Christian world – and I was just a squire. I trailed along with the squires.

I stopped at the holy water font by the door and took some, and Richard grabbed my arm.

I bowed.

He just looked at my face. He did so for long enough that other men clearly thought we were about to fight. A savoyard stepped between us. 'Messieurs!' he hissed. 'This is a place of God!'

Richard stuck by me.

Mass seemed to go on for ever. There was no way we could speak. Father Pierre Thomas consecrated the host with the local chaplain. Count Amadeus refused to take the host from Father Pierre Thomas, and I knew in a moment that our embassy, whatever it had been, had failed.

Fra Peter caught my eye and gave me a sign that said, 'Get ready to move.'

When Mass ended, the courtiers went for the great hall. A very pretty woman dropped me a splendid curtsey. 'Do you dance?' she asked.

'I do not,' I said.

She shook her head. 'Why are all the handsome men in orders?' she asked, and flounced away before I could disabuse her notion.

Richard was by me, and he said, 'You really are William Gold.'

I grinned and tried to embrace him.

He backed away. 'You are alive?' he said – three times. And his face was a study in conflict.

'William!' Fra Peter said. I turned and saw that he had Juan with him.

I turned to Richard. 'You are a knight,' I said. 'I congratulate you.'

'You are alive,' he breathed.

'Richard,' I said. 'It is all right.'

'William! Now!' Fra Peter called. I made a sketchy bow to Richard Musard and ran for my knight.

We gathered our men-at-arms in a hurry and got our horses. Fra Peter was tight-lipped, and Father Pierre Thomas looked as if he'd been struck.

'Get some sleep,' Fra Peter said. 'We ride at dawn.'

'Before the Green Count does something we'll regret,' Father Pierre Thomas said.

We did ride at dawn, but after two hours on the road, when we reached the turning point where the alpine passes stretch away to the east and the road runs down to the west into Provence and Avignon, Father Pierre Thomas had a brief conference with Fra Peter. He smiled at me, gave each of us a blessing, which all of us needed, and rode away west with only the men-at-arms he'd brought a week before.

Fra Peter watched him go, a rare look of indecision on his face.

'What happened?' I made bold to ask.

'The last hope for the crusade just behaved like an arrogant child,' Fra Peter said. Then he took a deep breath. 'William, please forget I said that. Father Pierre Thomas has to go straight to the Pope. I am going to John Hawkwood.'

We arrived at Romagnano in late October – probably as late as we could come before the high passes closed.

It was like coming home. Yet a different kind of home – new men, new whores, new children. The whole town was ours – that is, it was the property of the English Company. I rode through the streets, suddenly conscious of how I looked. I had been on the road for four weeks, and I was cleaner and neater than most of the men-at-arms I passed.

I saw more and more men I knew as I passed into the heart of the town, where the taverns were. I saw Andrew Belmont – he hadn't been at Brignais, but he had been at Poitiers. I saw John Thornbury, and he shocked me by running along the cobbled street and throwing his arms around me.

He pounded my back, despite my armour. 'Will Gold!' he said. 'By the good God, Will Gold! We heard you was dead!'

He bowed to Fra Peter. 'My lord. Pardon we poor Englishmen.'

Fra Peter extended a hand. 'I, too, am a poor Englishman. Poorer than you, I'll wager.'

Thornbury cast an eye over our ten lances. He grinned at Sam Bibbo, and reached to clasp hands with Bill Grice.

'Tell me these men are for us,' he said.

I probably had a grin as big as my face. 'Sir John said bring ten lances,' I said.

There was a whoop of epic proportions from a second-floor window, and John Hughes jumped from a narrow balcony into the streets. Alpine towns are high and narrow and clean, a perfect contract of white plaster and blackened beams. Town houses have high, narrow windows, but John Hughes got through the window, onto the balcony and down to the street faster than you can tell it. He pulled Sam Bibbo down from his horse.

Sam was grinning like a fool, but he said, 'Now, John, I ain't your girl. Put me down, you gowp.'

I was still mounted, but I looked down to find a neat young man, only a little shorter than my horse, holding my bridle. It took me a breath or two to realize this was Perkin. Master Smallwood, as I understood everyone called him now. He was dressed soberly, in black, and he looked ... like a man.

I dismounted and we embraced.

'I ...' He hung his head. 'I heard you was alive, but until a month ago we all thought you was dead.'

And then there were all my old mates: Robert Grandice, not seen in a year; Belier, looking like a man-at-arms; even the two wild Irishmen, Seamus and Kenneth, who I hadn't seen in three years. They no longer looked Irish, except for their facial hair. They had doublets and hose like civilized men.

I almost had my ribs crushed by Kenneth, who was bigger than me – few men are –and kept saying, 'Been too long!'

Then, while I was introducing men to Fra Peter, Sir John came down from his commanderie. He looked wealthy – his clothes were the best in the street, and that said something. He had gold on – a gold belt of plaques, a gold earring and gold on the mount of his dagger scabbard – and he carried a short staff, like a great noble.

He and Fra Peter exchanged bows.

'From the Pope?' he asked straightway.

Fra Peter nodded.

Sir John nodded. 'None too soon,' he said. He looked at me and smiled. 'William the cook, as I live and breathe.' His smile broke wider. 'These are your ten lances?'

My forty men – or Fra Peter's, as the case may be – filled the street. Streets in Alpine towns wind like snakes, and climb and drop like – never mind. They can be steep and the houses press close. It's like Cumbria, friends, except twice as steep, and on a cold day your iron-shod horse-hooves ring like an anvil against the cobbles as your horse climbs a street. My little column closed the town's main street to all traffic.

So I turned. I remember my chest being tight with pride at it. 'Yes, Sir John.'

'Well, we're full up at the moment.' He grinned. 'And I'll have to speak to the captain about you.'

Thornbury laughed. 'Our captain, Sir Albert Sterz.' He rolled his eyes. 'Full up, my arse. Look at their armour, John! That's Bill Grice, Bob Courtney and Sam Bibbo. Christ, these are proper soldiers.'

John Hawkwood met my eye and his eyes sparkled. 'Shut up, Master Thornbury. I'm negotiating.'

We settled on thirty florins a month within an hour.

I confess I was a trifle put out when Sir John took Fra Peter to his rooms and left the rest of us to drink wine. It reminded me of Chaucer and Master Hoo.

Juan sat by me. He pushed in when I was reminiscing with Perkin – in the main, I was reassuring him and my other former mates that I held them no ill-will for riding away when I was to be hanged.

'Please?' Juan asked politely.

Perkin frowned at him.

'What, Juan?' I asked.

He frowned back at Perkin.

'Gentlemen!' I said, and thumped my dagger on the table.

'Why is Fra Peter speaking to this Sir John?' he asked.

I shrugged and drank more good Piedmontese wine. It was a little lighter and thinner than the Provençal stuff I'd been drinking, but for all that, a better flavour. The blonde lass who waggled her hips as she walked away was pleasing as well. I liked the town, and I liked the sense of ... order that I got from the men I'd seen. There was more discipline here than de Badefol had ever managed.

'I don't know,' I admitted. 'But I'll guess, if it pleases you.'

Juan nodded. He slipped a glance at Perkin, who frowned.

I remember thinking, Sweet Christ, why can't they just get along?

'The Pope is at war with Milan. I assume that Fra Peter brought orders for the English Company.' I turned to Perkin. 'How many lances?' I asked.

'With yours added?' Perkin asked sweetly. 'About two thousand.'

I spat wine. 'Two thousand *lances*?' I asked. 'Eight thousand mounted men?'

Perkin nodded. 'We have every village around here crammed to the rafters. We purchased food from Genoa before the winter weather came.' He smiled. 'We raid into Savoy when we want sport.'

'Ever see Richard?' I asked.

Perkin smiled a lopsided smile. 'I hit him in the head not a week ago, but his helmet turned the blow, bad cess to it.' He drank. 'Fucking traitor.'

Six months with men of religion had had a certain effect on me. 'I'm not sure that's how he sees it,' I said.

'What?' Perkin asked. There were other men sitting around – don't imagine it was just me, Perkin and Juan, because there were sixty of us crammed in a little slope-sided auberge, trying to talk and listen and trade tales all at the same time.

I shrugged. 'Later,' I said.

Perkin leaned over. 'Tell me you are staying?' he asked.

'Up to my knight,' I said. 'Fra Peter.'

Later, after another round of introductions, reminiscences and war stories, we sat in another inn, the walls crowded with the heads of dead animals, and listened to a pair of musicians play. It was richer music than I'd heard in France – Avignon may have been full of whores, but there wasn't any music but church music – but these two were fine – a pleasure to hear – and then they sang together with a woman, and the three wove their voices together like a turkey carpet. I couldn't understand a word they said – it was Italian.

I had just introduced Fiore to Perkin, and he began interpreting the song – gradually the other voices fell away, though, as everyone became quiet because the music was so good.

Era il giorno ch'al sol si scoloraro
per la pietà del suo factore i rai,
quando ì fui preso, et non me ne guardai,
chè i bè vostr'occhi, donna, mi legaro.

Tempo non mi parea da far riparo
contra colpi d'Amor: però m'andai
secur, senza sospetto; onde i miei guai
nel commune dolor s'incominciaro.

Trovommi Amor del tutto disarmato
et aperta la via per gli occhi al core,
che di lagrime son fatti uscio et varco:

Però al mio parer non li fu honore
ferir me de saetta in quello stato,
a voi armata non mostrar pur l'arco.

It was the day the sun's rays had turned pale
with pity for the suffering of his Maker
when I was caught, and I put up no fight,
my lady, for your lovely eyes had bound me.

It seemed no time to be on guard against
Love's blows; therefore, I went my way
secure and fearless-so, all my misfortunes
began in midst of universal woe.

Love found me all disarmed and found the way
was clear to reach my heart down through the eyes
which have become the halls and doors of tears.

It seems to me it did him little honour
to wound me with his arrow in my state
and to you, armed, not show his bow at all.

Darkness fell outside, and when I went out into the sharp night air
to piss, I heard wolves. There's a moral there, I have no doubt.

When I went back into the inn, there was a boy from Sir John. I
went with him, and met the famous Albert Sterz.

Sterz was German, from Swabia, and as tall as me, if rather heavier
and older. I'd seen him of course – seen him at Pont-Saint-Esprit and

elsewhere – but he was a knight, and one of the commanders of the companies, and I was, well, a squire.

But he took my hand with every evidence of good will.

'I hier you haf a fine array of lances,' he said. I won't weary you with my attempt to imitate his Swabian accent, but he spoke fine English.

I stammered something.

'Your arrival couldn't have been better timed,' he said.

Fra Peter sat by the chimney on a stool. His face was blank.

The next morning, he had all his kit in the street at first light. I curried his horse from habit, fetched him some bread and wine from a surly girl whose night had clearly not ended early, and broke my fast with him. We prayed together, and then he went out and looked over his horse.

'I can't stay,' he said. He seemed to be talking to his saddle. 'William, these men are not …' He paused and took a breath. 'You like it here?'

'They are better than when I last saw them,' I said. 'Better disciplined. Better fed.'

He grimaced. 'They've turned every woman in the town into a whore, and every house into a wine shop. They are even now planning to descend into Lombardy and burn the fields and kill the peasants.' His eyes met mine. 'For their master, the Pope.' He looked away.

I understood. 'And you brought the orders,' I said.

'Orders from the Pope – *suggestions* from the King of England,' he said. 'Do you know that the Visconti of Milan are providing a great deal of the money for the King of France's ransom?'

I hadn't known. I tried to work it out.

Fra Peter smiled. 'I'll have pity on you. The Chancellor – of England – told me that as long as the King of France's ransom is unpaid, England keeps the rents and income of twenty counties and a hundred castles. And while that ransom is unpaid, and English garrisons sit in the mightiest fortresses of France, the King of France is powerless to end the truce, break the treaty, go to war *or* on crusade. You saw what the companies did to France.' He started to pack his mule, and I stepped to the other side of the animal to help. 'France is to be kept crippled.'

I bit my lip. 'Fra Peter, I'm sure they all have Christian souls, but I'm an Englishman. So, when we make war on Milan, we do it for

England?' I confess I grinned. 'I can't say I'm worse pleased.'

Fra Peter pulled a cord tight and tied it off. 'I'm an Englishman, too. But I'm a knight of the church – and watching the destruction of the riches of France sickens me. Is Italy now to be treated the same? I'm sworn to crusade, and without France, there will be no crusade.' He got one end of a forty-pound bag of grain, I got the other and we hoisted it over the panniers onto the mule and began to tie it down. 'Have I shown you this lashing, William?'

'Yes, Fra Peter.'

'Perhaps I'm just old, and sick of the whole thing. I'd like to fight other men like me, in an honourable way, in a good cause, and not rape anyone in the process.' He shrugged. 'I shouldn't tell you this, but Savoy demanded of Father Pierre Thomas that we order the English out of his province. He told Father Pierre Thomas that until the companies are gone, he will not swear to go on crusade.'

Well, I'd caught rumours of this at Turin.

'What did Father Pierre Thomas say?' I asked.

'Can you guess, William?' he asked. He smiled at me over the saddle.

'I guess he informed the Count that the crusade was an atonement for his sins and not a matter of political advantage,' I said.

Fra Peter snorted. 'You really are getting the hang of this,' he said. 'Of course, when Father Pierre Thomas speaks that way, he means every word.'

'But you just told Hawkwood to continue his fight against Milan,' I said.

He looked at every lashing, and then gave me a great hug. 'Go fight, William, but do your best to fight with honour. Protect the weak, war down the strong and help the poor.' He sprang into the saddle like a much younger man. 'When the order summons you, come. In the meantime, remember that you are not William Gold, mercenary bandit. You are William Gold, esquire, donat of the Order of St John the Baptist, and behave accordingly.'

I wept, but I rallied. 'Even when my opponents lie, cheat, steal and betray me?' I asked.

'Especially then. We practise chivalry because it is right, not because other men can be expected to do the same. The sword of justice – tempered with mercy.' He laughed. 'Remember what Father Pierre Thomas said of the church? Full of sinners? Imagine that the order of chivalry is entirely full of caitiffs trying to be knights.'

Those words stuck in my head, I can tell you. That's what we are. No one is without sin. No man is a perfect knight. We are caitiffs, but it is the striving that makes us better.

He mounted on the mounting block.

'Stay alive! My blessing on you, William Gold.'

He laid his hand on my head and rode off into the dawn.

Juan cried that he'd missed his master leaving.

Perkin mocked him for it, and the two of them stripped to their shirts and wrestled in the tiny inn yard. I let them.

Perkin was thrown first and hit his head, but he came back at Juan, and was put down again. Juan had been practising with Fiore, who was watching.

Perkin rose, rubbing his head. 'You have more wrestling tricks than a Cornishman,' he said.

Fiore laughed. 'I see I will have new students.'

We celebrated Christmas like gentlemen. It was my first proper Christmas in years, and I exchanged gifts with my friends, kissed a pretty whore under a sprig of greenery and went to Mass in a good church. I went blithely to confession, and said my beads – my new habits stuck.

We feasted with the town – Sterz had a fine notion of how to keep the townspeople on our side, and we brought in a herd of beef from the coast at our cost. Our company was now so large that we had armourers and basket-makers and butchers. This was not a nation of thieves like the Great Company of Brignais. This was an army, like the army of the Prince of Wales or the King of France. We had a seneschal and a marshal; laws and police. Men who pissed in the streets were punished. Two days after Christmas, an Englishman tried to force a girl in one of the villages – she put a knife into his thigh and escaped, and her father complained. Sir John oversaw a trial as if he was an English magistrate, and the man was found guilty, beaten with rods and his money given to the girl. Then he was dismissed from the company.

On New Year's day, we rode for Lombardy. We travelled for two days down a long pass, and then, in bleak midwinter, we descended into the fields of Lombardy. I remember my first sight of Italy, and I thought that it couldn't be a coincidence that we were leaving the Count of Savoy's land.

I remember thinking, with the old ways of a routier coming back, that it was the richest country I'd ever seen – even in winter.

We rode to the gates of Milan. Milan is a magnificent city, and should, you'd think, have been well-defended. It's well-walled, but the lords thereof are tyrants – I've fought for and against them, and I know whereof I speak. So they have a fortified palace inside the city to defend against their own citizens, and fortress walls to keep the likes of me out.

Our orders were exact and our discipline was excellent. We were to rob and burn our way to the gates, killing as few men as possible and outraging no women. Sterz summoned all the leading men on the night before we raided Milan, and stood by his camp table.

'What we want is to force Visconti to make peace,' he said. 'What we *do not want* is a lot of enraged Milanese demanding further war. Murder and rape won't get you a florin, lads. Rob them, burn them out, push their sorry arses into the walls. That's all it will take.' He smiled.

Sir John nodded. 'Enough angry Milanese inside his walls,' he said, 'and Galleazzo might find himself overthrown.'

We had assignments and guides – towns, monastries, fortified houses. Mine was written out, and I had a Milanese exile, a bitter old man named Bernabo Pieto. He led me through the cold winter's night, and we stormed a house full of soldiers – killed a couple, took the rest, and turned the noble family out into the cold, stripped of jewels and gold.

By morning, we'd struck to the very gates and posted the Pope's demands there; we had twenty senior Milanese officials to ransom and we hadn't lost a man. Milan did nothing in response – Galeazzo cowered in his palace and let his countryside burn.

If I felt a trifle dirty from the rampage, I had 300 florins in gold from my share.

He might have been slow on the battlefield, but he was quick enough, politically. Galeazzo reacted by hiring the most famous mercenary in Italy – the German captain, Konrad von Landau. That is, he was famous, but we'd never heard of him.

He brought a great company of German lances – almost 4,000. He arrived in early March, and drove us back into the hills – or perhaps Albert Sterz had always meant to retire. Certainly there was no haste to our movements.

Sterz was a good officer, but a harsh disciplinarian. When we camped, he would punish men for fouling the streets outside their tents – sensible, I confess, but not a way to win an archer's love. He never hesitated to apply punishments, and we had the impression that not only did he like to order punishment, he liked to see it carried out, too. Some men get drunk on authority. Sterz wasn't one of them. He merely liked the taste.

A company of Hungarians joined the Germans. Most of us had never seen a Hungarian, but we heard they had bows which they could shoot from horseback. The archers shook their heads and said they must be puny things that couldn't penetrate armour, and the handful of men who had fought the Turks said it was all horse shit.

All the fears and angers of the days before battle.

We were badly outnumbered, but we were confident. It worried me, the casual arrogance of the English.

We had a steady stream of Milanese ambassadors coming into our camp. I became the officer responsible for meeting them and bringing them to Sir Albert, because of my good manners and genteel air. They were really emissaries, often accompanied by heralds with all the trappings of chivalry, yet they came to spy. Their intention was to count our archers and look at our entrenchments and the shape of our camp.

So we greeted them each day with the same ten lances – mine – in full armour, and we rode them into our camp by different routes. This amused us more each day. One day, I showed them men-at-arms practising on horseback in groups of 100; the whole was an elaborate stage show, like a passion play, staged by Sir John. The next day they rode through an empty camp – the army, right down to our whores, was behind the next ridge.

And I was present as the Milanese offered Sir Albert and Sir John ever more elaborate bribes. I was even offered one myself.

After a week of this, I was with Sir John after we escorted a particularly unctuous Milanese churchman back to the Milanese lines. When he was gone, I turned to Sir John. 'If the French had offered us 20,000 florins to retreat the night before Brignais,' I said, 'Mechin would have taken it, split it with a half-dozen captains and ridden away.'

Sir John nodded. He had a hint of red to his beard and moustache, and I had seldom seen him look so much like a fox. 'That was a different *empris*,' he said. 'We had too many Gascons. Too many brigands.' He shrugged. 'Here, we are professional soldiers, and we have some faith in each other. I'm sure Albert would ride away and abandon the Pope for enough money.' His eyes twinkled. 'I would myself. A hundred thousand florins?'

'*Par dieu!*' I said, shocked. That was a King's ransom. Swearing was returning to my vocabulary.

'No,' he said. 'The world is changing, William. If we were someone's army – your friend the Green Count's, for example – and the Visconti offered him twenty thousand florins to go away, why, he'd take it. Twenty thousand florins is a fortune.' He nodded. 'But in our army, a *hundred* thousand florins is still only forty florins for each man-at-arms.' He shrugged. 'That's one month's pay – not enough to break the contract. It only makes it less likely the next bastard won't hire you, or play fair on the *condotta*.'

Condotta was the first word every Englishman learned in Italy. It means 'contract'.

Sir John reined in and looked back at the Milanese camp – the German and Hungarian camp. 'The thing is,' he said, 'this is the richest country in the world. The banks are here, William. All the money comes here from all over Christendom.' He watched as fires sprang into being, like the rising of the evening stars. My little company passed behind us, harness rattling.

'In France, we took grain from peasants,' he said as he turned and looked at me. 'Before we're done here, we'll take the gold from the banks.'

The next morning, a Flemish merchant came over the passes behind us. He sent a pair of his men-at-arms to negotiate with Sterz, who charged tolls like a lord, of course.

Perkin led one of the patrols, and told me that evening that the merchant had 200 mules loaded with wool – a fortune – and another 100 loaded with goods meant for us.

'Good English wool – undyed and white as virtue.' He laughed. 'And all the things we need: thread, bronze kettles, tin bottles, wool cloaks.' He showed me his new water bottle.

The next day, the merchant opened a small fair in Romagnano. Now that we were back at our base in the Count of Savoy's lands, I wondered how he was doing in his negotiations with the Pope.

I was slipping away from the life of a donat, and becoming an officer in a mercenary company.

At any rate, 2,000 lances of soldiers is a fair number of customers, and this man's company had many things we wanted – razors, for one. Cups, Flemish cloaks, goatskin boots, pewter chargers.

His wool shipment was for the dyers of Florence, but fashions spring up very quickly among soldiers. Andrew Belmont, who was a devilishly handsome fellow, bought three cloth yards of white wool and a tailor threw him off a fine surcoat in an hour – it didn't have to be lined, of course, because he wore it over his armour. The wool was beautiful and warm. A dozen of us saw him in his fine surcoat that evening – and laughed when he spilled red wine on it – and in the morning there were fifty of us, me included, in white surcoats. Three days after the Fleming arrived, he'd sold 4,000 cloth yards of his fine white wool.

Most soldiers can sew. I made my own coat; I hung my breast and backplate on a cross of wood and tailored the wool, coached by Perkin, who was working his own and teaching Fiore, while Juan emulated him from afar while pretending he wasn't involved. We had to send a boy to buy shears – from the Fleming.

I dagged my sleeves. Hah! There was a rumour that Sir John Hawkwood had been an apprentice tailor in London – not true, on my honour – but we had some tailors, and they taught us, so we were all popinjays.

At any rate, we were still retreating – very slowly – before von Landau's advance. But the same day the Fleming arrived, Sterz told the Milanese envoys that he saw no further point in their sending spies to his camp dressed as heralds – a mortal insult, even though the honest truth. And our German challenged their German to a contest of arms. He offered to meet von Landau on horse or foot, with lances, spears or swords – man to man, twenty against twenty, a hundred against a hundred, or army to army.

The very next morning, Konrad von Landau led his 12,000 men across two small streams and formed in close order by the castle of Canturino. We rode down the opposite ridge.

We were formed in six divisions and mine was commanded by Sir John. I had fifteen lances on the right flank of the centre battle.

I have some things to say that might matter to your account.

I was wearing the best armour I'd ever worn into a fight, and I was with better men then I'd ever had around me, except at Poitiers, and I didn't know anything, then. I trusted the men on my right and my left; I trusted the man leading my battle, and I trusted the man leading the *battle* to the left and to the right. I trusted Albert Sterz.

I ate well the night before the fight, the week before and the month before and, in fact, most of the year before. I was in the best physical state of my life, and I had slept well. I prayed, and was shriven by a priest.

I had changed. The order had changed me. But at the same time, the whole world of the companies had changed. These men around me were not routiers. Like me, some had been, but in Italy, they were professional soldiers, and war was about to become an entirely different affair.

When you ride at the enemy on a good horse, in good armour, surrounded by your friends and well rested and fed – truly, lads, you have to be a coward to fight badly. Or a fool, which may be the same.

We were all afraid – the Germans outnumbered us – but not with a fear that paralyses, but with a fear that pushes you to strive harder.

We stared at each other across the stream for half an hour.

Sterz rode down our front. 'Dismount!' he called. We dismounted in a orderly way – the pages came forward, took the archers' horses first, then the knights' chargers, and there was, I confess, a moment of chaos as every man sought his place in the ranks. Then, like a sword going home in the scabbard, we were set, with only a few unhandy sods still pushing.

Front rank: knights and men-at-arms.

Second rank: armoured squires and pages.

Third rank: archers.

Fourth rank: men with less armour.

In my lance, I stood in front, armed cap-a-pied. Behind me stood a new man, Richard Grimlace, both of us with heavy-headed seven-foot spears. Then Sam Bibbo. Then Arnaud, in a good jack and brigantine, with a second quiver of arrows for Sam and a spear and a sword and buckler, a basinet on his head. We had 2,000 of these little units.

Sir John stayed mounted, and so did Sterz, Belmont and a few other officers.

Sterz trotted to our front and waved his baton. 'Front!' he roared. 'Let's go!'

We moved forward to the very edge of the stream.

It was fairly full of ice-cold water, and I remember staring down into the depths of the stream at my feet. It was, of course, a mountain stream, filling its stone banks to the brim.

There was a trout in it.

The old Romans lived by signs – animals, birds – I was reading Ovid by then.

That trout made me absurdly happy.

'Ready!' called Sterz.

All along the third rank, the archers nocked arrows. Heavy, quarter-pounder war-bow arrows.

Opposite us, the Germans were 100 paces away, sitting on their horses, listening to a trio of Germans address them.

I had a long look at the Hungarians. They were moving; their horses fidgeted.

I pointed them out to Sir John, who was sitting on his charger just behind Arnaud.

'They're not happy and they haven't been paid,' Sir John said with infinite satisfaction. 'Watch and learn, William the Cook.'

'Draw!' called Sam Bibbo at my back. No one had named him master archer, but archers aren't men-at-arms: they have strange, craftsmanlike notions of leadership. Sam was widely held to be the best bow, and that made him master archer.

When you see 2,000 war bows bent in earnest, it stops your heart. The white bows go down, swooping like hawks, then they rise as the archers bend them, like a great flock of birds turning and rising together, and at the top of their flight—

'And *loose*!'

Two thousand shafts, loosed in the same breath.

They make a noise, like 100 nuns whispering at Mass.

'Nock!' Sam roared.

'Draw! And loose!'

There were horses down all along the German ranks, and a few men. Germans don't bard their horses like the French do.

Because unlike the French, they don't fight us.

Horses scream.

'Nock!' Sam screamed. He was out of practice and his voice broke a little.

'Draw! And loose!' Another 500 pounds of steel and wood went off to meet the Germans. Every war arrow weighs almost a quarter of a London pound.

The trio of German officers were yelling at the top of their lungs – you could tell that from their posture. As I watched, one took a clothyard of ash under his arm, right through his body, and fell.

'Nock!' Sam called.

'Draw!' The only noise from the English was the muscular grunt of 2,000 men drawing their great bows together.

'Loose!'

The Hungarians broke.

They turned and ran, their small, swift horses carrying them clear of the arrow fall. They were led by knights, who wavered longer, but the mounted archers were gone in as long as it takes to tell the story.

All 3,000 of them.

Sterz held up his baton.

Fingers reaching for shafts stopped, paused and reached instead for swords.

'Forward!' he called.

By the sweet and gentle Christ, my friends, and by all the saints, that water was cold. And it came to my hips. Ice water to your balls!

Every one of us gasped as we hit that water. It filled my sabatons, my greaves and my clothes.

But 8,000 men can break the force of any stream. It was six paces across, and our front was well dressed – that is, we were all level with each other. Back then, we never practised any such thing – then we were scrambing up the far bank. Men grabbed bushes and trees – it was a three-foot climb out of the icy torrent – men behind pushed.

Then we were up, and it felt as if I could reach out and touch the Germans.

Even then, I thought the Germans would charge and make a fight of it.

Konrad von Landau rode to the front and called something in German. I don't know what he was saying, but he sounded like he was saying, 'Stand! Stand!'

They were melting away.

We formed and we did it quickly – we're not the Legions of Heaven, or Old Romans, but we were a company and we had spirit. Then we started forward, spears held two-handed. The closer we got to the Germans, the faster we were going. Men stumbled and fell – I remember that field, and it looked as smooth as a tile in a Flemish bath, but it was covered with fist-sized rocks, left by the glaciers, and if you got one under your heel, down you went.

As is often the way, everything suddenly happened at once.

The Germans nearest von Landau charged, but they'd waited far too long, and we were closer than twenty paces, and their horses were unsure from their first steps whether to face our spears or not. Others among the Germans were running, or sitting where they were.

I'm going to guess they didn't trust the men to their right and left.

Fiore was three men to my left. I heard him say, quite distinctly, 'But we won't get to fight at all!'

The Germans came at us, but their horse flinched, and we charged into them rather than the other way round.

I hadn't faced another man in combat for a year – almost to a day.

I punched my spear into the armpit of the first German I met. He raised his sword to cut at me, and down he went, over the cantle of his saddle. I had to push past his horse to go on – the horse just stood its ground like an equine statue; I've never seen the like.

I remember the next man because I took him for ransom. He had a lance, which he endeavoured to use against me with both hands. I slammed it to earth with my spear and returned his stroke with a blow to his aventail, rocked him in the saddle and stabbed him three times in as many heartbeats. Each blow turned by his breastplate, but I had practised this at the pell – my point was looking for a weak joint and he couldn't shake me.

My fourth blow popped his visor and went into his helmet – by an odd twist of luck and armouring, it went over his head, between his head and the padding of his helmet. So instead of instant death, it stretched his spine and gaffed him from the saddle as his horse tried to turn, so that he was on his back. By ill luck, he hit one of the small stones and was knocked unconscious.

Or perhaps it was good luck. He lived.

My third German knight was trying to run. I killed his horse from behind, and left him for Robert or Arnaud. They took him.

I was now deep into the German lines and the battle was over. The Germans were running, except for a band of perhaps 100, gathered around their great knight, von Landau, and they were facing Sir John's men – and mine. I left off pursuing stragglers and ran at the rear of von Landaus's stand. Of course he didn't want to be taken, and he was still calling on his men to stand and not run. The English no longer had any order – everyone was going in all directions, looking for men to take and ransom.

War between mercenaries can be formulaic, but battle is always chaos and death.

The knot around von Landau grew smaller and smaller; it was very like the end at Poitiers. I faced a Milanese knight in superb armour, and he beat my spear aside with his sword; I caught his sword on my spear haft, and he cut into it, once, twice, and then the spear broke. I threw the shards at his horse to make it shy and drew my longsword. He came at me again, the horse pressing against me, so I dropped and went under the horse – got a nasty knock from the beast – and came up under his stirrup. I cut into the unarmoured back of his thigh and he yelled. Kenneth, the Irishman, got his other leg and pulled him out of his stirrups. He screamed – that must have pulled every muscle in his hips – and then he was dead, with Seamus's great axe through his head.

Waste of a ransom, in my opinion, but the Irish are mad.

I was one horse from von Landau. If I could kill him or take him, someone would knight me – I could feel it and it was all I wanted.

He was sword to sword with Fiore.

He hammered the man on foot, and Fiore covered himself, so that he seemed to live in a tent of steel – every blow fell like a hammer only to trail away. Some fell so hard on Fiore's sword that sparks flew in broad daylight. Blow after blow.

It is not done, even among mercenaries, to interrupt a fair fight between peers. So even though von Landau was mounted and a famous name, no one came forward to gut his horse.

Landau urged his mount into the Italian.

I prepared to put him down. But I'd have to do it in single combat, and I didn't want Fiore to die just so I could get my spurs.

Fiore's sword took another hammer blow and snapped.

He ducked under Landau's next blow, fell to one knee and picked up one of the fist-sized rocks.

As Landau's sword went back, Fiore threw. The stone hit just above the mercenary captain's open visor, and Landau fell as his horse reared.

He hit the ground stone dead.

Hah! True as the gospel, messieurs. It's in Villani! The best swordsman who ever lived killed Konrad von Landau with a rock.

That night, we were in a clean inn in Romagnano – not in a camp or a muddy tent, nor lying on the ground. I rather liked war in Italy, so far.

I was sitting at a decent oak table, drinking good wine.

Fiore and Juan were refighting the battle with Perkin and Robert, who'd managed to get his arm broken but was nonetheless in fine spirits because he'd picked up all my prisoners and made himself enough florins to buy a good horse and become a man-at-arms.

A Swiss girl with the face of a London urchin and the manners of a fine lady was hovering around, fussing over him. Smart lass. Tend a man when he's sick or wounded and you own him.

'Now you've seen a battle,' I said, only partly in jest. 'Does it affect your theories?'

He rocked his head back and forth. 'I killed an armoured knight with a rock,' he said. He sounded disappointed.

There was something in the way he said it – a combination of pride at having done it, wistfulness at having missed the ransom and annoyance at God's plan for having to use a rock and not a weapon requiring more skill – that made me burst out laughing, and all the others followed suit. The laughter spread, as laughter does – one man told another, one girl whispered and giggled, and the inn rafters rang with it.

He frowned for a moment, and then he had the grace to laugh with us, though I swear to you he didn't know why. Maestro Fiore, as we know him now, was not without humour, but in some ways he lived with the gods, not with mere men.

For example, he'd killed the enemy commander, he was young, exceptionally fit and rather handsome; he was the hero of the hour. He was, quite literally, surrounded by attractive young women – English, Italian, German, Swiss and Provençal. He did look at them from time to time, but I don't think he had any idea how to proceed beyond that.

I'm losing the thread here. We were laughing; he was laughing. And then, through the crowd of camp followers, came a young man. The pretty blonde girl I had been eyeing near the door suddenly flinched aside as she looked at the new man; her nose wrinkled in distaste.

The man had short, dark hair cut in the latest Italian fashion, a sort of bowl cut that went well under a helmet, and he had tight leather boots to the thigh, a neat blue doublet and a matching blue belt with a sheathed dagger – slim and long. He didn't look like anyone I knew, and my eyes passed over him.

Another girl glared at him and he glared back, then I knew who he was.

He was Milady.

Perkin saw her and shuddered. He knew trouble when he saw it.

I rose and bowed, and she smiled at me. 'I couldn't stay away,' she said. 'I gather I missed the battle.'

Fiore bowed. 'I haven't had the pleasure,' he said. 'Do you always dress as a man?'

That was Fiore, too. He watched people in a way that most men do not. He knew she was a woman instantly. Most men didn't, but many women did.

She smiled at him and offered her hand, like a woman. 'I do not dress like a man,' she said. 'I become a man, if I want to.' She tilted a head to one side. 'I missed you, William Gold.'

'Thanks, Janet.' I bowed. I hadn't missed her. Or I had?

I suspect I wore the same face that Richard wore when he saw me.

Why, though? She was a good companion, and what I had of gentle manners I owed to her. 'How's Richard?' I asked.

She smiled. 'Well, when I left him.'

That could mean anything.

'Are you ... visiting?' I asked.

She frowned. 'No, William. I plan to stay and lead a lance.' She looked around, daring us to protest.

Fiore bowed. 'May I be your squire, Madame?'

She snapped her fingers. 'No, messire. I have a lover – I couldn't possibly satisfy a second. Even in the most chaste and chivalrous way, men are tiresome. Except when you are one, and then men are a delight.' She looked up and her eyes met his.

He said, 'Do you have any skill with the sword?'

She shrugged expressively. 'I'm a better jouster,' she said, 'but I have been known to use the sword and the dagger.'

'Ah,' sighed Fiore. A woman who could use a sword.

We were all doomed.

We ate and drank, and in an hour she was part of us again. When Andrew Belmont came by to congratulate Fiore, he noticed her. He put an arm around her waist, and she dropped him on his arse.

Andrew was a true knight, for all his failings, which were many. He bounced to his feet and grinned. 'Horse or foot, messire,' he said. 'If you dress like a man, you'd best fight like one.'

She grinned. 'Horse,' she said.

Belmont paused. I think he still thought she was a whore playing dress-up, but he shrugged. 'Dawn, by the bridge,' he said.

We were young, and we were still awake when it was time to arm her. She had a fine harness – still some bits we'd picked up in the fight in Provence, which seemed ten years ago but was only two. She was drunk as a lord, and suddenly flirtatious and angry by turns. She kissed Fiore while he struggled to get her brigantine closed, which I promise you is not the best way to get your squires to arm you quickly, or well. On the other hand, it does seem to get devoted service.

It took three of us to get her on her horse, and I held the bridle all the way down to the bridge. Andy Belmont was there, and so was half the White Company, as we had taken to calling ourselves, drunk as only successful mercenaries – and sailors – can manage. The rumour had gone round that the handsome Belmont had run afoul of a whore who intended to fight him. Remember, to us there was nothing funnier than watching two cripples fight with sticks – an incontinent dwarf who could drink wine and piss it in the same action could keep a dozen men laughing for an hour. So a knight jousting with a whore?

The sun was just above the rim of the world.

Somehow I'd become the marshal. I had severe doubts about the whole thing – I was afraid for her, and afraid that someone would be killed. Both of them rode expensive horses, and a dead horse was both dishonour and financial ruin.

They set their chargers at either end of the course. We didn't have a barrier, but then, we did this for a living.

Andrew motioned to me, and I trotted to his stirrup.

'She's not a whore, is she?' he asked.

'She wishes to have a lance and fight,' I said. 'She used to fight. She's been with us before.'

He made a face. 'Very well,' he said. He was drunk, too. 'I won't hit her too hard.'

I went to my place and held my neck-cloth aloft. It fluttered in the cold wind and someone called, 'Get on with it!'

I let it go.

Andrew leaned forward slightly, and his horse gave a small rear, then began to head down the list.

Milady's horse came from a stand to a dead gallop in three steps, accelerating like an arrow from a bow.

His lance struck her in the shoulder and rocked her backwards. She was light, and so was her horse, and suddenly both of them were crashing to earth.

Her lance tip caught him dead in the centre of the breastplate, and even as she went down, her lance tip continued to track him, bursting the girth on his saddle and throwing him back over the rump of his horse.

Both of them crashed to earth.

We stood in shocked silence, broken only by the hoofbeats of Andrew's riderless horse galloping down the rest of the list.

Then Milady's small horse got to his feet. He shook like a dog and walked a few steps. Uninjured.

Milady sat up and said, 'Fuck.'

Andrew just lay there for a moment, then he rolled over to get a knee under him – most of us have to do that, in full armour – and he was laughing. He got to his feet, tottered over to her and extended a hand.

She looked up at him. 'Don't we have two more courses to ride?' she said.

'Absolutely not,' Belmont said, and we all burst into cheers.

Our victory over von Landau shocked Italy. Von Landau had been very famous, and we killed him.

After the battle, everyone called us the White Company. I don't know who started it – I'm sure it was the white surcoats, although I've met some useless bastards who say it was our spotless reputation – I sneer – or our shining armour – to which I'll attest that at Canturino, there were maybe fifty Englishmen in white harnesses. Five years later, we all had them, but that's another story.

We were famous.

In days, the envoys arrived, and Milan sued for peace with the Pope. We didn't even bother to burn their countryside again.

I wasn't knighted, but as I sat drinking wine with other men – Andrew Belmont, John Thornbury, Perkin and Fiore – I felt like a knight. We had fought well, for something reasonably worthy. I'd shown mercy and I hadn't done evil.

It was hardly great reknown, but it was a start.

By mid-June, the war was over. Crops were growing all over the plain of Lombardy, and Italy looked rich and at peace. We did *not* burn the peasants or rape their women.

Offers rolled in. We sat and practised, drilled and rode, read and played music. Fiore fell in love with Milady. It was so predictable, it was like one of the romances. He taught her his way of the sword, and they jousted, and he couldn't keep his eyes off her. She would turn to me after her third cup of wine and say, 'Would you keep the swordsman from following me like a puppy?'

In late June, there were ten rumours in camp about our next contract, but most of us who knew Sir John knew that the two highest bidders were Pisa and Florence, and since Florence was the richest, most secure state in Italy, we were pretty sure we'd be fighting for them.

I noted that if we accepted either contract, we would leave alpine Savoy. And the Green Count might have his deal with the Pope, after all.

That was the night that Fiore followed Milady out into the spring air, and came back with a handprint on the side of his face. He wouldn't talk about it. Someone had given him bad advice. Juan sat and talked with him.

Later, when I 'went for a walk' with one of the girls who had made herself available, I passed a couple by the stream – they weren't making love, merely talking, but for my money, they were Andrew Belmont and Janet – Milady – and they weren't particularly overdressed.

I don't tell you this so you can gossip. It's all relevant.

Two days later, a priest coming over the pass from Turin said he'd found a body. One of our archers had wandered a bit too far from town and been knifed.

The general verdict was that it was probably time we moved on.

The next morning, Sir John announced that we'd been hired – by Pisa.

Pisa hired us, not Florence. I didn't even know where Pisa was; it was only a matter of months since I'd found that Pisa was a place, not a man.

'Florence is our enemy,' Sir John said, with enormous, foxlike satisfaction.

We were going to Tuscany to make war on the banks. We were a professional army, and not one of us was a great lord. We were an army that bore every resemblance to a guild of craftsmen, and we were marching into the richest part of the Christian world.

The Florentines lost a battle to us before we even arrived. War in Italy, in general, was smarter than war in France – both sides used strategems worthy of the old Romans, and ambush and subterfuge were part of those battles. The most cunning general was held to be the best. It was the same with the way they did business – I'd seen that first hand. Italians admired sleight of hand. They admired you if you beat your opponent in such a way that showed you were smarter, rather than merely stronger.

Consequently, the moment Florence's envoys knew for sure that the White Company was off to serve Pisa, Florence hired a dozen small German bands close by and sent them to devastate the Pisan *contada* (countryside). The Germans moved quickly, crossing the frontier in just a week.

But the White Company had a fine reputation for fast marches, and we arrived in Pisa the night the Germans crossed the frontier. By the time they'd burned a dozen small farms, their scouts and spies brought them word of our 8,000 mounted men (and one woman) riding in triumph through the streets. We outnumbered them, and we had a high repute – a sovereign *preux*. The Germans retreated over the frontier, leaving so quickly they abandoned some of their food carts.

The cream of the jest is that we were still two weeks of hard marching to the north, but such was our repute that the Pisans mounted their best young men, armoured them, and had them ride all night – in one city gate and out another – wearing white surcoats. they fooled their own citizens well enough to fool the spies.

By late July we were in Pisa, where they gave us a parade in earnest – young women ran out of respectable houses to hand me cups of wine and kiss me. Ah, Italy! Making war in France is like having sex in a dirty room. Making war in Italy is like . . .

That was a good year, but we knew our business and the German captains knew theirs, so we manoeuvred and collected our thirty florins a month. My ransoms came in from Canturino. I took over a dozen lances from other men – a Scotsman who was going home, an Englishman who retired and married a rich Pisan woman.

I wanted to be a corporal.

I wanted to be knighted.

And despite being a junior officer in a company of mercenaries, I practised what I had learned.

Pisa didn't trust us, particularly, so were seldom inside the city walls, but Tuscany was beyond beautiful – magnificent, like a fine horse, a beautiful woman, a good bottle of wine and a choir singing all at the same time. The trees are tall, the farms perfectly managed, the sky a colour of blue that just doesn't occur in England. In Tuscany, I ate olives for the first time. I knew the oil, but the fruit itself ... Superb! And the wine – if French wines are good, and they are, and Piedmontese wines are better, and they are, the best vintages of Tuscany are, well ...

Perfect. If there is wine in heaven, it comes from Tuscany.

The bread is good, and the food is good, if you like garlic, and I do.

Tuscan woman know what they want. Many of them didn't want anything to do with me, but those who did – I very much preferred their manner of address, to steal one of Milady's phrases.

Janet was my entrée into polite society. Despite her past – perhaps because of it – and despite riding abroad dressed as a man – or perhaps because of that, too – young women of good family flocked to her. A few wanted to emulate her. Most did not, but wanted to be seen with her, or to be seen to approve of her. Gentlewomen in Italy – rich merchants' wives and daughters, and aristocrats – were sometimes cloistered and sometimes exceptionally free.

At any rate, they were well-educated and free enough to ride abroad in camps full of mercenary foreigners who leered at them – I leered as much as the next man, I promise you. No camp girl, not the prettiest, easiest or most free of them, can compete with a woman of the same age who has the advantage of clothes, posture, diet and a good horse.

At any rate, through Janet, I met Pamfilo di Frangioni, a young noblewoman of Pisa. Her family owned sixty or seventy farms, and she rode out to our camp most days with her brothers, all of whom were, in fact, gentlemen of Pisa and served with us by turns. They were decent men – a little odd-seeming and foreign to me, but good hearted, and they loved their sister. She could ride like a Turk, and she dressed – you know, she wore pearls in her hair every day I saw her, and she never wore the same clothes twice. It took me weeks to realize that she did this apurpose; that she was, in her sixteen-year-old way, *perfectly* aware that she had several hundred young Englishmen panting every time her horse skimmed along the road and she jumped the barricade into our camp.

From her, I learned a little of how to flirt.

Pamfilo was not going to run off to the bushes with a mercenary, no matter how attractively red-bearded. But she might discuss the matter – she would certainly allow the nape of her neck to be kissed on a warm evening, and she might, after a glass of wine, run her bare foot up your leg to the thigh under the table while chatting with her mother.

I am not sure whether I loved her or not, merely that she was great fun, and seeing her raised my heart every time.

From her I learned what Emile might have taught me of courtly love – about how love can make you a better knight.

We usually made camp within an hour's ride of the Frangioni castle, and many of us would then wait to see how many hours passed before we saw the tell-tale dust rising as, dressed in silk, she galloped her horse across the fields, her brothers trailing behind.

Twice that autumn we marched on Florence. Florence went so far as to recruit Rudolph von Hapsburg – another famous knight, this one with a name I'd heard, from one of the most powerful families in Swabia. He promised to catch us and – a nasty piece of work – crucify us.

Well. I find Englishmen love to be threatened by fools.

We marched and he marched, and the dust rose. I spent long days in the saddle, siting ambushes that were never sprung, looking for his supply convoys and watching his main force from scrubby trees at the edge of the largest wheat fields in Europe. I had one small feat of arms that fall – I met a German knight at a ford and unhorsed him. I let him go – he was a penniless adventurer – but my name gained a little lustre, and I made him go back to Florence and tell every lady he met that he was the slave of Pamfilo di Frangioni.

When Sir John heard of it, he summoned me to his tent.

'William, what are you playing at?' he asked.

I thought I was the wit of the world. 'Courtly love,' I said.

'By St George, young man, our business is war. Tup a ewe if you need to, but make war, sir. Good day.' He turned and went back to his letters.

I ignored him. To John Hawkwood, of course, war *was* a business.

In November the weather turned – even Tuscany gets cold rain, and that was the coldest winter anyone could remember. We headed south, but before we'd gone two days march, some of Sterz's German *barbutes* turned us from our usual campsites and we were sent west around the city and far from the Frangioni's.

It was the Plague.

Plague went through us like lettuce through a goose, and we lost men – not many, as most Englishmen were salted, by then – but a great many girls and some of the German men-at-arms. Juan's pretty lass died, and he never got it. To his immense credit, the Spaniard stayed by her side, moved her to his own tent and breathed her air until she passed. Then he paid for Masses for her soul.

We lost about 300 lances to the Plague.

I thought of my sister, and for the first time in a year, I sat down in an inn and wrote her a long letter, six pages on vellum that cost, each page, as much as the best woman you could buy in our camp.

I rode into Pisa with a safe conduct from Sir John, and purchased another manuscript, this one a selection of Latin recipes from Constantinople. I wrapped the letter and the book in Egyptian fustian and some fine silk, and sent it with a Florentine merchant bound for England. Despite being at war, we traded with Florence pretty freely.

The process of writing and sending my letter caused me to search my trunks – I had two – for wax. By now, even our French boys were men-at-arms, and Perkin commanded a lance, but I still asked him to find things for me. When I explained my problem, he struck himself in the face – a little over-dramatic, but he meant it.

'By the virgin, William!' he said. 'I have your … your things. From the factor.' He shook his head. 'Your old clothes and things.'

There followed a joyful searching through a chest unopened in almost two winters. My clothes were food for moths and worms, as they had been put away filthy. I lifted them from the old trunk with a knife, they were so dirty.

They smelled like old sins, but under the old sins lay one bright virtue.

The trunk held Emile's favour. I had long assumed it lost. I think I held it and stared at it for most of the time it took my companions to play a full game of piquet, which the Pisans were busy teaching us in order to lighten our wallets, little knowing that the companions had known it for five years. I tucked it into my doublet, walked to our local chapel and paid for a Mass for her soul.

The next day, I heard that Pamfila had died of the Plague. I was riding into Pisa to fetch new clothing, and I met her mother, dressed all in black. She was on a mule, and she rode up to me.

I knew immediately.

She took my hand and cried a little. I had almost no Italian back then, and I had to wait until Fiore came to translate.

She'd taken the Plague only two weeks earlier. She'd swelled for a day, breathed badly and died. But her mother said that before the pustules broke, a man came with a letter from a friend of hers in Florence to tell her the quaint story of having met a German knight who said he was her eternal slave because he'd been taken in a fair *empris*.

Fiore turned to me. 'She says, my daughter died with your name on her lips,' and she says, 'Always will our family see you as one of us.'

That, too, changed me. If you don't get why, well ...

Sir John Hawkwood was named captain of Pisa.

It was, in its way, as great a compliment as he could ever have received, and it moved him to the top of our profession. He had been Sterz's marshal for two years.

But I think it ruined his relations with Sir Albert. I agree that we – the White Company – were a little tired of Sterz's ways. We would sit in camp for weeks, but we had to rise at dawn every morning. We never slept in, and we never missed a day of lacing, cleaning ...

He was like that. But so was the Order of St John, so I didn't mind as much as men like William Grice did.

Or, as it turned out, Sir John Hawkwood. But the lads had the notion that Sir John would be easier – and they also knew he was English, while our enemies kept being German. All in all, I think Sir Albert was as good a captain as I ever served under – he was brave, he was careful, he planned well and men liked him. But he didn't have the – I can't describe it – the *sprezzatura* that Hawkwood had. Sir John seemed to do things well – without effort. He had wonderful spies and he used them to stay ahead in everything. He rode well, and he could joust, and he spent the autumn learning to use a hawk and hounds so that he could hunt or falcon with Italian noblemen. He learned these things because he saw it all as part of his profession.

At any rate, Hawkwood was made captain of Pisa. Directly he took the baton – I think it was February of the year of our lord 1364 – he led us on a raid across Tuscany, into Florentine lands in mid-winter.

It had worked against Milan, and I think it had been his idea. But we tried to go too far into the highlands, and the snow was the worst in fifty years – so much snow that the horses couldn't get grass and began to die. A dead war horse is the single most expensive corpse you'll ever see.

We passed Carmignano undetected, but the passes were blocked with snow, and after a particularly nasty skirmish at the gates of the Mugello – nasty because everything that hurts, hurts more in bitter cold, and I got knocked off my horse by a German I never saw – Sir John admitted we were beaten and we retreated.

We had no supplies and no baggage train.

Men started to die.

A battle is a crisis, if you like, but it is one for which you plan and train, and it isn't a surprise – one hopes. That march taxed all of us to, and beyond, our limits. And the strain didn't come all at once; it built day by day.

I was injured – not wounded, merely badly hurt. I'd fallen well, if falling off a tall horse is ever good, on my arse. I had a bruise as big as Lombardy and a roll of muscle that seemed like an internal wound, it hurt so badly, but I could ride and I could give orders.

Instead of fighting the enemy, we were foraging and building fires, and that became the limit of my command. Men would wander off in the snow and vanish and we'd never see them again. Except that when it was Juan, I turned my horse's head – still the war horse I'd taken from Father Pierre Thomas, in what seemed like a different world – and rode back along our trail until I found him.

'I'm sleepy,' he said.

I put him on my horse and pinned him against me until I reached Janet's fire.

'Some men will do anything to sleep with me,' she quipped, and put him in her blankets while her squire piled wood on her personal fire.

He lost all the toes on his left foot.

Richard Grimlace wasn't so lucky. He went into a stone barn and peasants killed him. We rode back to find him, and we killed the peasants – even though I knew that was wrong.

We made a fort of their barn and waited out the last of the snow there, with a fire in the corner. We had seventy men and one woman in that barn, and all of us lived to see Pisa.

I slept between Perkin and Milady. At some point in the night – you have to imagine us packed like salt herrings, so banish any salacious thought – I knew she was awake. In her ear, I said, 'Do you ever miss Richard Mussard?'

'No,' she said.

I paused. 'He wanted to marry you,' I said. 'I seem to remember.'

She rolled a quarter turn. 'We did marry,' she said. She shrugged, and John Hughes, sleeping on her other side, groaned. I suspect I groaned, too.

'He'll get over me,' she said.

I thought of Richard at Turin. It occurred to me that she'd already run away from him by then – and then he'd seen me. What would he think?

When the snow cleared, we rode for Pisa. We collected another twenty men on our way, but the White Company would have lost fewer men in a heavy defeat. The snow did to us what the Germans could not. We lost 400 lances and were half the size we'd been the summer before.

There was talk of taking the command from Sir John. I had never seen him so low – he slept too much, went to meetings with Pisans and spent too little time with men like Andrew Belmont and me.

The Pisans tightened their belts and hired another famous knight – one of the most famous: Hannekin Baumgarten. He was a Knight of the Holy Roman Empire, a member of two famous orders of chivalry and a dozen well-known tournament societies. He was a big, handsome man, and his Cologne German was less offensive to the English than Swabian. He was also a fine jouster.

He brought a small army of Germans. Each 'nation' had about 1,000 lances.

Spring came and seemed to dispel the last of the Plague. I received a letter from Fra Peter when the passes opened, and another, from my sister, in the same packet. They made me happy. I sat and wrote back to them the same day, and spent from my dwindling store of florins to send them to Avignon and London.

We had two incidents that spring, neither of which brought me any pleasure.

We marched on Florence in mid-April, as yet unpaid. We marched as far as Pistoia with Baumgarten, but our 8,000 cavalry was too much for one web of narrow roads, so we elected to go our separate ways. Sir John was back in command, and he sent Andrew Belmont to sieze Prato by night – the way we'd taken Pont-Saint-Esprit. We rode hard, caught them with the drawbridge down, and then everything went wrong and Andrew was badly wounded.

I got to him, pinned him to his saddle and got him clear of the crossbow bolts.

We tried again that night, but they were ready, and the only thing we could do was ride around the town, whooping like imps of Satan. While my men distracted the militia on the walls, I climbed down into the ditch and crawled to the main gate, where I stood up and pounded on it with my fists.

'I summon this town to surrender in the name of the White Company!' I roared.

It had no effect on the campaign, but was much talked about. When we returned to the army, Sir John summoned me.

'I'm appointing you corporal,' he said.

Corporals commanded fifty lances – 200 men.

I took Belmont's division while he went back to Pisa. It was a very left-handed way to achieve command, though, and it made me uneasy.

Janet was quick to congratulate me.

I was surprised. 'I thought you had a—'

She looked at me in such a way as to deprive me of the power of speech. 'Gentlemen don't say everything that comes to their minds,' she spat. 'Andrew Belmont is nothing to me.'

The second incident took place a few days later. It was not my day to patrol and I was in camp. A patrol of Rudolph von Hapsburg's encountered a patrol of ours – of mine. It was led by Perkin – Master Smallwood. They met at the corner of a wood and it was a surprise to both parties. A German officer – Sir Heinrich, as the heralds reported to us – charged. He was reported to me as being a giant mounted on an elephant, but those Germans beat my men so badly I couldn't get a straight story out of any of them.

Sir Heinrich's lance caught Perkin in the body armour. He didn't have a steel breastplate and the blow crushed his ribcage. He probably died when he hit the ground. Seamus died there, too, cut from the saddle by a German knight's axe.

Kenneth had been in camp with me, and his reaction was so violent I ordered his squire to watch him every minute – I was afeared he'd desert to try and kill a German. The Irish are the most fiery men on the face of the earth.

But Seamus and Perkin didn't die for nothing. I went with a herald and reclaimed their corpses, giving Hapsburg's camp a careful look as I did. The Swabians were contemptuous of us, and I met the giant

Heinrich in person – I'm a big man, and he over-topped me by a head. He didn't bother to conceal his camp, and he returned my friend to me with the trappings of chivalry, but few, if any, of the essentials.

'He was easy to put down,' Heinrich said in his heavily accented English. 'None of you English is any match for a knight.' He laughed. 'Pitiful.'

I turned to the German herald who accompanied us. 'Is this what passes for courtesy in Swabia?' I asked.

'Save your tears, Englishman,' Heinrich said. 'None of you are *knights*. We know what you are: peasants who have stolen armour. We are not afraid of your White Company.' He laughed.

Perhaps I could have said something inspired, or merely insulting, but instead, I marked their banners and penants as carefully as I might. I put Perkin and Seamus in carts, and Arnaud, who had driven a few carts in his life, helped me drive them back to our lines.

Courtesy and control. And perhaps, simply biding my time. Treating war as a business.

We buried them and our other dead that night and a priest said Mass. And then we slipped away. We retreated.

We left Rudolph von Hapsburg with nothing. He sat there for three days, waiting for us to attack him, so I'm going to guess that his Swabians weren't as sure of themselves as Heinrich sounded.

We pounded south, back to Prato, then we drove east, along the same path as Sir Hannekin. We broke up into smaller divisions to cover more ground, looting and burning across an empty countryside. We ate well, but something had gone out of me with Perkin's death.

I wanted to avenge him. I loved Father Pierre Thomas, but I was not going to turn the other cheek for the German bastard who'd killed my squire.

It had become more personal and less chivalrous in the Hapsburg camp.

Professional war is an odd thing, and personal animosity is not useful. As an example, when we passed through Prato the second time, we received reinforcements – both English and German. Erich von Landau joined us at Prato. The next night, at the fire, while our Italian servants cooked, Erich spoke to Fiore in German, and Fiore stood up carefully and nodded.

Erich said something in Italian.

Fiore nodded. Sadly, I think.

Erich went and shook his hand, and that was that. I don't *know* that they discussed that the Friulian had killed Erich's brother, but I assume that some accommodation was reached.

I was watching Milady as she was behaving oddly. The day after Perkin died, I found her in camp, dressed in a kirtle and gown. She looked down her nose at me and I rode on.

Perkin left a hole in my lances, and in my life – I couldn't find anything. I never had six pair of lace points that matched. I didn't have a squire just then, so I picked up the youngest man-at-arms to join us at Prato, an English boy still young enough to have pimples, who had come all the way out from England to fight in Italy. We were becoming famous. His name was Edward, and his father, he said, was a bishop.

Edward Bishop, he called himself. And with the same draft from England came a Scot – or an Irishman – Colin Campbell.

We rode further east and linked up with Baumgarten in the hills of Montughi, where we camped. Rudolph von Hapsburg had finally stopped waiting for us on the other side of the city and had retreated to Florence proper. All our marching hadn't got us clear of him, though. We could see his camp fires.

Beyond his fires, we could see Florence in the distance. Baumgarten and Hawkwood put their pavilions side by side, and we saw the two of them, sitting on camp stools, drinking wine.

We drank wine, too. Probably too much. We were angry – angry as soldiers are when they feel they have not been well led. Soldiers – professional soldiers – are like the men and boys who put on the passion plays at Clerkenwell. You work and work – make your costume, write and rewrite your lines, and then you put on your performance, and for a few days you are the toast of London. But then some other guild puts on their bit – they have a splendid King Herod, a fine Jesus who moves the women to tears – and your brilliant bit is forgotten. We'd had our moment at Canturino, but since then, we'd been defeated by snow and the Germans; the crowd no longer sang *our* praises, but those of the Germans. Our own Italians were deserting. We'd left Pisa with 2,000 lances of English and Germans, and another thousand Italian men-at-arms. Now we had just a few hundred.

I sat on a leather trunk, sewing a grommet. Grommets are the very sinews of armour – for every piece, there are a couple of grommets in your arming coat to hold the whole thing together. Sewing made me think of Perkin, who was, *sans doute*, the best squire I'd ever had. My new squire couldn't sew and clearly thought the whole thing beneath him, so I sat in the firelight with my arming doublet, trying to coax the torn out holes back into shape so I could lace on my leg harnesses the next day – if we were going to fight.

Perhaps I should have punished him. What I remember is being tired all the time. Tired with fatigue and – men tell you this often, monsieur? – tired of it all. When Perkin died, it was as if the whole game had no point. Let me tell you how it is. The more times you face the fight, and the more men you kill, the harder it is to smile, to laugh, to see the glory in the day. Even to have a friend or a lover. What comes easier is to drink hard, gamble and never, ever go inside your head to see what's there. Perhaps I should have punished my lazy, arrogant squire, but had I roused myself, I might simply have killed him, because that is where you go, when all you do and all you breathe is fighting and death.

Chivalry is the answer. Just as men have developed laws to protect us from greed – pale reflections of God's law, perhaps, but rules nonetheless – so we have chivalry to protect us from violence. So that if we must kill, we have rules.

I remember that night, because we were all there. Not Robert, killed by peasants, and not Seamus, killed by Germans, nor Perkin. But Janet was there, slim and blue, drinking from a Venetian glass and sitting in a broad chair her squire had stolen from a church. John Hughes was there, leaning over her, making a joke, and Sam Bibbo was quietly sharpening arrows. Fiore was watching her, but he was talking about feats of arms he'd heard of, and he had Juan's attention and William Grice's. Courtney was trying to shave in the dark, with a dozen men 'helping' by making suggestions, most of which would have made a Southwark girl blush. Arnaud was trying a pair of leg harnesses, and a patient armour merchant – a Florentine, no less – was making adjustments. John Thornbury was playing cards with de la Motte and a pair of Baumgarten's men-at-arms. Kenneth MacDonald was repairing his jupon – a great deerskin coat stuffed with sheep's wool – and trading Irish jibes with Colin Campbell.

I watched them all, and I thought of all the others. Ned Candleman. Chris Shippen. Richard.

Christ, I missed Richard.

And drinking and thinking about Perkin made me angry.

'Tomorrow,' I said, and everyone stopped. I must have sounded like a madman. Wode. Milady turned and looked at me, and her eyes were wide.

'Tomorrow, we should show the Germans what we are,' I said.

Fiore looked at me and smiled. 'Do you intend some feat of arms?' he asked.

'By God, that's just what I intend,' I said.

Just after dark, a boy came and fetched me to Sir John Hawkwood. He had his feet up, and he was holding a silver cup. He looked quite relaxed. Sir Hannekin was sitting by him.

'William,' he said and nodded.

'Sir John?' I asked.

'Hannekin, this is William Gold, whom I've known since he was a boy. He'll command Andrew Belmont's lances. William, we're going to try for the city. We won't take it – Florence has more people than we have grains of wheat in this camp – but I intend to drive in Hapsburg's outposts and break his barricades.'

'I'm in,' I said.

'You'd best be in, young William,' Sir John said. 'Your battle has the best armour. You are the vanguard. I want you to go first – right at their barricades.'

I nodded. 'Consider it done,' I said. Or something equally brash.

Baumgarten laughed. 'Quite the young cock,' he said. 'I offered my best German knights, but Sir John must have you. I'll have my eye on you, Master William.'

I was given wine. I tried not to sound too drunk, and after a little while, and some polite noises, I went back to my people.

They all looked at me.

'Tomorrow,' I said, 'I mean to avenge Seamus and Perkin. And win my spurs, or die trying.'

No one said a thing. The fire crackled and I went to my cloak.

I mean, what else was there?

I didn't have Richard, and I didn't have Emile, and I wasn't ever going to be a knight. I was full of anger. And I thought, Plague take them all. I'll just cut my way to the gates of hell.

We rose before dawn. I didn't have a hangover, and after two leather bottles of water, a cup of wine and some hard bread and honey, I felt ready to face my armour. It was the first of May. I remembered

May – the month of love. I took Emile's favour out of my clothes and attached it to the peak of my helmet.

'Let's get this done, Edward,' I said.

He sighed.

I put on a clean shirt and my arming doublet, the one I'd repaired the night before, over clean braes and my best red hose. He pointed my hose to my doublet. 'This is servant's work,' he muttered.

I said nothing.

Perkin used to lay all my harness out on dry blankets. Edward didn't know what to do – I think he'd only armed in dry castles and nice big pavilions. 'I didn't get much sleep last night,' he said.

'You attach the greave to the cuisse with the little key,' I said. 'Before you put it on my leg.'

'I know that,' he said, hurrying to do as I'd said, as if he'd known all along. He knew, at one level, but at another, he'd forget what he was doing.

He was afraid, of course.

He stopped to put my sabatons on, and he spent far too much time on just two buckles. Then he seated the left leg and closed the greave.

'I need more light,' he said.

I said nothing.

He took an aeon getting the buckles closed on the cuisse.

Then he tackled the second leg. I had time to think how easy he had it – Perkin had had to arrange different armour all the time, as I damaged a leg, or plundered something I liked better. He'd been shaping into a good knight.

I had only learned to be a squire under Fra Peter, and only after I'd been a man-at-arms for years.

I was lucky, I decided. I had a lump in my throat and I was close to tears.

'This belt is too stiff,' Edward said.

'Take a moment. Breathe. There's no rush,' I said.

Milady Janet pranced by, fully armed.

I laced my own points, cinching the points tight to the arming jacket. When you fight on foot, the worst thing that can happen is to have your leg harnesses slip down even a little.

'I can do that,' he insisted.

No you can't, I thought, but I didn't say so. I was kind enough to know he didn't need to face his first battle feeling like he'd failed me.

Of his own accord, he fetched me a stool. I sat, and John Hughes put a cup of hippocras into my hand. He smiled. He was Milady's archer again, and very happy with it.

Sam Bibbo came up. He was eating a sausage. The two of them counted over their shafts while I armed.

Edward came back with my Milanese breast and backplates.

'Unseat the lance rest,' I said. 'I won't need it today.'

That started a murmur.

'Sir John says we'll fight on foot. We're to go for the barricades.' I smiled. I felt better.

I sat and drank hippocras, and thought about May and love. And Emile. And Fra Peter, and Father Pierre Thomas. And Richard, and a lot of other things. Chivalry. Fear.

I rose and shrugged on my haubergeon, looted from Poitiers.

Edward and Sam put the breast and backplates around me and closed it like an oyster's shell – buckled it home and fetched the arms.

The left arm went on, and was laced to the haubergeon, and then the right. I flexed each one in turn.

Three of them put my white coat over my armour.

All around me, in the growing light, all the men I liked best were doing the same things – the gradual process of arming. A young woman came with a basket of rolls, warm from an oven somewhere, like a miracle of loaves and fishes brought to the White Company camp.

'For luck,' she said. Just for a moment, she looked like Emile.

I ate the roll; it was delicious.

Edward came with my gauntlets and helmet.

'Go get armed yourself,' I said. I had the wisdom to know that the worst fear of a young man-at-arms is the fear of being late.

Sam brought me my war sword – four feet of good steel, made in Germany. He belted it around my waist and buckled it.

Arnaud appeared with de Charny's dagger. 'You'll miss this, if you don't have it,' he said. We tied it to the sword belt, and I drew it a few times. A rondel dagger has to flow into your fist in a fight. When you want it, you have to know just where it is.

Men were pale shapes flitting like moths when I rose from my stool. I could see Sir John in his full, new harness, all steel, and the light made him a statue of molten silver, or the shape of an angel – a very incongrous shape for Sir John Hawkwood. I walked to my horse, and spent some precious spirit vaulting into the saddle. My men were watching.

Pierre, my warhorse, was eager. Edward had made him gleam. That, he was good at.

I sat on Pierre and watched my lances form. The sun was just going to crest the horizon.

They had to know we were coming.

Kenneth MacDonald sprang onto his charger. He looked very dull, in a leather jupon instead of a breastplate. He wore a great aventail as big as a cloak, hanging down from the most steeply pointed German basinet I'd ever seen. He looked like a great orange bird of prey.

Milady looked like a very small, sleek steel falcon.

Juan looked showy; he wore a red cloak and his lady's favour – a little beaten about – was pinned to his shoulder. Fiore was very plain; he didn't have a steel breast and backplate, but his white coat hid his poverty.

Pages scurried about, collecting spears we'd use if we dismounted, picking up last requests, handing out cups of wine – many men drink hard before a fight. My page was eating a winter apple with one hand while trying to manage a horse with the other.

Edward was the last man in my battle to mount his horse.

Around us, other battles were in the last stages of preparation. Thornbury had all veterans, and he was ready – his whole company sat on their mounts, mocking the latecomers. The Germans were much slower – I could see a German man-at-arms who didn't have his breast and backplates on yet.

Sir John rode up to me. He looked over the camp and the Field of Mars – the place where we formed. As I watched, he came to a decision.

'You decide how far you can go,' he said. 'This is mostly for honour. Hapsburg has too many men for us to win a real victory. I'd like a man to touch the barricades.'

It was an honour, in a chivalric fight, to have reached the enemy barricades. I knew this language.

You might ask, *mon dieu*, if Sir John Hawkwood was making war into a business, why should touching the enemy barricades matter.

Look you. We were an army of a few thousand men, facing a city with a population of a hundred times that, defended by an army four times our own size. Even if we obliterated our enemies, we couldn't take Florence.

But men are not clockwork. They are flesh and blood. Taunts sting us. Insults hurt us.

'I'll do it,' I said.

He tapped me on the shoulder with his steel-clad fist. 'I imagine you will, William.'

He looked around.

An Italian priest – doubtless a Pisan – came forward with a censer, and said a prayer over us. I said a paternoster. A boy handed me a clay cup of water and smiled.

'I want to be a knight when I grow up,' he said in pretty fair English.

'Good,' I said. 'Thanks for the water.'

I turned to my lance and raised my fist.

'On me,' I said.

We filed off, and I led the way out onto the road. A dozen exiled Florentines – gentlemen – were gathered there, and two of them left their ranks. They led us down the road almost two leagues, and then we went across farm fields for as long as it would take a nun to sing Mass.

In the distance, I could see the Florentine forces forming. I remember thinking, Sweet Virgin Mother, they've had all night, they know we're coming, and they still aren't ready. It lit a small fire of hope in me.

My gentleman guide pointed with his sword. 'The gate of San Gallo,' he said.

It was a great gate, big enough for ten men to ride in abreast, and in front of it were entrenchments and barricades. They were full of men – crossbowmen from the guilds and German men-at-arms. They were about 500 paces distant, and the ground was as clear as a farmer's field from us to them. It rose steadily, too.

But the men manning those makeshift walls weren't steady. They seethed like maggots on a wound. Some were still arming, and others ...

Who knows why men are late?

'Companions!' I called out, and all the muttering behind me died away. Something was forming in my head: Anger. And hope. I raised my hand again.

'The best way to do this is very quickly. We form a line right here on my command. We will ride to long crossbow shot and dismount,

443

as fast as lightning, and we will go forward to the barricades without stopping to dress our line or issue challenges or any other formality.'

I looked back. 'As soon as Sam finds the distance comfortable, the archers are to fall to the rear and loft over us – steadily.'

'Comfortable, is it?' Sam said.

'All the way to the barricades,' I said. 'And over them, into the town.'

I had fifty lances. There were 3,000 men at the barricades.

'All the banks in the world are here,' I said.

That got a happy grumble.

'Drink water!' I ordered.

I loosened my sword in its sheath and checked de Charny's dagger.

No one said, 'This is insane.'

No one suggested we should stop.

'Ready?' Men at the barricade were pointing at us. We were so few, I assume they thought we wouldn't attack. Indeed, militiamen were already trailing away, back into the town. Looking for breakfast, the lucky sods.

I drew de Charny's dagger from my belt. 'I took this from Geoffrey de Charny at Poitiers!' I roared.

Men cheered.

'I will give it to the first man to touch the barricades!' I called.

They roared.

'Let's go,' I said.

Twenty yards into the empty field, I raised my fist, and my lances flowed forward from the right and left. A well-trained company can array itself faster than most folk can imagine. I didn't finish the first five lines of my paternoster before they were ready.

'Forward!' I called. I turned to look back, and saw Sir John with Thornbury's battle coming up on my left.

I didn't wait. I was, I hoped, doing what I'd been told. And I thought, To hell with it. Hell was probably where I was destined.

The Germans looked half armed and asleep. All 2,000 of them.

We covered fifty paces at a fast trot. Then another fifty. Not a bolt was loosed at us. Another fifty. We were moving well – I was proud of my lances, because we were in good order and well-bunched up.

We crossed the line I'd imagined for crossbow range, and since we received no bolts, I let us go on. Every heartbeat ate another pace.

A dozen bolts came out of the barricades. I'd aligned my attack with the rising sun. I looked back – it was a red ball behind us.

Another flight of bolts, and most of them went well over me. Somewhere one struck with a nasty hollow metallic sound. A horse screamed.

The crossbowmen would be spanning.

'Halt!' I roared. And then, 'Dismount!'

I swung my leg over, turned sideways, put my breastplate against my saddle and slithered to the ground.

My page emerged from behind me, slipped past me and took Pierre, who gave me a look.

The page dropped my spear at my feet. I stooped to get it, rose and looked right and left. I turned back towards Florence and began to walk the last 200 paces to the barricade.

A bolt struck my left spaulder and skidded away. It felt like a heavy punch from a strong man. There was a rattle of bolts – a dozen must have struck – but as far as I could see, all my men were still moving forward. And, of course, when you are going forward, you can't see your dead.

I looked down at the ground beneath my feet. Green tufts were springing to life in the old cart track, and there were the remnants of a house, probably pulled down the night before.

There was another rattle of crossbow bolts and a long, joyless scream.

The crossbow bolts were coming faster now. I took one more look, right and left, and closed my visor.

I think I laughed. I was empty. Empty of need or desire. I didn't care about my next meal or about John Hawkwood's next plan or Emile or our saviour. I was going to touch the barricade.

The barricade was eighty paces away, a little lower than a man and lined with men in armour that lit up red in the sun.

War-bow shafts began to fall like wicked sleet on the barricade and the men behind it.

I hadn't intended to run, but I found myself trotting, and the line trotted to keep up with me.

There were shouts ahead.

I felt ... strong. There was no reason that a frontal assault on the barricades should be going this well, and I had time to consider that it was a trap – that there was cavalry concealed to my left. But my last glance at my men had shown Thornbury's battle coming up on my left and Thomas Biston's on my right. If it was a trap, their Germans would need a hell of a lot of cavalry.

Baumgarten was deploying behind me.

We were as well placed as we were going to be.

I was running – in sabatons. Somewhere in my line was a man cursing his squire, but that day it was not me. Our line was fair enough, and the rising sun turned the tips of our spears to fire.

The men behind the barricades were seething. Men ran back and forth – fifty voices were calling and, as I watched, a guildsman tried to force his way to the barricade to loose his weapon and was roughly forced back by a German man-at-arms.

I looked for the pennants I wanted.

Twenty paces from the barricade, I realized that unless God and his legion of angels came down to stop us, we'd make the barricade. The crossbows had been ill-aimed and desultory, for whatever reason.

Typically, when men fight at barricades – at least in the lists – men stand on either side of a waist-high wooden wall and exchange blows. You can't be hit below your breastplate and your opponent can't grapple.

I'd never fought at a barricade.

But I'd stormed a few towns, and I had a different notion of how to tackle the wall. I had no intention of giving any other man de Charny's dagger.

Five paces out, I lengthened my stride. There were half a dozen Germans waiting for me, jostling to be the one to face me across the barrier.

All or nothing.

I leaped.

I almost didn't make it, which would have shortened this tale immensely, but I got my left foot on the barricade, my spear struck something, and then ...

Ah, and then I fought.

I landed deep in their ranks. Armour protects you from the abrasions and cuts of small blows, and for the first few cuts, it was all I could do to get my feet under me. I was close in – I had a man right against my breast, and my spear shaft was already broken – no idea how. I drew de Charny's dagger and stabbed – one, two, three times, as fast as my hand would move. It came away bloody, then I turned and stabbed behind me. I put my left hand on the pommel of the dagger, received a great blow to my head that rang bells, and grappled close to a man. He got one hand on the dagger, but his other held his sword, and my two-handed grip overcame him. He had no visor, and my dagger went in over his nose.

I kicked out behind me on instinct, and then I had space. I stumbled and put my back against the barrier, and for three deep breaths the Germans stood back. I put the dagger back in my sheath – St George must have guided my hand – and drew my longsword.

I took the time to bow and salute them. And breathe.

And then, of course, I attacked them.

I put my sword down in one of Fiore's guards – the boar's tooth – and cut up at the first German's hands. He had heavy leather gloves rather than steel gauntlets, and he sprayed fingers and screamed. My down cut stopped on his arms and I pushed it into his face.

The other two hammered blows at me, but they were thrown too fast, with too much fear. Both hit – one dented my left rebrace, and the other fell on the peak of my helmet, cut away a portion of Emile's favour, and glanced off the overlapping plates of my right spaulder.

I cut at the second man's head. He had a red coat over his coat of plates, and a full helmet that covered his face. My adversary swatted heavily at my blade, and I allowed his blow to turn mine and hammered his faceplate with my pommel, knocking him back a step. He raised his hands. I passed my blade over his head and kicked him in the gut while I held him, and he dropped – neck broken or unconscious. Either way, down.

Blows hit me. Many blows. A man in armour can take all the blows that don't kill him. My armour was good.

There were voices calling in English all around me. I pushed forward, and my opponents backed away.

To their rear, I saw Rudolph von Hapsburg's banner go up.

All around me, men were calling, 'George! St George and England!' and I narrowly avoided putting my point into Milady's basinet – she, of all people, I should have known in a mêlée. I have no idea how she'd passed me, but I fought from behind her for as long as a man takes to mount a horse. I pinked some Florentine in the leg, stabbing down, and she slammed her sword into his head. I doubt he fell dead – I suspect he'd merely had enough.

I think by then my whole battle – my command – was over the barricade and in the muddy trench behind it. A few guildsmen stood, and a few local men-at-arms were ashamed to show fear in front of their ladies, who even then were on the walls behind them.

But most of the local men ran for the gate, leaving the Swabians to face a rising tide of Englishmen and Germans.

Rudolph von Hapsburg may have been proud and boastful – Messire Villani says he was – but he was brave. He led his knights in person, and he charged at us. But it is harder to charge through a rout of fleeing men than it is to charge through a deluge of arrows or crossbow bolts. His men were pushed aside – they came at us in packets.

I wanted the giant. I could see him – he was a head taller than any other man, his pennon was black and he had a spear and an axe – he was off to my right. I shamelessly stepped back from an opponent and left him to Edward, passed behind Fiore, got two more paces – it was like pushing through a crowd at a fair – and there he was, hammering at MacDonald with his axe. MacDonald caught all three of his heavy blows, then tripped on a corpse – all those war-bow shafts had reaped more than a few Florentines – and his fall kept him from the giant's smashing blow.

I stepped into the gap. I remember as I stepped up, seeing a flash of gold on the helmet hard by Sir Heinrich. It had to be a gold cornet, and that meant the next knight to the left was Rudolph.

Heinrich raised his axe and cut. Big men are supposed to be slow. He wasn't. The axe flicked back and shot forward – I cut it to the right with an underhand blow, and he turned the axe in mid air and cut back at me. I had to put my left hand on the blade of my sword to parry – a technique Fiore taught me. I made my sword a staff.

I was close to him, and I smashed my guard into his visor. It wasn't much of a hit, but every hit counts.

He stumbled back one step, and I cut at him from the shoulder, as hard and fast as I could.

He caught it on his axe blade.

A blow caught my helmet squarely and I stumbled.

Apparently, single combat is an Anglo-French convention. Rudolph's sword was pushing for my eye-slits, but I batted it down and my back cut only just saved me from the axe.

Rudolph's sword licked out again and slammed my hand, but I had good gauntlets. He broke my little finger and it hurt like fuck. He punched the point at my head as my guard weakened, and his point went in between the base of my helmet and the chin of my aventail – suddenly my mouth was full of blood.

I had a few breaths to live, if that. He'd cut open my mouth – look, this scar right here – I still have the devil's smile, as we call it.

I pivoted toward Rudolph, fought through the pain and cut down at his shoulder. Then I pushed in with my other foot, driving forward with my not-inconsiderable size, flinching in my head from the inevitable axe-blow. I wagered my life that I could get so far forward into Rudolph that Heinrich wouldn't be able to hit me. I had no choice. It was all or nothing.

I was mostly right, and the staff of the axe slammed into my shoulder plates as my blow deceived Rudolph and hit his arm just below his shoulder armour – it landed on mail, but it broke the arm. Heinrich's hit on my shoulder landed on my pauldrons. That hurt, but pain was just pain.

I thrust for Rudolph's face – my best blow. Halfway to the target, I dropped my point the width of his sword and changed the direction subtly, so his parry moved nothing but the wind. My point missed his face but got into the chain aventail at his neck, bit deep, through chain and padding, and came away red.

I caught that at the edge of my vision, because I was already turning to parry the axe. The giant cut, and I counter-cut at his hands. I hit first. I hit his hands so hard he voided his blow.

Kenneth MacDonald got to his feet. He, too, had an axe, and he raised it.

Heinrich rotated fully to face me. I'd cut away a finger and he bellowed like a bull, while MacDonald's axe slammed into his chest. It didn't cut through the heavy iron plates of his coat, but it must have broken ribs, and he sat down, falling back across his Prince.

A trumpet was sounding the recall.

I was breathing so hard I could hardly keep my point in line.

Heinrich bounced to his feet again, blood pouring from his left gauntlet.

I cut up from the boar's tooth again, and took off the giant's thumb. MacDonald passed behind me and cut at yet another man, probably saving my life, but that's a mêlée. I was utterly focused on my giant.

He had killed Perkin.

He leaped forward off Rudolph von Hapsburg and I cut down, into his exposed thigh. He pushed through it and kept his feet a heartbeat, but the leg wouldn't hold him, and I was reversing my sword, holding it with one hand on the hilt and the other at the point, as if it was a very short spear, or a shovel for digging.

As he tried to get his balance, I slammed it into his faceplate. The visor held.

The man fell back.

The Germans were retreating, but they were also just realizing that their lord was lying on the ground at my feet. Heinrich had fallen across him as he tried to rise, crushing him to the ground. He fell with his arms spread – he'd lost fingers on both hands, and there was blood coming from under his helmet.

I stepped on his right hand, pinning the axe hand to the ground. I could see his eyes. Not mad, or filled with hate.

Just blue.

I put the tip of my war sword against his throat, where the skin showed. He'd fallen with his head back, so his aventail didn't quite cover his chin.

I won't say the battle stopped, just that I could hear men screaming in Italian and German, but very few men moving and everyone watching me.

I put the slightest pressure on the pommel of my sword.

So he'd know that I was the better man.

'Yield!' I said. Like a knight.

'Ja!' he said.

They let us go from the barriers. For one terrifying moment, they thought I was going to kill their Prince, and when I accepted Heinrich's surrender, Rudolph 'graciously' allowed us to retire.

That's what knights do.

When they're badly beaten.

I had to have help to get over the barricades. With 15,000 people watching me from the walls and from our lines, I could barely walk without limping, because my left leg-harness had slipped a fraction and every step hurt.

I forced myself to walk like a gentleman, with all the time in the world. I had to get my visor up to spit blood – my mouth was full of it and my white coat was covered.

Baumgarten's knights were cheering like heroes. They'd covered the barricade behind us, and many of them had fought, so no discredit to them. They walked back with us, slapping us on our backplates and calling things, which Fiore, who was all but glowing, refused to translate.

'That was . . .' he said. He said it twice.

Baumgarten himself came forward, which seemed odd, since we were retreating. We'd made our point. In fact, we'd scared the piss out of Florence. Juan, Milady and Grice were apparently able to touch the gate before we retired.

The archers were yelling, 'George and England.'

Baumgarten headed straight for me. His armour sparkled, and he wore the gold belt of a Knight of the Empire. He looked like a king.

He opened his visor.

A few paces from me, he stopped and handed his squire the baton he carried.

'William Gold!' he roared, so that they could hear him in the squares of Florence.

I stopped in front of him, so utterly exhausted that I had lost the power of speech.

Sir John came up – he was all but running – and men-at-arms crowded in.

'William Gold,' Buamgarten said again. 'Kneel!'

Kneel?

Sweet saviour of man, I might never get up.

But I knelt.

Edward appeared from the crowd and began to fumble with my aventail. 'Oh my God!' he said. 'My God, sir!'

He got it over my head. There was a lot of blood in it from my mouth wound.

Baumgarten turned to Sir John. 'Do you wish to do this?' he said.

Sir John shook his head. 'If *you* do it here, in bowshot of the walls, no one will ever be able to question the making.'

Sir Hannekin Baumgarten drew his sword. 'William Gold – birth enobles, but nothing enobles like a life of arms. A deed such as I just witnessed—'

'Guildsmen coming. Winding their crossbows,' muttered a squire.

Sam Bibbo, I'm told, loosed a shaft then and there. I didn't see it, but men who did say it flew 300 paces and frightened the wits out of a trio of Florentine guildsmen. Or killed all three, if you believe some.

The sword smacked down on my right shoulder, a little too damned hard. 'I dub thee knight,' Baumgarten said.

'By St Nicholas! What was it all for?' cursed my lady Janet as we rode south.

The days after my knighting were not pleasant. I had a fever from my mouth wound, and it wouldn't heal. I got it stitched twice.

If I were telling you a set of stories, monsieur, I'd tell you some pleasant fiction: that Florence sent out emissaries to Sir John, and he drove a hard bargain and settled an honourable peace.

That sounds well, does it not?

But what Florence actually did while I lay in my tent and moaned, was to pay a number of men, including the Imperial Knight who's buffet had just enobled me in front of 20,000 onlookers. Florence paid them enormous bribes, and our army, victorious in the field, vanished like alpine mist under a Tuscan sun. The Germans left first, but the money went far – even into the White Company.

In a week, those of us who didn't sell out were retreating across the Florentine *contada*. Hawkwood was sanguine. I still don't know if he received money, or not. You must know he has a sovereign price – a fine reputation – but he loved money.

Any road, we retreated on Pisa. And Pisa, who had nearly bankrupted themselves to buy us, was none too happy. Neither were we happy. The men who'd been bought had ridden south – Andrew Belmont, who was angry over my elevation; Sterz himself, probably smarting that Pisa had chosen Hawkwood instead of him, and a dozen other officers. Belmont's little company actually changed sides to serve Florence.

Just north of Pisa, we made a camp – a walled camp covered by the Arno River. Hawkwood stayed in command, and began to buy a new army.

Across the river, Florentine agents competed with ours to buy every available lance. And Sir Walter Leslie, from France, no less, arrived to compete as well. He was bidding for the pope, or so I understood. For a crusade.

On our second night in the new camp, we threw a party. We had horse races and a military dance – a hundred of us danced in armour, in full sight of our adversaries. To show we were still the White Company. To thumb our noses at the men who had taken money to change sides.

I came back from the dancing tired, but feeling better than I had in a week, to find Fra Peter was having a cup of wine with Milady. She smiled at me – truly smiled. She was alight with happiness.

Fra Peter was wearing his scarlet surcoat, the uniform of his order. He stood up as I approached.

'William?' he said.

I grinned. 'Sir William, to you,' I said.

He threw his arms around me and *crushed* me. I thought he might collapse my breastplate. Then he held me at arms length. 'Well done,' he said. 'It sounds like a marvellous feat of arms.' He looked at me. 'You don't seem surprised to see me.'

I shrugged and grinned like a fool. Praise from Fra Peter was praise indeed. 'Leslie's recruiting for a crusade,' I said. 'Or so I hear. So I expected you.'

Fra Peter nodded. 'Come,' he said. 'Come and walk with me.'

'Are we going to pray?' I asked. I meant it as a jest.

'We might, at that,' he allowed. We walked a ways, stepping carefully over tent ropes and horse dung. I was still in armour and I had that bone-wrenching fatigue you can only experience from wearing iron on your body.

'That was ... a woman. In arming clothes, at your fire,' he said.

'Yes,' I agreed, instantly on my guard. 'She's a fine lance. She's won her place here.'

Fra Peter nodded again. 'Women can be trouble in war,' he said. 'But that's Sir John Hawkwood's business and none of mine.' We'd come a long way, by then, right to the bank of the river. It was a soft summer night in Tuscany, and we sat under a chestnut tree as doves cried their haunting cries.

'She is not my lover,' I said, with all the righteousness a young man can project.

There were campfires across the river – so close, in fact, that the conversations of the men at those fires carried. A loud voice proclaimed that someone was a 'fucking sodomite' and a 'son of a whore' in Thames-side English.

Fra Peter's craggy face – he had a big nose – was outlined against the firelight of the enemy camp, and he wasn't looking at me. He was looking across the river.

Finally, he spoke. 'Will you come on crusade?' he asked. 'The King of France has taken the cross. Father Thomas has even convinced the Green Count to take the cross.'

I thought that through. 'Because the pope got John Hawkwood to leave his lands?'

Fra Peter's head made an odd motion. 'Perhaps. I prefer to think that it was Pierre Thomas and his preaching.' He shrugged. 'You served with Hawkwood. What do you think of war in Italy?'

'I think it is much like being a routier. Except we behave a little better and we are paid a great deal more.' It was my turn to shrug.

'You are a corporal now. You have rank – men follow you.' Fra Peter turned, and his eyes were dark. 'Aye, tis possible that you have all you want here.' He continued to look at me, then he looked away. 'I am wasting time, I think. I want you to come with me on crusade, but before I ask you, I have to give you something. This thing ...' His dark eyes were on mine like the heavy blade of an adversary. 'This thing came into my hands without my seeking it. I think it may be wrong for me to give it to you. Father Thomas says no. He says that you must have your free will.'

He reached into the breast of his red coat with the white cross and handed me a small envelope. It was of coarse brown cloth, covered in oil, and inside was another envelope of heavy parchment.

I took an eating knife from my purse. 'Is it ...' I think my voice was full of hope. 'Is it from Richard?' I asked. 'Richard Musard?'

Fra Peter blinked. 'No, lad. Hah!' His laugh sounded grim. 'I'll have to call you Sir William soon. No, but it is from Turin. When I took Father Thomas back to Turin, I was at the Green Count's court for some days.'

I got my eating knife and carefully slit the old cloth to get at the parchment. There was a small seal.

Even in the dark, as soon as my thumb touched the seal, I suspected.

My heart beat as fast as it would have in combat. 'She sent me a letter before she died!' I said.

And Fra Peter shook his head. 'No, William. She is still alive.' He paused. 'I have seen her – and spoken to her.'

I ran. Wearing my armour, I ran to the nearest campfire, leaving the older man sitting with his back to a chestnut tree. I came up to a fire where a dozen servants sat – not men I knew. They scattered in real fear – fear of an armed man running at them for the darkness.

I knelt by the light of their fire and used my eating knife to break her seal. The parchment unfolded, slim and short, and there was a tiny enclosure, shaped like a sacred heart.

Dear William.

I have learned that you think I am dead. I am not. I have so much to tell you.

My husband, it would appear, used this story of my death to hurt you. I had a long recovery from my second child – I might have died – but – I smile to write this – I did not. In the last few days, at the court of the Green Count, I have learned many things, about you and about the Count d'Herblay and the part he has played. I have had opportunity to talk with Sir Richard Mussard.

Monsieur, my husband has done all in his power to destroy you. I think it is worth adding that short of physical violence he dares do nothing to me, as I am not only the mother of his children, but the holder of his purse strings. I have my own retainers, indeed, now I have my own household. And so it shall remain, this I promise you.

I send you this letter by means of the very good knight Fra Peter of London, in hopes that he will find you in good health – the way I imagine you every day – a true knight. Be all a knight should be, and if God so wills it, perhaps we will yet see a day.

But I will commit no more to this parchment. Nor will I say adieu. Only, let your deeds so shine before men that I will hear of them, and clap my hands together.

Emile d'Herblay

I read the letter five or six times. I remember trying to decide ... anything. It all went around like a meaningless whirl of words. She was alive.

Alive.

Apparently, I cared very much. I remember that letter the way I remember wounds I have taken – the shock of the pain, the shock of the blood.

I actually fell over. I was kneeling by the fire and I lost my balance and fell. I lay there as if I had taken a blow, and then, as I got to my feet, the heart-shaped scrap of parchment came out of the envelope and fluttered to the ground like a moth.

It was very small. On it, a fine hand had written, 'Perhaps I will go on a pilgrimage.' There was no signature.

Pilgrims, like crusades, went to the Holy Land by way of Venice. And Rhodes.

Fra Peter was standing a distance away.

I pushed the letter and the heart into my purse and went to him. 'I will go on crusade,' I said.

Fra Peter's eyes twinkled in the firelight. 'God works in mysterious ways,' he said.

Epilogue

Sir William smiled his half-smile at Master Chaucer, who was leaning his elbows on the table. Froissart was awake – wide-eyed, scribbling notes on a wax tablet. John de Blake couldn't take his eyes off his master. Aemilie had, at some point, acquired a stool and was asleep with her head against the wall.

'You came back, I see,' the knight said.

Chaucer grunted. 'What choice did I have, with your archers raising the roof?' He raised an eyebrow. 'Worse than satyrs, and louder.'

'Such a story!' Froissart said.

Chaucer's eyes met Gold's across the table. 'Some of it's even true,' he said. He said it with venom, but Gold threw back his head and laughed. He roared.

And Chaucer couldn't help it. He laughed, too.

Historical Note

I am not a professional historian. I'm a novelist. That caveat aside, I care deeply for authenticity. I'm a reenactor and a collector, a patron of craftsmanship, and an amateur martial artist. I ride horses, I shoot bows, I cook at campfires, and I listen to music and read the languages and even fish with the period fishing tackle.

That doesn't mean I get all of these things correct. But, since many of you will know me as a historical novelist who specializes in the Classical world, I feel I should state my credentials. I have a degree in Medieval History and I studied the fourteenth century and most especially the campaign of Poitiers before writing my honor's dissertation on retinue service in the Hundred Years War. I may have some terms wrong, and my theories of warfare are open to argument, but in many ways, this is a subject that I know better than Classical History. The mid- to late-fourteenth century was, if you like, my first love, and it has been a joy to return to the world of chivalry – good and bad.

It is essential to understand, when examining this world of stark contrasts and incredible passions, that people believed very strongly in ideas – like Islam, like Christianity, like chivalry. Piety – the devotional practice of Christianity – was such an essential part of life that even most 'atheists' practised all the forms of Christianity. Yet there were many flavours of belief. Theology had just passed one of its most important milestones with the works of Thomas Aquinas, but Roman Christianity had so many varieties of practice that it would require the birth of Protestantism and then the Counter-Reformation to establish orthodoxy. I mention all this to say that to describe the fourteenth century without reference to religion would be – completely ahistorical. I make no judgment on their beliefs – I merely try to represent them accurately.

The same should be said for chivalry. It is easy for the modern amoralist to sneer – The Black Prince massacred innocents and burned towns, Henry V ordered prisoners butchered. The period is decorated with hundreds, if not thousands of moments where the chivalric warriors fell from grace and behaved like monsters. I loveth chivalry, warts and all, and it is my take – and, I think, a considered one – that in chivalry we find the birth of the modern codes of war and of military justice, and that to merely state piously that 'war is hell' and that 'sometimes good men do bad things' is crap. War needs rules. Brutality needs limits. These were not amateur enthusiasts, conscripts, or draftees. They were full-time professionals who made for themselves a set of rules so that they could function – in and out of violence – as human beings. If the code of chivalry was abused – well, so are concepts like Liberty and Democracy abused. Cynicism is easy. Practice of the discipline of chivalry when your own life is in imminent danger is nothing less than heroic – it required then and still requires discipline and moral judgement, confidence in warrior skills and a strong desire to ameliorate the effects of war. I suspect that in addition to helping to control violence (and helping to promote it – a two-edged sword) the code and its reception in society did a great deal to ameliorate the effects of PTSD. I think that the current scholarship believes that, on balance, the practice of chivalry may have done more to promote violence than to quell it – but I've always felt that this is a massively ill-considered point of view – as if to suggest that the practice of democracy has been bad for peace, based on the casualty rates of the twentieth century.

And a word about the martial arts of the period. The world sees knights as illiterate thugs swinging heavy weapons and wearing hundreds of pounds of armour. In fact, the professionals wore armour that fitted like a tailored steel suit to the individual, and with weight evenly distributed over the body. We have several manuals of arms from this period, the most famous of which is by a character in this series – Fiore di Liberi, a northern Italian master who left us a magnificently illustrated step-by-step guide to the way to fight in and out of armour, unarmed, with a dagger, with a stick, with a sword, with a two-handed sword, with a spear, with a poleax, and mounted with a lance. The techniques are brutal, elegant and effective. They also pre-date any clear, unambiguous martial manual from the east, and are directly tied to combat, not remote reflections of it. I recommend their study, and the whole of Fiore's work in the Getty collection is available to your inspection at http://wiktenauer.com/wiki/Fior_di_Battaglia_MS_Ludwig_XV_13. If you'd like to learn more, I recommend the works of Rob Charrette and Guy Windsor. Guy's School is at http://swordschool.com/ and Rob Charrette's superb examination of Fiore's techniques is available at http://www.freelanceacademypress.com/. Fiore Di Liberi was a real man, and his passion for his art shines through the pages of his book.

Finally, Sir William Gold, like Arimnestos, was a real person. He was a lieutenant of the White Company and often, but not always, followed Sir John Hawkwood. He had a fascinating career, and I suspect I'll render it more exciting yet – but the events described, whether Poitiers and the dismemberment of France in the middle of the century, the Italian wars, or the Green Count's Crusade – all of them are real events. Most of the characters are real people, and when I've created characters, I've used sources like Chaucer's re-markable *Canterbury Tales* to make them live. Geoffrey Chaucer was a squire and a member of the Prince Lionel's household. He really was captured in France. He was, I think, the acerbic young man I describe, and I have tried to be faithful to what is known about his life. I hope that I have been faithful to the period and to the lives of these great men and women (great and terrible – Hawkwood was no man's hero) and I do hope that my readers learn things. I think a good historical novel should teach, and I'm unabashed to say it.

But I remain a novelist first, and I hope that I have taken the bones of history and made a good story.

Acknowledgements

My greatest thanks have to go, first and foremost, to the man to whom this work is dedicated – Richard Kaeuper of the University of Rochester. The finest professor I ever had – the most passionate, the most clear, the most brilliant – Dr Kaeuper's works on chivalry and the role of violence in society makes him, I think, the preeminent medievalist working today, and I have been lucky to be able to get his opinions and the wealth of his knowledge on many subjects great and small. Where I have gone astray, the fault is all mine.

Not far behind, I need to thank Guy Windsor, who introduced me to the Armizare of Fiore di Liberi and profoundly informed my notions of what late-Medieval warfare was like among the skilled. Guy runs a school in Finland and I recommend his books and his research and offer my thanks. I'd also like to thank all the people with whom I train and spar – the Companions of Saint Eustachios in Greece and Canada. Reenacting the Middle Ages has many faces, and immersion in that world may not ever be a perfectly authentic experience – but inasmuch as I have gotten 'right' the clothes, the armour, the food or the weapons – it is due to all my reenacting friends, including Chris Verwijmeren, master archer, and Leo Todeschini and JT Palikko and Peter Fuller, master craftsmen.

Throughout the writing of this series, I have used, as my standard reference to names, dates, and events, the works of Jonathan Sumption, whose books are, I think, the best unbiased summation of the causes, events and consequences of the war. I've never met him, but I'd like to offer him my thanks by suggesting that anyone who wants to follow the real events should buy Sumption's books!

As Dick Kaueper once suggested in a seminar, there would have been no Middle Ages as we know them without two things – the horse and Christianity. I owe my horsemanship skills largely to two people – Ridgely and Georgine Davis of Pennsylvania, both of whom are endlessly patient with teaching and with horseflesh in getting me to understand even the basics of mounted combat. And for my understanding of the church, I'd like first thank all the theologians I know – I'm virtually surrounded by people with degrees in theology – and second, the work of F. C. Copleston, whose work, *A History of Medieval Philosophy*, was essential to my writing and understanding of the period – as essential, in fact, as the writings of Chaucer and Boccaccio.

My sister-in-law, Nancy Watt, provided early comments, criticism, and copy-editing while I worked my way through the historical problems – and she worked her way through lung cancer. I very much value her commitment.

And, finally, I'd like to thank my friends who support my odd passions and my wife and child, who are tolerant, mocking, justly puzzled, delighted, and gracious by turns as I drag them from battlefield to castle and as we sew like fiends for a tournament in Italy.

William Gold is, I think, my favourite character. I hope you like him. He has a long way to go.

Christian Cameron
Toronto, 2013